DAVID HERBERT LAWRENCE was born on September 11, 1885, in the mining village of Eastwood, near Nottingham, England. His father was an uneducated miner; his mother, a former schoolteacher. *Sons and Lovers* (1913) reflects his boyhood, schooling, and strong attachment to his mother. Lawrence began his first novel, *The White Peacock* (1911), while attending Nottingham University. In 1912 he left his teaching job to devote himself to his writing. That same year he eloped with Frieda von Richthofen, wife of one of his professors. They were married in 1914. Suffering from tuberculosis, Lawrence was in constant flight from his ill health, traveling through Europe and around the world by way of Australia to Mexico, settling for a while in Taos, New Mexico. Lawrence and Frieda returned to Europe in 1929. Shortly after his death on March 2, 1930, in the south of France, E. M. Forster called him "the greatest imaginative novelist of our generation." During his life he had produced more than forty volumes of fiction, poetry, drama, criticism, philosophy, and travel writing. Among his most famous works are: *The Prussian Officer* (1914), *The Rainbow* (1915), *Women in Love* (1920), *Studies in Classic American Literature* (1923), *The Plumed Serpent* (1926), and *Lady Chatterley's Lover* (1928).

D. H. LAWRENCE

Women in Love

WITH AN INTRODUCTION BY
Louise DeSalvo

A SIGNET CLASSIC

SIGNET CLASSIC
Published by the Penguin Group
Penguin Books USA Inc., 375 Hudson Street,
New York, New York 10014, U.S.A.
Penguin Books Ltd, 27 Wrights Lane,
London W8 5TZ, England
Penguin Books Australia Ltd, Ringwood,
Victoria, Australia
Penguin Books Canada Ltd, 10 Alcorn Avenue
Toronto, Ontario, Canada M4V 3B2
Penguin Books (N.Z.) Ltd, 182–190 Wairau Road,
Auckland 10, New Zealand

Penguin Books Ltd, Registered Offices:
Harmondsworth, Middlesex, England

Published by Signet Classic, an imprint of Dutton Signet,
a division of Penguin Books USA Inc., by arrangement with Viking Penguin,
a division of Penguin USA Inc.

First Signet Classic Printing, January, 1995
10 9 8 7 6 5 4 3 2 1

 REGISTERED TRADEMARK—MARCA REGISTRADA

Library of Congress Catalog Card Number: 94–67398

Printed in the United States of America

BOOKS ARE AVAILABLE AT QUANTITY DISCOUNTS WHEN USED TO PROMOTE PRODUCTS OR
SERVICES. FOR INFORMATION PLEASE WRITE TO PREMIUM MARKETING DIVISION, PENGUIN
BOOKS USA INC., 375 HUDSON STREET, NEW YORK, NEW YORK 10014.

Contents

Introduction

At the end of October 1916, D. H. Lawrence packed up the last half of the handwritten draft of his novel *Women in Love* and sent it on to his agent, J. B. Pinker, for typing. "It is a terrible and horrible and wonderful novel," Lawrence wrote, in an enclosed letter. "You will hate it and nobody will publish it."[1]

Lawrence had good reason to suspect that his agent would have a hard time finding a publisher. Less than a year before, in November 1915, by court order, the public hangman of London had burned more than a thousand copies of Lawrence's previous work, *The Rainbow,* outside the Royal Exchange, because of an obscenity charge. The prosecutor had described the novel as "a mass of obscenity of thought, idea, and action" couched in an artistic language deliberately chosen by Lawrence to disguise its prurient content.[2] The court objected most strenuously to Lawrence's explicit descriptions of lovemaking; many of the offending passages were scenes between wives and their husbands. But the novel also included a suggestive lesbian scene, and love scenes between unmarried people.

The obscenity charge, though, might have been a smokescreen for the government's prosecution of Lawrence for his antiwar stance, articulated in "England, My England," which had appeared in October 1915 in the *English Review.* There were some who believed that Lawrence's views amounted to treason.[3] And Lawrence's insistence that the bonds of married love superseded loyalty to one's country even during war was surely a threat to a government committed to winning its battle with Germany, even if it meant the obliteration of an entire generation of young Englishmen.

Lawrence's fears that his novel would not see print proved prophetic. The publisher Methuen, which held the right of first refusal to the novel, turned down *Women in Love* after it was offered to them. By the end of January 1917, Duckworth (who had previously published Lawrence's work), Martin Secker, and Constable & Co. had all refused it. Constable criticized its "expressions of antipathy to England and all forms of English civilisation" and its "destructive philosophy . . . unwelcome at the present time."[4]

In composing *Women in Love,* Lawrence had repeated a lifelong habit in penning many vicious and vindictive satirical portraits of people with whom he had been intimate, but whom he had come to despise.[5] The continuing threat of libel suits from those he had offended, in addition to the radical nature of his novel, kept *Women in Love* out of print for years, until 1920.

Among those whom Lawrence attacked were important and influential members of England's ruling class. Lady Ottoline Morrell appears as Hermione Roddice; her husband, Philip Morrell, a Liberal member of Parliament, as Hermione's brother Salsie; and Bertrand Russell, as Sir Joshua Mattheson. He used fictive portraits of them to illustrate his belief in the decline, decay, and moral perversity of the ruling class, which he had witnessed firsthand in his visits to the Morrells' country estate, Garsington, depicted in *Women in Love* as Breadalby. Lawrence's satire of Garsington and its habitues, and, particularly, his writing of Ottoline/Hermione as a woman who represented the "Flux of Corruption," who resembled a "corpse," "vomit," and "offal," compelled the Morrells to threaten a libel suit if the novel were published.[6]

While he wrote *Women in Love,* Lawrence was living with his wife, Frieda, in Zennor, Cornwall, whose primeval and clean natural beauty calmed him. They had rented some isolated, whitewashed granite outbuildings under the moors, overlooking the sea and the setting sun. Lawrence, ever the homemaker, had prettied them up by painting his walls and furniture, by sewing and hanging yellow and green curtains, and by planting flowers. Often, he wrote out-of-doors, his notebook upon his knees, his back braced against a granite outcropping. He listened to the sounds of birds and the wind and the sea in those moments when he paused to gather his thoughts. When he needed relief from the tedium of composition, he went down to the sea to bathe. Often, he let the huge waves carry his naked body to shore, risking their hurling him against the rocks.

Lawrence composed *Women in Love* at a furious pace—on some days, he wrote as many as three thousand words—in just six months. He began the work about April 19, 1916, and he finished a version of it by October 1916, while war was being waged across the English Channel.[7]

Lawrence's ability to write a novel at this speed, during these troubling times, and given the fate of its predecessor, is surely testimony to his tenacity in the face of adversity, and to the indomitable nature of his creative spirit. In part, Lawrence was writing quickly because fiction had always been his major source of income, and he needed money.[8] In part, it proceeded apace because he knew where the work was going. Portions of the work had originally been included in *The Rainbow*, before Lawrence split that work in two: into *The Rainbow* (describing the Brangwen family history) and *Women in Love* (which brought the multigenerational saga up to the present).

But Lawrence's ability to work relentlessly was fueled, too, by anger—anger at England for censoring him; at Ottoline Morrell and Bertrand Russell for their liberal politics, which preached reform rather than revolution; at human beings for their corruption; at the war, which he viewed as a "monstrous disaster, the collapse of all human decency"; at his wife, Frieda, for refusing to submit to him in the ways he insisted; and at himself for not being able to squelch his homoerotic impulses. A few days before beginning work, he wrote "Soon I shall be like a lion raging after his prey, seeking whom he may devour."[9]

Soon after Lawrence began the novel, Katherine Mansfield and John Middleton Murry came to join the Lawrences in Cornwall in an experiment in communal living. Lawrence hoped that he could achieve an intimate, mystical union with Murry that would satisfy his need for a relationship with a

man. Murry, never sure of what Lawrence required from
him, could not comply. The communal experiment collapsed
when Murry heard Lawrence moaning invectives against
him, calling Murry an obscene bug sucking his life away.
Mansfield and Murry, too, were sickened by the physical violence of the Lawrences, by the "saucepans and frying pans
hurtling through the air," by the "atmosphere of HATE between them."[10] Lawrence proclaimed that the sadomasochistic love affair between Gudrun Brangwen and Gerald Crich
was based upon that of Mansfield and Murry. Murry, though,
believed it to be more like that of Lawrence and Frieda.

Lawrence had to abandon his dream of a communal life
with Murry and Mansfield. The experiment was a woeful
failure. Lawrence learned, too, that blood-brotherhood—the
relationship he proposed to Murry, his way of loving men
asexually—could not satisfy his powerful homosexual feelings. His desire for Murry, which he could not hide, ended
their friendship. Nor did taking a homosexual partner satisfy
him, because he believed that homosexual desire was by its
very nature corrupt and perverse.

Lawrence wrote *Women in Love* during one of the most
difficult emotional periods of his life—at times he was seriously suicidal—when his marriage was in serious jeopardy,
when he was confronting the irresistible nature of his homosexual desire. As Lawrence was penning his saga of the saving love Rupert Birkin (his alter ego) and Ursula Brangwen
(based upon Frieda) try to achieve, he and Frieda were living
through a physically violent and unfaithful period in their
marriage. *Women in Love,* in part, is Lawrence's urgent attempt to persuade himself that the love he and Frieda shared
was normal, that heterosexual love was good, and that he
could practice it in a life-enhancing way. Much about the
novel was fantasy and wish fulfillment.[11]

But much of the novel, too, traces the lethal quality of tyrannical love, and of sadomasochistic love and so replicates
features of the Lawrences' marriage. The love affairs of
Hermione Roddice and Rupert Birkin, of Gudrun Brangwen
and Gerald Crich (which results in Crich's death), of the
newly married couple who drown, of Halliday, of Loerke
and his lover—all explore what Lawrence himself was expe-

riencing, that love can be dangerous. Ursula and Gudrun, too, have experienced the love of their father as an extreme form of bullying. Ursula seems to escape somewhat unscathed; but Gudrun recreates the family drama in her affair with Gerald Crich.

Lawrence's lifelong preoccupation with charting the impact of violence, bullying, and the tyranny that exists within families originated in his own experience. He had grown up in Nottinghamshire, the son of Lydia and Arthur Lawrence. His father was a coal miner; his mother had been an apprentice teacher.

Lawrence described his parents' marriage as one lifelong "carnal bloody fight." Lawrence's mother had early turned the children against their father, inviting them to see him as an intruder in his own home.

Friends described Lydia Lawrence's affection for her son as that of a lover. Lawrence believed that his mother's attentions to him were excessive, a "final and fatal devotion" that he described as incestuous in his *Fantasia of the Unconscious*. Lawrence's view of over-ardent parental love, of incestuous love, as tyrannical was visionary; it was also an attempt to understand what had compromised his life and his ability to love. According to Frieda, Lawrence's mother had destroyed her son's potential to love any other woman. Surely, too, the fierce fighting that Lawrence witnessed in childhood formed his view of heterosexual love as a pitched battlefield.[12]

The events in *Women in Love* consist of a sequel to those in *The Rainbow*, Lawrence's celebration of the intricacies of heterosexual married love. It continues the theme of the Brangwen saga in exploring the sexual lives of Ursula and Gudrun Brangwen, daughters of Anna and Will Brangwen (whose marriage is described in *The Rainbow*), but with two significant differences. *Women in Love* does not celebrate heterosexual love. Its lovers torture and torment one another, vie for dominance and control, engage in sadistic and masochistic behavior, beat one another, and use love as a weapon for destruction. As Richard Aldington, a friend of Lawrence's, noted, the novel was misnamed: It should have been called *Everybody in Hate*. *Women in Love* also differs from its predecessor in the character Rupert Birkin's quest for same-sex love between men as a necessary adjunct to heterosexual love, and to marriage. Surely the novel's most erotic moments are those in which Rupert Birkin and Gerald Crich strip down and wrestle. In a prologue to the novel (not published in Lawrence's lifetime), Birkin speaks overtly of his "desire" for "the body" of "a strange Cornish type of man," of his preference for men, and of his having to force himself into heterosexuality that was "a real torture" for him. It was "for men that he felt the hot, flushing roused attraction which a man is supposed to feel for the other sex," Birkin admits to himself.[13]

In Cornwall, as Lawrence wrote of Rupert and Ursula fighting their way through to a mutually satisfying relationship, his marriage was faltering, and Lawrence took two lovers: the young farmer William Henry Hocking (with whom Lawrence was intimate throughout much of 1917), and the American journalist Esther Andrews. As he wrote of Rupert Birkin's need for a man, Lawrence entered a homosexual affair for the first time since his adolescence. Yielding to a form of love that he often described as perverse, surely was a prime cause of Lawrence's instability in Cornwall. In a later novel, *Kangaroo*, Lawrence wrote of his affair with Hocking as a "consciously willed destruction of his wife's being."[14]

Women in Love argued that the only way the world could be saved from degeneracy, decay, and destruction—from the fate of Sodom and Gomorrah—was if, "against a background of fetid corruption, a man and woman . . . discover each other." Women had to give up female tyranny; what men required from women was "an absolute surrender, unconditional." The proper sexual union of a woman and man established "the possibility of hope and salvation" and would be enough to save the world.[15] It is this love toward which Rupert/Lawrence and Ursula/Frieda struggle.

D. H. Lawrence would have to wait out the war before the publishing climate would change enough to be receptive to *Women in Love*. "Whilst President Wilson coos and preens in New York, whilst Ottoline stinks at Garsington, whilst Clemenceau spouts in France," he wrote a friend, "I am not worth a penny."[16]

After completing *Women in Love,* Lawrence's fortunes declined still further. He and his wife, Frieda, a German national, were accused of spying for the Germans. They were expelled from Cornwall, placed under surveillance as they made their way around England, living off the largesse of friends and family, and forbidden from leaving the country.[17] Lawrence continued to work, writing short stories, poetry, philosophy, history, drama, psychology, and essays on American literature and English novelists. But because only fiction could provide him with enough income to support himself and Frieda, his inability to get *Women in Love* published because of the English literary establishment's hostility to his work, and the government's singling out his work for censorship—cost him dearly. He no longer had the heart to write fiction. He no longer had the will to fight back.

By the end of the war, Lawrence's condition was desperate. He was "practically penniless, and possessed only a single pair of trousers, which through constant washing had shrunk to above his ankles."[18] His health was very poor; he was having trouble with his lungs. He had lost almost all his friends, and his literary reputation was at its nadir. The repeated illnesses he suffered, exacerbated by his poverty, surely shortened his life.

The novel was finally privately published in 1920 in the United States by Thomas Seltzer; and in 1921, in England, by Martin Secker. Though Lawrence celebrated by drinking a bottle of "beautiful Moselle to its luck," he also dreamed of "huge blue prosecution papers." Though Ottoline Morrell chose not to sue, another of Lawrence's targets in the novel, Philip Heseltine (who appears as the debauched Halliday), threatened a libel suit, and tried to get the novel suppressed by the Purity League. The dispute was resolved when Lawrence agreed to change Halliday's physical appearance, and some "hush-money" was paid.[19]

The *Times Literary Supplement* panned the novel, calling it a "dull, disappointing piece of work." Under the banner

"A BOOK THE POLICE SHOULD BAN. Loathsome Study of Sex Depravity—Misleading Youth to Unspeakable Disaster," *John Bull* scorched the work, said that it should be banned and burned because Lawrence's characters were perverted. *Westminster Gazette*'s review "poked fun"; *Time and Tide* noted the novel's incompetence; the *Observer* spoke of the book's "ravings." Rebecca West, though, writing in the *New Statesman* called it "a work of genius."[20] The negative reception of *Women in Love* in England broke Lawrence's spirit; he resolved to quit Europe, taking up Mabel Luhan's proposal that he move to New Mexico.[21]

But Lawrence's fortunes, and the reception of *Women in Love,* changed dramatically in 1922, after The New York Society for the Suppression of Vice took his American publisher Thomas Seltzer to court on obscenity charges. Not only did the judge not find the work obscene; instead, he called it "a distinct contribution to literature." Publicity from the trial "stimulated a huge demand for the novel." By the end of the year, there were 28,000 copies of the novel in print. For the first time in Lawrence's life he wasn't destitute or dependent on the generosity of his friends. He had stashed £500 in the bank, and was repaying his many loans. *Women in Love,* "his best, his favourite book, the one which contained the quintessence of his message to Mankind," at long last brought Lawrence the security that he had struggled so long to achieve, though he did not have many more years left to enjoy his changed fortunes.[22]

D. H. Lawrence died on March 2, 1930, of pulmonary tuberculosis. He was only forty-four years old. The years of persecution by the English government and the poverty and deprivation forced upon him because of his criticism of his native land had taken their toll, and had shortened his life. But through all the years of poverty and desperation, Lawrence never wavered in his critique of what he believed to be the faults with the English way of life, in his fight against tyranny, and in his belief that personal freedom was more important than devotion to country.

No matter what the cost, Lawrence told the truth as he saw it. And he suffered mightily for doing so. Yet the body of work that he left behind revolutionized English literature.

For Lawrence insisted that a writer who was born as an outsider to power, privilege, and position, could more clearly see, and more accurately criticize the faults of a system than those writers who profited from it.

No matter how furiously they fought, Frieda Lawrence remained staunch in her assessment that D. H. Lawrence's work was the only fruitful branch on the otherwise sterile tree of English literature. Among his disciples were Anaïs Nin and Henry Miller, who based their own literary explorations into the vagaries of love upon the example of his work. Virginia Woolf's private assessment, that Lawrence's work was "honest, and therefore he is one hundred times better than most of us,"[23] best sums up his contribution to English letters.

—Louise DeSalvo

NOTES

1. Herbert Davis, "*Women in Love:* A Corrected Typescript," *University of Toronto Quarterly* (27 October 1957), p. 35.

2. For accounts of the court order, see Emile Delavenay, *D. H. Lawrence: The Man and His Work, The Formative Years: 1885–1919,* trans. from the French by Katherine M. Delavenay (London: Heinemann, 1972); Jeffrey Meyers, *D. H. Lawrence: A Biography* (New York: Alfred A. Knopf, 1990), p. 189.

3. See the accounts in Paul Delany, *D. H. Lawrence's Nightmare: The Writer and His Circle in the Years of the Great War* (New York: Basic Books, 1978); Delavenay; Meyers; and the Introduction to D. H. Lawrence, *The Rainbow,* ed. by Mark Kinkead-Weekes (Cambridge: Cambridge University Press, 1989).

4. David Farmer, Introduction to D. H. Lawrence, *Women in Love,* edited by David Farmer, Lindeth Vasey, and John Worthen (Cambridge: Cambridge University Press, 1987), pp. xxxiii–xxxiv.

5. See Louise DeSalvo, *Conceived with Malice: Literature as Revenge in the Lives and Works of Virginia and Leonard Woolf, D. H. Lawrence, Djuna Barnes, and Henry Miller* (New York: Dutton, 1994).

6. D. H. Lawrence, *Women in Love,* Xerox of Typescript, The Thomas Fisher Rare Book Library, Robart's Library, The University of Toronto, p. 378, p. 210.

7. George Ford, *Double Measure* (New York: Holt, Rinehart & Winston, 1965), p. 165; Delany, p. 239.

8. Farmer, p. xxvii.

9. Frieda Lawrence, *"Not I, But the Wind ..."* (New York: Alfred A. Knopf, 1956), p. 73; D. H. Lawrence, *The Letters of D. H. Lawrence.* Volume II, June 1913–October 1916, ed. by George J. Zytaruk and James T. Boulton and Andrew Robertson (Cambridge: Cambridge University Press, 1981), p. 594.

10. Delany, p. 217, p. 220, p. 232, p. 230.

11. Delany, p. 226.

12. See, especially, John Middleton Murry, *Son of Woman: The Story of D. H. Lawrence* (New York: Jonathan Cape & Harrison Smith, 1931).

13. D. H. Lawrence "Prologue to *Women in Love*," quoted in Meyers, p. 214; D. H. Lawrence "Prologue to *Women in Love*" in *Phoenix II* (New York: The Viking Press, 1968), p. 99, pp. 104–5.

14. See Delavenay, p. 226; Meyers, p. 199 ff; Murry, p. 110.

15. Lawrence, Typescript of *Women in Love,* p. 244; see Meyers, p. 205; see Ford, p. 168.

16. D. H. Lawrence, *The Letters of D. H. Lawrence.* Volume III, October 1916–June 1921, ed. by James T. Boulton and Andrew Robertson (Cambridge: Cambridge University Press, 1987).

17. Farmer, p. xxxviii.

18. Robert Lucas, *Frieda Lawrence: The Story of Frieda von Richthofen and D. H. Lawrence,* translated from the German by Geoffrey Skelton (New York: The Viking Press, 1973), p. 157.

19. D. H. Lawrence, *The Letters of D. H. Lawrence.* Volume IV, June 1921–March 1924, ed. by Warren Roberts, James T. Boulton, and Elizabeth Mansfield (Cambridge: Cambridge University Press 1987), #2255; Edward Nehls, ed., *D. H. Lawrence: A Composite Biography,* Volume I, 1885–1919 (Madison: The University of Wisconsin Press, 1957), p. 593; Edward Nehls, ed., *D. H. Lawrence: A Composite Biography,* Volume II, 1919–1925 (Madison: The University of Wisconsin Press, 1958), pp. 91–2;

Richard Aldington, *Portrait of a Genius But . . .* (New York: Duell, Sloan and Pearce, 1950), p. 18.

20. Farmer, pp. lii–lv; Elaine Feinstein, *Lawrence and the Women: The Intimate Life of D. H. Lawrence* (New York: HarperCollins, 1993), p. 171.

21. Aldington, p. 283.

22. Lucas, p. 190; see Aldington.

23. Virginia Woolf, *The Question of Things Happening: The Letters of Virginia Woolf,* Volume II, 1912–1922, ed. by Nigel Nicolson and Joanne Trautmann (London: The Hogarth Press, 1976), p. 476.

1

Sisters

Ursula and Gudrun Brangwen sat one morning in the window-bay of their father's house in Beldover, working and talking. Ursula was stitching a piece of brightly coloured embroidery, and Gudrun was drawing upon a board which she held on her knee. They were mostly silent, talking as their thoughts strayed through their minds.

'Ursula,' said Gundrun, 'don't you *really want* to get married?' Ursula laid her embroidery in her lap and looked up. Her face was calm and considerate.

'I don't know,' she replied. 'It depends how you mean.'

Gudrun was slightly taken aback. She watched her sister for some moments.

'Well,' she said, ironically, 'it usually means one thing! But don't you think, anyhow, you'd be—' she darkened slightly—'in a better position than you are in now.'

A shadow came over Ursula's face.

'I might,' she said. 'But I'm not sure.'

Again Gudrun paused, slightly irritated. She wanted to be quite definite.

'You don't think one needs the *experience* of having been married?' she asked.

'Do you think it need *be* an experience?' replied Ursula.

'Bound to be, in some way or other,' said Gudrun, coolly. 'Possibly undesirable, but bound to be an experience of some sort.'

'Not really,' said Ursula. 'More likely to be the end of experience.'

Gudrun sat very still, to attend to this.

'Of course,' she said, 'there's *that* to consider.' This brought the conversation to a close. Gudrun, almost angrily, took up her rubber and began to rub out part of her drawing. Ursula stitched absorbedly.

'You wouldn't consider a good offer?' asked Gudrun.

'I think I've rejected several,' said Ursula.

'*Really!*' Gudrun flushed dark—'But anything really worth while? Have you *really*?'

'A thousand a year, and an awfully nice man. I liked him awfully,' said Ursula.

'Really! But weren't you fearfully tempted?'

'In the abstract but not in the concrete,' said Ursula. 'When it comes to the point, one isn't even tempted—oh, if I were tempted, I'd marry like a shot. I'm only tempted *not* to.' The faces of both sisters suddenly lit up with amusement.

'Isn't it an amazing thing,' cried Gudrun, 'how strong the temptation is, not to!' They both laughed, looking at each other. In their hearts they were frightened.

There was a long pause, whilst Ursula stitched and Gudrun went on with her sketch. The sisters were women, Ursula twenty-six, and Gudrun twenty-five. But both had the remote, virgin look of modern girls, sisters of Artemis rather than of Hebe. Gudrun was very beautiful, passive, soft-skinned, soft-limbed. She wore a dress of dark-blue silky stuff, with ruches of blue and green linen lace in the neck and sleeves; and she had emerald-green stockings. Her look of confidence and diffidence contrasted with Ursula's sensitive expectancy. The provincial people, intimidated by Gudrun's perfect *sang-froid* and exclusive bareness of manner, said of her: 'She is a smart woman.' She had just come back from London, where she had spent several years, working at an art-school, as a student, and living a studio life.

'I was hoping now for a man to come along,' Gudrun said, suddenly catching her underlip between her teeth, and making a strange grimace, half sly smiling, half anguish. Ursula was afraid.

'So you have come home, expecting him here?' she laughed.

'Oh my dear,' cried Gudrun, strident, 'I wouldn't go out of my way to look for him. But if there did happen to come along a highly attractive individual of sufficient means— well—' she tailed off ironically. Then she looked search-

ingly at Ursula, as if to probe her. 'Don't you find yourself
getting bored?' she asked of her sister. 'Don't you find, that
things fail to materialize? *Nothing materializes!* Everything
withers in the bud.'

'What withers in the bud?' asked Ursula.

'Oh, everything—oneself—things in general.' There was
a pause, whilst each sister vaguely considered her fate.

'It does frighten one,' said Ursula, and again there was a
pause. 'But do you hope to get anywhere by just marrying?'

'It seems to be the inevitable next step,' said Gudrun. Ursula pondered this, with a little bitterness. She was a class
mistress herself, in Willey Green Grammar School, as she
had been for some years.

'I know,' she said, 'it seems like that when one thinks in
the abstract. But really imagine it: imagine any man one
knows, imagine him coming home to one every evening, and
saying "Hello", and giving one a kiss—'

There was a blank pause.

'Yes,' said Gudrun, in a narrowed voice. 'It's just impossible. The man makes it impossible.'

'Of course there's children—' said Ursula doubtfully.

Gudrun's face hardened.

'Do you *really* want children, Ursula?' she asked coldly.
A dazzled, baffled look came on Ursula's face.

'One feels it is still beyond one,' she said.

'*Do* you feel like that?' asked Gudrun. 'I get no feeling
whatever from the thought of bearing children.'

Gudrun looked at Ursula with a mask-like, expressionless
face. Ursula knitted her brows.

'Perhaps it isn't genuine,' she faltered. 'Perhaps one
doesn't really want them, in one's soul—only superficially.'
A hardness came over Gudrun's face. She did not want to be
too definite.

'When one thinks of other people's children—' said Ursula.

Again Gudrun looked at her sister, almost hostile.

'Exactly,' she said, to close the conversation.

The two sisters worked on in silence. Ursula having always
that strange brightness of an essential flame that is caught,
meshed, contravened. She lived a good deal by herself, to

herself, working, passing on from day to day, and always thinking, trying to lay hold on life, to grasp it in her own understanding. Her active living was suspended, but underneath, in the darkness, something was coming to pass. If only she could break through the last integuments! She seemed to try and put her hands out, like an infant in the womb, and she could not, not yet. Still she had a strange prescience, an intimation of something yet to come.

She laid down her work and looked at her sister. She thought Gudrun so *charming,* so infinitely charming, in her softness and her fine, exquisite richness of texture and delicacy of line. There was a certain playfulness about her too, such a piquancy or ironic suggestion, such an untouched reserve. Ursula admired her with all her soul.

'Why did you come home, Prune?' she asked.

Gudrun knew she was being admired. She sat back from her drawing and looked at Ursula, from under her finely-curved lashes.

'Why did I come back, Ursula?' she repeated. 'I have asked myself a thousand times.'

'And don't you know?'

'Yes, I think I do. I think my coming back home was just *reculer pour mieux sauter.'*

And she looked with a long, slow look of knowledge at Ursula.

'I know!' cried Ursula, looking slightly dazzled and falsified, and as if she did *not* know. 'But where can one jump to?'

'Oh, it doesn't matter,' said Gudrun, somewhat superbly. 'If one jumps over the edge, one is bound to land somewhere.'

'But isn't it very risky?' asked Ursula.

A slow mocking smile dawned on Gudrun's face.

'Ah!' she said, laughing. 'What is it all but words!' And so again she closed the conversation. But Ursula was still brooding.

'And how do you find home, now you have come back to it?' she asked.

Gudrun paused for some moments, coldly, before answering. Then, in a cold truthful voice, she said:

'I find myself completely out of it.'

'And father?'

Gudrun looked at Ursula, almost with resentment, as if brought to bay.

'I haven't thought about him: I've refrained,' she said coldly.

'Yes,' wavered Ursula; and the conversation was really at an end. The sisters found themselves confronted by a void, a terrifying chasm, as if they had looked over the edge.

They worked on in silence for some time, Gudrun's cheek was flushed with repressed emotion. She resented its having been called into being.

'Shall we go out and look at that wedding?' she asked at length, in a voice that was too casual.

'Yes!' cried Ursula, too eagerly, throwing aside her sewing and leaping up, as if to escape something, thus betraying the tension of the situation and causing a friction of dislike to go over Gudrun's nerves.

As she went upstairs, Ursula was aware of the house, of her home round about her. And she loathed it, the sordid, too-familiar place! She was afraid at the depth of her feeling against the home, the milieu, the whole atmosphere and condition of this obsolete life. Her feeling frightened her.

The two girls were soon walking swiftly down the main road of Beldover, a wide street, part shops, part dwelling-houses, utterly formless and sordid, without poverty. Gudrun, new from her life in Chelsea and Sussex, shrank cruelly from this amorphous ugliness of a small colliery town in the Midlands. Yet forward she went, through the whole sordid gamut of pettiness, the long amorphous, gritty street. She was exposed to every stare, she passed on through a stretch of torment. It was strange that she should have chosen to come back and test the full effect of this shapeless, barren ugliness upon herself. Why had she wanted to submit herself to it, did she still want to submit herself to it, the insufferable torture of these ugly, meaningless people, this defaced countryside? She felt like a beetle toiling in the dust. She was filled with repulsion.

They turned off the main road, past a black patch of common-garden, where sooty cabbage stumps stood shameless. No one thought to be ashamed. No one was ashamed of it all.

'It is like a country in an underworld,' said Gudrun. 'The colliers bring it above-ground with them, shovel it up. Ursula, it's marvellous, it's really marvellous—it's really wonderful, another world. The people are all ghouls, and everything is ghostly. Everything is a ghoulish replica of the real world, a replica, a ghoul, all soiled, everything sordid. It's like being mad, Ursula.'

The sisters were crossing a black path through a dark, soiled field. On the left was a large landscape, a valley with collieries, and opposite hills with cornfields and woods, all blackened with distance, as if seen through a veil of crape. White and black smoke rose up in steady columns, magic within the dark air. Near at hand came the long rows of dwellings, approaching curved up the hill-slope, in straight lines along the brow of the hill. They were of darkened red brick, brittle, with dark slate roofs. The path on which the sisters walked was black, trodden-in by the feet of the recurrent colliers, and bounded from the field by iron fences; the stile that led again into the road was rubbed shiny by the moleskins of the passing miners. Now the two girls were going between some rows of dwellings, of the poorer sort. Women, their arms folded over their coarse aprons, standing gossiping at the end of their block, stared after the Brangwen sisters with that long, unwearying stare of aborigines; children called out names.

Gudrun went on her way half dazed. If this were human life, if these were human beings, living in a complete world, then what was her own world, outside? She was aware of her grass-green stockings, her large grass-green velour hat, her full soft coat, of a strong blue colour. And she felt as if she were treading in the air, quite unstable, her heart was contracted, as if at any minute she might be precipitated to the ground. She was afraid.

She clung to Ursula, who, through long usage, was inured to this violation of a dark, uncreated, hostile world. But all the time her heart was crying, as if in the midst of some ordeal: 'I want to go back, I want to go away, I want not to know it, not to know that this exists.' Yet she must go forward.

Ursula could feel her suffering.

'You hate this, don't you?' she asked.

'It bewilders me,' stammered Gudrun.

'You won't stay long,' replied Ursula.

And Gudrun went along, grasping at release.

They drew away from the colliery region, over the curve of the hill, into the purer country of the other side, towards Willey Green. Still the faint glamour of blackness persisted over the fields and the wooded hills, and seemed darkly to gleam in the air. It was a spring day, chill, with snatches of sunshine. Yellow celandines showed out from the hedge-bottoms, and in the cottage gardens of Willey Green, currant-bushes were breaking into leaf, and little flowers were coming white on the grey alyssum that hung over the stone walls.

Turning, they passed down the high-road, that went between high banks towards the church. There, in the lowest bend of the road, low under the trees, stood a little group of expectant people, waiting to see the wedding. The daughter of the chief mine-owner of the district, Thomas Crich, was getting married to a naval officer.

'Let us go back,' said Gudrun, swerving away. 'There are all those people.'

And she hung wavering in the road.

'Never mind them,' said Ursula, 'they're all right. They all know me, they don't matter.'

'But must we go through them?' asked Gudrun.

'They're quite all right, really,' said Ursula, going forward. And together the two sisters approached the group of uneasy, watchful common people. They were chiefly women, colliers' wives of the more shiftless sort. They had watchful, underworld faces.

The two sisters held themselves tense, and went straight towards the gate. The women made way for them, but barely sufficient, as if grudging to yield ground. The sisters passed in silence through the stone gateway and up the steps, on the red carpet, a policeman estimating their progress.

'What price the stockings!' said a voice at the back of Gudrun. A sudden fierce anger swept over the girl, violent and murderous. She would have liked them all annihilated, cleared away, so that the world was left clear for her. How she hated walking up the churchyard path, along the red carpet, continuing in motion, in their sight.

'I won't go into the church,' she said suddenly, with such final decision that Ursula immediately halted, turned round, and branched off up a small side path which led to the little private gate of the Grammar School, whose grounds adjoined those of the church.

Just inside the gate of the school shrubbery, outside the churchyard, Ursula sat down for a moment on the low stone wall under the laurel bushes, to rest. Behind her, the large red building of the school rose up peacefully, the windows all open for the holiday. Over the shrubs, before her, were the pale roofs and tower of the old church. The sisters were hidden by the foliage.

Gudrun sat down in silence. Her mouth was shut close, her face averted. She was regretting bitterly that she had ever come back. Ursula looked at her, and thought how amazingly beautiful she was, flushed with discomfiture. But she caused a constraint over Ursula's nature, a certain weariness. Ursula wished to be alone, freed from the tightness, the enclosure of Gudrun's presence.

'Are we going to stay here?' asked Gudrun.

'I was only resting a minute,' said Ursula, getting up as if rebuked. 'We will stand in the corner by the fives-court, we shall see everything from there.'

For the moment, the sunshine fell brightly into the churchyard, there was a vague scent of sap and of spring, perhaps of violets from off the graves. Some white daisies were out, bright as angels. In the air, the unfolding leaves of a copper-beech were blood-red.

Punctually at eleven o'clock, the carriages began to arrive. There was a stir in the crowd at the gate, a concentration as a carriage drove up, wedding guests were mounting up the steps and passing along the red carpet to the church. They were all gay and excited because the sun was shining.

Gudrun watched them closely with objective curiosity. She saw each one as a complete figure, like a character in a book, or a subject in a picture, or a marionette in a theatre,

a finished creation. She loved to recognize their various
characteristics, to place them in their true light, give them
their own surroundings, settle them for ever as they passed
before her along the path to the church. She knew them, they
were finished, sealed and stamped and finished with, for her.
There was none that had anything unknown, unresolved, until the Criches themselves began to appear. Then her interest
was piqued. Here was something not quite so preconcluded.

There came the mother, Mrs Crich, with her eldest son
Gerald. She was a queer unkempt figure, in spite of the at-
tempts that had obviously been made to bring her into line
for the day. Her face was pale, yellowish, with a clear, transparent skin, she leaned forward rather, her features were
strongly marked, handsome, with a tense, unseeing, preda-
tive look. Her colourless hair was untidy, wisps floating
down on to her sac coat of dark blue silk, from under her
blue silk hat. She looked like a woman with a monomania,
furtive almost, but heavily proud.

Her son was of a fair, sun-tanned type, rather above middle height, well-made, and almost exaggeratedly well-
dressed. But about him also was the strange, guarded look,
the unconscious glisten, as if he did not belong to the same
creation as the people about him. Gudrun lighted on him at
once. There was something northern about him that magne-
tized her. In his clear northern flesh and his fair hair was a
glisten like sunshine refracted through crystals of ice. And
he looked so new, unbroached, pure as an arctic thing. Perhaps he was thirty years old, perhaps more. His gleaming
beauty, maleness, like a young, good-humoured, smiling
wolf, did not blind her to the significant, sinister stillness in
his bearing, the lurking danger of his unsubdued temper.
'His totem is the wolf,' she repeated to herself. 'His mother
is an old, unbroken wolf.' And then she experienced a keen
paroxysm, a transport, as if she had made some incredible
discovery, known to nobody else on earth. A strange transport took possession of her, all her veins were in a paroxysm
of violent sensation. 'Good God!' she exclaimed to herself
'what is this?' And then, a moment after, she was saying as-
suredly, 'I shall know more of that man.' She was tortured
with desire to see him again, a nostalgia, a necessity to see

him again, to make sure it was not all a mistake, that she was not deluding herself, that she really felt this strange and overwhelming sensation on his account, this knowledge of him in her essence, this powerful apprehension of him. 'Am I *really* singled out for him in some way, is there really some pale gold, arctic light that envelops only us two?' she asked herself. And she could not believe it, she remained in a muse, scarcely conscious of what was going on around.

The bridesmaids were here, and yet the bridegroom had not come. Ursula wondered if something was amiss, and if the wedding would yet all go wrong. She felt troubled, as if it rested upon her. The chief bridesmaids had arrived. Ursula watched them come up the steps. One of them she knew, a tall, slow, reluctant woman with a weight of fair hair and a pale, long face. This was Hermione Roddice, a friend of the Criches. Now she came along, with her head held up, balancing an enormous flat hat of yellow velvet, on which were streaks of ostrich feathers, natural and grey. She drifted forward as if scarcely conscious, her long blanched face lifted up, not to see the world. She was rich. She wore a dress of silky, frail velvet, of pale yellow colour, and she carried a lot of small rose-coloured cyclamens. Her shoes and stockings were of brownish grey, like the feathers on her hat, her hair was heavy, she drifted along with a peculiar fixity of the hips, a strange unwilling motion. She was impresssive, in her lovely pale-yellow and brownish-rose, yet macabre, something repulsive. People were silent when she passed, impressed, roused, wanting to jeer, yet for some reason silenced. Her long, pale face, that she carried lifted up, somewhat in the Rossetti fashion, seemed almost drugged, as if a strange mass of thoughts coiled in the darkness within her, and she was never allowed to escape.

Ursula watched her with fascination. She knew her a little. She was the most remarkable woman in the Midlands. Her father was a Derbyshire Baronet of the old school, she was a woman of the new school, full of intellectuality, and heavy, nerve-worn with consciousness. She was passionately interested in reform, her soul was given up to the public cause. But she was a man's woman, it was the manly world that held her.

She had various intimacies of mind and soul with various men of capacity. Ursula knew, among these men, only Rupert Birkin, who was one of the school-inspectors of the county. But Gudrun had met others, in London. Moving with her artist friends in different kinds of society, Gudrun had already come to know a good many people of repute and standing. She had met Hermione twice, but they did not take to each other. It would be queer to meet again down here in the Midlands, where their social standing was so diverse, after they had known each other on terms of equality in the houses of sundry acquaintances in town. For Gudrun had been a social success, and had her friends among the slack aristocracy that keeps touch with the arts.

Hermione knew herself to be well-dressed; she knew herself to be the social equal, if not far the superior, of anyone she was likely to meet in Willey Green. She knew she was accepted in the world of culture and of intellect. She was a *Kulturäger,* a medium for the culture of ideas. With all that was highest, whether in society or in thought or in public action, or even in art, she was at one, she moved among the foremost, at home with them. No one could put her down, no one could make mock of her, because she stood among the first and those that were against her were below her, either in rank, or in wealth, or in high association of thought and progress and understanding. So, she was invulnerable. All her life, she had sought to make herself invulnerable, unassailable, beyond reach of the world's judgement.

And yet her soul was tortured, exposed. Even walking up the path to the church, confident as she was that in every respect she stood beyond all vulgar judgement, knowing perfectly that her appearance was complete and perfect, according to the first standards, yet she suffered a torture, under her confidence and her pride, feeling herself exposed to wounds and to mockery and to despite. She always felt vulnerable, vulnerable, there was always a secret chink in her armour. She did not know her self what it was. It was a lack of robust self, she had no natural sufficiency, there was a terrible void, a lack, a deficiency of being within her.

And she wanted someone to close up this deficiency, to close it up for ever. She craved for Rupert Birkin. When he was there, she felt complete, she was sufficient, whole. For the rest of time she was established on the sand, built over a chasm, and, in spite of all her vanity and securities, any common maid-servant of positive, robust temper could fling her down this bottomless pit of insufficiency, by the slightest movement of jeering or contempt. And all the while the pensive, tortured woman piled up her own defences of aesthetic knowledge, and culture, and world-visions, and disinterestedness. Yet she could never stop up the terrible gap of insufficiency.

If only Birkin would form a close and abiding connexion with her, she would be safe during this fretful voyage of life. He could make her sound and triumphant, triumphant over the very angels of heaven. If only he would do it! But she was tortured with fear, with misgivings. She made herself beautiful, she strove so hard to come to that degree of beauty and advantage, when he should be convinced. But always there was a deficiency.

He was perverse too. He fought her off, he always fought her off. The more she strove to bring him to her, the more he battled her back. And they had been lovers now, for years. Oh, it was so wearying, so aching; she was so tired. But still she believed in herself. She knew he was trying to leave her. She knew he was trying to break away from her finally, to be free. But still she believed in her strength to keep him, she believed in her own higher knowledge. His own knowledge was high, she was the central touchstone of truth. She only needed his conjunction with her.

And this, this conjunction with her, which was his highest fulfilment also, with the perverseness of a wilful child he wanted to deny. With the wilfulness of an obstinate child, he wanted to break the holy connexion that was between them.

He would be at this wedding; he was to be groom's man. He would be in the church, waiting. He would know when she came. She shuddered with nervous apprehension and desire as she went through the church-door. He would be there, surely he would see how beautiful her dress was, surely he would see how she had made herself beautiful for him. He would understand, he would be able to see how she was made for him, the first, how she was, for him, the highest.

Surely at last he would be able to accept his highest fate, he would not deny her.

In a little convulsion of too-tired yearning, she entered the church and looked slowly along her cheeks for him, her slender body convulsed with agitation. As best man, he would be standing beside the altar. She looked slowly, deferring in her certainty.

And then, he was not there. A terrible storm came over her, as if she were drowning. She was possessed by a devastating hopelessness. And she approached mechanically to the altar. Never had she known such a pang of utter and final hopelessness. It was beyond death, so utterly null, desert.

The bridegroom and the groom's man had not yet come. There was a growing consternation outside. Ursula felt almost responsible. She could not bear it that the bride should arrive and no groom. The wedding must not be a fiasco, it must not.

But here was the bride's carriage, adorned with ribbons and cockades. Gaily the grey horses curvetted to their destination at the church-gate, a laughter in the whole movement. Here was the quick of all laughter and pleasure. The door of the carriage was thrown open, to let out the very blossom of the day. The people on the roadway murmured faintly with the discontented murmuring of a crowd.

The father stepped out first into the air of the morning, like a shadow. He was a tall, thin, careworn man, with a thin black beard that was touched with grey. He waited at the door of the carriage patiently, self-obliterated.

In the opening of the doorway was a shower of fine foliage and flowers, a whiteness of satin and lace, and a sound of a gay voice saying:

'How do I get out?'

A ripple of satisfaction ran through the expectant people. They pressed near to receive her, looking with zest at the stooping blonde head with its flower buds, and at the delicate, white, tentative foot that was reaching down to the step of the carriage. There was a sudden foaming rush, and the bride like a sudden surf-rush, floating all white beside her father in the morning shadow of trees, her veil flowing with laughter.

'That's done it!' she said.

She put her hand on the arm of her careworn, sallow father, and frothing her light draperies, proceeded over the eternal red carpet. Her father, mute and yellowish, his black beard making him look more careworn, mounted the steps stiffly, as if his spirits were absent; but the laughing mist of the bride went along with him undiminished.

And no bridegroom had arrived! It was intolerable for her. Ursula, her heart strained with anxiety, was watching the hill beyond; the white, descending road, that should give sight of him. There was a carriage. It was running. It had just come into sight. Yes, it was he. Ursula turned towards the bride and the people, and, from her place of vantage, gave an inarticulate cry. She wanted to warn them that he was coming. But her cry was inarticulate and inaudible, and she flushed deeply, between her desire and her wincing confusion.

The carriage rattled down the hill, and drew near. There was a shout from the people. The bride, who had just reached the top of the steps, turned round gaily to see what was the commotion. She saw a confusion among the people, a cab pulling up, and her lover dropping out of the carriage, and dodging among the horses and into the crowd.

'Tibs! Tibs!' she cried in her sudden, mocking excitement, standing high on the path in the sunlight and waving her bouquet. He, dodging with his hat in his hand, had not heard.

'Tibs!' she cried again, looking down to him.

He glanced up, unaware, and saw the bride and her father standing on the path above him. A queer, startled look went over his face. He hesitated for a moment. Then he gathered himself together for a leap, to overtake her.

'Ah-h-h!' came her strange, intaken cry, as, on the reflex, she started, turned and fled, scudding with an unthinkable swift beating of her white feet and fraying of her white garments, towards the church. Like a hound the young man was after her, leaping the steps and swinging past her father, his supple haunches working like those of a hound that bears down on the quarry.

'Ay, after her!' cried the vulgar women below, carried suddenly into the sport.

She, her flowers shaken from her like froth, was steadying herself to turn the angle of the church. She glanced behind, and with a wild cry of laughter and challenge, veered, poised, and was gone beyond the grey stone buttress. In another instant the bridegroom, bent forward as he ran, had caught the angle of the silent stone with his hand, and had swung himself out of sight, his supple, strong loins vanishing in pursuit.

Instantly cries and exclamations of excitement burst from the crowd at the gate. And then Ursula noticed again the dark, rather stooping figure of Mr Crich, waiting suspended on the path, watching with expressionless face the flight to the church. It was over, and he turned round to look behind him, at the figure of Rupert Birkin, who at once came forward and joined him.

'We'll bring up the rear,' said Birkin, a faint smile on his face.

'Ay!' replied the father laconically. And the two men turned together up the path.

Birkin was as thin as Mr Crich, pale and ill-looking. His figure was narrow but nicely made. He went with a slight trail of one foot, which came only from self-consciousness. Although he was dressed correctly for his part, yet there was an innate incongruity which caused a slight ridiculousness in his appearance. His nature was clever and separate, he did not fit at all in the conventional occasion. Yet he subordinated himself to the common idea, travestied himself.

He affected to be quite ordinary, perfectly and marvelously commonplace. And he did it so well, taking the tone of his surroundings, adjusting himself quickly to his interlocutor and his circumstance, that he achieved a verisimilitude of ordinary commonplaceness that usually propitiated his onlookers for the moment, disarmed them from attacking his singleness.

Now he spoke quite easily and pleasantly to Mr Crich, as they walked along the path; he played with situations like a man on a tight-rope: but always on a tight-rope, pretending nothing but ease.

'I'm sorry we are so late,' he was saying. 'We couldn't

find a button-hook, so it took us a long time to button our boots. But you were to the moment.'

'We are usually to time,' said Mr Crich.

'And I'm always late,' said Birkin. 'But today I was *really* punctual, only accidentally not so. I'm sorry.'

The two men were gone, there was nothing more to see, for the time. Ursula was left thinking about Birkin. He piqued her, attracted her, and annoyed her.

She wanted to know him more. She had spoken with him once or twice, but only in his official capacity as inspector. She thought he seemed to acknowledge some kinship between her and him, a natural, tacit understanding, a using of the same language. But there had been no time for the understanding to develop. And something kept her from him, as well as attracted her to him. There was a certain hostility, a hidden ultimate reserve in him, cold and inaccessible.

Yet she wanted to know him.

'What do you think of Rupert Birkin?' she asked, a little reluctantly, of Gudrun. She did not want to discuss him.

'What do I think of Rupert Birkin?' repeated Gudrun. 'I think he's attractive—decidedly attractive. What I can't stand about him is his way with other people—his way of treating any little fool as if she were his greatest consideration. One feels so awfully sold, oneself.'

'Why does he do it?' said Ursula.

'Because he has no real critical faculty—of people, at all events,' said Gudrun. 'I tell you, he treats any little fool as he treats me or you—and it's such an insult.'

'Oh, it is,' said Ursula. 'One must discriminate.'

'One *must* discriminate,' repeated Gudrun. 'But he's a wonderful chap, in other respects—a marvellous personality. But you can't trust him.'

'Yes,' said Ursula vaguely. She was always forced to assent to Gudrun's pronouncements, even when she was not in accord altogether.

The sisters sat silent, waiting for the wedding party to come out. Gudrun was impatient of talk. She wanted to think about Gerald Crich. She wanted to see if the strong feeling she had got from him was real. She wanted to have herself ready.

Inside the church, the wedding was going on. Hermione Roddice was thinking only of Birkin. He stood near her. She seemed to gravitate physically towards him. She wanted to stand touching him. She could hardly be sure he was near her, if she did not touch him. Yet she stood subjected through the wedding service.

She had suffered so bitterly when he did not come, that still she was dazed. Still she was gnawed as by a neuralgia, tormented by his potential absence from her. She had awaited him in a faint delirium of nervous torture. As she stood bearing herself pensively, the rapt look on her face, that seemed spiritual, like the angels, but which came from torture, gave her a certain poignancy that tore his heart with pity. He saw her bowed head, her rapt face, the face of an almost demoniacal ecstatic. Feeling him looking, she lifted her face and sought his eyes, her own beautiful grey eyes flaring him a great signal. But he avoided her look, she sank her head in torment and shame, the gnawing at her heart going on. And he too was tortured with shame, and ultimate dislike, and with acute pity for her, because he did not want to meet her eyes, he did not want to receive her flare of recognition.

The bride and bridegroom were married, the party went into the vestry. Hermione crowded involuntarily up against Birkin, to touch him. And he endured it.

Outside, Gudrun and Ursula listened for their father's playing on the organ. He would enjoy playing a wedding march. Now the married pair were coming! The bells were ringing, making the air shake. Ursula wondered if the trees and the flowers could feel the vibration, and what they thought of it, this strange motion in the air. The bride was quite demure on the arm of the bridegroom, who stared up into the sky before him, shutting and opening his eyes unconsciously, as if he were neither here nor there. He looked rather comical, blinking and trying to be in the scene, when emotionally he was violated by his exposure to a crowd. He looked a typical naval officer, manly, and up to his duty.

Birkin came with Hermione. She had a rapt, triumphant look, like the fallen angels restored, yet still subtly demoniacal, now she held Birkin by the arm. And he was expressionless, neutralized, possessed by her as if it were his fate, without question.

Gerald Crich came, fair, good-looking, healthy, with a great reserve of energy. He was erect and complete, there was a strange stealth glistening through his amiable, almost happy appearance. Gudrun rose sharply and went away. She could not bear it. She wanted to be alone, to know this strange, sharp inoculation that had changed the whole temper of her blood.

2

Shortlands

The Brangwens went home to Beldover, the wedding party gathered at Shortlands, the Criches' home. It was a long, low old house, a sort of manor farm, that spread along the top of a slope just beyond the narrow little lake of Willey Water. Shortlands looked across a sloping meadow that might be a park, because of the large, solitary trees that stood here and there, across the water of the narrow lake, at the wooded hill that successfully hid the colliery valley beyond, but did not quite hide the rising smoke. Nevertheless, the scene was rural and picturesque, very peaceful, and the house had a charm of its own.

It was crowded now with the family and the wedding guests. The father, who was not well, withdrew to rest. Gerald was host. He stood in the homely entrance hall, friendly and easy, attending to the men. He seemed to take pleasure in his social functions, he smiled, and was abundant in hospitality.

The women wandered about in a little confusion, chased hither and thither by the three married daughters of the house. All the while there could be heard the characteristic, imperious voice of one Crich woman or another calling 'Helen, come here a minute,' 'Marjorie, I want you—here,' 'Oh, I say, Mrs Witham—' There was a great rustling of skirts, swift glimpses of smartly-dressed women, a child danced through the hall and back again, a maidservant came and went hurriedly.

Meanwhile the men stood in calm little groups, chatting, smoking, pretending to pay no heed to the rustling animation of the women's world. But they could not really talk, because of the glassy ravel of women's excited, cold laughter and running voices. They waited, uneasy, suspended, rather bored. But Gerald remained as if genial and happy, unaware that he was waiting or unoccupied, knowing himself the very pivot of the occasion.

Suddenly Mrs Crich came noiselessly into the room, peering about with her strong, clear face. She was still wearing her hat, and her sac coat of blue silk.

'What is it, mother?' said Gerald.

'Nothing, nothing!' she answered vaguely. And she went straight towards Birkin, who was talking to a Crich brother-in-law.

'How do you do, Mr Birkin,' she said, in her low voice, that seemed to take no count of her guests. She held out her hand to him.

'Oh Mrs Crich,' replied Birkin, in his readily-changing voice, 'I couldn't come to you before.'

'I don't know half the people here,' she said, in her low voice. Her son-in-law moved uneasily away.

'And you don't like strangers?' laughed Birkin. 'I myself can never see why one should take account of people, just because they happen to be in the room with one: why *should* I know they are there?'

'Why indeed, why indeed!' said Mrs Crich, in her low, tense voice. 'Except that they *are* there. *I* don't know people whom I find in the house. The children introduce them to me—"Mother, this is Mr So-and-so." I am no further. What has Mr So-and-so to do with his own name?—and what have I to do with either him or his name?'

She looked up at Birkin. She startled him. He was flattered too that she came to talk to him, for she took hardly any notice of anybody. He looked down at her tense clear face, with its heavy features, but he was afraid to look into her heavy-seeing blue eyes. He noticed instead how her hair looped in slack, slovenly strands over her rather beautiful ears, which were not quite clean. Neither was her neck perfectly clean. Even in that he seemed to belong to her, rather than to the rest of the company; though, he thought to himself, he was always well washed, at any rate at the neck and ears.

He smiled faintly, thinking these things. Yet he was tense, feeling that he and the elderly, estranged woman were conferring together like traitors, like enemies within the camp of the other people. He resembled a deer, that throws one ear back upon the trail behind, and one ear forward, to know what is ahead.

'People don't really matter,' he said, rather unwilling to continue.

The mother looked up at him with sudden, dark interrogation, as if doubting his sincerity.

'How do you mean, *matter*?' she asked sharply.

'Not many people are anything at all,' he answered, forced to go deeper than he wanted to. 'They jingle and giggle. It would be much better if they were just wiped out. Essentially, they don't exist, they aren't there.'

She watched him steadily while he spoke.

'But we don't imagine them,' she said sharply.

'There's nothing to imagine, that's why they don't exist.'

'Well,' she said, 'I would hardly go as far as that. There they are, whether they exist or no. It doesn't rest with me to decide on their existence. I only know that I can't be expected to take count of them all. You can't expect me to know them, just because they happen to be there. As far as *I* go they might as well not be there.'

'Exactly,' he replied.

'Mightn't they?' she asked again.

'Just as well,' he repeated. And there was a little pause.

'Except that they *are* there, and that's a nuisance,' she said. 'There are my sons-in-law,' she went on, in a sort of monologue. 'Now Laura's got married, there's another. And I really don't know John from James yet. They come up to me and call me mother. I know what they will say—"How are you, mother?" I ought to say, "I am not your mother, in any sense." But what is the use? There they are. I have had children of my own. I suppose I know them from another woman's children.'

'One would suppose so,' he said.

She looked at him, somewhat surprised, forgetting perhaps that she was talking to him. And she lost her thread.

She looked round the room, vaguely. Birkin could not guess what she was looking for, nor what she was thinking. Evidently she noticed her sons.

'Are my children all there?' she asked him abruptly.

He laughed, startled, afraid perhaps.

'I scarcely know them, except Gerald,' he replied.

'Gerald!' she exclaimed. 'He's the most wanting of them all. You'd never think it, to look at him now, would you?'

'No,' said Birkin.

The mother looked across at her eldest son, stared at him heavily for some time.

'Ay,' she said, in an incomprehensible monosyllable, that sounded profoundly cynical. Birkin felt afraid, as if he dared not realize. And Mrs Crich moved away, forgetting him. But she returned on her traces.

'I should like him to have a friend,' she said. 'He has never had a friend.'

Birkin looked down into her eyes, which were blue, and watching heavily. He could not understand them. 'Am I my brother's keeper?' he said to himself, almost flippantly.

Then he remembered, with a slight shock, that that was Cain's cry. And Gerald was Cain, if anybody. Not that he was Cain, either, although he had slain his brother. There was such a thing as pure accident, and the consequences did not attach to one, even though one had killed one's brother in such wise. Gerald as a boy had accidentally killed his brother. What then? Why seek to draw a brand and a curse across the life that had caused the accident? A man can live by accident, and die by accident. Or can he not? Is every man's life subject to pure accident, is it only the race, the genus, the species, that has a universal reference? Or is this not true, is there no such thing as pure accident? Has *everything* that happens a universal significance? Has it? Birkin, pondering as he stood there, had forgotten Mrs Crich, as she had forgotten him.

He did not believe that there was any such thing as accident. It all hung together, in the deepest sense.

Just as he had decided this, one of the Crich daughters came up, saying:

'Won't you come and take your hat off, mother dear? We shall be sitting down to eat in a minute, and it's a formal occasion, darling, isn't it?' She drew her arm through her mother's, and they went away. Birkin immediately went to talk to the nearest man.

The gong sounded for the luncheon. The men looked up,

but no move was made to the dining-room. The women of the house seemed not to feel that the sound had meaning for them. Five minutes passed by. The elderly manservant, Crowther, appeared in the doorway exasperatedly. He looked with appeal at Gerald. The latter took up a large, curved conch shell, that lay on a shelf, and without reference to anybody, blew a shattering blast. It was a strange rousing noise, that made the heart beat. The summons was almost magical. Everybody came running, as if at a signal. And then the crowd in one impulse moved to the dining-room.

Gerald waited a moment, for his sister to play hostess. He knew his mother would pay no attention to her duties. But his sister merely crowded to her seat. Therefore the young man, slightly too dictatorial, directed the guests to their places.

There was a moment's lull, as everybody looked at the *hors d' œuvres* that were being handed round. And out of this lull, a girl of thirteen or fourteen, with her long hair down her back, said in a clam, self-possessed voice:

'Gerald, you forget father, when you make that unearthly noise.'

'Do I?' he answered. And then, to the company, 'Father is lying down, he is not quite well.'

'How is he, really?' called one of the married daughters, peeping round the immense wedding cake that towered up in the middle of the table shedding its artificial flowers.

'He has no pain, but he feels tired,' replied Winifred, the girl with the hair down her back.

The wine was filled, and everybody was talking boisterously. At the far end of the table sat the mother, with her loosely-looped hair. She had Birkin for a neighbour. Sometimes she glanced fiercely down the rows of faces, bending forwards and staring unceremoniously. And she would say in a low voice to Birkin:

'Who is that young man?'

'I don't know,' Birkin answered discreetly.

'Have I seen him before?' she asked.

'I don't think so. *I* haven't,' he replied. And she was satisfied. Her eyes closed wearily, a peace came over her face, she looked like a queen in repose. Then she started, a little social smile came on her face, for a moment she looked the pleasant hostess. For a moment she bent graciously, as if everyone were welcome and delightful. And then immediately the shadow came back, a sullen, eagle look was on her face, she glanced from under her brows like a sinister creature at bay, hating them all.

'Mother,' called Diana, a handsome girl a little older than Winifred, 'I may have wine, mayn't I?'

'Yes, you may have wine,' replied the mother automatically, for she was perfectly indifferent to the question.

And Diana beckoned to the footman to fill her glass.

'Gerald shouldn't forbid me,' she said calmly, to the company at large.

'All right, Di,' said her brother amiably. And she glanced challenge at him as she drank from her glass.

There was a strange freedom, that almost amounted to anarchy, in the house. It was rather a resistance to authority, than liberty. Gerald had some command, by mere force of personality, not because of any granted position. There was a quality in his voice, amiable but dominant, that cowed the others, who were all younger than he.

Hermione was having a discussion with the bridegroom about nationality.

'No,' she said, 'I think that the appeal to patriotism is a mistake. It is like one house of business rivalling another house of business.'

'Well, you can hardly say that, can you?' exclaimed Gerald, who had a real *passion* for discussion. 'You couldn't call a race a business concern, could you?—and nationality roughly corresponds to race, I think. I think it is *meant* to.'

There was a moment's pause. Gerald and Hermione were always strangely but politely and evenly inimical.

'*Do* you think race corresponds with nationality?' she asked musingly, with expressionless indecision.

Birkin knew she was waiting for him to participate. And dutifully he spoke up.

'I think Gerald is right—race is the essential element in nationality, in Europe at least,' he said.

Again Hermione paused, as if to allow this statement to cool. Then she said with strange assumption of authority:

'Yes, but even so, is the patriotic appeal an appeal to the

racial instinct? Is it not rather an appeal to the proprietary instinct, the *commercial* instinct? And isn't this what we mean by nationality?'

'Probably,' said Birkin, who felt that such a discussion was out of place and out of time.

But Gerald was now on the scent of argument.

'A race may have its commercial aspect,' he said. 'In fact it must. It is like a family. You *must* make provision. And to make provision you have got to strive against other families, other nations. I don't see why you shouldn't.'

Again Hermione made a pause, domineering and cold, before she replied: 'Yes, I think it is always wrong to provoke a spirit of rivalry. It makes bad blood. And bad blood accumulates.'

'But you can't do away with the spirit of emulation altogether?' said Gerald. 'It is one of the necessary incentives to production and improvement."

'Yes,' came Hermione's sauntering response. 'I think you can do away with it.'

'I must say,' said Birkin, 'I detest the spirit of emulation.' Hermione was biting a piece of bread, pulling it from between her teeth with her fingers, in a slow, slightly derisive movement. She turned to Birkin.

'You do hate it, yes,' she said, intimate and gratified.

'Detest it,' he repeated.

'Yes,' she murmured, assured and satisfied.

'But,' Gerald insisted, 'you don't allow one man to take away his neighbour's living, so why should you allow one nation to take away the living from another nation?'

There was a long slow murmur from Hermione before she broke into speech, saying with a laconic indifference:

'It is not always a question of possessions, is it? It is not all a question of goods?'

Gerald was nettled by this implication of vulgar materialism.

'Yes, more or less,' he retorted. 'If I go and take a man's hat from off his head, that hat becomes a symbol of that man's liberty. When he fights me for his hat, he is fighting me for his liberty.'

Hermione was nonplussed.

'Yes,' she said, irritated. 'But that way of arguing by imaginary instances is not supposed to be genuine, is it? A man does *not* come and take my hat from off my head, does he?'

'Only because the law prevents him,' said Gerald.

'Not only,' said Birkin. 'Ninety-nine men out of a hundred don't want my hat.'

'That's a matter of opinion,' said Gerald.

'Or the hat,' laughed the bridegroom.

'And if he does want my hat, such as it is,' said Birkin, 'why, surely it is open to me to decide, which is a greater loss to me, my hat, or my liberty as a free and indifferent man. If I am compelled to offer fight, I lose the latter. It is a question which is worth more to me, my pleasant liberty of conduct, or my hat.'

'Yes,' said Hermione, watching Birkin strangely. 'Yes.'

'But would you let somebody come and snatch your hat off your head?' the bride asked of Hermione.

The face of the tall straight woman turned slowly and as if drugged to this new speaker.

'No,' she replied, in a low inhuman tone, that seemed to contain a chuckle. 'No, I shouldn't let anybody take my hat off my head.'

'How would you prevent it?' asked Gerald.

'I don't know,' replied Hermione slowly. 'Probably I should kill him.'

There was a strange chuckle in her tone, a dangerous and convincing humour in her bearing.

'Of course,' said Gerald, 'I can see Rupert's point. It is a question to him whether his hat or his peace of mind is more important.'

'Peace of body,' said Birkin.

'Well, as you like there,' replied Gerald. 'But how are you going to decide this for a nation?'

'Heaven preserve me,' laughed Birkin.

'Yes, but suppose you have to?' Gerald persisted.

'Then it is the same. If the national crown-piece is an old hat, then the thieving gent may have it.'

'But *can* the national or racial hat be an old hat?' insisted Gerald.

'Pretty well bound to be, I believe,' said Birkin.

'I'm not so sure,' said Gerald.

'I don't agree, Rupert,' said Hermione.

'All right,' said Birkin.

'I'm all for the old national hat,' laughed Gerald.

'And a fool you look in it,' cried Diana, his pert sister who was just in her teens.

'Oh, we're quite out of our depths with these old hats,' cried Laura Crich. 'Dry up now, Gerald. We're going to drink toasts. Let us drink toasts. Toasts—glasses, glasses—now then, toasts! Speech! Speech!'

Birkin, thinking about race or national death, watched his glass being filled with champagne. The bubbles broke at the rim, the man withdrew, and feeling a sudden thirst at the sight of the fresh wine, Birkin drank up his glass. A queer little tension in the room roused him. He felt a sharp constraint.

'Did I do it by accident, or on purpose?' he asked himself. And he decided that, according to the vulgar phrase, he had done it 'accidentally on purpose'. He looked round at the hired footman. And the hired footman came, with a silent step of cold servant-like disapprobation. Birkin decided that he detested toasts, and footmen, and assemblies, and mankind altogether, in most of its aspects. Then he rose to make a speech. But he was somehow disgusted.

At length it was over, the meal. Several men strolled out into the garden. There was a lawn, and flower-beds, and at the boundary an iron fence shutting off the little field or park. The view was pleasant; a highroad curving round the edge of a low lake, under the trees. In the spring air, the water gleamed and the opposite woods were purplish with new life. Charming Jersey cattle came to the fence, breathing hoarsely from their velvet muzzles at the human beings, expecting perhaps a crust.

Birkin leaned on the fence. A cow was breathing wet hotness on his hand.

'Pretty cattle, very pretty,' said Marshall, one of the brothers-in-law. 'They give the best milk you can have.'

'Yes,' said Birkin.

'Eh, my little beauty, eh, my beauty!' said Marshall, in a queer high falsetto voice, that caused the other man to have convulsions of laughter in his stomach.

'Who won the race, Lupton?' he called to the bridegroom, to hide the fact that he was laughing.

The bridegroom took his cigar from his mouth.

'The race?' he exclaimed. Then a rather thin smile came over his face. He did not want to say anything about the flight to the church door. 'We got there together. At least she touched first, but I had my hand on her shoulder.'

'What's this?' asked Gerald.

Birkin told him about the race of the bride and the bridegroom.

'H'm!' said Gerald, in disapproval. 'What made you late then?'

'Lupton would talk about the immortality of the soul,' said Birkin, 'and then he hadn't got a button-hook.'

'Oh, God!' cried Marshall. 'The immortality of the soul on your wedding day! Hadn't you got anything better to occupy your mind?'

'What's wrong with it?' asked the bridegroom, a clean-shaven naval man, flushing sensitively.

'Sounds as if you were going to be executed instead of married. *The immortality of the soul!*' repeated the brother-in-law, with most killing emphasis.

But he fell quite flat.

'And what did you decide?' asked Gerald, at once pricking up his ears at the thought of a metaphysical discussion.

'You don't want a soul today, my boy,' said Marshall. 'It'd be in your road.'

'Christ! Marshall, go and talk to somebody else,' cried Gerald, with sudden impatience.

'By God, I'm willing,' said Marshall, in a temper. 'Too much bloody soul and talk altogether—'

He withdrew in a dudgeon, Gerald staring after him with angry eyes, that grew gradually calm and amiable as the stoutly-built form of the other man passed into the distance.

'There's one thing, Lupton,' said Gerald, turning suddenly to the bridegroom. 'Laura won't have brought such a fool into the family as Lottie did.'

'Comfort yourself with that,' laughed Birkin.

'I take no notice of them,' laughed the bridegroom.

'What about this race then—who began it?' Gerald asked.

'We were late. Laura was at the top of the churchyard steps when our cab came up. She saw Lupton bolting towards her. And she fled. But why do you look so cross? Does it hurt your sense of the family dignity?'

'It does, rather,' said Gerald. 'If you're doing a thing, do it properly, and if you're not going to do it properly, leave it alone.'

'Very nice aphorism,' said Birkin.

'Don't you agree?' asked Gerald.

'Quite,' said Birkin. 'Only it bores me rather, when you become aphoristic.'

'Damn you, Rupert, you want all the aphorisms your own way,' said Gerald.

'No. I want them out of the way, and you're always shoving them in it.'

Gerald smiled grimly at this humorism. Then he made a little gesture of dismissal with his eyebrows.

'You don't believe in having any standard of behaviour at all, do you?' he challenged Birkin, censoriously.

'Standard—no. I hate standards. But they're necessary for the common ruck. Anybody who is anything can just be himself and do as he likes.'

'But what do you mean by being himself?' said Gerald. 'Is that an aphorism or a cliché?'

'I mean just doing what you want to do. I think it was perfect good form in Laura to bolt from Lupton to the church door. It was almost a masterpiece in good form. It's the hardest thing in the world to act spontaneously on one's impulses—and it's the only really gentlemanly thing to do—provided you're fit to do it.'

'You don't expect me to take you seriously, do you?' asked Gerald.

'Yes, Gerald, you're one of the very few people I do expect that of.'

'Then I'm afraid I can't come up to your expectations here, at any rate. You think people should just do as they like.'

'I think they always do. But I should like them to like the purely individual thing in themselves, which makes them act in singleness. And they only like to do the collective thing.'

'And I,' said Gerald grimly, 'shouldn't like to be in a

world of people who acted individually and spontaneously, as you call it. We should have everybody cutting everybody else's throat in five minutes.'

'That means *you* would like to be cutting everybody's throat,' said Birkin.

'How does that follow?' asked Gerald crossly.

'No man,' said Birkin, 'cuts another man's throat unless he wants to cut it, and unless the other man wants it cutting. This is a complete truth. It takes two people to make a murder: a murderer and a murderee. And a murderee is a man who is murderable. And a man who is murderable is a man who in a profound if hidden lust desires to be murdered.'

'Sometimes you talk pure nonsense,' said Gerald to Birkin. 'As a matter of fact, none of us wants our throat cut, and most other people would like to cut it for us—some time or other—'

'It's a nasty view of things, Gerald,' said Birkin, 'and no wonder you are afraid of yourself and your own unhappiness.'

'How am I afraid of myself?' said Gerald; 'and I don't think I am unhappy.'

'You seem to have a lurking desire to have your gizzard slit, and imagine every man has his knife up his sleeve for you,' Birkin said.

'How do you make that out?' said Gerald.

'From you,' said Birkin.

There was a pause of strange enmity between the two men, that was very near to love. It was always the same between them; always their talk brought them into a deadly nearness of contact, a strange, perilous intimacy which was either hate or love, or both. They parted with apparent unconcern, as if their going apart were a trivial occurrence. And they really kept it to the level of trivial occurrence. Yet the heart of each burned for the other. They burned with each other, inwardly. This they would never admit. They intended to keep their relationship a casual free-and-easy friendship, they were not going to be so unmanly and unnatural as to allow any heart-burning between them. They had not the faintest belief in deep relationship between men and men, and their disbelief prevented any development of their powerful but suppressed friendliness.

3

Class-room

A school-day was drawing to a close. In the class-room the last lesson was in progress, peaceful and still. It was elementary botany. The desks were littered with catkins, hazel and willow, which the children had been sketching. But the sky had come over dark, as the end of the afternoon approached: there was scarcely light to draw any more. Ursula stood in front of the class, leading the children by questions to understand the structure, and the meaning of the catkins.

A heavy, copper-coloured beam of light came in at the west window, gilding the outlines of the children's heads with red gold, and falling on the wall opposite in a rich, ruddy illumination. Ursula, however, was scarcely conscious of it. She was busy, the end of the day was here, the work went on as a peaceful tide that is at flood, hushed to retire.

This day had gone by like so many more, in an activity that was like a trance. At the end there was a little haste, to finish what was in hand. She was pressing the children with questions, so that they should know all they were to know, by the time the gong went. She stood in shadow in front of the class, with catkins in her hand, and she leaned towards the children, absorbed in the passion of instruction.

She heard, but did not notice the click of the door. Suddenly she started. She saw, in the shaft of ruddy, copper-coloured light near her, the face of a man. It was gleaming like fire, watching her, waiting for her to be aware. It startled her terribly. She thought she was going to faint. All her suppressed, subconscious fear sprang into being, with anguish.

'Did I startle you?' said Birkin, shaking hands with her. 'I thought you had heard me come in.'

'No,' she faltered, scarcely able to speak. He laughed, saying he was sorry. She wondered why it amused him.

'It is so dark,' he said. 'Shall we have the light?'

And moving aside, he switched on the strong electric lights. The class-room was distinct and hard, a strange place after the soft dim magic that filled it before he came. Birkin turned curiously to look at Ursula. Her eyes were round and wondering, bewildered, her mouth quivered slightly. She looked like one who is suddenly wakened. There was a living, tender beauty, like a tender light of dawn shining from her face. He looked at her with a new pleasure, feeling gay in his heart, irresponsible.

'You are doing catkins?' he asked, picking up a piece of hazel from a scholar's desk in front of him. 'Are they as far out as this? I hadn't noticed them this year.'

He looked absorbedly at the tassel of hazel in his hand.

'The red ones too!' he said, looking at the flickers of crimson that came from the female bud.

Then he went in among the desks, to see the scholars' books. Ursula watched his intent progress. There was a stillness in his motion that hushed the activities of her heart. She seemed to be standing aside in arrested silence, watching him move in another concentrated world. His presence was so quiet, almost like a vacancy in the corporate air.

Suddenly he lifted his face to her, and her heart quickened at the flicker of his voice.

'Give them some crayons, won't you?' he said, 'so that they can make the gynaecious flowers red, and the androgynous yellow. I'd chalk them in plain, chalk in nothing else, merely the red and the yellow. Outline scarcely matters in this case. There is just the one fact to emphasize.'

'I haven't any crayons,' said Ursula.

'There will be some somewhere—red and yellow, that's all you want.'

Ursula sent out a boy on a quest.

'It will make the books untidy,' she said to Birkin, flushing deeply.

'Not very,' he said. 'You must mark in these things obviously. It's the fact you want to emphasize, not the subjective impression to record. What's the fact?—red little spiky stigmas of the female flower, dangling yellow male catkin, yellow pollen flying from one to the other. Make a pictorial record of the fact, as a child does when drawing a face—two eyes, one nose, mouth with teeth—so—' And he drew a figure on the blackboard.

At that moment another vision was seen through the glass panels of the door. It was Hermione Roddice. Birkin went and opened to her.

'I saw your car,' she said to him. 'Do you mind my coming to find you? I wanted to see you when you were on duty.'

She looked at him for a long time, intimate and playful, then she gave a short little laugh. And then only she turned to Ursula, who, with all the class, had been watching the little scene between the lovers.

'How do you do, Miss Brangwen,' sang Hermione, in her low, odd, singing fashion, that sounded almost as if she were poking fun. 'Do you mind my coming in?'

Her grey, almost sardonic eyes rested all the while on Ursula, as if summing her up.

'Oh no,' said Ursula.

'Are you *sure*?' repeated Hermione, with complete sang froid, and an odd, half-bullying effrontery.

'Oh no, I like it awfully,' laughed Ursula, a little bit excited and bewildered, because Hermione seemed to be compelling her, coming very close to her, as if intimate with her; and yet, how could she be intimate?

This was the answer Hermione wanted. She turned satisfied to Birkin.

'What are you doing?' she sang, in her casual, inquisitive fashion.

'Catkins,' he replied.

'Really!' she said. 'And what do you learn about them?' She spoke all the while in a mocking, half teasing fashion, as if making game of the whole business. She picked up a twig of the catkin, piqued by Birkin's attention to it.

She was a strange figure in the class-room, wearing a large, old cloak of greenish cloth, on which was a raised pattern of dull gold. The high collar, and the inside of the cloak, was lined with dark fur. Beneath she had a dress of fine lavender-coloured cloth, trimmed with fur, and her hat was close-fitting, made of fur and of the dull, green-and-gold figured stuff. She was tall and strange, she looked as if she had come out of some new, bizarre picture.

'Do you know the little red ovary flowers, that produce the nuts? Have you ever noticed them?' he asked her. And he came close and pointed them out to her, on the sprig she held.

'No,' she replied. 'What are they?'

'Those are the little seed-producing flowers, and the long catkins, they only produce pollen, to fertilize them.'

'Do they, do they!' repeated Hermione, looking closely.

'From those little red bits, the nuts come; if they receive pollen from the long danglers.'

'Little red flames, little red flames,' murmured Hermione to herself. And she remained for some moments looking only at the small buds out of which the red flickers of the stigma issued.

'Aren't they beautiful? I think they're so beautiful,' she said, moving close to Birkin, and pointing to the red filaments with her long, white finger.

'Had you never noticed them before?' he asked.

'No, never before,' she replied.

'And now you will always see them,' he said.

'Now I shall always see them,' she repeated. 'Thank you so much for showing me. I think they're so beautiful—little red flames—'

Her absorption was strange, almost rhapsodic. Both Birkin and Ursula were suspended. The little red pistillate flowers had some strange, almost mystic-passionate attraction for her.

The lesson was finished, the books were put away, at last the class was dismissed. And still Hermione sat at the table, with her chin in her hand, her elbow on the table, her long white face pushed up, not attending to anything. Birkin had gone to the window, and was looking from the brilliantly-lighted room on to the grey, colourless outside, where rain was noiselessly falling. Ursula put away her things in the cupboard.

At length Hermione rose and came near to her.

'Your sister has come home?' she said.

'Yes,' said Ursula.

'And does she like being back in Beldover?'

'No,' said Ursula.

'No, I wonder she can bear it. It takes all my strength, to bear the ugliness of this district, when I stay here. Won't you come and see me? Won't you come with your sister to stay at Breadalby for a few days?—do—'

'Thank you very much,' said Ursula.

'Then I will write to you,' said Hermione. 'You think your sister will come? I should be so glad. I think she is wonderful. I think some of her work is really wonderful. I have two water-wagtails, carved in wood, and painted—perhaps you have seen it?'

'No,' said Ursula.

'I think it is perfectly wonderful—like a flash of instinct—'

'Her little carvings *are* strange,' said Ursula.

'Perfectly beautiful—full of primitive passion—'

'Isn't it queer that she always likes little things?—she must always work small things, that one can put between one's hands, birds, and tiny animals. She likes to look through the wrong end of the opera-glasses, and see the world that way—why is it, do you think?'

Hermione looked down at Ursula with that long, detached scrutinizing gaze that excited the younger woman.

'Yes,' said Hermione at length. 'It is curious. The little things seem to be more subtle to her—'

'But they aren't, are they? A mouse isn't any more subtle than a lion, is it?'

Again Hermione looked down at Ursula with that long scrutiny, as if she were following some train of thought of her own, and barely attending to the other's speech.

'I don't know,' she replied.

'Rupert, Rupert,' she sang mildly, calling him to her. He approached in silence.

'Are little things more subtle than big things?' she asked, with the odd grunt of laughter in her voice, as if she were making game of him in the question.

'Dunno,' he said.

'I hate subtleties,' said Ursula.

Hermione looked at her slowly.

'Do you?' she said.

'I always think they are a sign of weakness,' said Ursula, up in arms, as if her prestige were threatened.

Hermione took no notice. Suddenly her face puckered, her brow was knit with thought, she seemed twisted in troublesome effort for utterance.

'Do you really think, Rupert,' she asked, as if Ursula were not present, 'do you really think it is worth while? Do you really think the children are better for being roused to consciousness?'

A dark flash went over his face, a silent fury. He was hollow-cheeked and pale, almost unearthly. And the woman, with her serious, conscience-harrowing question tortured him on the quick.

'They are not roused to consciousness,' he said. 'Consciousness comes to them, willy-nilly.'

'But do you think they are better for having it quickened, stimulated? Isn't it better that they should remain unconscious of the hazel, isn't it better that they should see as a whole, without all this pulling to pieces, all this knowledge?'

'Would you rather, for yourself, know or not know, that the little red flowers are there, putting out for the pollen?' he asked harshly. His voice was brutal, scornful, cruel.

Hermione remained with her face lifted up, abstracted. He hung silent in irritation.

'I don't know,' she replied, balancing mildly. 'I don't know.'

'But knowing is everything to you, it is all your life,' he broke out. She slowly looked at him.

'Is it?' she said.

'To know, that is your all, that is your life—you have only this, this knowledge,' he cried. 'There is only one tree, there is only one fruit, in your mouth.'

Again she was some time silent.

'Is there?' she said at last, with the same untouched calm. And then in a tone of whimsical inquisitiveness: 'What fruit, Rupert?'

'The eternal apple,' he replied in exasperation, hating his own metaphors.

'Yes,' she said. There was a look of exhaustion about her. For some moments there was silence. Then, pulling herself together with a convulsed movement, Hermione resumed, in a sing-song, casual voice.

'But leaving me apart, Rupert; do you think the children are better, richer, happier, for all this knowledge; do you really think they are? Or is it better to leave them untouched, spontaneous. Hadn't they better be animals, simple animals, crude, violent, *anything*, rather than this self-consciousness, this incapacity to be spontaneous.'

They thought she had finished. But with a queer rumbling in her throat she resumed, 'Hadn't they better be anything than grow up crippled, crippled in their souls, crippled in their feelings—so thrown back—so turned back on themselves—incapable—' Hermione clenched her fist like one in a trance—'of any spontaneous action, always deliberate, always burdened with choice, never carried away.'

Again they thought she had finished. But just as he was going to reply, she resumed her queer rhapsody—'never carried away, out of themselves, always conscious, always self-conscious, always aware of themselves. Isn't *anything* better than this? Better be animals, mere animals with no mind at all, than this, this *nothingness*—'

'But do you think it is knowledge that makes us unliving and self-conscious?' he asked irritably.

She opened her eyes and looked at him slowly.

'Yes,' she said. She paused, watching him all the while, her eyes vague. Then she wiped her fingers across her brow, with a vague weariness. It irritated him bitterly. 'It is the mind,' she said, 'and that is death.' She raised her eyes slowly to him: 'Isn't the mind—' she said, with the convulsed movement of her body, 'isn't it our death? Doesn't it destroy all our spontaneity, all our instincts? Are not the young people growing up today, really dead before they have a chance to live?'

'Not because they have too much mind, but too little,' he said brutally.

'Are you *sure*?' she cried. 'It seems to me the reverse.

They are over-conscious, burdened to death with consciousness.'

'Imprisoned within a limited, false set of concepts,' he cried.

But she took no notice of this, only went on with her own rhapsodic interrogation.

'When we have knowledge, don't we lose everything but knowledge?' she asked pathetically. 'If I know about the flower, don't I lose the flower and have only the knowledge? Aren't we exchanging the substance for the shadow, aren't we forfeiting life for this dead quality of knowledge? And what does it mean to me after all? What does all this knowing mean to me? It means nothing.'

'You are merely making words,' he said; 'knowledge means everything to you. Even your animalism, you want it in your head. You don't want to *be* an animal, you want to observe your own animal functions, to get a mental thrill out of them. It is all purely secondary—and more decadent than the most hide-bound intellectualism. What is it but the worst and last form of intellectualism, this love of yours for passion and the animal instincts? Passion and the instincts—you want them hard enough, but through your head, in your consciousness. It all takes place in your head, under that skull of yours. Only you won't be conscious of what *actually* is: you want the lie that will match the rest of your furniture.'

Hermione set hard and poisonous against this attack. Ursula stood covered with wonder and shame. It frightened her, to see how they hated each other.

"It's all that Lady of Shalott business,' he said, in his strong abstract voice. He seemed to be charging her before the unseeing air. 'You've got that mirror, your own fixed will, your immortal understanding, your own tight conscious world, and there is nothing beyond it. There, in the mirror, you must have everything. But now you have come to all your conclusions, you want to go back and be like a savage, without knowledge. You want a life of pure sensation and "passion".'

He quoted the last word satirically against her. She sat convulsed with fury and violation, speechless, like a stricken pythoness of the Greek oracle.

'But your passion is a lie,' he went on violently. 'It isn't passion at all, it is your *will*. It's your bullying will. You want to clutch things and have them in your power. You want to have things in your power. And why? Because you haven't got any real body, any dark sensual body of life. You have no sensuality. You have only your will and your conceit of consciousness, and your lust for power, to *know*.'

He looked at her in mingled hate and contempt, also in pain because she suffered, and in shame because he knew he tortured her. He had an impulse to kneel and plead for forgiveness. But a bitterer red anger burned up to fury in him. He became unconscious of her, he was only a passionate voice speaking.

'Spontaneous!' he cried. 'You and spontaneity! You, the most deliberate thing that ever walked or crawled! You'd be verily deliberately spontaneous—that's you. Because you want to have everything in your own volition, your deliberate voluntary consciousness. You want it all in that loathsome little skull of yours, that ought to be cracked like a nut. For you'll be the same till it *is* cracked, like an insect in its skin. If one cracked your skull perhaps one might get a spontaneous, passionate woman out of you, with real sensuality. As it is, what you want is pornography—looking at yourself in mirrors, watching your naked animal actions in mirrors, so that you can have it all in your consciousness, make it all mental.'

There was a sense of violation in the air, as if too much was said, the unforgivable. Yet Ursula was concerned now only with solving her own problems, in the light of his words. She was pale and abstracted.

'But do you really *want* sensuality?' she asked puzzled.

Birkin looked at her, and became intent in his explanation.

'Yes,' he said, 'that and nothing else, at this point. It is a fulfillment—the great dark knowledge you can't have in your head—the dark involuntary being. It is death to one's self—but it is the coming into being of another.'

'But how? How can you have knowledge not in your head?' she asked, quite unable to interpret his phrases.

'In the blood,' he answered; 'when the mind and the known world is drowned in darkness—everything must go—

there must be the deluge. Then you find yourself in a palpable body of darkness, a demon—'

'But why should I be a demon—?' she asked.

' *"Woman wailing for her demon lover"*—' he quoted—'why, I don't know.'

Hermione roused herself as from a death—annihilation.

'He is such a *dreadful* satanist, isn't he?' she drawled to Ursula, in a queer resonant voice, that ended in a shrill little laugh of pure ridicule. The two women were jeering at him, jeering him into nothingness. The laugh of the shrill, triumphant female sounded from Hermione, jeering him as if he were a neuter.

'No,' he said. 'You are the real devil who won't let life exist.'

She looked at him with a long, slow look, malevolent, supercilious.

'You know all about it, don't you?' she said, with slow, cold, cunning mockery.

'Enough,' he replied, his face fixing fine and clear like steel. A horrible despair, and at the same time a sense of release, liberation, came over Hermione. She turned with a pleasant intimacy to Ursula.

'You are sure you will come to Breadalby?' she said, urging.

'Yes, I should like to very much,' replied Ursula.

Hermione looked down at her, gratified, reflecting, and strangely absent, as if possessed, as if not quite there.

'I'm so glad,' she said, pulling herself together. 'Some time in about a fortnight. Yes? I will write to you here, at the school, shall I? Yes. And you'll be sure to come? Yes. I shall be so glad. Good-bye! Good-bye!'

Hermione held out her hand and looked into the eyes of the other woman. She knew Ursula as an immediate rival, and the knowledge strangely exhilarated her. Also she was taking leave. It always gave her a sense of strength, advantage, to be departing and leaving the other behind. Moreover she was taking the man with her, if only in hate.

Birkin stood aside, fixed and unreal. But now, when it was his turn to bid good-bye, he began to speak again.

'There's the whole difference in the world,' he said, 'between the actual sensual being and the vicious mental deliberate profligacy our lot goes in for. In our night-time there's always the electricity switched on, we watch ourselves, we get it all in the head, really. You've got to lapse out before you can know what sensual reality is, lapse into unknowingness, and give up your volition. You've got to do it. You've got to learn not-to-be, before you can come into being.

'But we have got such a conceit of ourselves—that's where it is. We are so conceited, and so unproud. We've got no pride, we're all conceit, so conceited in our papier-mâché realized selves. We'd rather die than give up our little self-righteous self-opinionated self-will.'

There was silence in the room. Both women were hostile and resentful. He sounded as if he were addressing a meeting. Hermione merely paid no attention, stood with her shoulders tight in a shrug of dislike.

Ursula was watching him as if furtively, not really aware of what she was seeing. There was a great physical attractiveness in him—a curious hidden richness, that came through his thinness and his pallor like another voice, conveying another knowledge of him. It was in the curves of his brows and his chin, rich, fine, exquisite curves, the powerful beauty of life itself. She could not say what it was. But there was a sense of richness and of liberty.

'But we are sensual enough, without making ourselves so, aren't we?' she asked, turning to him with a certain golden laughter flickering under her greenish eyes, like a challenge. And immediately the queer, careless, terribly attractive smile came over his eyes and brows, though his mouth did not relax.

"No,' he said, 'we aren't. We're too full of ourselves.'

'Surely it isn't a matter of conceit,' she cried.

'That and nothing else.'

She was frankly puzzled.

'Don't you think that people are most conceited of all about their sensual powers?' she asked.

'That's why they aren't sensual—only sensuous—which is another matter. They're *always* aware of themselves—and they're so conceited, that rather than release themselves, and live in another world, from another centre, they'd—'

'You want your tea, don't you,' said Hermione, turning to Ursula with a gracious kindliness. 'You've worked all day—'

Birkin stopped short. A spasm of anger and chagrin went over Ursula. His face set. And he bade good-bye, as if he had ceased to notice her.

They were gone. Ursula stood looking at the door for some moments. Then she put out the lights. And having done so, she sat down again in her chair, absorbed and lost. And then she began to cry, bitterly, bitterly weeping: but whether for misery or joy, she never knew.

4

Diver

The week passed away. On the Saturday it rained, a soft drizzling rain that held off at times. In one of the intervals Gudrun and Ursula set out for a walk, going towards Willey Water. The atmosphere was grey and translucent, the birds sang sharply on the young twigs, the earth would be quickening and hastening in growth. The two girls walked swiftly, gladly, because of the soft, subtle rush of morning that filled the wet haze. By the road the blackthorn was in blossom, white and wet, its tiny amber grains burning faintly in the white smoke of blossom. Purple twigs were darkly luminous in the grey air, high hedges glowed like living shadows, hovering nearer, coming into creation. The morning was full of a new creation.

When the sisters came to Willey Water, the lake lay all grey and visionary, stretching into the moist, translucent vista of trees and meadow. Fine electric activity in sound came from the dumbles below the road, the birds piping one against the other, and water mysteriously plashing, issuing from the lake.

The two girls drifted swiftly along. In front of them, at the corner of the lake, near the road, was a mossy boat-house under a walnut tree, and a little landing-stage where a boat was moored, wavering like a shadow on the still grey water, below the green, decayed poles. All was shadowy with coming summer.

Suddenly, from the boat-house, a white figure ran out, frightening in its swift sharp transit, across the old landing-stage. It launched in a white arc through the air, there was a bursting of the water, and among the smooth ripples a swimmer was making out to space, in a centre of faintly heaving motion. The whole otherworld, wet and remote, he had to himself. He could move into the pure translucency of the grey, uncreated water.

Gudrun stood by the stone wall, watching.

'How I envy him,' she said, in low, desirous tones.

'Ugh!' shivered Ursula. 'So cold!'

'Yes, but how good, how really fine, to swim out there!' The sisters stood watching the swimmer move further into the grey, moist, full space of the water, pulsing with his own small, invading motion, and arched over with mist and dim woods.

'Don't you wish it were you?' asked Gudrun, looking at Ursula.

'I do,' said Ursula. 'But I'm not sure—it's so wet.'

'No,' said Gudrun, reluctantly. She stood watching the motion on the bosom of the water, as if fascinated. He, having swum a certain distance, turned round and was swimming on his back, looking along the water at the two girls by the wall. In the faint wash of motion, they could see his ruddy face, and could feel him watching them.

'It is Gerald Crich,' said Ursula.

'I know,' replied Gudrun.

And she stood motionless gazing over the water at the face which washed up and down on the flood, as he swam steadily. From his separate element he saw them and he exulted to himself because of his own advantage, his possession of a world to himself. He was immune and perfect. He loved his own vigorous, thrusting motion, and the violent impulse of the very cold water against his limbs, buoying him up. He could see the girls watching him a way off, outside, and that pleased him. He lifted his arm from the water, in a sign to them.

'He is waving,' said Ursula.

'Yes,' replied Gudrun. They watched him. He waved again, with a strange movement of recognition across the difference.

'Like a *Nibelung*,' laughed Ursula. Gudrun said nothing, only stood still looking over the water.

Gerald suddenly turned, and was swimming away swiftly, with a side stroke. He was alone now, alone and immune in the middle of the waters, which he had all to himself. He exulted in his isolation in the new element, unquestioned and unconditioned. He was happy, thrusting with his legs and all his body, without bond or connexion anywhere, just himself in the water world.

Gudrun envied him almost painfully. Even this momentary possession of pure isolation and fluidity seemed to her so terribly desirable that she felt herself as if damned, out there on the high-road.

'God, what it is to be a man!' she cried.

'What?' exclaimed Ursula in surprise.

'The freedom, the liberty, the mobility!' cried Gudrun, strangely flushed and brilliant. 'You're a man, you want to do a thing, you do it. You haven't the *thousand* obstacles a woman has in front of her.'

Ursula wondered what was in Gudrun's mind, to occasion this outburst. She could not understand.

'What do you want to do?' she asked.

'Nothing,' cried Gudrun, in swift refutation. 'But supposing I did. Supposing I want to swim up that water. It is impossible, it is one of the impossibilities of life, for me to take my clothes off now and jump in. But isn't it *ridiculous,* doesn't it simply prevent our living!'

She was so hot, so flushed, so furious, that Ursula was puzzled.

The two sisters went on, up the road. They were passing between the trees just below Shortlands. They looked up at the long, low house, dim and glamorous in the wet morning, its cedar trees slanting before the windows. Gudrun seemed to be studying it closely.

"Don't you think it's attractive, Ursula?' asked Gudrun.

'Very,' said Ursula. 'Very peaceful and charming.'

'It has form, too—it has a period.'

'What period?'

'Oh, eighteenth century, for certain; Dorothy Wordsworth and Jane Austen, don't you think?'

Ursula laughed.

'Don't you think so?' repeated Gudrun.

'Perhaps. But I don't think the Criches fit the period. I know Gerald is putting in a private electric plant, for lighting the house, and is making all kinds of latest improvements.'

Gudrun shrugged her shoulders swiftly.

'Of course,' she said, 'that's quite inevitable.'

'Quite,' laughed Ursula. 'He is several generations of youngness at one go. They hate him for it. He takes them all by the scruff of the neck, and fairly flings them along. He'll have to die soon, when he's made every possible improvement, and there will be nothing more to improve. He's got *go,* anyhow.'

'Certainly, he's got go,' said Gudrun. 'In fact I've never seen a man that showed signs of so much. The unfortunate thing is, where does his *go* go to, what becomes of it?'

'Oh I know,' said Ursula. 'It goes in applying the latest appliances!'

'Exactly,' said Gudrun.

'You know he shot his brother?' said Ursula.

'Shot his brother?' cried Gudrun, frowning, as if in disapprobation.

'Didn't you know? Oh yes!—I thought you knew. He and his brother were playing together with a gun. He told his brother to look down the gun, and it was loaded, and blew the top of his head off. Isn't it a horrible story?'

'How fearful!' cried Gudrun. 'But it is long ago?'

'Oh yes, they were quite boys,' said Ursula. 'I think it is one of the most horrible stories I know.'

'And he of course did not know that the gun was loaded?'

'Yes. You see it was an old thing that had been lying in the stable for years. Nobody dreamed it would ever go off, and of course, no one imagined it was loaded. But isn't it dreadful, that it should happen?'

'Frightful!' cried Gudrun. 'And isn't it horrible too to think of such a thing happening to one when one was a child, and having to carry the responsibility of it all through one's life. Imagine it, two boys playing together—then this comes upon them, for no reason whatever—out of the air. Ursula, it's very frightening! Oh, it's one of the things I can't bear. Murder, that is thinkable, because there's a will behind it. But a thing like that to *happen* to one—'

'Perhaps there *was* an unconscious will behind it,' said

Ursula. 'This playing at killing has some primitive *desire* for killing in it, don't you think?'

'Desire!' said Gudrun, coldly, stiffening a little. 'I can't see that they were even playing at killing. I suppose one boy said to the other, "You look down the barrel while I pull the trigger, and see what happens." It seems to me the purest form of accident.'

'No,' said Ursula. 'I couldn't pull the trigger of the emptiest gun in the world, not if someone were looking down the barrel. One instinctively doesn't do it—one can't.'

Gudrun was silent for some moments, in sharp disagreement.

'Of course,' she said coldly. 'If one is a woman, and grown up, one's instinct prevents one. But I cannot see how that applies to a couple of boys playing together.'

Her voice was cold and angry.

'Yes,' persisted Ursula. At that moment they heard a woman's voice a few yards off say loudly:

'Oh damn the thing!' They went forward and saw Laura Crich and Hermione Roddice in the field on the other side of the hedge, and Laura Crich struggling with the gate, to get out. Ursula at once hurried up and helped to lift the gate.

'Thanks so much,' said Laura, looking up flushed and amazon-like, yet rather confused. 'It isn't right on the hinges.'

'No,' said Ursula. 'And they're so heavy.'

'Surprising!' cried Laura.

'How do you do,' sang Hermione, from out of the field, the moment she could make her voice heard. 'It's nice now. Are you going for a walk? Yes. Isn't the young green beautiful? So beautiful—quite burning. Good morning—good morning—you'll come and see me? thank you so much—next week—yes—good-bye, g-o-o-d-b-y-e.'

Gudrun and Ursula stood and watched her slowly waving her head up and down, and waving her hand slowly in dismissal, smiling a strange affected smile, making a tall queer, frightening figure, with her heavy fair hair slipping to her eyes. Then they moved off, as if they had been dismissed like inferiors. The four women parted.

As soon as they had gone far enough, Ursula said, her cheeks burning:

'I do think she's impudent.'

'Who, Hermione Roddice?' asked Gudrun. 'Why?'

'The way she treats one—impudence!'

'Why, Ursula, what did you notice that was so impudent?' asked Gudrun rather coldly.

'Her whole manner. Oh, it's impossible, the way she tries to bully one. Pure bullying. She's an impudent woman. "You'll come and see me," as if we should be falling over ourselves for the privilege.'

'I can't understand, Ursula, what you are so much put out about,' said Gudrun, in some exasperation. 'One knows those women are impudent—these free women who have emancipated themselves from the aristocracy.'

'But it is so *unnecessary*—so vulgar,' cried Ursula.

'No, I don't see it. And if I did—*pour moi elle n'existe pas*. I don't grant her the power to be impudent to me.'

'Do you think she likes you?' asked Ursula.

'Well, no, I shouldn't think she did.'

'Then why does she ask you to go to Breadalby and stay with her?'

Gudrun lifted her shoulders in a low shrug.

'After all, she's got the sense to know we're not just the ordinary run,' said Gudrun. 'Whatever she is, she's not a fool. And I'd rather have somebody I detested than the ordinary woman who keeps to her own set. Hermione Roddice does risk herself in some respects.'

Ursula pondered this for a time.

'I doubt it,' she replied. 'Really she risks nothing. I suppose we ought to admire her for knowing she *can* invite us—school teachers—and risk nothing.'

'Precisely!' said Gudrun. 'Think of the myriads of women that daren't do it. She makes the most of her privileges—that's something. I suppose, really, we should do the same, in her place.'

'No,' said Ursula. 'No. It would bore me. I couldn't spend my time playing her games. It's *infra dig*.'

The two sisters were like a pair of scissors, snipping off

everything that came athwart them; or like a knife and a whetstone, the one sharpened against the other.

'Of course,' cried Ursula suddenly, 'she ought to thank her stars if we will go and see her. You are perfectly beautiful, a thousand times more beautiful than ever she is or was, and to my thinking, a thousand times more beautifully dressed, for she never looks fresh and natural, like a flower, always old, thought-out; and we are more intelligent than most people.'

'Undoubtedly!' said Gudrun.

'And it ought to be admitted, simply,' said Ursula.

'Certainly it ought,' said Gudrun. 'But you'll find that the really chic thing is to be so absolutely ordinary, so perfectly commonplace and like the person in the street, that you really are a masterpiece of humanity, not the person in the street actually, but the artistic creation of her—'

'How awful!' cried Ursula.

'Yes, Ursula, it *is* awful, in most respects. You daren't be anything that isn't amazingly *à terre,* so much *à terre* that it is the artistic creation of ordinariness.'

'It's very dull to create oneself into nothing better,' laughed Ursula.

'Very dull!' retorted Gudrun. 'Really, Ursula, it *is* dull, that's just the word. One longs to be high-flown, and make speeches like Corneille, after it.'

Gudrun was becoming flushed and excited over her own cleverness.

'Strut,' said Ursula. 'One wants to strut, to be a swan among geese.'

'Exactly,' cried Gudrun, 'a swan among geese.'

'They are all so busy playing the ugly duckling,' cried Ursula, with mocking laughter. 'And I don't feel a bit like a humble and pathetic ugly duckling. I do feel like a swan among geese—I can't help it. They make one feel so. And I don't care what *they* think of me. *Je m'en fiche.*'

Gudrun looked up at Ursula with a queer, uncertain envy and dislike.

'Of course, the only thing to do is to despise them all— just all,' she said.

The sisters went home again, to read and talk and work,

and wait for Monday, for school. Ursula often wondered what else she waited for, besides the beginning and end of the school week, and the beginning and end of the holidays. This was a whole life! Sometimes she had periods of tight horror, when it seemed to her that her life would pass away and be gone, without having been more than this. But she never really accepted it. Her spirit was active, her life like a shoot that is growing steadily, but which has not yet come above ground.

5

In the Train

One day at this time Birkin was called to London. He was not very fixed in his abode. He had rooms in Nottingham, because his work lay chiefly in that town. But often he was in London, or in Oxford. He moved about a great deal, his life seemed uncertain, without any definite rhythm, any organic meaning.

On the platform of the railway station he saw Gerald Crich, reading a newspaper, and evidently waiting for the train. Birkin stood some distance off, among the people. It was against his instinct to approach anybody.

From time to time, in a manner characteristic of him, Gerald lifted his head and looked round. Even though he was reading the newspaper closely, he must keep a watchful eye on his external surroundings. There seemed to be a dual consciousness running in him. He was thinking vigorously of something he read in the newspaper, and at the same time his eye ran over the surfaces of the life round him, and he missed nothing. Birkin, who was watching him, was irritated by his duality. He noticed too, that Gerald seemed always to be at bay against everybody, in spite of his queer, genial, social manner when roused.

Now Birkin started violently at seeing this genial look flash on to Gerald's face, at seeing Gerald approaching with hand outstretched.

'Hallo, Rupert, where are you going?'

'London. So are you, I suppose.'

'Yes—'

Gerald's eyes went over Birkin's face in curiosity.

'We'll travel together if you like,' he said.

'Don't you usually go first?' asked Birkin.

'I can't stand the crowd,' replied Gerald. 'But third'll be all right. There's a restaurant car, we can have some tea.'

The two men looked at the station clock, having nothing further to say.

'What were you reading in the paper?' Birkin asked.

Gerald looked at him quickly.

'Isn't it funny, what they *do* put in the newspapers,' he said. 'Here are two leaders—' he held out his *Daily Telegraph,* 'full of the ordinary newspaper cant—' he scanned the columns down—'and then there's this little—I dunno what you'd call it, essay, almost—appearing with the leaders, and saying there must arise a man who will give new values to things, give us new truths, a new attitude to life, or else we shall be a crumbling nothingness in a few years, a country in ruin—'

'I suppose that's a bit of newspaper cant, as well,' said Birkin.

'It sounds as if the man meant it, and quite genuinely,' said Gerald.

'Give it to me,' said Birkin, holding out his hand for the paper.

The train came, and they went on board, sitting on either side a little table, by the window, in the restaurant car. Birkin glanced over his paper, then looked up at Gerald, who was waiting for him.

'I believe the man means it,' he said, 'as far as he means anything.'

'And do you think it's true? Do you think we really want a new gospel?' asked Gerald.

Birkin shrugged his shoulders.

'I think the people who say they want a new religion are the last to accept anything new. They want novelty right enough. But to stare straight at this life that we've brought upon ourselves and rejected, absolutely smash up the old idols of ourselves, that we sh'll never do. You've got very badly to want to get rid of the old before anything new will appear—even in the self.'

Gerald watched him closely.

'You think we ought to break up this life, just start and let fly?' he asked.

'This life. Yes I do. We've got to bust it completely, or shrivel inside it, as in a tight skin. For it won't expand any more.'

There was a queer little smile in Gerald's eyes, a look of amusement, calm and curious.

'And how do you propose to begin? I suppose you mean, reform the whole order of society?' he asked.

Birkin had a slight, tense frown between the brows. He too was impatient of the conversation.

'I don't propose at all,' he replied. 'When we really want to go for something better, we shall smash the old. Until then, any sort of proposal, or making proposals, is no more than a tiresome game for self-important people.'

The little smile began to die out of Gerald's eyes, and he said, looking with a cool stare at Birkin:

'So you really think things are very bad?'

'Completely bad.'

The smile appeared again.

'In what way?'

'Every way,' said Birkin. 'We are such dreary liars. Our one idea is to lie to ourselves. We have an ideal of a perfect world, clean and straight and sufficient. So we cover the earth with foulness; life is a blotch of labour, like insects scurrying in filth, so that your collier can have a pianoforte in his parlour, and you can have a butler and a motor-car in your up-to-date house, and as a nation we can sport the Ritz, or the Empire, Gaby Deslys and the Sunday newspapers. It is very dreary.'

Gerald took a little time to re-adjust himself after this tirade.

'Would you have us live without houses—return to nature?' he asked.

'I would have nothing at all. People only do what they want to do—and what they are capable of doing. If they were capable of anything else, there would be something else.'

Again Gerald pondered. He was not going to take offence at Birkin.

'Don't you think the collier's *pianoforte,* as you call it, is a symbol for something very real, a real desire for something higher, in the collier's life?'

'Higher!' cried Birkin. 'Yes. Amazing heights of upright grandeur. It makes him so much higher in his neighbouring collier's eyes. He sees himself reflected in the neighbouring opinion, like in a Brocken mist, several feet taller on the strength of the pianoforte, and he is satisfied. He lives for the sake of that Brocken spectre, the reflection of himself in the human opinion. You do the same. If you are of high importance to humanity you are of high importance to yourself. That is why you work so hard at the mines. If you can produce coal to cook five thousand dinners a day, you are five thousand times more important than if you cooked only your own dinner.'

'I suppose I am,' laughed Gerald.

'Can't you see,' said Birkin, 'that to help my neighbour to eat is no more than eating myself. "I eat, thou eatest, he eats, we eat, you eat, they eat"—and what then? Why should every man decline the whole verb. First person singular is enough for me.'

'You've got to start with material things,' said Gerald. Which statement Birkin ignored.

'And we've got to live for *something,* we're not just cattle that can graze and have done with it,' said Gerald.

'Tell me,' said Birkin. 'What do you live for?'

Gerald's face went baffled.

'What do I live for?' he repeated. 'I suppose I live to work, to produce something, in so far as I am a purposive being. Apart from that, I live because I am living.'

'And what's your work? Getting so many more thousands of tons of coal out of the earth every day. And when we've got all the coal we want, and all the plush furniture, and pianofortes, and the rabbits are all stewed and eaten, and we're all warm and our bellies are filled and we're listening to the young lady performing on the pianoforte—what then? What then, when you've made a real fair start with your material things?'

Gerald sat laughing at the words and the mocking humour of the other man. But he was cogitating too.

'We haven't got there yet,' he replied. 'A good many people are still waiting for the rabbit and the fire to cook it.'

'So while you get the coal I must chase the rabbit?' said Birkin, mocking at Gerald.

'Something like that,' said Gerald.

Birkin watched him narrowly. He saw the perfect good-humoured callousness, even strange, glistening malice, in Gerald, glistening through the plausible ethics of productivity.

'Gerald,' he said, 'I rather hate you.'

'I know you do,' said Gerald. 'Why do you?'

Birkin mused inscrutably for some minutes.

'I should like to know if you are conscious of hating me,' he said at last. 'Do you ever consciously detest me—hate me with mystic hate? There are odd moments when I hate you starrily.'

Gerald was rather taken aback, even a little disconcerted. He did not quite know what to say.

'I may, of course, hate you sometimes,' he said. 'But I'm not aware of it—never acutely aware of it, that is.'

'So much the worse,' said Birkin.

Gerald watched him with curious eyes. He could not quite make him out.

'So much the worse is it?' he repeated.

There was a silence between the two men for some time, as the train ran on. In Birkin's face was a little irritable tension, a sharp knitting of the brows, keen and difficult. Gerald watched him warily, carefully, rather calculatingly, for he could not decide what he was after.

Suddenly Birkin's eyes looked straight and overpowering into those of the other man.

'What do you think is the aim and object of your life, Gerald?' he asked.

Again Gerald was taken aback. He could not think what his friend was getting at. Was he poking fun, or not?

'At this moment, I couldn't say off-hand,' he replied, with faintly ironic humour.

'Do you think to live is the be-all and the end-all of life?' Birkin asked, with direct, attentive seriousness.

'Of my own life?' said Gerald.

'Yes.'

There was a really puzzled pause.

'I can't say,' said Gerald. 'It hasn't been, so far.'

'What has your life been, so far?'

'Oh—finding out things for myself—and getting experiences—and making things *go*.'

Birkin knitted his brows like sharply moulded steel.

'I find,' he said, 'that one needs some one *really* pure single activity—I should call love a single pure activity. But I *don't* really love anybody—not now.'

'Have you ever really loved anybody?' asked Gerald.

'Yes and no,' replied Birkin.

'Not finally?' said Gerald.

'Finally—finally—no,' said Birkin.

'Nor I,' said Gerald.

'And do you want to?' said Birkin.

Gerald looked with a long, twinkling, almost sardonic look into the eyes of the other man.

'I don't know,' he said.

'I do—I want to love,' said Birkin.

'You do?'

'Yes. I want the finality of love.'

'The finality of love,' repeated Gerald. And he waited for a moment.

'Just one woman?' he added. The evening light, flooding yellow along the fields, lit up Birkin's face with a tense, abstract steadfastness. Gerald still could not make it out.

'Yes, one woman,' said Birkin.

But to Gerald it sounded as if he were insistent rather than confident.

'I don't believe a woman, and nothing but a woman, will ever make my life,' said Gerald.

'Not the centre and core of it—the love between you and a woman?' asked Birkin.

Gerald's eyes narrowed with a queer dangerous smile as he watched the other man.

'I never quite feel it that way,' he said.

'You don't? Then wherein does life centre, for you?'

'I don't know—that's what I want somebody to tell me.

As far as I can make out, it doesn't centre at all. It is artificially held *together* by the social mechanism.'

Birkin pondered as if he would crack something.

'I know,' he said, 'it just doesn't centre. The old ideals are dead as nails—nothing there. It seems to me there remains only this perfect union with a woman—sort of ultimate marriage—and there isn't anything else.'

'And you mean if there isn't the woman, there's nothing?' said Gerald.

'Pretty well that—seeing there's no God.'

'Then we're hard to put to it,' said Gerald. And he turned to look out of the window at the flying, golden landscape.

Birkin could not help seeing how beautiful and soldierly his face was, with a certain courage to be indifferent.

'You think it's heavy odds against us?' said Birkin.

'If we've got to make our life up out of a woman, one woman, woman only, yes, I do,' said Gerald. 'I don't believe I shall ever make up *my* life, at that rate.'

Birkin watched him almost angrily.

'You are a born unbeliever,' he said.

'I only feel what I feel,' said Gerald. And he looked again at Birkin almost sardonically, with his blue, manly, sharplighted eyes. Birkin's eyes were at the moment full of anger. But swiftly they became troubled, doubtful, then full of a warm, rich affectionateness and laughter.

'It troubles me very much, Gerald,' he said, wrinkling his brows.

'I can see it does,' said Gerald, uncovering his mouth in a manly, quick, soldierly laugh.

Gerald was held unconsciously by the other man. He wanted to be near him, he wanted to be within his sphere of influence. There was something very congenial to him in Birkin. But yet, beyond this, he did not take much notice. He felt that he, himself, Gerald, had harder and more durable truths than any the other man knew. He felt himself older, more knowing. It was the quick-changing warmth and vitality and brilliant warm utterance he loved in his friend. It was the rich play of words and quick interchange of feelings he enjoyed. The real content of the words he never really considered: he himself knew better.

Birkin knew this. He knew that Gerald wanted to be *fond* of him without taking him seriously. And this made him go hard and cold. As the train ran on, he sat looking at the land, and Gerald fell away, became as nothing to him.

Birkin looked at the land, at the evening, and was thinking: 'Well, if mankind is destroyed, if our race is destroyed like Sodom, and there is this beautiful evening with the luminous land and trees, I am satisfied. That which informs it all is there, and can never be lost. After all, what is mankind but just one expression of the incomprehensible. And if mankind passes away, it will only mean that this particular expression is completed and done. That which is expressed, and that which is to be expressed, cannot be diminished. There it is, in the shining evening. Let mankind pass away— time it did. The creative utterances will not cease, they will only be there. Humanity doesn't embody the utterance of the incomprehensible any more. Humanity is a dead letter. There will be a new embodiment, in a new way. Let humanity disappear as quick as possible.'

Gerald interrupted him by asking:

'Where are you staying in London?'

Birkin looked up.

'With a man in Soho. I pay part of the rent of a house, and stop there when I like.'

'Good idea—have a place more or less your own,' said Gerald.

'Yes. But I don't care for it much. I'm tired of the people I am bound to find there.'

'What kind of people?'

'Art—music—London Bohemia—the most pettifogging calculating Bohemia that ever reckoned its pennies. But there are a few decent people, decent in some respects. They are really very thorough rejecters of the world—perhaps they live only in the gesture of rejection and negation—but negatively something, at any rate.'

'What are they?—painters, musicians?'

'Painters, musicians, writers—hangers-on, models, advanced young people, anybody who is openly at outs with the conventions, and belongs to nowhere particularly. They

are often young fellows down from the University, and girls
who are living their own lives, as they say.'

'All loose?' said Gerald.

Birkin could see his curiosity roused.

'In one way. Most bound, in another. For all their shock-
ingness, all on one note.'

He looked at Gerald, and saw how his blue eyes were lit
up with a little flame of curious desire. He saw too how
good-looking he was. Gerald was attractive, his blood
seemed fluid and electric. His blue eyes burned with a keen,
yet cold light, there was a certain beauty, a beautiful passiv-
ity in all his body, his moulding.

'We might see something of each other—I am in London
for two or three days,' said Gerald.

'Yes,' said Birkin, 'I don't want to go to the theatre, or the
music-hall—you'd better come round and see what you can
make of Halliday and his crowd.'

'Thanks—I should like to,' laughed Gerald. 'What are
you doing tonight?'

'I promised to meet Halliday at the Pompadour. It's a bad
place, but there is nowhere else.'

'Where is it?' asked Gerald.

'Piccadilly Circus.'

'Oh yes—well, shall I come round there?'

'By all means, it might amuse you.'

The evening was falling. They had passed Bedford. Birkin
watched the country, and was filled with a sort of hopelessness. He always felt this, on approaching London. His dislike of mankind, of the mass of mankind, amounted almost
to an illness.

' "Where the quiet coloured end of evening smiles
        Miles and miles—" '

he was murmuring to himself, like a man condemned to
death. Gerald, who was very subtly alert, wary in all his
senses, leaned forward and asked smilingly:

'What were you saying?' Birkin glanced at him, laughed,
and repeated:

' "Where the quiet coloured end of evening smiles,
        Miles and miles,
Over pastures where the something something sheep
        Half asleep—" '

Gerald also looked now at the country. And Birkin, who, for some reason, was now tired and dispirited, said to him:

'I always feel doomed when the train is running into London. I feel such a despair, so hopeless, as if it were the end of the world.'

'Really!' said Gerald. 'And does the end of the world frighten you?'

Birkin lifted his shoulders in a slow shrug.

'I don't know,' he said. 'It does while it hangs imminent and doesn't fall. But people give me a bad feeling—very bad.'

There was a roused glad smile in Gerald's eyes.

'Do they?' he said. And he watched the other man critically.

In a few minutes the train was running through the disgrace of outspread London. Everybody in the carriage was on the alert, waiting to escape. At last they were under the huge arch of the station, in the tremendous shadow of the town. Birkin shut himself together—he was in now.

The two men went together in a taxi-cab.

'Don't you feel like one of the damned?' asked Birkin, as they sat in a little, swiftly-running enclosure, and watched the hideous great street.

'No,' laughed Gerald.

'It is real death,' said Birkin.

6

Crème de Menthe

They met again in the café several hours later. Gerald went through the push doors into the large, lofty room where the faces and heads of the drinkers showed dimly through the haze of smoke, reflected more dimly, and repeated *ad infinitum* in the great mirrors on the walls, so that one seemed to enter a vague, dim world of shadowy drinkers humming within an atmosphere of blue tobacco smoke. There was, however, the red plush of the seats to give substance within the bubble of pleasure.

Gerald moved in his slow, observant, glistening-attentive motion down between the tables and the people whose shadowy faces looked up as he passed. He seemed to be entering in some strange element, passing into an illuminated new region, among a host of licentious souls. He was pleased, and entertained. He looked over all the dim, evanescent, strangely illuminated faces that bent across the tables. Then he saw Birkin rise and signal to him.

At Birkin's table was a girl with bobbed, blonde hair cut short in the artist fashion, hanging straight and curving slightly inwards to her ears. She was small and delicately made, with fair colouring and large, innocent, blue eyes. There was a delicacy, almost a floweriness in all her form, and at the same time a certain attractive grossness of spirit, that made a little spark leap instantly alight in Gerald's eyes.

Birkin, who looked muted, unreal, his presence left out, introduced her as Miss Darrington. She gave her hand with a sudden, unwilling movement, looking all the while at Gerald with a dark, exposed stare. A glow came over him as he sat down.

The waiter appeared. Gerald glanced at the glasses of the

other two. Birkin was drinking something green, Miss Darrington had a small liqueur glass that was empty save for a tiny drop.

'Won't you have some more——?'

'Brandy,' she said, sipping her last drop and putting down the glass. The waiter disappeared.

'No,' she said to Birkin. 'He doesn't know I'm back. He'll be tewwified when he sees me here.'

She spoke her r's like w's, lisping with a slightly babyish pronunciation which was at once affected and true to her character. Her voice was dull and toneless.

'Where is he then?' asked Birkin.

'He's doing a private show at Lady Snellgrove's,' said the girl. 'Warens is there too.'

There was a pause.

'Well, then,' said Birkin, in a dispassionate protective manner, 'what do you intend to do?'

The girl paused sullenly. She hated the question.

'I don't intend to do anything,' she replied. 'I shall look for some sittings tomorrow.'

'Who shall you go to?' asked Birkin.

'I shall go to Bentley's first. But I believe he's angwy with me for running away.'

'That is from the Madonna?'

'Yes. And then if he doesn't want me, I know I can get work with Carmarthen.'

'Carmarthen?'

'Frederick Carmarthen—he does photographs.'

'Chiffon and shoulders—'

'Yes. But he's awfully decent.' There was a pause.

'And what are you going to do about Julius?' he asked.

'Nothing,' she said. 'I shall just ignore him.'

'You've done with him altogether?' But she turned aside her face sullenly, and did not answer the question.

Another young man came hurrying up to the table.

'Hallo, Birkin! Hallo, Minette, when did you come back?' he said eagerly.

'Today.'

'Does Halliday know?'

'I don't know. I don't care either.'

'Ha-ha! The wind still sits in that quarter, does it? Do you mind if I come over to this table?'

'I'm talking to Wupert, do you mind?' she replied, coolly and yet appealingly, like a child.

'Open confession—good for the soul, eh?' said the young man. 'Well, so long.'

And giving a sharp look at Birkin and at Gerald, the young man moved off, with a swing of his coat skirts.

All this time Gerald had been completely ignored. And yet he felt that the girl was physically aware of his proximity. He waited, listened, and tried to piece together the conversation.

'Are you staying at the house?' the girl asked, of Birkin.

'For three days,' replied Birkin. 'And you?'

'I don't know yet. I can always go to Bertha's.' There was a silence.

Suddenly the girl turned to Gerald, and said, in a rather formal, polite voice, with the distant manner of a woman who accepts her position as a social inferior, yet assumes intimate *camaraderie* with the male she addresses:

'Do you know London well?'

'I can hardly say,' he laughed. 'I've been up a good many times, but I was never in this place before.'

'You're not an artist, then?' she said, in a tone that placed him an outsider.

'No,' he replied.

'He's a soldier, and an explorer, and a Napoleon of industry,' said Birkin, giving Gerald his credentials for Bohemia.

'Are you a soldier?' asked the girl, with a cold yet lively curiosity.

'No, I resigned my commission,' said Gerald, 'some years ago.'

'He was in the last war,' said Birkin.

'Were you really?' said the girl.

'And then he explored the Amazon,' said Birkin, 'and now he is ruling over coal-mines.'

The girl looked at Gerald with steady, calm curiosity. He laughed, hearing himself described. He felt proud too, full of male strength. His blue, keen eyes were lit up with laughter, his ruddy face, with its sharp fair hair, was full of satisfaction, and glowing with life. He piqued her.

'How long are you staying?' she asked him.

'A day or two,' he replied. 'But there is no particular hurry.'

Still she stared into his face with that slow, full gaze which was so curious and so exciting to him. He was acutely and delightfully conscious of himself, of his own attractiveness. He felt full of strength, able to give off a sort of electric power. And he was aware of her blue, exposed-looking eyes upon him. She had beautiful eyes, flower-like, fully opened, naked in their looking at him. And on them there seemed to float a curious iridescence, a sort of film of disintegration, and sullenness, like oil on water. She wore no hat in the heated café, her loose, simple jumper was strung on a string round her neck. But it was made of rich yellow *crêpe-de-chine*, that hung heavily and softly from her young throat and her slender wrists. Her appearance was simple and complete, really beautiful, because of her regularity and form, her shiny yellow hair falling curved and level on either side of her head, her straight, small, softened features, provoking in the slight fullness of their curves, her slender neck and the simple, rich-coloured smock hanging on her slender shoulders. She was very still, almost null, in her manner, apart and watchful.

She appealed to Gerald strongly. He felt an awful, enjoyable power over her, an instinctive cherishing very near to cruelty. For she was a victim. He felt that she was in his power, and he was generous. The electricity was turgid and voluptuously rich, in his limbs. He would be able to destroy her utterly in the strength of his discharge. But she was waiting in her separation, given.

They talked banalities for some time. Suddenly Birkin said:

'There's Julius!' and he half rose to his feet, motioning to the newcomer. The girl, with a curious, almost evil motion, looked round over her shoulder without moving her body. Gerald watched her fair, close hair swing over her ears. He felt her watching intensely the man who was approaching, so he looked too. He saw a swarthy, slender young man with rather long, solid black hair hanging from under his black hat, moving cumbrously down the room, his face lit up with a smile at once naïve and warm, and vapid. He approached towards Birkin with a haste of welcome.

It was not till he was quite close that he perceived the girl. He recoiled, went green, and said, in a high squealing voice:

'Minette, what are *you* doing here?'

The café looked up like animals when they hear a cry. Halliday hung motionless, an almost imbecile smile flickering palely on his face. The girl only stared at him with an ice-cold look in which flared an unfathomable hell of knowledge, and a certain impotence. She was limited by him.

'Why have you come back?' repeated Halliday, in the same high, hysterical voice. 'I told you not to come back.'

The girl did not answer, only stared in the same ice-blank, heavy fashion, straight at him, as he stood recoiled, as if for safety, against the next table.

'You know you wanted her to come back—come and sit down,' said Birkin to him.

'No, I didn't want her to come back, and I told her not to come back. What have you come for, Minette?'

'For nothing from *you*,' she said in a heavy voice of resentment.

'Then why have you come back at *all*?' cried Halliday, his voice rising to a kind of squeal.

'She comes as she likes,' said Birkin. 'Are you going to sit down, or are you not?'

'No, I won't sit down with Minette,' cried Halliday.

'I won't hurt you, you needn't be afraid,' she said to him, very curtly, and yet with a sort of protectiveness towards him, in her voice.

Halliday came and sat at the table, putting his hand on his heart, and crying:

'Oh, it's given me such a turn! Minette, I wish you wouldn't do these thing. Why did you come back?'

'Not for anything from you,' she repeated.

'You've said that before,' he cried in a high voice.

She turned completely away from him, to Gerald Crich, whose eyes were shining with a subtle amusement.

'Were you ever vewy much afwaid of the savages?' she asked in her calm, dull, childish voice.

'No—never very much afraid. On the whole they're harmless—they're not born yet, you can't feel really afraid of them. You know you can manage them.'

'Do you weally? Aren't they very fierce?'

'Not very. There aren't many fierce things, as a matter of fact. There aren't many things, neither people nor animals, that have it in them to be really dangerous.'

'Except in herds,' interrupted Birkin.

'Aren't there really?' she said. 'Oh, I thought savages were all so dangerous, they'd have your life before you could look around.'

'Did you?' he laughed. 'They are over-rated, savages. They're too much like other people, not exciting, after the first acquaintance.'

'Oh, it's not so very wonderfully brave then, to be an explorer?'

'No. It's more a question of hardships than of terrors.'

'Oh! And weren't you ever afraid?'

'In my life? I don't know. Yes, I'm afraid of some things—of being shut up, locked up anywere—or being fastened. I'm afraid of being bound hand and foot.'

She looked at him steadily with her naïve eyes, that rested on him and roused him so deeply, that it left his upper self quite calm. It was rather delicious, to feel her drawing his self-revelations from him, as from the very innermost dark marrow of his body. She wanted to know. And her eyes seemed to be looking through into his naked organism. He felt, she was compelled to him, she was fated to come into contact with him, must have the seeing him and knowing him. And this roused a curious exultance. Also he felt, she must relinquish herself into his hands, and be subject to him. She was so profane, slave-like, watching him, absorbed by him. It was not that she was interested in what he said; she was absorbed by his self-revelation, by *him*, she wanted the secret of him, the experience of his male being.

Gerald's face was lit up with an uncanny smile, full of light and rousedness, yet unconscious. He sat with his arms on the table, his sun-browned, rather sinister hands, that were animal and yet very shapely and attractive, pushed forward towards her. And they fascinated her. And she knew, she watched her own fascination.

Other men had come to the table, to talk with Birkin and Halliday. Gerald said in a low voice, apart, to Minette:

'Where have you come back from?'

'From the country,' replied Minette, in a very low, yet fully resonant voice. Her face closed hard. Continually she glanced at Halliday, and then a flare came over her eyes. The heavy, fair young man ignored her completely; he was really afraid of her. For some moments she would be unaware of Gerald. He had not conquered her yet.

'And what has Halliday to do with it?' he asked, his voice still muted.

She would not answer for some seconds. Then she said, unwillingly:

'He made me go and live with him, and now he wants to throw me over. And yet he won't let me go to anybody else. He wants me to live hidden in the country. And then he says I persecute him, that he can't get rid of me.'

'Doesn't know his own mind,' said Gerald.

'He hasn't any mind, so he can't know it,' she said. 'He waits for what somebody tells him to do. He never does anything he wants to do himself—because he doesn't know what he wants. He's a perfect baby.'

Gerald looked at Halliday for some moments, watching the soft, rather degenerate face of the young man. Its very softness was an attraction; it was a soft, warm nature, into which one might plunge with gratification.

'But he has no hold over you, has he?' Gerald asked.

'You see he *made* me go and live with him, when I didn't want to,' she replied. 'He came and cried to me, tears, you never saw so many, saying *he couldn't* bear it unless I went back to him. And he wouldn't go away, he would have stayed for ever. He made me go back. Then every time he behaves in this fashion. And now I'm going to have a baby, he wants to give me a hundred pounds and send me into the country, so that he would never see me nor hear of me again. But I'm not going to do it, after—'

A queer look came over Gerald's face.

'Are you going to have a child?' he asked incredulous. It

seemed, to look at her, impossible, she was so young and so far in spirit from any childbearing.

She looked full into his face, and her blue, inchoate eyes had now a furtive look, and a look of a knowledge of evil, dark and indomitable. A flame ran secretly to his heart.

'Yes,' she said. 'Isn't it beastly?'

'Don't you want it?' he asked.

'I don't,' she replied emphatically.

'But—' he said, 'how long have you known?'

'Ten weeks,' she said.

All the time she kept her eyes full upon him. He remained silent, thinking. Then, switching off and becoming cold, he asked, in a voice full of considerate kindness:

'Is there anything we can eat here? Is there anything you would like?'

'Yes,' she said, 'I should adore some oysters.'

'All right,' he said. 'We'll have oysters.' And he beckoned to the waiter.

Halliday took no notice, until the little plate was set before her. Then suddenly he cried:

'Minette, you can't eat oysters when you're drinking brandy.'

'What has it got to do with you?' she asked.

'Nothing, nothing,' he cried. 'But you can't eat oysters when you're drinking brandy.'

'I'm not drinking brandy,' she replied, and she sprinkled the last drops of her liqueur over his face. He gave an odd squeal. She sat looking at him, as if indifferent.

'Minette, why do you do that?' he cried in panic. He gave Gerald the impression that he was terrified of her, and that he loved his terror. He seemed to relish his own horror and hatred of her, turn it over and extract every flavour from it, in real panic. Gerald thought him a strange fool, and yet piquant.

'But Minette,' said another man, in a very small, quick Eton voice, 'you promised not to hurt him.'

'I haven't hurt him,' she answered.

'What will you drink?' the young man asked. He was dark, and smooth-skinned, and full of a stealthy vigour.

'I don't like porter, Maxim,' she replied.

'You must ask for champagne,' came the whispering gentlemanly voice of the other.

Gerald suddenly realized that this was a hint to him.

'Shall we have champagne?' he asked, laughing.

'Yes, please, dwy,' she lisped childishly.

Gerald watched her eating the oysters. She was delicate and finicking in her eating, her fingers were fine and seemed very sensitive in the tips, so she put her food apart with fine, small motions, she ate carefully, delicately. It pleased him very much to see her, and it irritated Birkin. They were all drinking champagne. Maxim, the prim young Russian with the smooth, warm-coloured face and black, oiled hair, was the only one who seemed to be perfectly calm and sober. Birkin was white and abstract, unnatural, Gerald was smiling with a constant bright, amused, cold light in his eyes, leaning a little protectively towards Minette, who was very handsome, and soft, unfolded like some fair ice-flower in dreadful flowering nakedness, vainglorious now, flushed with wine and with the excitement of men. Halliday looked foolish. One glass of wine was enough to make him drunk and giggling. Yet there was always a pleasant, warm naïveté about him, that made him attractive.

'I'm not afwaid of anything except black-beetles,' said Minette, looking up suddenly and staring with her round eyes, on which there seemed an unseeing film of flame, fully upon Gerald. He laughed dangerously, from the blood. Her childish speech caressed his nerves, and her burning, filmed eyes, turned now full upon him, oblivious of all her antecedents, gave him a sort of licence.

'I'm not,' she protested. 'I'm not afraid of other things. But black-beetles—ugh!' She shuddered convulsively, as if the very thought were too much to bear.

'Do you mean,' said Gerald, with the punctiliousness of a man who has been drinking, 'that you are afraid of the sight of a black-beetle, or you are afraid of a black-beetle biting you, or doing you some harm?'

'Do they bite?' cried the girl.

'How perfectly loathsome!' exclaimed Halliday.

'I don't know,' replied Gerald, looking round the table.

'Do black-beetles bite? But that isn't the point. Are you afraid of their biting, or is it a metaphysical antipathy?'

The girl was looking full upon him all the time with inchoate eyes.

'Oh, I think they're beastly, they're horrid,' she cried. 'If I see one, it gives me the creeps all over. If one were to crawl on me, I'm *sure* I should die—I'm sure I should.'

'I hope not,' whispered the young Russian.

'I'm sure I should, Maxim,' she asseverated.

'Then one won't crawl on you,' said Gerald, smiling and knowing. In some strange way he understood her.

'It's metaphysical, as Gerald says,' Birkin stated.

There was a little pause of uneasiness.

'And are you afraid of nothing else, Minette?' asked the young Russian, in his quick, hushed, elegant manner.

'Not weally,' she said. 'I am afwaid of some things, but not weally the same. I'm not afwaid of *blood*.'

'Not afwaid of blood!' exclaimed a young man with a thick, pale, jeering face, who had just come to the table and was drinking whisky.

Minette turned on him a sulky look of dislike, low and ugly.

'Aren't you really afraid of blud?' the other persisted, a sneer all over his face.

'No, I'm not,' she retorted.

'Why, have you ever seen blood, except in a dentist's spittoon?' jeered the young man.

'I wasn't speaking to you,' she replied rather superbly.

'You can answer me, can't you?' he said.

For reply, she suddenly jabbed a knife across his thick, pale hand. He started up with a vulgar curse.

'Shows what you are,' said Minette in contempt.

'Curse you,' said the young man, standing by the table and looking down at her with acrid malevolence.

'Stop that,' said Gerald, in quick, instinctive command.

The young man stood looking down at her with sardonic contempt, a cowed, self-conscious look on his thick, pale face. The blood began to flow from his hand.

'Oh, how horrible, take it away!' squealed Halliday, turning green and averting his face.

'D'you feel ill?' asked the sardonic young man, in some

concern. 'Do you feel ill, Julius? Garn, it's nothing, man, don't give her the pleasure of letting her think she's performed a feat—don't give her the satisfaction, man—it's just what she wants.'

'Oh!' squealed Halliday.

'He's going to cat, Maxim,' said Minette warningly. The suave young Russian rose and took Halliday by the arm, leading him away. Birkin, white and diminished, looked on as if he were displeased. The wounded, sardonic young man moved away, ignoring his bleeding hand in the most conspicuous fashion.

'He's an awful coward, really,' said Minette to Gerald. 'He's got such an influence over Julius.'

'Who is he?' asked Gerald.

'He's a Jew, really. I can't bear him.'

'Well, he's quite unimportant. But what's wrong with Halliday?'

'Julius's the most awful coward you've ever seen,' she cried. 'He always faints if I lift a knife—he's tewwified of me.'

'H'm!' said Gerald.

'They're all afwaid of me,' she said. 'Only the Jew thinks he's going to show his courage. But he's the biggest coward of them all, really, because he's afwaid what people will think about him—and Julius doesn't care about that.'

'They've a lot of valour between them,' said Gerald good-humouredly.

Minette looked at him with a slow, slow smile. She was very handsome, flushed, and confident in dreadful knowledge. Two little points of light glinted on Gerald's eyes.

'Why do they call you Minette? Because you're like a cat?' he asked her.

'I expect so,' she said.

The smile grew more intense on his face.

'You are, rather;—or a young, female panther.'

'Oh God, Gerald!' said Birkin, in some disgust.

They both looked uneasily at Birkin.

'You're silent tonight, Wupert,' she said to him, with a slight insolence, being safe with the other man.

Halliday was coming back, looking forlorn and sick.

'Minette,' he said, 'I wish you wouldn't do these things—Oh!' He sank in his chair with a groan.

'You'd better go home,' she said to him.

'I *will* go home,' he said. 'But won't you all come along. Won't you come round to the flat?' he said to Gerald. 'I should be so glad if you would. Do—that'll be splendid. I say!' He looked round for a waiter. 'Get me a taxi.' Then he groaned again. 'Oh, I do feel—perfectly ghastly! Minette, you see what you do to me.'

'Then why are you such an idiot?' she said with sullen calm.

'But I'm not an idiot! Oh, how awful! Do come, everybody, it will be *so* splendid. Minette, you are coming. What? Oh, but you *must* come, yes, you must. What? Oh, my dear girl, don't make a fuss now, I feel perfectly—Oh, it's so ghastly—Ho!—er! Oh!'

'You know you can't drink,' she said to him, coldly.

'I tell you it isn't drink—it's your disgusting behaviour, Minette, it's nothing else. Oh, how awful! Libidnikov, do let us go.'

'He's only drunk one glass—only one glass,' came the rapid, hushed voice of the young Russian.

They all moved off to the door. The girl kept near to Gerald, and seemed to be at one in her motion with him. He was aware of this, and filled with demon-satisfaction that his motion held good for two. He held her in the hollow of his will, and she was soft, secret, invisible in her stirring there.

They crowded five of them into the taxi-cab. Halliday lurched in first, and dropped into his seat against the other window. Then Minette took her place, and Gerald sat next to her. They heard the young Russian giving orders to the driver, then they were all seated in the dark, crowded close together, Halliday groaning and leaning out of the window. They felt the swift, muffled motion of the car.

Minette sat near to Gerald, and she seemed to become soft, subtly to infuse herself into his bones, as if she were passing into him in a black, electric flow. Her being suffused into his veins like a magnetic darkness, and concentrated at the base of his spine like a fearful source of power. Meanwhile her voice sounded out reedy and nonchalant, as she talked indifferently with Birkin and with Maxim. Between her and Gerald was this silence and this black, electric comprehension in the darkness. Then she found his hand, and grasped it in her own firm, small clasp. It was so utterly dark, and yet such a naked statement, that rapid vibrations ran through his blood and over his brain, he was no longer responsible. Still her voice rang on like a bell, tinged with a tone of mockery. And as she swung her head, her fine mane of hair just swept his face, and all his nerves were on fire, as with a subtle friction of electricity. But the great centre of his force held steady, a magnificent pride to him, at the base of his spine.

They arrived at a street of quiet houses, went up a garden path, and presently a door was being opened for them by a dark-skinned servant. Gerald looked in surprise, wondering if he were a gentleman, one of the Orientals down from Oxford, perhaps. But no, he was the man-servant.

'Make tea, Hasan,' said Halliday.

'There is a room for me?' said Birkin.

To both of which questions the man grinned, and murmured.

He made Gerald uncertain, because, being tall and slender and reticent, he looked like a gentleman.

'Who is your servant?' he asked of Halliday. 'He looks a swell.'

'Oh yes—that's because he's dressed in another man's clothes. He's anything but a swell really. We found him in the road, starving. So I took him here, and another man gave him clothes. He's anything but what he seems to be—his only advantage is that he can't speak English and can't understand it, so he's perfectly safe.'

"He's very dirty,' said the young Russian swiftly and silently.

Directly, the man appeared in the doorway.

'What is it?' said Halliday.

The man grinned and murmured shyly:

'Want to speak to master.'

Gerald watched curiously. The fellow in the doorway was good-looking and clean-limbed, his bearing was calm, he looked elegant, aristocratic. Yet he was half a savage, grinning foolishly. Halliday went out into the corridor to speak with him.

'What?' they heard his voice. 'What? What do you say? Tell me again. What? Want money? Want *more* money? But what do you want money for?' There was the confused sound of the Arab's talking, then Halliday appeared in the room, smiling also foolishly, and saying:

'He says he wants money to buy underclothing. Can anybody lend me a shilling? Oh thanks, a shilling will do to buy all the underclothes he wants.' He took the money from Gerald and went out into the passage again, where they heard him saying, 'You can't want more money, you had three and six yesterday. You mustn't ask for any more. Bring the tea in quickly.'

Gerald looked round the room. It was an ordinary London sitting-room in a house evidently taken furnished, rather haphazard but pleasant. But there were several statues, woodcarvings from the West Pacific, strange and disturbing, the carved natives looked almost like the foetus of a human being. One was a woman sitting naked in a strange posture, and looking tortured, her abdomen stuck out. The young Russian explained that she was sitting in child-birth, clutching the ends of the band that hung from her neck, one in each hand, so that she could bear down, and help labour. The strange, transfixed, rudimentary face of the woman again reminded Gerald of a foetus, it was also rather wonderful, conveying the suggestion of the extreme of physical sensation, beyond the limits of mental consciousness.

'Aren't they rather obscene?' he asked, disapproving.

'I don't know,' murmured the other rapidly. 'I have never defined the obscene. I think they are very good.'

Gerald turned away. There were one or two new pictures in the room, in the Futurist manner; there was a large piano. And these, with some ordinary London lodging-house furniture of the better sort, completed the whole.

Minette had taken off her hat and coat, and was seated on the sofa. She was evidently quite at home in the house, but uncertain, suspended. She did not quite know her position. Her alliance for the time being was with Gerald, and she did not know how far this was admitted by any of the men. She was considering how she should carry off the situation. She was determined to have her experience. Now, at this eleventh hour, she was not to be baulked. Her face was flushed as with battle, her eye was brooding but inevitable.

The man came in with tea and a bottle of Kümmel. He set the tray on a little table before the couch.

'Minette,' said Halliday, 'pour out the tea.'

She did not move.

'Won't you do it?' Halliday repeated, in a state of nervous apprehension.

'I've not come back here as it was before,' she said. 'I only came because the others wanted me to, not for your sake.'

'My dear Minette, you know you are your own mistress. I don't want you to do anything but use the flat for your own convenience—you know it, I've told you so many times.'

She did not reply, but silently, reservedly reached for the tea-pot. They all sat round and drank tea. Gerald could feel the electric connexion between him and her so strongly, as she sat there quiet and withheld, that another set of conditions altogether had come to pass. Her silence and her immutability perplexed him. *How* was he going to come to her? And yet he felt it quite inevitable. He trusted completely to the current that held them. His perplexity was only superficial, new conditions reigned, the old were surpassed; here one did as one was possessed to do, no matter what it was.

Birkin rose. It was nearly one o'clock.

'I'm going to bed,' he said. 'Gerald, I'll ring you up in the morning at your place—or you ring me up here.'

'Right,' said Gerald, and Birkin went out.

When he was well gone, Halliday said in a stimulated voice, to Gerald:

'I say, won't you stay here—oh do!'

'You can't put everybody up,' said Gerald.

'Oh but I can, perfectly—there are three more beds besides mine—do stay, won't you. Everything is quite ready—there is always somebody here—I always put people up—I love having the house crowded.'

'But there are only two rooms,' said Minette, in a cold, hostile voice, 'now Rupert's here.'

'I know there are only two rooms,' said Halliday, in his

odd, high way of speaking. 'But what does that matter? There is the studio—'

He was smiling rather foolishly, and he spoke eagerly, with an insinuating determination.

'Julius and I will share one room,' said the Russian in his discreet, precise voice. Halliday and he were friends since Eton.

'It's very simple,' said Gerald, rising and pressing back his arms, stretching himself. Then he went again to look at one of the pictures. Every one of his limbs was turgid with electric force, and his back was tense like a tiger's with slumbering fire. He was very proud.

Minette rose. She gave a black look at Halliday, fierce and deadly, which brought the rather foolish, pleased smile to that young man's face. Then she went out of the room, with a cold Good-night to them all generally.

There was a brief interval, they heard a door close, then Maxim said, in his refined voice:

'That's all right.'

He looked significantly at Gerald, and said again, with a silent nod:

'That's all right—you're all right.'

Gerald looked at the smooth, ruddy, comely face, and at the strange, significant eyes, and it seemed as if the voice of the young Russian, so small and perfect, sounded in the blood rather than in the air.

'*I'm* all right then,' said Gerald.

'Yes! Yes! You're all right,' said the Russian.

Halliday continued to smile, and to say nothing.

Suddenly Minette appeared again in the door, her small, childish face looking sullen and vindictive.

'I know you want to catch me out,' came her cold, rather resonant voice. 'But I don't care, I don't care how much you catch me out.'

She turned and was gone again. She had been wearing a loose dressing-gown of purple silk, tied round her waist. She looked so small and childish and vulnerable, almost pitiful. And yet the looks of her eyes made Gerald feel drowned in some potent darkness that almost frightened him.

The men lit another cigarette and talked casually.

7

Totem

In the morning Gerald woke late. He had slept heavily. Minette was still asleep, sleeping childishly and pathetically. There was something small and curled up and defenceless about her, that roused an unsatisfied flame of passion in the young man's blood, a devouring avid pity. He looked at her again. But it would be too cruel to wake her. He subdued himself, and went away.

Hearing voices coming from the sitting-room, Halliday talking to Libidnikov, he went to the door and glanced in. He had on a silk wrap of a beautiful bluish colour, with an amethyst hem.

To his surprise he saw the two young men by the fire, stark naked. Halliday looked up, rather pleased.

'Good-morning,' he said. 'Oh—did you want towels?' And stark naked he went out into the hall, striding a strange, white figure between the unliving furniture. He came back with the towels, and took his former position, crouching seated before the fire on the fender.

'Don't you love to feel the fire on your skin?' he said.

'It *is* rather pleasant,' said Gerald.

'How perfectly splendid it must be to be in a climate where one could do without clothing altogether,' said Halliday.

'Yes,' said Gerald, 'if there weren't so many things that sting and bite.'

'That's a disadvantage,' murmured Maxim.

Gerald looked at him, and with a slight revulsion saw the human animal, golden skinned and bare, somehow humiliating. Halliday was different. He had a rather heavy, slack, broken beauty, dark and firm. He was like a Christ in a

Pietà. The animal was not there at all, only the heavy, broken beauty. And Gerald realized how Halliday's eyes were beautiful too, so hazel-yellow and warm and confused, broken also in their expression. The fireglow fell on his heavy, rather bowed shoulders, he sat slackly crouched on the fender, his face was uplifted, weak, perhaps slightly disintegrate, and yet with a moving beauty of its own.

'Of course,' said Maxim, 'you've been in hot countries where the people go about naked.'

'Oh really!' exclaimed Halliday. 'Where?'

'South America—Amazon,' said Gerald.

'Oh but how perfectly splendid! It's one of the things I want most to do—to live from day to day without *ever* putting on any sort of clothing whatever. If I could do that, I should feel I had lived.'

'But why?' said Gerald. 'I can't see that it makes so much difference.'

'Oh, I think it would be perfectly splendid. I'm sure life would be entirely another thing—entirely different, and perfectly wonderful.'

'But why?' asked Gerald. 'Why should it?'

'Oh—one would *feel* things instead of merely looking at them. I should feel the air move against me, and feel the things I touched, instead of having only to look at them. I'm sure life is all wrong because it has become much too visual—we can neither hear nor feel nor understand, we can only see. I'm sure that is entirely wrong.'

'Yes, that is true, that is true,' said the Russian.

Gerald glanced at him, and saw him, his suave, golden coloured body with the black hair growing fine and freely, like tendrils, and his limbs like smooth plant-stems. He was so healthy and well-made, why did he make one ashamed, why did one feel repelled? Why should Gerald even dislike it, why did it seem to him to detract from his own dignity. Was that all a human being amounted to? So uninspired! thought Gerald.

Birkin suddenly appeared in the doorway, in white pyjamas and wet hair, and a towel over his arm. He was aloof and white, and somehow evanescent.

'There's the bath-room now, if you want it,' he said generally, and was going away, when Gerald called:

'I say, Rupert!'

'What?' The single white figure appeared again, a presence in the room.

'What do you think of that figure there? I want to know,' Gerald asked.

Birkin, white and strangely ghostly, went over to the carved figure of the savage woman in labour. Her nude, protuberant body crouched in a strange, clutching posture, her hands gripping the ends of the ban, above her breast.

'It is art,' said Birkin.

'Very beautiful, it's very beautiful,' said the Russian.

They all drew near to look. Gerald looked at the group of men, the Russian golden and like a water-plant, Halliday tall and heavily, brokenly beautiful, Birkin very white and indefinite, not to be assigned, as he looked closely at the carven woman. Strangely elated, Gerald also lifted his eyes to the face of the wooden figure. And his heart contracted.

He saw vividly with his spirit the grey, forward-stretching face of the savage woman, dark and tense, abstracted in utter physical stress. It was a terrible face, void, peaked, abstracted almost into meaninglessness by the weight of sensation beneath. He saw Minette in it. As in a dream, he knew her.

'Why is it art?' Gerald asked, shocked, resentful.

'It conveys a complete truth,' said Birkin. 'It contains the whole truth of that state, whatever you feel about it.'

'But you can't call it *high* art,' said Gerald.

'High! There are centuries and hundreds of centuries of development in a straight line, behind that carving; it is an awful pitch of culture, of a definite sort.'

'What culture?' Gerald asked, in opposition. He hated the sheer barbaric thing.

'Pure culture in sensation, culture in the physical consciousness, really ultimate *physical* consciousness, mindless, utterly sensual. It is so sensual as to be final, supreme.'

But Gerald resented it. He wanted to keep certain illusions, certain ideas like clothing.

'You like the wrong things, Rupert,' he said, 'things against yourself.'

'Oh, I know, this isn't everything,' Birkin replied, moving away.

When Gerald went back to his room from the bath, he also carried his clothes. He was so conventional at home, that when he was really away, and on the loose, as now, he enjoyed nothing so much as full outrageousness. So he strode with his blue silk wrap over his arm and felt defiant.

Minette lay in her bed, motionless, her round, blue eyes like stagnant, unhappy pools. He could only see the dead, bottomless pools of her eyes. Perhaps she suffered. The sensation of her inchoate suffering roused the old sharp flame in him, a mordant pity, a passion almost of cruelty.

'You are awake now,' he said to her.

'What time is it?' came her muted voice.

She seemed to flow back, almost like liquid, from his approach, to sink helplessly away from him. Her inchoate look of a violated slave, whose fulfilment lies in her further and further violation, made his nerves quiver with acutely desirable sensation. After all, his was the only will, she was the passive substance of his will. He tingled with the subtle, biting sensation. And then he knew, he must go away from her, there must be pure separation between them.

It was a quiet and ordinary breakfast, the four men all looking very clean and bathed. Gerald and the Russian were both correct and *comme il faut* in appearance and manner, Birkin was gaunt and sick, and looked a failure in his attempt to be a properly dressed man, like Gerald and Maxim. Halliday wore tweeds and a green flannel shirt, and a rag of a tie, which was just right for him. The Arab brought in a great deal of soft toast, and looked exactly the same as he had looked the night before, statically the same.

At the end of the breakfast Minette appeared, in a purple silk wrap with a shimmering sash. She had recovered herself somewhat, but was mute and lifeless still. It was a torment to her when anybody spoke to her. Her face was like a small, fine mask, sinister too, masked with unwilling suffering. It was almost midday. Gerald rose and went away to his business, glad to get out. But he had not finished. He was coming back again at evening, they were all dining together, and had booked seats for the party, excepting Birkin, at a music-hall.

At night they came back to the house very late again, again flushed with drink. Again the Arab—who invariably disappeared between the hours of ten and twelve at night—came in silently and inscrutably with tea, bending in a slow, strange, leopard-like fashion to put the tray softly on the table. His face was immutable, aristocratic-looking, tinged slightly with grey under the skin; he was young and good-looking. But Birkin felt a slight sickness, looking at him, and feeling the slight greyness as an ash or a corruption, in the aristocratic inscrutability of expression a nauseating, bestial stupidity.

Again they talked cordially and rousedly together. But already a certain friability was coming over the party, Birkin was mad with irritation, Halliday was turning in an insane hatred against Gerald, Minette was becoming hard and cold, like a flint knife, and Halliday was laying himself out to her. And her intention, ultimately, was to capture Halliday, to have complete power over him.

In the morning they all stalked and lounged about again. But Gerald could feel a strange hostility to himself in the air. It roused his obstinacy, and he stood up against it. He hung on for two more days. The result was a nasty and insane scene with Halliday on the fourth evening. Halliday turned with absurd animosity upon Gerald, in the café. There was a row. Gerald was on the point of knocking-in Halliday's face; when he was filled with sudden disgust and indifference, and he went away, leaving Halliday in a foolish state of gloating triumph, Minette hard and established, and Maxim standing clear. Birkin was absent, he had gone out of town again.

Gerald was piqued because he had left without giving Minette money. It was true, he did not know whether she wanted money or not. But she might have been glad of ten pounds, and he would have been *very* glad to give them to her. Now he felt in a false position. He went away chewing his lips to get at the ends of his short clipped moustache. He knew Minette was merely glad to be rid of him. She had got her Halliday whom she wanted. She wanted him completely in her power. Then she would marry him. She wanted to marry him. She had set her will on marrying Halliday. She never wanted to hear of Gerald again; unless, perhaps, she were in difficulty; because after all, Gerald was what she called a man, and these others, Halliday, Libidnikov, Birkin, the whole Bohemian set, they were only half men. But it was half men she could deal with. She felt sure of herself with them. The real men, like Gerald, put her in her place too much.

Still, she respected Gerald, she really respected him. She had managed to get his address, so that she could appeal to him in time of distress. She knew he wanted to give her money. She would perhaps write to him on that inevitable rainy day.

8

Breadalby

Breadalby was a Georgian house with Corinthian pillars standing among the softer, greener hills of Derbyshire, not far from Cromford. In front, it looked over a lawn, over a few trees, down to a string of fish-ponds in the hollow of the silent park. At the back were trees, among which were to be found the stables, and the big kitchen garden, behind which was a wood.

It was a very quiet place, some miles from the high-road, back from the Derwent Valley, outside the show scenery. Silent and forsaken, the golden stucco showed between the trees, the house-front looked down the park, unchanged and unchanging.

Of late, however, Hermione had lived a good deal at the house. She had turned away from London, away from Oxford, towards the silence of the country. Her father was mostly absent, abroad, she was either alone in the house, with her visitors, of whom there were always several, or she had with her her brother, a bachelor, and a Liberal member of Parliament. He always came down when the House was not sitting, seemed always to be present in Breadalby, although he was most conscientious in his attendance to duty.

The summer was just coming in when Ursula and Gudrun went to stay the second time with Hermione. Coming along in the car, after they had entered the park, they looked across the dip, where the fish-ponds lay in silence, at the pillared front of the house, sunny and small like an English drawing of the old school, on the brow of the green hill, against the trees. There were small figures on the green lawn, women in lavender and yellow moving to the shade of the enormous, beautifully balanced cedar tree.

'Isn't it complete!' said Gudrun. 'It is as final as an old aquatint.' She spoke with some resentment in her voice, as if she were captivated unwillingly, as if she must admire against her will.

'Do you love it?' asked Ursula.

'I don't *love* it, but in its way, I think it is quite complete.'

The motor-car ran down the hill and up again in one breath, and they were curving to the side door. A parlour-maid appeared, and then Hermione, coming forward with her pale face lifted, and her hands outstretched, advancing straight to the new-comers, her voice singing:

'Here you are—I'm so glad to see you—' she kissed Gudrun—'so glad to see you—' she kissed Ursula and remained with her arm round her. 'Are you very tired?'

'Not at all tired,' said Ursula.

'Are you tired, Gudrun?'

'Not at all, thanks,' said Gudrun.

'No—' drawled Hermione. And she stood and looked at them. The two girls were embarrassed because she would not move into the house, but must have her little scene of welcome there on the path. The servants waited.

'Come in,' said Hermione at last, having fully taken in the pair of them. Gudrun was the more beautiful and attractive, she had decided again, Ursula was more physical, more womanly. She admired Gudrun's dress more. It was of green poplin, with a loose coat above it, of broad, dark-green and dark-brown stripes. The hat was of a pale, greenish straw, the colour of new hay, and it had a plaited ribbon of black and orange, the stockings were dark green, the shoes black. It was a good get-up, at once fashionable and individual. Ursula, in dark blue, was more ordinary, though she also looked well.

Hermione herself wore a dress of prune-coloured silk, with coral beads and coral-coloured stockings. But her dress was both shabby and soiled, even rather dirty.

'You would like to see your rooms now, wouldn't you! Yes. We will go up now, shall we?'

Ursula was glad when she could be left alone in her room. Hermione lingered so long, made such a stress on one. She stood so near to one, pressing herself near upon one, in a way that was most embarrassing and oppressive. She seemed to hinder one's workings.

Lunch was served on the lawn, under the great tree, whose thick, blackish boughs came down close to the grass. There were present a young Italian woman, slight and fashionable, a young, athletic-looking Miss Bradley, a learned, dry Baronet of fifty, who was always making witticisms and laughing at them heartily in a harsh, horse-laugh, there was Rupert Birkin, and then a woman secretary, a Fräulein März, young and slim and pretty.

The food was very good, that was one thing. Gudrun, critical of everything, gave it her full approval. Ursula loved the situation, the white table by the cedar tree, the scent of new sunshine, the little vision of the leafy park, with far-off deer feeding peacefully. There seemed a magic circle drawn about the place, shutting out the present, enclosing the delightful, precious past, trees and deer and silence, like a dream.

But in spirit she was unhappy. The talk went on like a rattle of small artillery, always slightly sententious, with a sententiousness that was only emphasized by the continual crackling of a witticism, the continual spatter of verbal jest, designed to give a tone of flippancy to a stream of conversation that was all critical and general, a canal of conversation rather than a stream.

The attitude was mental and very wearying. Only the elder sociologist, whose mental fibre was so tough as to be insentient, seemed to be thoroughly happy. Birkin was down in the mouth. Hermione appeared, with amazing persistence, to wish to ridicule him and make him look ignominious in the eyes of everybody. And it was surprising how she seemed to succeed, how helpless he seemed against her. He looked completely insignificant. Ursula and Gudrun, both very unused, were mostly silent, listening to the slow, rhapsodic sing-song of Hermione, or the verbal sallies of Sir Joshua, or the prattle of Fräulein, or the responses of the other two women.

Luncheon was over, coffee was brought out on the grass, the party left the table and sat about in lounge chairs, in the shade or in the sunshine as they wished. Fräulein departed

into the house, Hermione took up her embroidery, the little
Contessa took a book, Miss Bradley was weaving a basket
out of fine grass, and there they all were on the lawn in the
early summer afternoon, working leisurely and spattering
with half-intellectual, deliberate talk.

Suddenly there was the sound of the brakes and the shutting off of a motor-car.

'There's Salsie!' sang Hermione, in her slow, amusing
sing-song. And laying down her work, she rose slowly, and
slowly passed over the lawn, round the bushes, out of sight.

'Who is it?' asked Gudrun.

'Mr Roddice—Miss Roddice's brother—at least, I suppose it's he,' said Sir Joshua.

'Salsie, yes, it is her brother,' said the little Contessa, lifting her head for a moment from her book, and speaking as
if to give information, in her slightly deepened, guttural English.

They all waited. And then round the bushes came the tall
form of Alexander Roddice, striding romantically like a
Meredith hero who remembers Disraeli. He was cordial with
everybody, he was at once a host, with an easy, off-hand
hospitality that he had learned for Hermione's friends. He
had just come down from London, from the House. At once
the atmosphere of the House of Commons made itself felt
over the lawn: the Home Secretary had said such and such
a thing, and he, Roddice, on the other hand, thought such
and such a thing, and had said so-and-so to the P.M.

Now Hermione came round the bushes with Gerald Crich.
He had come along with Alexander. Gerald was presented to
everybody, was kept by Hermione for a few moments in full
view, then he was led away, still by Hermione. He was evidently her guest of the moment.

There had been a split in the Cabinet; the Minister for Education had resigned owing to adverse criticism. This started
a conversation on education.

'Of course,' said Hermione, lifting her face like a rhapso-
dist, 'there *can* be no reason, no *excuse* for education, except
the joy and beauty of knowledge in itself.' She seemed to
rumble and ruminate with subterranean thoughts for a min-

ute, then she proceeded: 'Vocational education *isn't* education, it is the close of education.'

Gerald, on the brink of discussion, sniffed the air with delight and prepared for action.

'Not necessarily,' he said. 'But isn't education really like gymnastics, isn't the end of education the production of a well-trained vigorous, energetic mind?'

'Just as athletics produce a healthy body, ready for anything,' cried Miss Bradley, in hearty accord.

Gudrun looked at her in silent loathing.

'Well—' rumbled Hermione, 'I don't know. To me the pleasure of knowing is *so* great, so *wonderful*—nothing has meant so much to me in all life, as certain knowledge—no, I am sure—nothing.'

'What knowledge, for example, Hermione?' asked Alexander.

Hermione lifted her face and rumbled—

'M—m—m—I don't know ... But one thing was the stars, when I really understood something about the stars. One feels so *uplifted,* so *unbounded ...*'

Birkin looked at her in a white fury.

'What do you want to feel unbounded for?' he said sarcastically. 'You don't want to *be* unbounded.'

Hermione recoiled in offence.

'Yes, but one does have that limitless feeling,' said Gerald. 'It's like getting on top of the mountain and seeing the Pacific.'

'Silent upon a peak in Dariayn,' murmured the Italian, lifting her face for a moment from her book.

'Not necessarily in Darien,' said Gerald, while Ursula began to laugh.

Hermione waited for the dust to settle, and then she said, untouched:

'Yes, it is the greatest thing in life—*to know*. It is really to be happy, to be *free*.'

'Knowledge is, of course, liberty,' said Mattheson.

'In compressed tabloids,' said Birkin, looking at the dry, stiff little body of the Baronet. Immediately Gudrun saw the famous sociologist as a flat bottle, containing tabloids of

compressed liberty. That pleased her. Sir Joshua was labelled
and placed for ever in her mind.

'What does that mean, Rupert?' sang Hermione, in a calm
snub.

'You can only have knowledge, strictly,' he replied, 'of
things concluded, in the past. It's like bottling the liberty of
last summer in the bottled gooseberries.'

'*Can* one have knowledge only of the past?' asked the
Baronet, pointedly. 'Could we call our knowledge of the
laws of gravitation for instance, knowledge of the past?'

'Yes,' said Birkin.

'There is a most beautiful thing in my book,' suddenly
piped the little Italian woman. 'It says the man came to the
door and threw his eyes down the street.'

There was a general laugh in the company. Miss Bradley
went and looked over the shoulder of the Contessa.

'See!' said the Contessa.

'Bazarov came to the door and threw his eyes hurriedly
down the street,' she read.

Again there was a loud laugh, the most startling of which
was the Baronet's, which rattled out like a clatter of falling
stones.

'What is the book?' asked Alexander, promptly.

'Fathers and Sons, by Turgenev,' said the little foreigner,
pronouncing every syllable distinctly. She looked at the
cover, to verify herself.

'An old American edition,' said Birkin.

'Ha!—of course—translated from the French,' said Alexander, with a fine declamatory voice. '*Bazarov ouvra la
porte et jeta les yeux dans la rue.*'

He looked brightly round the company.

'I wonder what the "hurriedly" was,' said Ursula.

They all began to guess.

And then, to the amazement of everybody, the maid came
hurrying with a large tea-tray. The afternoon had passed so
swiftly.

After tea, they were all gathered for a walk.

'Would you like to come for a walk?' said Hermione to
each of them, one by one. And they all said yes, feeling

somehow like prisoners marshalled for exercise. Birkin only refused.

'Will you come for a walk, Rupert?'

'No, Hermione.'

'But are you *sure*?'

'Quite sure.' There was a second's hesitation.

'And why not?' sang Hermione's question. It made her blood run sharp, to be thwarted in even so trifling a matter. She intended them all to walk with her in the park.

'Because I don't like trooping off in a gang,' he said.

Her voice rumbled in her throat for a moment. Then she said, with a curious stray calm:

'Then we'll leave a little boy behind, if he's sulky.'

And she looked really gay, while she insulted him. But it merely made him stiff.

She trailed off to the rest of the company, only turning to wave her handkerchief to him, and to chuckle with laughter, singing out:

'Good-bye, good-bye, little boy.'

'Good-bye, impudent hag,' he said to himself.

They all went through the park. Hermione wanted to show them the wild daffodils on a little slope. 'This way, this way,' sang her leisurely voice at intervals. And they had all to come this way. The daffodils were pretty, but who could see them? Ursula was stiff all over with resentment by this time, resentment of the whole atmosphere. Gudrun, mocking and objective, watched and registered everything.

They looked at the shy deer, and Hermione talked to the stag, as if he too were a boy she wanted to wheedle and fondle. He was male, so she must exert some kind of power over him. They trailed home by the fish-ponds, and Hermione told them about the quarrel of two male swans, who had striven for the love of the one lady. She chuckled and laughed as she told how the ousted lover had sat with his head buried under his wing, on the gravel.

When they arrived back at the house, Hermione stood on the lawn and sang out, in a strange, small, high voice that carried very far:

'Rupert! Rupert!' The first syllable was high and slow, the second dropped down. 'Roo-o-opert.'

But there was no answer. A maid appeared.

'Where is Mr Birkin, Alice?' asked the mild straying voice of Hermione. But under the straying voice, what a persistent, almost insane *will*!

'I think he's in his room, madame.'

'Is he?'

Hermione went slowly up the stairs, along the corridor, singing out in her high, small call:

'Ru-oo-pert! Ru-oo-pert!'

She came to his door, and tapped, still crying: 'Roo-pert.'

'Yes,' sounded his voice at last.

'What are you doing?'

The question was mild and curious.

There was no answer. Then he opened the door.

'We've come back,' said Hermione. 'The daffodils are *so* beautiful.'

'Yes,' he said, 'I've seen them.'

She looked at him with her long, slow, impassive look, along her cheeks.

'Have you?' she echoed. And she remained looking at him. She was stimulated above all things by this conflict with him, when he was like a sulky boy, helpless, and she had him safe at Breadalby. But underneath she knew the split was coming, and her hatred of him was subconscious and intense.

'What were you doing?' she reiterated, in her mild, indifferent tone. He did not answer, and she made her way, almost unconsciously into his room. He had taken a Chinese drawing of geese from the boudoir, and was copying it, with much skill and vividness.

'You are copying the drawing,' she said, standing near the table, and looking down at his work. 'Yes. How beautifully you do it! You like it very much, don't you?'

'It's a marvellous drawing,' he said.

'Is it? I'm so glad you like it, because I've always been fond of it. The Chinese Ambassador gave it me.'

'I know,' he said.

'But why do you copy it?' she asked, casual and singsong. 'Why not do something original?'

'I want to know it,' he replied. 'One gets more of China, copying this picture, than reading all the books.'

'And what do you get?'

She was at once roused, she laid as it were violent hands on him, to extract his secrets from him. She *must* know. It was a dreadful tyranny, an obsession in her, to know all he knew. For some time he was silent, hating to answer her. Then, compelled, he began:

'I know what centres they live from—what they perceive and feel—the hot, stinging centrality of a goose in the flux of cold water and mud—the curious bitter stinging heat of a goose's blood, entering their own blood like an inoculation of corruptive fire—fire of the cold-burning mud—the lotus mystery.'

Hermione looked at him along her narrow, pallid cheeks. Her eyes were strange and drugged, heavy under their heavy, drooping lids. Her thin bosom shrugged convulsively. He stared back at her, devilish and unchanging. With another strange, sick convulsion, she turned away, as if she were sick, could feel dissolution setting in in her body. For with her mind she was unable to attend to his words; he caught her, as it were, beneath all her defences, and destroyed her with some insidious occult potency.

'Yes,' she said, as if she did not know what she was saying. 'Yes,' and she swallowed, and tried to regain her mind. But she could not, she was witless, decentralized. Use all her will as she might, she could not recover. She suffered the ghastliness of dissolution, broken and gone in a horrible corruption. And he stood and looked at her unmoved. She strayed out, pallid and preyed-upon like a ghost, like one attacked by the tomb-influences which dog us. And she was gone like a corpse, that has no presence, no connexion. He remained hard and vindictive.

Hermione came down to dinner strange and sepulchral, her eyes heavy and full of sepulchral darkness, strength. She had put on a dress of stiff old greenish brocade, that fitted tight and made her look tall and rather terrible, ghastly. In the gay light of the drawing-room she was uncanny and oppressive. But seated in the half-light of the dining-room, sitting stiffly before the shaded candles on the table, she seemed a power, a presence. She listened and attended with a drugged attention.

The party was gay and extravagant in appearance, everybody had put on evening dress except Birkin and Joshua Mattheson. The little Italian Contessa wore a dress of tissue, of orange and gold and black velvet in soft wide stripes, Gudrun was emerald green with strange net-work, Ursula was in yellow with dull silver veiling, Miss Bradley was of grey, crimson and jet, Fräulein März wore pale blue. It gave Hermione a sudden convulsive sensation of pleasure, to see these rich colours under the candle-light. She was aware of the talk going on, ceaselessly, Joshua's voice dominating; of the ceaseless pitter-patter of women's light laughter and responses; of the brilliant colours and the white table and the shadow above and below; and she seemed in a swoon of gratification, convulsed with pleasure, and yet sick, like a *revenant*. She took very little part in the conversation, yet she heard it all, it was all hers.

They all went together into the drawing-room, as if they were one family, easily, without any attention to ceremony. Fräulein handed the coffee, everybody smoked cigarettes, or else long warden pipes of white clay, of which a sheaf was provided.

'Will you smoke?—cigarettes or pipe?' asked Fräulein prettily. There was a circle of people, Sir Joshua with his eighteenth-century appearance, Gerald the amused, handsome young Englishman, Alexander tall and the handsome politician, democratic and lucid, Hermione strange like a long Cassandra, and the women lurid with colour, all dutifully smoking their long white pipes, and sitting in a half-moon in the comfortable, soft-lighted drawing-room, round the logs that flickered on the marble hearth.

The talk was very often political or sociological, and interesting, curiously anarchistic. There was an accumulation of powerful force in the room, powerful and destructive. Everything seemed to be thrown into the melting-pot, and it seemed to Ursula they were all witches, helping the pot to bubble. There was an elation and a satisfaction in it all, but it was cruelly exhausting for the new-comers, this ruthless mental pressure, this powerful, consuming, destructive men-

tality that emanated from Joshua and Hermione and Birkin
and dominated the rest.

But a sickness, a fearful nausea gathered possession of
Hermione. There was a lull in the talk, as it was arrested by
her unconscious but all-powerful will.

'Salsie, won't you play something?' said Hermione,
breaking off completely. 'Won't somebody dance? Gudrun,
you will dance, won't you? I wish you would. *Anche tu, Palestra, ballerai?—sì, per piacere.* You too, Ursula.'

Hermione rose and slowly pulled the gold-embroidered
band that hung by the mantel, clinging to it for a moment,
then releasing it suddenly. Like a priestess she looked, unconscious, sunk in a heavy half-trance.

A servant came, and soon reappeared with armfuls of silk
robes and shawls and scarves, mostly Oriental, things that
Hermione, with her love for beautiful extravagant dress, had
collected gradually.

'The three women will dance together,' she said.

'What shall it be?' asked Alexander, rising briskly.

'*Vergini delle Rocchette,*' said the Contessa at once.

'They are so languid,' said Ursula.

'The three witches from Macbeth,' suggested Fräulein
usefully. It was finally decided to do Naomi and Ruth and
Orpah. Ursula was Naomi, Gudrun was Ruth, the Contessa
was Orpah. The idea was to make a little ballet, in the style
of the Russian Ballet of Pavlova and Nijinsky.

The Contessa was ready first, Alexander went to the piano, a space was cleared. Orpah, in beautiful Oriental
clothes, began slowly to dance the death of her husband.
Then Ruth came, and they wept together, and lamented, then
Naomi came to comfort them. It was all done in dumb show,
the women danced their emotion in gesture and motion. The
little drama went on for a quarter of an hour.

Ursula was beautiful as Naomi. All her men were dead, it
remained to her only to stand alone in indomitable assertion,
demanding nothing. Ruth, woman-loving, loved her. Orpah,
a vivid, sensational, subtle widow, would go back to the
former life, a repetition. The inter-play between the women
was real and rather frightening. It was strange to see how
Gudrun clung with heavy, desperate passion to Ursula, yet

smiled with subtle malevolence against her, how Ursula accepted silently, unable to provide any more either for herself or for the other, but dangerous and indomitable, refuting her grief.

Hermione loved to watch. She could see the Contessa's rapid, stoat-like sensationalism, Gudrun's ultimate but treacherous cleaving to the woman in her sister, Ursula's dangerous helplessness, as if she were helplessly weighted, and unreleased.

'That was very beautiful,' everybody cried with one accord. But Hermione writhed in her soul, knowing what she could not know. She cried out for more dancing, and it was her will that set the Contessa and Birkin moving mockingly in Malbrouk.

Gerald was excited by the desperate cleaving of Gudrun to Naomi. The essence of that female, subterranean recklessness and mockery penetrated his blood. He could not forget Gudrun's lifted, offered, cleaving, reckless, yet withal mocking weight. And Birkin, watching like a hermit crab from its hole, had seen the brilliant frustration and helplessness of Ursula. She was rich, full of dangerous power. She was like a strange unconscious bud of powerful womanhood. He was unconsciously drawn to her. She was his future.

Alexander played some Hungarian music, and they all danced, seized by the spirit. Gerald was marvellously exhilarated at finding himself in motion, moving towards Gudrun, dancing with feet that could not yet escape from the waltz and the two-step, but feeling his force stir along his limbs and his body, out of captivity. He did not know yet how to dance their convulsive, rag-time sort of dancing, but he knew how to begin. Birkin, when he could get free from the weight of the people present, whom he disliked, danced rapidly and with a real gaiety. And how Hermione hated him for this irresponsible gaiety.

'Now I see,' cried the Contessa excitedly, watching his purely gay motion, which he had all to himself. 'Mr Birkin, he is a changer.'

Hermione looked at her slowly, and shuddered, knowing that only a foreigner could have seen and have said this.

'*Cosa vuol'dire Palestra?*' she asked, sing-song.

'Look,' said the Contessa, in Italian. 'He is not a man, he is a chameleon, a creature of change.'

'He is not a man, he is treacherous, not one of us,' said itself over in Hermione's consciousness. And her soul writhed in the black subjugation to him, because of his power to escape, to exist, other than she did, because he was not consistent, not a man, less than a man. She hated him in a despair that shattered her and broke her down, so that she suffered sheer dissolution like a corpse, and was unconscious of everything save the horrible sickness of dissolution that was taking place within her, body and soul.

The house being full, Gerald was given the smaller room, really the dressing-room, communicating with Birkin's bedroom. When they all took their candles and mounted the stairs, where the lamps were burning subduedly, Hermione captured Ursula and brought her into her own bedroom, to talk to her. A sort of constraint came over Ursula in the big, strange bedroom. Hermione seemed to be bearing down on her, awful and inchoate, making some appeal. They were looking at some Indian silk shirts, gorgeous and sensual in themselves, their shape, their almost corrupt gorgeousness. And Hermione came near, and her bosom writhed, and Ursula was for a moment blank with panic. And for a moment Hermione's haggard eyes saw the fear on the face of the other, there was again a sort of crash, a crashing down. And Ursula picked up a shirt of rich red and blue silk, made for a young princess of fourteen, and was crying mechanically:

'Isn't it wonderful—who would dare to put those two strong colours together—'

Then Hermione's maid entered silently and Ursula, overcome with dread, escaped, carried away by powerful impulse.

Birkin went straight to bed. He was feeling happy, and sleepy. Since he had danced he was happy. But Gerald would talk to him. Gerald, in evening dress, sat on Birkin's bed when the other lay down, and must talk.

'Who are those two Brangwens?' Gerald asked.

'They live in Beldover.'

'In Beldover! Who are they then?'

'Teachers in the Grammar School.'

There was a pause.

'They are!' exclaimed Gerald at length. 'I thought I had seen them before.'

'It disappoints you?' said Birkin.

'Disappoints me! No—but how is it Hermione has them here?'

'She knew Gudrun in London—that's the younger one, the one with the darker hair—she's an artist—does sculpture and modelling.'

'She's not a teacher in the Grammar School, then—only the other?'

'Both—Gudrun art mistress, Ursula a class mistress.'

'And what's the father?'

'Handicraft instructor in the schools.'

'Really!'

'Class-barriers are breaking down!'

Gerald was always uneasy under the slightly jeering tone of the other.

'That their father is handicraft instructor in a school! What does it matter to me?'

Birkin laughed. Gerald looked at his face, as it lay there laughing and bitter and indifferent on the pillow, and he could not go away.

'I don't suppose you will see very much more of Gudrun at least. She is a restless bird, she'll be gone in a week or two,' said Birkin.

'Where will she go?'

'London, Paris, Rome—heaven knows. I always expect her to sheer off to Damascus or San Francisco; she's a bird of paradise. God knows what she's got to do with Beldover. It goes by contraries, like dreams.'

Gerald pondered for a few moments.

'How do you know her so well?' he asked.

'I knew her in London,' he replied, 'in the Algernon Strange set. She'll know about Minette and Libidnikov and the rest—even if she doesn't know them personally. She was never quite that set—more conventional, in a way. I've known her for two years, I suppose.'

'And she makes money, apart from her teaching?' asked Gerald.

'Some—irregularly. She can sell her models. She has a certain *réclame*.'

'How much for?'

'A guinea, ten guineas.'

'And are they good? What are they?'

'I think sometimes they are marvellously good. That is hers, those two wagtails in Hermione's boudoir—you've seen them—they are carved in wood and painted.'

'I thought it was savage carving again.'

'No, hers. That's what they are—animals and birds, sometimes odd small people in everyday dress, really rather wonderful when they come off. They have a sort of funniness that is quite unconscious and subtle.'

'She might be a well-known artist one day?' mused Gerald.

'She might. But I think she won't. She drops her art if anything else catches her. Her contrariness prevents her taking it seriously—she must never be too serious, she feels she might give herself away. And she won't give herself away—she's always on the defensive. That's what I can't stand about her type. By the way, how did things go off with Minette after I left you? I haven't heard anything.'

'Oh, rather disgusting. Halliday turned objectionable, and I only just saved myself from jumping in his stomach, in a real old-fashioned row.'

Birkin was silent.

'Of course,' he said, 'Julius is somewhat insane. On the one hand he's had religious mania, and on the other, he is fascinated by obscenity. Either he is a pure servant, washing the feet of Christ, or else he is making obscene drawings of Jesus—action and reaction—and between the two, nothing. He is really insane. He wants a pure lily, another girl, with a Botticelli face, on the one hand, and on the other, he *must* have Minette, just to defile himself with her.'

'That's what I can't make out,' said Gerald. 'Does he love her, Minette, or doesn't he?'

'He neither does nor doesn't. She is the harlot, the actual harlot of adultery to him. And he's got a craving to throw himself into the filth of her. Then he gets up and calls on the name of the lily of purity, the baby-faced girl, and so enjoys himself all round. It's the old story—action and reaction, and nothing between.'

'I don't know,' said Gerald, after a pause, 'that he does insult Minette so very much. She strikes me as being rather foul.'

'But I thought you liked her,' exclaimed Birkin. 'I always felt fond of her. I never had anything to do with her, personally, that's true.'

'I liked her all right, for a couple of days,' said Gerald. 'But a week of her would have turned me over. There's a certain smell, about the skin of those women, that in the end is sickening beyond words—even if you like it at first.'

'I know,' said Birkin. Then he added, rather fretfully, 'But go to bed, Gerald. God knows what time it is.'

Gerald looked at his watch, and at length rose off the bed, and went to his room. But he returned in a few minutes, in his shirt.

'One thing,' he said, seating himself on the bed again. 'We finished up rather stormily, and I never had time to give her anything.'

'Money?' said Birkin. 'She'll get what she wants from Halliday or from one of her acquaintances.'

'But then,' said Gerald, 'I'd rather give her her dues and settle the account.'

'She doesn't care.'

'No, perhaps not. But one feels the account is left open, and one would rather it were closed.'

'Would you?' said Birkin. He was looking at the white legs of Gerald, as the latter sat on the side of the bed in his shirt. They were white-skinned, full, muscular legs, handsome and decided. Yet they moved Birkin with a sort of pathos, tenderness, as if they were childish.

'I think I'd rather close the account,' said Gerald, repeating himself vaguely.

'It doesn't matter one way or another,' said Birkin.

'You always say it doesn't matter,' said Gerald, a little puzzled, looking down at the face of the other man affectionately.

'Neither does it,' said Birkin.

'But she was a decent sort, really—'

'Render unto Caesarina the things that are Caesarina's,' said Birkin, turning aside. It seemed to him Gerald was talking for the sake of talking. 'Go away, it wearies me—it's too late at night,' he said.

'I wish you'd tell me something that *did* matter,' said Gerald, looking down all the time at the face of the other man, waiting for something. But Birkin turned his face aside.

'All right then, go to sleep,' said Gerald, and he laid his hand affectionately on the other man's shoulder, and went away.

In the morning when Gerald awoke and heard Birkin move, he called out: 'I still think I ought to give Minette some money.'

'Oh, God!' said Birkin, 'don't be so matter-of-fact. Close the account in your own soul, if you like. It is there you can't close it.'

'How do you know I can't?'

'Knowing you.'

Gerald meditated for some moments.

'It seems to me the right thing to do, you know, with the Minettes, is to pay them.'

'And the right thing for mistresses: keep them. And the right thing for wives: live under the same roof with them. *Integer vitae scelerisque purus*—' said Birkin.

'There's no need to be nasty about it,' said Gerald.

'It bores me. I'm not interested in your peccadilloes.'

'And I don't care whether you are or not—I am.'

The morning was again sunny. The maid had been in and brought the water, and had drawn the curtains. Birkin, sitting up in bed, looked lazily and pleasantly out on the park, that was so green and deserted, romantic, belonging to the past. He was thinking how lovely, how sure, how formed, how final all the things of the past were—the lovely accomplished past—this house, so still and golden, the park slumbering its centuries of peace. And then, what a snare and a delusion, this beauty of static things—what a horrible, dead prison Breadalby really was, what an intolerable confinement, the peace! Yet it was better than the sordid scrambling conflict of the present. If only one might create the future after one's own heart—for a little pure truth, a little unflinching application of simple truth to life, the heart cried out ceaselessly.

'I can't see what you will leave me at all, to be interested in,' came Gerald's voice from the lower room. 'Neither the Minettes, nor the mines, nor anything else.'

'You be interested in what you can, Gerald. Only I'm not interested myself,' said Birkin.

'What am I to do at all, then?' came Gerald's voice.

'What you like. What am I to do myself?'

In the silence Birkin could feel Gerald musing this fact.

'I'm blest if I know,' came the good-humoured answer.

'You see,' said Birkin, 'part of you wants Minette, and nothing but Minette, part of you wants the mines, the business, and nothing but the business—and there you are—all in bits—'

'And part of me wants something else,' said Gerald, in a queer, quiet, real voice.

'What?' said Birkin, rather surprised.

'That's what I hoped you could tell me,' said Gerald.

There was a silence for some time.

'I can't tell you—I can't find my own way, let alone yours. You might marry,' Birkin replied.

'Who—Minette?' asked Gerald.

'Perhaps,' said Birkin. And he rose and went to the window.

'That is your panacea,' said Gerald. 'But you haven't even tried it on yourself yet, and you are sick enough.'

'iI am,' said Birkin. 'Still, I shall come right.'

'Through marriage?'

'Yes,' Birkin answered obstinately.

'And no,' added Gerald. 'No, no, no, my boy.'

There was a silence between them, and a strange tension of hostility. They always kept a gap, a distance between them, they wanted always to be free each of the other. Yet there was a curious heart-straining towards each other.

'*Salvator femininus,*' said Gerald, satirically.

'Why not?' said Birkin.

'No reason at all,' said Gerald, 'if it really works. But whom will you marry?'

'A woman,' said Birkin.

'Good,' said Gerald.

Birkin and Gerald were the last to come down to breakfast. Hermione liked everybody to be early. She suffered when she felt her day was diminished, she felt she had missed her life. She seemed to grip the hours by the throat, to force her life from them. She was rather pale and ghastly, as if left behind, in the morning. Yet she had her power, her will was strangely pervasive. With the entrance of the two young men a sudden tension was felt.

She lifted her face, and said, in her amused sing-song:

'Good morning! Did you sleep well? I'm so glad.'

And she turned away, ignoring them. Birkin, who knew her well, saw that she intended to discount his existence.

'Will you take what you want from the sideboard?' said Alexander, in a voice slightly suggesting disapprobation. 'I hope the things aren't cold. Oh no! Do you mind putting out the flame under the chafing-dish, Rupert? Thank you.'

Even Alexander was rather authoritative where Hermione was cool. He took his tone from her, inevitably. Birkin sat down and looked at the table. He was so used to this house, to this room, to this atmosphere, through years of intimacy, and now he felt in complete opposition to it all, it had nothing to do with him. How well he knew Hermione, as she sat there, erect and silent and somewhat bemused, and yet so potent, so powerful! He knew her statically, so finally, that it was almost like a madness. It was difficult to believe one was not mad, that one was not a figure in the hall of kings in some Egyptian tomb, where the dead all sat immemorial and tremendous. How utterly he knew Joshua Mattheson, who was talking in his harsh, yet rather mincing voice, endlessly, endlessly, always with a strong mentality working, always interesting, and yet always known, everything he said known beforehand, however novel it was, and clever. Alexander the up-to-date host, so bloodlessly free-and-easy, Fräulein so prettily chiming in just as she should, the little Italian Countess taking notice of everybody, only playing her little game, objective and cold, like a weasel watching everything, and extracting her own amusement, never giving herself in the slightest; then Miss Bradley, heavy and rather subservient, treated with cool, almost amused contempt by Hermione, and therefore slighted by everybody—how known it all was, like a game with the figures set out, the same figures, the Queen of chess, the knights, the pawns, the same now as they were hundreds of years ago, the same figures moving round in one of the innumerable permutations that make up the game. But the game is known, its going on is like a madness, it is so exhausted.

There was Gerald, an amused look on his face; the game pleased him. There was Gudrun, watching with steady, large, hostile eyes; the games fascinated her, and she loathed it. There was Ursula, with a slightly startled look on her face, as if she were hurt, and the pain were just outside her consciousness.

Suddenly Birkin got up and went out.

'That's enough,' he said to himself involuntarily.

Hermione knew his motion, though not in her consciousness. She lifted her heavy eyes and saw him lapse suddenly away, on a sudden, unknown tide, and the waves broke over her. Only her indomitable will remained static and mechanical, she sat at the table making her musing, stray remarks. But the darkness had covered her, she was like a ship that has gone down. It was finished for her too, she was wrecked in the darkness. Yet the unfailing mechanism of her will worked on, she had that activity.

'Shall we bathe this morning?' she said, suddenly looking at them all.

'Splendid,' said Joshua. 'It is a perfect morning.'

'Oh, it is beautiful,' said Fräulein.

'Yes, let us bathe,' said the Italian woman.

'We have no bathing-suits,' said Gerald.

'Have mine,' said Alexander. 'I must go to church and read the lessons. They expect me.'

'Are you a Christian?' asked the Italian Countess, with sudden interest.

'No,' said Alexander. 'I'm not. But I believe in keeping up the old institutions.'

'They are so beautiful,' said Fräulein daintily.

'Oh, they are,' cried Miss Bradley.

They all trailed out on to the lawn. It was a sunny, soft morning in early summer, when life ran in the world subtly,

like a reminiscence. The church bells were ringing a little
way off, not a cloud was in the sky, the swans were like lilies on the water below, the peacocks walked with long,
prancing steps across the shadow and into the sunshine of
the grass. One wanted to swoon into the by-gone perfection
of it all.

'Good-bye,' called Alexander, waving his gloves cheerily,
and he disappeared behind the bushes, on his way to church.

'Now,' said Hermione, 'shall we all bathe?'

'I won't,' said Ursula.

'You don't want to?' said Hermione, looking at her
slowly.

'No. I don't want to,' said Ursula.

'Nor I,' said Gudrun.

'What about my suit?' asked Gerald.

'I don't know,' laughed Hermione, with an odd, amused
intonation. 'Will a handkerchief do—a large handkerchief?'

'That will do,' said Gerald.

'Come along, then,' sang Hermione.

The first to run across the lawn was the little Italian, small
and like a cat, her white legs twinkling as she went, ducking
slightly her head, that was tied in a gold silk kerchief. She
tripped through the gate and down the grass, and stood, like
a tiny figure of ivory and bronze, at the water's edge, having
dropped off her toweling, watching the swans, which came
up in surprise. Then out ran Miss Bradley, like a large, soft
plum in her dark-blue suite. Then Gerald came, a scarlet silk
kerchief round his loins, his towels over his arms. He
seemed to flaunt himself a little in the sun, lingering and
laughing, strolling easily, looking white but natural in his
nakedness. Then came Sir Joshua, in an overcoat, and lastly
Hermione, striding with stiff grace from out of a great man-
tle of purple silk, her head tied up in purple and gold. Handsome was her stiff, long body, her straight-stepping white
legs, there was a static magnificence about her as she let the
cloak float loosely away from her striding. She crossed the
lawn like some strange memory, and passed slowly and
stately towards the water.

There were three ponds, in terraces descending the valley,
large and smooth and beautiful, lying in the sun. The water

ran over a little stone wall, over small rocks, splashing down from one pond to the level below. The swans had gone out on to the opposite bank, the reeds smelled sweet, a faint breeze touched the skin.

Gerald had dived in, after Sir Joshua, and had swum to the end of the pond. There he climbed out and sat on the wall. There was a dive, and the little Countess was swimming like a rat, to join him. They both sat in the sun, laughing and crossing their arms on their breasts. Sir Joshua swam up to them, and stood near them, up to his arm-pits in the water. Then Hermione and Miss Bradley swam over, and they sat in a row on the embankment.

'Aren't they terrifying? Aren't they really terrifying?' said Gudrun. 'Don't they look saurian? They are just like great lizards. Did you ever see anything like Sir Joshua? But really, Ursula, he belongs to the primeval world, when great lizards crawled about.'

Gudrun looked in dismay on Sir Joshua, who stood up to the breast in the water, his long, greyish hair washed down into his eyes, his neck set into thick, crude shoulders. He was talking to Miss Bradley, who, seated on the bank above, plump and big and wet, looked as if she might roll and slither in the water almost like one of the slithering sea-lions in the Zoo.

Ursula watched in silence. Gerald was laughing happily, between Hermione and the Italian. He reminded her of Dionysus, because his hair was really yellow, his figure so full and laughing. Hermione, in her large, stiff, sinister grace, leaned near him, frightening, as if she were not responsible for what she might do. He knew a certain danger in her, a convulsive madness. But he only laughed the more, turning often to the little Countess, who was flashing up her face at him.

They all dropped into the water, and were swimming together like a shoal of seals. Hermione was powerful and unconscious in the water, large and slow and powerful, Palestra was quick and silent as a water-rat. Gerald wavered and flickered, a white natural shadow. Then, one after the other, they waded out, and went up to the house.

But Gerald lingered a moment to speak to Gudrun.

'You don't like the water?' he said.

She looked at him with a long, slow inscrutable look, as he stood before her negligently, the water standing in beads all over his skin.

'I like it very much,' she replied.

He paused, expecting some sort of explanation.

'And you swim?'

'Yes, I swim.'

Still he would not ask her why she would not go in then. He could feel something ironic in her. He walked away, piqued for the first time.

'Why wouldn't you bathe?' he asked her again, later, when he was once more the properly-dressed young Englishman.

She hesitated a moment before answering, opposing his persistence.

'Because I didn't like the crowd,' she replied.

He laughed, her phrase seemed to re-echo in his consciousness. The flavour of her slang was piquant to him. Whether he would or not, she signified the real world to him. He wanted to come up to her standards, fulfil her expectations. He knew that her criterion was the only one that mattered. The others were all outsiders, instinctively, whatever they might be socially. And Gerald could not help it, he was bound to strive to come up to her criterion, fulfil her idea of a man and a human being.

After lunch, when all the others had withdrawn, Hermione and Gerald and Birkin lingered, finishing their talk. There had been some discussion, on the whole quite intellectual and artificial, about a new state, a new world of man. Supposing this old social state *were* broken and destroyed, then, out of the chaos, what then?

The great social idea, said Sir Joshua, was the *social* equality of man. No, said Gerald, the idea was, that every man was fit for his own little bit of a task—let him do that, and then please himself. The unifying principle was the work in hand. Only work, the business of production, held men together. It was mechanical, but then society *was* a mechanism. Apart from work they were isolated, free to do as they liked.

'Oh!' cried Gudrun. 'Then we shan't have names any more—we shall be like the Germans, nothing but Herr Obermeister and Herr Untermeister. I can imagine it—"I am Mrs Colliery-Manager Crich—I am Mrs Member-of-Parliament Roddice. I am Miss Art-Teacher Brangwen." Very pretty that.'

'Things would work very much better, Miss Art-Teacher Brangwen,' said Gerald.

'What things, Mr Colliery-Manager Crich? The relation between you and me, *par exemple*?'

'Yes, for example,' cried the Italian. 'That which is between men and women—!'

'That is non-social,' said Birkin, sarcastically.

'Exactly,' said Gerald. 'Between me and a woman, the social question does not enter. It is my own affair.'

'A ten-pound note on it,' said Birkin.

'You don't admit that a woman is a social being?' asked Ursula of Gerald.

'She is both,' said Gerald. 'She is a social being, as far as society is concerned. But for her own private self, she is a free agent, it is her own affair, what she does.'

'But won't it be rather difficult to arrange the two halves?' asked Ursula.

'Oh no,' replied Gerald. 'They arrange themselves naturally—we see it now, everywhere.'

'Don't you laugh so pleasantly till you're out of the wood,' said Birkin.

Gerald knitted his brows in momentary irritation.

'Was I laughing?' he said.

'*If*,' said Hermione at last, 'we could only realize that in the *spirit* we are all one, all equal in the spirit, all brothers there—the rest wouldn't matter, there would be no more of this carping and envy and this struggle for power, which destroys, only destroys.'

This speech was received in silence, and almost immediately the party rose from the table. But when the others had gone, Birkin turned round in bitter declamation, saying:

'It is just the opposite, just the contrary, Hermione. We are all different and unequal in spirit—it is only the *social* differences that are based on accidental material conditions. We are all abstractly or mathematically equal, if you like. Every man has hunger and thirst, two eyes, one nose and two legs. We're all the same in point of number. But spiritually there is pure difference and neither equality nor inequality counts. It is upon these two bits of knowledge that you must found a state. Your democracy is an absolute lie—your brotherhood of man is a pure falsity, if you apply it further than the mathematical abstraction. We all drank milk first, we all eat bread and meat, we all want to ride in motor-cars—therein lies the beginning and the end of the brotherhood of man. But no equality.

'But I, myself, who am myself, what have I to do with equality with any other man or woman? In the spirit, I am as separate as one star is from another, as different in quality and quantity. Establish a state on *that*. One man isn't any better than another, not because they are equal, but because they are intrinsically *other*, that there is no term of comparison. The minute you begin to compare, one man is seen to be far better than another, all the inequality you can imagine is there by nature. I want every man to have his share in the world's goods, so that I am rid of his importunity, so that I can tell him: "Now you've got what you want—you've got your fair share of the world's gear. Now, you one-mouthed fool, mind yourself and don't obstruct me." '

Hermione was looking at him with leering eyes, along her cheeks. He could feel violent waves of hatred and loathing of all he said coming out of her. It was dynamic hatred and loathing, coming strong and black out of the unconsciousness. She heard his words in her unconscious self, *consciously* she was as if deafened, she paid no heed to them.

'It *sounds* like megalomania, Rupert,' said Gerald, genially.

Hermione gave a queer, grunting sound. Birkin stood back.

'Yes, let it,' he said suddenly, the whole tone gone out of his voice, that had been so insistent, bearing everybody down. And he went away.

But he felt, later, a little compunction. He had been violent, cruel with poor Hermione. He wanted to recompense her, to make it up. He had hurt her, he had been vindictive. He wanted to be on good terms with her again.

He went into her boudoir, a remote and very cushiony place. She was sitting at her table writing letters. She lifted her face abstractedly when he entered, watched him go to the sofa, and sit down. Then she looked down at her paper again.

He took up a large volume which he had been reading before, and became minutely attentive to his author. His back was towards Hermione. She could not go on with her writing. Her whole mind was a chaos, darkness breaking in upon it, and herself struggling to gain control with her will, as a swimmer struggles with the swirling water. But in spite of her efforts she was borne down, darkness seemed to break over her, she felt as if her heart was bursting. The terrible tension grew stronger and stronger, it was most fearful agony, like being walled up.

And then she realized that his presence was the wall, his presence was destroying her. Unless she could break out, she must die most fearfully, walled up in horror. And he was the wall. She must break down the wall—she must break him down before her, the awful obstruction of him who obstructed her life to the last. It must be done, or she must perish most horribly.

Terrible shocks ran over her body, like shocks of electricity, as if many volts of electricity suddenly struck her down. She was aware of him sitting silently there, an unthinkable evil obstruction. Only this blotted out her mind, pressed out her very breathing, his silent, stooping back, the back of his head.

A terrible voluptuous thrill ran down her arms—she was going to know her voluptuous consummation. Her arms quivered and were strong, immeasurably and irresistibly strong. What delight, what delight in strength, what delirium of pleasure! She was going to have her consummation of voluptuous ecstasy at last. It was coming! In utmost terror and agony, she knew it was upon her now, in extremity of bliss. Her hand closed on a blue, beautiful ball of lapis lazuli that stood on her desk for a paper-weight. She rolled it round in her hand as she rose silently. Her heart was a pure flame in her breast, she was purely unconscious in ecstasy. She moved towards him and stood behind him for a moment in ecstasy. He, closed within the spell, remained motionless and unconscious.

Then swiftly, in a flame that drenched down her body like fluid lightning and gave her a perfect, unutterable consummation, unutterable satisfaction, she brought down the ball of jewel stone with all her force, crash on his head. But her fingers were in the way and deadened the blow. Nevertheless, down went his head on the table on which his book lay, the stone slid aside and over his ear, it was one convulsion of pure bliss for her, lit up by the crushed pain of her fingers. But it was not somehow complete. She lifted her arm high to aim once more, straight down on the head that lay dazed on the table. She must smash it, it must be smashed before her ecstasy was consummated, fulfilled for ever. A thousand lives, a thousand deaths mattered nothing now, only the fulfilment of this perfect ecstasy.

She was not swift, she could only move slowly. A strong spirit in him woke him and made him lift his face and twist to look at her. Her arm was raised, the hand clasping the ball of lapis lazuli. It was her left hand, he realized again with horror that she was left-handed. Hurriedly, with a burrowing motion, he covered his head under the thick volume of Thucydides, and the blow came down, almost breaking his neck, and shattering his heart.

He was shattered, but he was not afraid. Twisting round to face her he pushed the table over and got away from her. He was like a flask that is smashed to atoms, he seemed to himself that he was all fragments, smashed to bits. Yet his movements were perfectly coherent and clear, his soul was entire and unsurprised.

'No you don't, Hermione,' he said in a low voice. 'I don't let you.'

He saw her standing tall and livid and attentive, the stone clenched tense in her hand.

'Stand away and let me go,' he said, drawing near to her.

As if pressed back by some hand, she stood away, watching him all the time without changing, like a neutralized angel confronting him.

'It is no good,' he said, when he had gone past her. 'It isn't I who will die. You hear?'

He kept his face to her as he went out, lest she should strike again. While he was on his guard, she dared not move. And he was on his guard, she was powerless. So he had gone, and left her standing.

She remained perfectly rigid, standing as she was for a long time. Then she staggered to the couch and lay down, and went heavily to sleep. When she awoke, she remembered what she had done, but it seemed to her, she had only hit him, as any woman might do, because he tortured her. She was perfectly right. She knew that, spiritually, she was right. In her own infallible purity, she had done what must be done. She was right, she was pure. A drugged, almost sinister religious expression became permanent on her face.

Birkin, barely conscious, and yet perfectly direct in his motion, went out of the house and straight across the park, to the open country, to the hills. The brilliant day had become overcast, spots of rain were falling. He wandered on to a wild valley-side where were thickets of hazel, many flowers, tufts of heather, and little clumps of young fir-trees, budding with soft paws. It was rather wet everywhere, there was a stream running down at the bottom of the valley, which was gloomy, or seemed gloomy. He was aware that he could not regain his consciousness, that he was moving in a sort of darkness.

Yet he wanted something. He was happy in the wet hillside, that was overgrown and obscure with bushes and flowers. He wanted to touch them all, to saturate himself with the touch of them all. He took off his clothes, and sat down naked among the primroses, moving his feet softly among the primroses, his legs, his knees, his arms right up to the armpits, lying down and letting them touch his belly, his breasts. It was such a fine, cool, subtle touch all over him, he seemed to saturate himself with their contact.

But they were too soft. He went through the long grass to a clump of young fir-trees, that were no higher than a man. The soft sharp boughs beat upon him, as he moved in keen pangs against them, threw little cold showers of drops on his belly, and beat his loins with their clusters of soft-sharp nee-

dles. There was a thistle which pricked him vividly, but not
too much, because all his movements were too discriminate
and soft. To lie down and roll in the sticky, cool young hy-
acinths, to lie on one's belly and over one's back with hand-
fuls of fine wet grass, soft as a breath, soft and more delicate
and more beautiful than the touch of any woman; and then
to sting one's thigh against the living dark bristles of the fir-
boughs; and then to feel the light whip of the hazel on one's
shoulders, stinging, and then to clasp the silvery birch-trunk
against one's breast, its smoothness, its hardness, its vital
knots and ridges—this was good, this was all very good,
very satisfying. Nothing else would do, nothing else would
satisfy, except this coolness and subtlety of vegetation travelling into one's blood. How fortunate he was, that there was
this lovely, subtle, responsive vegetation, waiting for him, as
he waited for it; how fulfilled he was, how happy!

As he dried himself a little with his handkerchief, he
thought about Hermione and the blow. He could feel a pain
on the side of his head. But after all, what did it matter?
What did Hermione matter, what did people matter altogether? There was this perfect cool loneliness, so lovely and
fresh and unexplored. Really, what a mistake he had made,
thinking he wanted people, thinking he wanted a woman. He
did not want a woman—not in the least. The leaves and the
primroses and the trees, they were really lovely and cool and
desirable, they really came into the blood and were added on
to him. He was enrichened now immeasurably, and so glad.

It was quite right of Hermione to want to kill him. What
had he to do with her? Why should he pretend to have anything to do with human beings at all? Here was his world,
he wanted nobody and nothing but the lovely, subtle, responsive vegetation, and himself, his own living self.

It was necessary to go back into the world. That was true.
But that did not matter, so one knew where one belonged.
He knew now where he belonged. This was his place, his
marriage place. The world was extraneous.

He climbed out of the valley, wondering if he were mad.
But if so, he preferred his own madness, to the regular sanity. He rejoiced in his own madness, he was free. He did not
want that old sanity of the world, which was become so re-

pulsive. He rejoiced in the new-found world of his madness. It was so fresh and delicate and so satisfying.

As for the certain grief he felt at the same time, in his soul, that was only the remains of an old ethic, that bade a human being adhere to humanity. But he was weary of the old ethic, of the human being, and of humanity. He loved now the soft, delicate vegetation, that was so cool and perfect. He would overlook the old grief, he would put away the old ethic, he would be free in his new state.

He was aware of the pain in his head becoming more and more difficult every minute. He was walking now along the road to the nearest station. It was raining and he had no hat. But then plenty of cranks went out nowadays without hats, in the rain.

He wondered again how much of his heaviness of heart, a certain depression, was due to fear, fear lest anybody should have seen him naked lying against the vegetation. What a dread he had of mankind, of other people! It amounted almost to horror, to a sort of dream terror—his horror of being observed by some other people. If he were on an island, like Alexander Selkirk, with only the creatures and the trees, he would be free and glad, there would be none of this heaviness, this misgiving. He could love the vegetation and be quite happy and unquestioned, by himself.

He had better send a note to Hermione: she might trouble about him, and he did not want the onus of this. So at the station, he wrote saying:

I will go on to town—I don't want to come back to Breadalby for the present. But it is quite all right—I don't want you to mind having biffed me, in the least. Tell the others it is just one of my moods. You were quite right, to biff me—because I know you wanted to. So there's the end of it.

In the train, however, he felt ill. Every motion was insufferable pain, and he was sick. He dragged himself from the station into a cab, feeling his way step by step, like a blind man, and held up only by a dim will.

For a week or two he was ill, but he did not let Hermione

know, and she thought he was sulking; there was a complete estrangement between them. She became rapt, abstracted in her conviction of exclusive righteousness. She lived in and by her own self-esteem, conviction of her own rightness of spirit.

9

Coal-dust

Going home from school in the afternoon, the Brangwen girls descended the hill between the picturesque cottages of Willey Green till they came to the railway crossing. There they found the gate shut, because the colliery train was rumbling nearer. They could hear the small locomotive panting hoarsely as it advanced with caution between the embankments. The one-legged man in the little signal-hut by the road stared out from his security, like a crab from a snail-shell.

Whilst the two girls waited, Gerald Crich trotted up on a red Arab mare. He rode well and softly, pleased with the delicate quivering of the creature between his knees. And he was very picturesque, at least in Gudrun's eyes, sitting soft and close on the slender red mare, whose long tail flowed on the air. He saluted the two girls, and drew up at the crossing to wait for the gate, looking down the railway for the approaching train. In spite of her ironic smile at his picturesqueness, Gudrun liked to look at him. He was well set and easy, his face with its warm tan showed up his whitish, coarse moustache, and his blue eyes were full of sharp light as he watched the distance.

The locomotive chuffed slowly between the banks, hidden. The mare did not like it. She began to wince away, as if hurt by the unknown noise. But Gerald pulled her back and held her head to the gate. The sharp blasts of the chuffing engine broke with more and more force on her. The repeated sharp blows of unknown, terrifying noise struck through her till she was rocking with terror. She recoiled like a spring let go. But a glistening, half-smiling look came into Gerald's face. He brought her back again, inevitably.

The noise was released, the little locomotive with her clanking steel connecting-rod emerged on the highroad, clanking sharply. The mare rebounded like a drop of water from hot iron. Ursula and Gudrun pressed back into the hedge, in fear. But Gerald was heavy on the mare, and forced her back. It seemed as if he sank into her magnetically, and could thrust her back against herself.

'The fool!' cried Ursula loudly. 'Why doesn't he ride away till it's gone by?'

Gudrun was looking at him with black-dilated, spellbound eyes. But he sat glistening and obstinate, forcing the wheeling mare, which spun and swerved like a wind, and yet could not get out of the grasp of his will, nor escape from the mad clamour of terror that resounded through her, as the trucks thumped slowly, heavily, horrifying, one after the other, one pursuing the other, over the rails of the crossing.

The locomotive, as if wanting to see what could be done, put on the brakes, and back came the trucks rebounding on the iron buffers, striking like horrible cymbals, clashing nearer and nearer in frightful strident concussions. The mare opened her mouth and rose slowly, as if lifted up on a wind of terror. Then suddenly her fore-feet struck out, as she convulsed herself utterly away from the horror. Back she went, and the two girls clung to each other, feeling she must fall backwards on top of him. But he leaned forward, his face shining with fixed amusement, and at last he brought her down, sank her down, and was bearing her back to the mark. But as strong as the pressure of his compulsion was the repulsion of her utter terror, throwing her back away from the railway, so that she spun round and round on two legs, as if she were in the centre of some whirlwind. It made Gudrun faint with poignant dizziness, which seemed to penetrate to her heart.

'No—! No—! Let her go! Let her go, you fool, you *fool*—!' cried Ursula at the top of her voice, completely outside herself. And Gudrun hated her bitterly for being outside herself. It was unendurable that Ursula's voice was so powerful and naked.

A sharpened look came on Gerald's face. He bit himself down on the mare like a keen edge biting home, and *forced* her round. She roared as she breathed, her nostrils were two wide, hot holes, her mouth was apart, her eyes frenzied. It was a repulsive sight. But he held on her unrelaxed, with an almost mechanical relentlessness, keen as a sword pressing into her. Both man and horse were sweating with violence. Yet he seemed calm as a ray of cold sunshine.

Meanwhile the eternal trucks were rumbling on, very slowly, treading one after the other, one after the other, like a disgusting dream that has no end. The connecting chains were grinding and squeaking as the tension varied, the mare pawed and struck away mechanically now, her terror fulfilled in her, for now the man encompassed her; her paws were blind and pathetic as she beat the air, the man closed round her, and brought her down, almost as if she were part of his own physique.

'And she's bleeding! She's bleeding!' cried Ursula, frantic with opposition and hatred of Gerald. She alone understood him perfectly, in pure opposition.

Gudrun looked and saw the trickles of blood on the sides of the mare, and she turned white. And then on the very wound the bright spurs came down, pressing relentlessly. The world reeled and passed into nothingness for Gudrun, she could not know any more.

When she recovered, her soul was calm and cold, without feeling. The trucks were still rumbling by, and the man and the mare were still fighting. But she herself was cold and separate, she had no more feeling for them. She was quite hard and cold and indifferent.

They could see the top of the hooded guard's-van approaching, the sound of the trucks was diminishing, there was hope of relief from the intolerable noise. The heavy panting of the half-stunned mare sounded automatically, the man seemed to be relaxing confidently, his will bright and unstained. The guard's-van came up, and passed slowly, the guard staring out in his transition on the spectacle in the road. And, through the man in the closed wagon Gudrun could see the whole scene spectacularly, isolated and momentary, like a vision isolated in eternity.

Lovely, grateful silence seemed to trail behind the receding train. How sweet the silence is! Ursula looked with hatred on the buffers of the diminishing wagon. The gate-keeper stood ready at the door of his hut, to proceed to open the gate. But Gudrun sprang suddenly forward, in front of the struggling horse, threw off the latch and flung the gates asunder, throwing one-half to the keeper, and running with the other half forwards. Gerald suddenly let go the horse and leaped forwards, almost on to Gudrun. She was not afraid. As he jerked aside the mare's head, Gudrun cried, in a strange, high voice, like a gull, or like a witch screaming out from the side of the road:

'I should think you're proud.'

The words were distinct and formed. The man, twisting aside on his dancing horse, looked at her in some surprise, some wondering interest. Then the mare's hoofs had danced three times on the drum-like sleepers of the crossing, and man and horse were bounding springily, unequally up the road.

The two girls watched them go. The gate-keeper hobbled thudding over the logs of the crossing, with his wooden leg. He had fastened the gate. Then he also turned, and called to the girls:

'A masterful young jockey, that'll have his own road, if every anybody would.'

'Yes,' cried Ursula, in her hot, overbearing voice. 'Why couldn't he take the horse away, till the trucks had gone by? He's a fool, and a bully. Does he think it's manly, to torture a horse? It's a living thing, why should he bully it and torture it?'

There was a pause, then the gate-keeper shook his head, and replied:

'Yes, it's as nice a little mare as you could set eyes on— beautiful little thing, beautiful. Now you couldn't see his father treat any animal like that—not you. They're as different as they well can be, Gerald Crich and his father—two different men, different made.'

Then there was a pause.

'But why does he do it?' cried Ursula, 'why does he? Does he think he's grand, when he's bullied a sensitive creature, ten times as sensitive as himself?'

Again there was a cautious pause. Then again the man

shook his head, as if he would say nothing, but would think the more.

'I expect he's got to train the mare to stand to anything,' he replied. 'A pure-bred Harab—not the sort of breed as is used to round here—different sort from our sort altogether. They say as he got her from Constantinople.'

'He would!' said Ursula. 'He'd better have left her to the Turks, I'm sure they would have had more decency towards her.'

The man went in to drink his can of tea, the girls went on down the lane, that was deep in soft black dust. Gudrun was as if numbed in her mind by the sense of indomitable soft weight of the man, bearing down into the living body of the horse: the strong, indomitable thighs of the blond man clenching the palpitating body of the mare into pure control; a sort of soft white magnetic domination from the loins and thighs and calves, enclosing and encompassing the mare heavily into unutterable subordination, soft-blood-subordination, terrible.

On the left, as the girls walked silently, the coal-mine lifted its great mounds and its patterned head-stocks, the black railway with the trucks at rest looked like a harbour just below, a large bay of railroad with anchored wagons.

Near the second level-crossing, that went over many bright rails, was a farm belonging to the collieries, and a great round globe of iron, a disused boiler, huge and rusty and perfectly round, stood silently in a paddock by the road. The hens were pecking round it, some chickens were balanced on the drinking trough, wagtails flew away in among trucks, from the water.

On the other side of the wide crossing, by the roadside, was a heap of pale-grey stones for mending the roads, and a cart standing, and a middle-aged man with whiskers round his face was leaning on his shovel, talking to a young man in gaiters, who stood by the horse's head. Both men were facing the crossing.

They saw the two girls appear, small, brilliant figures in the near distance, in the strong light of the late afternoon. Both wore light, gay summer dresses. Ursula had an orange-coloured knitted coat, Gudrun a pale yellow. Ursula wore ca-

nary yellow stockings, Gudrun bright rose. The figures of
the two women seemed to glitter in progress over the wide
bay of the railway crossing, white and orange and yellow
and rose glittering in motion across a hot world silted with
coal-dust.

The two men stood quite still in the heat, watching. The
elder was a short, hard-faced energetic man of middle age,
the younger a labourer of twenty-three or so. They stood in
silence watching the advance of the sisters. They watched
whilst the girls drew near, and whilst they passed, and whilst
they receded down the dusty road, that had dwellings on one
side, and dusty young corn on the other.

Then the elder man, with the whiskers round his face, said
in a prurient manner to the young man:

'What price that, eh? She'll do, won't she?'

'Which?' asked the young man, eagerly, with a laugh.

'Her with the red stockings. What d' you say? I'd give my
week's wage for five minutes; what!—just for five minutes.'

Again the young man laughed.

'Your missis 'ud have summat to say to you,' he replied.

Gudrun had turned round and looked at the two men.
They were to her sinister creatures, standing watching after
her, by the heap of pale grey slag. She loathed the man with
whiskers round his face.

'You're first class, you are,' the man said to her, and to
the distance.

'Do you think it would be worth a week's wages?' said
the younger man, musing.

'Do I? I'd put 'em bloody-well down this second—'

The younger man looked after Gudrun and Ursula objectively, as if he wished to calculate what there might be, that
was worth his week's wages. He shook his head with fatal
misgiving.

'No,' he said. 'It's not worth that to me.'

'Isn't?' said the old man. 'By God, if it isn't to me!'

And he went on shovelling his stones.

The girls descended between the houses with slate roofs
and blackish brick walls. The heavy gold glamour of approaching sunset lay over all the colliery district, and the ugliness overlaid with beauty was like a narcotic to the senses.

On the roads silted with black dust, the rich light fell more warmly, more heavily, over all the amorphous squalor a kind of magic was cast, from the glowing close of day.

'It has a foul kind of beauty, this place,' said Gudrun, evidently suffering from fascination. 'Can't you feel in some way, a thick, hot attraction in it? I can. And it quite stupefies me.'

They were passing between blocks of miners' dwellings. In the back yards of several dwellings a miner could be seen washing himself in the open on this hot evening, naked down to the loins, his great trousers of moleskin slipping almost away. Miners already cleaned were sitting on their heels, with their backs near the walls, talking and silent in pure physical well-being, tired, and taking physical rest. Their voices sounded out with strong intonation, and the broad dialect was curiously caressing to the blood. It seemed to envelop Gudrun in a labourer's caress, there was in the whole atmosphere, a resonance of physical men, a glamorous thickness of labour and maleness, surcharged in the air. But it was universal in the district, and therefore unnoticed by the inhabitants.

To Gudrun, however, it was potent and half-repulsive. She could never tell why Beldover was so utterly different from London and the south, why one's whole feelings were different, why one seemed to live in another sphere. Now she realized that this was the world of powerful, underworld men who spent most of their time in the darkness. In their voices she could hear the voluptuous resonance of darkness, the strong, dangerous underworld, mindless, inhuman. They sounded also like strange machines, heavy, oiled. The voluptuousness was like that of machinery, cold and iron.

It was the same every evening when she came home, she seemed to move through a wave of disruptive force, that was given off from the presence of thousands of vigorous, underworld, half-automatized colliers, and which went to the brain and the heart, awaking a fatal desire, and a fatal callousness.

There came over her a nostalgia for the place. She hated it, she knew how utterly cut off it was, how hideous and how sickeningly mindless. Sometimes she beat her wings like a new Daphne, turning not into a tree but a machine. And yet she was overcome by the nostalgia. She struggled to get more and more into accord with the atmosphere of the place, she craved to get her satisfaction of it.

She felt herself drawn out at evening into the main street of the town, that was uncreated and ugly, and yet surcharged with this same potent atmosphere of intense, dark callousness. There were always miners about. They moved with their strange, distorted dignity, a certain beauty, and unnatural stillness in their bearing, a look of abstraction and half-resignation in their pale, often gaunt faces. They belonged to another world, they had a strange glamour, their voices were full of an intolerable deep resonance, like a machine's burring, a music more maddening than the sirens' long ago.

She found herself, with the rest of the common women, drawn out on Friday evenings to the little market. Friday was pay-day for the colliers, and Friday night was market night. Every woman was abroad, every man was out, shopping with his wife, or gathering with his pals. The pavements were dark for miles around with people coming in; the little market-place on the crown of the hill, and the main street of Beldover were black with thickly-crowded men and women.

It was dark, the market-place was hot with kerosene flares, which threw a ruddy light on the grave faces of the purchasing wives, and on the pale abstract faces of the men. The air was full of the sound of criers and of people talking, thick streams of people moved on the pavements towards the solid crowd of the market. The shops were blazing and packed with women, in the streets were men, mostly men, miners of all ages. Money was spent with almost lavish freedom.

The carts that came could not pass through. They had to wait, the driver calling and shouting, till the dense crowd would make way. Everywhere, young fellows from the outlying districts were making conversation with the girls, standing in the road and at the corners. The doors of the public-houses were open and full of light, men passed in and out in a continual stream, everywhere men were calling out to one another, or crossing to meet one another, or standing in little gangs and circles, discussing, endlessly discussing.

The sense of talk, buzzing, jarring, half-secret, the endless mining, and political wrangling, vibrated in the air like discordant machinery. And it was their voices which affected Gudrun almost to swooning. They aroused a strange, nostalgic ache of desire, something almost demoniacal, never to be fulfilled.

Like any other common girl of the district, Gudrun strolled up and down, up and down the length of the brilliant two hundred paces of the pavement nearest the market-place. She knew it was a vulgar thing to do; her father and mother could not bear it; but the nostalgia came over her, she must be among the people. Sometimes she sat among the louts in the cinema: rakish-looking, unattractive louts they were. Yet she must be among them.

And, like any other common lass, she found her 'boy'. It was an electrician, one of the electricians introduced according to Gerald's new scheme. He was an earnest, clever man, a scientist with a passion for sociology. He lived alone in a cottage, in lodgings, in Willey Green. He was a gentleman, and sufficiently well-to-do. His landlady spread the reports about him; he *would* have a large wooden tub in his bedroom, and every time he came in from work, he *would* have pails and pails of water brought up, to bathe in, then he put on clean shirt and under-clothing *every* day, and clean silk socks; fastidious and exacting he was in these respects, but in every other way, most ordinary and unassuming.

Gudrun knew all these things. The Brangwens' house was one to which the gossip came naturally and inevitably. Palmer was in the first place a friend of Ursula's. But in his pale, elegant, serious face there showed the same nostalgia that Gudrun felt. He too must walk up and down the street on Friday evening. So he walked with Gudrun, and a friendship was struck up between them. But he was not in love with Gudrun; he *really* wanted Ursula, but for some strange reason, nothing could happen between her and him. He liked to have Gudrun about, as a fellow-mind—but that was all. And she had no real feeling for him. He was a scientist, he had to have a woman to back him. But he was really impersonal, he had the fineness of an elegant piece of machinery. He was too cold, too destructive to care really for women, too great an egoist. He was polarized by the men. Individually he detested and despised them. In the mass they fascinated him, as machinery fascinated him. They were a new sort of machinery to him—but incalculable, incalculable.

So Gudrun strolled the streets with Palmer, or went to the cinema with him. And his long, pale, rather elegant face flickered as he made his sarcastic remarks. There they were, the two of them: two elegants in one sense: in the other sense, two units, absolutely adhering to the people, teeming with the distorted colliers. The same secret seemed to be working in the souls of all alike, Gudrun, Palmer, the rakish young bloods, the gaunt, middle-aged men. All had a secret sense of power, and of inexpressible destructiveness, and of fatal half-heartedness, a sort of rottenness in the will.

Sometimes Gudrun would start aside, see it all, see how she was sinking in. And then she was filled with a fury of contempt and anger. She felt she was sinking into one mass with the rest—all so close and intermingled and breathless. It was horrible. She stifled. She prepared for flight, feverishly she flew to her work. But soon she let go. She started off into the country—the darkish, glamorous country. The spell was beginning to work again.

10

Sketch-book

One morning the sisters were sketching by the side of Willey Water, at the remote end of the lake. Gudrun had waded out to a gravelly shoal, and was seated like a Buddhist, staring fixedly at the water-plants that rose succulent from the mud of the low shores. What she could see was mud, soft, oozy, watery mud, and from its festering chill, water-plants rose up, thick and cool and fleshy, very straight and turgid, thrusting out their leaves at right angles, and having dark lurid colours, dark green and blotches of black-purple and bronze. But she could feel their turgid fleshy structure as in a sensuous vision, she *knew* how they rose out of the mud, she *knew* how they thrust out from themselves, how they stood stiff and succulent against the air.

Ursula was watching the butterflies, of which there were dozens near the water, little blue ones suddenly snapping out of nothingness into a jewel-life, a large black-and-red one standing upon a flower and breathing with his soft wings, intoxicatingly, breathing pure, ethereal sunshine; two white ones wrestling in the low air; there was a halo round them; ah, when they came tumbling nearer they were orange-tips, and it was the orange that had made the halo. Ursula rose and drifted away, unconscious like the butterflies.

Gudrun, absorbed in a stupor of apprehension of surging water-plants, sat crouched on the shoal, drawing, not looking up for a long time, and then staring unconsciously, absorbedly at the rigid, naked, succulent stems. Her feet were bare, her hat lay on the bank opposite.

She started out of her trance, hearing the knocking of oars. She looked round. There was a boat with a gaudy Japanese parasol, and a man in white, rowing. The woman was

Hermione, and the man was Gerald. She knew it instantly.
And instantly she perished in the keen *frisson* of anticipation, an electric vibration in her veins, intense, much more
intense than that which was always humming low in the atmosphere of Beldover.

Gerald was her escape from the heavy slough of the pale,
underworld, automatic colliers. He started out of the mud.
He was master. She saw his back, the movement of his white
loins. But not that—it was the whiteness he seemed to enclose as he bent forwards, rowing. He seemed to stoop to
something. His glistening, whitish hair seemed like the electricity of the sky.

'There's Gudrun,' came Hermione's voice floating distinct
over the water. 'We will go and speak to her. Do you mind?'

Gerald looked round and saw the girl standing by the water's edge, looking at him. He pulled the boat towards her,
magnetically, without thinking of her. In his world, his conscious world, she was still nobody. He knew that Hermione
had a curious pleasure in treading down all the social differences, at least apparently, and he left it to her.

'How do you do, Gudrun?' sang Hermione, using the
Christian name in the fashionable manner. 'What are you
doing?'

'How do you do, Hermione? I *was* sketching.'

'Were you?' The boat drifted nearer, till the keel ground
on the bank. 'May we see? I should like to *so* much.'

It was no use resisting Hermione's deliberate intention.

'Well—' said Gudrun reluctantly, for she always hated to
have her unfinished work exposed—'there's nothing in the
least interesting.'

'Isn't there? But let me see, will you?'

Gudrun reached out the sketch-book, Gerald stretched
from the boat to take it. And as he did so, he remembered
Gudrun's last words to him, and her face lifted up to him as
he sat on the swerving horse. An intensification of pride
went over his nerves, because he felt, in some way she was
compelled by him. The exchange of feeling between them
was strong and apart from their consciousness.

And as if in a spell, Gudrun was aware of his body,
stretching and surging like the marsh-fire, stretching towards

her, his hand coming straight forward like a stem. Her voluptuous, acute apprehension of him made the blood faint in
her veins, her mind went dim and unconscious. And he
rocked on the water perfectly, like the rocking of phospho-
rescence. He looked round at the boat. It was drifting off a
little. He lifted the oar to bring it back. And the exquisite
pleasure of slowly arresting the boat, in the heavy-soft water, was complete as a swoon.

'That's what you have done,' said Hermione, looking
searchingly at the plants on the shore, and comparing with
Gudrun's drawing. Gudrun looked round in the direction of
Hermione's long, pointing finger. 'That is it, isn't it?' repeated Hermione needing confirmation.

'Yes,' said Gudrun automatically, taking no real heed.

'Let me look,' said Gerald, reaching forward for the book.
But Hermione ignored him, he must not presume, before she
had finished. But he, his will as unthwarted and as unflinching as hers, stretched forward till he touched the book. A little shock, a storm of revulsion against him, shook Hermione
unconsciously. She released the book when he had not properly got it, and it tumbled against the side of the boat and
bounced into the water.

'There!' sang Hermione, with a strange ring of malevolent
victory. 'I'm so sorry, so awfully sorry. Can't you get it,
Gerald?'

This last was said in a note of anxious sneering that made
Gerald's veins tingle with fine hate for her. He leaned far out
of the boat, reaching down into the water. He could feel his
position was ridiculous, his loins exposed behind him.

'It is of no importance,' came the strong, clanging voice
of Gudrun. She seemed to touch him. But he reached farther,
the boat swayed violently. Hermione, however, remained un-
perturbed. He grasped the book, under the water, and
brought it up, dripping.

'I'm so dreadfully sorry—dreadfully sorry,' repeated
Hermione. 'I'm afraid it was all my fault.'

'It's of no importance—really, I assure you—it doesn't
matter in the least,' said Gudrun loudly, with emphasis, her
face flushed scarlet. And she held out her hand impatiently

for the wet book, to have done with the scene. Gerald gave it to her. He was not quite himself.

'I'm so dreadfully sorry,' repeated Hermione, till both Gerald and Gudrun were exasperated. 'Is there nothing that can be done?'

'In what way?' asked Gudrun, with cool irony.

'Can't we save the drawings?'

There was a moment's pause, wherein Gudrun made evident all her refutation of Hermione's persistence.

'I assure you,' said Gudrun, with cutting distinctness, 'the drawings are quite as good as ever they were, for my purpose. I want them only for reference.'

'But can't I give you a new book? I wish you'd let me do that. I feel so truly sorry. I feel it was all my fault.'

'As far as I saw,' said Gudrun, 'it wasn't your fault at all. If there was any *fault,* it was Mr Crich's. But the whole thing is *entirely* trivial, and it really is ridiculous to take any notice of it.'

Gerald watched Gudrun closely, whilst she repulsed Hermione. There was a body of cold power in her. He watched her with an insight that amounted to clairvoyance. He saw her a dangerous, hostile spirit, that could stand undiminished and unabated. It was so finished, and of such perfect gesture, moreover.

'I'm awfully glad if it doesn't matter,' he said; 'if there's no real harm done.'

She looked back at him, with her fine blue eyes, and signalled full into his spirit, as she said, her voice ringing with intimacy almost caressive now it was addressed to him:

'Of course, it doesn't matter in the *least.'*

The bond was established between them, in that look, in her tone. In her tone, she made the understanding clear—they were of the same kind, he and she, a sort of diabolic free-masonry subsisted between them. Henceforward, she knew, she had her power over him. Wherever they met, they would be secretly associated. And he would be helpless in the association with her. Her soul exulted.

'Good-bye! I'm so glad you forgive me. Gooood-bye!'

Hermione sang her farewell, and waved her hand. Gerald automatically took the oar and pushed off. But he was looking all the time, with a glimmering, subtly-smiling admiration in his eyes, at Gudrun, who stood on the shoal shaking the wet book in her hand. She turned away and ignored the receding boat. But Gerald looked back as he rowed, beholding her, forgetting what he was doing.

'Aren't we going too much to the left?' sang Hermione, as she sat ignored under her coloured parasol.

Gerald looked round without replying, the oars balanced and glancing in the sun.

'I think it's all right,' he said good-humouredly, beginning to row again without thinking of what he was doing. And Hermione disliked him extremely for his good-humoured obliviousness, she was nullified, she could not regain ascendancy.

11

An Island

Meanwhile Ursula had wandered on from Willey Water along the course of the bright little stream. The afternoon was full of larks' singing. On the bright hill-sides was a subdued smoulder of gorse. A few forget-me-nots flowered by the water. There was a rousedness and a glancing everywhere.

She strayed absorbedly on, over the brooks. She wanted to go to the mill-pond above. The big mill-house was deserted, save for a labourer and his wife who lived in the kitchen. So she passed through the empty farm-yard and through the wilderness of a garden, and mounted the bank by the sluice. When she got to the top, to see the old, velvety surface of the pond before her, she noticed a man on the bank, tinkering with a punt. It was Birkin sawing and hammering away.

She stood at the head of the sluice, looking at him. He was unaware of anybody's presence. He looked very busy, like a wild animal, active and intent. She felt she ought to go away, he would not want her. He seemed to be so much occupied. But she did not want to go away. Therefore she moved along the bank till he would look up.

Which he soon did. The moment he saw her, he dropped his tools and came forward, saying:

'How do you do? I'm making the punt water-tight. Tell me if you think it is right.'

She went along with him.

'You are your father's daughter, so you can tell me if it will do,' he said.

She bent to look at the patched punt.

'I am sure I am my father's daughter,' she said, fearful of

having to judge. 'But I don't know anything about carpentry. It *looks* right, don't you think?'

'Yes, I think. I hope it won't let me to the bottom, that's all. Though even so, it isn't a great matter, I should come up again. Help me to get it into the water, will you?'

With combined efforts they turned over the heavy punt and set it afloat.

'Now,' he said, 'I'll try it and you can watch what happens. Then if it carries, I'll take you over to the island.'

'Do,' she cried, watching anxiously.

The pond was large, and had that perfect stillness and the dark lustre of very deep water. There were two small islands overgrown with bushes and a few trees, towards the middle. Birkin pushed himself off, and veered clumsily in the pond. Luckily the punt drifted so that he could catch hold of a willow bough, and pull it to the island.

'Rather overgrown,' he said, looking into the interior, 'but very nice. I'll come and fetch you. The boat leaks a little.'

In a moment he was with her again, and she stepped into the wet punt.

'It'll float us all right,' he said, and manoeuvred again to the island.

They landed under a willow tree. She shrank from the little jungle of rank plants before her, evil-smelling figwort and hemlock. But he explored into it.

'I shall mow this down,' he said, 'and then it will be romantic—like Paul et Virginie.'

'Yes, one could have lovely Watteau picnics here,' cried Ursula with enthusiasm.

His face darkened.

'I don't want Watteau picnics here,' he said.

'Only your Virginie,' she laughed.

'Virginie enough,' he smiled wryly. 'No, I don't want her either.'

Ursula looked at him closely. She had not seen him since Breadalby. He was very thin and hollow, with a ghastly look in his face.

'You have been ill, haven't you?' she asked, rather repulsed.

'Yes,' he replied coldly.

They had sat down under the willow tree, and were looking at the pond, from their retreat on the island.

'Has it made you frightened?' she asked.

'What of?' he asked, turning his eyes to look at her.
Something in him, inhuman and unmitigated, disturbed her,
and shook her out of her ordinary self.

'It *is* frightening to be very ill, isn't it?' she said.

'It isn't pleasant,' he said. 'Whether one is really afraid of
death or not, I have never decided. In one mood, not a bit,
in another, very much.'

'But doesn't it make you feel ashamed? I think it makes
one so ashamed, to be ill—illness is so terribly humiliating,
don't you think?'

He considered for some minutes.

'Maybe,' he said. 'Though one knows all the time one's
life isn't really right, at the source. That's the humiliation. I
don't see that the illness counts so much, after that. One is
ill because one doesn't live properly—can't. It's the failure
to live that makes one ill, and humiliates one.'

'But do you fail to live?' she asked, almost jeering.

'Why, yes—I don't make much of a success of my days.
One seems always to be bumping one's nose against the
blank wall ahead.'

Ursula laughed. She was frightened, and when she was
frightened she always laughed and pretended to be jaunty.

'Your poor nose!' she said, looking at that feature of his
face.

'No wonder it's ugly,' he replied.

She was silent for some minutes, struggling with her own
self-deception. It was an instinct in her, to deceive herself.

'But *I'm* happy—I think life is *awfully* jolly,' she said.

'Good,' he answered, with a certain cold indifference.

She reached for a bit of paper which had wrapped a small
piece of chocolate she had found in her pocket, and began
making a boat. He watched her without heeding her. There
was something strangely pathetic and tender in her moving,
unconscious finger-tips, that were agitated and hurt, really.

'I *do* enjoy things—don't you?' she asked.

'Oh yes! But it infuriates me that I can't get right, at the
really growing part of me. I feel all tangled and messed up,

and I *can't* get straight anyhow. I don't know what really to *do*. One must do something somewhere.'

'Why should you always be *doing*?' she retorted. 'It is so plebeian. I think it is much better to be really patrician, and to do nothing but just be oneself, like a walking flower.'

'I quite agree,' he said, 'if one has burst into blossom. But I can't get my flower to blossom anyhow. Either it is blighted in the bud, or has got the smother-fly, or it isn't nourished. Curse it, it isn't even a bud. It is a contravened knot.'

Again she laughed. He was so very fretful and exasperated. But she was anxious and puzzled. How was one to get out, anyhow. There must be a way out somewhere.

There was a silence, wherein she wanted to cry. She reached for another bit of chocolate paper, and began to fold another boat.

'And why is it,' she asked at length, 'that there is no flowering, no dignity of human life now?'

'The whole idea is dead. Humanity itself is dry-rotten, really. There are myriads of human beings hanging on the bush—and they look very nice and rosy, your healthy young men and women. But they are apples of Sodom, as a matter of fact, Dead Sea Fruit, gall-apples. It isn't true that they have any significance—their insides are full of bitter, corrupt ash.'

'But there *are* good people,' protested Ursula.

'Good enough for the life of today. But mankind is a dead tree, covered with fine brilliant galls of people.'

Ursula could not help stiffening herself against this, it was too picturesque and final. But neither could she help making him go on.

'And if it is so, *why* is it?' she asked, hostile. They were rousing each other to a fine passion of opposition.

'Why, why are people all balls of bitter dust? Because they won't fall off the tree when they're ripe. They hang on to their old positions when the position is overpast, till they become infested with little worms and dry-rot.'

There was a long pause. His voice had become hot and very sarcastic. Ursula was troubled and bewildered, they were both oblivious of everything but their own immersion.

'But even if everybody is wrong—where are *you* right?' she cried, 'where are you any better?'

'I?—I'm not right,' he cried back. 'At least my only rightness lies in the fact that I know it. I detest what I am, outwardly. I loathe myself as a human being. Humanity is a huge aggregate lie, and a huge lie is less than a small truth. Humanity is less, far less than the individual, because the individual may sometimes be capable of truth, and humanity is a tree of lies. And they say that love is the greatest thing; they persist in *saying* this, the foul liars, and just look at what they do! Look at all the millions of people who repeat every minute that love is the greatest, and charity is the greatest—and see what they are doing all the time. By their works ye shall know them, for dirty liars and cowards, who daren't stand by their own actions, much less by their own words.'

'But,' said Ursula sadly, 'that doesn't alter the fact that love is the greatest, does it? What they *do* doesn't alter the truth of what they say, does it?'

'Completely, because if what they say *were* true, then they couldn't help fulfilling it. But they maintain a lie, and so they run amok at last. It's a lie to say that love is the greatest. You might as well say that hate is the greatest, since the opposite of everything balances. What people want is hate—hate and nothing but hate. And in the name of righteousness and love, they get it. They distil themselves with nitroglycerine, all the lot of them, out of very love. It's the lie that kills. If we want hate, let us have it—death, murder, torture, violent destruction—let us have it: but not in the name of love. But I abhor humanity, I wish it was swept away. It could go, and there would be no *absolute* loss, if every human being perished tomorrow. The reality would be untouched. Nay, it would be better. The real tree of life would then be rid of the most ghastly, heavy crop of Dead Sea Fruit, the intolerable burden of myriad simulacra of people, an infinite weight of mortal lies.'

'So you'd like everybody in the world destroyed?' said Ursula.

'I should indeed.'

'And the world empty of people?'

'Yes truly. You yourself, don't you find it a beautiful clean thought, a world empty of people, just uninterrupted grass, and a hare sitting up?'

The pleasant sincerity of his voice made Ursula pause to consider her own proposition. And really it *was* attractive: a clean, lovely, humanless world. It was the *really* desirable. Her heart hesitated, and exulted. But still, she was dissatisfied with *him*.

'But,' she objected, 'you'd be dead yourself, so what good would it do you?'

'I would die like a shot, to know that the earth would really be cleaned of all the people. It is the most beautiful and freeing thought. Then there would *never* be another foul humanity created, for a universal defilement.'

'No,' said Ursula, 'there would be nothing.'

'What! Nothing? Just because humanity was wiped out? You flatter yourself. There'd be everything.'

'But how, if there were no people?'

'Do you think that creation depends on *man*! It merely doesn't. There are the trees and the grass and birds. I much prefer to think of the lark rising up in the morning upon a humanless world. Man is a mistake, he must go. There is the grass, and hares and adders, and the unseen hosts, actual angels that go about freely when a dirty humanity doesn't interrupt them—and good pure-tissued demons: very nice.'

It pleased Ursula, what he said, pleased her very much, as a fantasy. Of course it was only a pleasant fancy. She herself knew too well the actuality of humanity, its hideous actuality. She knew it could not disappear so cleanly and conveniently. It had a long way to go yet, a long and hideous way. Her subtle, feminine, demoniacal soul knew it well.

'If only man was swept off the face of the earth, creation would go on so marvelously, with a new start, non-human. Man is one of the mistakes of creation—like the ichthyosauri. If only he were gone again, think what lovely things would come out of the liberated days;—things straight out of the fire.'

'But man will never be gone,' she said, with insidious, diabolical knowledge of the horrors of persistence. 'The world will go with him.'

'Ah no,' he answered, 'not so. I believe in the proud angels and the demons that are our fore-runners. They will destroy us, because we are not proud enough. The ichthyosauri were not proud: they crawled and floundered as we do. And besides, look at elder-flowers and bluebells—they are a sign that pure creation takes place—even the butterfly. But humanity never gets beyond the caterpillar stage—it rots in the chrysalis, it never will have wings. It is anti-creation, like monkeys and baboons.'

Ursula watched him as he talked. There seemed a certain impatient fury in him, all the while, and at the same time a great amusement in everything, and a final tolerance. And it was this tolerance she mistrusted, not the fury. She saw that, all the while, in spite of himself, he would have to be trying to save the world. And this knowledge, whilst it comforted her heart somewhere with a little self-satisfaction, stability, yet filled her with a certain sharp contempt and hate of him. She wanted him to herself, she hated the Salvator Mundi touch. It was something diffuse and generalized about him, which she could not stand. He would behave in the same way, say the same things, give himself as completely to anybody who came along, anybody and everybody who liked to appeal to him. It was despicable, a very insidious form of prostitution.

'But,' she said, 'you believe in individual love, even if you don't believe in loving humanity—?'

'I don't believe in love at all—that is, any more than I believe in hate, or in grief. Love is one of the emotions like all the others—and so it is all right whilst you feel it. But I can't see how it becomes an absolute. It is just part of human relationships, no more. And it is only part of *any* human relationship. And why one should be required *always* to feel it, any more than one always feels sorrow or distant joy, I cannot conceive. Love isn't a desideratum—it is an emotion you feel or you don't feel, according to circumstance.'

'Then why do you care about people at all?' she asked, 'if you don't believe in love? Why do you bother about humanity?'

'Why do I? Because I can't get away from it.'

'Because you love it,' she persisted.

It irritated him.

'If I do love it,' he said, 'it is my disease.'

'But it is a disease you don't want to be cured of,' she said, with some cold sneering.

He was silent now, feeling she wanted to insult him.

'And if you don't believe in love, what *do* you believe in?' she asked, mocking. 'Simply in the end of the world, and grass?'

He was beginning to feel a fool.

'I believe in the unseen hosts,' he said.

'And nothing else? You believe in nothing visible, except grass and birds? Your world is a poor show.'

'Perhaps it is,' he said, cool and superior now he was offended, assuming a certain insufferable aloof superiority, and withdrawing into his distance.

Ursula disliked him. But also she felt she had lost something. She looked at him as he sat crouched on the bank. There was a certain priggish Sunday-school stiffness over him, priggish and detestable. And yet, at the same time, the moulding of him was so quick and attractive, it gave such a great sense of freedom: the moulding of his brows, his chin, his whole physique, something so alive, somewhere, in spite of the look of sickness.

And it was this duality in feeling which he created in her, that made a fine hate of him quicken in her bowels. There was his wonderful, desirable life-rapidity, the rare quality of an utterly desirable man; and there was at the same time this ridiculous, mean effacement into a Salvator Mundi and a Sunday-school teacher, a prig of the stiffest type.

He looked up at her. He saw her face strangely enkindled, as if suffused from within by a powerful sweet fire. His soul was arrested in wonder. She was enkindled in her own living fire. Arrested in wonder and in pure, perfect attraction, he moved towards her. She sat like a strange queen, almost supernatural in her glowing smiling richness.

'The point about love,' he said, his consciousness quickly adjusting itself, 'is that we hate the word because we have vulgarized it. It ought to be proscribed, tabooed from utterance, for many years, till we get a new, better idea.'

There was a beam of understanding between them.

'But it always means the same thing,' she said.

'Ah, God, no, let it not mean that any more,' he cried. 'Let the old meanings go.'

'But still it is love,' she persisted. A strange, wicked yellow light shone at him in her eyes.

He hesitated, baffled, withdrawing.

'No,' he said, 'it isn't. Spoken like that, never in the world. You've no business to utter the word.'

'I must leave it to you, to take it out of the Ark of the Covenant at the right moment,' she mocked.

Again they looked at each other. She suddenly sprang up, turned her back to him, and walked away. He too rose slowly and went to the water's edge, where, crouching, he began to amuse himself unconsciously. Picking a daisy he dropped it on the pond, so that the stem was a keel, the flower floated like a little water-lily, staring with its open face up to the sky. It turned slowly round, in a slow, slow Dervish dance, as it veered away.

He watched it, then dropped another daisy into the water, and after that another, and sat watching them with bright, absolved eyes, crouching near on the bank. Ursula turned to look. A strange feeling possessed her, as if something were taking place. But it was all intangible. And some sort of control was being put on her. She could not know. She could only watch the brilliant little discs of the daisies veering slowly in travel on the dark, lustrous water. The little flotilla was drifting into the light, a company of white specks in the distance.

'Do let us go to the shore, to follow them,' she said, afraid of being any longer imprisoned on the island. And they pushed off in the punt.

She was glad to be on the free land again. She went along the bank towards the sluice. The daisies were scattered broadcast on the pond, tiny radiant things, like an exaltation, points of exaltation here and there. Why did they move her so strongly and mystically?

'Look,' he said, 'your boat of purple paper is escorting them, and they are a convoy of rafts.'

Some of the daisies came slowly towards her, hesitating,

making a shy bright little cotillon on the dark clear water. Their gay bright candour moved her so much as they came near, that she was almost in tears.

'Why are they so lovely,' she cried. 'Why do I think them so lovely?'

'They are nice flowers,' he said, her emotional tones putting a constraint on him.

'You know that a daisy is a company of florets, a concourse, become individual. Don't the botanists put it highest in the line of development? I believe they do.'

'The compositae, yes, I think so,' said Ursula, who was never very sure of anything. Things she knew perfectly well, at one moment, seemed to become doubtful the next.

'Explain it so, then,' he said. 'The daisy is a perfect little democracy, so it's the highest of flowers, hence its charm.'

'No,' she cried, 'no—never. It isn't democratic.'

'No,' he admitted. 'It's the golden mob of the proletariat, surrounded by a showy white fence of the idle rich.'

'How hateful—your hateful social orders!' she cried.

'Quite! It's a daisy—we'll leave it alone.'

'Do. Let it be a dark horse for once,' she said: 'if anything can be a dark horse to you,' she added satirically.

They stood aside, forgetful. As if a little stunned, they both were motionless, barely conscious. The little conflict into which they had fallen had torn their consciousness and left them like two impersonal forces, there in contact.

He became aware of the lapse. He wanted to say something, to get on to a new more ordinary footing.

'You know,' he said, 'that I am having rooms here at the mill? Don't you think we can have some good times?'

'Oh, are you?' she said, ignoring all his implication of admitted intimacy.

He adjusted himself at once, became normally distant.

'If I find I can live sufficiently by myself,' he continued, 'I shall give up my work altogether. It has become dead to me. I don't believe in the humanity I pretend to be part of, I don't care a straw for the social ideals I live by, I hate the dying organic form of social mankind—so it can't be anything but trumpery, to work at education. I shall drop it as soon as I am clear enough—tomorrow perhaps—and be by myself.'

'Have you enough to live on?' asked Ursula.

'Yes—I've about four hundred a year. That makes it easy for me.'

There was a pause.

'And what about Hermione?' asked Ursula.

'That's over, finally—a pure failure, and never could have been anything else.'

'But you still know each other?'

'We could hardly pretend to be strangers, could we?'

There was a stubborn pause.

'But isn't that a half-measure?' asked Ursula at length.

'I don't think so,' he said. 'You'll be able to tell me if it is.'

Again there was a pause of some minutes' duration. He was thinking.

'One must throw everything away, everything—let everything go, to get the one last thing one wants,' he said.

'What thing?' she asked in challenge.

'I don't know—freedom together,' he said.

She had wanted him to say 'love'.

There was heard a loud barking of the dogs below. He seemed disturbed by it. She did not notice. Only she thought he seemed uneasy.

'As a matter of fact,' he said, in rather a small voice, 'I believe that is Hermione come now, with Gerald Crich. She wanted to see the rooms before they are furnished.'

'I know,' said Ursula. 'She will superintend the furnishing for you.'

'Probably. Does it matter?'

'Oh no, I should think not,' said Ursula. 'Though personally, I can't bear her. I think she is a lie, if you like, you who are always talking about lies.' Then she ruminated for a moment, when she broke out: 'Yes, and I do mind if she furnishes your rooms—I do mind. I mind that you keep her hanging on at all.'

He was silent now, frowning.

'Perhaps,' he said. 'I don't *want* her to furnish the rooms here—and I don't keep her hanging on. Only, I needn't be churlish to her, need I? At any rate, I shall have to go down and see them now. You'll come, won't you?'

'I don't think so,' she said coldly and irresolutely.

'Won't you? Yes, do. Come and see the rooms as well. Do come.'

12

Carpeting

He set off down the bank, and she went unwillingly with him. Yet she would not have stayed away, either.

'We know each other well, you and I, already,' he said. She did not answer.

In the large darkish kitchen of the mill, the labourer's wife was talking shrilly to Hermione and Gerald, who stood, he in white and she in a glistening bluish foulard, strangely luminous in the dusk of the room; whilst from the cages on the walls, a dozen or more canaries sang at the top of their voices. The cages were all placed round a small square window at the back, where the sunshine came in, a beautiful beam, filtering through green leaves of a tree. The voice of Mrs Salmon shrilled against the noise of the birds, which rose ever more wild and triumphant, and the woman's voice went up and up against them, and the birds replied with wild animation.

'Here's Rupert!' shouted Gerald in the midst of the din. He was suffering badly, being very sensitive in the ear.

'O-o-h them birds, they won't let you speak—!' shrilled the labourer's wife in disgust. 'I'll cover them up.'

And she darted here and there, throwing a duster, an apron, a towel, a table-cloth over the cages of the birds.

'Now will you stop it, and let a body speak for your row,' she said, still in a voice that was too high.

The party watched her. Soon the cages were covered, they had a strange funereal look. But from under the towels odd defiant trills and bubblings still shook out.

'Oh, they won't go on,' said Mrs Salmon reassuringly. 'They'll go to sleep now.'

'Really,' said Hermione politely.

'They will,' said Gerald. 'They will go to sleep automatically, now the impression of evening is produced.'

'Are they so easily deceived?' cried Ursula.

'Oh yes,' replied Gerald. 'Don't you know the story of Fabre, who, when he was a boy, put a hen's head under her wing, and she straight away went to sleep? It's quite true.'

'And did that make him a naturalist?' asked Birkin.

'Probably,' said Gerald.

Meanwhile Ursula was peeping under one of the cloths. There sat the canary in a corner, bunched and fluffed up for sleep.

'How ridiculous!' she cried. 'It really thinks the night has come! How absurd! Really, how can one have any respect for a creature that is so easily taken in!'

'Yes,' sang Hermione, coming also to look. She put her hand on Ursula's arm and chuckled a low laugh. 'Yes, doesn't he look comical?' she chuckled. 'Like a stupid husband.'

Then, with her hand still on Ursula's arm, she drew her away, saying, in her mild sing-song:

'How did you come here? We saw Gudrun too.'

'I came to look at the pond,' said Ursula, 'and I found Mr Birkin there.'

'Did you? This is quite a Brangwen land, isn't it?'

'I'm afraid I hoped so,' said Ursula. 'I ran here for refuge, when I saw you down the lake, just putting off.'

'Did you! And now we've run you to earth.'

Hermione's eyelids lifted with an uncanny movement, amused but overwrought. She had always her strange, rapt look, unnatural and irresponsible.

'I was going on,' said Ursula. 'Mr Birkin wanted me to see the rooms. Isn't it delightful to live here? It is perfect.'

'Yes,' said Hermione, abstractedly. Then she turned right away from Ursula, ceased to know her existence.

'How do you feel, Rupert?' she sang in a new, affectionate tone to Birkin.

'Very well,' he replied.

'Were you quite comfortable?' The curious, sinister, rapt look was on Hermione's face, she shrugged her bosom in a convulsed movement, and seemed like one half in a trance.

'Quite comfortable,' he replied.

There was a long pause, whilst Hermione looked at him for a long time, from under her heavy, drugged eyelids.

'And you think you'll be happy here?' she said at last.

'I'm sure I shall.'

'I'm sure I shall do anything for him as I can,' said the labourer's wife. 'And I'm sure our mester will; so I *hope* as he'll find himself comfortable.'

Hermione turned and looked at her slowly.

'Thank you so much,' she said, and then she turned completely away again. She recovered her position, and lifting her face towards him, and addressing him exclusively, she said:

'Have you measured the rooms?'

'No,' he said, 'I've been mending the punt.'

'Shall we do it now?' she said slowly, balanced and dispassionate.

'Have you got a tape measure, Mrs Salmon?' he said, turning to the woman.

'Yes, sir, I think I can find one,' replied the woman, bustling immediately to a basket. "This is the only one I've got, if it will do.'

Hermione took it, though it was offered to him.

'Thank you so much,' she said. 'It will do very nicely. Thank you so much.' Then she turned to Birkin, saying with a little gay movement: 'Shall we do it now, Rupert?'

'What about the others, they'll be bored,' he said reluctantly.

'Do you mind?' said Hermione, turning to Ursula and Gerald vaguely.

'Not in the least,' they replied.

'Which room shall we do first?' she said, turning again to Birkin, with the same gaiety, now she was going to *do* something with him.

'We'll take them as they come,' he said.

'Should I be getting your teas ready, while you do that?' said the labourer's wife, also gay because *she* had something to do.

'Would you?' said Hermione, turning to her with the curious motion of intimacy that seemed to envelop the woman, draw her almost to Hermione's breast, and which left the others standing apart. 'I should be so glad. Where shall we have it?'

'Where would you like it? Shall it be in here, or out on the grass?'

'Where shall we have tea?' sang Hermione to the company at large.

'On the bank by the pond. And *we'll* carry the things up, if you'll just get them ready, Mrs Salmon,' said Birkin.

'All right,' said the pleased woman.

The party moved down the passage into the front room. It was empty, but clean and sunny. There was a window looking on to the tangled front garden.

'This is the dining-room,' said Hermione. 'We'll measure it this way, Rupert—you go down there—'

'Can't I do it for you,' said Gerald, coming to take the end of the tape.

'No, thank you,' cried Hermione, stooping to the ground in her bluish, brilliant foulard. It was a great joy to her to *do* things, and to have the ordering of the job, with Birkin. He obeyed her subduedly. Ursula and Gerald looked on. It was a peculiarity of Hermione's, that at every moment, she had one intimate, and turned all the rest of those present into on-lookers. This raised her into a state of triumph.

They measured and discussed in the dining-room, and Hermione decided what the floor coverings must be. It sent her into a strange, convulsed anger, to be thwarted. Birkin always let her have her way, for the moment.

Then they moved across, through the hall, to the other front room, that was a little smaller than the first.

'This is the study,' said Hermione. 'Rupert, I have a rug that I want you to have for here. Will you let me give it to you? Do—I want to give it you.'

'What is it like?' he asked ungraciously.

'You haven't seen it. It is chiefly rose red, then blue, a metallic, mid-blue, and a very soft dark blue. I think you would like it. Do you think you would?'

'It sounds very nice,' he replied. 'What is it? Oriental? With a pile?'

'Yes. Persian! It is made of camel's hair, silky. I think it is called Bergamos—twelve feet by seven—Do you think it will do?'

'It would *do*,' he said. 'But why should you give me an expensive rug? I can manage perfectly well with my old Oxford Turkish.'

'But may I give it to you? Do let me.'

'How much did it cost?'

She looked at him, and said:

'I don't remember. It was quite cheap.'

He looked at her, his face set.

'I don't want to take it, Hermione,' he said.

'Do let me give it to the rooms,' she said, going up to him and putting her hand on his arm lightly, pleadingly. 'I shall be so disappointed.'

'You know I don't want you to give me things,' he repeated helplessly.

'I don't want to give you *things*,' she said teasingly. 'But will you have this?'

'All right,' he said, defeated, and she triumphed.

They went upstairs. There were two bedrooms to correspond with the rooms downstairs. One of them was half furnished, and Birkin had evidently slept there. Hermione went round the room carefully, taking in every detail, as if absorbing the evidence of his presence, in all the inanimate things. She felt the bed and examined the coverings.

'Are you *sure* you were quite comfortable?' she said, pressing the pillow.

'Perfectly,' he replied coldly.

'And were you warm? There is no down quilt. I am sure you need one. You mustn't have a great pressure of clothes.'

'I've got one,' he said. 'It is coming down.'

They measured the rooms, and lingered over every consideration. Ursula stood at the window and watched the woman carrying the tea up the bank to the pond. She hated the palaver Hermione made, she wanted to drink tea, she wanted anything but this fuss and business.

At last they all mounted the grassy bank, to the picnic. Hermione poured out tea. She ignored now Ursula's presence. And Ursula, recovering from her ill-humour, turned to Gerald saying:

'Oh, I hated you so much the other day, Mr Crich.'

'What for?' said Gerald, wincing slightly away.

'For treating your horse so badly. Oh, I hated you so much!'

'What did he do?' sang Hermione.

'He made his lovely sensitive Arab horse stand with him at the railway-crossing whilst a horrible lot of trucks went by; and the poor thing, she was in a perfect frenzy, a perfect agony. It was the most horrible sight you can imagine.'

'Why did you do it, Gerald?' asked Hermione, calm and interrogative.

'She must learn to stand—what use is she to me in this country if she shies and goes off every time an engine whistles.'

'But why inflict unnecessary torture?' said Ursula. 'Why make her stand all that time at the crossing? You might just as well have ridden back up the road, and saved all that horror. Her sides were bleeding where you had spurred her. It was too horrible—!'

Gerald stiffened.

'I have to use her,' he replied. 'And if I'm going to be sure of her at *all,* she'll have to learn to stand noises.'

'Why should she?' cried Ursula in a passion. 'She is a living creature, why should she stand anything, just because you choose to make her? She had as much right to her own being, as you have to yours.'

'There I disagree,' said Gerald. 'I consider that mare is there for my use. Not because I bought her, but because that is the natural order. It is more natural for a man to take a horse and use it as he likes, than for him to go down on his knees to it, begging it to do as it wishes, and to fulfil its own marvellous nature.'

Ursula was just breaking out, when Hermione lifted her face and began, in her musing sing-song:

'I do think—I do really think we must have the *courage* to use the lower animal life for our needs. I do think there is something wrong, when we look on every living creature as if it were ourselves. I do feel, that it is false to project our own feelings on every animate creature. It is a lack of discrimination, a lack of criticism.'

'Quite,' said Birkin sharply. 'Nothing is so detestable as the maudlin attributing of human feelings and consciousness to animals.'

'Yes,' said Hermione wearily, 'we must really take a position. Either we are going to use the animals, or they will use us.'

'That's a fact,' said Gerald. 'A horse has got a will like a man, though it had no *mind*, strictly. And if your will isn't master, then the horse is master of you. And this is a thing I can't help. I can't help being master of the horse.'

'If only we could learn how to use our will,' said Hermione, 'we could do anything. The will can cure anything, and put anything right. That I am convinced of—if only we use the will properly, intelligibly.'

'What do you mean by using the will properly?' said Birkin.

'A very great doctor taught me,' she said, addressing Ursula and Gerald vaguely. 'He told me, for instance, that to cure oneself of a bad habit, one should *force* oneself to do it, when one would not do it;—make oneself do it—and then the habit would disappear.'

'How do you mean?' said Gerald.

'If you bite your nails, for example. Then, when you don't want to bite your nails, bite them, make yourself bite them. And you would find the habit was broken.'

'Is that so?' said Gerald.

'Yes. And in so many things, I have *made* myself well. I was a very queer and nervous girl. And by learning to use my will, simply by using my will, I *made* myself right.'

Ursula looked all the while at Hermione, as she spoke in her slow, dispassionate, and yet strangely tense voice. A curious thrill went over the younger woman. Some strange, dark, convulsive power was in Hermione, fascinating and repelling.

'It is fatal to use the will like that,' cried Birkin harshly, 'disgusting. Such a will is an obscenity.'

Hermione looked at him for a long time, with her shadowed, heavy eyes. Her face was soft and pale and thin, almost phosphorescent, her jaw was lean.

'I'm sure it isn't,' she said at length. There always seemed an interval, a strange split between what she seemed to feel and experience, and what she actually said and thought. She seemed to catch her thoughts at length from off the surface of a maelstrom of chaotic black emotions and reactions, and Birkin was always filled with repulsion, she caught so infallibly, her will never failed her. Her voice was always dispassionate and tense, and perfectly confident. Yet she shuddered with a sense of nausea, a sort of sea-sickness that always threatened to overwhelm her mind. But her mind remained unbroken, her will was still perfect. It almost sent Birkin mad. But he would never, never dare to break her will, and let loose the maelstrom of her subconsciousness, and see her in her ultimate madness. Yet he was always striking at her.

'And of course,' he said to Gerald, 'horses *haven't* got a complete will, like human beings. A horse has no *one* will. Every horse, strictly, has two wills. With one will, it wants to put itself in the human power completely—and with the other, it wants to be free, wild. The two wills sometimes lock—you know that, if ever you've felt a horse bolt, while you've been driving it.'

'I have felt a horse bolt while I was driving it,' said Gerald, 'but it didn't make me know it had two wills. I only knew it was frightened.'

Hermione had ceased to listen. She simply became oblivious when these subjects were started.

'Why should a horse want to put itself in the human power?' asked Ursula. 'That is quite incomprehensible to me. I don't believe it ever wanted it.'

'Yes it did. It's the last, perhaps highest, love-impulse: resign your will to the higher being,' said Birkin.

'What curious notions you have of love,' jeered Ursula.

'And woman is the same as horses: two wills act in opposition inside her. With one will, she wants to subject herself utterly. With the other she wants to bolt, and pitch her rider to perdition.'

'Then I'm a bolter,' said Ursula, with a burst of laughter.

'It's a dangerous thing to domesticate even horses, let alone women,' said Birkin. 'The dominant principle has some rare antagonists.'

'Good thing too,' said Ursula.

'Quite,' said Gerald, with a faint smile. 'There's more fun.'

Hermione could bear no more. She rose, saying in her easy sing-song:

'Isn't the evening beautiful! I get filled sometimes with such a great sense of beauty, that I feel I can hardly bear it.'

Ursula, to whom she had appealed, rose with her, moved to the last impersonal depths. And Birkin seemed to her almost a monster of hateful arrogance. She went with Hermione along the bank of the pond, talking of beautiful, soothing things, picking the gentle cowslips.

'Wouldn't you like a dress,' said Ursula to Hermione, 'of this yellow spotted with orange—a cotton dress?'

'Yes,' said Hermione, stopping and looking at the flower, letting the thought come home to her and soothe her. 'Wouldn't it be pretty? I should *love* it.'

And she turned smiling to Ursula, in a feeling of real affection.

But Gerald remained with Birkin, wanting to probe him to the bottom, to know what he meant by the dual will in horses. A flicker of excitement danced on Gerald's face.

Hermione and Ursula strayed on together, united in a sudden bond of deep affection and closeness.

'I really do not want to be forced into all this criticism and analysis of life. I really *do* want to see things in their entirety, with their beauty left to them, and their wholeness, their natural holiness. Don't you feel it, don't you feel you *can't* be tortured into any more knowledge?' said Hermione, stopping in front of Ursula, and turning to her with clenched fists thrust downwards.

'Yes,' said Ursula. 'I do. I am sick of all this poking and prying.'

'I'm so glad you are. Sometimes,' said Hermione, again stopping arrested in her progress and turning to Ursula, 'sometimes I wonder if I *ought* to submit to all this realization, if I am not being weak in rejecting it. But I feel I *can't*—I *can't*. It seems to destroy *everything*. All the beauty and the—and the true holiness is destroyed—and I feel I can't live without them.'

'And it would be simply wrong to live without them,'

cried Ursula. 'No, it is so *irreverent* to think that everything must be realized in the head. Really, something must be left to the Lord, there always is and always will be.'

'Yes,' said Hermione, reassured like a child, 'it should, shouldn't it? And Rupert—' she lifted her face to the sky, in a muse—'he *can* only tear things to pieces. He really *is* like a boy who must pull everything to pieces to see how it is made. And I can't think it is right—it does seem so irreverent, as you say.'

'Like tearing open a bud to see what the flower will be like,' said Ursula.

'Yes. And that kills everything, doesn't it? It doesn't allow any possibility of flowering.'

'Of course not,' said Ursula. 'It is purely destructive.'

'It is, isn't it!'

Hermione looked long and slow at Ursula, seeming to accept confirmation from her. Then the two women were silent. As soon as they were in accord, they began mutually to mistrust each other. In spite of herself, Ursula felt herself recoiling from Hermione. It was all she could do to restrain her revulsion.

They returned to the men, like two conspirators who have withdrawn to come to an agreement. Birkin looked up at them. Ursula hated him for his cold watchfulness. But he said nothing.

'Shall we be going?' said Hermione. 'Rupert, you are coming to Shortlands to dinner? Will you come at once, will you come now, with us?'

'I'm not dressed,' replied Birkin. 'And you know Gerald stickles for convention.'

'I don't stickle for it,' said Gerald. 'But if you'd got as sick as I have of rowdy go-as-you-please in the house, you'd prefer it if people were peaceful and conventional, at least at meals.'

'All right,' said Birkin.

'But can't we wait for you while you dress?' persisted Hermione.

'If you like.'

He rose to go indoors. Ursula said she would take her leave.

'Only,' she said, turning to Gerald, 'I must say that, however man is lord of the beast and the fowl, I still don't think he has any right to violate the feelings of the inferior creation. I still think it would have been much more sensible and nice of you if you'd trotted back up the road while the train went by, and been considerate.'

'I see,' said Gerald, smiling, but somewhat annoyed. 'I must remember another time.'

'They all think I'm an interfering female,' thought Ursula to herself, as she went away. But she was in arms against them.

She ran home plunged in thought. She had been very much moved by Hermione, she had really come into contact with her, so that there was a sort of league between the two women. And yet she could not bear her. But she put the thought away. 'She's really good,' she said to herself. 'She really wants what is right.' And she tried to feel at one with Hermione, and to shut off from Birkin. She was strictly hostile to him. But she was held to him by some bond, some deep principle. This at once irritated her and saved her.

Only now and again, violent little shudders would come over her, out of her subconsciousness, and she knew it was the fact that she had stated her challenge to Birkin, and he had, consciously or unconsciously, accepted. It was a fight to the death between them—or to new life: though in what the conflict lay, no one could say.

13

Mino

The days went by, and she received no sign. Was he going to ignore her, was he going to take no further notice of her secret? A dreary weight of anxiety and acrid bitterness settled on her. And yet Ursula knew she was only deceiving herself, and that he *would* proceed. She said no word to anybody.

Then, sure enough, there came a note from him, asking if she would come to tea, with Gudrun, to his rooms in town.

'Why does he ask Gudrun as well?' she asked herself at once. 'Does he want to protect himself, or does he think I would not go alone?'

She was tormented by the thought that he wanted to protect himself. But at the end of all, she only said to herself:

'I don't want Gudrun to be there, because I want him to say something more to me. So I shan't tell Gudrun anything about it, and I shall go alone. Then I shall know.'

She found herself sitting on the tram-car, mounting up the hill going out of the town, to the place where he had his lodging. She seemed to have passed into a kind of dream world, absolved from the conditions of actuality. She watched the sordid streets of the town go by beneath her, as if she were a spirit disconnected from the material universe. What had it all to do with her? She was palpitating and formless within the flux of the ghost life. She could not consider any more, what anybody would say of her or think about her. People had passed out of her range, she was absolved. She had fallen strange and dim, out of the sheath of the material life, as a berry falls from the only world it has ever known, down out of the sheath on to the real unknown.

Birkin was standing in the middle of the room, when she

was shown in by the landlady. He too was moved outside
himself. She saw him agitated and shaken, a frail, unsubstantial body silent like the node of some violent force, that
came out from him and shook her almost into a swoon.

'You are alone?' he said.

'Yes—Gudrun could not come.'

He instantly guessed why.

And they were both seated in silence, in the terrible tension of the room. She was aware that it was a pleasant room,
full of light and very restful in its form—aware also of a
fuchsia tree, with dangling scarlet and purple flowers.

'How nice the fuchsias are!' she said, to break the silence.

'Aren't they! Did you think I had forgotten what I said?'

A swoon went over Ursula's mind.

'I don't want you to remember it—if you don't want to,'
she struggled to say, through the dark mist that covered her.

There was silence for some moments.

'No,' he said. 'It isn't that. Only—if we are going to
know each other, we must pledge ourselves for ever. If we
are going to make a relationship, even of friendship, there
must be something final and irrevocable about it.'

There was a clang of mistrust and almost anger in his
voice. She did not answer. Her heart was too much contracted. She could not have spoken.

Seeing she was not going to reply, he continued, almost
bitterly, giving himself away:

'I can't say it is love I have to offer—and it isn't love I
want. It is something much more impersonal and harder—
and rarer.'

There was a silence, out of which she said:

'You mean you don't love me?'

She suffered furiously, saying that.

'Yes, if you like to put it like that. Though perhaps that
isn't true. I don't know. At any rate, I don't feel the emotion
of love for you—no, and I don't want to. Because it gives
out in the last issues.'

'Love gives out in the last issues?' she asked, feeling
numb to the lips.

'Yes, it does. At the very last, one is alone, beyond the influence of love. There is a real impersonal me, that is be-

yond love, beyond any emotional relationship. So it is with you. But we want to delude ourselves that love is the root. It isn't. It is only the branches. The root is beyond love, a naked kind of isolation, an isolated me, that does *not* meet and mingle, and never can.'

She watched him with wide, troubled eyes. His face was incandescent in its abstract earnestness.

'And you mean you can't love?' she asked, in trepidation.

'Yes if you like. I have loved. But there is a beyond, where there is not love.'

She could not submit to this. She felt it swooning over her. But she could not submit.

'But how do you know—if you have never *really* loved?' she asked.

'It is true what I say; there is a beyond, in you, in me, which is further than love, beyond the scope, as stars are beyond the scope of vision, some of them,'

'Then there is no love,' cried Ursula.

'Ultimately, no, there is something else. But, ultimately, there *is* no love.'

Ursula was given over to this statement for some moments. Then she half rose from her chair, saying, in a final, repellant voice:

'Then let me go home—what am I doing here?'

'There is the door,' he said. 'You are a free agent.'

He was suspended finely and perfectly in this extremity. She hung motionless for some seconds, then she sat down again.

'If there is no love, what is there?' she cried, almost jeering.

'Something,' he said, looking at her, battling with his soul, with all his might.

'What?'

He was silent for a long time, unable to be in communication with her while she was in this state of opposition.

'There is,' he said, in a voice of pure abstraction, 'a final me which is stark and impersonal and beyond responsibility. So there is a final you. And it is there I would want to meet you—not in the emotional, loving plane—but there beyond, where there is no speech and no terms of agreement. There we are two stark, unknown beings, two utterly strange creatures, I would want to approach you, and you me. And there could be no obligation, because there is no standard for action there, because no understanding has been reaped from that plane. It is quite inhuman—so there can be no calling to book, in any form whatsoever—because one is outside the pale of all that is accepted, and nothing known applies. One can only follow the impulse, taking that which lies in front, and responsible for nothing, asked for nothing, giving nothing, only each taking according to the primal desire.'

Ursula listened to this speech, her mind dumb and almost senseless, what he said was so unexpected and so untoward.

'It is just purely selfish,' she said.

'If it is pure, yes. But it isn't selfish at all. Because I don't *know* what I want of you. I deliver *myself* over to the unknown, in coming to you, I am without reserves or defences, stripped entirely, into the unknown. Only there needs the pledge between us, that we will both cast off everything, cast off ourselves even, and cease to be, so that that which is perfectly ourselves can take place in us.'

She pondered along her own line of thought.

'But it is because you love me, that you want me?' she persisted.

'No it isn't. It is because I believe in you—if I *do* believe in you.'

'Aren't you sure?' she laughed, suddenly hurt.

He was looking at her steadfastly, scarcely heeding what she said.

'Yes, I must believe in you, or else I shouldn't be here saying this,' he replied. 'But that is all the proof I have. I don't feel any very strong belief at this particular moment.'

She disliked him for this sudden relapse into weariness and faithlessness.

'But don't you think me good-looking?' she persisted in a mocking voice.

He looked at her, to see if he felt that she was good-looking.

'I don't *feel* that you're good-looking,' he said.

'Not even attractive?' she mocked, bitingly.

He knitted his brows in sudden exasperation.

'Don't you see that it's not a question of visual appreciation in the least,' he cried. 'I don't *want* to see you. I've seen plenty of women, I'm sick and weary of seeing them. I want a woman I don't see.'

'I'm sorry I can't oblige you by being invisible,' she laughed.

'Yes,' he said, 'you are invisible to me, if you don't force me to be visually aware of you. But I don't want to see you or hear you.'

'What did you ask me to tea for, then?' she mocked.

But he would take no notice of her. He was talking to himself.

'I want to find you, where you don't know your own existence, the you that your common self denies utterly. But I don't want your good looks, and I don't want your womanly feelings, and I don't want your thoughts nor opinions nor your ideas—they are all bagatelles to me.'

'You are very conceited, Monsieur,' she mocked. 'How do you know what my womanly feelings are, or my thoughts or my ideas? You don't even know what I think of you now.'

'Nor do I care in the slightest.'

'I think you are very silly. I think you want to tell me you love me, and you go all this way round to do it.'

'All right,' he said, looking up with sudden exasperation. 'Now go away then, and leave me alone. I don't want any more of your meretricious persiflage.'

'Is it really persiflage?' she mocked, her face really relaxing into laughter. She interpreted it, that he had made a deep confession of love to her. But he was so absurd in his words, also.

They were silent for many minutes, she was pleased and elated like a child. His concentration broke, he began to look at her simply and naturally.

'What I want is a strange conjunction with you—' he said quietly; '—not meeting and mingling;—you are quite right:—but an equilibrium, a pure balance of two single beings:—as the stars balance each other.'

She looked at him. He was very earnest, and earnestness was always rather ridiculous, commonplace, to her. It made her feel unfree and uncomfortable. Yet she liked him so much. But why drag in the stars.

'Isn't this rather sudden?' she mocked.

He began to laugh.

'Best to read the terms of the contract, before we sign,' he said.

A young grey cat that had been sleeping on the sofa jumped down and stretched, rising on its long legs, and arching its slim back. Then it sat considering for a moment, erect and kingly. And then, like a dart, it had shot out of the room, through the open window-doors, and into the garden.

'What's he after?' said Birkin, rising.

The young cat trotted lordly down the path, waving his tail. He was an ordinary tabby with white paws, a slender young gentleman. A crouching, fluffy, brownish-grey cat was stealing up the side of the fence. The Mino walked statelily up to her, with manly nonchalance. She crouched before him and pressed herself on the ground in humility, a fluffy soft outcast, looking up at him with wild eyes that were green and lovely as great jewels. He looked casually down on her. So she crept a few inches further, proceeding on her way to the back door, crouching in a wonderful, soft, self-obliterating manner, and moving like a shadow.

He, going statelily on his slim legs, walked after her, then suddenly, for pure excess, he gave her a light cuff with his paw on the side of her face. She ran off a few steps, like a blown leaf along the ground, then crouched unobtrusively, in submissive, wild patience. The Mino pretended to take no notice of her. He blinked his eyes superbly at the landscape. In a minute she drew herself together and moved softly, a fleecy brown-grey shadow, a few paces forward. She began to quicken her pace, in a moment she would be gone like a dream, when the young grey lord sprang before her, and gave her a light handsome cuff. She subsided at once, submissively.

'She is a wild cat,' said Birkin. 'She has come in from the woods.'

The eyes of the stray cat flared round for a moment, like great green fires staring at Birkin. Then she had rushed in a soft swift rush, half-way down the garden. Then she paused

to look round. The Mino turned his face in pure superiority
to his master, and slowly closed his eyes, standing in statu-
esque young perfection. The wild cat's round, green, wondering eyes were staring all the while like uncanny fires.
Then again, like a shadow, she slid towards the kitchen.

In a lovely springing leap, like a wind, the Mino was upon
her, and had boxed her twice, very definitely, with a white,
delicate fist. She sank and slid back, unquestioning. He
walked after her, and cuffed her once or twice, leisurely,
with sudden little blows of his magic white paws.

'Now why does he do that?' cried Ursula in indignation.

'They are on intimate terms,' said Birkin.

'And is that why he hits her?'

'Yes,' laughed Birkin, 'I think he wants to make it quite
obvious to her.'

'Isn't it horrid of him!' she cried; and going out into the
garden she called to the Mino:

'Stop it, don't bully. Stop hitting her.'

The stray cat vanished like a swift, invisible shadow. The
Mino glanced at Ursula, then looked from her disdainfully to
his master.

'Are you a bully, Mino?' Birkin asked.

The young slim cat looked at him, and slowly narrowed
its eyes. Then it glanced away at the landscape, looking into
the distance as if completely oblivious of the two human beings.

'Mino,' said Ursula, 'I don't like you. You are a bully like
all males.'

'No,' said Birkin, 'he is justified. He is not a bully. He is
only insisting to the poor stray that she shall acknowledge
him as a sort of fate, her own fate: because you can see she
is fluffy and promiscuous as the wind. I am with him entirely. He wants superfine stability.'

'Yes, I know!' cried Ursula. 'He wants his own way—I
know what your fine words work down to—bossiness, I call
it, bossiness.'

The young cat again glanced at Birkin in disdain of the
noisy woman.

'I quite agree with you, Miciotto,' said Birkin to the cat.
'Keep your male dignity, and your higher understanding.'

Again the Mino narrowed his eyes as if he were looking at the sun. Then, suddenly affecting to have no connexion at all with the two people, he went trotting off, with assumed spontaneity and gaiety, his tail erect, his white feet blithe.

'Now he will find the *belle sauvage* once more, and entertain her with his superior wisdom,' laughed Birkin.

Ursula looked at the man who stood in the garden with his hair blowing and his eyes smiling ironically, and she cried:

'Oh, it makes me so cross, the assumption of male superiority! And it is such a lie! One wouldn't mind if there were any justification for it.'

'The wild cat,' said Birkin, 'doesn't mind. She perceives that it is justified.'

'Does she!' cried Ursula. 'And tell it to the Horse Marines.'

'To them also.'

'It is just like Gerald Crich with his horse—a lust for bullying—a real *Wille zur Macht*—so base, so petty.'

'I agree that the *Wille zur Macht* is a base and petty thing. But with the Mino, it is the desire to bring this female cat into a pure stable equilibrium, a transcendent and abiding *rapport* with the single male. Whereas without him, as you see, she is a mere stray, a fluffy sporadic bit of chaos. It is a *volonté de pouvoir*, if you like, a will to ability, taking *pouvoir* as a verb.'

'Ah—! Sophistries! It's the old Adam.'

'Oh yes. Adam kept Eve in the indestructible paradise, when he kept her single with himself, like a star in its orbit.'

'Yes—yes—' cried Ursula, pointing her finger at him. 'There you are—a star in its orbit! A satellite—a satellite of Mars—that's what she is to be! There—there—you've given yourself away! You want a satellite, Mars and his satellite! You've said it—you've said it—you've dished yourself!'

He stood smiling in frustration and amusement and irritation and admiration and love. She was so quick, and so lambent, like discernible fire, and so vindictive, and so rich in her dangerous flamy sensitiveness.

'I've not said it at all,' he replied, 'if you will give me a chance to speak.'

'No, no!' she cried. 'I won't let you speak. You've said it, a satellite, you're not going to wriggle out of it. You've said it.'

'You'll never believe now that I *haven't* said it,' he answered. 'I neither implied nor indicated nor mentioned a satellite, nor intended a satellite, never.'

'*You prevaricator!*' she cried, in real indignation.

'Tea is ready, sir,' said the landlady from the doorway.

They both looked at her, very much as the cats had looked at them, a little while before.

'Thank you, Mrs Daykin.'

An interrupted silence fell over the two of them, a moment of breach.

'Come and have tea,' he said.

'Yes, I should love it,' she replied, gathering herself together.

They sat facing each other across the tea table.

'I did not say, nor imply, a satellite. I meant two single equal stars balanced in conjunction—'

'You gave yourself away, you gave away your little game completely,' she cried, beginning at once to eat. He saw that she would take no further heed of his expostulation, so he began to pour the tea.

'What *good* things to eat!' she cried.

'Take your own sugar,' he said.

He handed her her cup. He had everything so nice, such pretty cups and plates, painted with mauve-lustre and green, also shapely bowls and glass plates, and old spoons, on a woven cloth of pale grey and black and purple. It was very rich and fine. But Ursula could see Hermione's influence.

'Your things are so lovely!' she said, almost angrily.

'*I* like them. It gives me real pleasure to use things that are attractive in themselves—pleasant things. And Mrs Daykin is good. She thinks everything is wonderful, for my sake.'

'Really,' said Ursula, 'landladies are better than wives, nowadays. They certainly *care* a great deal more. It is much more beautiful and complete here now, than if you were married.'

'But think of the emptiness within,' he laughed.

'No,' she said. 'I am jealous that men have such perfect

landladies and such beautiful lodgings. There is nothing left them to desire.'

'In the housekeeping way, we'll hope not. It is disgusting, people marrying for a home.'

'Still,' said Ursula, 'a man has very little need for a woman now, has he?'

'In outer things, maybe—except to share his bed and bear his children. But essentially, there is just the same need as there ever was. Only nobody takes the trouble to be essential.'

'How essential?' she said.

'I do think,' he said, 'that the world is only held together by the mystic conjunction, the ultimate unison between people—a bond. And the immediate bond is between man and woman.'

'But it's such old hat,' said Ursula. 'Why should love be a bond? No, I'm not having any.'

'If you are walking westward,' he said, 'you forfeit the northern and eastward and southern direction. If you admit a unison, you forfeit all the possibilities of chaos.'

'But love is freedom,' she declared.

'Don't cant to me,' he replied. 'Love is a direction which excludes all other directions. It's a freedom *together,* if you like.'

'No,' she said, 'love includes everything.'

'Sentimental cant,' he replied. 'You want the state of chaos, that's all. It is ultimate nihilism, this freedom-in-love business, this freedom which is love and love which is freedom. As a matter of fact, if you enter into a pure unison, it is irrevocable, and it is one way, like the path of a star.'

'Ha!' she cried bitterly. 'It is the old dead morality.'

'No,' he said, 'it is the law of creation. One is committed. One must commit oneself to a conjunction with the other—forever. But it is not selfless—it is a maintaining of the self in mystic balance and integrity—like a star balanced with another star.'

'I don't trust you when you drag in the stars,' she said. 'If you were quite true, it wouldn't be necessary to be so far-fetched.'

'Don't trust me then,' he said, angry. 'It is enough that I trust myself.'

'And that is where you make another mistake,' she replied. 'You *don't* trust yourself. You don't fully believe yourself what you are saying. You don't really want this conjunction, otherwise you wouldn't talk so much about it, you'd get it.'

He was suspended for a moment, arrested.

'How?' he said.

'By just loving,' she retorted in defiance.

He was still a moment in anger. Then he said:

'I tell you, I don't believe in love like that. I tell you, you want love to administer to your egoism, to subserve you. Love is a process of subservience with you—and with everybody. I hate it.'

'No,' she cried, pressing back her head like a cobra, her eyes flashing. 'It is a process of pride—I want to be proud—'

'Proud and subservient, proud and subservient, I know you,' he retorted dryly. 'Proud and subservient, then subservient to the proud—I know you and your love. It is a tick-tack, tick-tack, a dance of opposites.'

'Are you sure?' she mocked wickedly, 'what my love is?'

'Yes, I am,' he retorted.

'So cocksure!' she said. 'How can anybody ever be right, who is so cocksure? It shows you are wrong.'

He was silent in chagrin.

They had talked and struggled till they were both wearied out.

'Tell me about yourself and your people,' he said.

And she told him about the Brangwens, and about her mother, and about Skrebensky, her first love, and about her later experiences. He sat very still, watching her as she talked. And he seemed to listen with reverence. Her face was beautiful and full of baffled light as she told him all the things that had hurt her or perplexed her so deeply. He seemed to warm and comfort his soul at the beautiful light of her nature.

'If she *really* could pledge herself,' he thought to himself, with passionate insistence but hardly any hope. Yet a curious little irresponsible laughter appeared in his heart.

'We have all suffered so much,' he mocked, ironically.

She looked up at him, and a flash of wild gaiety went over her face, a strange flash of yellow light coming from her eyes.

'Haven't we!' she cried, in a high, reckless cry. 'It is almost absurd, isn't it?'

'Quite absurd,' he said. 'Suffering bores me, any more.'

'So it does me.'

He was almost afraid of the mocking recklessness of her splendid face. Here was one who would go to the whole lengths of heaven or hell, whichever she had to go. And he mistrusted her, he was afraid of a woman capable of such abandon, such dangerous thoroughness of destructivity. Yet he chuckled within himself also.

She came over to him and put her hand on his shoulder, looking down at him with strange golden-lighted eyes, very tender, but with a curious devilish look lurking underneath.

'Say you love me, say "my love" to me,' she pleaded.

He looked back into her eyes, and saw. His face flickered with sardonic comprehension.

'I love you right enough,' he said grimly. 'But I want it to be something else.'

'But why? But why?' she insisted, bending her wonderful luminous face to him, 'Why isn't it enough?'

'Because we can go one better,' he said, putting his arms round her.

'No, we can't,' she said, in a strong, voluptuous voice of yielding. 'We can only love each other. Say "my love" to me, say it, say it.'

She put her arms round his neck. He enfolded her, and kissed her subtly, murmuring in a subtle voice of love, and irony, and submission:

'Yes—my love, yes—my love. Let love be enough then. I love you then—I love you. I'm bored by the rest.'

'Yes,' she murmured, nestling very sweet and close to him.

14

Water-Party

Every year Mr Crich gave a more or less public water-party on the lake. There was a little pleasure-launch on Willey Water and several rowing-boats, and guests could take tea either in the marquee that was set up in the grounds of the house, or they could picnic in the shade of the great walnut tree at the boat-house by the lake. This year the staff of the Grammar School was invited, along with the chief officials of the firm. Gerald and the younger Criches did not care for this party, but it had become customary now, and it pleased the father, as being the only occasion when he could gather some people of the district together in festivity with him. For he loved to give pleasures to his dependents and to those poorer than himself. But his children preferred the company of their equals in wealth. They hated their inferiors' humility or gratitude or awkwardness.

Nevertheless they were willing to attend at this festival, as they had done almost since they were children, the more so, as they all felt a little guilty now, and unwilling to thwart their father any more, since he was so ill in health. Therefore, quite cheerfully Laura prepared to take her mother's place as hostess, and Gerald assumed responsibility for the amusements on the water.

Birkin had written to Ursula saying he expected to see her at the party, and Gudrun, although she scorned the patronage of the Criches, would nevertheless accompany her mother and father if the weather were fine.

The day came blue and full of sunshine, with little wafts of wind. The sisters both wore dresses of white crêpe, and hats of soft grass. But Gudrun had a sash of brilliant black and pink and yellow colour wound broadly round her waist, and she had pink silk stockings, and black and pink and yellow decoration on the brim of her hat, weighing it down a little. She carried also a yellow silk coat over her arm, so that she looked remarkable, like a painting from the Salon. Her appearance was a sore trial to her father, who said angrily:

'Don't you think you might as well get yourself up for a Christmas cracker, an' ha' done with it?'

But Gudrun looked handsome and brilliant, and she wore her clothes in pure defiance. When people stared at her, and giggled after her, she made a point of saying loudly, to Ursula:

'Regarde, regarde ces gens-lá! Ne sont-ils pas de hiboux incroyables?' And with the words of French in her mouth, she would look over her shoulder at the giggling party.

'No, really, it's impossible!' Ursula would reply distinctly. And so the two girls took it out of their universal enemy. But their father became more and more enraged.

Ursula was all snowy white, save that her hat was pink, and entirely without trimming, and her shoes were dark red, and she carried an orange-coloured coat. And in this guise they were walking all the way to Shortlands, their father and mother going in front.

They were laughing at their mother, who, dressed in a summer material of black and purple stripes, and wearing a hat of purple straw, was setting forth with much more of the shyness and trepidation of a young girl than her daughters ever felt, walking demurely beside her husband, who, as usual, looked rather crumpled in his best suit, as if he were the father of a young family and had been holding the baby whilst his wife got dressed.

'Look at the young couple in front,' said Gudrun calmly. Ursula looked at her mother and father, and was suddenly seized with uncontrollable laughter. The two girls stood in the road and laughed till the tears ran down their faces, as they caught sight again of the shy, unworldly couple of their parents going on ahead.

'We are roaring at you, mother,' called Ursula, helplessly following after her parents.

Mrs Brangwen turned round with a slightly puzzled exasperated look. 'Oh indeed!' she said. 'What is there so very funny about *me,* I should like to know?'

She could not understand that there could be anything amiss with her appearance. She had a perfect calm sufficiency, an easy indifference to any criticism whatsoever, as if she were beyond it. Her clothes were always rather odd, and as a rule slip-shod, yet she wore them with a perfect ease and satisfaction. Whatever she had on, so long as she was barely tidy, she was right, beyond remark; such an aristocrat she was by instinct.

'You look so stately, like a country Baroness,' said Ursula, laughing with a little tenderness at her mother's naïve puzzled air.

'*Just* like a country Baroness!' chimed in Gudrun. Now the mother's natural hauteur became self-conscious, and the girls shrieked again.

'Go home, you pair of idiots, great giggling idiots!' cried the father inflamed with irritation.

'Mm-m-er!' booed Ursula, pulling a face at his crossness. The yellow lights danced in his eyes, he leaned forward in real rage.

'Don't be so silly as to take any notice of the great gabies,' said Mrs Brangwen, turning on her way.

'I'll see if I'm going to be followed by a pair of giggling, yelling jackanapes—' he cried vengefully.

The girls stood still, laughing helplessly at his fury, upon the path beside the hedge.

'Why you're as silly as they are, to take any notice,' said Mrs Brangwen also becoming angry now he was really enraged.

'There are some people coming, father,' cried Ursula, with mocking warning. He glanced round quickly, and went on to join his wife, walking stiff with rage. And the girls followed, weak with laughter.

When the people had passed by, Brangwen cried in a loud, stupid voice:

'I'm going back home if there's any more of this. I'm damned if I'm going to be made a fool of in this fashion, in the public road.'

He was really out of temper. At the sound of his blind,

vindictive voice, the laughter suddenly left the girls, and
their hearts contracted with contempt. They hated his words
'in the public road'. What did they care for the public road?
But Gudrun was conciliatory.

'But we weren't laughing to *hurt* you,' she cried, with an
uncouth gentleness which made her parents uncomfortable.
'We were laughing because we're fond of you.'

'We'll walk on in front, if they are *so* touchy,' said Ursula, angry. And in this wise they arrived at Willey Water.
The lake was blue and fair, the meadows sloped down in
sunshine on one side, the thick dark woods dropped steeply
on the other. The little pleasure-launch was fussing out from
the shore, twanging its music, crowded with people, flapping
its paddles. Near the boat-house was a throng of gaily-
dressed persons, small in the distance. And on the high-road,
some of the common people were standing along the hedge,
looking at the festivity beyond, enviously, like souls not admitted to paradise.

'My eye!' said Gudrun, *sotto voce,* looking at the motley
of guests, 'there's a pretty crowd if you like! Imagine yourself in the midst of that, my dear.'

Gudrun's apprehensive horror of people in the mass unnerved Ursula. 'It looks rather awful,' she said anxiously.

'And imagine what they'll be like—*imagine!*' said
Gudrun, still in that unnerving, subdued voice. Yet she advanced determinedly.

'I suppose we can get away from them,' said Ursula anxiously.

'We're in a pretty fix if we can't,' said Gudrun. Her
extreme ironic loathing and apprehension was very trying to
Ursula.

'We needn't stay,' she said.

'I certainly shan't stay five minutes among that little lot,'
said Gudrun. They advanced nearer, till they saw policemen
at the gates.

'Policemen to keep you in, too!' said Gudrun. 'My word,
this is a beautiful affair.'

'We'd better look after father and mother,' said Ursula
anxiously.

'Mother's *perfectly* capable of getting through this little celebration,' said Gudrun with some contempt.

But Ursula knew that her father felt uncouth and angry and unhappy, so she was far from her ease. They waited outside the gate till their parents came up. The tall, thin man in his crumpled clothes was unnerved and irritable as a boy, finding himself on the brink of this social function. He did not feel a gentleman, he did not feel anything except pure exasperation.

Ursula took her place at his side, they gave their tickets to the policeman, and passed in on to the grass, four abreast; the tall, hot, ruddy-dark man with his narrow boyish brow drawn with irritation, the fresh-faced, easy woman, perfectly collected though her hair was slipping on one side, then Gudrun, her eyes round and dark and staring, her full soft face impassive, almost sulky, so that she seemed to be backing away in antagonism even whilst she was advancing; and then Ursula, with the odd, brilliant, dazzled look on her face, that always came when she was in some false situation.

Birkin was the good angel. He came smiling to them with his affected social grace, that somehow was never *quite* right. But he took off his hat and smiled at them with a real smile in his eyes, so that Brangwen cried out heartily in relief:

'How do you do? You're better, are you?'

'Yes, I'm better. How do you do, Mrs Brangwen? I know Gudrun and Ursula very well.'

His eyes smiled full of natural warmth. He had a soft, flattering manner with women, particularly with women who were not young.

'Yes,' said Mrs Brangwen, cool but yet gratified. 'I have heard them speak of you often enough.'

He laughed. Gudrun looked aside, feeling she was being belittled. People were standing about in groups, some women were sitting in the shade of the walnut tree, with cups of tea in their hands, a waiter in evening dress was hurrying round, some girls were simpering with parasols, some young men, who had just come in from rowing, were sitting cross-legged on the grass, coatless, their shirt-sleeves rolled up in manly fashion, their hands resting on their white flan-

nel trousers, their gaudy ties floating about, as they laughed
and tried to be witty with the young damsels.

'Why,' thought Gudrun churlishly, 'don't they have the
manners to put their coats on, and not to assume such intimacy in their appearance.'

She abhorred the ordinary young man, with his hair plastered back, and his easy-going chumminess.

Hermione Roddice came up, in a handsome gown of white
lace, trailing an enormous silk shawl blotched with great
embroidered flowers, and balancing an enormous plain hat
on her head. She looked striking, astonishing, almost macabre, so tall, with the fringe of her great cream-coloured
vividly-blotched shawl trailing on the ground after her, her
thick hair coming low over her eyes, her face strange and
long and pale, and the blotches of brilliant colour drawn
round her.

'Doesn't she look *weird!*' Gudrun heard some girls titter
behind her. And she could have killed them.

'How do you do!' sang Hermione, coming up very kindly,
and glancing slowly over Gudrun's father and mother. It was
a trying moment, exasperating for Gudrun. Hermione was
really so strongly entrenched in her class superiority, she
could come up and know people out of simple curiosity, as
if they were creatures on exhibition. Gudrun would do the
same herself. But she resented being in the position when
somebody might do it to her.

Hermione, very remarkable, and distinguishing the
Brangwens very much, led them along to where Laura Crich
stood receiving the guests.

'This is Mrs Brangwen,' sang Hermione, and Laura, who
wore a stiff embroidered linen dress, shook hands and said
she was glad to see her. Then Gerald came up, dressed in
white, with a black and brown blazer, and looking handsome. He too was introduced to the Brangwen parents, and
immediately he spoke to Mrs Brangwen as if she were a
lady, and to Brangwen as if he were *not* a gentleman. Gerald
was so obvious in his demeanour. He had to shake hands
with his left hand, because he had hurt his right, and carried
it, bandaged up, in the pocket of his jacket. Gudrun was *very*

thankful that none of her party asked him what was the matter with the hand.

The steam launch was fussing in, all its music jingling, people calling excitedly from on board. Gerald went to see to the debarkation, Birkin was getting tea for Mrs Brangwen, Brangwen had joined a Grammar School group, Hermione was sitting down by their mother, the girls went to the landing-stage to watch the launch come in.

She hooted and tooted gaily, then her paddles were silent, the ropes were thrown ashore, she drifted in with a little bump. Immediately the passengers crowded excitedly to come ashore.

'Wait a minute, wait a minute,' shouted Gerald in sharp command.

They must wait till the boat was tight on the ropes, till the small gangway was put out. Then they streamed ashore, clamouring as if they had come from America.

'Oh, it's *so* nice!' the young girls were crying. 'It's quite lovely.'

The waiters from on board ran out to the boat-house with baskets, the captain lounged on the little bridge. Seeing all safe, Gerald came to Gudrun and Ursula.

'You wouldn't care to go on board for the next trip, and have tea there?' he asked.

'No, thanks,' said Gudrun coldly.

'You don't care for the water?'

'For the water? Yes, I like it very much.'

He looked at her, his eyes searching.

'You don't care for going on a launch, then?'

She was slow in answering, and then she spoke slowly.

'No,' she said. 'I can't say that I do.' Her colour was high, she seemed angry about something.

'*Un peu trop de monde,*' said Ursula, explaining.

'Eh? *Trop de monde!*' He laughed shortly. 'Yes, there's a fair number of 'em.'

Gudrun turned on him brilliantly.

'Have you ever been from Westminster Bridge to Richmond on one of the Thames steamers?' she cried.

'No,' he said. 'I can't say I have.'

'Well, it's one of the most *vile* experiences I've ever had.'

She spoke rapidly and excitedly, the colour high in her cheeks. 'There was absolutely nowhere to sit down, nowhere, a man just above sang "Rocked in the Cradle of the Deep" the *whole* way; he was blind and he had a small organ, one of those portable organs, and he expected money; so you can imagine what *that* was like; there came a constant smell of luncheon from below, and puffs of hot oily machinery; the journey took hours and hours and hours; and for miles, literally for miles, dreadful boys ran with us on the shore, in that *awful* Thames mud, going in *up to the waist*—they had their trousers turned back, and they went up to their hips in that indescribable Thames mud, their faces always turned to us, and screaming, exactly like carrion creatures, screaming " 'Ere y'are sir, 'ere y'are sir, 'ere y'are sir", exactly like some foul carrion objects, perfectly obscene; and paterfamilias on board, laughing when the boys went right down in that awful mud, occasionally throwing them a ha'penny. And if you'd seen the intent look on the faces of these boys, and the way they darted in the filth when a coin was flung—really, no vulture or jackal could dream of approaching them, for foulness. I *never* would go on a pleasure boat again—never.'

Gerald watched her all the time she spoke, his eyes glittering with faint rousedness. It was not so much what she said; it was she herself who roused him, roused him with a small, vivid pricking.

'Of course,' he said, 'every civilized body is bound to have its vermin.'

'Why?' cried Ursula. '*I* don't have vermin.'

'And it's not that—it's the *quality* of the whole thing—paterfamilias laughing and thinking its sport, and throwing the ha'pennies, and materfamilias spreading her fat little knees and eating, continually eating—' replied Gudrun.

'Yes,' said Ursula. 'It isn't the boys so much who are vermin; it's the people themselves, the whole body politic, as you call it.'

Gerald laughed.

'Never mind,' he said. 'You shan't go on the launch.'

Gudrun flushed quickly at his rebuke.

There were a few moments of silence. Gerald, like a sentinel, was watching the people who were going on to the boat. He was very good-looking and self-contained, but his air of soldierly alertness was rather irritating.

'Will you have tea here then, or go across to the house, where there's a tent on the lawn?' he asked.

'Can't we have a rowing-boat, and get out?' asked Ursula, who was always rushing in too fast.

'To get out?' smiled Gerald.

'You see,' said Gudrun, flushing at Ursula's outspoken rudeness, 'we don't know the people, we are almost *complete* strangers here.'

'Oh, I can soon set you up with a few acquaintances,' he said easily.

Gudrun looked at him, to see if it were ill-meant. Then she smiled at him.

'Ah,' she said, 'you know what we mean. Can't we go up there, and explore that coast?' She pointed to a grove on the hillock of the meadow-side, near the shore, half-way down the lake. 'That looks perfectly lovely. We might even bathe. Isn't it beautiful in this light! Really, it's like one of the reaches of the Nile—as one imagines the Nile.'

Gerald smiled at her factitious enthusiasm for the distant spot.

'You're sure it's far enough off?' he asked ironically, adding at once: 'Yes, you might go there, if we could get a boat. They seem to be all out.'

He looked round the lake and counted the rowing-boats on its surface.

'How lovely it would be!' cried Ursula wistfully.

'And don't you want tea?' he said.

'Oh,' said Gudrun, 'we could just drink a cup and be off.'

He looked from one to the other, smiling. He was somewhat offended—yet sporting.

'Can you manage a boat pretty well?' he asked.

'Yes,' replied Gudrun coldly, 'pretty well.'

'Oh yes,' cried Ursula. 'We can both of us row like water-spiders.'

'You can? There's a light little canoe of mine, that I didn't take out for fear somebody should drown themselves. Do you think you'd be safe in that?'

'Oh, perfectly,' said Gudrun.

'What an angel!' cried Ursula.

'Don't, for *my* sake, have an accident—because I'm responsible for the water.'

'Sure,' pledged Gudrun.

'Besides, we can both swim quite well,' said Ursula.

'Well—then I'll get them to put you up a tea-basket, and you can picnic all to yourselves—that's the idea, isn't it?'

'How fearfully good! How frightfully nice if you could!' cried Gudrun warmly, her colour flushing up again. It made the blood stir in his veins, the subtle way she turned to him and infused her gratitude into his body.

'Where's Birkin?' he said, his eyes twinkling. 'He might help me to get it down.'

'But what about your hand? Isn't it hurt?' asked Gudrun, rather muted, as if avoiding the intimacy. This was the first time the hurt had been mentioned. The curious way she skirted round the subject sent a new, subtle caress through his veins. He took his hand out of his pocket. It was bandaged. He looked at it, then put it in his pocket again. Gudrun quivered at the sight of the wrapped-up paw.

'Oh, I can manage with one hand. The canoe is as light as a feather,' he said. 'There's Rupert!—Rupert!'

Birkin turned from his social duties and came towards them.

'What have you done to it?' asked Ursula, who had been aching to put the question for the last half-hour.

'To my hand?' said Gerald. 'I trapped it in some machinery.'

'Ugh!' said Ursula. 'And did it hurt much?'

'Yes,' he said. 'It did at the time. It's getting better now. It crushed the fingers.'

'Oh,' cried Ursula, as if in pain, 'I hate people who hurt themselves. I can *feel* it.' And she shook her hand.

'What do you want?' said Birkin.

The two men carried down the slim brown boat, and set it on the water.

'You're quite sure you'll be safe in it?' Gerald asked.

'Quite sure,' said Gudrun. 'I wouldn't be so mean as to

take it, if there was the slightest doubt. But I've had a canoe at Arundel, and I assure you I'm perfectly safe.'

So saying, having given her word like a man, she and Ursula entered the frail craft, and pushed gently off. The two men stood watching them. Gudrun was paddling. She knew the men were watching her, and it made her slow and rather clumsy. The colour flew in her face like a flag.

'Thanks awfully,' she called back to him, from the water, as the boat slid away. 'It's lovely—like sitting in a leaf.'

He laughed at the fancy. Her voice was shrill and strange, calling from the distance. He watched her as she paddled away. There was something childlike about her, trustful and deferential, like a child. He watched her all the while, as she rowed. And to Gudrun it was a real delight, in make-belief, to be the childlike, clinging woman to the man who stood there on the quay, so good-looking and efficient in his white clothes, and moreover the most important man she knew at the moment. She did not take any notice of the wavering, indistinct, lambent Birkin, who stood at his side. One figure at a time occupied the field of her attention.

The boat rustled lightly along the water. They passed the bathers whose striped tents stood between the willows of the meadow's edge, and drew along the open shore, past the meadows that sloped golden in the light of the already late afternoon. Other boats were stealing under the wooded shore opposite, they could hear people's laughter and voices. But Gudrun rowed on towards the clump of trees that balanced perfect in the distance, in the golden light.

The sisters found a little place where a tiny stream flowed into the lake, with reeds and flowery march of pink willow herb, and a gravelly bank to the side. Here they ran delicately ashore, with their frail boat, the two girls took off their shoes and stockings and went through the water's edge to the grass. The tiny ripples of the lake were warm and clear, they lifted their boat on to the bank, and looked round with joy. They were quite alone in a forsaken little stream-mouth, and on the knoll just behind was the clump of trees.

'We will bathe just for a moment,' said Ursula, 'and then we'll have tea.'

They looked round. Nobody could notice them, or could

come up in time to see them. In less than a minute Ursula had thrown off her clothes and had slipped naked into the water, and was swimming out. Quickly, Gudrun joined her. They swam silently and blissfully for a few minutes, circling round their little stream-mouth. Then they slipped ashore and ran into the grove again, like nymphs.

'How lovely it is to be free,' said Ursula, running swiftly here and there between the tree-trunks, quite naked, her hair blowing loose. The grove was of beech-trees, big and splendid, a steel-grey scaffolding of trunks and boughs, with level sprays of strong green here and there, whilst through the northern side the distance glimmered open as through a window.

When they had run and danced themselves dry, the girls quickly dressed and sat down to the fragrant tea. They sat on the northern side of the grove, in the yellow sunshine facing the slope of the grassy hill, alone in a little wild world of their own. The tea was hot and aromatic, there were delicious little sandwiches of cucumber and of caviare, and winy cakes.

'Are you happy, Prune?' cried Ursula in delight, looking at her sister.

'Ursula, I'm perfectly happy,' replied Gudrun gravely, looking at the westering sun.

'So am I.'

When they were together, doing the things they enjoyed, the two sisters were quite complete in a perfect world of their own. And this was one of the perfect moments of freedom and delight, such as children alone know, when all seems a perfect and blissful adventure.

When they had finished tea, the two girls sat on, silent and serene. Then Ursula, who had a beautiful strong voice, began to sing to herself, softly: *'Annchen von Tharau.'* Gudrun listened, as she sat beneath the trees, and the yearning came into her heart. Ursula seemed so peaceful and sufficient unto herself, sitting there unconsciously crooning her song, strong and unquestioned at the centre of her own universe. And Gudrun felt herself outside. Always this desolating, agonized feeling, that she was outside of life, an onlooker, whilst Ursula was a partaker, caused Gudrun to suffer from a sense of her own negation, and made her, that she must always demand the other to be aware of her, to be in connexion with her.

'Do you mind if I do Dalcroze to that tune, Hurtler?' she asked in a curious muted tone, scarce moving her lips.

'What did you say?' asked Ursula, looking up in peaceful surprise.

'Will you sing while I do Dalcroze?' said Gudrun, suffering at having to repeat herself.

Ursula thought a moment, gathering her straying wits together.

'While you do——?' she asked vaguely.

'Dalcroze movements,' said Gudrun, suffering tortures of self-consciousness, even because of her sister.

'Oh, Dalcroze! I couldn't catch the name. *Do*—I should love to see you,' cried Ursula, with childish surprised brightness. 'What shall I sing?'

'Sing anything you like, and I'll take the rhythm from it.'

But Ursula could not for her life think of anything to sing. However, she suddenly began, in a laughing, teasing voice:

'My love—is a high-born lady——'

Gudrun, looking as if some invisible chain weighed on her hands and feet, began slowly to dance in the eurhythmic manner, pulsing and fluttering rhythmically with her feet making slower, regular gestures with her hands and arms, now spreading her arms wide, now raising them above her head, now flinging them softly apart, and lifting her face, her feet all the time beating and running to the measure of the song, as if it were some strange incantation, her white, rapt form drifting here and there in a strange impulsive rhapsody, seeming to be lifted on a breeze of incantation, shuddering with strange little runs. Ursula sat on the grass, her mouth open in her singing, her eyes laughing as if she thought it was a great joke, but a yellow light flashing up in them, as she caught some of the unconscious ritualistic suggestion of the complex shuddering and waving and drifting of her sister's white form, that was clutched in pure, mindless, tossing rhythm, and a will set powerful in a kind of hypnotic influence.

'My love is a high-born lady—She is-s-s—rather dark than shady——' rang out Ursula's laughing, satiric song, and

quicker, fiercer went Gudrun in the dance, stamping as if she
were trying to throw off some bond, flinging her hands suddenly and stamping again, then rushing with face uplifted
and throat full and beautiful, and eyes half closed, sightless.
The sun was low and yellow, sinking down, and in the sky
floated a thin, ineffectual moon.

Ursula was quite absorbed in her song, when suddenly
Gudrun stopped and said mildly, ironically:

'Ursula!'

'Yes?' said Ursula, opening her eyes out of the trance.

Gudrun was standing still and pointing, a mocking smile
on her face, towards the side.

'Ugh!' cried Ursula in sudden panic, starting to her feet.

'They're quite all right,' rang out Gudrun's sardonic
voice.

On the left stood a little cluster of Highland cattle, vividly
coloured and fleecy in the evening light, their horns branching into the sky, pushing forward their muzzles inquisitively,
to know what it was all about. Their eyes glittered through
their tangle of hair, their naked nostrils were full of shadow.

'Won't they do anything?' cried Ursula in fear.

Gudrun, who was usually frightened of cattle, now shook
her head in a queer, half-doubtful, half-sardonic motion, a
faint smile round her mouth.

'Don't they look charming, Ursula?' cried Gudrun, in a
high, strident voice, something like the scream of a sea-gull.

'Charming,' cried Ursula in trepidation. 'But won't they
do anything to us?'

Again Gudrun looked back at her sister with an enigmatic
smile, and shook her head.

'I'm sure they won't,' she said, as if she had to convince
herself also, and yet, as if she were confident of some secret
power in herself, and had to put it to the test. 'Sit down and
sing again,' she called in her high, strident voice.

'I'm frightened,' cried Ursula, in a pathetic voice, watching the group of sturdy short cattle, that stood with their
knees planted, and watched with their dark, wicked eyes,
through the matted fringe of their hair. Nevertheless, she
sank down again, in her former posture.

'They are quite safe,' came Gudrun's high call. 'Sing something, you've only to sing something.'

It was evident she had a strange passion to dance before the sturdy, handsome cattle.

Ursula began to sing, in a false quavering voice:

'Way down in Tennessee—'

She sounded purely anxious. Nevertheless, Gudrun, with her arms outspread and her face uplifted, went in a strange palpitating dance towards the cattle, lifting her body towards them as if in a spell, her feet pulsing as if in some little frenzy of unconscious sensation, her arms, her wrists, her hands stretching and heaving and falling and reaching and reaching and falling, her breasts lifted and shaken towards the cattle, her throat exposed as in some voluptuous ecstasy towards them, whilst she drifted imperceptibly nearer, an uncanny white figure, towards them, carried away in its own rapt trance, ebbing in strange fluctuations upon the cattle, that waited, and ducked their heads a little in sudden contraction from her, watching all the time as if hypnotized, their bare horns branching in the clear light, as the white figure of the women ebbed upon them, in the slow, hypnotizing convulsion of the dance. She could feel them just in front of her, it was as if she had the electric pulse from their breasts running into her hands. Soon she would touch them, actually touch them. A terrible shiver of fear and pleasure went through her. And all the while Ursula, spell-bound, kept up her high-pitched thin, irrelevant song, which pierced the fading evening like an incantation.

Gudrun could hear the cattle breathing heavily with helpless fear and fascination. Oh, they were brave little beasts, these wild Scotch bullocks, wild and fleecy. Suddenly one of them snorted, ducked its head, and backed.

'Hue! Hi-eee!' came a sudden loud shout from the edge of the grove. The cattle broke and fell back quite spontaneously, went running up the hill, their fleece waving like fire to their motion. Gudrun stood suspended out on the grass, Ursula rose to her feet.

It was Gerald and Birkin come to find them, and Gerald had cried out to frighten off the cattle.

'What do you think you're doing?' he now called, in a high, wondering vexed tone.

'Why have you come?' came back Gudrun's strident cry of anger.

'What do you think you were doing?' Gerald repeated, automatically.

'We were doing eurhythmics,' laughed Ursula, in a shaken voice.

Gudrun stood aloof looking at them with large dark eyes of resentment, suspended for a few moments. Then she walked away up the hill, after the cattle, which had gathered in a little, spell-bound cluster higher up.

'Where are you going?' Gerald called after her. And he followed her up the hill-side. The sun had gone behind the hill, and shadows were clinging to the earth, the sky above was full of travelling light.

'A poor song for a dance,' said Birkin to Ursula, standing before her with a sardonic, flickering laugh on his face. And in another second, he was singing softly to himself, and dancing a grotesque step-dance in front of her, his limbs and body shaking loose, his face flickering palely, a constant thing, whilst his feet beat a rapid mocking tattoo, and his body seemed to hang all loose and quaking in between, like a shadow.

'I think we've all gone mad,' she said, laughing rather frightened.

'Pity we aren't madder,' he answered, as he kept up the incessant shaking dance. Then suddenly he leaned up to her and kissed her fingers lightly, putting his face to hers and looking into her eyes with a pale grin. She stepped back, affronted.

'Offended—?' he asked ironically, suddenly going quite still and reserved again. 'I thought you liked the light fantastic.'

'Not like that,' she said, confused and bewildered, almost affronted. Yet somewhere inside her she was fascinated by the sight of his loose, vibrating body, perfectly abandoned to its own dropping and swinging, and by the pallid, sardonic-smiling face above. Yet automatically she stiffened herself away, and disapproved. It seemed almost an obscenity, in a man who talked as a rule so very seriously.

'Why not like that?' he mocked. And immediately he dropped again into the incredibly rapid, slack-waggling dance, watching her malevolently. And moving in the rapid, stationary dance he came a little nearer, and reached forward with an incredibly mocking, satiric gleam on his face, and would have kissed her again, had she not started back.

'No, don't!' she cried really afraid.

'Cordelia after all,' he said satirically. She was stung, as if this were an insult. She knew he intended it as such, and it bewildered her.

'And you,' she cried in retort, 'why do you always take your soul in your mouth, so frightfully full?'

'So that I can spit it out the more readily,' he said, pleased by his own retort.

Gerald Crich, his face narrowing to an intent gleam, followed up the hill with quick strides, straight after Gudrun. The cattle stood with their noses together on the brow of a slope, watching the scene below, the men in white hovering about the white forms of the women, watching above all Gudrun, who was advancing slowly towards them. She stood a moment, glancing back at Gerald, and then at the cattle.

Then in a sudden motion, she lifted her arms and rushed sheer upon the long-horned bullocks, in shuddering irregular runs, pausing for a second and looking at them, then lifting her hands and running forward with a flash, till they ceased pawing the ground, and gave way, snorting with terror, lifting their heads from the ground and flinging themselves away, galloping off into the evening, becoming tiny in the distance, and still not stopping.

Gudrun remained staring after them, with a mask-like defiant face.

'Why do you want to drive them mad?' asked Gerald, coming up with her.

She took no notice of him, only averted her face from him.

'It's not safe, you know,' he persisted. 'They're nasty, when they do turn.'

'Turn where? Turn away?' she mocked loudly.

'No,' he said, 'turn against you.'

'Turn against *me*?' she mocked.

He could make nothing of this.

'Anyway, they gored one of the farmer's cows to death the other day,' he said.

'What do I care?' she said.

'*I* cared though,' he replied, 'seeing that they're my cattle.'

'How are they yours! You haven't swallowed them. Give me one of them now,' she said, holding out her hand.

'You know where they are,' he said, pointing over the hill. 'You can have one if you'd like it sent to you later on.'

She looked at him inscrutably.

'You think I'm afraid of you and your cattle, don't you?' she asked.

His eyes narrowed dangerously. There was a faint domineering smile on his face.

'Why should I think that?' he said.

She was watching him all the time with her dark, dilated, inchoate eyes. She leaned forward and swung round her arm, catching him a light blow on the face with the back of her hand.

'That's why,' she said, mocking.

And she felt in her soul an unconquerable desire for deep violence against him. She shut off the fear and dismay that filled her conscious mind. She wanted to do as she did, she was not going to be afraid.

He recoiled from the slight blow on his face. He became deadly pale, and a dangerous flame darkened his eyes. For some seconds he could not speak, his lungs were so suffused with blood, his heart stretched almost to bursting with a great gush of ungovernable emotion. It was as if some reservoir of black emotion had burst within him, and swamped him.

'You have struck the first blow,' he said at last, forcing the words from his lungs, in a voice so soft and low, it sounded like a dream within her, not spoken in the outer air.

'And I shall strike the last,' she retorted involuntarily, with confident assurance. He was silent, he did not contradict her.

She stood negligently, staring away from him, into the distance. On the edge of her consciousness the question was asking itself, automatically:

'Why *are* you behaving in this *impossible* and ridiculous fashion.' But she was sullen, she half shoved the question out of herself. She could not get it clean away, so she felt self-conscious.

Gerald, very pale, was watching her closely. His eyes were lit up with intent lights, absorbed and gleaming. She turned suddenly on him.

'It's you who make me behave like this, you know,' she said, almost suggestive.

'I? How?' he said.

But she turned away, and set off towards the lake. Below, on the water, lanterns were coming alight, faint ghosts of warm flame floating in the pallor of the first twilight. The earth was spread with darkness, like lacquer, overhead was a pale sky, all primrose, and the lake was pale as milk in one part. Away at the landing-stage, tiniest points of coloured rays were stringing themselves in the dusk. The launch was being illuminated. All round, shadow was gathering from the trees.

Gerald, white like a presence in his summer clothes, was following down the open grassy slope. Gudrun waited for him to come up. Then she softly put out her hand and touched him, saying softly:

'Don't be angry with me.'

A flame flew over him, and he was unconscious. Yet he stammered:

'I'm not angry with you. I'm in love with you.'

His mind was gone, he grasped for sufficient mechanical control, to save himself. She laughed a silvery little mockery, yet intolerably caressive.

'That's one way of putting it,' she said.

The terrible swooning burden on his mind, the awful swooning, the loss of all his control, was too much for him. He grasped her arm in his one hand, as if his hand were iron.

'It's all right, then, is it?' he said, holding her arrested.

She looked at the face with the fixed eyes, set before her, and her blood ran cold.

'Yes, it's all right,' she said softly, as if drugged, her voice crooning and witch-like.

He walked on beside her, a striding, mindless body. But he recovered a little as he went. He suffered badly. He had killed his brother when a boy, and was set apart, like Cain.

They found Birkin and Ursula sitting together by the boats, talking and laughing. Birkin had been teasing Ursula.

'Do you smell this little marsh?' he said, sniffing the air. He was very sensitive to scents, and quick in understanding them.

'It's rather nice,' she said.

'No,' he replied, 'alarming.'

'Why alarming?' she laughed.

'It seethes and seethes, a river of darkness,' he said, 'putting forth lilies and snakes, and the *ignis fatuus,* and rolling all the time onward. That's what we never take into account—that it rolls onwards.'

'What does?'

'The other river, the black river. We always consider the silver river of life, rolling on and quickening all the world to a brightness, on and on to heaven, flowing into a bright eternal sea, a heaven of angels thronging. But the other is our real reality—'

'But what other? I don't see any other,' said Ursula.

'It is your reality, nevertheless,' he said; 'that dark river of dissolution. You see it rolls in us just as the other rolls—the black river of corruption. And our flowers are of this—our sea-born Aphrodite, all our white phosphorescent flowers of sensuous perfection, all our reality, nowadays.'

'You mean that Aphrodite is really deathly?' asked Ursula.

'I mean she is the flowering mystery of the death-process, yes,' he replied. 'When the stream of synthetic creation lapses, we find ourselves part of the inverse process, the blood of destructive creation. Aphrodite is born in the first spasm of universal dissolution—then the snakes and swans and lotus—marsh-flowers—and Gudrun and Gerald—born in the process of destructive creation.'

'And you and me—?' she asked.

'Probably,' he replied. 'In part, certainly. Whether we are that, *in toto,* I don't yet know.'

'You mean we are flowers of dissolution—*fleurs du mal*? I don't feel as if I were,' she protested.

He was silent for a time.

'I don't feel as if we were, *altogether*,' he replied. 'Some people are pure flowers of dark corruption—lilies. But there ought to be some roses, warm and flamy. You know Herakleitos says "a dry soul is best". I know so well what that means. Do you?'

'I'm not sure,' Ursula replied. 'But what if people *are* all flowers of dissolution—when they're flowers at all—what difference does it make?'

'No difference—and all the difference. Dissolution rolls on, just as production does,' he said. 'It is a progressive process—and it ends in universal nothing—the end of the world, if you like. But why isn't the end of the world as good as the beginning?'

'I suppose it isn't,' said Ursula, rather angry.

'Oh yes, ultimately,' he said. 'It means a new cycle of creation after—but not for us. If it is the end, then we are of the end—*fleurs du mal,* if you like. If we are *fleurs du mal,* we are not roses of happiness, and there you are.'

'But I think I am,' said Ursula. 'I think I am a rose of happiness.'

'Ready-made?' he asked ironically.

'No—real,' she said, hurt.

'If we are the end, we are not the beginning,' he said.

'Yes, we are,' she said. 'The beginning comes out of the end.'

'After it, not out of it. After us, not out of us.'

'You are a devil, you know, really,' she said. 'You want to destroy our hope. You *want* us to be deathly.'

'No,' he said, 'I only want us to *know* what we are.'

'Ha!' she cried in anger. 'You only want us to know death.'

'You're quite right,' said the soft voice of Gerald, out of the dusk behind.

Birkin rose. Gerald and Gudrun came up. They all began to smoke, in the moments of silence. One after another,

Birkin lighted their cigarettes. The match flickered in the twilight, and they were all smoking peacefully by the water-side. The lake was dim, the light dying from off it, in the midst of the dark land. The air all round was intangible, neither here nor there, and there was an unreal noise of banjoes, or suchlike music.

As the golden swim of light overhead died out, the moon gained brightness, and seemed to begin to smile forth her ascendancy. The dark woods on the opposite shore melted into universal shadow. And amid this universal under-shadow, there was a scattered intrusion of lights. Far down the lake were fantastic pale strings of colour, like beads of wan fire, green and red and yellow. The music came out in a little puff, as the launch, all illuminated, veered into the great shadow, stirring her outlines of half-living lights, puffing out her music in little drifts.

All were lighting up. Here and there, close against the faint water, and at the far end of the lake, where the water lay milky in the last whiteness of the sky, and there was no shadow, solitary, frail flames of lanterns floated from the unseen boats. There was a sound of oars, and a boat passed from the pallor into the darkness under the wood, where her lanterns seemed to kindle into fire, hanging in ruddy lovely globes. And again, in the lake, shadowy red gleams hovered in reflection about the boat. Everywhere were these noiseless ruddy creatures of fire drifting near the surface of the water, caught at by the rarest, scarce visible reflections.

Birkin brought the lanterns from the bigger boat, and the four shadowy white figures gathered round, to light them. Ursula held up the first, Birkin lowered the light from the rosy, glowing cup of his hands, into the depths of the lantern. It was kindled, and they all stood back to look at the great blue moon of light that hung from Ursula's hand, casting a strange gleam on her face. It flickered, and Birkin went bending over the well of light. His face shone out like an apparition, so unconscious, and again, something demoniacal. Ursula was dim and veiled, looming over him.

'That is all right,' said his voice softly.

She held up the lantern. It had a flight of storks streaming through a turquoise sky of light, over a dark earth.

'This is beautiful,' she said.

'Lovely,' echoed Gudrun, who wanted to hold one also and lift it up full of beauty.

'Light one for me,' she said. Gerald stood by her, incapacitated. Birkin lit the lantern she held up. Her heart beat with anxiety, to see how beautiful it would be. It was primrose yellow, with tall straight flowers growing darkly from their dark leaves, lifting their heads into the primrose day, while butterflies hovered about them, in the pure clear light.

Gudrun gave a little cry of excitement, as if pierced with delight.

'Isn't it beautiful, oh, isn't it beautiful!'

Her soul was really pierced with beauty, she was translated beyond herself. Gerald leaned near to her, into her zone of light, as if to see. He came close to her, and stood touching her, looking with her at the primrose-shining globe. And she turned her face to his, that was faintly bright in the light of the lantern, and they stood together in one luminous union, close together and ringed round with light, all the rest excluded.

Birkin looked away, and went to light Ursula's second lantern. It had a pale ruddy sea-bottom, with black crabs and sea-weed moving sinuously under a transparent sea, that passed into flamy ruddiness above.

'You've got the heavens above, and the waters under the earth,' said Birkin to her.

'Anything but the earth itself,' she laughed, watching his live hands that hovered to attend to the light.

'I'm dying to see what my second one is,' cried Gudrun, in a vibrating rather strident voice, that seemed to repel the others from her.

Birkin went and kindled it. It was of a lovely deep blue colour, with a red floor, and a great white cuttle-fish flowing in white soft streams all over it. The cuttle-fish had a face that stared straight from the heart of the light, very fixed and coldly intent.

'How truly terrifying!' exclaimed Gudrun, in a voice of horror. Gerald, at her side, gave a low laugh.

'But isn't it really fearful!' she cried in dismay.

Again he laughed, and said:

'Change it with Ursula, for the crabs.'

Gudrun was silent for a moment.

'Ursula,' she said, 'could you bear to have this fearful thing?'

'I think the colouring is *lovely*,' said Ursula.

'So do I,' said Gudrun. 'But could you *bear* to have it swinging to your boat? Don't you want to destroy it *at once*?'

'Oh no,' said Ursula. 'I don't want to destroy it.'

'Well, do you mind having it instead of the crabs? Are you sure you don't mind?'

Gudrun came forward to exchange lanterns.

'No,' said Ursula, yielding up the crabs and receiving the cuttle-fish.

Yet she could not help feeling rather resentful at the way in which Gudrun and Gerald should assume a right over her, a precedence.

'Come then,' said Birkin. 'I'll put them on the boats.'

He and Ursula were moving away to the big boat.

'I suppose you'll row me back, Rupert,' said Gerald, out of the pale shadow of the evening.

'Won't you go with Gudrun in the canoe?' said Birkin. 'It'll be more interesting.'

There was a moment's pause. Birkin and Ursula stood dimly, with their swinging lanterns, by the water's edge. The world was all illusive.

'Is that all right?' said Gudrun to him.

'It'll suit *me* very well,' he said. 'But what about you, and the rowing? I don't see why you should pull me.'

'Why not?' she said. 'I can pull you as well as I could pull Ursula.'

By her tone he could tell she wanted to have him in the boat to herself, and that she was subtly gratified that she should have power over them both. He gave himself, in a strange, electric submission.

She handed him the lanterns, whilst she went to fix the cane at the end of the canoe. He followed after her, and stood with the lanterns dangling against his white-flannelled thighs, emphasizing the shadow around.

'Kiss me before we go,' came his voice softly from out of the shadow above.

She stopped her work in real, momentary astonishment.

'But why?' she exclaimed, in pure surprise.

'Why?' he echoed ironically.

And she looked at him fixedly for some moments. Then she leaned forward and kissed him, with a slow, luxurious kiss, lingering on the mouth. And then she took the lanterns from him, while he stood swooning with the perfect fire that burned in all his joints.

They lifted the canoe into the water, Gudrun took her place, and Gerald pushed off.

'Are you sure you don't hurt your hand, doing that?' she asked, solicitous. 'Because I could have done it *perfectly.*'

'I don't hurt myself,' he said in a low, soft voice, that caressed her with inexpressible beauty.

And she watched him as he sat near her, very near to her, in the stern of the canoe, his legs coming towards hers, his feet touching hers. And she paddled softly, lingeringly, longing for him to say something meaningful to her. But he remained silent.

'You like this, do you?' she said, in a gentle, solicitous voice.

He laughed shortly.

'There is a space between us,' he said, in the same low, unconscious voice, as if something were speaking out of him. And she was as if magically aware of their being balanced in separation, in the boat. She swooped with acute comprehension and pleasure.

'But I'm very near,' she said caressively, gaily.

'Yet distant, distant,' he said.

Again she was silent with pleasure, before she answered, speaking with a reedy, thrilled voice:

'Yet we cannot very well change, whilst we are on the water.' She caressed him subtly and strangely, having him completely at her mercy.

A dozen or more boats on the lake swung their rosy and moon-like lanterns low on the water, that reflected as from a fire. In the distance, the steamer twanged and thrummed and washed with her faintly-splashing paddles, trailing her strings of coloured lights, and occasionally lighting up the whole scene luridly with an effusion of fireworks, Roman candles and sheaves of stars and other simple effects, illuminating the surface of the water, and showing the boats creeping round, low down. Then the lovely darkness fell again, the lanterns and the little threaded lights glimmered softly, there was a muffled knocking of oars and a waving of music.

Gudrun paddled almost imperceptibly. Gerald could see, not far ahead, the rich blue and the rose globes of Ursula's lanterns swaying softly cheek to cheek as Birkin rowed, and iridescent, evanescent gleams chasing in the wake. He was aware, too, of his own delicately coloured lights casting their softness behind him.

Gudrun rested her paddle and looked round. The canoe lifted with the lightest ebbing of the water. Gerald's white knees were very near to her.

'Isn't it beautiful!' she said softly, as if reverently.

She looked at him, as he leaned back against the faint crystal of the lantern-light. She could see his face, although it was a pure shadow. But it was a piece of twilight. And her breast was keen with passion for him, he was so beautiful in his male stillness and mystery. It was a certain pure effluence of maleness, like an aroma from his softly, firmly moulded contours, a certain rich perfection of his presence, that touched her with an ecstasy, a thrill of pure intoxication. She loved to look at him. For the present she did not want to touch him, to know the further, satisfying substance of his living body. He was purely intangible, yet so near. Her hands lay on the paddle like slumber, she only wanted to see him, like a crystal shadow, to feel his essential presence.

'Yes,' he said vaguely. 'It is very beautiful.'

He was listening to the faint near sounds, the dropping of water-drops from the oar-blades, the slight drumming of the lanterns behind him, as they rubbed against one another, the occasional rustling of Gudrun's full skirt, an alien land noise. His mind was almost submerged, he was almost transfused, lapsed out for the first time in his life, into the things about him. For he always kept such a keen attentiveness, concentrated and unyielding in himself. Now he had let go, imperceptibly he was melting into oneness with the whole. It was like pure, perfect sleep, his first great sleep of life. He had been so insistent, so guarded, all his life. But here was sleep, and peace, and perfect lapsing out.

'Shall I row to the landing-stage?' asked Gudrun wistfully.

'Anywhere,' he answered. 'Let it drift.'

'Tell me then, if we are running into anything,' she replied, in that very quiet, toneless voice of sheer intimacy.

'The lights will show,' he said.

So they drifted almost motionless, in silence. He wanted silence, pure and whole. But she was uneasy yet for some word, for some assurance.

'Nobody will miss you?' she asked, anxious for some communication.

'Miss me?' he echoed. 'No! Why?'

'I wondered if anybody would be looking for you.'

'Why should they look for me?' And then he remembered his manners. 'But perhaps you want to get back,' he said, in a changed voice.

'No, I don't want to get back,' she replied. 'No, I assure you.'

'You're quite sure it's all right for you?'

'Perfectly all right.'

And again they were still. The launch twanged and hooted, somebody was singing. Then as if the night smashed, suddenly there was a great shout, a confusion of shouting, warring on the water, then the horrid noise of paddles reversed and churned violently.

Gerald sat up, and Gudrun looked at him in fear.

'Somebody in the water,' he said, angrily, and desperately, looking keenly across the dusk. 'Can you row up?'

'Where, to the launch?' asked Gudrun, in nervous panic. 'Yes.'

'You'll tell me if I don't steer straight,' she said, in nervous apprehension.

'You keep pretty level,' he said, and the canoe hastened forward.

The shouting and the noise continued, sounding horrid through the dusk, over the surface of the water.

'Wasn't this *bound* to happen?' said Gudrun, with heavy hateful irony. But he hardly heard, and she glanced over her shoulder to see her way. The half-dark waters were sprinkled with lovely bubbles of swaying lights, the launch did not look far off. She was rocking her lights in the early night. Gudrun rowed as hard as she could. But now that it was a serious matter, she seemed uncertain and clumsy in her stroke, it was difficult to paddle swiftly. She glanced at his face. He was looking fixedly into the darkness, very keen and alert and single in himself, intrumental. Her heart sank, she seemed to die a death. 'Of course,' she said to herself, 'nobody will be drowned. Of course they won't. It would be too extravagant and sensational.' But her heart was cold, because of his sharp impersonal face. It was as if he belonged naturally to dread and catastrophe, as if he were himself again.

Then there came a child's voice, a girl's high, piercing shriek:

'Di—Di—Di—Di—Oh Di—Oh Di—Oh Di!'

The blood ran cold in Gudrun's veins.

'It's Diana, is it,' muttered Gerald. 'The young monkey, she'd have to be up to some of her tricks.'

And he glanced again at the paddle, the boat was not going quickly enough for him. It made Gudrun almost helpless at the rowing, this nervous stress. She kept up with all her might. Still the voices were calling and answering.

'Where, where? There you are—that's it. Which? No— No-o-o. Damn it all, here, *here*—' Boats were hurrying from all directions to the scene, coloured lanterns could be seen waving close to the surface of the lake, reflections swaying after them in uneven haste. The steamer hooted again, for some unknown reason. Gudrun's boat was travelling quickly, the lanterns were swinging behind Gerald.

And then again came the child's high, screaming voice, with a note of weeping and impatience in it now:

'Di—Oh Di—Oh Di—Di—!'

It was a terrible sound, coming through the obscure air of the evening.

'You'd be better if you were in bed, Winnie,' Gerald muttered to himself.

He was stooping unlacing his shoes, pushing them off with the foot. Then he threw his soft hat into the bottom of the boat.

'You can't go into the water with your hurt hand,' said Gudrun, panting, in a low voice of horror.

'What? It won't hurt.'

He had struggled out of his jacket, and had dropped it between his feet. He sat bare-headed, all in white now. He felt the belt at his waist. They were nearing the launch, which stood still big above them, her myriad lamps making lovely darts, and sinuous running tongues of ugly red and green and yellow light on the lustrous dark water, under the shadow.

'Oh get her out! Oh Di, *darling*! Oh get her out! Oh Daddy, Oh Daddy!' moaned the child's voice, in distraction. Somebody was in the water, with a lifebelt. Two boats paddled near, their lanterns swinging ineffectually, the boats nosing round.

'Hi there—Rockley!—hi there!'

'Mr Gerald!' came the captain's terrified voice. 'Miss Diana's in the water.'

'Anybody gone in for her?' came Gerald's sharp voice.

'Young Doctor Brindell, sir.'

'Where?'

'Can't see no signs of them, sir. Everybody's looking, but there's nothing so far.'

There was a moment's ominous pause.

'Where did she go in?'

'I think—about where that boat is,' came the uncertain answer, 'that one with red and green lights.'

'Row there,' said Gerald quietly to Gudrun.

'Get her out, Gerald, oh get her out,' the child's voice was crying anxiously. He took no heed.

'Lean back that way,' said Gerald to Gudrun, as he stood up in the frail boat. 'She won't upset.'

In another moment, he had dropped clean down, soft and plumb, into the water. Gudrun was swaying violently in her boat, the agitated water shook with transient lights, she realized that it was faintly moonlight, and that he was gone. So it was possible to be gone. A terrible sense of fatality robbed her of all feeling and thought. She knew he was gone out of the world, there was merely the same world, and absence, his absence. The night seemed large and vacuous. Lanterns swayed here and there, people were talking in an undertone on the launch and in the boats. She could hear Winifred moaning: *'Oh do find her Gerald, do find her,'* and someone trying to comfort the child. Gudrun paddled aimlessly here and there. The terrible, massive, cold, boundless surface of the water terrified her beyond words. Would he never come back? She felt she must jump into the water too, to know the horror also.

She started, hearing someone say: 'There he is.' She saw the movement of his swimming, like a water-rat. And she rowed involuntarily to him. But he was near another boat, a bigger one. Still she rowed towards him. She must be very near. She saw him—he looked like a seal. He looked like a seal as he took hold of the side of the boat. His fair hair was washed down on his round head, his face seemed to glisten suavely. She could hear him panting.

Then he clambered into the boat. Oh, and the beauty of the subjection of his loins, white and dimly luminous as he climbed over the side of the boat, made her want to die, to die. The beauty of his dim and luminous loins as he climbed into the boat, his back rounded and soft—ah, this was too much for her, too final a vision. She knew it, and it was fatal. The terrible hopelessness of fate, and of beauty, such beauty!

He was not like a man to her, he was an incarnation, a great phase of life. She saw him press the water out of his face, and look at the bandage on his hand. And she knew it was all no good, and that she would never go beyond him, he was the final approximation of life to her.

'Put the lights out, we shall see better,' came his voice, sudden and mechanical and belonging to the world of man. She could scarcely believe there was a world of man. She leaned round and blew out her lanterns. They were difficult to blow out. Everywhere the lights were gone save the coloured points on the sides of the launch. The bluey-grey, early night spread level around, the moon was overhead, there were shadows of boats here and there.

Again there was a splash, and he was gone under. Gudrun

sat, sick at heart, frightened of the great, level surface of the water, so heavy and deadly. She was so alone, with the level, unliving field of the water stretching beneath her. It was not a good isolation, it was a terrible, cold separation of suspense. She was suspended upon the surface of the insidious reality until such time as she also should disappear beneath it.

Then she knew, by a stirring of voices, that he had climbed out again, into a boat. She sat wanting connexion with him. Strenuously she claimed her connexion with him, across the invisible space of the water. But round her heart was an isolation unbearable, through which nothing would penetrate.

'Take the launch in. It's no use keeping her there. Get lines for the dragging,' came the decisive, instrumental voice, that was full of the sound of the world.

The launch began gradually to beat the waters.

'Gerald! Gerald!' came the wild crying voice of Winifred. He did not answer. Slowly the launch drifted round in a pathetic, clumsy circle, and slunk away to the land, retreating into the dimness. The wash of her paddles grew duller. Gudrun rocked in her light boat, and dipped the paddle automatically to steady herself.

'Gudrun?' called Ursula's voice.

'Ursula!'

The boats of the two sisters pulled together.

'Where is Gerald?' said Gudrun.

'He's dived again,' said Ursula plaintively. 'And I know he ought not, with his hurt hand and everything.'

'I'll take him in home this time,' said Birkin.

The boats swayed again from the wash of steamer. Gudrun and Ursula kept a look-out for Gerald.

'There he is!' cried Ursula, who had the sharpest eyes. He had not been long under. Birkin pulled towards him, Gudrun following. He swam slowly, and caught hold of the boat with his wounded hand. It slipped, and he sank back.

'Why don't you help him?' cried Ursula sharply.

He came again, and Birkin leaned to help him into the boat. Gudrun again watched Gerald climb out of the water, but this time slowly, heavily, with the blind clambering motions of an amphibious beast, clumsy. Again the moon shone with faint luminosity on his white wet figure, on the stooping back and the rounded loins. But it looked defeated now, his body, it clambered and fell with slow clumsiness. He was breathing hoarsely too, like an animal that is suffering. He sat slack and motionless in the boat, his head blunt and blind like a seal's, his whole appearance inhuman, unknowing. Gudrun shuddered as she mechanically followed his boat. Birkin rowed without speaking to the landing-stage.

'Where are you going?' Gerald asked suddenly, as if just waking up.

'Home,' said Birkin.

'Oh no!' said Gerald imperiously. 'We can't go home while they're in the water. Turn back again, I'm going to find them.' The women were frightened, his voice was so imperative and dangerous, almost mad, not to be opposed.

'No,' said Birkin. 'You can't.' There was a strange fluid compulsion in his voice. Gerald was silent in a battle of wills. It was as if he would kill the other man. But Birkin rowed evenly and unswerving, with an inhuman inevitability.

'Why should you interfere?' said Gerald, in hate.

Birkin did not answer. He rowed towards the land. And Gerald sat mute, like a dumb beast, panting, his teeth chattering, his arms inert, his head like a seal's head.

They came to the landing-stage. Wet and naked looking, Gerald climbed up the few steps. There stood his father, in the night.

'Father!' he said.

'Yes, my boy? Go home and get those things off.'

'We shan't save them, father,' said Gerald.

'There's hope yet, my boy.'

'I'm afraid not. There's no knowing where they are. You can't find them. And there's a current, as cold as hell.'

'We'll let the water out,' said the father. 'Go home you and look to yourself. See that he's looked after, Rupert,' he added in a neutral voice.

'Well, father, I'm sorry. I'm sorry. I'm afraid it's my fault. But it can't be helped; I've done what I could for the mo-

ment. I could go on diving, of course—not much, though—
and not much use—'

He moved away barefoot, on the planks of the platform.
Then he trod on something sharp.

'Of course, you've got no shoes on,' said Birkin.

'His shoes are here!' cried Gudrun from below. She was
making fast her boat.

Gerald waited for them to be brought to him. Gudrun
came with them. He pulled them on his feet.

'If you once die,' he said, 'Then when it's over, it's finished. Why come to life again? There's room under that
water there for thousands.'

'Two is enough,' she said, murmuring.

He dragged on his second shoe. He was shivering violently and his jaw shook as he spoke.

'That's true,' he said, 'maybe. But it's curious how much
room there seems, a whole universe under there; and as cold
as hell, you're as helpless as if your head was cut off.' He
could scarcely speak, he shook so violently. 'There's one
thing about our family, you know,' he continued. 'Once anything goes wrong, it can never be put right again—not with
us. I've noticed it all my life—you can't put a thing right,
once it has gone wrong.'

They were walking across the high-road to the house.

'And do you know, when you are down there, it is so
cold, actually, and so endless, so different really from what
it is on top, so endless—you wonder how it is so many are
alive, why we're up here. Are you going? I shall see you
again, shan't I? Good-night, and thank you. Thank you very
much.'

The two girls waited a while, to see if there were any
hope. The moon shone clearly overhead, with almost impertinent brightness, the small dark boats clustered on the water, there were voices and subdued shouts. But it was all to
no purpose. Gudrun went home when Birkin returned.

He was commissioned to open the sluice that let out the
water from the lake, which was pierced at one end, near the
high-road, thus serving as a reservoir to supply with water
the distant mines, in case of necessity. 'Come with me,' he

said to Ursula, 'and then I will walk home with you, when I've done this.'

He called at the water-keeper's cottage and took the key of the sluice. They went through a little gate from the high-road, to the head of the water, where was a great stone basin which received the overflow, and a flight of stone steps descended into the depths of the water itself. At the head of the steps was the lock of the sluice-gate.

The night was silver-grey and perfect, save for the scattered restless sound of voices. The grey sheen of the moonlight caught the stretch of water, dark boats plashed and moved. But Ursula's mind ceased to be receptive, everything was unimportant and unreal.

Birkin fixed the iron handle of the sluice, and turned it with a wrench. The cogs began slowly to rise. He turned and turned, like a slave, his white figure became distinct. Ursula looked away. She could not bear to see him winding heavily and laboriously, bending and rising mechanically like a slave, turning the handle.

Then, a real shock to her, there came a loud splashing of water from out of the dark, tree-filled hollow beyond the road, a splashing that deepened rapidly to a harsh roar, and then became a heavy, booming noise of a great body of water falling solidly all the time. It occupied the whole of the night, this great steady booming of water, everything was drowned within it, drowned and lost. Ursula seemed to have to struggle for her life. She put her hands over her ears, and looked at the high bland moon.

'Can't we go now?' she cried to Birkin, who was watching the water on the steps, to see if it would get any lower. It seemed to fascinate him. He looked at her and nodded.

The little dark boats had moved nearer, people were crowding curiously along the hedge by the high-road, to see what was to be seen. Birkin and Ursula went to the cottage with the key, then turned their backs on the lake. She was in great haste. She could not bear the terrible crushing boom of the escaping water.

'Do you think they are dead?' she cried in a high voice, to make herself heard.

'Yes,' he replied.

'Isn't it horrible!'

He paid no heed. They walked up the hill, farther and farther away from the noise.

'Do you mind very much?' she asked him.

'I don't mind about the dead,' he said, 'once they are dead. The worst of it is, they cling on to the living, and won't let go!'

She pondered for a time.

'Yes,' she said. 'The *fact* of death doesn't really seem to matter much, does it?'

'No,' he said. 'What does it matter if Diana Crich is alive or dead?'

'Doesn't it?' she said, shocked.

'No, why should it? Better she were dead—she'll be much more real. She'll be positive in death. In life she was a fretting, negated thing.'

'You are rather horrible,' murmured Ursula.

'No! I'd rather Diana Crich were dead. Her living somehow was all wrong. As for the young man, poor devil—he'll find his way out quickly instead of slowly. Death is all right—nothing better.'

'Yet you don't want to die,' she challenged him.

He was silent for a time. Then he said, in a voice that was frightening to her in its change:

'I should like to be through with it—I should like to be through with the death process.'

'And aren't you?' asked Ursula nervously.

They walked on for some way in silence, under the trees. Then he said slowly, as if afraid:

'There is life which belongs to death, and there is life which isn't death. One is tired of the life that belongs to death—our kind of life. But whether it is finished, God knows. I want love that is like sleep, like being born again, vulnerable as a baby that just comes into the world.'

Ursula listened, half attentive, half avoiding what he said. She seemed to catch the drift of his statement, and then she drew away. She wanted to hear, but she did not want to be implicated. She was reluctant to yield there, where he wanted her, to yield as it were her very identity.

'Why should love be like sleep?' she asked sadly.

'I don't know. So that it is like death—I *do* want to die from this life—and yet it is more than life itself. One is delivered over like a naked infant from the womb, all the old defences, and the old body gone, and new air around one, that has never been breathed before.'

She listened, making out what he said. She knew, as well as he knew, that words themselves do not convey meaning, that they are but a gesture we make, a dumb show like any other. And she seemed to feel his gesture through her blood, and she drew back, even though her desire sent her forward.

'But,' she said gravely, 'didn't you say you wanted something that was *not* love—something beyond love?'

He turned in confusion. There was always confusion in speech. Yet it must be spoken. Whichever way one moved, if one were to move forwards, one must break a way through. And to know, to give utterance, was to break a way through the walls of the prison as the infant in labour strives through the walls of the womb. There is no new movement now, without the breaking through of the old body, deliberately, in knowledge, in the struggle to get out.

'I don't want love,' he said. 'I don't want to know you. I want to be gone out of myself, and you to be lost to yourself, so we are found different. One shouldn't talk when one is tired and wretched. One Hamletizes, and it seems a lie. Only believe me when I show you a bit of healthy pride and insouciance. I hate myself serious.'

'Why shouldn't you be serious?' she said.

He thought for a minute, then he said sulkily:

'I don't know.' Then they walked on in silence, at outs. He was vague and lost.

'Isn't it strange,' she said, suddenly putting her hand on his arm, with a loving impulse, 'how we always talk like this! I suppose we do love each other in some way.'

'Oh yes,' he said; 'too much.'

She laughed almost gaily.

'You'd have to have it your own way, wouldn't you?' she teased. 'You could never take it on trust.'

He changed, laughed softly, and turned and took her in his arms, in the middle of the road.

'Yes,' he said softly.

And he kissed her face and brow, slowly, gently, with a sort of delicate happiness which surprised her extremely, and to which she could not respond. They were soft, blind kisses, perfect in their stillness. Yet she held back from them. It was like strange moths, very soft and silent, settling on her from the darkness of her soul. She was uneasy. She drew away.

'Isn't somebody coming?' she said.

So they looked down the dark road, then set off again walking towards Beldover. Then suddenly, to show him she was no shallow prude, she stopped and held him tight, hard against her, and covered his face with hard, fierce kisses of passion. In spite of his otherness, the old blood beat up in him.

'Not this, not this,' he whimpered to himself, as the first perfect mood of softness and sleep-loveliness ebbed back away from the rushing of passion that came up to his limbs and over his face as she drew him. And soon he was a perfect hard flame of passionate desire for her. Yet in the small core of the flame was an unyielding anguish of another thing. But this also was lost; he only wanted her, with an extreme desire that seemed inevitable as death, beyond question.

Then, satisfied and shattered, fulfilled and destroyed, he went home away from her, drifting vaguely through the darkness, lapsed into the old fire of burning passion. Far away, far away, there seemed to be a small lament in the darkness. But what did it matter? What did it matter, what did anything matter save this ultimate and triumphant experience of physical passion, that had blazed up anew like a new spell of life. 'I was becoming quite dead-alive, nothing but a word-bag,' he said in triumph, scorning his other self. Yet somewhere far off and small, the other hovered.

The men were still dragging the lake when he got back. He stood on the bank and heard Gerald's voice. The water was still booming in the night, the moon was fair, the hills beyond were elusive. The lake was sinking. There came the raw smell of the banks, in the night air.

Up at Shortlands there were lights in the windows, as if nobody had gone to bed. On the landing-stage was the old doctor, the father of the young man who was lost. He stood quite silent, waiting. Birkin also stood and watched, Gerald came up in a boat.

'You still here, Rupert?' he said. 'We can't get them. The bottom slopes, you know, very steep. The water lies between two very sharp slopes, with little branch valleys, and God knows where the drift will take you. It isn't as if it was a level bottom. You never know where you are, with the dragging.'

'Is there any need for you to be working?' said Birkin. 'Wouldn't it be much better if you went to bed?'

'To bed! Good God, do you think I should sleep? We'll find 'em, before I go away from here.'

'But the men would find them just the same without you—why should you insist?'

Gerald looked up at him. Then he put his hand affectionately on Birkin's shoulder, saying:

'Don't you bother about me, Rupert. If there's anybody's health to think about, it's yours, not mine. How do you feel yourself?'

'Very well. But you, you spoil your own chance of life—you waste your best self.'

Gerald was silent for a moment. Then he said:

'Waste it? What else is there to do with it?'

'But leave this, won't you? You force yourself into horrors, and put a mill-stone of beastly memories round your neck. Come away now.'

'A mill-stone of beastly memories!' Gerald repeated. Then he put his hand again affectionately on Birkin's shoulder. 'God, you've got such a telling way of putting things, Rupert, you have.'

Birkin's heart sank. He was irritated and weary of having a telling way of putting things.

'Won't you leave it? Come over to my place'—he urged as one urges a drunken man.

'No,' said Gerald coaxingly, his arm across the other man's shoulder. 'Thanks very much, Rupert—I shall be glad to come tomorrow, if that'll do. You understand, don't you? I want to see this job through. But I'll come tomorrow, right enough. Oh, I'd rather come and have a chat with you

than—than do anything else, I verily believe. Yes, I would.
You mean a lot to me, Rupert, more than you know.'

'What do I mean, more than I know?' asked Birkin irritably. He was acutely aware of Gerald's hand on his shoulder.
And he did not want this altercation. He wanted the other
man to come out of the ugly misery.

'I'll tell you another time,' said Gerald coaxingly.

'Come along with me now—I want you to come,' said
Birkin.

There was a pause, intense and real. Birkin wondered why
his own heart beat so heavily. Then Gerald's fingers gripped
hard and communicative into Birkin's shoulder, as he said:

'No, I'll see this job through, Rupert. Thank you—I know
what you mean. We're all right, you know, you and me.'

'I may be all right, but I'm sure you're not, mucking
about here,' said Birkin. And he went away.

The bodies of the dead were not recovered till towards
dawn. Diana had her arms tight round the neck of the young
man, choking him.

'She killed him,' said Gerald.

The moon sloped down the sky and sank at last. The lake
was sunk to quarter size, it had horrible raw banks of clay,
that smelled of raw rottenish water. Dawn roused faintly behind the eastern hill. The water still boomed through the
sluice.

As the birds were whistling for the first morning, and
the hills at the back of the desolate lake stood radiant with
the new mists, there was a straggling procession up to
Shortlands, men bearing the bodies on a stretcher, Gerald
going beside them, the two grey-bearded fathers following
in silence. Indoors the family was all sitting up, waiting.
Somebody must go to tell the mother, in her room. The doctor in secret struggled to bring back his son, till he himself
was exhausted.

Over all the outlying district was a hush of dreadful excitement on that Sunday morning. The colliery people felt as
if this catastrophe had happened directly to themselves, indeed they were more shocked and frightened than if their
own men had been killed. Such a tragedy in Shortlands, the
high home of the district! One of the young mistresses, per-

sisting in dancing on the cabin roof of the launch, wilful young madam, drowned in the midst of the festival, with the young doctor! Everywhere on the Sunday morning, the colliers wandered about, discussing the calamity. At all the Sunday dinners of the people, there seemed a strange presence. It was as if the angel of death were very near, there was a sense of the supernatural in the air. The men had excited, startled faces, the women looked solemn, some of them had been crying. The children enjoyed the excitement at first. There was an intensity in the air, almost magical. Did all enjoy it? Did all enjoy the thrill?

Gudrun had wild ideas of rushing to comfort Gerald. She was thinking all the time of the perfect comforting, reassuring thing to say to him. She was shocked and frightened, but she put that away, thinking of how she should deport herself with Gerald: act her part. That was the real thrill: how she should act her part.

Ursula was deeply and passionately in love with Birkin, and she was capable of nothing. She was perfectly callous about all the talk of the accident, but her estranged air looked like trouble. She merely sat by herself, whenever she could, and longed to see him again. She wanted him to come to the house—she would not have it otherwise, he must come at once. She was waiting for him. She stayed indoors all day, waiting for him to knock at the door. Every minute, she glanced automatically at the window. He would be there.

15

Sunday Evening

A s the day wore on, the life-blood seemed to ebb away from Ursula, and within the emptiness a heavy despair gathered. Her passion seemed to bleed to death, and there was nothing. She sat suspended in a state of complete nullity, harder to bear than death.

'Unless something happens,' she said to herself, in the perfect lucidity of final suffering, 'I shall die. I am at the end of my line of life.'

She sat crushed and obliterated in a darkness that was the border of death. She realized how all her life she had been drawing nearer and nearer to this brink, where there was no beyond, from which one had to leap like Sappho into the unknown. The knowledge of the imminence of death was like a drug. Darkly, without thinking at all, she knew that she was near to death. She had travelled all her life along the line of fulfillment, and it was nearly concluded. She knew all she had to know, she had experienced all she had to experience, she was fulfilled in a kind of bitter ripeness, there remained only to fall from the tree into death. And one must fulfil one's development to the end, must carry the adventure to its conclusion. And the next step was over the border into death. So it was then! There was a certain peace in the knowledge.

After all, when one was fulfilled, one was happiest in falling into death, as a bitter fruit plunges in its ripeness downwards. Death is a great consummation, a consummating experience. It is a development from life. That we know, while we are yet living. What then need we think for further? One can never see beyond the consummation. It is enough that death is a great and conclusive experience. Why should we ask what comes after the experience, when the experience is still unknown to us? Let us die, since the great experience is the one that follows now upon all the rest, death, which is the next great crisis in front of which we have arrived. If we wait, if we baulk the issue, we do but hang about the gates in undignified uneasiness. There it is, in front of us, as in front of Sappho, the illimitable space. Thereinto goes the journey. Have we not the courage to go on with our journey, must we cry 'I daren't'? On ahead we will go, into death, and whatever death may mean. If a man can see the next step to be taken, why should he fear the next but one? Why ask about the next but one? Of the next step we are certain. It is the step into death.

'I shall die—I shall quickly die,' said Ursula to herself, clear as if in a trance, clear, calm, and certain beyond human certainty. But somewhere behind, in the twilight, there was a bitter weeping and a hopelessness. That must not be attended to. One must go where the unfaltering spirit goes, there must be no baulking the issue, because of fear. No baulking the issue, no listening to the lesser voices. If the deepest desire be now, to go on into the unknown of death, shall one forfeit the deepest truth for one more shallow?

'Then let it end,' she said to herself. It was a decision. It was not a question of taking one's life—she would *never* kill herself, that was repulsive and violent. It was a question of *knowing* the next step. And the next step led into the space of death. Did it?—or was there—?

Her thoughts drifted into unconsciousness, she sat as if asleep beside the fire. And then the thought came back. The space of death! Could she give herself to it? Ah, yes—it was a sleep. She had had enough. So long she had held out and resisted. Now was the time to relinquish, not to resist any more.

In a kind of spiritual trance, she yielded, she gave way, and all was dark. She could feel, within the darkness, the terrible assertion of her body, the unutterable anguish of dissolution, the only anguish that is too much, the far-off awful nausea of dissolution set in within the body.

'Does the body correspond so immediately with the spirit?' she asked herself. And she knew, with the clarity of ultimate knowledge, that the body is only one of the manifestations of the spirit, the transmutation of the integral spirit is the transmutation of the physical body as well. Unless I set my will, unless I absolve myself from the rhythm of life, fix myself and remain static, cut off from living, absolved within my own will. But better die than live mechanically a life that is a repetition of repetitions. To die is to move on with the invisible. To die is also a joy, a joy of submitting to that which is greater than the known; namely, the pure unknown. That is a joy. But to live mechanized and cut off within the motion of the will, to live as an entity absolved from the unknown, that is shameful and ignominious. There is no ignominy in death. There is complete ignominy in an unreplenished, mechanized life. Life indeed may be ignominious, shameful to the soul. But death is never a shame. Death itself, like the illimitable space, is beyond our sullying.

Tomorrow was Monday. Monday, the beginning of another school-week! Another shameful, barren school-week, mere routine and mechanical activity. Was not the adventure of death infinitely preferable? Was not death infinitely more lovely and noble than such a life? A life of barren routine, without inner meaning, without any real significance. How sordid life was, how it was a terrible shame to the soul, to live now! How much cleaner and more dignified to be dead! One could not bear any more of this shame of sordid routine and mechanical nullity. One might come to fruit in death. She had had enough. For where was life to be found? No flowers grow upon busy machinery, there is no sky to a routine, there is no space to a rotary motion. And all life was a rotary motion, mechanized, cut off from reality. There was nothing to look for from life—it was the same in all countries and all peoples. The only window was death. One could look out on to the great dark sky of death with emotion, as one had looked out of the class-room window as a child, and seen perfect freedom in the outside. Now one was not a child, and one knew that the soul was a prisoner within this sordid vast edifice of life, and there was no escape, save in death.

But what a joy! What a gladness to think that whatever

humanity did, it could not seize hold of the kingdom of death, to nullify that. The sea they turned into a murderous alley and a soiled road of commerce, disputed like the dirty land of a city every inch of it. The air they claimed too, shared it up, parcelled it out to certain owners, they trespassed in the air to fight for it. Everything was gone, walled in, with spikes on top of the walls, and one must ignominiously creep between the spiky walls through a labyrinth of life.

But the great dark, illimitable kingdom of death, there humanity was put to scorn. So much they could do upon earth, the multifarious little gods that they were. But the kingdom of death put them all to scorn, they dwindled into their true vulgar silliness in face of it.

How beautiful, how grand and perfect death was, how good to look forward to. There one would wash off all the lies and ignominy and dirt that had been put upon one here, a perfect bath of cleanness and glad refreshment, and go unknown, unquestioned, unabased. After all, one was rich, if only in the promise of perfect death. It was a gladness above all, that this remained to look forward to, the pure inhuman otherness of death.

Whatever life might be, it could not take away death, the inhuman transcendent death. Oh, let us ask no question of it, what it is or is not. To know is human, and in death we do not know, we are not human. And the joy of this compensates for all the bitterness of knowledge and the sordidness of our humanity. In death we shall not be human, and we shall not know. The promise of this is our heritage, we look forward like heirs to their majority.

Ursula sat quite still and quite forgotten, alone by the fire in the drawing-room. The children were playing in the kitchen, all the others were gone to church. And she was gone into the ultimate darkness of her own soul.

She was startled by hearing the bell ring, away in the kitchen, the children came scudding along the passage in delicious alarm.

'Ursula, there's somebody.'

'I know. Don't be silly,' she replied. She too was startled, almost frightened. She dared hardly go to the door.

Birkin stood on the threshold, his rain-coat turned up to his ears. He had come now, now she was gone far away. She was aware of the rainy night behind him.

'Oh, is it you?' she said.

'I am glad you are at home,' he said in a low voice, entering the house.

'They are all gone to church.'

He took off his coat and hung it up. The children were peeping at him round the corner.

'Go and get undressed now, Billy and Dora,' said Ursula. 'Mother will be back soon, and she'll be disappointed if you're not in bed.'

The children, in a sudden angelic mood, retired without a word. Birkin and Ursula went into the drawing-room. The fire burned low. He looked at her and wondered at the luminous delicacy of her beauty, and the wide shining of her eyes. He watched from a distance, with wonder in his heart, she seemed transfigured with light.

'What have you been doing all day?' he asked her.

'Only sitting about,' she said.

He looked at her. There was a change in her. But she was separate from him. She remained apart, in a kind of brightness. They both sat silent in the soft light of the lamp. He felt he ought to go away again, he ought not to have come. Still he did not gather enough resolution to move. But he was *de trop*, her mood was absent and separate.

Then there came the voices of the two children calling shyly outside the door, softly, with self-excited timidity:

'Ursula! Ursula!'

She rose and opened the door. On the threshold stood the two children in their long nightgowns, with wide-eyed, angelic faces. They were being very good for the moment, playing the role perfectly of two obedient children.

'Shall you take us to bed!' said Billy, in a loud whisper.

'Why, you *are* angels tonight,' she said softly. 'Won't you come and say good night to Mr Birkin?'

The children merged shyly into the room, on bare feet. Billy's face was wide and grinning, but there was a great solemnity of being good in his round blue eyes. Dora, peeping from the floss of her fair hair, hung back like some tiny Dryad, that has no soul.

'Will you say good night to me?' asked Birkin, in a voice that was strangely soft and smooth. Dora drifted away at once, like a leaf lifted on a breath of wind. But Billy went softly forward, slow and willing, lifting his pinched-up mouth implicitly to be kissed. Ursula watched the full, gathered lips of the man gently touch those of the boy, so gently. Then Birkin lifted his fingers and touched the boy's round, confiding cheek, with a faint touch of love. Neither spoke. Billy seemed angelic like a cherub boy, or like an acolyte, Birkin was a tall, grave angel looking down to him.

'Are you going to be kissed?' Ursula broke in, speaking to the little girl. But Dora edged away like a tiny Dryad that will not be touched.

'Won't you say good night to Mr Birkin? Go, he's waiting for you,' said Ursula. But the girl-child only made a little motion away from him.

'Silly Dora, silly Dora!' said Ursula.

Birkin felt some mistrust and antagonism in the small child. He could not understand it.

'Come then,' said Ursula. 'Let us go before mother comes.'

'Who'll hear us say our prayers?' asked Billy anxiously.

'Whom you like.'

'Won't you?'

'Yes, I will.'

'Ursula?'

'Well, Billy?'

'Is it *whom* you like?'

'That's it.'

'Well, what is *whom*?'

'It's the accusative of who.'

There was a moment's contemplative silence, then the confiding:

'Is it?'

Birkin smiled to himself as he sat by the fire. When Ursula came down he sat motionless, with his arms on his knees. She saw him, how he was motionless and ageless, like some crouching idol, some image of a deathly religion. He looked round at her, and his face, very pale and unreal, seemed to gleam with a whiteness almost phosphorescent.

'Don't you feel well?' she asked, in indefinable repulsion.

'I hadn't thought about it.'

'But don't you know without thinking about it?'

He looked at her, his eyes dark and swift, and he saw her revulsion. He did not answer her question.

'Don't you know whether you are unwell or not, without thinking about it?' she persisted.

'Not always,' he said coldly.

'But don't you think that's very wicked?'

'Wicked?'

'Yes. I think it's *criminal* to have so little connexion with your own body that you don't even know when you are ill.'

He looked at her darkly.

'Yes,' he said.

'Why don't you stay in bed when you are seedy? You look perfectly ghastly.'

'Offensively so?' he asked ironically.

'Yes, quite offensive. Quite repelling.'

'Ah!! Well, that's unfortunate.'

'And it's raining, and it's a horrible night. Really, you shouldn't be forgiven for treating your body like it—you *ought* to suffer, a man who takes as little notice of his body as that.'

'—takes as little notice of his body as that,' he echoed mechanically.

This cut her short, and there was silence.

The others came in from church, and the two had the girls to face, then the mother and Gudrun, and then the father and the boy.

'Good-evening,' said Brangwen, faintly surprised. 'Came to see me, did you?'

'No,' said Birkin, 'not about anything in particular, that is. The day was dismal, and I thought you wouldn't mind if I called in.'

'It *has* been a depressing day,' said Mrs Brangwen sympathetically. At that moment the voices of the children were heard calling from upstairs: 'Mother! Mother!' She lifted her face and answered mildly into the distance: 'I shall come up to you in a minute, Doysie,' Then to Birkin: 'There is nothing fresh at Shortlands, I suppose? Ah,' she sighed, 'no, poor things, I should think not.'

'You've been over there today, I suppose?' asked the father.

'Gerald came round to tea with me, and I walked back with him. The house is over-excited and unwholesome, I thought.'

'I should think they were people who hadn't much restraint,' said Gudrun.

'Or too much,' Birkin answered.

'Oh yes, I'm sure,' said Gudrun, almost vindictively, 'one or the other.'

'They all feel they ought to behave in some unnatural fashion,' said Birkin. 'When people are in grief, they would do better to cover their faces and keep in retirement, as in the old days.'

'Certainly!' cried Gudrun, flushed and inflammable. 'What can be worse than this public grief—what is more horrible, more false! If *grief* is not private, and hidden, what is?'

'Exactly,' he said. 'I felt ashamed when I was there and they were all going about in a lugubrious false way, feeling they must not be natural or ordinary.'

'Well—' said Mrs Brangwen, offended at this criticism, 'it isn't so easy to bear a trouble like that.'

And she went upstairs to the children.

He remained only a few minutes longer, then took his leave. When he was gone Ursula felt such a poignant hatred of him, that all her brain seemed turned into a sharp crystal of fine hatred. Her whole nature seemed sharpened and intensified into a pure dart of hate. She could not imagine what it was. It merely took hold of her, the most poignant and ultimate hatred, pure and clear and beyond thought. She could not think of it at all, she was translated beyond herself. It was like a possession. She felt she was possessed. And for several days she went about possessed by this exquisite force of hatred against him. It surpassed anything she had ever known before, it seemed to throw her out of the world into some terrible region where nothing of her old life held good. She was quite lost and dazed, really dead to her own life.

It was so completely incomprehensible and irrational. She did not know *why* she hated him, her hate was quite abstract. She had only realized with a shock that stunned her, that she was overcome by this pure transportation. He was the enemy, fine as a diamond, and as hard and jewel-like, the quintessence of all that was inimical.

She thought of his face, white and purely wrought, and of his eyes that had such a dark, constant will of assertion, and she touched her own forehead, to feel if she were mad, she was so transfigured in white flame of essential hate.

It was not temporal, her hatred, she did not hate him for this or for that; she did not want to do anything to him, to have any connexion with him. Her relation was ultimate and utterly beyond words, the hate was so pure and gem-like. It was as if he were a beam of essential enmity, a beam of light that did not only destroy her, but denied her altogether, revoked her whole world. She saw him as a clear stroke of uttermost contradiction, a strange gem-like being whose existence defined her own non-existence. When she heard he was ill again, her hatred only intensified itself a few degrees, if that were possible. It stunned her and annihilated her, but she could not escape it. She could not escape this transfiguration of hatred that had come upon her.

16

Man to Man

He lay sick and unmoved, in pure opposition to everything. He knew how near to breaking was the vessel that held his life. He knew also how strong and durable it was. And he did not care. Better a thousand times take one's chance with death, than accept a life one did not want. But best of all to persist and persist, and persist for ever, till one were satisfied in life.

He knew that Ursula was referred back to him. He knew his life rested with her. But he would rather not live than accept the love she proffered. The old way of love seemed a dreadful bondage, a sort of conscription. What it was in him he did not know, but the thought of love, marriage, and children, and a life lived together, in the horrible privacy of domestic and connubial satisfaction, was repulsive. He wanted something clearer, more open, cooler, as it were. The hot narrow intimacy between man and wife was abhorrent. The way they shut their doors, these married people, and shut themselves into their own exclusive alliance with each other, even in love, disgusted him. It was a whole community of mistrustful couples insulated in private houses or private rooms, always in couples, and no further life, no further immediate, no disinterested relationship admitted: a kaleidoscope of couples, disjoined, separatist, meaningless entities of married couples. True, he hated promiscuity even worse than marriage, and a liaison was only another kind of coupling, reactionary from the legal marriage. Reaction was a greater bore than action.

On the whole, he hated sex, it was such a limitation. It was sex that turned a man into a broken half of a couple, the woman into the other broken half. And he wanted to be single in himself, the woman single in herself. He wanted sex to revert to the level of the other appetites, to be regarded as a functional process, not as a fulfilment. He believed in sex marriage. But beyond this, he wanted a further conjunction, where man had being and woman had being, two pure beings, each constituting the freedom of the other, balancing each other like two poles of one force, like two angels, or two demons.

He wanted so much to be free, not under the compulsion of any need for unification, or tortured by unsatisfied desire. Desire and aspiration should find their object without all this torture, as now, in a world of plenty of water, simple thirst is inconsiderable, satisfied almost unconsciously. And he wanted to be with Ursula as free as with himself, single and clear and cool, yet balanced, polarized with her. The merging, the clutching, the mingling of love was become madly abhorrent to him.

But it seemed to him, woman was always so horrible and clutching, she had such a lust for possession, a greed of self-importance in love. She wanted to have, to own, to control, to be dominant. Everything must be referred back to her, to Woman, the Great Mother of everything, out of whom proceeded everything and to whom everything must finally be rendered up.

It filled him with almost insane fury, this calm assumption of the Magna Mater, that all was hers, because she had borne it. Man was hers because she had borne him. A Mater Dolorosa, she had borne him, a Magna Mater, she now claimed him again, soul and body, sex, meaning, and all. He had a horror of the Magna Mater, she was detestable.

She was on a very high horse again was woman, the Great Mother. Did he not know it in Hermione. Hermione, the humble, the subservient, what was she all the while but the Mater Dolorosa, in her subservience, claiming with horrible, insidious arrogance and female tyranny, her own again, claiming back the man she had borne in suffering. By her very suffering and humility she bound her son with chains, she held him her everlasting prisoner.

And Ursula, Ursula was the same—or the inverse. She too was the awful, arrogant queen of life, as if she were a queen

bee on whom all the rest depended. He saw the yellow flare
in her eyes, he knew the unthinkable overweening assumption of primacy in her. She was unconscious of it herself.
She was only too ready to knock her head on the ground before a man. But this was only when she was so certain of her
man, that she could worship him as a woman worships her
own infant, with a worship of perfect possession.

It was intolerable, this possession at the hands of woman.
Always a man must be considered as the broken-off fragment of a woman, and the sex was the still aching scar of the
laceration. Man must be added on to a woman, before he had
any real place or wholeness.

And why? Why should we consider ourselves, men and
women, as broken fragments of one whole? It is not true. We
are not broken fragments of one whole. Rather we are the
singling away into purity and clear being, of things that were
mixed. Rather the sex is that which remains in us of the
mixed, the unresolved. And passion is the further separating
of this mixture, that which is manly being taken into the being of the man, that which is womanly passing to the
woman, till the two are clear and whole as angels, the ad-
mixture of sex in the highest sense surpassed, leaving two
single beings constellated together like two stars.

In the old age, before sex was, we were mixed, each one
a mixture. The process of singling into individuality resulted
into the great polarization of sex. The womanly drew to one
side, the manly to the other. But the separation was imper-
fect even then. And so our world-cycle passes. There is now
to come the new day, when we are beings each of us, fulfilled in difference. The man is pure man, the woman pure
woman, they are perfectly polarized. But there is no longer
any of the horrible merging, mingling self-abnegation of
love. There is only the pure duality of polarization, each one
free from any contamination of the other. In each, the individual is primal, sex is subordinate, but perfectly polarized.
Each has a single, separate being, with its own laws. The
man has his pure freedom, the woman hers. Each acknowl-
edges the perfection of the polarized sex-circuit. Each admits the different nature in the other.

So Birkin meditated whilst he was ill. He liked sometimes

to be ill enough to take to his bed. For then he got better very quickly, and things came to him clear and sure.

Whilst he was laid up, Gerald came to see him. The two men had a deep, uneasy feeling for each other. Gerald's eyes were quick and restless, his whole manner tense and impatient, he seemed strung up to some activity. According to conventionality, he wore black clothes, he looked formal, handsome, and *comme il faut*. His hair was fair almost to whiteness, sharp like splinters of light, his face was keen and ruddy, his body seemed full of northern energy.

Gerald really loved Birkin, though he never quite believed in him. Birkin was too unreal;—clever, whimsical, wonderful, but not practical enough. Gerald felt that his own understanding was much sounder and safer. Birkin was delightful, a wonderful spirit, but after all, not to be taken seriously, not quite to be counted as a man among men.

'Why are you laid up again?' he asked kindly, taking the sick man's hand. It was always Gerald who was protective, offering the warm shelter of his physical strength.

'For my sins, I suppose,' Birkin said, smiling a little ironically.

'For your sins? Yes, probably that is so. You should sin less, and keep better in health?'

'You'd better teach me.'

He looked at Gerald with ironic eyes.

'How are things with you?' asked Birkin.

'With me?' Gerald looked at Birkin, saw he was serious, and a warm light came into his eyes.

'I don't know that they're any different. I don't see how they could be. There's nothing to change.'

'I suppose you are conducting the business as successfully as ever, and ignoring the demand of the soul.'

'That's it,' said Gerald. 'At least as far as the business is concerned. I couldn't say about the soul, I'm sure.'

'No.'

'Surely you don't expect me to?' laughed Gerald.

'No. How are the rest of your affairs progressing, apart from the business?'

'The rest of my affairs? What are those? I couldn't say; I don't know what you refer to.'

'Yes, you do,' said Birkin. 'Are you gloomy or cheerful? And what about Gudrun Brangwen?'

'What about her?' A confused look came over Gerald. 'Well,' he added, 'I don't know. I can only tell you she gave me a hit over the face last time I saw her.'

'A hit over the face! What for?'

'That I couldn't tell you, either.'

'Really! But when?'

'The night of the party—when Diana was drowned. She was driving the cattle up the hill, and I went after her—you remember.'

'Yes, I remember. But what made her do that? You didn't definitely ask her for it, I suppose?'

'I? No, not that I know of. I merely said to her that it was dangerous to drive those Highland bullocks—as it *is*. She turned in such a way, and said—"I suppose you think I'm afraid of you and your cattle, don't you?" So I asked her "why?" and for answer she flung me a back-hander across the face.'

Birkin laughed quickly, as if it pleased him. Gerald looked at him, wondering, and began to laugh as well, saying:

'I didn't laugh at the time, I assure you. I was never so taken aback in my life.'

'And weren't you furious?'

'Furious? I should think I was. I'd have murdered her for two pins.'

'H'm!' ejaculated Birkin. 'Poor Gudrun, wouldn't she suffer afterwards for having given herself away!' He was hugely delighted.

'Would she suffer?' asked Gerald, also amused now.

Both men smiled in malice and amusement.

'Badly, I should think; seeing how self-conscious she is.'

'She is self-conscious, is she? Then what made her do it? For I certainly think it was quite uncalled-for, and quite unjustified.'

'I suppose it was a sudden impulse.'

'Yes, but how do you account for her having such an impulse? I'd done her no harm.'

Birkin shook his head.

'The Amazon suddenly came up in her, I suppose,' he said.

'Well,' replied Gerald, 'I'd rather it had been the Orinoco.'

They both laughed at the poor joke. Gerald was thinking how Gudrun had said she would strike the last blow too. But some reserve made him keep this back from Birkin.

'And you resent it?' Birkin asked.

'I don't resent it. I don't care a tinker's curse about it.' He was silent a moment, then he added, laughing, 'No, I'll see it through, that's all. She seemed sorry afterwards.'

'Did she? You've not met since that night?'

Gerald's face clouded.

'No,' he said. 'We've been—you can imagine how it's been, since the accident.'

'Yes. Is it calming down?'

'I don't know. It's a shock, of course. But I don't believe mother minds. I really don't believe she takes any notice. And what's so funny, she used to be all for the children— nothing mattered, nothing whatever mattered but the children. And now, she doesn't take any more notice than if it was one of the servants.'

'No? Did it upset *you* very much?'

'It's a shock. But I don't feel it very much, really. I don't feel any different. We've all got to die, and it doesn't seem to make any great difference, anyhow, whether you die or not. I can't feel any *grief,* you know. It leaves me cold. I can't quite account for it.'

'You don't care if you die or not?' asked Birkin.

Gerald looked at him with eyes blue as the blue-fibred steel of a weapon. He felt awkward, but different. As a matter of fact, he did care terribly, with a great fear.

'Oh,' he said, 'I don't want to die, why should I? But I never trouble. The question doesn't seem to be on the carpet for me at all. It doesn't interest me, you know.'

'*Timor mortis conturbat me,*' quoted Birkin, adding—'No, death doesn't really seem the point any more. It curiously doesn't concern me. It's like an ordinary tomorrow.'

Gerald looked closely at his friend. The eyes of the two men met, and an unspoken understanding was exchanged.

Gerald narrowed his eyes, his face was cool and unscrupulous as he looked at Birkin, impersonally, with a vision that ended in a point in space, strangely keen-eyed and yet blind.

'If death isn't the point,' he said, in a strangely abstract, cold, fine voice—'what is?' He sounded as if he had been found out.

'What is?' re-echoed Birkin. And there was a mocking silence.

'There's a long way to go, after the point of intrinsic death, before we disappear,' said Birkin.

'There is,' said Gerald. 'But what sort of way?' He seemed to press the other man for knowledge which he himself knew far better than Birkin did.

'Right down the slopes of degeneration—mystic, universal degeneration. There are many stages of pure degradation to go through: age-long. We live on long after our death, and progressively, in progressive devolution.'

Gerald listened with a faint, fine smile on his face, all the time, as if, somewhere, he knew so much better than Birkin, all about this: as if his own knowledge were direct and personal, whereas Birkin's was a matter of observation and inference, not quite hitting the nail on the head:—though aiming near enough at it. But he was not going to give himself away. If Birkin could get at the secrets, let him. Gerald would never help him. Gerald would be a dark horse to the end.

'Of course,' he said, with a startling change of conversation, 'it is father who really feels it. It will finish him. For him the world collapses. All his care now is for Winnie—he must save Winnie. He says she ought to be sent away to school, but she won't hear of it, and he'll never do it. Of course she *is* in rather a queer way. We're all of us curiously bad at living. We can do things—but we can't get on with life at all. It's curious—a family failing.'

'She oughtn't to be sent away to school,' said Birkin, who was considering a new proposition.

'She oughtn't? Why?'

'She's a queer child—a special child, more special even than you. And in my opinion special children should never be sent away to school. Only moderately ordinary children should be sent to school—so it seems to me.'

'I'm inclined to think just the opposite. I think it would probably make her more normal if she went away and mixed with other children.'

'She wouldn't mix, you see. *You* never really mixed, did you? And she wouldn't be willing even to pretend to. She's proud, and solitary, and naturally apart. If she has a single nature, why do you want to make her gregarious?'

'No, I don't want to make her anything. But I think school would be good for her.'

'Was it good for you?'

Gerald's eyes narrowed uglily. School had been torture to him. Yet he had not questioned whether one should go through this torture. He seemed to believe in education through subjection and torment.

'I hated it at the time, but I can see it was necessary,' he said. 'It brought me into line a bit—and you can't live unless you do come into line somewhere.'

'Well,' said Birkin, 'I begin to think that you can't live unless you keep entirely out of the line. It's no good trying to toe the line, when your one impulse is to smash up the line. Winnie is a special nature, and for special natures you must give a special world.'

'Yes, but where's your special world?' said Gerald.

'Make it. Instead of chopping yourself down to fit the world, chop the world down to fit yourself. As a matter of fact, two exceptional people make another world. You and I, we make another, separate world. You don't *want* a world same as your brothers-in-law. It's just the special quality you value. Do you *want* to be normal or ordinary? It's a lie. You want to be free and extraordinary, in an extraordinary world of liberty.'

Gerald looked at Birkin with subtle eyes of knowledge. But he would never openly admit what he felt. He knew more than Birkin, in one direction—much more. And this gave him his gentle love for the other man, as if Birkin were in some way young, innocent, child-like; so amazingly clever, but incurably innocent.

'Yet you are so banal as to consider me chiefly a freak,' said Birkin pointedly.

'A freak!' exclaimed Gerald, startled. And his face opened suddenly, as if lighted with simplicity, as when a flower opens out of the cunning bud. 'No—I never consider you a freak.' And he watched the other man with strange eyes, that Birkin could not understand. 'I feel,' Gerald continued, 'that there is always an element of uncertainty about you—perhaps you are uncertain about yourself. But I'm never sure of you. You can go away and change as easily as if you had no soul.'

He looked at Birkin with penetrating eyes. Birkin was amazed. He thought he had all the soul in the world. He stared in amazement. And Gerald, watching, saw the amazing attractive goodliness of his eyes, a young, spontaneous goodness that attracted the other man infinitely, yet filled him with bitter chagrin, because he mistrusted it so much. He knew Birkin could do without him—could forget, and not suffer. This was always present in Gerald's consciousness, filling him with bitter unbelief: this consciousness of the young, animal-like spontaneity of detachment. It seemed almost like hypocrisy and lying, sometimes, oh, often, on Birkin's part, to talk so deeply and importantly.

Quite other things were going through Birkin's mind. Suddenly he saw himself confronted with another problem—the problem of love and eternal conjunction between two men. Of course this was necessary—it had been a necessity inside himself all his life—to love a man purely and fully. Of course he had been loving Gerald all along, and all along denying it.

He lay in the bed and wondered, whilst his friend sat beside him, lost in brooding. Each man was gone in his own thoughts.

'You know how the old German knights used to swear a *Blutbrüderschaft*,' he said to Gerald, with quite a new happy activity in his eyes.

'Make a little wound in their arms, and rub each other's blood into the cut?' said Gerald.

'Yes—and swear to be true to each other, of one blood, all their lives. That is what we ought to do. No wounds, that is obsolete. But we ought to swear to love each other, you and I, implicitly, and perfectly, finally, without any possibility of going back on it.'

He looked at Gerald with clear, happy eyes of discovery. Gerald looked down at him, attracted, so deeply bondaged in fascinated attraction, that he was mistrustful, resenting the bondage, hating the attraction.

'We will swear to each other, one day, shall we?' pleaded Birkin. 'We will swear to stand by each other—be true to each other—ultimately—infallibly—given to each other, organically—without possibility of taking back.'

Birkin sought hard to express himself. But Gerald hardly listened. His face shone with a certain luminous pleasure. He was pleased. But he kept his reserve. He held himself back.

'Shall we swear to each other, one day?' said Birkin, putting out his hand towards Gerald.

Gerald just touched the extended fine, living hand, as if withheld and afraid.

'We'll leave it till I understand it better,' he said, in a voice of excuse.

Birkin watched him. A little sharp disappointment, perhaps a touch of contempt came into his heart.

'Yes,' he said. 'You must tell me what you think, later. You know what I mean? Not sloppy emotionalism. An impersonal union that leaves one free.'

They lapsed both into silence. Birkin was looking at Gerald all the time. He seemed now to see, not the physical, animal man, which he usually saw in Gerald, and which usually he liked so much, but the man himself, complete, and as if fated, doomed, limited. This strange sense of fatality in Gerald, as if he were limited to one form of existence, one knowledge, one activity, a sort of fatal halfness, which to himself seemed wholeness, always overcame Birkin after their moments of passionate approach, and filled him with a sort of contempt, or boredom. It was the insistence on the limitation which so bored Birkin in Gerald. Gerald could never fly away from himself, in real indifferent gaiety. He had a clog, a sort of monomania.

There was silence for a time. Then Birkin said, in a lighter tone, letting the stress of the contact pass:

'Can't you get a good governess for Winifred?—somebody exceptional?'

'Hermione Roddice suggested we should ask Gudrun to teach her to draw and to model in clay. You know Winnie is astonishingly clever with that plasticine stuff. Hermione declares she is an artist.' Gerald spoke in the usual animated, chatty manner, as if nothing unusual had passed. But Birkin's manner was full of reminder.

'Really! I didn't know that Oh well then, if Gudrun *would* teach her, it would be perfect—couldn't be anything better—if Winifred is an artist. Because Gudrun somewhere is one. And every true artist is the salvation of every other.'

'I thought they got on so badly, as a rule.'

'Perhaps. But only artists produce for each other the world that is fit to live in. If you can arrange *that* for Winifred, it is perfect.'

'But you think she wouldn't come?'

'I don't know. Gudrun is rather self-opinionated. She won't go cheap anywhere. Or if she does, she'll pretty soon take herself back. So whether she would condescend to do private teaching, particularly here, in Beldover, I don't know. But it would be just the thing. Winifred has got a special nature. And if you can put into her way the means of being self-sufficient, that is the best thing possible. She'll never get on with the ordinary life. You find it difficult enough yourself, and she is several skins thinner than you are. It is awful to think what her life will be like unless she does find a means of expression, some way of fulfillment. You can see what mere leaving it to fate brings. You can see how much marriage is to be trusted to—look at your own mother.'

'Do you think mother is abnormal?'

'No! I think she only wanted something more, or other than the common run of life. And not getting it, she has gone wrong perhaps.'

'After producing a brood of wrong children,' said Gerald gloomily.

'No more wrong than any of the rest of us,' Birkin replied. 'The most normal people have the worst subterranean selves, take them one by one.'

'Sometimes I think it is a curse to be alive,' said Gerald, with sudden impotent anger.

'Well,' said Birkin, 'why not! Let it be a curse sometimes to be alive—at other times it is anything but a curse. You've got plenty of zest in it really.'

'Less than you'd think,' said Gerald, revealing a strange poverty in his look at the other man.

There was silence, each thinking his own thoughts.

'I don't see what she has to distinguish between teaching at the Grammar School and coming to teach Win,' said Gerald.

'The difference between a public servant and a private one. The only nobleman today, king and only aristocrat, is the public, the public. You are quite willing to serve the public—but to be a private tutor—'

'I don't want to serve either—'

'No! And Gudrun will probably feel the same.'

Gerald thought for a few minutes. Then he said:

'At all events, father won't make her feel like a private servant. He will be fussy and grateful enough.'

'So he ought. And so ought all of you. Do you think you can hire a woman like Gudrun Brangwen with money? She is your equal like anything—probably your superior.'

'Is she?' said Gerald.

'Yes, and if you haven't the guts to know it, I hope she'll leave you to your own devices.'

'Nevertheless,' said Gerald, 'if she is my equal, I wish she weren't a teacher, because I don't think teachers as a rule are my equal.'

'Nor do I, damn them. But am I a teacher because I teach, or a parson because I preach?'

Gerald laughed. He was always uneasy on this score. He did not *want* to claim social superiority, yet he *would* not claim intrinsic personal superiority, because he would never base his standard of values on pure being. So he wobbled upon a tacit assumption of social standing. Now Birkin wanted him to accept the fact of intrinsic difference between human beings, which he did not intend to accept. It was against his social honour, his principle. He rose to go.

'I've been neglecting my business all this while,' he said, smiling.

'I ought to have reminded you before,' Birkin replied, laughing and mocking.

'I knew you'd say something like that,' laughed Gerald, rather uneasily.

'Did you?'

'Yes, Rupert. It wouldn't do for us all to be like you are—we should soon be in the cart. When I am above the world, I shall ignore all businesses.'

'Of course, we're not in the cart now,' said Birkin, satirically.

'Not as much as you make out. At any rate, we have enough to eat and drink—'

'And be satisfied,' added Birkin.

Gerald came near the bed and stood looking down at Birkin whose throat was exposed, whose tossed hair fell attractively on the warm brow, above the eyes that were so unchallenged and still in the satirical face. Gerald, full-limbed and turgid with energy, stood unwilling to go, he was held by the presence of the other man. He had not the power to go away.

'So,' said Birkin. 'Good-bye.' And he reached out his hand from under the bed-clothes, smiling with a glimmering look.

'Good-bye,' said Gerald, taking the warm hand of his friend in a firm grasp. 'I shall come again. I miss you down at the mill.'

'I'll be there in a few days,' said Birkin.

The eyes of the two men met again. Gerald's, that were keen as a hawk's, were suffused now with warm light and with unadmitted love, Birkin looked back as out of a darkness, unsounded and unknown, yet with a kind of warmth, that seemed to flow over Gerald's brain like a fertile sleep.

'Good-bye then. There's nothing I can do for you?'

'Nothing, thanks.'

Birkin watched the black-clothed form of the other man move out of the door, the bright head was gone, he turned over to sleep.

17

The Industrial Magnate

In Beldover, there was both for Ursula and for Gudrun an interval. It seemed to Ursula as if Birkin had gone out of her for the time, he had lost his significance, he scarcely mattered in her world. She had her own friends, her own activities, her own life. She turned back to the old ways with zest, away from him.

And Gudrun, after feeling every moment in all her veins conscious of Gerald Crich, connected even physically with him, was now almost indifferent to the thought of him. She was nursing new schemes for going away and trying a new form of life. All the time, there was something in her urging her to avoid the final establishing of a relationship with Gerald. She felt it would be wiser and better to have no more than a casual acquaintance with him.

She had a scheme for going to St Petersburg, where she had a friend who was a sculptor like herself, and who lived with a wealthy Russian whose hobby was jewel-making. The emotional, rather rootless life of the Russians appealed to her. She did not want to go to Paris. Paris was dry, and essentially boring. She would like to go to Rome, Munich, Vienna, or to St Petersburg or Moscow. She had a friend in St Petersburg and a friend in Munich. To each of these she wrote, asking about rooms.

She had a certain amount of money. She had come home partly to save, and now she had sold several pieces of work, she had been praised in various shows. She knew she could become quite the 'go' if she went to London. But she knew London, she wanted something else. She had seventy pounds, of which nobody knew anything. She would move soon, as soon as she heard from her friends. Her nature, in spite of her apparent placidity and calm, was profoundly restless.

The sisters happened to call in a cottage in Willey Green to buy honey. Mrs Kirk, a stout, pale, sharp-nosed woman, sly, honied, with something shrewish and cat-like beneath, asked the girls into her too cosy, too tidy kitchen. There was a cat-like comfort and cleanliness everywhere.

'Yes, Miss Brangwen,' she said, in her slightly whining, insinuating voice, 'and how do you like being back in the old place, then?'

Gudrun, whom she addressed, hated her at once.

'I don't care for it,' she replied abruptly.

'You don't? Ay, well, I suppose you found a difference from London. You like life, and big, grand places. Some of us has to be content with Willey Green and Beldover. And what do you think of our Grammar School, as there's so much talk about?'

'What do I think of it?' Gudrun looked round at her slowly. 'Do you mean, do I think it's a good school?'

'Yes. What is your opinion of it?'

'I *do* think it's a good school.'

Gudrun was very cold and repelling. She knew the common people hated the school.

'Ay, you do, then! I've heard so much, one way and the other. It's nice to know what those that's in it feel. But opinions vary, don't they? Mr Crich up at Highclose is all for it. Ay, poor man, I'm afraid he's not long for this world. He's very poorly.'

'Is he worse?' asked Ursula.

'Eh, yes—since they lost Miss Diana. He's gone off to a shadow. Poor man, he's had a world of trouble.'

'Has he?' asked Gudrun, faintly ironic.

'He has, a world of trouble. And as nice and kind a gentleman as ever you could wish to meet. His children don't take after him.'

'I suppose they take after their mother?' said Ursula.

'In many ways.' Mrs Kirk lowered her voice a little. 'She was a proud haughty lady when she came into these parts—my word, she was that! She mustn't be looked at, and

it was worth your life to speak to her.' The woman made a
dry, sly face.

'Did you know her when she was first married?'

'Yes, I knew her. I nursed three of her children. And
proper little terrors they were, little fiends—that Gerald was
a demon if ever there was one, a proper demon, ay, at six
months old.' A curious malicious, sly tone came into the
woman's voice.

'Really,' said Gudrun.

'That wilful, masterful—he'd mastered one nurse at six
months. Kick, and scream, and struggle like a demon.
Many's the time I've pinched his little bottom for him, when
he was a child in arms. Ay, and he'd have been better if he'd
had it pinched oftener. But she wouldn't have them
corrected—no-o, wouldn't hear of it. I can remember the
rows she had with Mr Crich, my word. When he'd got
worked up, properly worked up till he could stand no more,
he'd lock the study door and whip them. But she paced up
and down all the while like a tiger outside, like a tiger, with
very murder in her face. She had a face that could *look*
death. And when the door was opened, she'd go in with her
hands lifted—"What have you been doing to *my* children,
you coward." She was like one out of her mind. I believe he
was frightened of her; he had to be driven mad before he'd
lift a finger. Didn't the servants have a life of it! And didn't
we used to be thankful when one of them caught it. They
were the torment of your life.'

'Really!' said Gudrun.

'In every possible way. If you wouldn't let them smash
their pots on the table, if you wouldn't let them drag the kitten about with a string round its neck, it you wouldn't give
them whatever they asked for, every mortal thing—then
there was a shine on, and their mother coming in asking—
"What's the matter with him? What have you done to him?
What is it, darling?" And then she'd turn on you as if she'd
trample you under her feet. But she didn't trample on me. I
was the only one that could do anything with her demons—
for she wasn't going to be bothered with them herself. No,
she took no trouble for them. But they must just have their
way, they mustn't be spoken to. And Master Gerald was the

beauty. I left when he was a year and a half, I could stand
no more. But I pinched his little bottom for him when he
was in arms, I did, when there was no holding him, and I'm
not sorry I did—'

Gudrun went away in fury and loathing. The phrase, 'I
pinched his little bottom for him', sent her into a white,
stony fury. She could not bear it, she wanted to have the
woman taken out at once and strangled. And yet there the
phrase was lodged in her mind for ever, beyond escape.
She felt, one day, she would *have* to tell him, to see how he
took it. And she loathed herself for the thought.

But at Shortlands the life-long struggle was coming to a
close. The father was ill and was going to die. He had bad
internal pains, which took away all his attentive life, and left
him with only a vestige of his consciousness. More and
more a silence came over him, he was less and less acutely
aware of his surroundings. The pain seemed to absorb his
activity. He knew it was there, he knew it would come
again. It was like something lurking in the darkness within
him. And he had not the power, or the will, to seek it out
and to know it. There it remained in the darkness, the great
pain, tearing him at times, and then being silent. And when
it tore him he crouched in silent subjection under it, and
when it left him alone again, he refused to know of it. It was
within the darkness, let it remain unknown. So he never admitted it, except in a secret corner of himself, where all his
never-revealed fears and secrets were accumulated. For the
rest, he had a pain, it went away, it made no difference. It
even stimulated him, excited him.

But it gradually absorbed his life. Gradually it drew away
all his potentiality, it bled him into the dark, it weaned him
of life and drew him away into the darkness. And in this twilight of his life little remained visible to him. The business,
his work, that was gone entirely. His public interests had disappeared as if they had never been. Even his family had become extraneous to him, he could only remember, in some
slight non-essential part of himself, that such and such were
his children. But it was historical fact, not vital to him. He
had to make an effort to know their relation to him. Even his
wife barely existed. She indeed was like the darkness, like

the pain within him. By some strange association, the darkness that contained the pain and the darkness that contained his wife were identical. All his thoughts and understandings became blurred and fused, and now his wife and the consuming pain were the same dark secret power against him, that he never faced. He never drove the dread out of its lair within him. He only knew that there was a dark place, and something inhabiting this darkness which issued from time to time and rent him. But he dared not penetrate and drive the beast into the open. He had rather ignore its existence. Only, in his vague way, the dread was his wife, the destroyer, and it was the pain, the destruction, a darkness which was one and both.

He very rarely saw his wife. She kept her room. Only occasionally she came forth, with her head stretched forward, and in her low, possessed voice, she asked him how he was. And he answered her, in the habit of more than thirty years: 'Well, I don't think I'm any the worse, dear.' But he was frightened of her, underneath this safeguard of habit, frightened almost to the verge of death.

But all his life, he had been so constant to his lights, he had never broken down. He would die even now without breaking down, without knowing what his feelings were, towards her. All his life, he had said: 'Poor Christiana, she has such a strong temper.' With unbroken will, he had stood by this position with regard to her, he had substituted pity for all his hostility, pity had been his shield and his safeguard, and his infallible weapon. And still, in his consciousness, he was sorry for her, her nature was so violent and so impatient.

But now his pity, with his life, was wearing thin, and the dread almost amounting to horror was rising into being. But before the armour of his pity really broke, he would die, as an insect when its shell is cracked. This was his final resource. Others would live on, and know the living death, the ensuing process of hopeless chaos. He would not. He denied death its victory.

He had been so constant to his lights, so constant to charity, and to his love for his neighbour. Perhaps he had loved his neighbour even better than himself—which is going one further than the commandment. Always, this flame had burned in his heart, sustaining him through everything, the welfare of the people. He was a large employer of labour, he was a great mine-owner. And he had never lost this from his heart, that in Christ he was one with his workmen. Nay, he had felt inferior to them, as if they through poverty and labour were nearer to God than he. He had always the unacknowledged belief that it was his workmen, the miners, who held in their hands the means of salvation. To move nearer to God, he must move towards his miners, his life must gravitate towards theirs. They were, unconsciously, his idol, his God made manifest. In them he worshipped the highest, the great, sympathetic, mindless Godhead of humanity.

And all the while, his wife had opposed him like one of the great demons of hell. Strange, like a bird of prey, with the fascinating beauty and abstraction of a hawk, she had beat against the bars of his philanthropy, and like a hawk in a cage, she had sunk into silence. By force of circumstance, because all the world combined to make the cage unbreakable, he had been too strong for her, he had kept her prisoner. And because she was his prisoner, his passion for her had always remained keen as death. He had always loved her, loved her with intensity. Within the cage, she was denied nothing, she was given all licence.

But she had gone almost mad. Of wild and overweening temper, she could not bear the humiliation of her husband's soft, half-appealing kindness to everybody. He was not deceived by the poor. He knew they came and sponged on him, and whined to him, the worst sort; the majority, luckily for him, were much too proud to ask for anything, much too independent to come knocking at his door. But in Beldover, as everywhere else, there were the whining, parasitic, foul human beings who come crawling after charity, and feeding on the living body of the public like lice. A kind of fire would go over Christiana Crich's brain, as she saw two more pale-faced, creeping women in objectionable black clothes, cringing lugubriously up the drive to the door. She wanted to set the dogs on them, 'Hi Rip! Hi Ring! Ranger! At 'em, boys, set 'em off.' But Crowther, the butler, with all the rest of the servants, was Mr Crich's man. Nevertheless, when her husband was away, she would come down like a wolf on the crawling supplicants: 'What do you people want? There is nothing for you here. You have no business on the drive at all. Simpson, drive them away and let no more of them through the gate.'

The servants had to obey her. And she would stand watching with an eye like the eagle's, whilst the groom in clumsy confusion drove the lugubrious persons down the drive, as if they were rusty fowls, scuttling before him.

But they learned to know, from the lodge-keeper, when Mr Crich was away, and they timed their visits. How many times, in the first years, would Crowther knock softly at the door: 'Person to see you, sir.'

'What name?'

'Grocock, sir.'

'What do they want?' The question was half impatient, half gratified. He liked hearing appeals to his charity.

'About a child, sir.'

'Show them into the library, and tell them they shouldn't come after eleven o'clock in the morning.'

'Why do you get up from dinner?—send them off,' his wife would say abruptly.

'Oh, I can't do that. It's no trouble just to hear what they have to say.'

'How many more have been here today? Why don't you establish open house for them? They would soon oust me and the children.'

'You know, dear, it doesn't hurt me to hear what they have to say. And if they really are in trouble—well, it is my duty to help them out of it.'

'It's your duty to invite all the rats in the world to gnaw at your bones.'

'Come, Christiana, it isn't like that. Don't be uncharitable.'

But she suddenly swept out of the room, and out to the study. There sat the meagre charity-seekers, looking as if they were at the doctor's.

'Mr Crich can't see you. He can't see you at this hour. Do you think he is your property, that you can come whenever you like? You must go away, there is nothing for you here.'

The poor people rose in confusion. But Mr Crich, pale and black-bearded and deprecating, came behind her, saying:

'Yes, I don't like you coming as late as this. I'll hear any of you in the morning part of the day, but I can't really do with you after. What's amiss then, Gittens. How is your Missis?'

'Why, she's sunk very low, Mester Crich, she's a'most gone, she is—'

Sometimes, it seemed to Mrs Crich as if her husband were some subtle funeral bird, feeding on the miseries of the people. It seemed to her he was never satisfied unless there was some sordid tale being poured out to him, which he drank in with a sort of mournful, sympathetic satisfaction. He would have no *raison d'être* if there were no lugubrious miseries in the world, as an undertaker would have no meaning if there were no funerals.

Mrs Crich recoiled back upon herself, she recoiled away from this world of creeping democracy. A band of tight, baleful exclusion fastened round her heart, her isolation was fierce and hard, her antagonism was passive but terribly pure, like that of a hawk in a cage. As the years went on, she lost more and more count of the world, she seemed rapt in some glittering abstraction, almost purely unconscious. She would wander about the house and about the surrounding country, staring keenly and seeing nothing. She rarely spoke, she had no connexion with the world. And she did not even think. She was consumed in a fierce tension of opposition, like the negative pole of a magnet.

And she bore many children. For, as time went on, she never opposed her husband in word or deed. She took no notice of him, externally. She submitted to him, let him take what he wanted and do as he wanted with her. She was like a hawk that sullenly submits to everything. The relation between her and her husband was wordless and unknown, but it was deep, awful, a relation of utter interdestruction. And he, who triumphed in the world, he became more and more hollow in his vitality, the vitality was bled from within him, as by some haemorrhage. She was hulked like a hawk in a cage, but her heart was fierce and undiminished within her, though her mind was destroyed.

So to the last he would go to her and hold her in his arms sometimes, before his strength was all gone. The terrible white, destructive light that burned in her eyes only excited and roused him. Till he was bled to death, and then he dreaded her more than anything. But he always said to himself, how happy he had been, how he had loved her with a pure and consuming love ever since he had known her. And he thought of her as pure, chaste; the white flame which was known to him alone, the flame of her sex, was a white flower of snow to his mind. She was a wonderful white snow-flower, which he had desired infinitely. And now he was dying with all his ideas and interpretations intact. They would only collapse when the breath left his body. Till then they would be pure truths for him. Only death would show the perfect completeness of the lie. Till death, she was his white snow-flower. He had subdued her, and her subjugation was to him an infinite chastity in her, a virginity which he could never break, and which dominated him as by a spell.

She had let go the outer world, but within herself she was unbroken and unimpaired. She only sat in her room like a moping, dishevelled hawk, motionless, mindless. Her children, for whom she had been so fierce in her youth, now meant scarcely anything to her. She had lost all that, she was quite by herself. Only Gerald, the gleaming, had some existence for her. But of late years, since he had become head of the business, he too was forgotten. Whereas the father, now he was dying, turned for compassion to Gerald. There had always been opposition between the two of them. Gerald had feared and despised his father, and to a great extent had avoided him all through boyhood and young manhood. And the father had felt very often a real dislike of his eldest son, which, never wanting to give way to, he had refused to acknowledge. He had ignored Gerald as much as possible, leaving him alone.

Since, however, Gerald had come home and assumed responsibility in the firm, and had proved such a wonderful director, the father, tired and weary of all outside concerns, had put all his trust of these things in his son, implicitly, leaving everything to him, and assuming a rather touching dependence on the young enemy. This immediately roused a poignant pity and allegiance in Gerald's heart, always shadowed by contempt and by unadmitted enmity. For Gerald was in reaction against Charity; and yet he was dominated by it, it assumed supremacy in the inner life, and he could not confute it. So he was partly subject to that which his father stood for, but he was in reaction against it. Now he could not save himself. A certain pity and grief and tenderness for his father overcame him, in spite of the deeper, more sullen hostility.

The father won shelter from Gerald through compassion. But for love he had Winifred. She was his youngest child, she was the only one of his children whom he had ever closely loved. And her he loved with all the great, overweening, sheltering love of a dying man. He wanted to shelter her infinitely, infinitely, to wrap her in warmth and love and shelter, perfectly. It he could save her she should never know one pain, one grief, one hurt. He had been so right all his life, so constant in his kindness and his goodness. And this was his last passionate righteousness, his love for the child Winifred. Some things troubled him yet. The world had passed away from him, as his strength ebbed. There were no more poor and injured and humble to protect and succour. These were all lost to him. There were no more sons and daughters to trouble him, and to weigh on him as an unnatural responsibility. These too had faded out of reality. All these things had fallen out of his hands, and left him free.

There remained the covert fear and horror of his wife, as she sat mindless and strange in her room, or as she came forth with slow, prowling step, her head bent forward. But this he put away. Even his life-long righteousness, however, would not quite deliver him from the inner horror. Still, he could keep it sufficiently at bay. It would never break forth openly. Death would come first.

Then there was Winifred! If only he could be sure about her, if only he could be sure. Since the death of Diana, and the development of his illness, his craving for surety with regard to Winifred amounted almost to obsession. It was as if, even dying, he must have some anxiety, some responsibility of love, of Charity, upon his heart.

She was an odd, sensitive, inflammable child, having her father's dark hair and quiet bearing, but being quite detached, momentaneous. She was like a changeling indeed, as if her feelings did not matter to her, really. She often seemed to be talking and playing like the gayest and most childish of children, she was full of the warmest, most delightful affection for a few things—for her father, and for her animals in particular. But if she heard that her beloved kitten Leo had been run over by the motor-car she put her head on one side, and replied, with a faint contraction like resentment on her face: 'Has he?' Then she took no more notice. She only disliked the servant who would force bad news on her, and wanted her to be sorry. She wished not to know, and that seemed her chief motive. She avoided her mother, and most of the members of her family. She *loved* her Daddy, because he wanted her always to be happy, and because he seemed to become young again, and irresponsible in her presence. She liked Gerald, because he was so self-contained. She loved people who would make life a game for her. She had an amazing instinctive critical faculty, and was a pure anarchist, a pure aristocrat at once. For she accepted her equals wherever she found them, and she ignored with blithe indifference her inferiors, whether they were her brothers and sisters, or whether they were wealthy guests of the house, or whether they were the common people or the servants. She was quite single and by herself, deriving from nobody. It was as if she were cut off from all purpose or continuity, and existed simply moment by moment.

The father, as by some strange final illusion, felt as if all his fate depended on his ensuring to Winifred her happiness. She who could never suffer, because she never formed vital connexions, she who could lose the dearest things of her life and be just the same the next day, the whole memory dropped out, as if deliberately, she whose will was so strangely and easily free, anarchistic, almost nihilistic, who like a soulless bird flits on its own will, without attachment or responsibility beyond the moment, who in her every motion snapped the threads of serious relationship with blithe, free hands, really nihilistic, because never troubled, she must be the object of her father's final passionate solicitude.

When Mr Crich heard that Gudrun Brangwen might come to help Winifred with her drawing and modelling he saw a road to salvation for his child. He believed that Winifred had talent, he had seen Gudrun, he knew that she was an exceptional person. He could give Winifred into her hands as into the hands of a right being. Here was a direction and a positive force to be lent to his child, he need not leave her directionless and defenceless. If he could but graft the girl on to some tree of utterance before he died, he would have fulfilled his responsibility. And here it could be done. He did not hesitate to appeal to Gudrun.

Meanwhile, as the father drifted more and more out of life, Gerald experienced more and more a sense of exposure. His father after all had stood for the living world to him. Whilst his father lived Gerald was not responsible for the world. But now his father was passing away, Gerald found himself left exposed and unready before the storm of living, like the mutinous first mate of a ship that has lost his captain, and who sees only a terrible chaos in front of him. He did not inherit an established order and a living idea. The whole unifying idea of mankind seemed to be dying with his father, the centralizing force that had held the whole together seemed to collapse with his father, the parts were ready to go asunder in terrible disintegration. Gerald was as if left on board of a ship that was going asunder beneath his feet, he was in charge of a vessel whose timbers were all coming apart.

He knew that all his life he had been wrenching at the frame of life to break it apart. And now, with something of the terror of a destructive child, he saw himself on the point of inheriting his own destruction. And during the last months, under the influence of death, and of Birkin's talk, and of Gudrun's penetrating being, he had lost entirely that mechanical certainty that had been his triumph. Sometimes spasms of hatred came over him, against Birkin and Gudrun and that whole set. He wanted to go back to the dullest conservatism, to the most strictest Toryism. But the desire did not last long enough to carry him into action.

During his childhood and his boyhood he had wanted a sort of savagedom. The days of Homer were his ideal, when a man was chief of an army of heroes, or spent his years in wonderful Odyssey. He hated remorselessly the circumstances of his own life, so much that he never really saw Beldover and the colliery valley. He turned his face entirely away from the blackened mining region that stretched away on the right hand of Shortlands, he turned entirely to the country and the woods beyond Willey Water. It was true that the panting and rattling of the coal-mines could always be heard at Shortlands. But from his earliest childhood, Gerald had paid no heed to this. He had ignored the whole of the industrial sea which surged in coal-blackened tides against the grounds of the house. The world was really a wilderness where one hunted and swam and rode. He rebelled against all authority. Life was a condition of savage freedom.

Then he had been sent away to school, which was so much death to him. He refused to go to Oxford, choosing a German university. He had spent a certain time at Bonn, at Berlin, and at Frankfurt. There, a curiosity had been aroused in his mind. He wanted to see and to know, in a curious objective fashion, as if it were an amusement to him. Then he must try war. Then he must travel into the savage regions that had so attracted him.

The result was, he found humanity very much alike everywhere, and to a mind like his, curious and cold, the savage was duller, less exciting than the European. So he took hold of all kinds of sociological ideas, and ideas of reform. But they never went more than skin-deep, they were never more than a mental amusement. Their interest lay chiefly in the reaction against the positive order, the destructive reaction.

He discovered at last a real adventure in the coal-mines. His father asked him to help in the firm. Gerald had been educated in the science of mining, and it had never interested him. Now, suddenly, with a sort of exultation, he laid hold of the world.

There was impressed photographically on his consciousness the great industry. Suddenly, it was real, he was part of it. Down the valley ran the colliery railway, linking mine with mine. Down the railway ran the trains, short trains of heavily laden trucks, long trains of empty wagons, each one bearing in big white letters the initials:

'C. B. & Co.'

These white letters on all the wagons he had seen since his first childhood, and it was as if he had never seen them, they were so familiar, and so ignored. Now at last he saw his own name written on the wall. Now he had a vision of power.

So many wagons, bearing his initial, running all over the country. He saw them as he entered London in the train, he saw them at Dover. So far his power ramified. He looked at Beldover, at Selby, at Whatmore, at Lethley Bank, the great colliery villages which depended entirely on his mines. They were hideous and sordid, during his childhood they had been sores in his consciousness. And now he saw them with pride. Four raw new towns, and many ugly industrial hamlets were crowded under his dependence. He saw the stream of miners flowing along the causeways from the mines at the end of the afternoon, thousands of blackened, slightly distorted human beings with red mouths, all moving subjugate to his will. He pushed slowly in his motor-car through the little market-top on Friday nights in Beldover, through a solid mass of human beings that were making their purchases and doing their weekly spending. They were all subordinate to him. They were ugly and uncouth, but they were his instruments. He was the God of the machine. They made way for his motorcar automatically, slowly.

He did not care whether they made way with alacrity, or grudgingly. He did not care what they thought of him. His vision had suddenly crystallized. Suddenly he had conceived the pure instrumentality of mankind. There had been so much humanitarianism, so much talk of sufferings and feelings. It was ridiculous. The sufferings and feelings of individuals did not matter in the least. They were mere conditions, like the weather. What mattered was the pure instrumentality of the individual. As a man as of a knife: does it cut well? Nothing else mattered.

Everything in the world has its function, and is good or not good in so far as it fulfils this function more or less perfectly. Was a miner a good miner? Then he was complete. Was a manager a good manager. That was enough. Gerald himself, who was responsible for all this industry, was he a good director? If he were, he had fulfilled his life. The rest was by-lay.

The mines were there, they were old. They were giving out, it did not pay to work the seams. There was talk of closing down two of them. It was at this point that Gerald arrived on the scene.

He looked around. There lay the mines. They were old, obsolete. They were like old lions, no more good. He looked again. Pah! the mines were nothing but the clumsy efforts of impure minds. There they lay, abortions of a half-trained mind. Let the idea of them be swept away. He cleared his brain of them, and thought only of the coal in the under earth. How much was there?

There was plenty of coal. The old workings could not get at it, that was all. Then break the neck of the old workings. The coal lay there in its seams, even though the seams were thin. There it lay, inert matter, as it had always lain, since the beginning of time, subject to the will of man. The will of man was the determining factor. Man was the arch-god of earth. His mind was obedient to serve his will. Man's will was the absolute, the only absolute.

And it was his will to subjugate Matter to his own ends. The subjugation itself was the point, the fight was the be-all, the fruits of victory were mere results. It was not for the sake of money that Gerald took over the mines. He did not care about money, fundamentally. He was neither ostentatious nor luxurious, neither did he care about social position, not finally. What he wanted was the pure fulfilment of his own will in the struggle with the natural conditions. His will was now, to take the coal out of the earth, profitably. The profit was merely the condition of victory, but the victory itself lay in the feat achieved. He vibrated with zest before the challenge. Every day he was in the mines, examining, testing, he consulted experts, he gradually gathered the whole situation into his mind, as a general grasps the plan of his campaign.

Then there was need for a complete break. The mines were run on an old system, an obsolete idea. The initial idea had been, to obtain as much money from the earth as would make the owners comfortably rich, would allow the workmen sufficient wages and good conditions, and would increase the wealth of the country altogether. Gerald's father, following in the second generation, having a sufficient fortune, had thought only of the men. The mines, for him, were primarily great fields to produce bread and plenty for all the hundreds of human beings gathered about them. He had lived and striven with his fellow owners to benefit the men every time. And the men had been benefited in their fashion. There were few poor, and few needy. All was plenty, because the mines were good and easy to work. And the miners, in those days, finding themselves richer than they might have expected, felt glad and triumphant. They thought themselves well off, they congratulated themselves on their good fortune, they remembered how their fathers had starved and suffered, and they felt that better times had come. They were grateful to those others, the pioneers, the new owners, who had opened out the pits, and let forth this stream of plenty.

But man is never satisfied, and so the miners, from gratitude to their owners, passed on to murmuring. Their sufficiency decreased with knowledge, they wanted more. Why should the master be so out-of-all-proportion rich?

There was a crisis when Gerald was a boy, when the Masters' Federation closed down the mines because the men would not accept a reduction. This lock-out had forced home the new conditions to Thomas Crich. Belonging to the Federation, he had been compelled by his honour to close the pits against his men. He, the father, the Patriarch, was forced to deny the means of life to his sons, his people. He, the rich man who would hardly enter heaven because of his possessions, must now turn upon the poor, upon those who were nearer Christ than himself, those who were humble and despised and closer to perfection, those who were manly and noble in their labours, and must say to them: 'Ye shall neither labour nor eat bread.'

It was this recognition of the state of war which really broke his heart. He wanted his industry to be run on love. Oh, he wanted love to be the directing power even of the mines. And now, from under the cloak of love, the sword was cynically drawn, the sword of mechanical necessity.

This really broke his heart. He must have the illusion and

now the illusion was destroyed. The men were not against *him*, but they were against the masters. It was war, and willy-nilly he found himself on the wrong side, in his own conscience. Seething masses of miners met daily, carried away by a new religious impulse. The idea flew through them: 'All men are equal on earth,' and they would carry the idea to its material fulfilment. After all, is it not the teaching of Christ? And what is an idea, if not the germ of action in the material word. 'All men are equal in spirit, they are all sons of God. Whence then this obvious *disquality*?' It was a religious creed pushed to its material conclusion. Thomas Crich at least had no answer. He could but admit, according to his sincere tenets, that the disquality was wrong. But he could not give up his goods, which were the stuff of disquality. So the men would fight for their rights. The last impulses of the last religious passion left on earth, the passion for equality, inspired them.

Seething mobs of men marched about, their faces lighted up as for holy war, with a smoke of cupidity. How disentangle the passion for equality from the passion of cupidity, when begins the fight for equality of possessions? But the God was the machine. Each man claimed equality in the Godhead of the great productive machine. Every man equally was part of this Godhead. But somehow, somewhere, Thomas Crich knew this was false. When the machine is the Godhead, and production or work is worship, then the most mechanical mind is purest and highest, the representative of God on earth. And the rest are subordinate, each according to his degree.

Riots broke out. Whatmore pit-head was in flames. This was the pit farthest in the country, near the woods. Soldiers came. From the windows of Shortlands, on that fatal day, could be seen the flare of fire in the sky not far off, and now the little colliery train, with the workmen's carriages which were used to convey the miners to the distant Whatmore, was crossing the valley full of soldiers, full of red-coats. Then there was the far-off sound of firing, then the later news that the mob was dispersed, one man was shot dead, the fire was put out.

Gerald, who was a boy, was filled with the wildest excitement and delight. He longed to go with the soldiers to shoot the men. But he was not allowed to go out of the lodge gates. At the gates were stationed sentries with guns. Gerald stood near them in delight, whilst gangs of derisive miners strolled up and down the lanes, calling and jeering:

'Now then, three ha'porth o' coppers, let's see thee shoot thy gun.' Insults were chalked on the walls and the fences, the servants left.

And all this while Thomas Crich was breaking his heart, and giving away hundreds of pounds in charity. Everywhere there was free food, a surfeit of free food. Anybody could have bread for asking, and a loaf cost only three-ha'pence. Every day there was a free tea somewhere, the children had never had so many treats in their lives. On Friday afternoon great basketfuls of buns and cakes were taken into the schools, and great pitchers of milk, the schoolchildren had what they wanted. They were sick with eating too much cake and milk.

And then it came to an end, and the men went back to work. But it was never the same as before. There was a new situation created, a new idea reigned. Even in the machine, there should be equality. No part should be subordinate to any other part: all should be equal. The instinct for chaos had entered. Mystic equality lies in abstraction, not in having or in doing, which are processes. In function and process, one man, one part, must of necessity be subordinate to another. It is a condition of being. But the desire for chaos had risen, and the idea of mechanical equality was the weapon of disruption which should execute the will of men, the will for chaos.

Gerald was a boy at the time of the strike, but he longed to be a man, to fight the colliers. The father, however, was trapped between two half-truths, and broken. He wanted to be a pure Christian, one and equal with all men. He even wanted to give away all he had, to the poor. Yet he was a great promoter of industry, and he knew perfectly that he must keep his goods and keep his authority. This was as divine a necessity in him, as the need to give away all he possessed—more divine, even, since this was the necessity he acted upon. Yet because he did *not* act on the other ideal, it dominated him, he was dying of chagrin because he must forfeit it. He wanted to be a father of loving kindness and sacrificial benevolence. The colliers shouted to him about his thousands a year. They would not be deceived.

When Gerald grew up in the ways of the world, he shifted the position. He did not care about the equality. The whole Christian attitude of love and self-sacrifice was old hat. He knew that position and authority were the right thing in the world, and it was useless to cant about it. They were the right thing, for the simple reason that they were functionally necessary. They were not the be-all and the end-all. It was like being part of a machine. He himself happened to be a controlling, central part, the masses of men were the parts variously controlled. This was merely as it happened. As well get excited because a central hub drives a hundred outer wheels—or because the whole universe wheels round the sun. After all, it would be mere silliness to say that the moon and the earth and Saturn and Jupiter and Venus have just as much right to be the centre of the universe, each of them separately, as the sun. Such an assertion is made merely in the desire of chaos.

Without bothering to *think* to a conclusion, Gerald jumped to a conclusion. He abandoned the whole democratic-equality problem as a problem of silliness. What mattered was the great social productive machine. Let that work perfectly, let it produce a sufficiency of everything, let every man be given a rational portion, greater or less according to his functional degree or magnitude, and then, provision made, let the devil supervene, let every man look after his own amusements and appetites, so long as he interfered with nobody.

So Gerald set himself to work, to put the great industry in order. In his travels, and in his accompanying readings, he had come to the conclusion that the essential secret of life was harmony. He did not define to himself at all clearly what harmony was. The word pleased him, he felt he had come to his own conclusions. And he proceeded to put his philosophy into practice by forcing order into the established world, translating the mystic word harmony into the practical word organization.

Immediately he *saw* the firm, he realized what he could do. He had a fight to fight with Matter, with the earth and the coal it enclosed. This was the sole idea, to turn upon the inanimate matter of the underground, and reduce it to his will. And for this fight with matter, one must have perfect instruments in perfect organization, a mechanism so subtle and harmonious in its workings that it represents the single mind of man, and by its relentless repetition of given movement, will accomplish a purpose irresistibly, inhumanly. It was this inhuman principle in the mechanism he wanted to construct that inspired Gerald with an almost religious exaltation. He, the man, could interpose a perfect, changeless, godlike medium between himself and the Matter he had to subjugate. There were two opposites, his will and the resistant Matter of the earth. And between these he could establish the very expression of his will, the incarnation of his power, a great and perfect machine, a system, an activity of pure order, pure mechanical repetition, repetition *ad infinitum*, hence eternal and infinite. He found his eternal and his infinite in the pure, complex, infinitely repeated motion, like the spinning of a wheel; but a productive spinning, as the revolving of the universe may be called a productive spinning, a productive repetition through eternity, to infinity. And this is the God-motion, this productive repetition *ad infinitum*. And Gerald was the God of the machine, *Deus ex Machina*. And the whole productive will of man was the Godhead.

He had his life-work now, to extend over the earth a great and perfect system in which the will of man ran smooth and unthwarted, timeless, a Godhead in process. He had to begin with the mines. The terms were given: first the resistant Matter of the underground; then the instruments of its subjugation, instruments human and metallic; and finally his own pure will, his own mind. It would need a marvellous adjustment of myriad instruments, human, animal, metallic, kinetic, dynamic, a marvellous casting of myriad tiny wholes into one great perfect entirety. And then, in this case there was perfection attained, the will of the highest was perfectly fulfilled, the will of mankind was perfectly enacted; for was not mankind mystically contradistinguished against inanimate Matter, was not the history of mankind just the history of the conquest of the one by the other?

The miners were overreached. While they were still in the toils of divine equality of man, Gerald had passed on, granted essentially their case, and proceeded in his quality of human being to fulfil the will of mankind as a whole. He merely represented the miners in a higher sense when he perceived that the only way to fulfil perfectly the will of man was to establish the perfect, inhuman machine. But he represented them very essentially, they were far behind, out of date, squabbling for their material equality. The desire had already transmuted into this new and greater desire, for a perfect intervening mechanism between man and Matter, the desire to translate the Godhead into pure mechanism.

As soon as Gerald entered the firm, the convulsion of death ran through the old system. He had all his life been tortured by a furious and destructive demon, which possessed him sometimes like an insanity. This temper now entered like a virus into the firm, and there were cruel eruptions. Terrible and inhuman were his examinations into every detail; there was no privacy he would spare, no old sentiment but he would turn it over. The old grey managers, the old grey clerks, the doddering old pensioners, he looked at them, and removed them as so much lumber. The whole concern seemed like a hospital of invalid employees. He had no emotional qualms. He arranged what pensions were necessary, he looked for efficient substitutes, and when these were found, he substituted them for the old hands.

'I've a pitiful letter here from Letherington,' his father would say, in a tone of deprecation and appeal. 'Don't you think the poor fellow might keep on a little longer. I always fancied he did very well.'

'I've got a man in his place now, father. He'll be happier out of it, believe me. You think his allowance is plenty, don't you?'

'It is not the allowance that he wants, poor man. He feels it very much, that he is superannuated. Says he thought he had twenty more years of work in him yet.'

'Not of this kind of work I want. He doesn't understand.'

The father sighed. He wanted not to know any more. He

believed the pits would have to be overhauled if they were to go on working. And after all, it would be worst in the long run for everybody, if they must close down. So he could make no answer to the appeals of his old and trusty servants, he could only repeat 'Gerald says'.

So the father drew more and more out of the light. The whole frame of the real life was broken for him. He had been right according to his lights. And his lights had been those of the great religion. Yet they seemed to have become obsolete, to be superseded in the world. He could not understand. He only withdrew with his lights into an inner room, into the silence. The beautiful candles of belief, that would not do to light the world any more, they would still burn sweetly and sufficiently in the inner room of his soul, and in the silence of his retirement.

Gerald rushed into the reform of the firm, beginning with the office. It was needful to economize severely, to make possible the great alterations he must introduce.

'What are these widows' coals?' he asked.

'We have always allowed all widows of men who worked for the firm a load of coals every three months.'

'They must pay cost price henceforward. The firm is not a charity institution, as everybody seems to think.'

Widows, these stock figures of sentimental humanitarianism, he felt a dislike at the thought of them. They were almost repulsive. Why were they not immolated on the pyre of the husband, like the sati in India? At any rate, let them pay the cost of their coals.

In a thousand ways he cut down the expenditure, in ways so fine as to be hardly noticeable to the men. The miners must pay for the cartage of their coals, heavy cartage too; they must pay for their tools, for the sharpening, for the care of lamps, for the many trifling things that made the bill of charges against every man mount up to a shilling or so in the week. It was not grasped very definitely by the miners, though they were sore enough. But it saved hundreds of pounds every week for the firm.

Gradually Gerald got hold of everything. And then began the great reform. Expert engineers were introduced in every department. An enormous electric plant was installed, both for lighting and for haulage underground, and for power. The electricity was carried into every mine. New machinery was brought from America, such as the miners had never seen before, great iron men, as the cutting machines were called, and unusual appliances. The working of the pits was thoroughly changed, all the control was taken out of the hands of the miners, the butty system was abolished. Everything was run on the most accurate and delicate scientific method, educated and expert men were in control everywhere, the miners were reduced to mere mechanical instruments. They had to work hard, much harder than before, the work was terrible and heart-breaking in its mechanicalness.

But they submitted to it all. The joy went out of their lives, the hope seemed to perish as they became more and more mechanized. And yet they accepted the new conditions. They even got a further satisfaction out of them. At first they hated Gerald Crich, they swore to do something to him, to murder him. But as time went on, they accepted everything with some fatal satisfaction. Gerald was their high priest, he represented the religion they really felt. His father was forgotten already. There was a new world, a new order, strict, terrible, inhuman, but satisfying in its very destructiveness. The men were satisfied to belong to the great and wonderful machine, even whilst it destroyed them. It was what they wanted. It was the highest that man had produced, the most wonderful and superhuman. They were exalted by belonging to this great and superhuman system which was beyond feeling or reason, something really godlike. Their hearts died within them, but their souls were satisfied. It was what they wanted. Otherwise Gerald could never have done what he did. He was just ahead of them in giving them what they wanted, this participation in a great and perfect system that subjected life to pure mathematical principles. This was a sort of freedom, the sort they really wanted. It was the first great step in undoing, the first great phase of chaos, the substitution of the mechanical principle for the organic, the destruction of the organic purpose, the organic unity, and the subordination of every organic unit to the great mechanical purpose. It was pure organic disintegration and pure mechanical organization. This is the first and finest state of chaos.

Gerald was satisfied. He knew the colliers said they hated him. But he had long ceased to hate them. When they streamed past him at evening, their heavy boots slurring on the pavement wearily, their shoulders slightly distorted, they took no notice of him, they gave him no greeting whatever, they passed in a grey-black stream of unemotional acceptance. They were not important to him, save as instruments, nor he to them, save as a supreme instrument of control. As miners they had their being, he had his being as director. He admired their qualities. But as men, personalities, they were just accidents, sporadic little unimportant phenomena. And tacitly, the men agreed to this. For Gerald agreed to it in himself.

He had succeeded. He had converted the industry into a new and terrible purity. There was a greater output of coal than ever, the wonderful and delicate system ran almost perfectly. He had a set of really clever engineers, both mining and electrical, and they did not cost much. A highly educated man cost very little more than a workman. His managers, who were all rare men, were no more expensive than the old bungling fools of his father's days, who were merely colliers promoted. His chief manager, who had twelve hundred a year, saved the firm at least five thousand. The whole system was now so perfect that Gerald was hardly necessary any more.

It was so perfect that sometimes a strange fear came over him, and he did not know what to do. He went on for some years in a sort of trance of activity. What he was doing seemed supreme, he was almost like a divinity. He was a pure and exalted activity.

But now he had succeeded—he had finally succeeded. And once or twice lately, when he was alone in the evening and had nothing to do, he had suddenly stood up in terror, not knowing what he was. And he went to the mirror and looked long and closely at his own face, at his own eyes, seeking for something. He was afraid, in mortal dry fear, but he knew not what of. He looked at his own face. There it was, shapely and healthy and the same as ever, yet somehow, it was not real, it was a mask. He dared not touch it, for fear it should prove to be only a composition mask. His eyes were blue and keen as ever, and as firm in their sockets. Yet he was not sure that they were not blue false bubbles that would burst in a moment and leave clear annihilation. He could see the darkness in them, as if they were only bubbles of darkness. He was afraid that one day he would break down and be a purely meaningless babble lapping round a darkness.

But his will yet held good, he was able to go away and read, and think about things. He liked to read books about the primitive man, books of anthropology, and also works of speculative philosophy. His mind was very active. But it was like a bubble floating in the darkness. At any moment it might burst and leave him in chaos. He would not die. He knew that. He would go on living, but the meaning would have collapsed out of him, his divine reason would be gone. In a strangely indifferent, sterile way, he was frightened. But he could not react even to the fear. It was as if his centres of feeling were drying up. He remained calm, calculative and healthy, and quite freely deliberate, even whilst he felt, with faint, small but final sterile horror, that his mystic reason was breaking, giving way now, at this crisis.

And it was a strain. He knew there was no equilibrium. He would have to go in some direction, shortly, to find relief. Only Birkin kept the fear definitely off him, saved him his quick sufficiency in life, by the odd mobility and changeableness which seemed to contain the quintessence of faith. But then Gerald must always come away from Birkin, as from a Church service, back to the outside real world of work and life. There it was, it did not alter, and words were futilities. He had to keep himself in reckoning with the world of work and material life. And it became more and more difficult, such a strange pressure was upon him, as if the very middle of him were a vacuum, and outside were an awful tension.

He had found his most satisfactory relief in women. After a debauch with some desperate woman, he went on quite easy and forgetful. The devil of it was, it was so hard to keep up his interest in women nowadays. He didn't care about them any more. A Pussum was all right in her way, but she was an exceptional case, and even she mattered extremely little. No, women, in that sense, were useless to him any more. He felt that his *mind* needed acute stimulation, before he could be physically roused.

18

Rabbit

Gudrun knew that it was a critical thing for her to go to Shortlands. She knew it was equivalent to accepting Gerald Crich as a lover. And though she hung back, disliking the condition, yet she knew she would go on. She equivocated. She said to herself, in torment recalling the blow and the kiss, 'After all, what is it? What is a kiss? What even is a blow? It is an instant, vanished at once. I can go to Shortlands just for a time, before I go away, if only to see what it is like.' For she had an insatiable curiosity to see and to know everything.

She also wanted to know what Winifred was really like. Having heard the child calling from the steamer in the night, she felt some mysterious connexion with her.

Gudrun talked with the father in the library. Then he sent for his daughter. She came accompanied by Mademoiselle.

'Winnie, this is Miss Brangwen, who will be so kind as to help you with your drawing and making models of your animals,' said the father.

The child looked at Gudrun for a moment with interest, before she came forward, and with face averted offered her hand. There was a complete *sang froid* and indifference under Winifred's childish reserve, a certain irresponsible callousness.

'How do you do?' said the child, not lifting her face.

'How do you do?' said Gudrun.

Then Winifred stood aside, and Gudrun was introduced to Mademoiselle.

'You have a fine day for your walk,' said Mademoiselle, in a bright manner.

'*Quite* fine,' said Gudrun.

Winifred was watching from her distance. She was as if amused, but rather unsure as yet what this new person was like. She saw so many new persons, and so few who became real to her. Mademoiselle was of no account whatever, the child merely put up with her, calmly and easily, accepting her little authority with faint scorn, compliant out of childish arrogance of indifference.

'Well, Winifred,' said the father, 'aren't you glad Miss Brangwen has come? She makes animals and birds in wood and in clay, that the people in London write about in the papers, praising them to the skies.'

Winifred smiled slightly.

'Who told you, Daddie?' she asked.

'Who told me? Hermione told me, and Rupert Birkin.'

'Do you know them?' Winifred asked of Gudrun, turning to her with faint challenge.

'Yes,' said Gudrun.

Winifred readjusted herself a little. She had been ready to accept Gudrun as a sort of servant. Now she saw it was on terms of friendship they were intended to meet. She was rather glad. She had so many half inferiors, whom she tolerated with perfect good humour.

Gudrun was very calm. She also did not take these things very seriously. A new occasion was mostly spectacular to her. However, Winifred was a detached, ironic child, she would never attach herself. Gudrun liked her and was intrigued by her. The first meetings went off with a certain humiliating clumsiness. Neither Winifred nor her instructress had any social grace.

Soon, however, they met in a kind of make-believe world. Winifred did not notice human beings unless they were like herself, playful and slightly mocking. She would accept nothing but the world of amusement, and the serious people of her life were the animals she had for pets. On those she lavished, almost ironically, her affection and her companionship. To the rest of the human scheme she submitted with a faint bored indifference.

She had a Pekinese dog called Looloo, which she loved.

'Let us draw Looloo,' said Gudrun, 'and see if we can get his Looliness, shall we?'

'Darling!' cried Winifred, rushing to the dog, that sat with contemplative sadness on the hearth, and kissing its bulging brow. 'Darling one, will you be drawn? Shall its mummy draw its portrait?' Then she chuckled gleefully, and turning to Gudrun, said: 'Oh, let's!'

They proceeded to get pencils and paper, and were ready.

'Beautifullest,' cried Winifred, hugging the dog, 'sit still while its mummy draws its beautiful portrait.' The dog looked up at her with grievous resignation in its large, prominent eyes. She kissed it fervently, and said: 'I wonder what mine will be like. It's sure to be awful.'

As she sketched she chuckled to herself, and cried out at times:

'Oh, darling, you're so beautiful!'

And again chuckling, she rushed to embrace the dog, in penitence, as if she were doing him some subtle injury. He sat all the time with the resignation and fretfulness of ages on his dark velvety face. She drew slowly, with a wicked concentration in her eyes, her head on one side, an intense stillness over her. She was as if working the spell of some enchantment. Suddenly she had finished. She looked at the dog, and then at her drawing, and then cried, with real grief for the dog, and at the same time with a wicked exultation:

'My beautiful, why did they?'

She took her paper to the dog, and held it under his nose. He turned his head aside as in chagrin and mortification, and she impulsively kissed his velvety bulging forehead.

''s a Loolie, 's a little Loozie! Look at his portrait, darling, look at his portrait, that his mother has done of him.' She looked at her paper and chuckled. Then, kissing the dog once more, she rose and came gravely to Gudrun, offering her the paper.

It was a grotesque little diagram of a grotesque little animal, so wicked and so comical, a slow smile came over Gudrun's face, unconsciously. And at her side Winifred chuckled with glee, and said:

'It isn't like him, is it? He's much lovelier than that. He's *so* beautiful—mmm, Looloo, my sweet darling.' And she flew off to embrace the chagrined little dog. He looked up at her with reproachful, saturnine eyes, vanquished in his extreme agedness of being. Then she flew back to her drawing, and chuckled with satisfaction.

'It isn't like him, is it?' she said to Gudrun.

'Yes, it's very like him,' Gudrun replied.

The child treasured her drawing, carried it about with her, and showed it, with a silent embarrassment, to everybody.

'Look,' she said, thrusting the paper into her father's hand.

'Why, that's Looloo!' he exclaimed. And he looked down in surprise, hearing the almost inhuman chuckles of the child at his side.

Gerald was away from home when Gudrun first came to Shortlands. But the first morning he came back he watched for her. It was a sunny, soft morning, and he lingered in the garden paths, looking at the flowers that had come our during his absence. He was clean and fit as ever, shaven, his fair hair scrupulously parted at the side, bright in the sunshine, his short, fair moustache closely clipped, his eyes with their humorous kind twinkle, which was so deceptive. He was dressed in black, his clothes sat well on his well-nourished body. Yet as he lingered before the flower-beds in the morning sunshine, there was a certain isolation, a fear about him, as of something wanting.

Gudrun came up quickly, unseen. She was dressed in blue, with woollen yellow stockings, like the Bluecoat boys. He glanced up in surprise. Her stockings always disconcerted him, the pale-yellow stockings and the heavy, heavy black shoes. Winifred, who had been playing about the garden with Mademoiselle and the dogs, came flitting towards Gudrun. The child wore a dress of black-and-white stripes. Her hair was rather short, cut round and hanging level in her neck.

'We're going to do Bismarck, aren't we?' she said, linking her hand through Gudrun's arm.

'Yes, we're going to do Bismarck. Do you want to?'

'Oh yes—oh, I do! I want most awfully to do Bismarck. He looks *so* splendid this morning, so *fierce*. He's almost as big as a lion.' And the child chuckled sardonically at her own hyperbole. 'He's a real king, he really is.'

'*Bonjour, Mademoiselle,*' said the little French governess, wavering up with a slight bow, a bow of the sort that Gudrun loathed, insolent.

'*Winifred veut tant faire le portrait de Bismarck—! Oh, mais toute la matinée*—"We will do Bismarck this morning!"—*Bismarck, Bismarck, toujours Bismarck! C'est un lapin, n'est-ce pas, mademoiselle?*'

'*Oui, c'est un grand lapin blanc et noir. Vous ne l'avez pas vu?*' said Gudrun in her good, but rather heavy French.

'*Non, mademoiselle, Winifred n'a jamais voulu me le faire voir. Tant de fois je le lui ai demandé, "Qu'est-ce donc que ce Bismarck, Winifred?" Mais elle n'a pas voulu me le dire. Son Bismarck, c'était un mystère.*'

'*Oui, c'est un mystère, vraiment un mystère!* Miss Brangwen, say that Bismarck is a mystery,' cried Winifred.

'Bismarck is a mystery, *Bismarck, c'est un mystère, der Bismarck, er ist ein Wunder,*' said Gudrun, in mocking incantation.

'*Ja, er ist ein Wunder,*' repeated Winifred, with odd seriousness, under which lay a wicked chuckle.

'*Ist er auch ein Wunder?*' came the slightly insolent sneering of Mademoiselle.

'*Doch!*' said Winifred briefly, indifferent.

'*Doch ist er nicht ein König.* Beesmarck, he was not a king, Winifred, as you have said. He was only—*il n'était que chancelier.*'

'*Qu'est-ce qu'un chancelier?*' said Winifred, with slightly contemptuous indifference.

'A *chancelier* is a chancellor, and a chancellor is, I believe, a sort of judge,' said Gerald, coming up and shaking hands with Gudrun. 'You'll have made a song of Bismarck soon,' said he.

Mademoiselle waited, and discreetly made her inclination, and her greeting.

'So they wouldn't let you see Bismarck, Mademoiselle?' he said.

'*Non, Monsieur.*'

'Ay, very mean of them. What are you going to do to him, Miss Brangwen? I want him sent to the kitchen and cooked.'

'Oh no,' cried Winifred.

'We're going to draw him,' said Gudrun.

'Draw him and quarter him and dish him up,' he said, being purposely fatuous.

'Oh no,' cried Winifred with emphasis, chuckling.

Gudrun detected the tang of mockery in him, and she looked up and smiled into his face. He felt his nerves caressed. Their eyes met in knowledge.

'How do you like Shortlands?' he asked.

'Oh, very much,' she said, with nonchalance.

'Glad you do. Have you noticed these flowers?'

He led her along the path. She followed intently. Winifred came, and the governess lingered in the rear. They stopped before some veined salpiglossis flowers.

'Aren't they wonderful?' she cried, looking at them absorbedly. Strange how her reverential, almost ecstatic admiration of the flowers caressed his nerves. She stooped down, and touched the trumpets, with infinitely fine and delicate-touching finger-tips. It filled him with ease to see her. When she rose, her eyes, hot with the beauty of the flowers, looked into his.

'What are they?' she asked.

'Sort of petunia, I suppose,' he answered. 'I don't really know them.'

'They are quite strangers to me,' she said.

They stood together in a false intimacy, a nervous contact. And he was in love with her.

She was aware of Mademoiselle standing near, like a little French beetle, observant and calculating. She moved away with Winifred, saying they would go to find Bismarck.

Gerald watched them go, looking all the while at the soft, full, still body of Gudrun, in its silky cashmere. How silky and rich and soft her body must be. An excess of appreciation came over his mind, she was the all-desirable, the all-beautiful. He wanted only to come to her, nothing more. He was only this, this being that should come to her, and be given to her.

At the same time he was finely and acutely aware of Mademoiselle's neat, brittle finality of form. She was like some elegant beetle with thin ankles, perched on her high heels, her glossy black dress perfectly correct, her dark hair done high and admirably. How repulsive her completeness and her finality was! He loathed her.

Yet he did admire her. She was perfectly correct. And it did rather annoy him, that Gudrun came dressed in startling colours, like a macaw, when the family was in mourning. Like a macaw she was! He watched the lingering way she took her feet from the ground. And her ankles were pale yellow, and her dress a deep blue. Yet it pleased him. It pleased him very much. He felt the challenge in her very attire—she challenged the whole world. And he smiled as to the note of a trumpet.

Gudrun and Winifred went through the house to the back, where were the stables and the out-buildings. Everywhere was still and deserted. Mr Crich had gone out for a short drive, the stable-man had just led round Gerald's horse. The two girls went to the hutch that stood in a corner, and looked at the great black-and-white rabbit.

'Isn't he beautiful! Oh, do look at him listening! Doesn't he look silly!' she laughed quickly, then added: 'Oh, do let's do him listening, do let us, he listens with so much of himself;—don't you, darling Bismarck?'

'Can we take him out?' said Gudrun.

'He's very strong. He really is extremely strong.' She looked at Gudrun, her head on one side, in odd calculating mistrust.

'But we'll try, shall we?'

'Yes, if you like. But he's a fearful kicker!'

They took the key to unlock the door. The rabbit exploded in a wild rush round the hutch.

'He scratches most awfully sometimes,' cried Winifred in excitement. 'Oh, do look at him, isn't he wonderful!' The rabbit tore round the hutch in a flurry. 'Bismarck!' cried the child, in rousing excitement. 'How *dreadful* you are! You are beastly.' Winifred looked up at Gudrun with some misgiving in her wild excitement. Gudrun smiled sardonically with her mouth. Winifred made a strange crooning noise of unaccountable excitement. 'Now he's still!' she cried, seeing the rabbit settled down in a far corner of the hutch. 'Shall we take him now?' she whispered excitedly, mysteriously, looking up at Gudrun and edging very close. 'Shall we get him now?—' she chuckled wickedly to herself.

They unlocked the door of the hutch. Gudrun thrust in her arm and seized the great, lusty rabbit as it crouched still, she grasped its long ears. It set its four feet flat, and thrust back. There was a long scraping sound as it was hauled forward, and in another instant it was in mid-air, lunging wildly, its body flying like a spring coiled and released, as it lashed out, suspended from the ears. Gudrun held the black-and-white tempest at arms' length, averting her face. But the rabbit was magically strong, it was all she could do to keep her grasp. She almost lost her presence of mind.

'Bismarck, Bismarck, you are behaving terribly,' said Winifred in a rather frightened voice. 'Oh, do put him down, he's beastly.'

Gudrun stood for a moment astounded by the thunderstorm that had sprung into being in her grip. Then her colour came up, a heavy rage came over her like a cloud. She stood shaken as a house in a storm, and utterly overcome. Her heart was arrested with fury at the mindlessness and the bestial stupidity of this struggle, her wrists were badly scored by the claws of the beast, a heavy cruelty welled up in her.

Gerald came round as she was trying to capture the flying rabbit under her arm. He saw, with subtle recognition, her sullen passion of cruelty.

'You should let one of the men do that for you,' he said, hurrying up.

'Oh, he's *so* horrid!' cried Winifred, almost frantic.

He held out his nervous, sinewy hand and took the rabbit by the ears from Gudrun.

'It's most *fearfully* strong,' she cried in a high voice, like the crying of a seagull, strange and vindictive.

The rabbit made itself into a ball in the air and lashed out, flinging itself into a bow. It really seemed demoniacal. Gudrun saw Gerald's body tighten, saw a sharp blindness come into his eyes.

'I know these beggars of old,' he said.

The long, demon-like beast lashed out again, spread on the air as if it were flying, looking something like a dragon, then closing up again, inconceivably powerful and explosive. The man's body, strung to its efforts, vibrated strongly. Then a sudden sharp, white-edged wrath came up in him. Swift as lightning he drew back and brought his free hand down like a hawk on the neck of the rabbit. Simultaneously, there came the unearthly abhorrent scream of a rabbit in the fear of death. It made one immense writhe, tore his wrists and his sleeves in a final convulsion, all its belly flashed white in a whirlwind of paws, and then he had slung it round and had it under his arm, fast. It cowered and skulked. His face was gleaming with a smile.

'You wouldn't think there was all that force in a rabbit,' he said, looking at Gudrun. And he saw her eyes black as night in her pallid face, she looked almost unearthly. The scream of the rabbit, after the violent tussle, seemed to have torn the veil of her consciousness. He looked at her, and the whitish, electric gleam in his face intensified.

'I don't really like him,' Winifred was crooning. 'I don't care for him as I do for Loozie. He's hateful really.'

A smile twisted Gudrun's face as she recovered. She knew she was revealed.

'Don't they make the most fearful noise when they scream?' she cried, the high note in her voice like a seagull's cry.

'Abominable,' he said.

'He shouldn't be so silly when he has to be taken out,' Winifred was saying, putting out her hand and touching the rabbit tentatively, as it skulked under his arm, motionless as if it were dead.

'He's not dead, is he, Gerald?' she asked.

'No, he ought to be,' he said.

'Yes, he ought!' cried the child, with a sudden flush of amusement. And she touched the rabbit with more confidence. 'His heart is beating *so* fast. Isn't he funny? He really is.'

'Where do you want him?' asked Gerald.

'In the little green court,' she said.

Gudrun looked at Gerald with strange, darkened eyes, strained with underworld knowledge, almost supplicating, like those of a creature which is at his mercy, yet which is his ultimate victor. He did not know what to say to her. He felt the mutual hellish recognition. And he felt he ought to say something to cover it. He had the power of lightning in his nerves, she seemed like a soft recipient of his magical, hideous white fire. He was unconfident, he had qualms of fear.

'Did he hurt you?' he asked.

'No,' she said.

'He's an insensible beast,' he said, turning his face away.

They came to the little court, which was shut in by old red walls in whose crevices wallflowers were growing. The grass was soft and fine and old, a level floor carpeting the court, the sky was blue overhead. Gerald tossed the rabbit down. It crouched still and would not move. Gudrun watched it with faint horror.

'Why doesn't it move?' she cried.

'It's skulking,' he said.

She looked up at him, and a slight sinister smile contracted her white face.

'Isn't it a *fool*!' she cried. 'Isn't it a sickening *fool*?' The vindictive mockery in her voice made his brain quiver. Glancing up at him, into his eyes, she revealed again the mocking, white-cruel recognition. There was a league between them, abhorrent to them both. They were implicated with each other in abhorrent mysteries.

'How many scratches have you?' he asked, showing his hard forearm, white and hard and torn in red gashes.

'How really vile!' she cried, flushing with a sinister vision. 'Mine is nothing.'

She lifted her arm and showed a deep red score down the silken white flesh.

'What a devil!' he exclaimed. But it was as if he had had knowledge of her in the long red rent of her forearm, so silken and soft. He did not want to touch her. He would have to make himself touch her, deliberately. The long, shallow red rip seemed torn across his own brain, tearing the surface of his ultimate consciousness, letting through the for ever unconscious, unthinkable red ether of the beyond, the obscene beyond.

'It doesn't hurt you very much, does it?' he asked, solicitous.

'Not at all,' she cried.

And suddenly the rabbit, which had been crouching as if
it were a flower, so still and soft, suddenly burst into life.
Round and round the court it went, as if shot from a gun,
round and round like a furry meteorite, in a tense hard circle
that seemed to bind their brains. They all stood in amazement, smiling uncannily, as if the rabbit were obeying some
unknown incantation. Round and round it flew, on the grass
under the old red walls like a storm.

And then quite suddenly it settled down, hobbled among
the grass, and sat considering, its nose twitching like a bit of
fluff in the wind. After having considered for a few minutes, a soft bunch with a black, open eye, which perhaps was
looking at them, perhaps was not, it hobbled calmly forward
and began to nibble the grass with that mean motion of a
rabbit's quick eating.

'It's mad,' said Gudrun. 'It is most decidedly mad.'

He laughed.

'The question is,' he said, 'what is madness? I don't suppose it is rabbit-mad.'

'Don't you think it is?' she asked.

'No. That's what it is to be a rabbit.'

There was a queer, faint, obscene smile over his face. She
looked at him and was him, and knew that he was initiate as
she was initiate. This thwarted her, and contravened her, for
the moment.

'God be praised we aren't rabbits,' she said in a high,
shrill voice.

The smile intensified a little on his face.

'Not rabbits?' he said, looking at her fixedly.

Slowly her face relaxed into a smile of obscene recognition.

'Ah, Gerald,' she said in a strong, slow, almost man-like
way. '—All that, and more.' Her eyes looked up at him with
shocking nonchalance.

He felt again as if she had hit him across the face—or
rather as if she had torn him across the breast, dully, finally.
He turned aside.

'Eat, eat, my darling!' Winifred was softly conjuring the rabbit, and creeping forward to touch it. It hobbled away from her. 'Let its mother stroke its fur then, darling, because it is so mysterious—'

19

Moony

After his illness Birkin went to the south of France for a time. He did not write, nobody heard anything of him. Ursula, left alone, felt as if everything were lapsing out. There seemed to be no hope in the world. One was a tiny little rock with the tide of nothingness rising higher and higher. She herself was real, and only herself—just like a rock in a wash of flood-water. The rest was all nothingness. She was hard and indifferent, isolated in herself.

There was nothing for it now, but contemptuous, resistant indifference. All the world was lapsing into a grey wish-wash of nothingness, she had no contact and no connexion anywhere. She despised and detested the whole show. From the bottom of her heart, from the bottom of her soul, she despised and detested people, adult people. She loved only children and animals: children she loved passionately, but coldly. They made her want to hug them, to protect them, to give them life. But this very love, based on pity and despair, was only a bondage and a pain to her. She loved best of all the animals, that were single and unsocial as she herself was. She loved the horses and cows in the field. Each was single and to itself, magical. It was not referred away to some detestable social principle. It was incapable of soulfulness and tragedy, which she detested so profoundly.

She could be very pleasant and flattering, almost subservient, to people she met. But no one was taken in. Instinctively each felt her contemptuous mockery of the human being in himself, or herself. She had a profound grudge against the human being. That which the word 'human' stood for was despicable and repugnant to her.

Mostly her heart was closed in this hidden, unconscious

strain of contemptuous ridicule. She thought she loved, she thought she was full of love. This was her idea of herself. But the strange brightness of her presence, a marvellous radiance of intrinsic vitality, was a luminousness of supreme repudiation, nothing but repudiation.

Yet, at moments, she yielded and softened, she wanted pure love, only pure love. This other, this state of constant unfailing repudiation, was a strain, a suffering also. A terrible desire for pure love overcame her again.

She went out one evening, numbed by this constant essential suffering. Those who are timed for destruction must die now. The knowledge of this reached a finality, a finishing in her. And the finality released her. If fate would carry off in death or downfall all those who were timed to go, why need she trouble, why repudiate any further? She was free of it all, she could seek a new union elsewhere.

Ursula set off to Willey Green, towards the mill. She came to Willey Water. It was almost full again, after its period of emptiness. Then she turned off through the woods. The night had fallen, it was dark. But she forgot to be afraid, she who had such great sources of fear. Among the trees, far from any human beings, there was a sort of magic peace. The more one could find a pure loneliness, with no taint of people, the better one felt. She was in reality terrified, horrified in her apprehension of people.

She started, noticing something on her right hand, between the tree-trunks. It was like a great presence, watching her, dodging her. She started violently. It was only the moon, risen through the thin trees. But it seemed so mysterious, with its white and deathly smile. And there was no avoiding it. Night or day, one could not escape the sinister face, triumphant and radiant like this moon, with a high smile. She hurried on, cowering from the white planet. She would just see the pond at the mill before she went home.

Not wanting to go through the yard, because of the dogs, she turned off along the hillside to descend on the pond from above. The moon was transcendent over the bare, open space, she suffered from being exposed to it. There was a glimmer of nightly rabbits across the ground. The night was as clear as crystal, and very still. She could hear a distant coughing of a sheep.

So she swerved down to the steep, tree-hidden bank above the pond, where the alders twisted their roots. She was glad to pass into the shade out of the moon. There she stood, at the top of the fallen-away bank, her hand on the rough trunk of a tree, looking at the water, that was perfect in its stillness, floating the moon upon it. But for some reason she disliked it. It did not give her anything. She listened for the hoarse rustle of the sluice. And she wished for something else out of the night, she wanted another night, not this moon-brilliant hardness. She could feel her soul crying out in her, lamenting desolately.

She saw a shadow moving by the water. It would be Birkin. He had come back then, unawares. She accepted it without remark, nothing mattered to her. She sat down among the roots of the alder tree, dim and veiled, hearing the sound of the sluice like dew distilling audibly into the night. The islands were dark and half revealed, the reeds were dark also, only some of them had a little frail fire reflection. A fish leaped secretly, revealing the light in the pond. This fire of the chill night breaking constantly on to the pure darkness, repelled her. She wished it were perfectly dark, perfectly, and noiseless and without motion. Birkin, small and dark also, his hair tinged with moonlight, wandered nearer. He was quite near, and yet he did not exist in her. He did not know she was there. Supposing he did something he would not wish to be seen doing, thinking he was quite private? But there, what did it matter? What did the small privacies matter? How could it matter, what he did? How can there be any secrets, we are all the same organisms? How can there be any secrecy, when everything is known to all of us?

He was touching unconsciously the dead husks of flowers as he passed by, and talking disconnectedly to himself.

'You can't go away,' he was saying. 'There *is* no away. You only withdraw upon yourself.'

He threw a dead flower-husk on to the water.

'An antiphony—they lie, and you sing back to them.

There wouldn't have to be any truth, if there weren't any
lies. Then one needn't assert anything—'

He stood still, looking at the water, and throwing upon it
the husks of the flowers.

'Cybele—curse her! The accursed *Syria Dea*! Does one
begrudge it her! What else is there—?'

Ursula wanted to laugh loudly and hysterically, hearing
his isolated voice speaking out. It was so ridiculous.

He stood staring at the water. Then he stooped and picked
up a stone, which he threw sharply at the pond. Ursula was
aware of the bright moon leaping and swaying, all distorted,
in her eyes. It seemed to shoot out arms of fire like a cuttle-
fish, like a luminous polyp, palpitating strongly before her.

And his shadow on the border of the pond was watching
for a few moments, then he stooped and groped on the
ground. Then again there was a burst of sound, and a burst
of brilliant light, the moon had exploded on the water, and
was flying asunder in flakes of white and dangerous fire.
Rapidly, like white birds, the fires all broken rose across the
pond, fleeing in clamorous confusion, battling with a flock
of dark waves that were forcing their way in. The furthest
waves of light, fleeing out, seemed to be clamouring against
the shore for escape, the waves of darkness came in heavily,
running under towards the centre. But at the centre, the heart
of all, was still a vivid, incandescent quivering of a white
moon not quite destroyed, a white body of fire writhing and
striving and not even now broken open, not yet violated. It
seemed to be drawing itself together with strange, violent
pangs, in blind effort. It was getting stronger, it was reas-
serting itself, the inviolable moon. And the rays were hastening in in thin lines of light, to return to the strengthened
moon, that shook upon the water in triumphant reassump-
tion.

Birkin stood and watched, motionless, till the pond was
almost calm, the moon was almost serene. Then, satisfied of
so much, he looked for more stones. She felt his invisible tenacity. And in a moment again, the broken lights scattered in
explosion over her face, dazzling her; and then, almost immediately, came the second shot. The moon leapt up white
and burst through the air. Darts of bright light shot asunder,

darkness swept over the centre. There was no moon, only a battlefield of broken lights and shadows, running close together. Shadows, dark and heavy, struck again and again across the place where the heart of the moon had been, obliterating it altogether. The white fragments pulsed up and down, and could not find where to go, apart and brilliant on the water like the petals of a rose that a wind has blown far and wide.

Yet again, they were flickering their way to the centre, finding the path blindly, enviously. And again, all was still, as Birkin and Ursula watched. The waters were loud on the shore. He saw the moon regathering itself insidiously, saw the heart of the rose intertwining vigorously and blindly, calling back the scattered fragments, winning home the fragments, in a pulse and in effort of return.

And he was not satisfied. Like a madness, he must go on. He got large stones, and threw them, one after the other, at the white-burning centre of the moon, till there was nothing but a rocking of hollow noise, and a pond surged up, no moon any more, only a few broken flakes tangled and glittering broadcast in the darkness, without aim or meaning, a darkened confusion, like a black and white kaleidoscope tossed at random. The hollow night was rocking and crashing with noise, and from the sluice came sharp, regular flashes of sound. Flakes of light appeared here and there, glittering tormented among the shadows, far off, in strange places; among the dripping shadow of the willow on the island. Birkin stood and listened and was satisfied.

Ursula was dazed, her mind was all gone. She felt she had fallen to the ground and was spilled out, like water on the earth. Motionless and spent she remained in the gloom. Though even now she was aware, unseeing, that in the darkness was a little tumult of ebbing flakes of light, a cluster dancing secretly in a round, twining and coming steadily together. They were gathering a heart again, they were coming once more into being. Gradually the fragments caught together reunited, heaving, rocking, dancing, falling back as in panic, but working their way home again persistently, making semblance of fleeing away when they had advanced, but always flickering nearer, a little closer to the mark, the cluster growing mysteriously larger and brighter, as gleam after gleam fell in with the whole, until a ragged rose, a distorted, frayed moon was shaking upon the waters again, reasserted, renewed, trying to recover from its convulsion, to get over the disfigurement and the agitation, to be whole and composed, at peace.

Birkin lingered vaguely by the water. Ursula was afraid that he would stone the moon again. She slipped from her seat and went down to him, saying:

'You won't throw stones at it any more, will you?'

'How long have you been there?'

'All the time. You won't throw any more stones, will you?'

'I wanted to see if I could make it be quite gone off the pond,' he said.

'Yes, it was horrible, really. Why should you hate the moon? It hasn't done you any harm, has it?'

'Was it hate?' he said.

And they were silent for a few minutes.

'When did you come back?' she said.

'Today.'

'Why did you never write?'

'I could find nothing to say.'

'Why was there nothing to say?'

'I don't know. Why are there no daffodils now?'

'No.'

Again there was a space of silence. Ursula looked at the moon. It had gathered itself together, and was quivering slightly.

'Was it good for you to be alone?' she asked.

'Perhaps. Not that I know much. But I got over a good deal. Did you do anything important?'

'No. I looked at England, and thought I'd done with it.'

'Why England?' he asked in surprise.

'I don't know, it came like that.'

'It isn't a question of nations,' he said. 'France is far worse.'

'Yes, I know. I felt I'd done with it all.'

They went and sat down on the roots of the trees, in the shadow. And being silent, he remembered the beauty of her eyes, which were sometimes filled with light, like spring, suffused with wonderful promise. So he said to her, slowly, with difficulty:

'There is a golden light in you, which I wish you would give me.' It was as if he had been thinking of this for some time.

She was startled, she seemed to leap clear of him. Yet also she was pleased.

'What kind of a light?' she asked.

But he was shy, and did not say any more. So the moment passed for this time. And gradually a feeling of sorrow came over her.

'My life is unfulfilled,' she said.

'Yes,' he answered briefly, not wanting to hear this.

'And I feel as if nobody could ever really love me,' she said.

But he did not answer.

'You think, don't you,' she said slowly, 'that I only want physical things? It isn't true. I want you to serve my spirit.'

'I know you do. I know you don't want physical things by themselves. But, I want you to give me—to give your spirit to me—that golden light which is you—which you don't know—give it me—'

After a moment's silence she replied:

'But how can I, you don't love me! You only want your own ends. You don't want to serve *me*, and yet you want me to serve you. It is so one-sided!'

It was a great effort to him to maintain this conversation, and to press for the thing he wanted from her, the surrender of her spirit.

'It is different,' he said. 'The two kinds of service are so different. I serve you in another way—not through *yourself*—somewhere else. But I want us to be together without bothering about ourselves—to be really together because we *are* together, as if it were a phenomenon, not a thing we have to maintain by our own effort.'

'No,' she said, pondering. 'You are just egocentric. You never have any enthusiasm, you never come out with any spark towards me. You want yourself, really, and your own affairs. And you want me just to be there, to serve you.'

But this only made him shut off from her.

'Ah well,' he said, 'words make no matter, anyway. The thing *is* between us, or it isn't.'

'You don't even love me,' she cried.

'I do,' he said angrily. 'But I want—' His mind saw again the lovely golden light of spring transfused through her eyes, as through some wonderful window. And he wanted her to be with him there, in this world of proud indifference. But what was the good of telling her he wanted this company in proud indifference. What was the good of talking, anyway? It must happen beyond the sound of words. It was merely ruinous to try to work her by conviction. This was a paradisal bird that could never be netted, it must fly by itself to the heart.

'I always think I am going to be loved—and then I am let down. You *don't* love me, you know. You don't want to serve me. You only want yourself.'

A shiver of rage went over his veins, at this repeated: 'You don't want to serve me.' All the paradisal disappeared from him.

'No,' he said, irritated, 'I don't want to serve you, because there is nothing there to serve. What you want me to serve is nothing, mere nothing. It isn't even you, it is your mere female quality. And I wouldn't give a straw for your female ego—it's a rag doll.'

'Ha!' she laughed in mockery. 'That's all you think of me, is it? And then you have the impudence to say you love me!'

She rose in anger, to go home.

'You want the paradisal unknowing,' she said, turning round on him as he still sat half visible in the shadow. 'I know what that means, thank you. You want me to be your thing, never to criticize you or to have anything to say for myself. You want me to be a mere *thing* for you! No, thank you! *If* you want that, there are plenty of women who will give it to you. There are plenty of women who will lie down for you to walk over them—*go* to them then, if that's what you want—go to them.'

'No,' he said, outspoken with anger. 'I want you to drop your assertive *will*, your frightened apprehensive self-insistence, that is what I want. I want you to trust yourself so implicitly that you can let yourself go.'

'Let myself go!' she re-echoed in mockery. '*I* can let myself go easily enough. It is you who can't let yourself go, it is you who hang on to yourself as if it were your only treasure. *You*—*you* are the Sunday school teacher—*You*—you preacher.'

The amount of truth that was in this made him stiff and unheeding of her.

'I don't mean let yourself go in the Dionysic ecstatic way,' he said. 'I know you can do that. But I hate ecstasy, Dionysic or any other. It's like going round in a squirrel cage, I want you not to care about yourself, just to be there and not to care about yourself, not to insist—be glad and sure and indifferent.'

'Who insists?' she mocked. 'Who is it that keeps on insisting? It isn't *me*!'

There was a weary, mocking bitterness in her voice. He was silent for some time.

'I know,' he said. 'While ever either of us insists to the other, we are all wrong. But there we are, the accord doesn't come.'

They sat in stillness under the shadow of the trees by the bank. The night was white around them, they were in the darkness, barely conscious.

Gradually, the stillness and peace came over them. She put her hand tentatively on his. Their hands clasped softly and silently in peace.

'Do you really love me?' she said.

He laughed.

'I call that your war-cry,' he replied, amused.

'Why!' she cried, amused and really wondering.

'Your insistence—Your war-cry—"A Brangwen, A Brangwen"—an old battle-cry. Yours is "Do you love me? Yield knave, or die" '

'No,' she said, pleading, 'not like that. Not like that. But I must know that you love me, mustn't I?'

'Well then, know it and have done with it.'

'But do you?'

'Yes, I do. I love you, and I know it's final. It is final, so why say any more about it.'

She was silent for some moments, in delight and doubt.

'Are you sure?' she said, nestling happily near to him.

'Quite sure—so now have done—accept it and have done.'

She was nestled quite close to him.

'Have done with what?' she murmured happily.

'With bothering,' he said.

She clung nearer to him. He held her close, and kissed her softly, gently. It was such peace and heavenly freedom, just to fold her and kiss her gently, and not to have any thoughts or any desires or any will, just to be still with her, to be perfectly still and together, in a peace that was not sleep, but content in bliss. To be content in bliss, without desire or insistence anywhere, this was heaven: to be together in happy stillness.

For a long time she nestled to him, and he kissed her softly, her hair, her face, her ears, gently, softly, like dew falling. But this warm breath on her ears disturbed her again, kindled the old destructive fires. She cleaved to him, and he could feel his blood changing like quicksilver.

'But we'll be still, shall we?' he said.

'Yes,' she said, as if submissively.

And she continued to nestle against him.

But in a little while she drew away and looked at him.

'I must be going home,' she said.

"Must you—how sad,' he replied.

She leaned forward and put up her mouth to be kissed.

'Are you really sad?' she murmured, smiling.

'Yes,' he said, 'I wish we could stay as we were, always.'

'Always! Do you?' she murmured, as he kissed her. And then, out of a full throat, she crooned: 'Kiss me! Kiss me!' And she cleaved close to him. He kissed her many times. But he too had his idea and his will. He wanted only gentle communion, no other, no passion now. So that soon she drew away, put on her hat and went home.

The next day, however, he felt wistful and yearning. He thought he had been wrong, perhaps. Perhaps he had been wrong to go to her with an idea of what he wanted. Was it really only an idea, or was it the interpretation of a profound yearning? If the latter, how was it he was always talking about sensual fulfilment? The two did not agree very well.

Suddenly he found himself face to face with a situation. It was as simple as this: fatally simple. On the one hand, he knew he did not want a further sensual experience—something deeper, darker, than ordinary life could give. He remembered the African fetishes he had seen at Halliday's so often. There came back to him one, a statuette about two feet high, a tall, slim, elegant figure from West Africa, in dark wood, glossy and suave. It was a woman, with hair dressed high, like a melon-shaped dome. He remembered her vividly: she was one of his soul's intimates. Her body was long and elegant, her face was crushed tiny like a beetle's, she had rows of round heavy collars, like a column of quoits, on her neck. He remembered her: her astonishing cultured elegance, her diminished, beetle face, the astounding long elegant body, on short, ugly legs, with such protuberant buttocks, so weighty and unexpected below her slim long loins. She knew what he himself did not know. She had thousands of years of purely sensual, purely unspiritual knowledge behind her. It must have been thousands of years since her race had died, mystically: that is, since the relation between the senses and the outspoken mind had broken, leaving the experience all in one sort, mystically sensual. Thousands of years ago, that which was imminent in himself must have taken place in these Africans: the goodness, the holiness, the desire for creation and productive happiness must have lapsed, leaving the single impulse for knowledge in one sort, mindless progressive knowledge through the senses, knowledge arrested and ending in the senses, mystic knowledge in disintegration and dissolution, knowledge such as the beetles have, which live purely within the world of corruption and cold dissolution. This was why her face looked like a beetle's: this was why the Egyptians worshipped the ball-rolling scarab: because of the principle of knowledge in dissolution and corruption.

There is a long way we can travel, after the death-break: after that point when the soul in intense suffering breaks, breaks away from its organic hold like a leaf that falls. We fall from the connexion with life and hope, we lapse from pure integral being, from creation and liberty, and we fall

into the long, long African process of purely sensual understanding, knowledge in the mystery of dissolution.

He realized now that this is a long process—thousands of
years it takes, after the death of the creative spirit. He realized that there were great mysteries to be unsealed, sensual,
mindless, dreadful mysteries, far beyond the phallic cult.
How far, in their inverted culture, had these West Africans
gone beyond phallic knowledge? Very, very far. Birkin recalled again the female figure: the elongated, long, long
body, the curious unexpected heavy buttocks, the long, imprisoned neck, the face with tiny features like a beetle's.
This was far beyond any phallic knowledge, sensual subtle
realities far beyond the scope of phallic investigation.

There remained this way, this awful African process, to be
fulfilled. It would be done differently by white races. The
white races, having the Arctic north behind them, the vast
abstraction of ice and snow, would fulfil a mystery of ice-
destructive knowledge, snow-abstract annihilation. Whereas
the West Africans, controlled by the burning death-
abstraction of the Sahara, had been fulfilled in sun-
destruction, the putrescent mystery of sun-rays.

Was this then all that remained? Was there left now nothing but to break off from the happy creative being, was the
time up? Is our day of creative life finished? Does there remain to us only the strange, awful afterwards of the knowledge in dissolution, the African knowledge, but different in
us, who are blond and blue-eyed from the north?

Birkin thought of Gerald. He was one of these strange
white wonderful demons from the north, fulfilled in the destructive frost mystery. And was he fated to pass away in
this knowledge, this one process of frost-knowledge, death
by perfect cold? Was he a messenger, an omen of the universal dissolution into whiteness and snow?

Birkin was frightened. He was tired too, when he had
reached this length of speculation. Suddenly his strange,
strained attention gave way, he could not attend to these
mysteries any more. There was another way, the way of
freedom. There was the paradisal entry into pure, single being, the individual soul taking precedence over love and desire for union, stronger than any pangs of emotion, a lovely

state of free proud singleness, which accepted the obligation of the permanent connexion with others, and with the other, submits to the yoke and leash of love, but never forfeits its own proud individual singleness, even while it loves and yields.

There was the other way, the remaining way. And he must run to follow it. He thought of Ursula, how sensitive and delicate she really was, her skin so over-fine, as if one skin were wanting. She was really so marvellously gentle and sensitive. Why did he ever forget it? He must go to her at once. He must ask her to marry him. They must marry at once, and so make a definite pledge, enter into a definite communion. He must set out at once and ask her, this moment. There was no moment to spare.

He drifted on swiftly to Beldover, half unconscious of his own movement. He saw the town on the slope of the hill, not straggling, but as if walled-in with the straight, final streets of miners' dwellings, making a great square, and it looked like Jerusalem to his fancy. The world was all strange and transcendent.

Rosalind opened the door to him. She started slightly, as a young girl will, and said:

'Oh, I'll tell father.'

With which she disappeared, leaving Birkin in the hall, looking at some reproductions from Picasso, lately introduced by Gudrun. He was admiring the almost wizard, sensuous apprehension of the earth, when Will Brangwen appeared, rolling down his shirt-sleeves.

'Well,' said Brangwen, 'I'll get a coat.' And he too disappeared for a moment. Then he returned and opened the door of the drawing-room, saying:

'You must excuse me, I was just doing a bit of work in the shed. Come inside, will you?'

Birkin entered and sat down. He looked at the bright, reddish face of the other man, at the narrow brow and the very bright eyes, and at the rather sensual lips that unrolled wide and expansive under the black cropped moustache. How curious it was that this was a human being! What Brangwen thought himself to be, how meaningless it was, confronted with the reality of him. Birkin could see only a strange, in-

explicable, almost patternless collection of passions and desires and suppressions and traditions and mechanical ideas,
all cast unfused and disunited into this slender, bright-faced
man of nearly fifty, who was as unresolved now as he was
at twenty, and as uncreated. How could he be the parent of
Ursula, when he was not created himself? He was not a parent. A slip of living flesh had been transmitted through him,
but the spirit had not come from him. The spirit had not
come from any ancester, it had come out of the unknown. A
child is the child of the mystery, or it is uncreated.

'The weather's not so bad as it has been,' said Brangwen,
after waiting a moment. There was no connexion between
the two men.

'No,' said Birkin. 'It was full moon two days ago.'

'Oh! You believe in the moon then, affecting the
weather?'

'No, I don't think I do. I don't really know enough about
it.'

'You know what they say? The moon and the weather
may change together, but the change of the moon won't
change the weather.'

'Is that it?' said Birkin. 'I hadn't heard it.'

There was a pause. Then Birkin said:

'Am I hindering you? I called to see Ursula, really. Is she
at home?'

'I don't believe she is. I believe she's gone to the library.
I'll just see.'

Birkin could hear him inquiring in the dining-room.

'No,' he said, coming back. 'But she won't be long. You
wanted to speak to her?'

Birkin looked across at the other man with curious calm,
clear eyes.

'As a matter of fact,' he said, 'I wanted to ask her to
marry me.'

A point of light came on the golden-brown eyes of the elder man.

'O-oh?' he said, looking at Birkin, then dropping his eyes
before the calm, steadily watching look of the other. 'Was
she expecting you then?'

'No,' said Birkin.

'No? I didn't know anything of this sort was on foot—' Brangwen smiled awkwardly.

Birkin looked back at him, and said to himself: 'I wonder why it should be "on foot"!' Aloud he said:

'No, it's perhaps rather sudden.' At which, thinking of his relationship with Ursula, he added—'but I don't know—'

'Quite sudden, is it? Oh!' said Brangwen, rather baffled and annoyed.

'In one way,' replied Birkin, '—not in another.'

There was a moment's pause, after which Brangwen said:

'Well, she pleases herself—'

'Oh yes!' said Birkin calmly.

A vibration came into Brangwen's strong voice as he replied:

'Though I shouldn't want her to be in too big a hurry, either. It's no good looking round afterwards, when it's too late.'

'Oh, it need never be too late,' said Birkin, 'as far as that goes.'

'How do you mean?' asked the father.

'If one repents being married, the marriage is at an end,' said Birkin.

'You think so?'

'Yes.'

'Ay, well, that may be your way of looking at it.'

Birkin, in silence, thought to himself: 'So it may. As for *your* way of looking at it, William Brangwen, it needs a little explaining.'

'I suppose,' said Brangwen, 'you know what sort of people we are? What sort of a bringing-up she's had?'

' "She",' thought Birkin to himself, remembering his childhood's corrections, 'is the cat's mother.'

'Do I know what sort of a bringing-up she's had?' he said aloud.

He seemed to annoy Brangwen intentionally.

'Well,' he said, 'she's had everything that's right for a girl to have—as far as possible, as far as we could give it her.'

'I'm sure she has,' said Birkin, which caused a perilous full-stop. The father was becoming exasperated. There was something naturally irritant to him in Birkin's mere presence.

'And I don't want to see her going back on it all,' he said, in a clanging voice.

'Why?' said Birkin.

This monosyllable exploded in Brangwen's brain like a shot.

'Why! I don't believe in your new-fangled ways and new-fangled ideas—in and out like a frog in a gallipot. It would never do for me.'

Birkin watched him with steady emotionless eyes. The radical antagonism in the two men was rousing.

'Yes, but are my ways and ideas new-fangled?' asked Birkin.

'Are they?' Brangwen caught himself up. 'I'm not speaking of you in particular,' he said. 'What I mean is that my children have been brought up to think and do according to the religion I was brought up in myself, and I don't want to see them going away from *that*.'

There was a dangerous pause.

'And beyond that—?' asked Birkin.

The father hesitated, he was in a nasty position.

'Eh? What do you mean? All I want to say is that my daughter'—he tailed off into silence, overcome by futility. He knew that in some way he was off the track.

'Of course,' said Birkin, 'I don't want to hurt anybody or influence anybody. Ursula does exactly as she pleases.'

There was a complete silence, because of the utter failure in mutual understanding. Birkin felt bored. Her father was not a coherent human being, he was a roomful of old echoes. The eyes of the younger man rested on the face of the elder. Brangwen looked up, and saw Birkin looking at him. His face was covered with inarticulate anger and humiliation and sense of inferiority in strength.

'And as for beliefs, that's one thing,' he said. 'But I'd rather see my daughters dead tomorrow than that they should be at the beck and call of the first man that likes to come and whistle for them.'

A queer painful light came into Birkin's eyes.

'As to that,' he said, 'I only know that it's much more

likely that it's I who am the beck and call of the woman, than she at mine.'

Again there was a pause. The father was somewhat bewildered.

'I know,' he said, 'she'll please herself—she always has done. I've done my best for them, but that doesn't matter. They've got themselves to please, and if they can help it they'll please nobody *but* themselves. But she's a right to consider her mother, and me as well—'

Brangwen was thinking his own thoughts.

'And I tell you this much, I would rather bury them than see them getting into a lot of loose ways such as you see everywhere nowadays. I'd rather bury them—'

'Yes, but, you see,' said Birkin slowly, rather wearily, bored again by this new turn, 'they won't give either you or me the chance to bury them, because they're not to be buried.'

Brangwen looked at him in a sudden flare of impotent anger.

'Now, Mr Birkin,' he said, 'I don't know what you're asking for. But my daughters are my daughters—and it's *my* business to look after them while I can.'

Birkin's brows knitted suddenly, his eyes concentrated in mockery. But he remained perfectly stiff and still. There was a pause.

'I've nothing against your marrying Ursula,' Brangwen began at length. 'It's got nothing to do with me, she'll do as she likes, me or no me.'

Birkin turned away, looking out of the window and letting go his consciousness. After all, what good was this? It was hopeless to keep it up. He would sit on till Ursula came home, then speak to her, then go away. He would not accept trouble at the hands of her father. It was all unnecessary, and he himself need not have provoked it.

The two men sat in complete silence, Birkin almost unconscious of his own whereabouts. He had come to ask her to marry him—well then, he would wait on, and ask her. As for what she said, whether she accepted or not, he did not think about it. He would say what he had come to say, and that was all he was conscious of. He accepted the complete insignificance of this household for him. But everything now was as if fated. He could see one thing ahead, and no more. From the rest, he was absolved entirely for the time being. It had to be left to fate and chance to resolve the issues.

At length they heard the gate. They saw her coming up the steps with a bundle of books under her arm. Her face was bright and abstracted as usual, with the abstraction, that look of being not quite *there,* not quite present to the facts of reality, that galled her father so much. She had a maddening faculty of assuming a light of her own, which excluded the reality, and within which she looked radiant as if in sunshine.

They heard her go into the dining-room and drop her armful of books on the table.

'Did you bring me that Girl's Own?' cried Rosalind.

'Yes, I brought it. But I forgot which one it was you wanted.'

'You would,' cried Rosalind angrily. 'It's right for a wonder.'

Then they heard her say something in a lowered tone.

'Where?' cried Ursula.

Again her sister's voice was muffled.

Brangwen opened the door and called in his strong, brazen voice:

'Ursula.'

She appeared in a moment, wearing her hat.

'Oh, how do you do!' she cried, seeing Birkin, and all dazzled as if taken by surprise. He wondered at her, knowing she was aware of his presence. She had her queer, radiant, breathless manner, as if confused by the actual world, unreal to it, having a complete bright world of her self alone.

'Have I interrupted a conversation?' she asked.

'No, only a complete silence,' said Birkin.

'Oh,' said Ursula vaguely, absent. Their presence was not vital to her, she was withheld, she did not take them in. It was a subtle insult that never failed to exasperate her father.

'Mr Birkin came to speak to *you,* not to me,' said her father.

'Oh, did he!' she exclaimed vaguely, as if it did not concern her. Then, recollecting herself, she turned to him rather radiantly, but still quite superficially, and said: 'Was it anything special?'

'I hope so,' he said ironically.

'—To propose to you, according to all accounts,' said her father.

'Oh,' said Ursula.

'Oh,' mocked her father, imitating her. 'Have you nothing more to say?'

She winced as if violated.

'Did you really come to propose to me?' she asked of Birkin, as if it were a joke.

'Yes,' he said. 'I suppose I came to propose.' He seemed to fight shy of the last word.

'Did you?' she cried, with her vague radiance. He might have been saying anything whatsoever. She seemed pleased.

'Yes,' he answered. 'I wanted to—I wanted you to agree to marry me.'

She looked at him. His eyes were flickering with mixed lights, wanting something of her, yet not wanting it. She shrank a little, as if she were exposed to his eyes, and as if it were a pain to her. She darkened, her soul clouded over, she turned aside. She had been driven out of her own radiant, single world. And she dreaded contact, it was almost unnatural to her at these times.

'Yes,' she said vaguely, in a doubting, absent voice.

Birkin's heart contracted swiftly, in a sudden fire of bitterness. It all meant nothing to her. He had been mistaken again. She was in some self-satisfied world of her own. He and his hopes were accidentals, violations to her. It drove her father to a pitch of mad exasperation. He had had to put up with this all his life from her.

'Well, what do you say!' he cried.

She winced. Then she glanced down at her father, half frightened, and she said:

'I didn't speak, did I?' as if she were afraid she might have committed herself.

'No,' said her father, exasperated. 'But you needn't look like an idiot. You've got your wits, haven't you?'

She ebbed away in silent hostility.

'I've got my wits, what does that mean?' she repeated in a sullen voice of antagonism.

'You heard what was asked you, didn't you?' cried her father in anger.

'Of course I heard.'

'Well then, can't you answer?' thundered her father.

'Why should I?'

At the impertinence of this retort, he went stiff. But he said nothing.

'No,' said Birkin, to help out the occasion, 'there's no need to answer at once. You can say when you like.'

Her eyes flashed with a powerful light.

'Why should I say anything?' she cried. 'You do this off your *own* bat, it has nothing to do with me. Why do you both want to bully me?'

'Bully you! Bully you!' cried her father in bitter, rancorous anger. 'Bully you! Why, it's a pity you can't be bullied into some sense and decency. Bully you! *You'll* see to that, you self-willed creature.'

She stood suspended in the middle of the room, her face glimmering and dangerous. She was set in satisfied defiance. Birkin looked up at her. He too was angry.

'But no one is bullying you,' he said in a very soft dangerous voice also.

'Oh yes,' she cried. 'You both want to force me into something.'

'That is an illusion of yours,' he said ironically.

'Illusion!' cried her father. 'A self-opinionated fool, that's what she is.'

Birkin rose, saying:

'However, we'll leave it for the time being.'

And without another word, he walked out of the house.

'You fool! You fool!' her father cried to her, with extreme bitterness. She left the room, and went upstairs, singing to herself. But she was terribly fluttered, as after some dreadful fight. From her window, she could see Birkin going up the road. He went in such a blithe drift of rage that her mind wondered over him. He was ridiculous, but she was afraid of him. She was as if escaped from some danger.

Her father sat below, powerless in humiliation and chagrin. It was as if he were possessed with all the devils, after one of these unaccountable conflicts with Ursula. He hated her as if his only reality were in hating her to the last degree. He had all hell in his heart. But he went away, to escape himself. He knew he must despair, yield, give in to despair, and have done.

Ursula's face closed, she completed herself against them all. Recoiling upon herself, she became hard and self-completed, like a jewel. She was bright and invulnerable, quite free and happy, perfectly liberated in her self-possession. Her father had to learn not to see her blithe obliviousness, or it would have sent him mad. She was so radiant with all things in her possession of perfect hostility.

She would go on now for days like this, in this bright frank state of seemingly pure spontaneity, so essentially oblivious of the existence of anything but herself, but so ready and facile in her interest. Ah, it was a bitter thing for a man to be near her, and her father cursed his fatherhood. But he must learn not to see her, not to know.

She was perfectly stable in resistance when she was in this state: so bright and radiant and attractive in her pure opposition, so very pure, and yet mistrusted by everybody, disliked on every hand. It was her voice, curiously clear and repellant, that gave her away. Only Gudrun was in accord with her. It was at these times that the intimacy between the two sisters was most complete, as if their intelligence were one. They felt a strong, bright bond of understanding between them, surpassing everything else. And during all these days of blind bright abstraction and intimacy of his two daughters, the father seemed to breathe an air of death, as if he were destroyed in his very being. He was irritable to madness, he could not rest, his daughters seemed to be destroying him. But he was inarticulate and helpless against them. He was forced to breathe the air of his own death. He cursed them in his soul, and only wanted that they should be removed from him.

They continued radiant in their easy female transcendency, beautiful to look at. They exchanged confidences, they were intimate in their revelations to the last degree, giving each other at last every secret. They withheld nothing, they told everything, till they were over the border of evil. And they armed each other with knowledge, they extracted the subtlest flavours from the apple of knowledge. It was curious how their knowledge was complementary, that of each to that of the other.

Ursula saw her men as sons, pitied their yearning and admired their courage, and wondered over them as a mother wonders over her child, with a certain delight in their novelty. But to Gudrun, they were the opposite camp. She feared them and despised them, and respected their activities even overmuch.

'Of course,' she said easily, 'there is a quality of life in Birkin which is quite remarkable. There is an extraordinary rich spring of life in him, really amazing, the way he can give himself to things. But there are so many things in life that he simply doesn't know. Either he is not aware of their existence at all or he dismissed them as merely negligible—things which are vital to the other person. In a way, he is not clever enough, he is too intense in spots.'

'Yes,' cried Ursula, 'too much of a preacher. He is really a priest.'

'Exactly! He can't hear what anybody else has to say—he simply cannot hear. His own voice is so loud.'

'Yes. He cries you down.'

'He cries you down,' repeated Gudrun. 'And by mere force of violence. And of course it is hopeless. Nobody is convinced by violence. It makes talking to him impossible—and living with him I should think would be more than impossible.'

'You don't think one could live with him?' asked Ursula.

'I think it would be too wearing, too exhausting. One would be shouted down every time, and rushed into his way without any choice. He would want to control you entirely. He cannot allow that there is any other mind than his own. And then the real clumsiness of his mind is its lack of self-criticism. No, I think it would be perfectly intolerable.'

'Yes,' assented Ursula vaguely. She only half agreed with Gudrun. 'The nuisance is,' she said, 'that one would find almost any man intolerable after a fortnight.'

'It's perfectly dreadful,' said Gudrun. 'But Birkin—he is

too positive. He couldn't bear it if you called your soul your own. Of him that is strictly true.'

'Yes,' said Ursula. 'You must have *his* soul.'

'Exactly! And what can you conceive more deadly?' This was all so true, that Ursula felt jarred to the bottom of her soul with ugly distaste.

She went on, with the discord jarring and jolting through her, in the most barren of misery.

Then there started a revulsion from Gudrun. She finished life off so thoroughly, she made things so ugly and so final. As a matter of fact, even if it were as Gudrun said, about Birkin, other things were true as well. But Gudrun would draw two lines under him and cross him out like an account that is settled. There he was, summed up, paid for, settled, done with. And it was such a lie. This finality of Gudrun's, this dispatching of people and things in a sentence, it was all such a lie. Ursula began to revolt from her sister.

One day as they were walking along the lane, they saw a robin sitting on the top twig of a bush, singing shrilly. The sisters stood to look at him. An ironical smile flickered on Gudrun's face.

'Doesn't he feel important?' smiled Gudrun.

'Doesn't he?' exclaimed Ursula, with a little ironical grimace. 'Isn't he a little Lloyd George of the air!'

'Isn't he! Little Lloyd George of the air! That's just what they are,' cried Gudrun in delight. Then for days, Ursula saw the persistent, obtrusive birds as stout, short politicians lifting up their voices from the platform, little men who must make themselves heard at any cost.

But even from this there came the revulsion. Some yellowhammers suddenly shot along the road in front of her. And they looked to her so uncanny and inhuman, like flaring yellow barbs shooting through the air on some weird, living errand, that she said to herself: 'After all, it is impudence to call them little Lloyd Georges. They are really unknown to us, they are the unknown forces. It is impudence to look at them as if they were the same as human beings. They are of another world. How stupid anthropomorphism is! Gudrun is really impudent, insolent, making herself the measure of everything, making everything come down to human standards. Rupert is quite right, human beings are boring, painting the universe with their own image. The universe is non-human, thank God.' It seemed to her irreverence, destructive of all true life, to make little Lloyd Georges of the birds. It was such a lie towards the robins, and such a defamation. Yet she had done it herself. But under Gudrun's influence: so she exonerated herself.

So she withdrew away from Gudrun and from that which she stood for, she turned in spirit towards Birkin again. She had not seen him since the fiasco of his proposal. She did not want to, because she did not want the question of her acceptance thrust upon her. She knew what Birkin meant when he asked her to marry him; vaguely, without putting it into speech, she knew. She knew what kind of love, what kind of surrender he wanted. And she was not at all sure that this was the kind of love that she herself wanted. She was not at all sure that it was this mutual unison in separateness that she wanted. She wanted unspeakable intimacies. She wanted to have him, utterly, finally to have him as her own, oh, so unspeakably, in intimacy. To drink him down—ah, like a life-draught. She made great professions, to herself, of her willingness to warm his foot-soles between her breasts, after the fashion of the nauseous Meredith poem. But only on condition that he, her lover, loved her absolutely, with complete self-abandon. And subtly enough, she knew he would never abandon himself *finally* to her. He did not believe in final self-abandonment. He said it openly. It was his challenge. She was prepared to fight him for it. For she believed in an absolute surrender to love. She believed that love far surpassed the individual. He said the individual was *more* than love, or than any relationship. For him, the bright, single soul accepted love as one of its conditions, a condition of its own equilibrium. She believed that love was *everything*. Man must render himself up to her. He must be quaffed to the dregs by her. Let him be *her man* utterly, and she in return would be his humble slave—whether she wanted it or not.

20

Gladiatorial

After the fiasco of the proposal, Birkin had hurried blindly away from Beldover, in a whirl of fury. He felt he had been a complete fool, that the whole scene had been a farce of the first water. But that did not trouble him at all. He was deeply, mockingly angry that Ursula persisted always in this old cry: 'Why do you want to bully me?' and in her bright, insolent abstraction.

He went straight to Shortlands. There he found Gerald standing with his back to the fire, in the library, as motionless as a man is who is completely and emptily restless, utterly hollow. He had done all the work he wanted to do—and now there was nothing. He could go out in the car, he could run to town. But he did not want to go out in the car, he did not want to run to town, he did not want to call on the Thirlbys. He was suspended motionless, in an agony of inertia, like a machine that is without power.

This was very bitter to Gerald, who had never known what boredom was, who had gone from activity to activity, never at a loss. Now, gradually, everything seemed to be stopping in him. He did not want any more to do the things that offered. Something dead within him just refused to respond to any suggestion. He cast over in his mind what it would be possible to do to save himself from this misery of nothingness, relieve the stress of this hollowness. And there were only three things left that would rouse him, make him live. One was to drink or smoke hashish, the other was to be soothed by Birkin, and the third was women. And there was no one for the moment to drink with. Nor was there a woman. And he knew Birkin was out. So there was nothing to do but to bear the stress of his own emptiness.

When he saw Birkin his face lit up in a sudden, wonderful smile.

'By God, Rupert,' he said, 'I'd just come to the conclusion that nothing in the world mattered except somebody to take the edge off one's being alone: the right somebody.'

The smile in his eyes was very astonishing as he looked at the other man. It was the pure gleam of relief. His face was pallid and even haggard.

'The right woman, I suppose you mean,' said Birkin spitefully.

'Of course, for choice. Failing that, an amusing man.'

He laughed as he said it. Birkin sat down near the fire.

'What were you doing?' he asked.

'I? Nothing. I'm in a bad way just now, everything's on edge, and I can neither work nor play. I don't know whether it's a sign of old age, I'm sure.'

'You mean you are bored?'

'Bored, I don't know. I can't apply myself. And I feel the devil is either very present inside me or dead.'

Birkin glanced up and looked in his eyes.

'You should try hitting something,' he said.

Gerald smiled.

'Perhaps,' he said. 'So long as it was something worth hitting.'

'Quite!' said Birkin in his soft voice. There was a long pause during which each could feel the presence of the other.

'One has to wait,' said Birkin.

'Ah, God! Waiting! What are we waiting for?'

'Some old Johnny says there are three cures for *ennui*, sleep, drink, and travel,' said Birkin.

'All cold eggs,' said Gerald. 'In sleep, you dream, in drink you curse, and in travel you yell at a porter. No, work and love are the two. When you're not at work you should be in love.'

'Be it then,' said Birkin.

'Give me the object,' said Gerald. 'The possibilities of love exhaust themselves.'

'Do they? And then what?'

'Then you die,' said Gerald.

'So you ought,' said Birkin.

'I don't see it,' replied Gerald. He took his hands out of his trousers pockets and reached for a cigarette. He was tense and nervous. He lit the cigarette over a lamp, reaching forward and drawing steadily. He was dressed for dinner, as usual in the evening, although he was alone.

'There's a third one even to your two,' said Birkin. 'Work, love, and fighting. You forget the fight.'

'I suppose I do,' said Gerald. 'Did you ever do any boxing—?'

'No, I don't think I did,' said Birkin.

'Ay—' Gerald lifted his head and blew the smoke slowly into the air.

'Why?' said Birkin.

'Nothing. I thought we might have a round. It is perhaps true that I want something to hit. It's a suggestion.'

'So you think you might as well hit me?' said Birkin.

'You? Well—! Perhaps—! In a friendly kind of way, of course.'

'Quite!' said Birkin bitingly.

Gerald stood leaning back against the mantelpiece. He looked down at Birkin, and his eyes flashed with a sort of terror like the eyes of a stallion, that are bloodshot and over-wrought, turned glancing backwards in a stiff terror.

'I feel that if I don't watch myself, I shall find myself doing something silly,' he said.

'Why not do it?' said Birkin coldly.

Gerald listened with quick impatience. He kept glancing down at Birkin, as if looking for something from the other man.

'I used to do some Japanese wrestling,' said Birkin. 'A Jap lived in the same house with me in Heidelberg, and he taught me a little. But I was never much good at it.'

'You did!' exclaimed Gerald. 'That's one of the things I've never ever seen done. You mean jiu-jitsu, I suppose?'

'Yes. But I am no good at those things—they don't interest me.'

'They don't? They do me. What's the start?'

'I'll show you what I can, if you like,' said Birkin.

'You will?' A queer, smiling look tightened Gerald's face for a moment as he said, 'Well, I'd like it very much.'

'Then we'll try jiu-jitsu. Only you can't do much in a starched shirt.'

'Then let us strip, and do it properly. Hold a minute—' He rang the bell and waited for the butler.

'Bring a couple of sandwiches and a syphon,' he said to the man, 'and then don't trouble me any more tonight—or let anybody else.'

The man went. Gerald turned to Birkin with his eyes lighted.

'And you used to wrestle with a Jap?' he said. 'Did you strip?'

'Sometimes.'

'You did! What was he like then, as a wrestler?'

'Good, I believe. I am no judge. He was very quick and slippery and full of electric fire. It is a remarkable thing what a curious sort of fluid force they seem to have in them, those people—not like a human grip—like a polyp—'

Gerald nodded.

'I should imagine so,' he said, 'to look at them. They repel me, rather.'

'Repel and attract, both. They are very repulsive when they are cold, and they look grey. But when they are hot and roused, there is a definite attraction—a curious kind of full electric fluid—like eels.'

'Well—, yes—, probably.'

The man brought in the tray and set it down.

'Don't come in any more,' said Gerald.

The door closed.

'Well then,' said Gerald; 'shall we strip and begin? Will you have a drink first?'

'No, I don't want one.'

'Neither do I.'

Gerald fastened the door and pushed the furniture aside. The room was large, there was plenty of space, it was thickly carpeted. Then he quickly threw off his clothes and waited for Birkin. The latter, white and thin, came over to him. Birkin was more a presence than a visible object; Gerald was aware of him completely, but not really visually. Whereas Gerald himself was concrete and noticeable, a piece of pure final substance.

'Now,' said Birkin, 'I will show you what I learned, and what I remember. You let me take you so—' And his hands closed on the naked body of the other man. In another moment, he had Gerald swung over lightly and balanced against his knee, head downwards. Relaxed, Gerald sprang to his feet with eyes glittering.

'That's smart,' he said. 'Now try again.'

So the two men began to struggle together. They were very dissimilar. Birkin was tall and narrow, his bones were very thin and fine. Gerald was much heavier and more plastic. His bones were strong and round, his limbs were rounded, all his contours were beautifully and fully moulded. He seemed to stand with a proper, rich weight on the face of the earth, whilst Birkin seemed to have the centre of gravitation in his own middle. And Gerald had a rich, frictional kind of strength, rather mechanical, but sudden and invincible, whereas Birkin was abstract as to be almost intangible. He impinged invisibly upon the other man, scarcely seeming to touch him, like a garment, and then suddenly piercing in a tense fine grip that seemed to penetrate into the very quick of Gerald's being.

They stopped, they discussed methods, they practised grips and throws, they became accustomed to each other, to each other's rhythm, they got a kind of mutual physical understanding. And then again they had a real struggle. They seemed to drive their white flesh deeper and deeper against each other, as if they would break into a oneness. Birkin had a great subtle energy, that would press upon the other man with an uncanny force, weigh him like a spell put upon him. Then it would pass, and Gerald would heave free, with white, heaving, dazzling movements.

So the two men entwined and wrestled with each other, working nearer and nearer. Both were white and clear, but Gerald flushed smart red where he was touched, and Birkin remained white and tense. He seemed to penetrate into Gerald's more solid, more diffuse bulk, to interfuse his body through the body of the other, as if to bring it subtly into subjection, always seizing with some rapid necromantic foreknowledge every motion of the other flesh, converting and counteracting it, playing upon the limbs and trunk of

Gerald like some hard wind. It was as if Birkin's whole
physical intelligence interpenetrated into Gerald's body, as if
his fine, sublimated energy entered into the flesh of the
fuller man, like some potency, casting a fine net, a prison,
through the muscles into the very depths of Gerald's physical being.

So they wrestled swiftly, rapturously, intent and mindless
at last, two essential white figures working into a tighter,
closer oneness of struggle, with a strange, octopus-like knot-
ting and flashing of limbs in the subdued light of the room;
a tense white knot of flesh gripped in silence between the
walls of old brown books. Now and again came a sharp gasp
of breath, or a sound like a sigh, then the rapid thudding of
movement on the thickly-carpeted floor, then the strange
sound of flesh escaping under flesh. Often, in the white in-
terlaced knot of violent living being that swayed silently,
there was no head to be seen, only the swift, tight limbs, the
solid white backs, the physical junction of two bodies
clinched into oneness. Then would appear the gleaming, ruffled head of Gerald, as the struggle changed, then for a moment the dun-coloured, shadowlike head of the other man
would lift up from the conflict, the eyes wide and dreadful
and sightless.

At length Gerald lay back inert on the carpet, his breast rising
in great slow panting, whilst Birkin kneeled over him, almost
unconscious. Birkin was much more exhausted. He caught little,
short breaths, he could scarcely breathe any more. The earth
seemed to tilt and sway, and a complete darkness was coming
over his mind. He did not know what happened. He slid forward quite unconscious over Gerald, and Gerald did not notice.
Then he was half conscious again, aware only of the strange tilt-
ing and sliding of the world. The world was sliding, everything
was sliding off into the darkness. And he was sliding, endlessly,
endlessly away.

He came to consciousness again, hearing an immense
knocking outside. What could be happening, what was it, the
great hammer-stroke resounding through the house? He did
not know. And then it came to him that it was his own heart
beating. But that seemed impossible, the noise was outside.
No, it was inside himself, it was his own heart. And the

beating was painful, so strained, surcharged. He wondered if Gerald heard it. He did not know whether he were standing or lying or falling.

When he realized that he had fallen prostrate upon Gerald's body he wondered, he was surprised. But he sat up, steadying himself with his hand and waiting for his heart to become stiller and less painful. It hurt very much, and took away his consciousness.

Gerald, however, was still less conscious than Birkin. They waited dimly, in a sort of not-being, for many uncounted, unknown minutes.

'Of course—' panted Gerald, 'I didn't have to be rough— with you—I had to keep back—my force—'

Birkin heard the sound as if his own spirit stood behind him, outside him, and listened to it. His body was in a trance of exhaustion, his spirit heard thinly. His body could not answer. Only he knew his heart was getting quieter. He was divided entirely between his spirit, which stood outside, and knew, and his body, that was a plunging, unconscious stroke of blood.

'I could have thrown you—using violence—' panted Gerald. 'But you beat me right enough.'

'Yes,' said Birkin, hardening his throat and producing the words in the tension there, 'you're much stronger than I—you could beat me—easily.'

Then he relaxed again to the terrible plunging of his heart and his blood.

'It surprised me,' panted Gerald, 'what strength you've got. Almost supernatural.'

'For a moment,' said Birkin.

He still heard as if it were his own disembodied spirit hearing, standing at some distance behind him. It drew nearer, however, his spirit. And the violent striking of blood in his chest was sinking quieter, allowing his mind to come back. He realized that he was leaning with all his weight on the soft body of the other man. It startled him, because he thought he had withdrawn. He recovered himself and sat up. But he was still vague and unestablished. He put out his hand to steady himself. It touched the hand of Gerald, that was lying out on the floor. And Gerald's hand closed warm and sudden over Birkin's, they remained exhausted and breathless, the one hand clasped closely over the other. It was Birkin whose hand, in swift response, had closed in a strong, warm clasp over the hand of the other. Gerald's clasp had been sudden and momentaneous.

The normal consciousness, however, was returning, ebbing back. Birkin could breathe almost naturally again. Gerald's hand slowly withdrew, Birkin slowly, dazedly rose to his feet and went towards the table. He poured out a whiskey and soda. Gerald also came for a drink.

'It was a real set-to, wasn't it?' said Birkin, looking at Gerald with darkened eyes.

'God, yes,' said Gerald. He looked at the delicate body of the other man, and added: 'It wasn't too much for you, was it?'

'No. One ought to wrestle and strive and be physically close. It makes one sane.'

'You do think so?'

'I do. Don't you?'

'Yes,' said Gerald.

There were long spaces of silence between their words. The wrestling had some deep meaning to them—an unfinished meaning.

'We are mentally, spiritually intimate, therefore we should be more or less physically intimate too—it is more whole.'

'Certainly it is,' said Gerald. Then he laughed pleasantly, adding: 'It's rather wonderful to me.' He stretched out his arms handsomely.

'Yes,' said Birkin. 'I don't know why one should have to justify oneself.'

'No.'

The two men began to dress.

'I think also that you are beautiful,' said Birkin to Gerald, 'and that is enjoyable too. One should enjoy what is given.'

'You think I am beautiful—how do you mean, physically?' asked Gerald, his eyes glistening.

'Yes. You have a northern kind of beauty, like light refracted from snow—and a beautiful, plastic form. Yes, that is there to enjoy as well. We should enjoy everything.'

Gerald laughed in his throat, and said:

'That's certainly one way of looking at it. I can say this much, I feel better. It has certainly helped me. Is this the Brüderschaft you wanted?'

'Perhaps. Do you think this pledges anything?'

'I don't know,' laughed Gerald.

'At any rate, one feels freer and more open now—and that is what we want.'

'Certainly,' said Gerald.

They drew to the fire, with the decanters and the glasses and the food.

'I always eat a little before I go to bed,' said Gerald. 'I sleep better.'

'I should not sleep so well,' said Birkin.

'No? There you are, we are not alike. I'll put a dressing-gown on.' Birkin remained alone, looking at the fire. His mind had reverted to Ursula. She seemed to return again into his consciousness. Gerald came down wearing a gown of broad-barred, thick black-and-green silk, brilliant and striking.

'You are very fine,' said Birkin, looking at the full robe.

'It was a caftan in Bokhara,' said Gerald. 'I like it.'

'I like it too.'

Birkin was silent, thinking how scrupulous Gerald was in his attire, how expensive too. He wore silk socks, and studs of fine workmanship, and silk underclothing, and silk braces. Curious! This was another of the differences between them. Birkin was careless and unimaginative about his own appearance.

'Of course you,' said Gerald, as if he had been thinking; 'there's something curious about you. You're curiously strong. One doesn't expect it, it is rather surprising.'

Birkin laughed. He was looking at the handsome figure of the other man, blond and comely in the rich robe, and he was half thinking of the difference between it and himself—so different; as far, perhaps, apart as man from woman, yet in another direction. But really it was Ursula, it was the woman who was gaining ascendance over Birkin's being at this moment. Gerald was becoming dim again, lapsing out of him.

'Do you know,' he said suddenly, 'I went and proposed to Ursula Brangwen tonight, that she should marry me.'

He saw the blank shining wonder come over Gerald's face.

'You did?'

'Yes. Almost formally—speaking first to her father, as it should be, in the world—though that was accident—or mischief.'

Gerald only stared in wonder, as if he did not grasp.

'You don't mean to say that you seriously went and asked her father to let you marry her?'

'Yes,' said Birkin, 'I did.'

'What, had you spoken to her before about it, then?'

'No, not a word. I suddenly thought I would go there and ask her—and her father happened to come instead of her—so I asked him first.'

'If you could have her?' concluded Gerald.

'Ye-es, that.'

'And you didn't speak to her?'

'Yes. She came in afterwards. So it was put to her as well.'

'It was! And what did she say then? You're an engaged man?'

'No—she only said she didn't want to be bullied into answering.'

'She what?'

'Said she didn't want to be bullied into answering.'

' "Said she didn't want to be bullied into answering!" Why, what did she mean by that?'

Birkin raised his shoulders. 'Can't say,' he answered. 'Didn't want to be bothered just then, I suppose.'

'But is this really so? And what did you do then?'

'I walked out of the house and came here.'

'You came straight here?'

'Yes.'

Gerald stared in amazement and amusement. He could not take it in.

'But is this really true, as you say it now?'

'Word for word.'

'It is?'

He leaned back in his chair, filled with delight and amusement.

'Well, that's good,' he said. 'And so you came here to wrestle with your good angel, did you?'

'Did I?' said Birkin.

'Well, it looks like it. Isn't that what you did?'

Now Birkin could not follow Gerald's meaning.

'And what's going to happen?' said Gerald. 'You're going to keep open the proposition, so to speak.'

'I suppose so. I vowed to myself I would see them all to the devil. But I suppose I shall ask her again, in a little while.'

Gerald watched him steadily.

'So you're fond of her then?' he asked.

'I think—I love her,' said Birkin, his face going very still and fixed.

Gerald glistened for a moment with pleasure, as if it were something done specially to please him. Then his face assumed a fitting gravity, and he nodded his head slowly.

'You know,' he said, 'I always believed in love—true love. But where does one find it nowadays?'

'I don't know,' said Birkin.

'Very rarely,' said Gerald. Then, after a pause, 'I've never felt it myself—not what I should call love. I've gone after women—and been keen enough over some of them. But I've never felt *love*. I don't believe I've ever felt as much *love* for a woman as I have for you—not *love*. You understand what I mean?'

'Yes. I'm sure you've never loved a woman.'

'You feel that, do you? And do you think I ever shall? You understand what I mean?' He put his hand to his breast, closing his fist there, as if he would draw something out. 'I mean that—that—I can't express what it is, but I know it.'

'What is it, then?' asked Birkin.

'You see, I can't put it into words. I mean, at any rate, something abiding, something that can't change—'

His eyes were bright and puzzled.

'Now do you think I shall ever feel that for a woman?' he said anxiously.

Birkin looked at him and shook his head.

'I don't know,' he said. 'I could not say.'

Gerald had been on the *qui vive,* as awaiting his fate. Now he drew back in his chair.

'No,' he said, 'and neither do I, and neither do I.'

'We are different, you and I,' said Birkin. 'I can't tell your life.'

'No,' said Gerald, 'no more can I. But I tell you—I begin to doubt it.'

'That you will ever love a woman?'

'Well—yes—what you would truly call love—'

'You doubt it?'

'Well—I begin to.'

There was a long pause.

'Life has all kinds of things,' said Birkin. 'There isn't only one road.'

'Yes, I believe that too. I believe it. And mind you, I don't care how it is with me—I don't care how it is—so long as I don't feel—' he paused, and a blank, barren look passed over his face, to express his feeling—'so long as I feel I've *lived,* somehow—and I don't care how it is—but I want to feel that—'

'Fulfilled,' said Birkin.

'We-ell, perhaps it is fulfilled; I don't use the same words as you.'

'It is the same.'

21

Threshold

G udrun was away in London, having a little show of her work with a friend, and looking round, preparing for flight from Beldover. Come what might, she would be on the wing in a very short time. She received a letter from Winifred Crich, ornamented with drawings.

'Father also has been to London, to be examined by the doctors. It made him very tired. They say he must rest a very great deal, so he is mostly in bed. He brought me a lovely tropical parrot in faience, of Dresden ware, also a man ploughing, and two mice climbing up a stalk, also in faience. The mice were Copenhagen ware. They are the best, but mice don't shine so much, otherwise they are very good, their tails are slim and long. They all shine nearly like glass. Of course it is the glaze, but I don't like it. Gerald likes the man ploughing the best, his trousers are torn, he is ploughing with an ox, being, I suppose, a German peasant. It is all grey and white, white shirt and grey trousers, but very shiny and clean. Mr Birkin likes the girl best, under the hawthorn blossom, with a lamb, and with daffodils painted on her skirts, in the drawing-room. But that is silly, because the lamb is not a real lamb, and she is silly too.

'Dear Miss Brangwen, are you coming back soon, you are very much missed here. I enclose a drawing of father sitting up in bed. He says he hopes you are not going to forsake us. Oh dear, Miss Brangwen, I am sure you won't. Do come back and draw the ferrets, they are the most lovely noble darlings in the world. We might carve them in holly-wood, playing against a background of green leaves. Oh, do let us, for they are most beautiful.

'Father says we might have a studio. Gerald says we could easily have a beautiful one over the stables, it would only need windows to be put in the slant of the roof, which is a simple matter. Then you could stay here all day and work, and we could live in the studio, like two real artists, like the man in the picture in the hall, with the frying-pan and the walls all covered with drawings. I long to be free, to live the free life of an artist. Even Gerald told father that only an artist is free, because he lives in a creative world of his own—'

Gudrun caught the drift of the family intentions, in this letter. Gerald wanted her to be attached to the household at Shortlands, he was using Winifred as his stalking-horse. The father thought only of his child, he saw a rock of salvation in Gudrun. And Gudrun admired him for his perspicacity. The child, moreover, was really exceptional. Gudrun was quite content. She was quite willing, given a studio, to spend her days at Shortlands. She disliked the Grammar School already thoroughly, she wanted to be free. If a studio were provided, she would be free to go on with her work, she would await the turn of events with complete serenity. And she was really interested in Winifred, she would be quite glad to understand the girl.

So there was quite a little festivity on Winifred's account, the day Gudrun returned to Shortlands.

'You should make a bunch of flowers to give to Miss Brangwen when she arrives,' Gerald said, smiling to his sister.

'Oh no,' cried Winifred, 'it's silly.'

'Not at all. It is a very charming and ordinary attention.'

'Oh, it *is* silly,' protested Winifred, with all the extreme *mauvaise honte* of her years. Nevertheless, the idea appealed to her. She wanted very much to carry it out. She flitted round the green-houses and the conservatory looking wistfully at the flowers on their stems. And the more she looked, the more she *longed* to have a bunch of the blossoms she saw, the more fascinated she became with her little vision of ceremony, and the more consumedly shy and self-conscious she grew, till she was almost beside herself. She could not get the idea out of her mind. It was as if some haunting challenge prompted her, and she had not enough courage to take it up. So again she drifted into the green-houses, looking at the lovely roses in their pots, and at the virginal cyclamens, and at the mystic white clusters of a creeper. The beauty, oh, the beauty of them, and oh, the paradisal bliss, if she should have a perfect bouquet and could give it to Gudrun the next day. Her passion and her complete indecision almost made her ill.

At last she slid to her father's side.

'Daddie—' she said.

'What, my precious?'

But she hung back, the tears almost coming to her eyes, in her sensitive confusion. Her father looked at her, and his heart ran hot with tenderness, an anguish of poignant love.

'What do you want to say to me, my love?'

'Daddie—!' her eyes smiled laconically—'isn't it silly if I give Miss Brangwen some flowers when she comes?'

The sick man looked at the bright, knowing eyes of his child, and his heart burned with love.

'No, darling, that's not silly. It's what they do to queens.'

This was not very reassuring to Winifred. She half suspected that queens in themselves were a silliness. Yet she so wanted her little romantic occasion.

'Shall I then?' she asked.

'Give Miss Brangwen some flowers? Do, Birdie. Tell Wilson I say you are to have what you want.'

The child smiled a small, subtle, unconscious smile to herself, in anticipation of her way.

'But I won't get them till tomorrow,' she said.

'Not till tomorrow, Birdie. Give me a kiss then—'

Winifred silently kissed the sick man, and drifted out of the room. She again went the round of the green-houses and the conservatory, informing the gardener, in her high, peremptory, simple fashion, of what she wanted, telling him all the blooms she had selected.

'What do you want these for?' Wilson asked.

'I want them,' she said. She wished servants did not ask questions.

'Ay, you've said as much. But what do you want them for, for decoration, or to send away, or what?'

'I want them for a presentation bouquet.'

'A presentation bouquet! Who's coming then?—the Duchess of Portland?'

'No.'

'Oh, not her? Well, you'll have a rare poppy-show if you put all the things you've mentioned into your bouquet.'

'Yes, I want a rare poppy-show.'

'You do! Then there's no more to be said.'

The next day Winifred, in a dress of silvery velvet and holding a gaudy bunch of flowers in her hand, waited with keen impatience in the schoolroom, looking down the drive for Gudrun's arrival. It was a wet morning. Under her nose was the strange fragrance of hot-house flowers, the bunch was like a little fire to her, she seemed to have a strange new fire in her heart. This slight sense of romance stirred her like an intoxicant.

At last she saw Gudrun coming, and she ran downstairs to warn her father and Gerald. They, laughing at her anxiety and gravity, came with her into the hall. The man-servant came hastening to the door, and there he was, relieving Gudrun of her umbrella, and then of her raincoat. The welcoming party hung back till their visitor entered the hall.

Gudrun was flushed with the rain, her hair was blown in loose little curls, she was like a flower just opened in the rain, the heart of the blossom just newly visible, seeming to emit a warmth of retained sunshine. Gerald winced in spirit, seeing her so beautiful and unknown. She was wearing a soft blue dress, and her stockings were of dark red.

Winifred advanced with odd, stately formality.

'We are so glad you've come back,' she said. 'These are your flowers.' She presented the bouquet.

'Mine!' cried Gudrun. She was suspended for a moment, then a vivid flush went over her, she was as if blinded for a moment with a flame of pleasure. Then her eyes, strange and flaming, lifted and looked at the father, and at Gerald. And again Gerald shrank in spirit, as if it would be more than he could bear, as her hot, exposed eyes rested on him. There was something so revealed, she was revealed beyond bearing, to his eyes. He turned his face aside. And he felt he would not be able to avert her. And he writhed under the imprisonment.

Gudrun put her face into the flowers.

'But how beautiful they are!' she said, in a muffled voice. Then, with a strange, suddenly revealed passion, she stooped and kissed Winifred.

Mr Crich went forward with his hand held out to her.

'I was afraid you were going to run away from us,' he said playfully.

Gudrun looked up at him with a luminous, roguish, unknown face.

'Really!' she replied. 'No, I didn't want to stay in London.'

Her voice seemed to imply that she was glad to get back to Shortlands, her tone was warm and subtly caressing.

'That is a good thing,' smiled the father. 'You see, you are very welcome here among us.'

Gudrun only looked into his face with dark-blue, warm, shy eyes. She was unconsciously carried away by her own power.

'And you look as if you came home in every possible triumph,' Mr Crich continued, holding her hand.

'No,' she said, glowing strangely. 'I haven't had any triumph till I came here.'

'Ah, come, come! We're not going to hear any of those tales. Haven't we read notices in the newspaper, Gerald?'

'You came off pretty well,' said Gerald to her, shaking hands. 'Did you sell anything?'

'No,' she said, 'not much.'

'Just as well,' he said.

She wondered what he meant. But she was all aglow with her reception, carried away by this little flattering ceremonial on her behalf.

'Winifred,' said the father, 'have you a pair of shoes for Miss Brangwen? You had better change at once—'

Gudrun went out with her bouquet in her hand.

'Quite a remarkable young woman,' said the father to Gerald, when she had gone.

'Yes,' replied Gerald briefly, as if he did not like the observation.

Mr Crich liked Gudrun to sit with him for half an hour. Usually he was ashy and wretched, with all the life gnawed

out of him. But as soon as he rallied, he liked to make believe that he was just as before, quite well and in the midst
of life—not of the outer world, but in the midst of a strong
essential life. And to this belief, Gudrun contributed perfectly. With her, he could get by stimulation those precious
half-hours of strength and exaltation and pure freedom,
when he seemed to live more than he had ever lived.

She came to him as he lay propped up in the library. His
face was like yellow wax, his eyes darkened, as it were
sightless. His black beard, now streaked with grey, seemed
to spring out of the waxy flesh of a corpse. Yet the atmosphere about him was energetic and playful. Gudrun sub-
scribed to this perfectly. To her fancy, he was just an
ordinary man. Only his rather terrible appearance was pho-
tographed upon her soul, away beneath her consciousness.
She knew that, in spite of his playfulness, his eyes could not
change from their darkened vacancy, they were the eyes of
a man who is dead.

'Ah, this is Miss Brangwen,' he said, suddenly rousing as
she entered, announced by the man-servant. 'Thomas, put
Miss Brangwen a chair here—that's right.' He looked at her
soft, fresh face with pleasure. It gave him the illusion of life.
'Now, you will have a glass of sherry and a little piece of
cake. Thomas—'

'No, thank you,' said Gudrun. And as soon as she had
said it, her heart sank horribly. The sick man seemed to fall
into a gap of death, at her contradiction. She ought to play
up to him, not to contravene him. In an instant she was smiling her rather roguish smile.

'I don't like sherry very much,' she said. 'But I like almost anything else.'

The sick man caught at this straw instantly.

'Not sherry! No! Something else! What then? What is
there, Thomas?'

'Port wine—curaçao—'

'I would love curaçao—' said Gudrun, looking at the sick
man confidingly.

'You would. Well then, Thomas, curaçao—and a little
cake or a biscuit?'

'A biscuit,' said Gudrun. She did not want anything, but she was wise.

'Yes.'

He waited till she was settled with her little glass and her biscuit. Then he was satisfied.

'You have heard the plan,' he said with some excitement, 'for a studio for Winifred over the stables?'

'No!' exclaimed Gudrun, in mock wonder.

'Oh!—I thought Winnie wrote it to you in her letter!'

'Oh—yes—of course. But I thought perhaps it was only her own little idea—' Gudrun smiled subtly, indulgently. The sick man smiled also, elated.

'Oh no. It is a real project. There is a good room under the roof of the stables—with sloping rafters. We had thought of converting it into a studio.'

'How *very* nice that would be!' cried Gudrun, with excited warmth. The thought of the rafters stirred her.

'You think it would? Well, it can be done.'

'But how perfectly splendid for Winifred! Of course, it is just what is needed, if she is to work at all seriously. One must have one's workshop, otherwise one never ceases to be an amateur.'

'Is that so? Yes. Of course, I should like you to share it with Winifred.'

'Thank you *so* much.'

Gudrun knew all these things already, but she must look shy and very grateful, as if overcome.

'Of course, what I should like best would be if you could give up your work at the Grammar School and just avail yourself of the studio, and work there—well, as much or as little as you liked—'

He looked at Gudrun with dark, vacant eyes. She looked back at him as if full of gratitude. These phrases of a dying man were so complete and natural, coming like echoes through his dead mouth.

'And as to your earnings—you don't mind taking from me what you have taken from the Education Committee, do you? I don't want you to be a loser.'

'Oh,' said Gudrun, 'if I can have the studio and work there, I can earn money enough, really I can.'

'Well,' he said, pleased to be the benefactor, 'we can see about all that. You wouldn't mind spending your days here?'

'If there were a studio to work in,' said Gudrun, 'I could ask for nothing better.'

'Is that so?'

He was really very pleased. But already he was getting tired. She could see the grey, awful semi-consciousness of mere pain and dissolution coming over him again, the torture coming into the vacancy of his darkened eyes. It was not over yet, this process of death. She rose softly, saying:

'Perhaps you will sleep. I must look for Winifred.'

She went out, telling the nurse that she had left him. Day by day the tissue of the sick man was further and further reduced, nearer and nearer the process came, towards the last knot which held the human being in its unity. But this knot was hard and unrelaxed, the will of the dying man never gave way. He might be dead in nine-tenths, yet the remaining tenth remained unchanged, till it too was torn apart. With his will he held the unit of himself firm, but the circle of his power was ever and ever reduced, it would be reduced to a point at last, then swept away.

To adhere to life, he must adhere to human relationships, and he caught at every straw. Winifred, the butler, the nurse, Gudrun, these were the people who meant all to him, in these last resources. Gerald, in his father's presence, stiffened with repulsion. It was so, to a less degree, with all the other children except Winifred. They could not see anything but the death, when they looked at their father. It was as if some subterranean dislike overcame them. They could not see the familiar face, hear the familiar voice. They were overwhelmed by the antipathy of visible and audible death. Gerald could not breathe in his father's presence. He must get out at once. And so, in the same way, the father could not bear the presence of his son. It sent a final irritation through the soul of the dying man.

The studio was made ready, Gudrun and Winifred moved in. They enjoyed so much the ordering and the appointing of it. And now they need hardly be in the house at all. They had their meals in the studio, they lived there safely. For the house was becoming dreadful. There were two nurses in white, flitting silently about, like heralds of death. The father was confined to his bed, there was a come and go of *sotto-voce* sisters and brothers and children.

Winifred was her father's constant visitor. Every morning, after breakfast, she went into his room when he was washed and propped up in bed, to spend half an hour with him.

'Are you better, Daddie?' she asked him invariably.

And invariably he answered:

'Yes, I think I'm a little better, pet.'

She held his hand in both her own, lovingly and protectively. And this was very dear to him.

She ran in again as a rule at lunch-time, to tell him the course of events, and every evening, when the curtains were drawn, and his room was cosy, she spent a long time with him. Gudrun was gone home, Winifred was alone in the house; she liked best to be with her father. They talked and prattled at random, he always as if he were well, just the same as when he was going about. So that Winifred, with a child's subtle instinct for avoiding the painful things, behaved as if nothing serious was the matter. Instinctively, she withheld her attention, and was happy. Yet in her remoter soul, she knew as well as the adults knew: perhaps better.

Her father was quite well in his make-believe with her. But when she went away, he relapsed under the misery of his dissolution. But still there were these bright moments, though as his strength waned, his faculty for attention grew weaker, and the nurse had to send Winifred away, to save him from exhaustion.

He never admitted that he was going to die. He knew it was so, he knew it was the end. Yet even to himself he did not admit it. He hated the fact, mortally. His will was rigid. He could not bear being overcome by death. For him there was no death. And yet, at times, he felt a great need to cry out and to wail and complain. He would have liked to cry aloud to Gerald, so that his son should be horrified out of his composure. Gerald was instinctively aware of this, and he recoiled, to avoid any such thing. This uncleanness of death repelled him too much. One should die quickly, like the Romans, one should be master of one's fate in dying as in living. He was convulsed in the clasp of this death of his father's, as in the coils of the great serpent of Laocoön. The

great serpent had got the father, and the son was dragged
into the embrace of horrifying death along with him. He resisted always. And in some strange way he was a tower of
strength to his father.

The last time the dying man asked to see Gudrun he was
grey with near death. Yet he must see someone, he must, in
the intervals of consciousness, catch into connexion with the
living world, lest he should have to accept his own situation.
Fortunately he was most of his time dazed and half gone.
And he spent many hours dimly thinking of the past, as it
were, dimly re-living his old experiences. But there were
times even to the end when he was capable of realizing what
was happening to him in the present, the death that was on
him. And these were the times when he called in outside
help, no matter whose. For to realize this death that he was
dying was a death beyond death, never to be borne. It was
an admission never to be made.

Gudrun was shocked by his appearance, and by the darkened, almost disintegrated eyes, that still were unconquered
and firm.

'Well,' he said in his weakened voice, 'and how are you
and Winifred getting on?'

'Oh, very well indeed,' replied Gudrun.

There were slight dead gaps in the conversation, as if the
ideas called up were only elusive straws floating on the dark
chaos of the sick man's dying.

'The studio answers all right?' he said.

'Splendid. It couldn't be more beautiful and perfect,' said
Gudrun.

She waited for what he would say next.

'And you think Winifred has the makings of a sculptor?'

It was strange how hollow the words were, meaningless.

'I'm sure she has. She will do good things one day.'

'Ah! Then her life won't be altogether wasted, you think?'

Gudrun was rather surprised.

'Sure it won't!' she exclaimed softly.

'That's right.'

Again Gudrun waited for what he would say.

'You find life pleasant, it is good to live, isn't it?' he

asked, with a pitiful faint smile that was almost too much for Gudrun.

'Yes,' she smiled—she would lie at random—'I get a pretty good time, I believe.'

'That's right. A happy nature is a great asset.'

Again Gudrun smiled, though her soul was dry with repulsion. Did one have to die like this—having the life extracted forcibly from one, whilst one smiled and made conversation to the end? Was there no other way? Must one go through all the horror of this victory over death, the triumph of the integral will, that would not be broken till it disappeared utterly? One must, it was the only way. She admired the self-possession and the control of the dying man exceedingly. But she loathed the death itself. She was glad the everyday world held good, and she need not recognize anything beyond.

'You are quite all right here?—nothing we can do for you?—nothing you find wrong in your position?'

'Except that you are too good to me,' said Gudrun.

'Ah, well, the fault of that lies with yourself,' he said, and he felt a little exultation, that he had made this speech. He was still so strong and living! But the nausea of death began to creep back on him, in reaction.

Gudrun went away, back to Winifred. Mademoiselle had left, Gudrun stayed a good deal at Shortlands, and a tutor came in to carry on Winifred's education. But he did not live in the house, he was connected with the Grammar School.

One day, Gudrun was to drive with Winifred and Gerald and Birkin to town in the car. It was a dark, showery day. Winifred and Gudrun were ready and waiting at the door. Winifred was very quiet, but Gudrun had not noticed. Suddenly the child asked, in a voice of unconcern:

'Do you think my father's going to die, Miss Brangwen?'

Gudrun started.

'I don't know,' she replied.

'Don't you truly?'

'Nobody knows for certain. He *may* die, of course.'

The child pondered for a few moments, then she asked:

'But do you *think* he will die?'

It was put almost like a question in geography or science,

insistent, as if she would force an admission from the adult. The watchful, slightly triumphant child was almost diabolical.

'Do I think he will die?' repeated Gudrun. 'Yes, I do.'

But Winifred's large eyes were fixed on her, and the girl did not move.

'He is very ill,' said Gudrun.

A small smile came over Winifred's face, subtle and sceptical.

'*I* don't believe he will,' the child asserted mockingly, and she moved away into the drive. Gudrun watched the isolated figure, and her heart stood still. Winifred was playing with a little rivulet of water, absorbedly as if nothing had been said.

'I've made a proper dam,' she said, out of the moist distance.

Gerald came to the door from out of the hall behind.

'It is just as well she doesn't choose to believe it,' he said.

Gudrun looked at him. Their eyes met; and they exchanged a sardonic understanding.

'Just as well,' said Gudrun.

He looked at her again, and a fire flickered up in his eyes.

'Best to dance while Rome burns, since it must burn, don't you think?' he said.

She was rather taken aback. But, gathering herself together, she replied:

'Oh—better dance than walk, certainly.'

'So I think.'

And they both felt the subterranean desire to let go, to fling away everything and lapse into a sheer unrestraint, brutal and licentious. A strange black passion surged up pure in Gudrun. She felt strong. She felt her hands so strong, as if she could tear the world asunder with them. She remembered the abandonments of Roman licence, and her heart grew hot. She knew she wanted this herself also—or something, something equivalent. Ah, if that which was unknown and suppressed in her were once let loose, what an orgiastic and satisfying event it would be. And she wanted it, she trembled slightly from the proximity of the man, who stood just behind her, suggestive of the same black licentiousness that rose in herself. She wanted it with him, this unacknowledged frenzy. For a moment the clear perception of this preoccupied her, distinct and perfect in its final reality. Then she shut it off completely, saying:

'We might as well go down to the lodge after Winifred—we can get in the car there.'

'So we can,' he answered, going with her.

They found Winifred at the lodge admiring the litter of pure-bred white puppies. The girl looked up, and there was a rather ugly, unseeing cast in her eyes as she turned to Gerald and Gudrun. She did not want to see them.

'Look!' she cried. 'Three new puppies! Marshall says this one seems perfect. Isn't it a sweetling? But it isn't so nice as its mother.' She turned to caress the fine white bull-terrier bitch that stood uneasily near her.

'My dearest Lady Crich,' she said, 'you are beautiful as an angel on earth. Angel—angel—don't you think she's good enough and beautiful enough to go to heaven, Gudrun? They will be in heaven, won't they—and *especially* my darling Lady Crich! Mrs Marshall, I say!'

'Yes, Miss Winifred?' said the woman, appearing at the door.

'Oh, do call this one Lady Winifred, if she turns out perfect, will you? Do tell Marshall to call it Lady Winifred.'

'I'll tell him—but I'm afraid that's a gentleman puppy, Miss Winifred.'

'Oh *no!*' There was the sound of a car. 'There's Rupert!' cried the child, and she ran to the gate.

Birkin, driving his car, pulled up outside the lodge gate.

'We're ready!' cried Winifred. 'I want to sit in front with you, Rupert. May I?'

'I'm afraid you'll fidget about and fall out,' he said.

'No, I won't. I do want to sit in front next to you. It makes my feet so lovely and warm, from the engines.'

Birkin helped her up, amused at sending Gerald to sit by Gudrun in the body of the car.

'Have you any news, Rupert?' Gerald called, as they rushed along the lanes.

'News?' exclaimed Birkin.

'Yes.' Gerald looked at Gudrun, who sat by his side, and

he said, his eyes narrowly laughing, 'I want to know
whether I ought to congratulate him, but I can't get anything
definite out of him.'

Gudrun flushed deeply.

'Congratulate him on what?' she asked.

'There was some mention of an engagement—at least, he
said something to me about it.'

Gudrun flushed darkly.

'You mean with Ursula?' she said, in challenge.

'Yes. That is so, isn't it?'

'I don't think there's any engagement,' said Gudrun
coldly.

'That so? Still no developments, Rupert?' he called.

'Where? Matrimonial? No.'

'How's that?' called Gudrun.

Birkin glanced quickly round. There was irritation in his
eyes also.

'Why?' he replied. 'What do you think of it, Gudrun?'

'Oh,' she cried, determined to fling her stone also into the
pool, since they had begun, 'I don't think she wants an engagement. Naturally, she's a bird that prefers the bush.'
Gudrun's voice was clear and gong-like. It reminded Rupert
of her father's, so strong and vibrant.

'And I,' said Birkin, his face playful but yet determined,
'I want a binding contract, and am not keen on love, particularly free love.'

They were both amused. *Why* this public avowal? Gerald
seemed suspended a moment, in amusement.

'Love isn't good enough for you?' he called.

'No!' shouted Birkin.

'Ha, well, that's being over-refined,' said Gerald, and the
car ran through the mud.

'What's the matter, really?' said Gerald, turning to Gudrun.

This was an assumption of a sort of intimacy that irritated
Gudrun almost like an affront. It seemed to her that Gerald
was deliberately insulting her, and infringing on the decent
privacy of them all.

"What is it?' she said, in her high, repellent voice. 'Don't ask me!—I know nothing about *ultimate* marriage, I assure you: or even penultimate.'

'Only the ordinary unwarrantable brand!' replied Gerald. 'Just so—same here. I am no expert on marriage and degrees of ultimateness. It seems to be a bee that buzzes loudly in Rupert's bonnet.'

'Exactly! But that is his trouble, exactly! Instead of wanting a woman for herself, he wants his *ideas* fulfilled. Which, when it comes to actual practice, is not good enough.'

'Oh no. Best go slap for what's womanly in woman, like a bull at a gate.' Then he seemed to glimmer in himself. 'You think love is the ticket, do you?' he asked.

'Certainly, while it lasts—you only can't insist on permanency,' came Gudrun's voice, strident above the noise.

'Marriage or no marriage, ultimate or penultimate or just so-so?—take the love as you find it.'

'As you please, or as you don't please,' she echoed. 'Marriage is a social arrangement, I take it, and has nothing to do with the question of love.'

His eyes were flickering on her all the time. She felt as if he were kissing her freely and malevolently. It made the colour burn in her cheeks, but her heart was quite firm and unfailing.

'You think Rupert is off his head a bit?' Gerald asked.

Her eyes flashed with acknowledgement.

'As regards a woman, yes,' she said, 'I do. There *is* such a thing as two people being in love for the whole of their lives—perhaps. But marriage is neither here nor there, even then. If they are in love, well and good. If not—why break eggs about it!'

'Yes,' said Gerald. 'That's how it strikes me. But what about Rupert?'

'I can't make out—neither can he nor anybody. He seems to think that if you marry you can get through marriage into a third heaven, or something—all very vague.'

'Very! And who wants a third heaven? As a matter of fact, Rupert has a great yearning to be *safe*—to tie himself to the mast.'

'Yes. It seems to me he's mistaken there too,' said Gudrun. 'I'm sure a mistress is more likely to be faithful than a wife—just because she is her *own* mistress. No—he says he believes that a man and wife can go further than any other two beings—but *where,* is not explained. They can know each other, heavenly and hellish but particularly hellish, so perfectly that they go beyond heaven and hell—into—there it all breaks down—into nowhere.'

'Into Paradise, he says,' laughed Gerald.

Gudrun shrugged her shoulders. '*Je m'en fiche* of your Paradise!' she said.

'Not being a Mohammedan,' said Gerald. Birkin sat motionless, driving the car, quite unconscious of what they said. And Gudrun, sitting immediately behind him, felt a sort of ironic pleasure in thus exposing him.

'He says,' she added, with a grimace of irony, 'that you can find an eternal equilibrium in marriage, if you accept the unison, and still leave yourself separate, don't try to fuse.'

'Doesn't inspire me,' said Gerald.

'That's just it,' said Gudrun.

'I believe in love, in a real *abandon,* if you're capable of it,' said Gerald.

'So do I,' said she.

'And so does Rupert, too—though he is always shouting.'

'No,' said Gudrun. 'He won't abandon himself to the other person. You can't be sure of him. That's the trouble, I think.'

'Yet he wants marriage! Marriage—*et puis?*'

'*Le paradis!*' mocked Gudrun.

Birkin, as he drove, felt a creeping of the spine, as if somebody were threatening his neck. But he shrugged with indifference. It began to rain. Here was a change. He stopped the car and got down to put up the hood.

22

Woman to Woman

They came to the town, and left Gerald at the railway station. Gudrun and Winifred were to come to tea with Birkin, who expected Ursula also. In the afternoon, however, the first person to turn up was Hermione. Birkin was out, so she went in the drawing-room, looking at his books and papers, and playing on the piano. Then Ursula arrived. She was surprised, unpleasantly so, to see Hermione, of whom she had heard nothing for some time.

'It is a surprise to see you,' she said.

'Yes,' said Hermione—'I've been away at Aix—'

'Oh, for your health?'

'Yes.'

The two women looked at each other. Ursula resented Hermione's long, grave, downward-looking face. There was something of the stupidity and the unenlightened self-esteem of a horse in it. 'She's got a horse-face,' Ursula said to herself, 'she runs between blinkers.' It did seem as if Hermione, like the moon, had only one side to her penny. There was no obverse. She started out all the time on the narrow, but to her, complete world of the extant consciousness. In the darkness, she did not exist. Like the moon, one half of her was lost to life. Her self was all in her head, she did not know what it was spontaneously to run or move, like a fish in the water, or a weasel on the grass. She must always *know*.

But Ursula only suffered from Hermione's one-sidedness. She only felt Hermione's cool evidence, which seemed to put her down as nothing. Hermione, who brooded and brooded till she was exhausted with the ache of her effort at consciousness, spent and ashen in her body, who gained so slowly and with such effort her final and barren conclusions of knowledge, was apt, in the presence of other women, whom she thought simply female, to wear the conclusions of her bitter assurance like jewels which conferred on her an unquestionable distinction, established her in a higher order of life. She was apt, mentally, to condescend to women such as Ursula, whom she regarded as purely emotional. Poor Hermione, it was her one possession, this aching certainty of hers, it was her only justification. She must be confident here, for God knows, she felt rejected and deficient enough elsewhere. In the life of thought, of the spirit, she was one of the elect. And she wanted to be universal. But there was a devastating cynicism at the bottom of her. She did not believe in her own universals—they were sham. She did not believe in the inner life—it was a trick, not a reality. She did not believe in the spiritual world—it was an affectation. In the last resort, she believed in Mammon, the flesh, and the devil—these at least were not sham. She was a priestess without belief, without conviction, suckled in a creed outworn, and condemned to the reiteration of mysteries that were not divine to her. Yet there was no escape. She was a leaf upon a dying tree. What help was there then, but to fight still for the old, withered truths, to die for the old, outworn belief, to be a sacred and inviolate priestess of desecrated mysteries? The old great truths *had* been true. And she was a leaf of the old great tree of knowledge that was withering now. To the old and last truth then she must be faithful even though cynicism and mockery took place at the bottom of her soul.

'I am so glad to see you,' she said to Ursula, in her slow voice, that was like an incantation. 'You and Rupert have become quite friends?'

'Oh yes,' said Ursula. 'He is always somewhere in the background.'

Hermione paused before she answered. She saw perfectly well the other woman's vaunt: it seemed truly vulgar.

'Is he?' she said slowly, and with perfect equanimity. 'And do you think you will marry?'

The question was so calm and mild, so simple and bare and dispassionate that Ursula was somewhat taken aback, rather attracted. It pleased her almost like a wickedness. There was some delightful naked irony in Hermione.

'Well,' replied Ursula, '*he* wants to, awfully, but I'm not so sure.'

Hermione watched her with slow, calm eyes. She noted this new expression of vaunting. How she envied Ursula a certain unconscious positivity! even her vulgarity!

'Why aren't you sure?' she asked, in her easy sing-song. She was perfectly at her ease, perhaps even rather happy in this conversation. 'You don't really love him?'

Ursula flushed a little at the mild impertinence of this question. And yet she could not definitely take offence. Hermione seemed so calmly and sanely candid. After all, it was rather great to be able to be so sane.

'He says it isn't love he wants,' she replied.

'What is it then?' Hermione was slow and level.

'He wants me really to accept him in marriage.'

Hermione was silent for some time, watching Ursula with slow, pensive eyes.

'Does he?' she said at length, without expression. Then, rousing, 'And what is it you don't want? You don't want marriage?'

'No—I don't—not really. I don't want to give the sort of *submission* he insists on. He wants me to give myself up—and I simply don't feel that I *can* do it.'

Again there was a long pause before Hermione replied:

'Not if you don't want to.' Then again there was silence. Hermione shuddered with a strange desire. Ah, if only he had asked *her* to subserve him, to be his slave! She shuddered with desire.

'You see, I can't—'

'But exactly in what does—'

They had both begun at once, they both stopped. Then Hermione, assuming priority of speech, resumed as if wearily:

'To what does he want you to submit?'

'He says he wants me to accept him non-emotionally, and finally—I really don't know *what* he means. He says he wants the demon part of himself to be mated—physically—not the human being. You see, he says one thing one day, and another the next—and he always contradicts himself—'

'And always thinks about himself, and his own dissatisfaction,' said Hermione slowly.

'Yes,' cried Ursula. 'As if there were no one but himself concerned. That makes it so impossible.'

But immediately she began to retract.

'He insists on my accepting God knows what in *him*,' she resumed. 'He wants me to accept *him* as—as an absolute—But it seems to me he doesn't want to *give* anything. He doesn't want real warm intimacy—he won't have it—he rejects it. He won't let me think, really, and he won't let me *feel*—he hates feelings.'

There was a long pause, bitter for Hermione. Ah, if only he would have made this demand of her! Her he *drove* into thought, drove inexorably into knowledge—and then execrated her for it.

'He wants me to sink myself,' Ursula resumed, 'not to have any being of my own—'

'Then why doesn't he marry an odalisk?' said Hermione in her mild sing-song, 'if it is that he wants.' Her long face looked sardonic and amused.

'Yes,' said Ursula vaguely. After all, the tiresome thing was, he did not want an odalisk, he did not want a slave. Hermione would have been his slave—there was in her a horrible desire to prostrate herself before a man—a man who worshipped her, however, and admitted her as the supreme thing. He did not want an odalisk. He wanted a woman to *take* something from him, to give herself up so much that she could take the last realities of him, the last facts, the last physical facts, physical and unbearable.

And if she did, would he acknowledge her? Would he be able to acknowledge her through everything, or would he use her just as his instrument, use her for his own private satisfaction, not admitting her? That was what the other men had done. They had wanted their own show, and they would not admit her, they turned all she was into nothingness. Just as Hermione now betrayed herself as a woman. Hermione was like a man, she believed only in men's things. She betrayed the woman in herself. And Birkin, would he acknowledge, or would he deny her?

'Yes,' said Hermione, as each woman came out of her

own separate reverie. 'It would be a mistake—I think it would be a mistake—'

'To marry him?' asked Ursula.

'Yes,' said Hermione slowly—'I think you need a man—soldierly, strong-willed—' Hermione held out her hand and clenched it with rhapsodic intensity. 'You should have a man like the old heroes—you need to stand behind him as he goes into battle, you need to *see* his strength, and to *hear* his shout—You need a man physically strong, and virile in his will, *not* a sensitive man—' There was a break, as if the pythoness had uttered the oracle, and now the woman went on, in a rhapsody-wearied voice: 'And you see, Rupert isn't this, he isn't. He is frail in health and body, he needs great, great care. Then he is so changeable and unsure of himself—it requires the greatest patience and understanding to help him. And I don't think you are patient. You would have to be prepared to suffer—dreadfully. I can't *tell* you how much suffering it would take to make him happy. He lives an *intensely* spiritual life, at times—too, too wonderful. And then come the reactions. I can't speak of what I have been through with him. We have been together so long, I really do know him, I *do* know what he is. And I feel I must say it; I feel it would be perfectly *disastrous* for you to marry him—for you even more than for him.' Hermione lapsed into bitter reverie. 'He is so uncertain, so unstable—he wearies, and then reacts. I couldn't *tell* you what his reactions are. I couldn't *tell* you the agony of them. That which he affirms and loves one day—a little later he turns on it in a fury of destruction. He is never constant, always this awful, dreadful reaction. Always the quick change from good to bad, bad to good. And nothing is so devastating, nothing—'

'Yes,' said Ursula humbly, 'you must have suffered.'

An unearthly light came on Hermione's face. She clenched her hand like one inspired.

'And one must be willing to suffer—willing to suffer for him hourly, daily—if you are going to help him, if he is to keep true to anything at all—'

'And I don't *want* to suffer hourly and daily,' said Ursula. 'I don't, I should be ashamed. I think it is degrading not to be happy.'

Hermione stopped and looked at her a long time.

'Do you?' she said at last. And this utterance seemed to her a mark of Ursula's far distance from herself. For to Hermione suffering was the greatest reality, come what might. Yet she too had a creed of happiness.

'Yes,' she said. 'One *should* be happy—' But it was a matter of will.

'Yes,' said Hermione, listlessly now, 'I can only feel that it would be disastrous, disastrous—at least, to marry in a hurry. Can't you be together without marriage? I do feel that marriage would be fatal for both of you. I think for you even more than for him—and I think of his health—'

'Of course,' said Ursula, '*I* don't care about marriage—it isn't really important to me—it's he who wants it.'

'It is his idea for the moment,' said Hermione, with that weary finality and a sort of *si jeunesse savait* infallibility.

There was a pause. Then Ursula broke into faltering challenge.

'You think I'm merely a physical woman, don't you?'

'No, indeed,' said Hermione. 'No, indeed! But I think you are vital and young—it isn't a question of years, or even of experience—it is almost a question of race. Rupert is race-old, he comes of an old race—and you seem to me so young, you come of a young, inexperienced race.'

'Do I!' said Ursula. 'But I think he is awfully young, on one side.'

'Yes, perhaps—childish in many respects. Nevertheless—'

They both lapsed into silence. Ursula was filled with deep resentment and a touch of hopelessness. 'It isn't true,' she said to herself, silently addressing her adversary. 'It isn't true. And it is *you* who want a physically strong, bullying man, not I. It is you who want an unsensitive man, not I. You *don't* know anything about Rupert, not really, in spite of the years you have had with him. You don't give him a woman's love, you give him an ideal love, and that is why he reacts away from you. You don't know. You only know the dead things. Any kitchen-maid would know something about him, you don't know. What do you think your knowledge is but dead understanding, that doesn't mean a thing. You are so false, and untrue, how could you know anything?

What is the good of your talking about love—you untrue spectre of a woman! How can you know anything, when you don't believe? You don't believe in yourself and your own womanhood, so what good is your conceited, shallow cleverness—!'

The two women sat on in antagonistic silence. Hermione felt injured, that all her good intention, all her offering, only left the other woman in vulgar antagonism. But then, Ursula could not understand, never would understand, could never be more than the usual jealous and unreasonable female, with a good deal of powerful female emotion, female attraction, and a fair amount of female understanding, but no mind. Hermione had decided long ago that where there was no mind, it was useless to appeal for reason—one had merely to ignore the ignorant. And Rupert—he had now reacted towards the strongly female, healthy, selfish woman—it was his reaction for the time being—there was no helping it all. It was all a foolish backward and forward, a violent oscillation that would at length be too violent for his coherency, and he would smash and be dead. There was no saving him. This violent and directionless reaction between animalism and spiritual truth would go on in him till he tore himself in two between the opposite directions, and disappeared meaninglessly out of life. It was no good—he too was without unity, without *mind,* in the ultimate stages of living; not quite man enough to make a destiny for a woman.

They sat on till Birkin came in and found them together. He felt at once the antagonism in the atmosphere, something radical and insuperable, and he bit his lip. But he affected a bluff manner.

'Hello, Hermione, are you back again? How do you feel?'

'Oh, better. And how are you—you don't look well—'

'Oh!—I believe Gudrun and Winnie Crich are coming in to tea. At least they said they were. We shall be a tea-party. What train did you come by, Ursula?'

It was rather annoying to see him trying to placate both women at once. Both women watched him, Hermione with deep resentment and pity for him. Ursula very impatient. He was nervous and apparently in quite good spirits, chattering

the conventional commonplaces. Ursula was amazed and in-
dignant at the way he made small talk; he was adept as any
fat in Christendom. She became quite stiff, she would not
answer. It all seemed to her so false and so belittling. And
still Gudrun did not appear.

'I think I shall go to Florence for the winter,' said
Hermione at length.

'Will you?' he answered. 'But it is so cold there.'

'Yes, but I shall stay with Palestra. It is quite comfortable.'

'What takes you to Florence?'

'I don't know,' said Hermione slowly. Then she looked at
him with her slow, heavy gaze. 'Barnes is starting his school
of aesthetics, and Olandese is going to give a set of dis-
courses on the Italian national policy—'

'Both rubbish,' he said.

'No, I don't think so,' said Hermione.

'Which do you admire, then?'

'I admire both. Barnes is a pioneer. And then I am interested in Italy, in her coming to national consciousness.'

'I wish she'd come to something different from national
consciousness, then,' said Birkin; 'especially as it only
means a sort of commercial-industrial consciousness. I hate
Italy and her national rant. And I think Barnes is an amateur.'

Hermione was silent for some moments, in a state of hostility. But yet, she had got Birkin back again into her world!
How subtle her influence was, she seemed to start his irritable attention into her direction exclusively, in one minute.
He was her creature.

'No,' she said, 'you are wrong.' Then a sort of tension
came over her, she raised her face like the pythoness inspired with oracles, and went on in rhapsodic manner: *'Il
Sandro mi scrive che ha accolto il più grande entusiasmo,
tutti i giovani, e fanciulle e ragazzi, sono tutti—'* She went
on in Italian, as if, in thinking of the Italians she thought in
their language.

He listened with a shade of distaste to her rhapsody, then
he said:

'For all that, I don't like it. Their nationalism is just industrialism—that and a shallow jealousy I detest so much.'

'I think you are wrong—I think you are wrong—' said Hermione. 'It seems to me purely spontaneous and beautiful, the modern Italian's *passion,* for it is a passion, for Italy, *l'Italia*—'

'Do you know Italy well?' Ursula asked of Hermione. Hermione hated to be broken in upon in this manner. Yet she answered mildly:

'Yes, pretty well. I spent several years of my girlhood there with my mother. My mother died in Florence.'

'Oh.'

There was a pause, painful to Ursula and to Birkin. Hermione, however, seemed abstracted and calm. Birkin was white, his eyes glowed as if he were in a fever, he was far too overwrought. How Ursula suffered in this tense atmosphere of strained wills! Her head seemed bound round by iron bands.

Birkin rang the bell for tea. They could not wait for Gudrun any longer. When the door was opened, the cat walked in.

'Micio! Micio!' called Hermione in her slow, deliberate sing-song. The young cat turned to look at her, then, with his slow and stately walk he advanced to her side.

'*Vieni—vieni quá,*' Hermione was saying in her strange caressive, protective voice, as if she were always the elder, the mother superior. '*Vieni dire Buon' Giorno alla zia. Mi ricordi, mi ricordi bene—non è vero, piccolo? È vero che mi ricordi? È vero?*' And slowly she rubbed his head, slowly and with ironic indifference.

'Does he understand Italian?' said Ursula, who knew nothing of the language.

'Yes,' said Hermione at length. 'His mother was Italian. She was born in my waste-paper basket in Florence on the morning of Rupert's birthday. She was his birthday present.'

Tea was brought in. Birkin poured out for them. It was strange how inviolable was the intimacy which existed between him and Hermione. Ursula felt that she was an outsider. The very tea-cups and the old silver was a bond between Hermione and Birkin. It seemed to belong to an old, past world which they had inhabited together, and in which Ursula was a foreigner. She was almost a parvenue in their old cultured milieu. Her convention was not their convention, their standards were not her standards. But theirs were established, they had the sanction and the grace of age. He and she together, Hermione and Birkin, were people of the same old tradition, the same withered deadening culture. And she, Ursula, was an intruder. So they always made her feel.

Hermione poured a little cream into a saucer. The simple way she assumed her rights in Birkin's room maddened and discouraged Ursula. There was a fatality about it, as if it were bound to be. Hermione lifted the cat and put the cream before him. He planted his two paws on the edge of the table and bent his gracious young head to drink.

'*Sicuro che capisce italiano,*' sang Hermione, '*non l'avrà dimenticato, la lingua della Mamma.*'

She lifted the cat's head with her long, slow, white fingers, not letting him drink, holding him in her power. It was always the same, this joy in power she manifested, peculiarly in power over any male being. He blinked forbearingly, with a male, bored expression, licking his whiskers. Hermione laughed in her short, grunting fashion.

'*Ecco, il bravo ragazzo, com' è superbo, questo!*'

She made a vivid picture, so calm and strange with the cat. She had a true static impressiveness, she was a social artist in some ways.

The cat refused to look at her, indifferently avoided her fingers, and began to drink again, his nose down to the cream, perfectly balanced, as he lapped with his odd little click.

'It's bad for him, teaching him to eat at table,' said Birkin.

'Yes,' said Hermione, easily assenting.

Then, looking down at the cat, she resumed her old, mocking, humorous sing-song.

'*Ti imparano fare brutte cose, brutte cose—*'

She lifted the Mino's white chin on her forefinger slowly. The young cat looked round with a supremely forbearing air, avoided seeing anything, withdrew his chin, and began to wash his face with his paw. Hermione grunted her laughter, pleased.

'*Bel giovanetto*—' she said.

The cat reached forward again and put his fine white paw on the edge of the saucer. Hermione lifted it down with delicate slowness. This deliberate, delicate carefulness of movement reminded Ursula of Gudrun.

'*No! Non è permesso di mettere il zampino nel tondinetto. Non piace al babbo. Un signor gatto così selvatico*—!'

And she kept her finger on the softly planted paws of the cat, and her voice had the same whimsical, humorous note of bullying.

Ursula had her nose out of joint. She wanted to go away now. It all seemed no good. Hermione was established for ever, she herself was ephemeral and had not yet even arrived.

'I will go now,' she said suddenly.

Birkin looked at her almost in fear—he so dreaded her anger. 'But there is no need for such hurry,' he said.

'Yes,' she answered. 'I will go.' And turning to Hermione, before there was time to say any more, she held out her hand and said 'Good-bye.'

'Good-bye—' sang Hermione, detaining the hand. 'Must you really go now?'

'Yes, I think I'll go,' said Ursula, her face set and averted from Hermione's eyes.

'You think you will—'

But Ursula had got her hand free. She turned to Birkin with a quick, almost jeering 'Good-bye', and she was opening the door before he had time to do it for her.

When she got outside the house she ran down the road in fury and agitation. It was strange, the unreasoning rage and violence Hermione roused in her, by her very presence. Ursula knew she gave herself away to the other woman, she knew she looked ill-bred, uncouth, exaggerated. But she did not care. She only ran up the road, lest she should go back and jeer in the faces of the two she had left behind. For they outraged her.

23

Excurse

Next day Birkin sought Ursula out. It happened to be the half-day at the Grammar School. He appeared towards the end of the morning, and asked her, would she drive with him in the afternoon. She consented. But her face was closed and unresponding, and his heart sank.

The afternoon was fine and dim. He was driving the motorcar, and she sat beside him. But still her face was closed against him, unresponding. When she became like this, like a wall against him, his heart contracted.

His life now seemed so reduced that he hardly cared any more. At moments it seemed to him he did not care a straw whether Ursula or Hermione or anybody else existed or did not exist. Why bother! Why strive for a coherent, satisfied life? Why not drift on in a series of accidents—like a picaresque novel? Why not? Why bother about human relationships? Why take them seriously—male or female? Why form any serious connexions at all? Why not be casual, drifting along, taking all for what it was worth?

And yet, still, he was damned and doomed to the old effort at serious living.

'Look,' he said, 'what I bought.' The car was running along a broad white road between autumn trees.

He gave her a little bit of screwed-up paper. She took it and opened it.

'How lovely,' she cried.

She examined the gift.

'How perfectly lovely!' she cried again. 'But why do you give them me?' She put the question offensively.

His face flickered with bored irritation. He shrugged his shoulders slightly.

'I wanted to,' he said coolly.

'But why? Why should you?'

'Am I called on to find reasons?' he asked.

There was a silence, whilst she examined the rings that had been screwed up in the paper.

'I think they are *beautiful*,' she said, 'especially this. This is wonderful—'

It was a round opal, red and fiery, set in a circle of tiny rubies.

'You like that best?' he said.

'I think I do.'

'I like the sapphire,' he said.

'This?'

It was a rose-shaped, beautiful sapphire, with small brilliants.

'Yes,' she said, 'it is lovely.' She held it in the light. 'Yes, perhaps it *is* the best—'

'The blue—' he said.

'Yes, wonderful—'

He suddenly swung the car out of the way of a farm-cart. It tilted on the bank. He was a careless driver, yet very quick. But Ursula was frightened. There was always that something regardless in him which terrified her. She suddenly felt he might kill her, by making some dreadful accident with the motor-car. For a moment she was stony with fear.

'Isn't it rather dangerous, the way you drive?' she asked him.

'No, it isn't dangerous,' he said. And then, after a pause: 'Don't you like the yellow ring at all?'

It was a squarish topaz set in a frame of steel, or some other similar mineral, finely wrought.

'Yes,' she said, 'I do like it. But why did you buy these rings?'

'I wanted them. They are second-hand.'

'You bought them for yourself?'

'No. Rings look wrong on my hands.'

'Why did you buy them then?'

'I bought them to give to you.'

'But why? Surely you ought to give them to Hermione! You belong to her.'

He did not answer. She remained with the jewels shut in her hand. She wanted to try them on her fingers, but something in her would not let her. And, moreover, she was afraid her hands were too large, she shrank from the mortification of a failure to put them on any but her little finger. They travelled in silence through the empty lanes.

Driving in a motor-car excited her, she forgot his presence even.

'Where are we?' she asked suddenly.

'Not far from Worksop.'

'And where are we going?'

'Anywhere.'

It was the answer she liked.

She opened her hand to look at the rings. They gave her *such* pleasure, as they lay, the three circles, with their knotted jewels, entangled in her palm. She would have to try them on. She did so secretly, unwilling to let him see, so that he should not know her finger was too large for them. But he saw, nevertheless. He always saw, if she wanted him not to. It was another of his hateful, watchful characteristics.

Only the opal, with its thin wire loop, would go on her ring finger. And she was superstitious. No, there was ill-portent enough, she would not accept this ring from him in pledge.

'Look,' she said, putting forward her hand, that was half closed and shrinking. 'The others don't fit me.'

He looked at the red-glinting, soft stone on her over-sensitive skin.

'Yes,' he said.

'But opals are unlucky, aren't they?' she said wistfully.

'No. I prefer unlucky things. Luck is vulgar. Who wants what *luck* would bring? I don't.'

'But why?' she laughed.

And, consumed with a desire to see how the other rings would look on her hand, she put them on her little finger.

'They can be made a little bigger,' he said.

'Yes,' she replied doubtfully. And she sighed. She knew that, in accepting the rings, she was accepting a pledge. Yet fate seemed more than herself. She looked again at the jewels. They were very beautiful to her eyes—not as ornament, or wealth, but as tiny fragments of loveliness.

'I'm glad you bought them,' she said, putting her hand, half unwillingly, gently on his arm.

He smiled slightly. He wanted her to come to him. But he was angry at the bottom of his soul, and indifferent. He knew she had a passion for him, really. But it was not finally interesting. There were depths of passion when one became impersonal and indifferent, unemotional. Whereas Ursula was still at the emotional personal level—always so abominably personal. He had taken her as he had never been taken himself. He had taken her at the roots of her darkness and shame—like a demon, laughing over the fountain of mystic corruption which was one of the sources of her being, laughing, shrugging, accepting, accepting finally. As for her, when would she so much go beyond herself as to accept him at the quick of death?

She now became quite happy. The motor-car ran on, the afternoon was soft and dim. She talked with lively interest, analysing people and their motives—Gudrun, Gerald. He answered vaguely. He was not very much interested any more in personalities and in people—people were all different, but they were all enclosed nowadays in a definite limitation, he said; there were only about two great ideas, two great streams of activity remaining, with various forms of reaction therefrom. The reactions were all varied in various people, but they followed a few great laws, and intrinsically there was no difference. They acted and reacted involuntarily according to a few great laws, and once the laws, the great principles, were known, people were no longer mystically interesting. They were all essentially alike, the differences were only variations on a theme. None of them transcended the given terms.

Ursula did not agree—people were still an adventure to her—but—perhaps not as much as she tried to persuade herself. Perhaps there was something mechanical, now, in her interest. Perhaps also her interest was destructive, her analysing was a real tearing to pieces. There was an under-space in her where she did not care for people and their idiosyncrasies, even to destroy them. She seemed to touch for a moment this under-silence in herself, she became still, and she turned for a moment purely to Birkin.

'Won't it be lovely to go home in the dark?' she said. 'We might have tea rather late—shall we?—and have high tea? Wouldn't that be rather nice?'

'I promised to be at Shortlands for dinner,' he said.

'But—it doesn't matter—you can go tomorrow—'

'Hermione is there,' he said, in rather an uneasy voice. 'She is going away in two days. I suppose I ought to say good-bye to her. I shall never see her again.'

Ursula drew away, closed in a violent silence. He knitted his brows, and his eyes began to sparkle again in anger.

'You don't mind, do you?' he asked irritably.

'No, I don't care. Why should I? Why should I mind?' her tone was jeering and offensive.

'That's what I ask myself,' he said; 'why *should* you mind! But you seem to.' His brows were tense with violent irritation.

'I *assure* you I don't, I don't mind in the least. Go where you belong—it's what I want you to do.'

'Ah, you fool!' he cried, 'with your "go where you belong". It's finished between Hermione and me. She means much more to *you,* if it comes to that, than she does to me. For you can only revolt in pure reaction from her—and to be her opposite is to be her counterpart.'

'Ah, opposite!' cried Ursula. 'I know your dodges. I am not taken in by your word-twisting. You belong to Hermione and her dead show. Well, if you do, you do. I don't blame you. But then you've nothing to do with me.'

In his inflamed, overwrought exasperation he stopped the car, and they sat there, in the middle of the country lane, to have it out. It was a crisis of war between them, so they did not see the ridiculousness of their situation.

'If you weren't a fool, if only you weren't a fool,' he cried in bitter despair, 'you'd see that one could be decent, even when one has been wrong. I *was* wrong to go on all those years with Hermione—it was a deathly process. But after all, one can have a little human decency. But no, you would tear

my soul out with your jealousy at the very mention of Hermione's name.'

'I jealous! *I*—jealous! You *are* mistaken if you think that.
I'm not jealous in the least of Hermione, she is nothing to
me, not *that*!' And Ursula snapped her fingers. 'No, it's you
who are a liar. It's you who must return, like a dog to his
vomit. It is what Hermione *stands* for that I *hate*. I *hate* it.
It is lies, it is false, it is death. But you want it, you can't
help it, you can't help yourself. You belong to that old,
deathly way of living—then go back to it. But don't come to
me, for I've nothing to do with it.'

And in the stress of her violent emotion, she got down
from the car and went to the hedgerow, picking unconsciously some flesh-pink spindleberries, some of which were
burst, showing their orange seeds.

'Ah, you are a fool,' he cried bitterly, with some contempt.

'Yes, I am. I *am* a fool. And thank God for it. I'm too big
a fool to swallow your cleverness. God be praised. You go
to your women—go to them—they are your sort—you've always had a string of them trailing after you—and you always will. Go to your spiritual brides—but don't come to
me as well, because I'm not having any, thank you. You're
not satisfied, are you? Your spiritual brides can't give you
what you want, they aren't common and fleshy enough for
you, aren't they? So you come to me, and keep them in the
background! You will marry me for daily use. But you'll
keep yourself well provided with spiritual brides in the
background. I know your dirty little game.' Suddenly a
flame ran over her, and she stamped her foot madly on the
road, and he winced, afraid that she would strike him. 'And
I, I'm not spiritual enough, *I'm* not as spiritual as that
Hermione—!' Her brows knitted, her eyes blazed like a tiger's. 'Then *go* to her, that's all I say, *go* to her, *go*. Ha, she
spiritual—*spiritual,* she! A dirty materialist as she is. *She*
spiritual? What does she care for, what is her spirituality?
What *is* it?' Her fury seemed to blaze out and burn his face.
He shrank a little. 'I tell you it's *dirt, dirt,* and nothing *but*
dirt. And it's dirt you want, you crave for it. Spiritual! Is
that spiritual, her bullying, her conceit, her sordid, material-

ism? She's a fishwife, a fishwife, she is such a materialist. And all so sordid. What does she work out to, in the end, with all her social passion, as you call it. Social passion— what social passion has she?—show it me!—where is it? She wants petty, immediate *power,* she wants the illusion that she is a great woman, that is all. In her soul she's a devilish unbeliever, common as dirt. That's what she is at the bottom. And all the rest is pretence—but you love it. You love the sham spirituality, it's your food. And why? Because of the dirt underneath. Do you think I don't know the foulness of your sex life—and hers?—I do. And it's that foulness you want, you liar. Then have it, have it. You're such a liar.'

She turned away, spasmodically tearing the twigs of spindleberry from the hedge, and fastening them, with vibrating fingers, in the bosom of her coat.

He stood watching in silence. A wonderful tenderness burned in him at the sight of her quivering, so sensitive fingers: and at the same time he was full of rage and callousness.

'This is a degrading exhibition,' he said coolly.

'Yes, degrading indeed,' she said. 'But more to me than to you.'

'Since you choose to degrade yourself,' he said. Again the flash came over her face, the yellow lights concentrated in her eyes.

'*You!*' she cried. 'You! You truth-lover! You puritymonger! It *stinks,* your truth and your purity. It stinks of the offal you feed on, you scavenger dog, you eater of corpses. You are foul, *foul*—and you must know it. Your purity, your candour, your goodness—yes, thank you, we've had some. What you are is a foul, deathly thing, obscene, that's what you are, obscene and perverse. You, and love! You may well say, you don't want love. No, you want *yourself,* and dirt and death—that's what you want. You are so *perverse,* so death-eating. And then—'

'There's a bicycle coming,' he said, writhing under her loud denunciation.

She glanced down the road.

'I don't care,' she cried.

Nevertheless she was silent. The cyclist, having heard the voices raised in altercation, glanced curiously at the man and the woman, and at the standing motor-car as he passed.

'—Afternoon,' he said cheerfully.

'Good afternoon,' replied Birkin coldly.

They were silent as the man passed into the distance.

A clearer look had come over Birkin's face. He knew she was in the main right. He knew he was perverse, so spiritual on the one hand, and in some strange way, degraded on the other. But was she herself any better? Was anybody any better?

'It may all be true, lies and stink and all,' he said. 'But Hermione's spiritual intimacy is no rottener than your emotional-jealous intimacy. One can preserve the decencies, even to one's enemies: for one's own sake. Hermione is my enemy—to her last breath! That's why I must bow her off the field.'

'You! You and your enemies and your bows! A pretty picture you make of yourself. But it takes nobody in but yourself. I *jealous*! *I*! What I say,' her voice sprang into flame, 'I say because it is *true*, do you see, because you are *you*, a foul and false liar, a whited sepulchre. That's why I say it. And *you* hear it.'

'And be grateful,' he added, with a satirical grimace.

'Yes,' she cried, 'and if you have a spark of decency in you, be grateful.'

'Not having a spark of decency, however—' he retorted.

'No,' she cried, 'you haven't a *spark*. And so you can go your way, and I'll go mine. It's no good, not the slightest. So you can leave me now, I don't want to go any farther with you—leave me—'

'You don't even know where you are,' he said.

'Oh, don't bother, I assure you I shall be all right. I've got ten shillings in my purse, and that will take me back from anywhere *you* have brought me to.' She hesitated. The rings were still on her fingers, two on her little finger, one on her ring finger. Still she hesitated.

'Very good,' he said. 'The only hopeless thing is a fool.'

'You are quite right,' she said.

Still she hesitated. Then an ugly, malevolent look came

over her face, she pulled the rings from her fingers and tossed them at him. One touched his face, the others hit his coat, and they scattered into the mud.

'And take your rings,' she said, 'and go and buy yourself a female elsewhere—there are plenty to be had, who will be quite glad to share your spiritual mess—or to have your physical mess, and leave your spiritual mess to Hermione.'

With which she walked away, desultorily, up the road. He stood motionless, watching her sullen, rather ugly walk. She was sullenly picking and pulling at the twigs of the hedge as she passed. She grew smaller, she seemed to pass out of his sight. A darkness came over his mind. Only a small, mechanical speck of consciousness hovered near him.

He felt tired and weak. yet also he was relieved. He gave up his old position. He went and sat on the bank. No doubt Ursula was right. It was true, really, what she said. He knew that his spirituality was concomitant of a process of depravity, a sort of pleasure in self-destruction. There really *was* a certain stimulant in self-destruction, for him—especially when it was translated spiritually. But then he knew it—he knew it, and had done. And was not Ursula's way of emotional intimacy, emotional and physical, was it not just as dangerous as Hermione's abstract spiritual intimacy? Fusion, fusion, this horrible fusion of two beings, which every woman and most men insisted on, was it not nauseous and horrible anyhow, whether it was a fusion of the spirit or of the emotional body? Hermione saw herself as the perfect Idea, to which all men must come: and Ursula was the perfect Womb, the bath of birth, to which all men must come! And both were horrible. Why could they not remain individuals, limited by their own limits? Why this dreadful all-comprehensiveness, this hateful tyranny? Why not leave the other being free, why try to absorb, or melt, or merge? One might abandon oneself utterly to the *moments,* but not to any other being.

He could not bear to see the rings lying in the pale mud of the road. He picked them up and wiped them unconsciously on his hands. They were the little tokens of the reality of beauty, the reality of happiness in warm creation. But he had made his hands all dirty and gritty.

There was a darkness over his mind. The terrible knot of consciousness that had persisted there like an obsession was broken, gone, his life was dissolved in darkness over his limbs and his body. But there was a point of anxiety in his heart now. He wanted her to come back. He breathed lightly and regularly like an infant, that breathes innocently, beyond the touch of responsibility.

She was coming back. He saw her drifting desultorily under the high hedge, advancing towards him slowly. He did not move, he did not look again. He was as if asleep, at peace, slumbering and utterly relaxed.

She came up and stood before him, hanging her head.

'See what a flower I found you,' she said, wistfully holding a piece of purple-red bell-heather under his face. He saw the clump of coloured bells, and the tree-like, tiny branch: also her hands, with their over-fine, over-sensitive skin.

'Pretty!' he said, looking up at her with a smile, taking the flower. Everything had become simple again, quite simple, the complexity gone into nowhere. But he badly wanted to cry: except that he was weary and bored by emotion.

Then a hot passion of tenderness for her filled his heart. He stood up and looked into her face. It was new, and oh, so delicate in its luminous wonder and fear. He put his arms round her, and she hid her face on his shoulder.

It was peace, just simple peace, as he stood folding her quietly there on the open lane. It was peace at last. The old, detestable world of tension had passed away at last, his soul was strong and at ease.

She looked up at him. The wonderful yellow light in her eyes now was soft and yielded, they were at peace with each other. He kissed her softly, many, many times. A laugh came into her eyes.

'Did I abuse you?' she asked.

He smiled too, and took her hand, that was so soft and given.

'Never mind,' she said, 'it is all for the good.' He kissed her again, softly, many times.

'Isn't it?' she said.

'Certainly,' he replied. 'Wait! I shall have my own back.'

She laughed suddenly, with a wild catch in her voice, and flung her arms around him.

'You are mine, my love, aren't you?' she cried, straining him close.

'Yes,' he said softly.

His voice was so soft and final, she went very still, as if under a fate which had taken her. Yes, she acquiesced—but it was accomplished without her acquiescence. He was kissing her quietly, repeatedly, with a soft, still happiness that almost made her heart stop beating.

'My love!' she cried, lifting her face and looking with frightened, gentle wonder of bliss. Was it all real? But his eyes were beautiful and soft and immune from stress or excitement, beautiful and smiling lightly to her, smiling with her. She hid her face on his shoulder, hiding before him, because he could see her so completely. She knew he loved her, and she was afraid, she was in a strange element, a new heaven round about her. She wished he were passionate, because in passion she was at home. But this was so still and frail, as space is more frightening than force.

Again, quickly, she lifted her head.

'Do you love me?' she said quickly, impulsively.

'Yes,' he replied, not heeding her motion, only her stillness.

She knew it was true. She broke away.

'So you ought,' she said, turning round to look at the road. 'Did you find the rings?'

'Yes.'

'Where are they?'

'In my pocket.'

She put her hand into his pocket and took them out.

She was restless.

'Shall we go?' she said.

'Yes,' he answered. And they mounted to the car once more, and left behind them this memorable battlefield.

They drifted through the wild, late afternoon in a beautiful motion that was smiling and transcendent. His mind was sweetly at ease, the life flowed through him as from some new fountain, he was as if born out of the cramp of a womb.

'Are you happy?' she asked him, in her strange, delighted way.

'Yes,' he said.

'So am I,' she cried in sudden ecstasy, putting her arm round him and clutching him violently against her, as he steered the motor-car.

'Don't drive much more,' she said. 'I don't want you to be always doing something.'

'No,' he said. 'We'll finish this little trip, and then we'll be free.'

'We will, my love, we will,' she cried in delight, kissing him as he turned to her.

He drove on in a strange new wakefulness, the tension of his consciousness broken. He seemed to be conscious all over, all his body awake with a simple, glimmering awareness, as if he had just come awake, like a thing that is born, like a bird when it comes out of an egg, into a new universe.

They dropped down a long hill in the dusk, and suddenly Ursula recognized on her right hand, below in the hollow, the form of Southwell Minster.

'Are we here!' she cried with pleasure.

The rigid, sombre, ugly cathedral was settling under the gloom of the coming night, as they entered the narrow town, the golden lights showed like slabs of revelation in the shop-windows.

'Father came here with mother,' she said, 'when they first knew each other. He loves it—he loves the Minster. Do you?'

'Yes. It looks like quartz crystals sticking up out of the dark hollow. We'll have our high tea at the Saracen's Head.'

As they descended, they heard the Minster bells playing a hymn, when the hour had struck six.

Glory to thee my God this night
For all the blessings of the light—

So, to Ursula's ear, the tune fell out, drop by drop, from the unseen sky on to the dusky town. It was like dim, bygone centuries sounding. It was all so far off. She stood in the old yard of the inn, smelling of straw and stables and petrol.

Above, she could see the first stars. What was it all? This was no actual world, it was the dream-world of one's childhood—a great circumscribed reminiscence. The world had become unreal. She herself was a strange, transcendent reality.

They sat together in a little parlour by the fire.

'Is it?' she plied, laughing, but unassured.

'What?'

'Everything—is everything true?'

'The best is true,' he said, grimacing at her.

'Is it?' she replied, laughing, but unassured.

She looked at him. He seemed still so separate. New eyes were opened in her soul. She saw a strange creature from another world in him. It was as if she were enchanted, and everything were metamorphosed. She recalled again the old magic of the Book of Genesis, where the sons of God saw the daughters of men, that they were fair. And he was one of these, one of these strange creatures from the beyond, looking down at her, and seeing she was fair.

He stood on the hearth-rug looking at her, at her face that was upturned exactly like a flower, a fresh, luminous flower, glinting faintly golden with the dew of the first light. And he was smiling faintly as if there were no speech in the world, save the silent delight of flowers in each other. Smilingly they delighted in each other's presence, pure presence, not to be thought of, even known. But his eyes had a faintly ironical contraction.

And she was drawn to him strangely, as in a spell. Kneeling on the hearth-rug before him, she put her arms round his loins, and put her face against his thighs. Riches! Riches! She was overwhelmed with a sense of a heavenful of riches.

'We love each other,' she said in delight.

'More than that,' he answered, looking down at her with his glimmering, easy face.

Unconsciously, with her sensitive finger-tips, she was tracing the back of his thighs, following some mysterious lifeflow there. She had discovered something, something more than wonderful, more wonderful than life itself. It was the strange mystery of his life-motion, there, at the back of the thighs, down the flanks. It was a strange reality of his

being, the very stuff of being, there in the straight downflow
of the thighs. It was here she discovered him one of the sons
of God such as were in the beginning of the world, not a
man, something other, something more.

This was release at last. She had had lovers, she had
known passion. But this was neither love nor passion. It was
the daughters of men coming back to the sons of God, the
strange inhuman sons of God who are in the beginning.

Her face was now one dazzle of released, golden light, as
she looked up at him and laid her hands full on his thighs,
behind, as he stood before her. He looked down at her with
a rich bright brow like a diadem above his eyes. She was
beautiful as a new marvellous flower opened at his knees, a
paradisal flower she was, beyond womanhood, such a flower
of luminousness. Yet something was tight and unfree in him.
He did not like this crouching, this radiance—not altogether.

It was all achieved for her. She had found one of the sons
of God from the Beginning, and he had found one of the
first most luminous daughters of men.

She traced with her hands the line of his loins and thighs,
at the back, and a living fire ran through her, from him,
darkly. It was a dark flood of electric passion she released
from him, drew into herself. She had established a rich new
circuit, a new current of passional electric energy, between
the two of them, released from the darkest poles of the body
and established in perfect circuit. It was a dark fire of electricity that rushed from him to her, and flooded them both
with rich peace, satisfaction.

'My love,' she cried, lifting her face to him, her eyes, her
mouth open in transport.

'My love,' he answered, bending and kissing her, always
kissing her.

She closed her hands over the full, rounded body of his
loins, as he stooped over her, she seemed to touch the quick
of the mystery of darkness that was bodily him. She seemed
to faint beneath, and he seemed to faint, stooping over her.
It was a perfect passing away for both of them, and at the
same time the most intolerable accession into being, the
marvellous fullness of immediate gratification, overwhelming, outflooding from the source of the deepest life-force,

the darkest, deepest, strangest life-source of the human body, at the back and base of the loins.

After a lapse of stillness, after the rivers of strange dark fluid richness had passed over her, flooding, carrying away her mind and flooding down her spine and down her knees, past her feet, a strange flood, sweeping away everything and leaving her an essential new being, she was left quite free, she was free in complete ease, her complete self. So she rose, stilly and blithe, smiling at him. He stood before her, glimmering, so awfully real, that her heart almost stopped beating. He stood there in his strange, whole body, that had its marvellous fountains, like the bodies of the sons of God who were in the beginning. There were strange fountains of his body, more mysterious and potent than any she had imagined or known, more satisfying, ah, finally, mystically-physically satisfying. She had thought there was no source deeper than the phallic source. And now, behold, from the smitten rock of the man's body, from the strange marvellous flanks and thighs, deeper, further in mystery than the phallic source, came the floods of ineffable darkness and ineffable riches.

They were glad, and they could forget perfectly. They laughed and went to the meal provided. There was a venison pasty, of all things, a large broad-faced cut ham, eggs and cresses and red beetroot, and medlars and apple-tart, and tea.

'What *good* things!' she cried with pleasure. 'How noble it looks!—shall I pour out the tea?—'

She was usually nervous and uncertain at performing these public duties, such as giving tea. But today she forgot, she was at her ease, entirely forgetting to have misgivings. The tea-pot poured beautifully from a proud slender spout. Her eyes were warm with smiles as she gave him his tea. She had learned at last to be still and perfect.

'Everything is ours,' she said to him.

'Everything,' he answered.

She gave a queer little crowing sound of triumph.

'I'm so glad!' she cried, with unspeakable relief.

'So am I,' he said. 'But I'm thinking we'd better get out of our responsibilities as quick as we can.'

'What responsibilities?' she asked, wondering.

'We must drop our jobs, like a shot.'

A new understanding dawned into her face.

'Of course,' she said, 'there's that.'

'We must get out,' he said. 'There's nothing for it but to get out, quick.'

She looked at him doubtfully across the table.

'But where?' she said.

'I don't know,' he said. 'We'll just wander about for a bit.'

Again she looked at him quizzically.

'I should be perfectly happy at the Mill,' she said.

'It's very near the old thing,' he said. 'Let us wander a bit.'

His voice could be so soft and happy-go-lucky, it went through her veins like an exhilaration. Nevertheless, she dreamed of a valley, and wild gardens, and peace. She had a desire too for splendour—an aristocratic extravagant splendour. Wandering seemed to her like restlessness, dissatisfaction.

'Where will you wander to?' she asked.

'I don't know. I feel as if I would just meet you and we'd set off—just towards the distance.'

'But where can one go?' she asked anxiously. 'After all, there *is* only the world, and none of it is very distant.'

'Still,' he said, 'I should like to go with you—nowhere. It would be rather wandering just to nowhere. That's the place to get to—nowhere. One wants to wander away from the world's somewheres, into our own nowhere.'

Still she meditated.

'You see, my love,' she said, 'I'm so afraid that while we are only people, we've got to take the world that's given— because there isn't any other.'

'Yes, there is,' he said. 'There's somewhere where we can be free—somewhere where one needn't wear much clothes—none even—where one meets a few people who have gone through enough, and can take things for granted—where you can be yourself, without bothering. There is somewhere—there are one or two people—'

'But where—?' she sighed.

'Somewhere—anywhere. Let's wander off. That's the thing to do—let's wander off.'

'Yes—' she said, thrilled at the thought of travel. But to her it was only travel.

'To be free,' he said. 'To be free, in a free place, with a few other people!'

'Yes,' she said wistfully. Those 'few other people' depressed her.

'It isn't really a locality, though,' he said. 'It's a perfected relation between you and me, and others—the perfect relation—so that we are free together.'

'It is, my love, isn't it,' she said. 'It's you and me. It's you and me, isn't it?' She stretched out her arms to him. He went across and stooped to kiss her face. Her arms closed round him again, her hands spread upon his shoulders, moving slowly there, moving slowly on his back, down his back slowly, with a strange recurrent, rhythmic motion, yet moving slowly down, pressing mysteriously over his loins, over his flanks. The sense of the awfulness of riches that could never be impaired flooded her mind like a swoon, a death in most marvellous possession, mystic-sure. She possessed him so utterly and intolerably that she herself lapsed out. And yet she was only sitting still in the chair, with her hands pressed upon him, and lost.

Again he softly kissed her.

'We shall never go apart again,' he murmured quietly. And she did not speak, but only pressed her hands firmer down upon the source of darkness in him.

They decided, when they woke again from the pure swoon, to write their resignations from the world of work there and then. She wanted this.

He rang the bell and ordered note-paper without a printed address. The waiter cleared the table.

'Now then,' he said, 'yours first. Put your home address, and the date—then "Director of Education, Town Hall—Sir—" Now then!—I don't know how one really stands—I suppose one could get out of it in less than a month—Anyhow, "Sir—I beg to resign my post as class-mistress in the Willey Green Grammar School. I should be very grateful if you would liberate me as soon as possible, without waiting for the expiration of the month's notice." That'll do. Have you got it? Let me look. "Ursula Brangwen." Good! Now I'll write mine. I ought to give them three months, but I can plead health. I can arrange it all right.'

He sat and wrote out his formal resignation.

'Now,' he said, when the envelopes were sealed and addressed, 'shall we post them here, both together? I know Jackie will say, "Here's a coincidence!" when he receives them in all their identity. Shall we let him say it, or not?'

'I don't care,' she said.

'No—?' he said, pondering.

'It doesn't matter, does it?' she said.

'Yes,' he replied. 'Their imaginations shall not work on us. I'll post yours here, mine after. I cannot be implicated in their imaginings.'

He looked at her with his strange, non-human singleness.

'Yes, you are right,' she said.

She lifted her face to him, all shining and open. It was as if he might enter straight into the source of her radiance. His face became a little distracted.

"Shall we go?' he said.

'As you like,' she replied.

They were soon out of the little town and running through the uneven lanes of the country. Ursula nestled near him, into his constant warmth, and watched the pale-lit revelation racing ahead, the visible night. Sometimes it was a wide old road, with grass-spaces on either side, flying magic and elfin in the greenish illumination, sometimes it was trees looming overhead, sometimes it was bramble bushes, sometimes the walls of a crew-yard and the butt of a barn.

'Are you going to Shortlands to dinner?' Ursula asked him suddenly. He started.

'Good God!' he said. 'Shortlands! Never again. Not that. Besides, we should be too late.'

'Where are we going then—to the Mill?'

'If you like. Pity to go anywhere on this good dark night. Pity to come out of it, really. Pity we can't stop in the good darkness. It is better than anything ever would be—this good immediate darkness.'

She sat wondering. The car lurched and swayed. She

knew there was no leaving him, the darkness held them both and contained them, it was not to be surpassed. Besides, she had a full mystic knowledge of his suave loins of darkness, dark-clad and suave, and in this knowledge there was some of the inevitability and the beauty of fate, fate which one asks for, which one accepts in full.

He sat still like an Egyptian Pharaoh, driving the car. He felt as if he were seated in immemorial potency, like the great carven statues of real Egypt, as real and as fulfilled with subtle strength, as these are, with a vague inscrutable smile on the lips. He knew what it was to have the strange and magical current of force in his back and loins, and down his legs, force so perfect that it stayed him immobile, and left his face subtly, mindlessly smiling. He knew what it was to be awake and potent in that other basic mind, the deepest physical mind. And from this source he had a pure and magic control, magical, mystical, a force in darkness, like electricity.

It was very difficult to speak, it was so perfect to sit in this pure living silence, subtle, full of unthinkable knowledge and unthinkable force, upheld immemorially in timeless force, like the immobile, supremely potent Egyptians, seated for ever in their living, subtle silence.

'We need not go home,' he said. 'This car has seats that let down and make a bed, and we can lift the hood.'

She was glad and frightened. She cowered near to him.

'But what about them at home?' she said.

'Send a telegram.'

Nothing more was said. They ran on in silence. But with a sort of second consciousness he steered the car towards a destination. For he had the free intelligence to direct his own ends. His arms and his breast and his head were rounded and living like those of the Greek, he had not the unawakened straight arms of the Egyptian, nor the sealed, slumbering head. A lambent intelligence played secondarily above his pure Egyptian concentration in darkness.

They came to a village that lined along the road. The car crept slowly along, until he saw the post office. Then he pulled up.

'I will send a telegram to your father,' he said. 'I will merely say "Spending the night in town", shall I?'

'Yes,' she answered. She did not want to be disturbed into taking thought.

She watched him move into the post office. It was also a shop, she saw. Strange, he was. Even as he went into the lighted, public place he remained dark and magic, the living silence seemed the body of reality in him, subtle, potent, indiscoverable. There he was! In a strange uplift of elation she saw him, the being never to be revealed, awful in its potency, mystic and real. This dark, subtle reality of him, never to be translated, liberated her into perfection, her own perfect being. She too was dark and fulfilled in silence.

He came out, throwing some packages into the car.

'There is some bread, and cheese, and raisins, and apples, and hard chocolate,' he said, in his voice that was as if laughing, because of the unblemished stillness and force which was the reality in him. She would have to touch him. To speak, to see, was nothing. It was a travesty to look and to comprehend the man there. Darkness and silence must fall perfectly on her, then she could know mystically, in unrevealed touch. She must lightly, mindlessly connect with him, have the knowledge which is death of knowledge, the reality of surety in not knowing.

Soon they had run on again into the darkness. She did not ask where they were going, she did not care. She sat in a fullness and a pure potency that was like apathy, mindless and immobile. She was next to him, and hung in a pure rest, as a star is hung, balanced unthinkably. Still there remained a dark lambency of anticipation. She would touch him. With perfect fine finger-tips of reality she would touch the reality in him, the suave, pure, untranslatable reality of his loins of darkness. To touch, mindlessly in darkness to come in pure touching upon the living reality of him, his suave perfect loins and thighs of darkness, this was her sustaining anticipation.

And he too waited in the magical steadfastness of suspense, for her to take this knowledge of him as he had taken it of her. He knew her darkly, with the fullness of dark knowledge. Now she would know him, and he too would be

liberated. He would be night-free, like an Egyptian, steadfast in
perfectly suspended equilibrium, pure mystic nodality of physical being. They would give each other this star-equilibrium
which alone is freedom.

She saw that they were running among trees—great old
trees with dying bracken undergrowth. The palish, gnarled
trunks showed ghostly, and like old priests in the hovering
distance, the fern rose magical and mysterious. It was a
night all darkness, with low cloud. The motor-car advanced
slowly.

'Where are we?' she whispered.

'In Sherwood Forest.'

It was evident he knew the place. He drove softly, watching. Then they came to a green road between the trees. They
turned cautiously round, and were advancing between the
oaks of the forest, down a green lane. The green lane wid-
ened into a little circle of grass, where there was a small
trickle of water at the bottom of a sloping bank. The car
stopped.

'We will stay here,' he said, 'and put out the lights.'

He extinguished the lamps at once, and it was pure night,
with shadows of trees like realities of other nightly being.
He threw a rug on to the bracken, and they sat in stillness
and mindless silence. There were faint sounds from the
wood, but no disturbance, no possible disturbance, the world
was under a strange ban, a new mystery had supervened.
They threw off their clothes, and he gathered her to him, and
found her, found the pure lambent reality of her for ever invisible flesh. Quenched, inhuman, his fingers upon her unrevealed nudity were the fingers of silence upon silence, the
body of mysterious night upon the body of mysterious night,
the night masculine and feminine, never to be seen with the
eye, or known with the mind, only known as a palpable revelation of living otherness.

She had her desire of him, she touched, she received the
maximum of unspeakable communication in touch, dark,
subtle, positively silent, a magnificent gift and give again, a
perfect acceptance and yielding, a mystery, the reality of that
which can never be known, vital, sensual reality that can
never be transmuted into mind content, but remains outside,

living body of darkness and silence and subtlety, the mystic body of reality. She had her desire fulfilled. He had his desire fulfilled. For she was to him what he was to her, the immemorial magnificence of mystic, palpable, real otherness.

They slept the chilly night through under the hood of the car, a night of unbroken sleep. It was already high day when he awoke. They looked at each other and laughed, then looked away, filled with darkness and secrecy. Then they kissed and remembered the magnificence of the night. It was so magnificent, such an inheritance of a universe of dark reality, that they were afraid to seem to remember. They hid away the remembrance and the knowledge.

24

Death and Love

Thomas Crich died slowly, terribly slowly. It seemed impossible to everybody that the thread of life could be drawn out so thin, and yet not break. The sick man lay unutterably weak and spent, kept alive by morphia and by drinks, which he sipped slowly. He was only half conscious—a thin strand of consciousness linking the darkness of death with the light of day. Yet his will was unbroken, he was integral, complete. Only he must have perfect stillness about him.

Any presence but that of the nurses was a strain and an effort to him now. Every morning Gerald went into the room, hoping to find his father passed away at last. Yet always he saw the transparent face, the same dread dark hair on the waxen forehead, and the awful, inchoate dark eyes, which seemed to be decomposing into formless darkness, having only a tiny grain of vision within them.

And always, as the dark, inchoate eyes turned to him, there passed through Gerald's bowels a burning stroke of revolt, that seemed to resound through his whole being, threatening to break his mind with its clangour, and making him mad.

Every morning, the son stood there, erect and taut with life, gleaming in his blondness. The gleaming blondness of his strange, imminent being put the father into a fever of fretful irritation. He could not bear to meet the uncanny, downward look of Gerald's blue eyes. But it was only for a moment. Each on the brink of departure, the father and son looked at each other, then parted.

For a long time Gerald preserved a perfect *sang froid,* he remained quite collected. But at last, fear undermined him.

He was afraid of some horrible collapse in himself. He had to stay and see this thing through. Some perverse will made him watch his father drawn over the borders of life. And yet, now, every day, the great red-hot stroke of horrified fear through the bowels of the son struck a further inflammation. Gerald went about all day with a tendency to cringe, as if there were the point of a sword of Damocles pricking the nape of his neck.

There was no escape—he was bound up with his father, he had to see him through. And the father's will never relaxed or yielded to death. It would have to snap when death at last snapped it—if it did not persist after a physical death. In the same way, the will of the son never yielded. He stood firm and immune, he was outside this death and this dying.

It was a trial by ordeal. Could he stand and see his father slowly dissolve and disappear in death, without once yielding his will, without once relenting before the omnipotence of death? Like a Red Indian undergoing torture, Gerald would experience the whole process of slow death without wincing or flinching. He even triumphed in it. He somehow *wanted* this death, even forced it. It was as if he himself were dealing the death, even when he most recoiled in horror. Still, he would deal it, he would triumph through death.

But in the stress of this ordeal, Gerald too lost his hold on the outer, daily life. That which was much to him, came to mean nothing. Work, pleasure—it was all left behind. He went on more or less mechanically with his business, but this activity was all extraneous. The real activity was this ghastly wrestling for death in his own soul. And his own will should triumph. Come what might, he would not bow down or submit or acknowledge a master. He had no master in death.

But as the fight went on, and all that he had been and was continued to be destroyed, so that life was a hollow shell all round him, roaring and clattering like the sound of the sea, a noise in which he participated externally, and inside this hollow shell was all the darkness and fearful space of death, he knew he would have to find reinforcements, otherwise he would collapse inwards upon the great dark void which circled at the centre of his soul. His will held his outer life, his outer mind, his outer being unbroken and unchanged. But the pressure was too great. He would have to find something to make good the equilibrium. Something must come with him into the hollow void of death in his soul, fill it up, and so equalize the pressure within to the pressure without. For day by day he felt more and more like a bubble filled with darkness, round which whirled the iridescence of his consciousness, and upon which the pressure of the outer world, the outer life, roared vastly.

In this extremity his instinct led him to Gudrun. He threw away everything now—he only wanted the relation established with her. He would follow her to the studio, to be near her, to talk to her. He would stand about the room, aimlessly picking up the implements, the lumps of clay, the little figures she had cast—they were whimsical and grotesque—looking at them without perceiving them. And she felt him following her, dogging her heels like a doom. She held away from him, and yet she knew he drew always a little nearer, a little nearer.

'I say,' he said to her one evening, in an odd, unthinking, uncertain way, 'won't you stay to dinner tonight? I wish you would.'

She started slightly. He spoke to her like a man making a request of another man.

'They'll be expecting me at home,' she said.

'Oh, they won't mind, will they?' he said. 'I should be awfully glad if you'd stay.'

Her long silence gave consent at last.

'I'll tell Thomas, shall I?' he said.

'I must go almost immediately after dinner,' she said.

It was a dark, cold evening. There was no fire in the drawing-room, they sat in the library. He was mostly silent, absent, and Winifred talked little. But when Gerald did rouse himself, he smiled and was pleasant and ordinary with her. Then there came over him again the long blanks, of which he was not aware.

She was very much attracted by him. He looked so preoccupied, and his strange, blank silences, which she could not read, moved her and made her wonder over him, made her feel reverential towards him.

But he was very kind. He gave her the best things at the table, he had a bottle of slightly sweet, delicious golden wine brought out for dinner, knowing she would prefer it to the burgundy. She felt herself esteemed, needed almost.

As they took coffee in the library, there was a soft, very soft knocking at the door. He started, and called, 'Come in.' The timbre of his voice, like something vibrating at high pitch, unnerved Gudrun. A nurse in white entered, half hovering in the doorway like a shadow. She was very good-looking, but strangely enough, shy and self-mistrusting.

'The doctor would like to speak to you, Mr Crich,' she said in her low, discreet voice.

'The doctor!' he said, starting up. 'Where is he?'

'He is in the dining-room.'

'Tell him I'm coming.'

He drank up his coffee and followed the nurse, who had dissolved like a shadow.

'Which nurse was that?' asked Gudrun.

'Miss Inglis—I like her best,' replied Winifred.

After a while Gerald came back, looking absorbed by his own thoughts, and having some of that tension and abstraction which is seen in a slightly drunken man. He did not say what the doctor had wanted him for, but stood before the fire, with his hands behind his back, and his face open and as if rapt. Not that he was really thinking—he was only arrested in pure suspense inside himself, and thoughts wafted through his mind without order.

'I must go now and see Mama,' said Winifred, 'and see Dadda before he goes to sleep.'

She bade them both good night.

Gudrun also rose to take her leave.

'You needn't go yet, need you?' said Gerald, glancing quickly at the clock. 'It is early yet. I'll walk down with you when you go. Sit down, don't hurry away.'

Gudrun sat down, as if, absent as he was, his will had power over her. She felt almost mesmerized. He was strange to her, something unknown. What was he thinking, what was he feeling, as he stood there so rapt, saying nothing? He kept her—she could feel that. He would not let her go. She watched him in humble submissiveness.

'Had the doctor anything new to tell you?' she asked softly, at length, with that gentle, timid sympathy which touched a keen fibre in his heart. He lifted his eyebrows with a negligent, indifferent expression.

'No—nothing new,' he replied, as if the question were quite casual, trivial. 'He says the pulse is very weak indeed, very intermittent—but that doesn't necessarily mean much, you know'

He looked down at her. Her eyes were dark and soft and unfolded, with a stricken look that roused him.

'No,' she murmured at length. 'I don't understand anything about these things.'

'Just as well not,' he said. 'I say, won't you have a cigarette?—do!' He quickly fetched the box and held her a light. Then he stood before her on the hearth again.

'No,' he said, 'we've never had much illness in the house, either—not till father.' He seemed to meditate a while. Then looking down at her, with strangely communicative blue eyes that filled her with dread, he continued: 'It's something you don't reckon with, you know, till it is there. And then you realize that it was there all the time—it was always there—you understand what I mean?—the possibility of this incurable illness, this slow death.'

He moved his feet uneasily on the marble hearth and put his cigarette to his mouth, looking up at the ceiling.

'I know,' murmured Gudrun: 'it is dreadful.'

He smoked without knowing. Then he took the cigarette from his lips, bared his teeth, and putting the tip of his tongue between his teeth, spat off a grain of tobacco, turning slightly aside, like a man who is alone, or who is lost in thought.

'I don't know what the effect actually *is* on one,' he said, and again he looked down at her. Her eyes were dark and stricken with knowledge, looking into his. He saw her submerged, and he turned aside his face. 'But I absolutely am not the same. There's nothing left, if you understand what I mean. You seem to be clutching at the void yourself. And so you don't know what to *do*.'

'No,' she murmured. A heavy thrill ran down her nerves,

heavy, almost pleasure, almost pain. 'What can be done?'
she added.

He turned and flipped the ash from his cigarette on to the
great marble hearth-stones, that lay bare in the room, without fender or bar.

'I don't know, I'm sure,' he replied. 'But I do think
you've got to find some way of resolving the situation—not
because you want to, but because you've *got* to, otherwise
you're done. The whole of everything, and yourself included, is just on the point of caving in. and you are just
holding it up with your hands. Well, it's a situation that obviously can't continue. You can't stand holding the roof up
with your hands for ever. You know that sooner or later
you'll *have* to let go. Do you understand what I mean? And
so something's got to be done, or there's a universal
collapse—as far as you yourself are concerned.'

He shifted slightly on the hearth, crunching a cinder under
his heel. He looked down at it. Gudrun was aware of the
beautiful old marble panels of the fireplace, swelling softly
carved, round him and above him. She felt as if she were
caught at last by fate, imprisoned in some horrible and fatal
trap.

'But what *can* be done?' she murmured humbly. 'You
must see me if I can be of any help at all—but how can I?
I don't see how I *can* help you.'

He looked down at her critically.

'I don't want you to *help*,' he said, slightly irritated, 'because there's nothing to be *done*. I only want sympathy, do
you see: I want somebody I can talk to sympathetically. That
eases the strain. And there *is* nobody to talk to sympathetically. That's the curious thing. There *is* nobody. There's
Rupert Birkin. But then he *isn't* sympathetic, he wants to
dictate. And that is no use whatsoever.'

She was caught in a strange snare. She looked down at her
hands.

Then there was the sound of the door softly opening. Gerald started. He was chagrined. It was his starting that really
startled Gudrun. Then he went forward, with quick, graceful,
intentional courtesy.

'Oh, mother!' he said. 'How nice of you to come down. How are you?'

The elderly woman, loosely and bulkily wrapped in a purple gown, came forward silently, slightly hulked, as usual. Her son was at her side. He pushed her up a chair, saying: 'You know Miss Brangwen, don't you?'

The mother glanced at Gudrun indifferently.

'Yes,' she said. Then she turned her wonderful, forget-me-not blue eyes up to her son, as she slowly sat down in the chair he had brought her.

'I came to ask you about your father,' she said, in her rapid, scarcely audible voice. 'I didn't know you had company.'

'No? Didn't Winifred tell you? Miss Brangwen stayed to dinner to make us a little more lively—'

Mrs Crich turned slowly round to Gudrun and looked at her, but with unseeing eyes.

'I'm afraid it would be no treat to her.' Then she turned again to her son. 'Winifred tells me the doctor had something to say about your father. What is it?'

'Only that the pulse is very weak—misses altogether a good many times—so that he might not last the night out,' Gerald replied.

Mrs Crich sat perfectly impassive, as if she had not heard. Her bulk seemed hunched in the chair, her fair hair hung slack over her ears. But her skin was clear and fine, her hands, as she sat with them forgotten and folded, were quite beautiful, full of potential energy. A great mass of energy seemed decaying up in that silent, hulking form.

She looked up at her son as he stood, keen and soldierly, near to her. Her eyes were most wonderfully blue, bluer than forget-me-nots. She seemed to have a certain confidence in Gerald, and to feel a certain motherly mistrust of him.

'How are *you*?' she muttered in her strangely quiet voice, as if nobody should hear but him. 'You're not getting into a state, are you? You're not letting it make you hysterical?'

The curious challenge in the last words startled Gudrun.

'I don't think so, mother,' he answered, rather coldly cheery. 'Somebody's got to see it through, you know.'

'Have they? Have they?' answered his mother rapidly.

'Why should *you* take it on yourself? What have you got to do, seeing it through. It will see itself through. You are not needed.'

'No, I don't suppose I can do any good,' he answered. 'It's just how it affects us, you see.'

'You like to be affected—don't you? It's quite nuts for you? You would have to be important. You have no need to stop at home. Why don't you go away!'

These sentences, evidently the ripened grain of many dark hours, took Gerald by surprise.

'I don't think it's any good going away now, mother, at the last minute,' he said coldly.

'You take care,' replied his mother. 'You mind *yourself*— that's your business. You take too much on yourself. You mind yourself, or you'll find yourself in Queer Street, that's what will happen to you. You're hysterical, always were.'

'I'm all right, mother,' he said. 'There's no need to worry about *me,* I assure you.'

'Let the dead bury their dead—don't go and bury yourself along with them—that's what I tell you. I know you well enough.'

He did not answer this, not knowing what to say. The mother sat bunched up in silence, her beautiful white hands, that had no rings whatsoever, clasping the pommels of her arm-chair.

'You can't do it,' she said, almost bitterly. 'You haven't the nerve. You're as weak as a cat, really—always were. Is this young woman staying here?'

'No,' said Gerald. 'She is going home tonight.'

'Then she'd better have the dog-cart. Does she go far?'

'Only to Beldover.'

'Ah!' The elderly woman never looked at Gudrun, yet she seemed to take knowledge of her presence.

'You are inclined to take too much on yourself, Gerald,' said the mother, pulling herself to her feet, with a little difficulty.

'Will you go, mother?' he asked politely.

'Yes, I'll go up again,' she replied. Turning to Gudrun, she bade her 'Good night'. Then she went slowly to the door, as if she were unaccustomed to walking. At the door she lifted her face to him implicitly. He kissed her.

'Don't come any further with me,' she said in her barely audible voice. 'I don't want you any further.'

He bade her good night, watched her cross to the stairs and mount slowly. Then he closed the door and came back to Gudrun. Gudrun rose also, to go.

'A queer being, my mother,' he said.

'Yes,' replied Gudrun.

'She has her own thoughts.'

'Yes,' said Gudrun.

Then they were silent.

'You want to go?' he asked. 'Half a minute, I'll just have a horse put in—'

'No,' said Gudrun. 'I want to walk.'

He had promised to walk with her down the long, lonely mile of drive, and she wanted this.

'You might *just* as well drive,' he said.

'I'd *much rather* walk,' she asserted, with emphasis.

'You would! Then I will come along with you. You know where your things are? I'll put boots on.'

He put on a cap and an overcoat over his evening dress. They went out into the night.

'Let us light a cigarette,' he said, stopping in a sheltered angle of the porch. 'You have one too.'

So, with the scent of tobacco on the night air, they set off down the dark drive that ran between close-cut hedges through sloping meadows.

He wanted to put his arm round her. If he could put his arm round her, and draw her against him as they walked, he would equilibrate himself. For now he felt like a pair of scales, the half of which tips down and down into an indefinite void. He must recover some sort of balance. And here was the hope and the perfect recovery.

Blind to her, thinking only of himself, he slipped his arm softly round her waist, and drew her to him. Her heart fainted, feeling herself taken. But then, his arm was so strong, she quailed under its powerful close grasp. She died a little death, and was drawn against him as they walked down the stormy darkness. He seemed to balance her perfectly in opposition to himself, in their dual motion of walking. So, suddenly, he was liberated and perfect, strong, heroic.

He put his hand to his mouth and threw his cigarette away, a gleaming point, into the unseen hedge. Then he was quite free to balance her.

'That's better,' he said, with exultancy.

The exultation in his voice was like a sweetish, poisonous drug to her. Did she then mean so much to him! She sipped the poison.

'Are you happier?' she asked wistfully.

'Much better,' he said in the same exultant voice, 'and I was rather far gone.'

She nestled against him. He felt her all soft and warm, she was the rich, lovely substance of his being. The warmth and motion of her walk suffused through him wonderfully.

'I'm *so* glad if I help you,' she said.

'Yes,' he answered. 'There's nobody else could do it, if you wouldn't.'

'That is true,' she said to herself, with a thrill of strange, fatal elation.

As they walked, he seemed to lift her nearer and nearer to himself, till she moved upon the firm vehicle of his body. He was so strong, so sustaining, and he could not be opposed. She drifted along in a wonderful interfusion of physical motion, down the dark, blowy hill-side. Far across shone the little yellow lights of Beldover, many of them, spread in a thick patch on another dark hill. But he and she were walking in perfect, isolated darkness, outside the world.

'But how much do you care for me!' came her voice, almost querulous. 'You see, I don't know, I don't understand!'

'How much!' His voice rang with a painful elation. 'I don't know either—but everything.' He was startled by his own declaration. It was true. So he stripped himself of every safeguard, in making this admission to her. He cared everything for her—she was everything.

'But I can't believe it,' said her low voice, amazed, trembling. She was trembling with doubt and exultance. This was the thing she wanted to hear, only this. Yet now she heard it, heard the strange clapping vibration of truth in his voice as he said it, she could not believe. She could not believe—she did not believe. Yet she believed, triumphantly, with fatal exultance.

'Why not?' he said. 'Why don't you believe it? It's true. It is true, as we stand at this moment—' he stood still with her in the wind; 'I care for nothing on earth, or in heaven, outside this spot where we are. And it isn't my own presence I care about, it is all yours. I'd sell my soul a hundred times—but I couldn't bear not to have you here. I couldn't bear to be alone. My brain would burst. It is true.' He drew her closer to him, with definite movement.

'No,' she murmured, afraid. Yet this was what she wanted. Why did she so lose courage?

They resumed their strange walk. They were such strangers—and yet they were so frightfully, unthinkably near. It was like a madness. Yet it was what she wanted, it was what she wanted. They had descended the hill, and now they were coming to the square arch where the road passed under the colliery railway. The arch, Gudrun knew, had walls of squared stone, mossy on one side with water that trickled down, dry on the other side. She had stood under it to hear the train rumble thundering over the logs overhead. And she knew that under this dark and lonely bridge the young colliers stood in the darkness with their sweethearts, in rainy weather. And so she wanted to stand under the bridge with *her* sweetheart, and be kissed under the bridge in the invisible darkness. Her steps dragged as she drew near.

So, under the bridge, they came to a standstill, and he lifted her upon his breast. His body vibrated taut and powerful as he closed upon her and crushed her, breathless and dazed and destroyed, crushed her upon his breast. Ah, it was terrible, and perfect. Under this bridge, the colliers pressed their lovers to their breast. And now, under the bridge, the master of them all pressed her to himself! And how much more powerful and terrible was his embrace than theirs, how much more concentrated and supreme his love was, than theirs in the same sort! She felt she would swoon, die, under the vibrating, inhuman tension of his arms and his body— she would pass away. Then the unthinkable high vibration slackened and became more undulating. He slackened and drew her with him to stand and his back to the wall.

She was almost unconscious. So the colliers' lovers would stand with their backs to the walls, holding their sweethearts and kissing them as she was being kissed. Ah, but would their kisses be fine and powerful as the kisses of the firm-mouthed master? Even the keen, short-cut moustache—the colliers would not have that.

And the colliers' sweethearts would, like herself, hang their heads back limp over their shoulder, and look out from the dark archway at the close patch of yellow lights on the unseen hill in the distance, or at the vague form of trees, and at the buildings of the colliery wood-yard, in the other direction.

His arms were fast around her, he seemed to be gathering her into himself, her warmth, her softness, her adorable weight, drinking in the suffusion of her physical being, avidly. He lifted her, and seemed to pour her into himself, like wine into a cup.

'This is worth everything,' he said in a strange, penetrating voice.

So she relaxed, and seemed to melt, to flow into him, as if she were some infinitely warm and precious suffusion filling into his veins, like an intoxicant. Her arms were round his neck, he kissed her and held her perfectly suspended, she was all slack and flowing into him, and he was the firm, strong cup that receives the wine of her life. So she lay cast upon him, stranded, lifted up against him, melting and melting under his kisses, melting into his limbs and bones, as if he were soft iron becoming surcharged with her electric life.

Till she seemed to swoon, gradually her mind went, and she passed away, everything in her was melted down and fluid, and she lay still, become contained by him, sleeping in him as lightning sleeps in a pure, soft stone. So she was passed away and gone in him, and he was perfected.

When she opened her eyes again and saw the patch of lights in the distance, it seemed to her strange that the world still existed, that she was standing under the bridge resting her head on Gerald's breast. Gerald—who was he? He was the exquisite adventure, the desirable unknown to her.

She looked up, and in the darkness saw his face above her, his shapely, male face. There seemed a faint, white light emitted from him, a white aura, as if he were a visitor from the unseen. She reached up, like Eve reaching to the apples on the tree of knowledge, and she kissed him, though her passion was a transcendent fear of the thing he was, touching his face with her infinitely delicate, encroaching, wondering fingers. Her fingers went over the mould of his face, over his features. How perfect and foreign he was—ah, how dangerous! Her soul thrilled with complete knowledge. This was the glistening forbidden apple, this face of a man. She kissed him, putting her fingers over his face, his eyes, his nostrils, over his brows and his ears, to his neck, to know him, to gather him in by touch. He was so firm and shapely, with such satisfying, inconceivable shapeliness, strange yet unutterably clear. He was such an unutterable enemy, yet glistening with uncanny white fire. She wanted to touch him and touch him and touch him, till she had him all in her hands, till she had strained him into her knowledge. Ah, if she could have the precious *knowledge* of him, she would be filled, and nothing could deprive her of this. For he was so unsure, so risky in the common world of day.

'You are so *beautiful*,' she murmured in her throat.

He wondered, and was suspended. But she felt him quiver, and she came down involuntarily nearer upon him. He could not help himself. Her fingers had him under their power. The fathomless, fathomless desire they could evoke in him was deeper than death, where he had no choice.

But she knew now, and it was enough. For the time, her soul was destroyed with the exquisite shock of his invisible fluid lightning. She knew. And this knowledge was a death from which she must recover. How much more of him was there to know? Ah, much, much, many days' harvesting for her large, yet perfectly subtle and intelligent hands upon the field of his living, radio-active body. Ah, her hands were eager, greedy for knowledge. But for the present it was enough, enough, as much as her soul could bear. Too much, and she would shatter herself, she would fill the fine vial of her soul too quickly, and it would break. Enough now— enough for the time being. There were all the after days when her hands, like birds, could feed upon the fields of his mystical plastic form—till then enough.

And even he was glad to be checked, rebuked, held back. For to desire is better than to possess, the finality of the end was dreaded as deeply as it was desired.

They walked on towards the town, towards where the lamps threaded singly, at long intervals, down the dark highroad of the valley. They came at length to the gate of the drive.

'Don't come any further,' she said.

'You'd rather I didn't?' he asked, relieved. He did not want to go up the public streets with her, his soul all naked and alight as it was.

'Much rather—good night.' She held out her hand. He grasped it, then touched the perilous, potent fingers with his lips.

'Good night,' he said. 'Tomorrow.'

And they parted. He went home full of the strength and the power of living desire.

But the next day, she did not come, she sent a note that she was kept indoors by a cold. Here was a torment! But he possessed his soul in some sort of patience, writing a brief answer, telling her how sorry he was not to see her.

The day after this, he stayed at home—it seemed so futile to go down to the office. His father could not live the week out. And he wanted to be at home, suspended.

Gerald sat on a chair by the window in his father's room. The landscape outside was black and winter-sodden. His father lay grey and ashen on the bed, a nurse moved silently in her white dress, neat and elegant, even beautiful. There was a scent of eau-de-Cologne in the room. The nurse went out of the room, Gerald was alone with death, facing the winter-black landscape.

'Is there much more water in Denley?' came the faint voice, determined and querulous, from the bed. The dying man was asking about a leakage from Willey Water into one of the pits.

'Some more—we shall have to run off the lake,' said Gerald.

'Will you?' The faint voice filtered to extinction. There was dead stillness. The grey-faced, sick man lay with eyes closed, more dead than death. Gerald looked away. He felt his heart was seared, it would perish if this went on much longer.

Suddenly he heard a strange noise. Turning round, he saw his father's eyes wide open, strained and rolling in a frenzy of inhuman struggling. Gerald started to his feet, and stood transfixed in horror.

"Wha-a-ah-h-h!' came a horrible choking rattle from his father's throat, the fearful, frenzied eye, rolling awfully in its wild, fruitless search for help, passed blindly over Gerald, then up came the dark blood and mess pumping over the face of the agonized being. The tense body relaxed, the head fell aside, down the pillow.

Gerald stood transfixed, his soul echoing in horror. He would move, but he could not. He could not move his limbs. His brain seemed to re-echo like a pulse.

The nurse in white softly entered. She glanced at Gerald, then at the bed.

'Ah!' came her soft whimpering cry, and she hurried forward to the dead man. 'Ah-h!' came the slight sound of her agitated distress, as she stood bending over the bedside. Then she recovered, turned, and came for towel and sponge. She was wiping the dead face carefully, and murmuring, almost whimpering, very softly: 'Poor Mr Crich!—Poor Mr Crich!—Oh, poor Mr Crich!'

'Is he dead?' clanged Gerald's sharp voice.

'Oh, yes, he's gone,' replied the soft, moaning voice of the nurse, as she looked up at Gerald's face. She was young and beautiful and quivering. A strange sort of grin went over Gerald's face, over the horror. And he walked out of the room.

He was going to tell his mother. On the landing he met his brother Basil.

'He's gone, Basil,' he said, scarcely able to subdue his voice, not to let an unconscious, frightening exultation sound through.

'What?' cried Basil, going pale.

Gerald nodded. Then he went on to his mother's room. She was sitting in her purple gown, sewing, very slowly sewing, putting in a stitch, then another stitch. She looked up at Gerald with her blue, undaunted eyes.

'Father's gone,' he said.

'He's dead? Who says so?'

'Oh, you know, mother, if you see him.'

She put her sewing down and slowly rose.

'Are you going to see him?' he asked.

'Yes,' she said.

By the bedside the children already stood in a weeping group.

'Oh, mother!' cried the daughters, almost in hysterics, weeping loudly.

But the mother went forward. The dead man lay in repose, as if gently asleep, so gently, so peacefully, like a young man sleeping in purity. He was still warm. She stood looking at him in gloomy, heavy silence for some time.

'Ay,' she said bitterly, at length, speaking as if to the unseen witnesses of the air. 'You're dead.' She stood for some minutes in silence, looking down. 'Beautiful,' she asserted, 'beautiful as if life had never touched you—never touched you. God send I look different. I hope I shall look my years when I am dead. Beautiful, beautiful,' she crooned over him. 'You can see him in his teens, with his first beard on his face. A beautiful soul, beautiful—' Then there was a tearing in her voice as she cried: 'None of you look like this when you are dead! Don't let it happen again.' It was a strange, wild command from out of the unknown. Her children moved unconsciously together, in a nearer group, at the dreadful command in her voice. The colour was flushed bright in her cheek, she looked awful and wonderful. 'Blame me, blame me if you like, that he lies there like a lad in his teens, with his first beard on his face. Blame me if you like. But you none of you know.' She was silent in intense silence. Then there came in a low, tense voice: 'If I thought that the children I bore would lie looking like that in death, I'd strangle them when they were infants, yes—'

'No, mother,' came the strange, clarion voice of Gerald from the background, 'we are different, we don't blame you.'

She turned and looked full in his eyes. Then she lifted her hands in a strange half-gesture of mad despair.

'Pray!' she said strongly. 'Pray for yourselves to God, for there's no help for you from your parents.'

'Oh, mother!' cried her daughters wildly.

But she had turned and gone, and they all went quickly away from each other.

When Gudrun heard that Mr Crich was dead, she felt rebuked. She had stayed away lest Gerald should think her too easy of winning. And now, he was in the midst of trouble, whilst she was cold.

The following day she went up as usual to Winifred, who was glad to see her, glad to get away into the studio. The girl had wept, and then, too frightened, had turned aside to avoid any more tragic eventuality. She and Gudrun resumed work as usual in the isolation of the studio, and this seemed an immeasurable happiness, a pure world of freedom, after the aimlessness and misery of the house. Gudrun stayed on till evening. She and Winifred had dinner brought up to the studio, where they ate in freedom, away from all the people in the house.

After dinner Gerald came up. The great high studio was full of shadow and a fragrance of coffee. Gudrun and Winifred had a little table near the fire at the far end, with a white lamp whose light did not travel far. They were a tiny world to themselves, the two girls surrounded by lovely shadows, the beams and rafters shadowy overhead, the benches and implements shadowy down the studio.

'You are cosy enough here,' said Gerald, going up to them.

There was a low brick fireplace, full of fire, an old blue Turkish rug, the little oak table with the lamp and the white-and-blue cloth and the dessert, and Gudrun making coffee in an old brass coffee-maker, and Winifred scalding a little milk in a tiny saucepan.

'Have you had coffee?' said Gudrun.

'I have, but I'll have some more with you,' he replied.

'Then you must have it in a glass—there are only two cups,' said Winifred.

'It is the same to me,' he said, taking a chair and coming

into the charmed circle of the girls. How happy they were, how cosy and glamorous it was with them, in a world of lofty shadows! The outside world, in which he had been transacting funeral business all the day, was completely wiped out. In an instant he snuffed glamour and magic.

They had all their things very dainty, two odd and lovely little cups, scarlet and solid gilt, and a little black jug with scarlet discs, and the curious coffee machine, whose spirit-flame flowed steadily, almost invisibly. There was the effect of rather sinister richness, in which Gerald at once escaped himself.

They all sat down, and Gudrun carefully poured out the coffee.

'Will you have milk?' she asked calmly, yet nervously poising the little black jug with its big red dots. She was always so completely controlled, yet so bitterly nervous.

'No, I won't,' he replied.

So, with a curious humility, she placed him the little cup of coffee, and herself took the awkward tumbler. She seemed to want to serve him.

'Why don't you give me the glass—it is so clumsy for you,' he said. He would much rather have had it, and seen her daintily served. But she was silent, pleased with the disparity, with her self-abasement.

'You are quite *en ménage,*' he said.

'Yes. We aren't really at home to visitors,' said Winifred.

'You're not? Then I'm an intruder?'

For once he felt his conventional dress was out of place, he was an outsider.

Gudrun was very quiet. She did not feel drawn to talk to him. At this stage, silence was best—or mere light words. It was best to leave serious things aside. So they talked gaily and lightly till they heard the man below lead out the horse, and call it to 'Back-back!' into the dog-cart that was to take Gudrun home. So she put on her things and shook hands with Gerald, without once meeting his eyes. And she was gone.

The funeral was detestable. Afterwards, at the tea-table, the daughters kept saying—'He was a good father to us—the best father in the world'—or else—'We shan't easily find another man as good as father was.'

Gerald acquiesced in all this. It was the right conventional attitude, and, as far as the world went, he believed in the conventions. He took it as a matter of course. But Winifred hated everything, and hid in the studio, and cried her heart out, and wished Gudrun would come.

Luckily everybody was going away. The Criches never stayed long at home. By dinner-time, Gerald was left quite alone. Even Winifred was carried off to London for a few days with her sister Laura.

But when Gerald was really left alone, he could not bear it. One day passed by, and another. And all the time he was like a man hung in chains over the edge of an abyss. Struggle as he might, he could not turn himself to the solid earth, he could not get footing. He was suspended on the edge of a void, writhing. Whatever he thought of, was the abyss—whether it were friends or strangers, or work or play, it all showed him only the same bottomless void, in which his heart swung perishing. There was no escape, there was nothing to grasp hold of. He must writhe on the edge of the chasm, suspended in chains of invisible physical life.

At first he was quiet, he kept still, expecting the extremity to pass away, expecting to find himself released into the world of the living, after this extremity of penance. But it did not pass, and a crisis gained upon him.

As the evening of the third day came on, his heart rang with fear. He could not bear another night. Another night was coming on, for another night he was to be suspended in chain of physical life, over the bottomless pit of nothingness. And he could not bear it. He could not bear it. He was frightened deeply, and coldly, frightened in his soul. He did not believe in his own strength any more. He could not fall into this infinite void and rise again. If he fell, he would be gone for ever. He must withdraw, he must seek reinforcements. He did not believe in his own single self any further than this.

After dinner, faced with the ultimate experience of his own nothingness, he turned aside. He pulled on his boots, put on his coat, and set out to walk in the night.

It was dark and misty. He went through the wood, stumbling and feeling his way to the Mill. Birkin was away. Good—he was half glad. He turned up the hill, and stumbled blindly over the wild slopes, having lost the path in the complete darkness. It was boring. Where was he going? No matter. He stumbled on till he came to a path again. Then he went on through another wood. His mind became dark, he went on automatically. Without thought or sensation, he stumbled unevenly on, out into the open again, fumbling for stiles, losing the path, and going along the hedges of the fields till he came to the outlet.

And at last he came to high road. It had distracted him to struggle blindly through the maze of darkness. But now, he must take a direction. And he did not even know where he was. But he must take a direction now. Nothing would be resolved by merely walking, walking away. He had to take a direction.

He stood still on the road that was high in the utterly dark night, and he did not know where he was. It was a strange sensation, his heart beating, and ringed round with the utterly unknown darkness. So he stood for some time.

Then he heard footsteps, and saw a small, swinging light. He immediately went towards this. It was a miner.

'Can you tell me,' he said, 'where this road goes?'

'Road? Ay, it goes ter Whatmore.'

'Whatmore? Oh, thank you, that's right. I thought I was wrong. Good night.'

'Good night,' replied the broad voice of the miner.

Gerald guessed where he was. At least, when he came to Whatmore, he would know. He was glad to be on a high road. He walked forward as in a sleep of decision.

That was Whatmore Village—? Yes, the King's Head—and there the hall gates. He descended the steep hill almost running. Winding through the hollow, he passed the Grammar School, and came to Willey Green Church. The churchyard! He halted.

Then in another moment he had clambered up the wall and was going among the graves. Even in this darkness he could see the heaped pallor of old white flowers at his feet. This then was the grave. He stooped down. The flowers were cold and clammy. There was a raw scent of chrysanthemums and tube-roses, deadened. He felt the clay beneath, and shrank, it was so horribly cold and sticky. He stood away in revulsion.

Here was one centre then, here in the complete darkness beside the unseen, raw grave. But there was nothing for him here. No, he had nothing to stay here for. He felt as if some of the clay were sticking cold and unclean on his heart. No, enough of this.

Where then?—home? Never! It was no use going there. That was less than no use. It could not be done. There was somewhere else to go. Where?

A dangerous resolve formed in his heart, like a fixed idea. There was Gudrun—she would be safe in her home. But he could get at her—he would get at her. He would not go back tonight till he had come to her, if it cost him his life. He staked his all on this throw.

He set off walking straight across the fields towards Beldover. It was so dark, nobody could ever see him. His feet were wet and cold, heavy with clay. But he went on persistently, like a wind, straight forward, as if to his fate. There were great gaps in his consciousness. He was conscious that he was at Winthorpe hamlet, but quite unconscious how he had got there. And then, as in a dream, he was in the long street of Beldover, with its street-lamps.

There was a noise of voices, and of a door shutting loudly, and being barred, and of men talking in the night. The 'Lord Nelson' had just closed, and the drinkers were going home. He had better ask one of these where she lived—for he did not know the side streets at all.

'Can you tell me where Somerset Drive is?' he asked of one of the uneven men.

'Where what?' replied the tipsy miner's voice.

'Somerset Drive.'

'Somerset Drive!—I've heard o' such a place, but I couldn't for my life say where it is. Who might you be wanting?'

'Mr Brangwen—William Brangwen.'

'William Brangwen—?'

'Who teaches at the Grammar School at Willey Green— his daughter teaches there too."

'O-o-o-oh, Brangwen! *Now* I've got you. Of *course,* William Brangwen! Yes, yes, he's got two lasses as teachers, aside hisself. Ay, that's him—that's him! Why, certainly I know where he lives, back you life I do! Yi—*what* place do they ca' it?'

'Somerset Drive,' repeated Gerald patiently. He knew his own colliers fairly well.

'Somerset Drive, for certain!' said the collier, swinging his arm as if catching something up. 'Somerset Drive—yi! I couldn't for my life lay hold o' the lercality o' the place. Yis, I know the place, to be sure I do—'

He turned unsteadily on his feet and pointed up the dark, nigh-deserted road.

'You go up theer—an' you ta'e th' first—yi, th' first turnin' on your left—o' that side—past Withamses tuffy shop—'

'*I* know,' said Gerald.

'Ay! You go down a bit, past wheer th' water-man lives— and then Somerset Drive, as they ca' it, branches off on t' right hand side—an' there's nowt but three houses in it, no more than three, I believe—an' I'm a'most certain as theirs is th' last—th' last o' th' three—you see—'

'Thank you very much,' said Gerald. 'Good night.'

And he started off, leaving the tipsy man there standing rooted.

Gerald went past the dark shops and houses, most of them sleeping now, and twisted round to the little blind road that ended on a field of darkness. He slowed down as he neared his goal, not knowing how he should proceed. What if the house were closed in darkness?

But it was not. He saw a big lighted window, and heard voices, then a gate banged. His quick ears caught the sound of Birkin's voice, his keen eyes made out Birkin, with Ursula standing in a pale dress on the step of the garden path. Then Ursula stepped down and came along the road, holding Birkin's arm.

Gerald went across into the darkness and they dawdled past him, talking happily. Birkin's voice low, Ursula's high and distinct. Gerald went quickly to the house.

The blinds were drawn before the big lighted window of

the dining-room. Looking up the path at the side he could see the door left open, shedding a soft, coloured light from the hall lamp. He went quickly and silently up the path, and looked up into the hall. There were pictures on the walls, and the antlers of a stag—and the stairs going up on one side—and just near the foot of the stairs the half opened door of the dining-room.

With heart drawn fine, Gerald stepped into the hall, whose floor was of coloured tiles, went quickly and looked into the large, pleasant room. In a chair by the fire, the father sat asleep, his head tilted back against the side of the big oak chimney-piece, his ruddy face seen foreshortened, the nostrils open, the mouth fallen a little. It would take the merest sound to wake him.

Gerald stood a second suspended. He glanced down the passage behind him. It was all dark. Again he was suspended. Then he went swiftly upstairs. His senses were so finely, almost supernaturally keen, that he seemed to cast his own will over the half-unconscious house.

He came to the first landing. There he stood, scarcely breathing. Again, corresponding to the door below, there was a door again. That would be the mother's room. He could hear her moving about in the candle-light. She would be expecting her husband to come up. He looked along the dark landing.

Then, silently, on infinitely careful feet, he went along the passage, feeling the wall with the extreme tips of his fingers. There was a door. He stood and listened. He could hear two people's breathing. It was not that. He went stealthily forward. There was another door, slightly open. The room was in darkness. Empty. Then there was the bathroom, he could smell the soap and the heat. Then at the end another bedroom—one soft breathing. This was she.

With an almost occult carefulness he turned the door-handle and opened the door an inch. It creaked slightly. Then he opened it another inch—then another. His heart did not beat, he seemed to create a silence about himself, an obliviousness.

He was in the room. Still the sleeper breathed softly. It was very dark. He felt his way forward inch by inch, with his feet and hands. He touched the bed, he could hear the sleeper. He drew nearer, bending close as if his eyes would disclose whatever there was. And then, very near to his face, to his fear, he saw the round, dark head of a boy.

He recovered, turned round, saw the door afar, a faint light revealed. And he retreated swiftly, drew the door to without fastening it, and passed rapidly down the passage. At the head of the stairs he hesitated. There was still time to flee.

But it was unthinkable. He would maintain his will. He turned past the door of the parental bedroom like a shadow, and was climbing the second flight of stairs. They creaked under his weight—it was exasperating. Ah, what disaster, if the mother's door opened just beneath him, and she saw him! It would have to be, if it were so. He held the control still.

He was not quite up these stairs when he heard a quick running of feet below, the outer door was closed and locked, he heard Ursula's voice, then the father's sleepy exclamation. He pressed on swiftly to the upper landing.

Again a door was ajar, a room was empty. Feeling his way forward, with the tips of his fingers, travelling rapidly, like a blind man, anxious lest Ursula should come upstairs, he found another door. There, with his preternaturally fine senses alert, he listened. He heard someone moving in bed. This would be she.

Softly now, like one who has only one sense, the tactile sense, he turned the latch. It clicked. He held still. The bedclothes rustled. His heart did not beat. Then again he drew the latch back, and very gently pushed the door. It made a sticking noise as it gave.

'Ursula?' said Gudrun's voice, frightened. He quickly opened the door and pushed it behind him.

'Is it you, Ursula?' came Gudrun's frightened voice. He heard her sitting up in bed. In another moment she would scream.

'No, it's me,' he said, feeling his way towards her. 'It is I, Gerald.'

She sat motionless in her bed in sheer astonishment. She

was too astonished, too much taken by surprise, even to be afraid.

'Gerald!' she echoed, in blank amazement. He had found his way to the bed, and his outstretched hand touched her warm breast blindly. She shrank away.

'Let me make a light,' she said, springing out.

He stood perfectly motionless. He heard her touch the match-box, he heard her fingers in their movement. Then he saw her in the light of a match, which she held to the candle. The light rose in the room, then sank to a small dimness, as the flame sank down on the candle, before it mounted again.

She looked at him as he stood near the other side of the bed. His cap was pulled low over his brow, his black overcoat was buttoned close up to his chin. His face was strange and luminous. He was inevitable as a supernatural being. When she had seen him, she knew. She knew there was something fatal in the situation, and she must accept it. Yet she must challenge him.

'How did you come up?' she asked.

'I walked up the stairs—the door was open.'

She looked at him.

'I haven't closed this door, either,' he said. She walked swiftly across the room and closed her door softly, and locked it. Then she came back.

She was wonderful, with startled eyes and flushed cheeks, and her plait of hair rather short and thick down her back, and her long, fine white night-dress falling to her feet.

She saw that his boots were all clayey, even his trousers were plastered with clay. And she wondered if he had made footprints all the way up. He was a very strange figure, standing in her bedroom, near the tossed bed.

'Why have you come?' she asked, almost querulous.

'I wanted to,' he replied.

And this she could see from his face. It was fate.

'You are so muddy,' she said in distaste, but gently.

He looked down at his feet.

'I was walking in the dark,' he replied. But he felt vividly elated. There was a pause. He stood on one side of the tumbled bed, she on the other. He did not even take his cap from his brows.

'And what do you want of me?' she challenged.

He looked aside and did not answer. Save for the extreme beauty and mystic attractiveness of this distinct, strange face, she would have sent him away. But his face was too wonderful and undiscovered to her. It fascinated her with the fascination of pure beauty, cast a spell on her, like nostalgia, an ache.

'What do you want of me?' she repeated in an estranged voice.

He pulled off his cap in a movement of dream-liberation and went across to her. But he could not touch her because she stood barefoot in her night-dress, and he was muddy and damp. Her eyes, wide and large and wondering, watched him, and asked him the ultimate question.

'I came—because I must,' he said. 'Why do you ask?'

She looked at him in doubt and wonder.

'I must ask,' she said.

He shook his head slightly.

'There is no answer,' he replied, with strange vacancy.

There was about him a curious and almost godlike air of simplicity and naïve directness. He reminded her of an apparition, the young Hermes.

'But why did you come to me?' she persisted.

'Because—it has to be so. If there weren't you in the world, then *I* shouldn't be in the world, either.'

She stood looking at him with large, wide, wondering, stricken eyes. His eyes were looking steadily into hers all the time, and he seemed fixed in an odd supernatural steadfastness. She sighed. She was lost now. She had no choice.

'Won't you take off your boots?' she said. 'They must be wet.'

He dropped his cap on a chair, unbuttoned his overcoat, lifting up his chin to unfasten the throat buttons. His short, keen hair was ruffled. He was so beautifully blond, like wheat. He pulled off his overcoat.

Quickly he pulled off his jacket, pulled loose his black tie, and was unfastening his studs, which were headed each with a pearl. She listened, watching, hoping no one would hear the starched linen crackle. It seemed to snap like pistol-shots.

He had come for vindication. She let him hold her in his arms, clasp her close against him. He found in her an infinite relief. Into her he poured all his pent-up darkness and corrosive death, and he was whole again. It was wonderful, marvellous, it was a miracle. This was the ever-recurrent miracle of his life, at the knowledge of which he was lost in an ecstasy of relief and wonder. And she, subject, received him as a vessel filled with his bitter potion of death. She had no power at this crisis to resist. The terrible frictional violence of death filled her, and she received it in an ecstasy of subjection, in throes of acute, violent sensation.

As he drew nearer to her, he plunged deeper into her enveloping soft warmth, a wonderful creative heat that penetrated his veins and gave him life again. He felt himself dissolving and sinking to rest in the bath of her living strength. It seemed as if her heart in her breast were a second unconquerable sun, into the glow and creative strength of which he plunged farther and farther. All his veins, that were murdered and lacerated, healed softly as life came pulsing in, stealing invisibly into him as if it were the all-powerful effluence of the sun. His blood, which seemed to have been drawn back into death, came ebbing on the return, surely, beautifully, powerfully.

He felt his limbs growing fuller and flexible with life, his body gained an unknown strength. He was a man again, strong and rounded. And he was a child, so soothed and restored and full of gratitude.

And she, she was the great bath of life, he worshipped her. Mother and substance of all life she was. And he, child and man, received of her and was made whole. His pure body was almost killed. But the miraculous, soft effluence of her breast suffused over him, over his seared, damaged brain, like a healing lymph, like a soft, soothing flow of life itself, perfect as if he were bathed in the womb again.

His brain was hurt, seared, the tissue was as if destroyed. He had not known how hurt he was, how his tissue, the very tissue of his brain was damaged by the corrosive flood of death. Now, as the healing lymph of her effluence flowed through him, he knew how destroyed he was, like a plant whose tissue is burst from inwards by a frost.

He buried his small, hard head between her breasts and pressed her breasts against him with his hands. And she with quivering hands pressed his head against her, as he lay suffused out, and she lay fully conscious. The lovely creative warmth flooded through him like a sleep of fecundity within the womb. Ah, if only she would grant him the flow of this living effluence, he would be restored, he would be complete again. He was afraid she would deny him before it was finished. Like a child at the breast, he cleaved intensely to her, and she could not put him away. And his seared, ruined membrane relaxed, softened, that which was seared and stiff and blasted yielded again, became soft and flexible, palpitating with new life. He was infinitely grateful, as to God, or as an infant is at its mother's breast. He was glad and grateful like a delirium, as he felt his own wholeness come over him again, as he felt the full, unutterable sleep coming over him, the sleep of complete exhaustion and restoration.

But Gudrun lay wide awake, destroyed into perfect consciousness. She lay motionless, with wide eyes staring motionless into the darkness, whilst he was sunk away in sleep, his arms round her.

She seemed to be hearing waves break on a hidden shore, long, slow, gloomy waves, breaking with the rhythm of fate, so monotonously that it seemed eternal. This endless breaking of slow, sullen waves of fate held her life a possession, whilst she lay with dark, wide eyes looking into the darkness. She could see so far, as far as eternity—yet she saw nothing. She was suspended in perfect consciousness—and of what was she conscious?

This mood of extremity, when she lay staring into eternity, utterly suspended, and conscious of everything, to the last limits, passed and left her uneasy. She had lain so long motionless. She moved, she became self-conscious. She wanted to look at him, to see him.

But she dared not make a light, because she knew he would wake, and she did not want to break his perfect sleep, that she knew he had got of her.

She disengaged herself softly and rose up a little to look at him. There was a faint light, it seemed to her, in the room. She could just distinguish his features, as he slept the perfect sleep. In this darkness, she seemed to see him so distinctly. But he was far off, in another world. Ah, she could shriek with torment, he was so far off, and perfected, in another world. She seemed to look at him as at a pebble far away under clear dark water. And here was she, left with all the anguish of consciousness, whilst he was sunk deep into the other element of mindless, remote, living shadow-gleam. He was beautiful, far off, and perfected. They would never be together. Ah, this awful, inhuman distance which would always be interposed between her and the other being!

There was nothing to do but to lie still and endure. She felt an overwhelming tenderness for him, and a dark, understirring of jealous hatred, that he should lie so perfect and immune, in another world, whilst she was tormented with violent wakefulness, cast out in the outer darkness.

She lay in intense and vivid consciousness, an exhausting superconsciousness. The church clock struck the hours, it seemed to her, in quick succession. She heard them distinctly in the tension of her vivid consciousness. And he slept as if time were one moment, unchanging and unmoving.

She was exhausted, wearied. Yet she must continue in this state of violent active superconsciousness. She was conscious of everything—her childhood, her girlhood, all the forgotten incidents, all the unrealized influences and all the happenings she had not understood, pertaining to herself, to her family, to her friends, her lovers, her acquaintances, everybody. It was as if she drew a glittering rope of knowledge out of the sea of darkness, drew and drew and drew it out of the fathomless depths of the past, and still it did not come to an end, there was no end to it, she must haul and haul at the rope of glittering consciousness, till she was weary, aching, exhausted, and fit to break, and yet she had not done.

Ah, if only she might wake him! She turned uneasily. When could she rouse him and send him away? When could she disturb him? And she relapsed into her activity of automatic consciousness, that would never end.

But the time was drawing near when she could wake him. It was like a release. The clock had struck four, outside in the night. Thank God the night had passed almost away. At five he must go, and she would be released. Then she could relax and fill her own place. Now she was driven up against his perfect sleeping motion like a knife white-hot on a grindstone. There was something monstrous about him, about his juxtaposition against her.

The last hour was the longest. And yet, at last it passed. Her heart leapt with relief—yes, there was the slow, strong stroke of the church clock—at last, after this night of eternity. She waited to catch each slow, fatal reverberation. 'Three—four—five!' There, it was finished. A weight rolled off her.

She raised herself, leaned over him tenderly, and kissed him. She was sad to wake him. After a few moments, she kissed him again. But he did not stir. The darling, he was so deep in sleep! What a shame to take him out of it. She let him lie a little longer. But he must go—he must really go.

With full over-tenderness she took his face between her hands and kissed his eyes. The eyes opened, he remained motionless, looking at her. Her heart stood still. To hide her face from his dreadful opened eyes, in the darkness, she bent down and kissed him, whispering:

'You must go, my love.'

But she was sick with terror, sick.

He put his arms round her. Her heart sank.

'But you must go, my love. It's late.'

'What time is it?' he said.

Strange, his man's voice. She quivered. It was an intolerable oppression to her.

'Past five o'clock,' she said.

But he only closed his arms round her again. Her heart cried with her in torture. She disengaged herself firmly.

'You really must go,' she said.

'Not for a minute,' he said.

She lay still, nestling against him, but unyielding.

'Not for a minute,' he repeated, clasping her closer.

'Yes,' she said, unyielding. 'I'm afraid if you stay any longer.'

There was a certain coldness in her voice that made him

release her, and she broke away, rose and lit the candle. That then was the end.

He got up. He was warm and full of life and desire. Yet he felt a little bit ashamed, humiliated, putting on his clothes before her, in the candle-light. For he felt revealed, exposed to her, at a time when she was in some way against him. It was all very difficult to understand. He dressed himself quickly, without collar or tie. Still he felt full and complete, perfected. She thought it humiliating to see a man dressing: the ridiculous shirt, the ridiculous trousers and braces. But again an idea saved her.

'It is like a workman getting up to go to work,' thought Gudrun. 'And I am like a workman's wife.' But an ache like nausea was upon her: a nausea of him.

He pushed his collar and tie into his overcoat pocket. Then he sat down and pulled on his boots. They were sodden, as were his socks and trouser-bottoms. But he himself was quick and warm.

'Perhaps you ought to have put your boots on downstairs,' she said.

At once, without answering, he pulled them off again and stood holding them in his hand. She had thrust her feet into slippers, and flung a loose robe around her. She was ready. She looked at him as he stood waiting, his black coat buttoned to the chin, his cap pulled down, his boots in his hand. And the passionate almost hateful fascination revived in her for a moment. It was not exhausted. His face was so warm-looking, wide-eyed and full of newness, so perfect. She felt old, old. She went to him heavily to be kissed. He kissed her quickly. She wished his warm, expressionless beauty did not so fatally put a spell on her, compel her and subjugate her. It was a burden upon her, that she resented, but could not escape. Yet when she looked at his straight man's brows, and at his rather small, well-shaped nose, and at his blue, indifferent eyes, she knew her passion for him was not yet satisfied, perhaps never could be satisfied. Only now she was weary, with an ache like nausea. She wanted him gone.

They went downstairs quickly. It seemed they made a prodigious noise. He followed her as, wrapped in her vivid green wrap, she preceded him with the light. She suffered badly with fear lest her people should be roused. He hardly cared. He did not care now who knew. And she hated this in him. One *must* be cautious. One must preserve oneself.

She led the way to the kitchen. It was neat and tidy, as the woman had left it. He looked up at the clock—twenty minutes past five! Then he sat down on a chair to put on his boots. She waited, watching his every movement. She wanted it to be over, it was a great nervous strain on her.

He stood up—she unbolted the back door and looked out. A cold, raw night, not yet dawn, with a piece of a moon in the vague sky. She was glad she need not go out.

'Good-bye then,' he murmured.

'I'll come to the gate,' she said.

And again she hurried on in front, to warn him of the steps. And at the gate, once more she stood on the step whilst he stood below her.

'Good-bye,' she whispered.

He kissed her dutifully and turned away.

She suffered torments hearing his firm tread going so distinctly down the road. Ah, the insensitiveness of that firm tread!

She closed the gate and crept quickly and noiselessly back to bed. When she was in her room, and the door closed, and all safe, she breathed freely, and a great weight fell off her. She nestled down in bed, in the groove his body had made, in the warmth he had left. And excited, worn out, yet still satisfied, she fell soon into a deep, heavy sleep.

Gerald walked quickly through the raw darkness of the coming dawn. He met nobody. His mind was beautifully still and thoughtless, like a still pool, and his body full and warm and rich. He went quickly along towards Shortlands in a grateful self-sufficiency.

25

Marriage or Not

The Brangwen family was going to move from Beldover. It was necessary now for the father to be in town.

Birkin had taken out a marriage licence, yet Ursula deferred from day to day. She would not fix any definite time—she still wavered. Her month's notice to leave the Grammar School was in its third week. Christmas was not far off.

Gerald waited for the Ursula-Birkin marriage. It was something crucial to him.

'Shall we make it a double-barrelled affair?' he said to Birkin one day.

'Who for the second shot?' asked Birkin.

'Gudrun and me,' said Gerald, the venturesome twinkle in his eyes.

Birkin looked at him steadily, as if somewhat taken aback.

'Serious—or joking?' he asked.

'Oh, serious. Shall I? Shall Gudrun and I rush in along with you?'

'Do by all means,' said Birkin. 'I didn't know you'd got that length.'

'What length?' said Gerald, looking at the other man, and laughing.

'Oh yes, we've gone all the lengths.'

'There remains to put it on a broad social basis, and to achieve a high moral purpose,' said Birkin.

'Something like that: the length and breadth and height of it,' replied Gerald, smiling.

'Oh well,' said Birkin, 'it's a very admirable step to take, I should say.'

Gerald looked at him closely.

'Why aren't you enthusiastic?' he asked. 'I thought you were such dead nuts on marriage.'

Birkin lifted his shoulders.

'One might as well be dead nuts on noses. There are all sorts of noses, snub and otherwise—'

Gerald laughed.

'And all sorts of marriage, also snub and otherwise?' he said.

'That's it.'

'And you think if I marry, it will be snub?' asked Gerald quizzically, his head a little on one side.

Birkin laughed quickly.

'How do I know what it will be!' he said. 'Don't lambaste me with my own parallels—'

Gerald pondered a while.

'But I should like to know your opinion, exactly,' he said.

'On your marriage?—or marrying? Why should you want my opinion? I've got no opinions. I'm not interested in legal marriage, one way or another. It's a mere question of convenience.'

Still Gerald watched him closely.

'More than that, I think,' he said seriously. 'However, you may be bored by the ethics of marriage, yet really to marry, in one's own personal case, is something critical, final—'

"You mean there is something final in going to the registrar with a woman?"

'If you're coming back with her, I do,' said Gerald. 'It is in some way irrevocable.'

'Yes, I agree,' said Birkin.

'No matter how one regards legal marriage, yet to enter into the married state, in one's own personal instance, is final—'

'I believe it is,' said Birkin, 'somewhere.'

'The question remains, then, should one do it,' said Gerald.

Birkin watched him narrowly, with amused eyes.

'You are like Lord Bacon, Gerald,' he said. 'You argue it like a lawyer—or like Hamlet's to-be-or-not-to-be. If I were you I would *not* marry: but ask Gudrun, not me. You're not marrying me, are you?'

Gerald did not heed the latter part of this speech.

'Yes,' he said, 'one must consider it coldly. It is something critical. One comes to the point where one must take a step in one direction or another. And marriage is one direction—'

'And what is the other?' asked Birkin quickly.

Gerald looked up at him with hot, strangely-conscious eyes, that the other man could not understand.

'I can't say,' he replied. 'If I knew *that*—' He moved uneasily on his feet and did not finish.

'You mean if you knew the alternative?' asked Birkin. 'And since you don't know it, marriage is a *pis aller*.'

Gerald looked up at Birkin with the same hot, constrained eyes.

'One does have the feeling that marriage is a *pis aller*,' he admitted.

'Then don't do it,' said Birkin. 'I tell you,' he went on, 'the same as I've said before, marriage in the old sense seems to me repulsive. *Égoïsme à deux* is nothing to it. It's a sort of tacit hunting in couples: the world all in couples, each couple in its own little house, watching its own little interests, and stewing in its own little privacy—it's the most repulsive thing on earth.'

'I quite agree,' said Gerald. 'There's something inferior about it. But as I say, what's the alternative.'

'One should avoid this *home* instinct. It's not an instinct, it's a habit of cowardliness. One should never have a *home*.'

'I agree really,' said Gerald. 'But there's no alternative.'

'We've got to find one. I do believe in a permanent union between a man and a woman. Chopping about is merely an exhaustive process. But a permanent relation between a man and a woman isn't the last word—it certainly isn't.'

'Quite,' said Gerald.

'In fact,' said Birkin, 'because the relation between man and woman is made the supreme and exclusive relationship, that's where all the tightness and meanness and insufficiency comes in.'

'Yes, I believe you,' said Gerald.

'You've got to take down the love-and-marriage ideal from its pedestal. We want something broader. I believe in the *additional* perfect relationship between man and man—additional to marriage.'

'I can never see how they can be the same,' said Gerald.

'Not the same—but equally important, equally creative, equally sacred, if you like.'

'I know,' said Gerald, 'you believe something like that. Only I can't *feel* it, you see.' He put his hand on Birkin's arm, with a sort of deprecating affection. And he smiled as if triumphantly.

He was ready to be doomed. Marriage was like a doom to him. He was willing to condemn himself in marriage, to become like a convict condemned to the mines of the underworld, living no life in the sun, but having a dreadful subterranean activity. He was willing to accept this. And marriage was the seal of his condemnation. He was willing to be sealed thus in the underworld, like a soul damned but living for ever in damnation. But he would not make any pure relationship with any other soul. He could not. Marriage was not the committing of himself into a relationship with Gudrun. It was a committing of himself in acceptance of the established world, he would accept the established order, in which he did not livingly believe, and then he would retreat to the underworld for his life. This he would do.

The other way was to accept Rupert's offer of alliance, to enter into the bond of pure trust and love with the other man, and then subsequently with the woman. If he pledged himself with the man he would later be able to pledge himself with the woman: not merely in legal marriage, but in absolute, mystic marriage.

Yet he could not accept the offer. There was a numbness upon him, a numbness either of unborn, absent volition or of atrophy. Perhaps it was the absence of volition. For he was strangely elated at Rupert's offer. Yet he was still more glad to reject it, not to be committed.

26

A Chair

There was a jumble market every Monday afternoon in the old market-place in town. Ursula and Birkin strayed down there one afternoon. They had been talking of furniture, and they wanted to see if there was any fragment they would like to buy, amid the heaps of rubbish collected on the cobblestones.

The old market-square was not very large, a mere bare patch of granite sets, usually with a few fruit-stalls under a wall. It was in a poor quarter of the town. Meagre houses stood down one side, there was a hosiery factory, a great blank with myriad oblong windows at the end, a street of little shops with flagstone pavement down the other side, and, for a crowning monument, the public baths, of new red brick, with a clock-tower. The people who moved about seemed stumpy and sordid, the air seemed to smell rather dirty, there was a sense of many mean streets ramifying off into the warrens of meanness. Now and again a great chocolate-and-yellow tram-car ground round a difficult bend under the hosiery factory.

Ursula was superficially thrilled when she found herself out among the common people, in the jumbled place piled with old bedding, heaps of old iron, shabby crockery in pale lots, muffled lots of unthinkable clothing. She and Birkin went unwillingly down the narrow aisle between the rusty wares. He was looking at the goods, she at the people.

She excitedly watched a young woman who was going to have a baby, and who was turning over a mattress and making a young man, down-at-heel and dejected, feel it also. So secretive and active and anxious the young woman seemed, so reluctant, slinking, the young man. He was going to marry her because she was having a child.

When they had felt the mattress, the young woman asked the old man seated on a stool among his wares how much it was. He told her, and she turned to the young man. The latter was ashamed and self-conscious. He turned his face away, though he left his body standing there, and muttered aside. And again the woman anxiously and actively fingered the mattress and added up in her mind and bargained with the old, unclean man. All the while the young man stood by, shamefaced and down-at-heel, submitting.

'Look,' said Birkin, 'there is a pretty chair.'

'Charming!' cried Ursula. 'Oh, charming.'

It was an arm-chair of simple wood, probably birch, but of such fine delicacy of grace, standing there on the sordid stones, it almost brought tears to the eyes. It was square in shape, of the purest, slender lines, and four short lines of wood in the back, that reminded Ursula of harp-strings.

'It was once,' said Birkin, 'gilded—and it had a cane seat. Somebody has nailed this wooden seat in. Look, here is a trifle of the red that underlay the gilt. The rest is all black, except where the wood is worn pure and glossy. It is the fine unity of the lines that is so attractive. Look, how they run and meet and counteract. But of course the wooden seat is wrong—it destroys the perfect lightness and unity in tension the cane gave. I like it though—'

'Ah yes,' said Ursula, 'so do I.'

'How much is it?' Birkin asked the man.

'Ten shillings.'

'And you will send it—?'

It was bought.

'So beautiful, so pure!' Birkin said. 'It almost breaks my heart.' They walked along between the heaps of rubbish. 'My beloved country—it had something to express even when it made that chair.'

'And hasn't it now?' asked Ursula. She was always angry when he took this tone.

'No, it hasn't. When I see that clear, beautiful chair, and I think of England, even Jane Austen's England—it had living thoughts to unfold even then, and pure happiness in unfolding them. And now, we can only fish among the rubbish-heaps for the remnants of their old expression. There is no production in us now, only sordid and foul mechanicalness.'

'It isn't true,' cried Ursula. 'Why must you always praise the past at the expense of the present? *Really,* I don't think so much of Jane Austen's England. It was materialistic enough, if you like—'

'It could afford to be materialistic,' said Birkin, 'because it had the power to be something other—which we haven't. We are materialistic because we haven't the power to be anything else—try as we may, we can't bring off anything but materialism: mechanism, the very soul of materialism.'

Ursula was subdued into angry silence. She did not heed what he said. She was rebelling against something else.

'And I hate your past. I'm sick of it,' she cried. 'I believe I even hate that old chair, though it *is* beautiful. It isn't *my* sort of beauty. I wish it had been smashed up when its day was over, not left to preach the beloved past to us. I'm sick of the beloved past.'

'Not so sick as I am of the accursed present,' he said.

'Yes, just the same. I hate the present—but I don't want the past to take its place—I don't want that old chair.'

He was rather angry for a moment. Then he looked at the sky shining beyond the tower of the public baths, and he seemed to get over it all. He laughed.

'All right,' he said, 'then let us not have it. I'm sick of it all, too. At any rate, one can't go on living on the old bones of beauty.'

'One can't,' she cried. 'I *don't* want old things.'

'The truth is, we don't want things at all,' he replied. 'The thought of a house and furniture of my own is hateful to me.'

This startled her for a moment. Then she replied:

'So it is to me. But one must live somewhere.'

'Not somewhere—anywhere,' he said. 'One should just live anywhere—not have a definite place. I don't want a definite place. As soon as you get a room, and it is *complete,* you want to run from it. Now my rooms at the Mill are quite complete, I want them at the bottom of the sea. It is a horrible tyranny of a fixed milieu, where each piece of furniture is a commandment-stone.'

She clung to his arm as they walked away from the market.

'But what are we going to do?' she said. 'We must live somehow. And I do want some beauty in my surroundings. I want a sort of natural *grandeur* even, *splendour*.'

'You'll never get it in houses and furniture—or even clothes. Houses and furniture and clothes, they are all terms of an old base world, a detestable society of man. And if you have a Tudor house and old, beautiful furniture, it is only the past perpetuated on top of you, horrible. And if you have a perfect modern house done for you by Poiret, it is something else perpetuated on top of you. It is all horrible. It is all possessions, possessions, bullying you and turning you into a generalization. You have to be like Rodin, Michael Angelo, and leave a piece of raw rock unfinished to your figure. You must leave your surroundings sketchy, unfinished, so that you are never contained, never confined, never dominated from the outside.'

She stood in the street contemplating.

'And we are never to have a complete place of our own— never a home?' she said.

'Pray God, in this world, no,' he answered.

'But there's only this world,' she objected.

He spread out his hands with a gesture of indifference.

'Meanwhile, then, we'll avoid having things of our own,' he said.

'But you've just bought a chair,' she said.

'I can tell the man I don't want it,' he replied.

She pondered again. Then a queer little movement twitched her face.

'No,' she said, 'we don't want it. I'm sick of old things.'

'New ones as well,' he said.

They retraced their steps.

There—in front of some furniture, stood the young couple, the woman who was going to have a baby and the narrow-faced youth. She was fair, rather short, stout. He was of medium height, attractively built. His dark hair fell sideways over his brow from under his cap, he stood strangely aloof, like one of the damned.

'Let us give it to *them*' whispered Ursula. 'Look, they are getting a home together.'

'I won't aid and abet them in it,' he said petulantly, instantly sympathizing with the aloof, furtive youth, against the active, procreant female.

'Oh yes,' cried Ursula. 'It's right for them—there's nothing else for them.'

'Very well,' said Birkin, 'you offer it to them. I'll watch.'

Ursula went rather nervously to the young couple who were discussing an iron washstand—or rather, the man was glancing furtively and wonderingly, like a prisoner, at the abominable article, whilst the woman was arguing.

'We bought a chair,' said Ursula, 'and we don't want it. Would you have it? We should be glad if you would.'

The young couple looked round at her, not believing that she could be addressing them.

'Would you care for it?' repeated Ursula. 'It's really *very* pretty—but—but—' she smiled rather dazzlingly.

The young couple only stared at her, and looked significantly at each other to know what to do. And the man curiously obliterated himself, as if he could make himself invisible as a rat can.

'We wanted to *give* it to you,' explained Ursula, now overcome with confusion and dread of them. She was attracted by the young man. He was a still, mindless creature, hardly a man at all, a creature that the towns have produced, strangely pure-bred and fine in one sense, furtive, quick, subtle. His lashes were dark and long and fine over his eyes, that had no mind in them, only a dreadful kind of subject, inward consciousness, glazed and dark. His dark brows and all his lines were finely drawn. He would be a dreadful, but wonderful lover to a woman, so marvellously contributed. His legs would be marvellously subtle and alive, under the shapeless trousers, he had some of the fineness and stillness and silkiness of a dark-eyed, silent rat.

Ursula had apprehended him with a fine *frisson* of attraction. The full-built woman was staring offensively. Again Ursula forgot him.

'Won't you have the chair?' she said. The man looked at her with a sideways look of appreciation, yet far off, almost

insolent. The woman drew herself up. There was a certain
costermonger richness about her. She did not know what Ursula was after, she was on her guard, hostile. Birkin approached, smiling wickedly at seeing Ursula so nonplussed
and frightened.

'What's the matter?' he said, smiling. His eyelids had
dropped slightly, there was about him the same suggestive
mocking secrecy that was in the bearing of the two city creatures. The man jerked his head a little on one side, indicating
Ursula, and said, with curious amiable, jeering warmth:

'What she warnt?—eh?' An odd smile writhed his lips.

Birkin looked at him from under his slack, ironical eyelids.

'To give you a chair—that—with the label on it,' he said,
pointing.

The man looked at the object indicated. There was a curious hostility in male, outlawed understanding between the
two men.

'What's she warnt to give it *us* for, guv'nor,' he replied in
a tone of free intimacy that insulted Ursula.

'Thought you'd like it—it's a pretty chair. We bought it
and don't want it. No need for you to have it, don't be
frightened,' said Birkin, with a wry smile.

The man glanced up at him, half inimical, half recogniz-
ing.

'Why don't you want it for yourselves, if you've just
bought it?' asked the woman coolly. ' 'Taint good enough
for you, now you've had a look at it. Frightened it's got
something in it, eh?'

She was looking at Ursula admiringly, but with some resentment.

'I'd never thought of that,' said Birkin. "But no, the
wood's too thin everywhere.'

'You see,' said Ursula, her face luminous and pleased.
'*We* are just going to get married, and we thought we'd buy
things. Then we decided just now, that we wouldn't have
furniture, we'd go abroad.'

The full-built, slightly blowsy city girl looked at the fine
face of the other woman with appreciation. They appreciated
each other. The youth stood aside, his face expressionless

and timeless, the thin line of the black moustache drawn strangely suggestive over his rather wide, closed mouth. He was impassive, abstract, like some dark suggestive presence, a gutter presence.

'It's all right to be some folks,' said the city girl, turning to her own young man. He did not look at her, but he smiled with the lower part of his face, putting his head aside in an odd gesture of assent. His eyes were unchanging, glazed with darkness.

'Cawsts something to chynge your mind,' he said in an incredibly low accent.

'Only ten shillings this time,' said Birkin.

The man looked up at him with a grimace of a smile, furtive, unsure.

'Cheap at 'arf a quid, guv'nor,' he said. 'Not like getting divawced.'

'We're not married yet,' said Birkin.

'No, no more aren't we,' said the young woman loudly. 'But we shall be a Saturday.'

Again she looked at the young man with a determined, protective look, at once overbearing and very gentle. He grinned sicklily, turning away his head. She had got his manhood, but Lord, what did he care! He had a strange furtive pride and slinking singleness.

'Good luck to you,' said Birkin.

'Same to you,' said the young woman. Then, rather tentatively: 'When's yours coming off, then?'

Birkin looked round at Ursula.

'It's for the lady to say,' he replied. 'We go to the registrar the moment she's ready.'

Ursula laughed, covered with confusion and bewilderment.

'No 'urry,' said the young man, grinning suggestive.

'Oh, don't break your neck to get there,' said the young woman. ' 'Slike when you're dead—you're a long time married.'

The young man turned aside as if this hit him.

'The longer the better, let us hope,' said Birkin.

'That's it, guv'nor,' said the young man admiringly. 'Enjoy it while it larsts—niver whip a dead donkey.'

'Only when he's shamming dead,' said the young woman, looking at her young man with caressive tenderness of authority.

'Aw, there's a difference,' he said satirically.

'What about the chair?' said Birkin.

'Yes, all right,' said the woman.

They trailed off to the dealer, the handsome but abject young fellow hanging a little aside.

'That's it,' said Birkin. 'Will you take it with you or have the address altered?'

'Oh, Fred can carry it. Make him do what he can for the dear old 'ome.'

'Mike use of 'im,' said Fred, grimly humourous, as he took the chair from the dealer. His movements were graceful, yet curiously abject, slinking.

' 'Ere's mother's cosy chair,' he said. 'Warnts a cushion.' And he stood it down on the market stones.

'Don't you think it's pretty?' laughed Ursula.

'Oh, I do,' said the young woman.

' 'Ave a sit in it, you'll wish you'd kept it,' said the young man.

Ursula promptly sat down in the middle of the market-place.

'Awfully comfortable,' she said. 'But rather hard. You try it.' She invited the young man to a seat. But he turned uncouthly, awkwardly aside, glancing up at her with quick bright eyes, oddly suggestive, like a quick, live rat.

'Don't spoil him,' said the young woman. 'He's not used to arm-chairs, 'e isn't.'

The young man turned away and said, with averted grin: 'Only warnts legs on 'is.'

The four parted. The young woman thanked them.

'Thank you for the chair—it'll last till it gives way.'

'Keep it for an ornyment,' said the young man.

'Good afternoon—good afternoon,' said Ursula and Birkin.

'Goo'-luck to you,' said the young man, glancing and avoiding Birkin's eyes as he turned aside his head.

The two couples went asunder, Ursula clinging to Birkin's arm. When they had gone some distance, she glanced back and saw the young man going beside the full, easy young woman. His trousers sank over his heels, he moved with a sort of slinking evasion, more crushed with odd self-consciousness now he had the slim old arm-chair to carry, his arm over the back, the four fine, square tapering legs swaying perilously near the granite sett of the pavement. And yet he was somewhere indomitable and separate, like a quick, vital rat. He had a queer, subterranean beauty, repulsive too.

'How strange they are!' said Ursula.

'Children of men,' he said. 'They remind me of Jesus: "The meek shall inherit the earth." '

'But they aren't the meek,' said Ursula.

'Yes, I don't know why, but they are,' he replied.

They waited for the tram-car. Ursula sat on top and looked out on the town. The dusk was just dimming the hollows of crowded houses.

'And are they going to inherit the earth?' she said.

'Yes—they.'

'Then what are we going to do?' she asked. 'We're not like them—are we? We're not the meek?'

'No. We've got to live in the chinks they leave us.'

'How horrible!' cried Ursula. 'I don't want to live in chinks.'

'Don't worry,' he said. 'They are the children of men, they like market-places and street corners best. That leaves plenty of chinks.'

'All the world,' she said.

'Ah, no—but some room.'

The tram-car mounted slowly up the hill, where the ugly winter-grey masses of houses looked like a vision of hell that is cold and angular. They sat and looked. Away in the distance was an angry redness of sunset. It was all cold, somehow small, crowded, and like the end of the world.

'I don't mind it even then,' said Ursula, looking at the repulsiveness of it all. 'It doesn't concern me.'

'No more it does,' he replied, holding her hand. 'One needn't see. One goes one's way. In my world it is sunny and spacious—'

'It is, my love, isn't it?' she cried, hugging near to him on the top of the tram-car, so that the other passengers stared at them.

'And we will wander about on the face of the earth,' he said, 'and we'll look at the world beyond just this bit.'

There was a long silence. Her face was radiant like gold as she sat thinking.

'I don't want to inherit the earth,' she said. 'I don't want to inherit anything.'

He closed his hand over hers.

'Neither do I. I want to be disinherited.'

She clasped his fingers closely.

'We won't care about *anything*,' she said.

He sat still and laughed.

'And we'll be married, and have done with them,' she added.

Again he laughed.

'It's one way of getting rid of everything,' she said, 'to get married.'

'And one way of accepting the whole world,' he added.

'A whole other world, yes,' she said happily.

'Perhaps there's Gerald—and Gudrun—' he said.

'If there is there is, you see,' she said. 'It's no good our worrying. We can't really alter them, can we?'

'No,' he said. 'One has no right to try—not with the best intentions in the world.'

'Do you try to force them?' she asked.

'Perhaps,' he said. 'Why should I want him to be free, if is isn't his business?'

She paused for a time.

'We can't *make* him happy, anyhow,' she said. 'He'd have to be it of himself.'

'I know,' he said. 'But we want other people with us, don't we?'

'Why should we?' she asked.

'I don't know,' he said uneasily. 'One has a hankering after a sort of further fellowship.'

'But why?' she insisted. 'Why should you hanker after other people? Why should you need them?'

This hit him right on the quick. His brows knitted.

'Does it end with just our two selves?' he asked, tense.

'Yes—what more do you want? If anybody likes to come along, let them. But why must you run after them?'

His face was tense and unsatisfied.

'You see,' he said, 'I always imagine our being really happy with some few other people—a little freedom with people.'

She pondered for a moment.

'Yes, one does want that. But it must *happen*. You can't do anything for it with your will. You always seem to think you can *force* the flowers to come out. People must love us because they love us—you can't *make* them.'

'I know,' he said. 'But must one take no steps at all? Must one just go as if one were alone in the world—the only creature in the world?'

'You've got me,' she said. 'Why should you *need* others? Why must you force people to agree with you? Why can't you be single by yourself, as you are always saying? You try to bully Gerald—as you tried to bully Hermione. You must learn to be alone. And it's so horrid of you. You've got me. And you want to force other people to love you as well. You do try to bully them to love you. And even then you don't want their love.'

His face was full of real perplexity.

'Don't I?' he said. 'It's the problem I can't solve. I *know* I want a perfect and complete relationship with you: and we've nearly got it—we really have. But beyond that. *Do* I want a real, ultimate relationship with Gerald? Do I want a final, almost extra-human relationship with him—a relationship in the ultimate of me and him—or don't I?'

She looked at him for a long time with strange bright eyes, but she did not answer.

27

Flitting

That evening Ursula returned home very bright-eyed and wondrous—which irritated her people. Her father came home at supper-time, tired after the evening class, and the long journey home. Gudrun was reading, the mother sat in silence.

Suddenly Ursula said to the company at large in a bright voice: 'Rupert and I are going to be married tomorrow.'

Her father turned round stiffly.

'You what?' he said.

'Tomorrow!' echoed Gudrun.

'Indeed!' said the mother.

But Ursula only smiled wonderfully and did not reply.

'Married tomorrow!' cried her father harshly. 'What are you talking about?'

'Yes,' said Ursula. 'Why not?' Those two words from her always drove him mad. 'Everything is all right—we shall go to the registrar's office—'

There was a second's hush in the room after Ursula's blithe vagueness.

'*Really,* Ursula!' said Gudrun.

'Might we ask why there has been all this secrecy?' demanded the mother, rather superbly.

'But there hasn't,' said Ursula. 'You knew.'

'Who knew?' now cried the father. 'Who knew? What do you mean by your "you knew"?'

He was in one of his stupid rages, she instantly closed against him.

'Of course you knew,' she said coolly. 'You knew we were going to get married.'

There was a dangerous pause.

'We knew you were going to get married, did we? Knew! Why, does anybody know anything about *you*, you shifty bitch!'

'Father!' cried Gudrun, flushing deep in violent remonstrance. Then in a cold but gentle voice, as if to remind her sister to be tractable: 'But isn't it a *fearfully* sudden decision, Ursula?' she asked.

'No, not really,' replied Ursula, with the same maddening cheerfulness. 'He's been *wanting* me to agree for weeks—he's had the license ready. Only I—I wasn't ready in myself. Now I am ready—is there anything to be disagreeable about?'

'Certainly not,' said Gudrun, but in a tone of cold reproof. 'You are perfectly free to do as you like.'

' "Ready in yourself"—*yourself*, that's all that matters, isn't it! "I wasn't ready in myself",' he mimicked her phrase offensively. 'You and *yourself*, you're of some importance, aren't you?'

She drew herself up and set back her throat, her eyes shining yellow and dangerous.

'I am to myself,' she said, wounded and mortified. 'I know I am not to anybody else. You only wanted to *bully* me—you never cared for my happiness.'

He was leaning forward watching her, his face intense like a spark.

'Ursula, what are you saying? Keep your tongue still,' cried her mother.

Ursula swung round and the lights in her eyes flashed.

'No, I won't,' she cried. 'I won't hold my tongue and be bullied. What does it matter which day I get married—what does it *matter*! It doesn't affect anybody but myself.'

Her father was tense and gathered together like a cat about to spring.

'Doesn't it?' he cried, coming nearer to her. She shrank away.

'No, how can it?' she replied, shrinking but stubborn.

'It doesn't matter to *me*, then, what you do—what becomes of you?' he cried, in a strange voice like a cry.

The mother and Gudrun stood back as if hypnotized.

'No,' stammered Ursula. Her father was very near to her. 'You only want to—'

She knew it was dangerous, and she stopped. He was gathered together, every muscle ready.

'What?' he challenged.

'Bully me,' she muttered, and even as her lips were moving, his hand had caught her smack at the side of the face and she was sent up against the door.

'Father!' cried Gudrun in a high voice, 'it is impossible!'

He stood unmoving. Ursula recovered, her hand was on the door-handle. She slowly drew herself up. He seemed doubtful now.

'It's true,' she declared, with brilliant tears in her eyes, her head lifted up in defiance. 'What has your love meant, what did it ever mean?—bullying and denial—it did—'

He was advancing again with strange, tense movements, and clenched fist, and the face of a murderer. But swift as lightning she had flashed out of the door, and they heard her running upstairs.

He stood for a moment looking at the door. Then, like a defeated animal, he turned and went back to his seat by the fire.

Gudrun was very white. Out of the intense silence the mother's voice was heard saying, cold and angry:

'Well, you shouldn't take so much notice of her.'

Again the silence fell, each followed a separate set of emotions and thoughts.

Suddenly the door opened again: Ursula, dressed in hat and furs, with a small valise in her hand:

'Good-bye!' she said in her maddening, bright, almost mocking tone. 'I'm going.'

And in the next instant the door was closed, they heard the outer door, then her quick steps down the garden path, then the gate banged, and her light footfall was gone. There was a silence like death in the house.

Ursula went straight to the station, hastening heedlessly on winged feet. There was no train, she must walk on to the junction. As she went through the darkness, she began to cry, and she wept bitterly, with a dumb, heart-broken, child's anguish, all the way on the road, and in the train. Time passed unheeded and unknown, she did not know where she was, nor what was taking place. Only she wept from fathomless depths of hopeless, hopeless grief, the terrible grief of a child, that knows no extenuation.

Yet her voice had the same defensive brightness as she spoke to Birkin's landlady at the door.

'Good evening! Is Mr Birkin in? Can I see him?'

'Yes, he's in. He's in his study.'

Ursula slipped past the woman. His door opened. He had heard her voice.

'Hello!' he exclaimed in surprise, seeing her standing there with the valise in her hand, and marks of tears on her face. She was one who wept without showing many traces, like a child.

'Do I look a sight?' she said, shrinking.

'No—why? Come in.' He took the bag from her hand and they went into the study.

There—immediately, her lips began to tremble like those of a child that remembers again, and the tears came rushing up.

'What's the matter?' he asked, taking her in his arms. She sobbed violently on his shoulder whilst he held her still, waiting.

'What's the matter?' he said again, when she was quieter. But she only pressed her face farther into his shoulder, in pain, like a child that cannot tell.

'What is it, then?' he asked.

Suddenly she broke away, wiped her eyes, regained her composure, and went and sat in a chair.

'Father hit me,' she announced, sitting bunched up, rather like a ruffled bird, her eyes very bright.

'What for?' he said.

She looked away and would not answer. There was a pitiful redness about her sensitive nostrils and her quivering lips.

'Why?' he repeated in his strange, soft, penetrating voice.

She looked round at him rather defiantly.

'Because I said I was going to be married tomorrow, and he bullied me.'

'Why did he bully you?'

Her mouth dropped again, she remembered the scene once more, the tears came up.

'Because I said he didn't care—and he doesn't it's only his domineeringness that's hurt—' she said, her mouth pulled awry by her weeping all the time she spoke, so that he almost smiled, it seemed so childish. Yet it was not childish, it was a mortal conflict, a deep wound.

'It isn't quite true,' he said. 'And even so, you shouldn't *say* it.'

'It *is* true—it *is* true,' she wept, 'and I won't be bullied by his pretending it's love—when it *isn't*—he doesn't care, how can he—no, he can't—'

He sat in silence. She moved him beyond himself.

'Then you shouldn't rouse him, if he can't,' replied Birkin quietly.

'And I *have* loved him, I have,' she wept. 'I've loved him always, and he's always done this to me, he has—'

'It's been a love of opposition, then,' he said. 'Never mind—it will be all right. It's nothing desperate.'

'Yes,' she wept, 'it is, it is.'

'Why?'

'I shall never see him again—'

'Not immediately. Don't cry, you had to break with him, it had to be—don't cry.'

He went over to her and kissed her fine, fragile hair, touching her wet cheeks gently.

'Don't cry,' he repeated, 'don't cry any more.'

He held her head close against him, very close and quiet.

At last she was still. Then she looked up, her eyes wide and frightened.

'Don't you want me?' she asked.

'Want you?' His darkened, steady eyes puzzled her and did not give her play.

'Do you wish I hadn't come?' she asked, anxious now again for fear she might be out of place.

'No,' he said. 'I wish there hadn't been the violence—so much ugliness—but perhaps it was inevitable.'

She watched him in silence. He seemed deadened.

'But where shall I stay?' she asked, feeling humiliated.

He thought for a moment.

'Here, with me,' he said. 'We're married as much today as we shall be tomorrow.'

'But—'

'I'll tell Mrs Varley,' he said. 'Never mind now.'

He sat looking at her. She could feel his darkened steady eyes looking at her all the time. It made her a little bit frightened. She pushed her hair off her forehead nervously.

'Do I look ugly?' she said.

And she blew her nose again.

A small smile came round his eyes.

'No,' he said, 'fortunately.'

And he went across to her and gathered her like a belonging in his arms. She was so tenderly beautiful, he could not bear to see her, he could only bear to hide her against himself. Now, washed all clean by her tears, she was new and frail like a flower just unfolded, a flower so new, so tender, so made perfect by inner light, that he could not bear to look at her, he must hide her against himself, cover his eyes against her. She had the perfect candour of creation, something translucent and simple, like a radiant, shining flower that moment unfolded in primal blessedness. She was so new, so wonder-clear, so undimmed. And he was so old, so steeped in heavy memories. Her soul was new, undefined and glimmering with the unseen. And his soul was dark and gloomy, it had only one grain of living hope, like a grain of mustard seed. But this one living grain in him matched the perfect youth in her.

'I love you,' he whispered as he kissed her, and trembled with pure hope, like a man who is born again to a wonderful, lively hope far exceeding the bounds of death.

She could not know how much it meant to him, how much he meant by the few words. Almost childish, she wanted proof, and statement, even over-statement, for everything seemed still uncertain, unfixed to her.

But the passion of gratitude with which he received her into his soul, the extreme, unthinkable gladness of knowing himself living and fit to unite with her, he, who was so nearly dead, who was so near to being gone with the rest of his race down the slope of mechanical death, could never be understood by her. He worshipped her as age worships youth, he gloried in her because, in his one grain of faith, he was young as she, he was her proper mate. This marriage with her was his resurrection and his life.

All this she could not know. She wanted to be made much of, to be adored. There were infinite distances of silence between them. How could he tell her of the immanence of her beauty, that was not form, or weight, or colour, but something like a strange, golden light! How could he know himself what her beauty lay in, for him. He said: 'Your nose is beautiful, your chin is adorable.' But it sounded like lies, and she was disappointed, hurt. Even when he said, whispering with truth, 'I love you, I love you,' it was not the real truth. It was something beyond love, such a gladness of having surpassed oneself, of having transcended the old existence. How could he say 'I' when he was something new and unknown, not himself at all? This I, this old formula of the age, was a dead letter.

In the new, superfine bliss, a peace superseding knowledge, there was no I and you, there was only the third, unrealized wonder, the wonder of existing not as oneself, but in a consummation of my being and of her being in a new one, a new, paradisal unit regained from the duality. How can I say 'I love you' when I have ceased to be, and you have ceased to be: we are both caught up and transended into a new oneness where everything is silent, because there is nothing to answer, all is perfect and at one. Speech travels between the separate parts. But in the perfect One there is perfect silence of bliss.

They were married by law on the next day, and she did as he bade her, she wrote to her father and mother. Her mother replied, not her father.

She did not go back to school. She stayed with Birkin in his rooms, or at the Mill, moving with him as he moved. But she did not see anybody, save Gudrun and Gerald. She was all strange and wondering as yet, but relieved as by dawn.

Gerald sat talking to her one afternoon in the warm study down at the Mill. Rupert had not yet come home.

'You are happy?' Gerald asked her, with a smile.

'Very happy!' she cried, shrinking a little in her brightness.

'Yes, one can see it.'

'Can one?' cried Ursula in surprise.

He looked up at her with a communicative smile.

'Oh yes, plainly.'

She was pleased. She meditated a moment.

'And can you see that Rupert is happy as well?'

He lowered his eyelids and looked aside.

'Oh yes,' he said.

'Really!'

'Oh yes.'

He was very quiet, as if it were something not to be talked about by him. He seemed sad.

She was very sensitive to suggestion. She asked the question he wanted her to ask.

'Why don't you be happy as well?' she said. 'You could be just the same.'

He paused a moment.

'With Gudrun?' he asked.

'Yes!' she cried, her eyes glowing. But there was a strange tension, an emphasis, as if they were asserting their wishes, against the truth.

'You think Gudrun would have me, and we should be happy?' he said.

'Yes, I'm *sure*!' she cried.

Her eyes were round with delight. Yet underneath she was constrained, she knew her own insistence.

'Oh, I'm *so* glad,' she added.

He smiled.

'What makes you glad?' he said.

'For *her* sake,' she replied. 'I'm sure you'd—you're the right man for her.'

'You are?' he said. 'And do you think she would agree with you?'

'Oh yes!' she exclaimed hastily. Then, upon reconsideration, very uneasy: 'Though Gudrun isn't so very simple, is she? One doesn't know her in five minutes, does one? She's not like me in that.' She laughed at him with her strange, open, dazzled face.

'You think she's not much like you?' Gerald asked.

She knitted her brows.

'Oh, in many ways she is. But I never know what she will do when anything new comes.'

'You don't?' said Gerald. He was silent for some moments. Then he moved tentatively. 'I was going to ask her, in any case, to go away with me at Christmas,' he said in a very small, cautious voice.

'Go away with you? For a time, you mean?'

'As long as she likes,' he said, with a deprecating movement.

They were both silent for some minutes.

'Of course,' said Ursula at last, 'she *might* just be willing to rush into marriage. You can see.'

'Yes,' smiled Gerald. 'I can see. But in case she won't—do you think she would go abroad with me for a few days—or for a fortnight?'

'Oh yes,' said Ursula. 'I'd ask her.'

'Do you think we might all go together?'

'All of us?' Again Ursula's face lighted up. 'It would be rather fun, don't you think?'

'Great fun,' he said.

'And then you could see,' said Ursula.

'What?'

'How things went. I think it is best to take the honeymoon before the wedding—don't you?'

She was pleased with this *mot*. He laughed.

'In certain cases,' he said. 'I'd rather it were so in my own case.'

'Would you!' exclaimed Ursula. Then doubtingly, 'Yes, perhaps you're right. One should please oneself.'

Birkin came in a little later, and Ursula told him what had been said.

'Gudrun!' exclaimed Birkin. 'She's a born mistress, just as Gerald is a born lover—*amant en titre*. If as somebody says all women are either wives or mistresses, then Gudrun is a mistress.'

'And all men either lovers or husbands,' cried Ursula. 'But why not both?'

'The one excludes the other,' he laughed.

'Then I want a lover,' cried Ursula.

'No, you don't,' he said.

'But I do,' she wailed.

He kissed her and laughed.

It was two days after this that Ursula was to go to fetch her things from the house in Beldover. The removal had taken place, the family had gone. Gudrun had rooms in Willey Green.

Ursula had not seen her parents since her marriage. She wept over the rupture, yet what was the good of making it up! Good or not good, she could not go to them. So her things had been left behind and she and Gudrun were to walk over for them in the afternoon.

It was a wintry afternoon, with red in the sky, when they arrived at the house. The windows were dark and blank, already the place was frightening. A stark, void entrance-hall struck a chill to the hearts of the girls.

'I don't believe I dare have come in alone,' said Ursula. 'It frightens me.'

'Ursula!' cried Gudrun. 'Isn't it amazing! Can you believe you lived in this place and never felt it? How I lived here a day without dying of terror, I cannot conceive!'

They looked in the big dining-room. It was a good-sized room, but now a cell would have been lovelier. The large bay windows were naked, the floor was stripped, and a border of dark polish went round the tract of pale boarding. In the faded wall-paper were dark patches where furniture had stood, where pictures had hung. The sense of walls, dry, thin, flimsy-seeming walls, and a flimsy flooring, pale with its artificial black edges, was neutralizing to the mind. Everything was null to the senses, there was enclosure without substance, for the walls were dry and papery. Where were they standing, on earth, or suspended in some cardboard box? In the hearth was burnt paper and scraps of half-burnt paper.

'Imagine that we passed our days here!' said Ursula.

'I know,' cried Gudrun. 'It is too appalling. What must we be like, if we are the contents of *this*!'

'Vile!' said Ursula. 'It really is.'

And she recognized half-burnt covers of *Vogue*—half-burnt representations of women in gowns—lying under the grate.

They went to the drawing-room. Another piece of shut-in air; without weight or substance, only a sense of intolerable papery imprisonment in nothingness. The kitchen did look more substantial, because of the red-tiled floor and the stove, but it was cold and horrid.

The two girls tramped hollowly up the bare stairs. Every sound re-echoed under their hearts. They tramped down the bare corridor. Against the wall of Ursula's bedroom were her things—a trunk, a work-basket, some books, loose coats, a hat-box, standing desolate in the universal emptiness of the dusk.

'A cheerful sight, aren't they?' said Ursula, looking down at her forsaken possessions.

'Very cheerful,' said Gudrun.

The two girls set to, carrying everything down to the front door. Again and again they made the hollow, re-echoing transit. The whole place seemed to resound about them with a noise of hollow, empty futility. In the distance the empty, invisible rooms sent forth a vibration almost of obscenity. They almost fled with the last articles into the out-of-door.

But it was cold. They were waiting for Birkin, who was coming with the car. They went indoors again, and upstairs to their parents' front bedroom, whose windows looked down on the road, and across the country at the black-barred sunset, black and red barred, without light.

They sat down in the window-seat to wait. Both girls were looking over the room. It was void, with a meaninglessness that was almost dreadful.

'Really,' said Ursula, 'this room *couldn't* be sacred, could it?'

Gudrun looked over it with slow eyes.

'Impossible,' she replied.

'When I think of their lives—father's and mother's, their love, and their marriage, and all of us children, and our bringing-up—would you have such a life, Prune?'

'I wouldn't, Ursula.'

'It all seems so *nothing*—their two lives—there's no meaning in it. Really, if they had *not* met, and *not* married, and not lived together—it wouldn't have mattered, would it?'

'Of course—you can't tell,' said Gudrun.

'No. But if I thought my life was going to be like it—Prune,' she caught Gudrun's arm, 'I should run.'

Gudrun was silent for a few moments.

'As a matter of fact, one cannot contemplate the ordinary life—one cannot contemplate it,' replied Gudrun. 'With you, Ursula, it is quite different. You will be out of it all, with Birkin. He's a special case. But with the ordinary man, who has his life fixed in one place, marriage is just impossible. There may be, and there *are,* thousands of women who want it, and could conceive of nothing else. But the very thought of it sends me *mad.* One must be free, above all, one must be free. One may forfeit everything else, but one must be free—one must not become 7 Pinchbeck Street—or Somerset Drive—or Shortlands. No man will be sufficient to make that good—no man! To marry, one must have a free lance or nothing, a comrade-in-arms, a *Glücksritter.* A man with a position in the social world—well, it is just impossible, impossible!'

'What a lovely word—a *Glücksritter*!' said Ursula. 'So much nicer than a soldier of fortune.'

'Yes, isn't it?' said Gudrun. 'I'd tilt the world with a *Glücksritter.* But a home, an establishment! Ursula, what would it mean?—think!'

'I know,' said Ursula. 'We've had one home—that's enough for me.'

'Quite enough,' said Gudrun.

'The little grey home in the west,' quoted Ursula ironically.

'Doesn't it sound grey, too,' said Gudrun grimly.

They were interrupted by the sound of the car. There was Birkin. Ursula was surprised that she felt so lit up, that she became suddenly so free from the problems of grey homes in the west.

They heard his heels click on the hall pavement below.

'Hello!' he called, his voice echoing alive through the house. Ursula smiled to herself. *He* was frightened of the place too.

'Hello! Here we are,' she called downstairs. And they heard him quickly running up.

'This is a ghostly situation,' he said.

'These houses don't have ghosts—they've never had any personality, and only a place with personality can have a ghost,' said Gudrun.

'I suppose so. Are you both weeping over the past?'

'We are,' said Gudrun, grimly.

Ursula laughed.

'Not weeping that it's gone, but weeping that it ever *was*,' she said.

'Oh,' he replied, relieved.

He sat down for a moment. There was something in his presence, Ursula thought, lambent and alive. It made even the impertinent structure of this null house disappear.

'Gudrun says she could not bear to be married and put into a house,' said Ursula meaningful—they knew this referred to Gerald.

He was silent for some moments.

'Well,' he said, 'if you know beforehand you couldn't stand it, you're safe.'

'Quite!' said Gudrun.

'Why *does* every woman think her aim in life is to have a hubby and a little grey home in the west? Why is this the goal of life? Why should it be?' said Ursula.

'*Il faut avoir le respect de ses bêtises,*' said Birkin.

'But you needn't have the respect for the *bêtise* before you've committed it,' laughed Ursula.

'Ah then, *des bêtises du papa*?'

'*Et de la maman,*' added Gudrun satirically.

'*Et des voisins,*' said Ursula.

They all laughed, and rose. It was getting dark. They carried the things to the car. Gudrun locked the door of the empty house. Birkin had lighted the lamps of the automobile. It all seemed very happy, as if they were setting out.

'Do you mind stopping at Coulsons. I have to leave the key there,' said Gudrun.

'Right,' said Birkin, and they moved off.

They stopped in the main street. The shops were just lighted, the last miners were passing home along the causeways, half-visible shadows in their grey pit-dirt, moving through the blue air. But their feet rang harshly in manifold sound, along the pavement.

How pleased Gudrun was to come out of the shop, and enter the car, and be borne swiftly away into the down-hill of palpable dusk, with Ursula and Birkin! What an adventure life seemed at this moment! How deeply, how suddenly she envied Ursula! Life for her was so quick, and an open door—so reckless as if not only this world, but the world that was gone and the world to come were nothing to her. Ah, if she could be *just like that,* it would be perfect.

For always, except in her moments of excitement, she felt a want within herself. She was unsure. She had felt that now, at last, in Gerald's strong and violent love, she was living fully and finally. But when she compared herself with Ursula, already her soul was jealous, unsatisfied. She was not satisfied—she was never to be satisfied.

What was she short of now? It was marriage—it was the wonderful stability of marriage. She did want it, let her say what she might. She had been lying. The old idea of marriage was right even now—marriage and the home. Yet her mouth gave a little grimace at the words. She thought of Gerald and Shortlands—marriage and the home! Ah well, let it rest! He meant a great deal to her—but—! Perhaps it was not in her to marry. She was one of life's outcasts, one of the drifting lives that have no root. No, no—it could not be so. She suddenly conjured up a rosy room, with herself in a beautiful gown, and a handsome man in evening dress who held her in his arms in the firelight, and kissed her. This picture she entitled 'Home'. It would have done for the Royal Academy.

'Come with us to tea—*do,*' said Ursula, as they ran nearer to the cottage of Willey Green.

'Thanks awfully—but I *must* go in—' said Gudrun. She wanted very much to go on with Ursula and Birkin. That seemed like life indeed to her. Yet a certain perversity would not let her.

'Do come—yes, it would be so nice,' pleaded Ursula.

'I'm awfully sorry—I should love to—but I can't—really—'

She descended from the car in trembling haste.

'Can't you really!' came Ursula's regretful voice.

'No, really I can't,' responded Gudrun's pathetic, cha-grined words out of the dusk.

'All right, are you?' called Birkin.

'Quite!' said Gudrun. 'Good night!'

'Good night,' they called.

'Come whenever you like, we shall be glad,' called Bir-kin.

'Thank you very much,' called Gudrun, in the strange, twanging voice of lonely chagrin that was very puzzling to him. She turned away to her cottage gate, and they drove on. But immediately she stood to watch them, as the car ran vague into the distance. And as she went up the path to her strange house, her heart was full of incomprehensible bitter-ness.

In her parlour was a long-case clock, and inserted into its dial was a ruddy, round, slant-eyed, joyous-painted face, that wagged over with the most ridiculous ogle when the clock ticked, and back again with the same absurd glad-eye at the next tick. All the time the absurd smooth, brown-ruddy face gave her an obtrusive 'glad-eye.' She stood for minutes, watching it, till a sort of maddened disgust overcame her, and she laughed at herself hollowly. And still it rocked, and gave her the glad-eye from one side, then from the other, from one side, then from the other. Ah, how unhappy she was! In the midst of her most active happiness, ah, how un-happy she was! She glanced at the table. Gooseberry jam, and the same homemade cake with too much soda in it! Still, gooseberry jam was good, and one so rarely got it.

All the evening she wanted to go to the Mill. But she coldly refused to allow herself. She went the next afternoon instead. She was happy to find Ursula alone. It was a lovely, intimate secluded atmosphere. They talked endlessly and de-lightedly. 'Aren't you *fearfully* happy here?' said Gudrun to her sister glancing at her own bright eyes in the mirror. She always envied, almost with resentment, the strange positive fullness that subsided in the atmosphere around Ursula and Birkin.

'How really beautifully this room is done,' she said aloud.

'This hard plaited matting—what a lovely colour it is, the colour of cool light!'

And it seemed to her perfect.

'Ursula,' she said at length, in a voice of question and detachment, 'did you know that Gerald Crich had suggested our going away all together at Christmas?'

'Yes, he's spoken to Rupert.'

A deep flush dyed Gudrun's cheek. She was silent a moment, as if taken aback, and not knowing what to say.

'But don't you think,' she said at last, 'it is *amazingly cool!*'

Ursula laughed.

'I like him for it,' she said.

Gudrun was silent. It was evident that, whilst she was almost mortified by Gerald's taking the liberty of making such a suggestion to Birkin, yet the idea itself attracted her strongly.

'There's a rather lovely simplicity about Gerald, I think,' said Ursula, 'so defiant, somehow! Oh, I think he's *very* lovable.'

Gudrun did not reply for some moments. She had still to get over the feeling of insult at the liberty taken with her freedom.

'What did Rupert say—do you know?' she asked.

'He said it would be most awfully jolly,' said Ursula.

Again Gudrun looked down, and was silent.

'Don't you think it would?' said Ursula, tentatively. She was never quite sure how many defences Gudrun was having round herself.

Gudrun raised her face with difficulty and held it averted.

'I think it *might* be awfully jolly, as you say,' she replied. 'But don't you think it was an unpardonable liberty to take—to talk of such things to Rupert—who after all—you see what I mean, Ursula—they might have been two men arranging an outing with some little *type* they'd picked up. Oh, I think it's unforgivable, quite!' She used the French word *'type.'*

Her eyes flashed, her soft face was flushed and sullen. Ursula looked on, rather frightened, frightened most of all because she thought Gudrun seemed rather common, really like a little *type*. But she had not the courage quite to think this—not right out.

'Oh no,' she cried, stammering. 'Oh no—not at all like that—oh no! No, I think it's rather beautiful, the friendship between Rupert and Gerald. They just are simple—they say anything to each other, like brothers.'

Gudrun flushed deeper. She could not *bear* it that Gerald gave her away—even to Birkin.

'But do you think even brothers have any right to exchange confidences of that sort?' she asked, with deep anger.

'Oh, yes,' said Ursula. 'There's never anything said that isn't perfectly straightforward. No, the thing that's amazed me most in Gerald—how perfectly simple and direct he can be! And you know, it takes rather a big man. Most of them *must* be indirect, they are such cowards.'

But Gudrun was still silent with anger. She wanted the absolute secrecy kept, with regard to her movements.

'Won't you go?' said Ursula. 'Do, we might all be so happy! There is something I *love* about Gerald—he's *much* more lovable than I thought him. He's free, Gudrun, he really is.'

Gudrun's mouth was still closed, sullen and ugly. She opened it at length.

'Do you know where he proposes to go?' she asked.

'Yes—to the Tyrol, where he used to go when he was in Germany—a lovely place where students go, small and rough and lovely, for winter sport!'

Through Gudrun's mind went the angry thought—'they know everything.'

'Yes,' she said aloud, 'about forty kilometres from Innsbruck, isn't it?'

'I don't know exactly where—but it would be lovely, don't you think, high in the perfect snow—?'

'Very lovely!' said Gudrun, sarcastically.

Ursula was put out.

'Of course,' she said, 'I think Gerald spoke to Rupert so that it shouldn't seem like an outing with a *type*—'

'I know, of course,' said Gudrun, 'that he quite commonly does take up with that sort.'

'Does he!' said Ursula. 'Why how do you know?'

'I know of a model in Chelsea,' said Gudrun coldly.

Now Ursula was silent.

'Well,' she said at last, with a doubtful laugh, 'I hope he has a good time with her.' At which Gudrun looked more glum.

28

Gudrun in the Pompadour

Christmas drew near, all four prepared for flight. Birkin and Ursula were busy packing their few personal things, making them ready to be sent off, to whatever country and whatever place they might choose at last. Gudrun was very much excited. She loved to be on the wing.

She and Gerald, being ready first, set off via London and Paris to Innsbruck, where they would meet Ursula and Birkin. In London they stayed one night. They went to the music-hall, and afterwards to the Pompadour Café.

Gudrun hated the Café, yet she always went back to it, as did most of the artists of her acquaintance. She loathed its atmosphere of petty vice and petty jealousy and petty art. Yet she always called in again, when she was in town. It was as if she *had* to return to this small, slow central whirlpool of disintegration and dissolution: just give it a look.

She sat with Gerald drinking some sweetish liqueur, and staring with black, sullen looks at the various groups of people at the tables. She would greet nobody, but young men nodded to her frequently, with a kind of sneering familiarity. She cut them all. And it gave her pleasure to sit there, cheeks flushed, eyes black and sullen, seeing them all objectively, as put away from her, like creatures in some menagerie of apish degraded souls. God, what a foul crew they were! Her blood beat black and thick in her veins with rage and loathing. Yet she must sit and watch, watch. One or two people came to speak to her. From every side of the Café, eyes turned half furtively, half jeeringly at her, men looking over their shoulders, women under their hats.

The old crowd was there, Carlyon in his corner with his pupils and his girl, Halliday and Libidnikov and the

Pussum—they were all there. Gudrun watched Gerald. She watched his eyes linger a moment on Halliday, on Halliday's party. These last were on the look-out—they nodded to him, he nodded again. They giggled and whispered among themselves. Gerald watched them with the steady twinkle in his eyes. They were urging Minette to something.

She at last rose. She was wearing a curious dress of dark silk with long pale rays, a curious rayed effect. She was thinner, her eyes were perhaps wider, more disintegrated. Otherwise she was just the same. Gerald watched her with the same steady twinkle in his eyes as she came across. She held out her thin fair hand to him.

'How are you?' she said.

He shook hands with her, but remained seated, and let her stand near him, against the table. She nodded coldly to Gudrun, whom she did not know to speak to, but well enough by sight and reputation.

'I am very well,' said Gerald. 'And you?'

'Oh I'm all wight. What about Wupert?'

'Rupert? He's very well, too.'

'Yes, I don't mean that. What about him being married?'

'Oh—yes, he is married.'

Minette's eyes had a hot flash.

'Oh, he's weally bwought it off then, has he? When was he married?'

'A week or two ago.'

'Weally! He's never written.'

'No.'

'No. Don't you think it's too bad?'

This last was in a tone of challenge. Minette let it be known by her tone, that she was aware of Gudrun's listening.

'I suppose he didn't feel like it,' replied Gerald.

'But why didn't he?' pursued Minette.

This was received in silence. There was an ugly, mocking persistence in the small, beautiful figure of the short-haired girl, as she stood near Gerald.

'Are you staying in town long?' she asked.

'Tonight only.'

'Oh, only tonight. Are you coming over to speak to Julius?'

'Not tonight.'

'Oh very well. I'll tell him then.' Then came her touch of diablerie. 'You're looking awf'lly fit.'

'Yes—I feel it.' Gerald was quite calm and easy, a spark of satiric amusement in his eye.

'Are you having a good time?'

This was a direct blow for Gudrun, spoken in a level, toneless voice of callous ease.

'Yes,' he replied, quite colourlessly.

'I'm awf'lly sorry you aren't coming round. You aren't very faithful to your friends.'

'Not very,' he said.

She nodded them both 'Good night', and went back slowly to her own set. Gudrun watched her curious walk, stiff and jerking at the loins. They heard her level, toneless voice distinctly.

'He won't come over;—he is otherwise engaged,' it said. There was more laughter and lowered voices and mockery at the table.

'Is she a friend of yours?' said Gudrun, looking calmly at Gerald.

'I've stayed at Halliday's with Birkin,' he said, meeting her slow, calm eyes. And she knew that Minette was one of his mistresses—and he knew she knew.

She looked round, and called for the waiter. She wanted an iced cocktail, of all things. This amused Gerald—he wondered what was up.

The Halliday party was tipsy, and malicious. They were talking out loudly about Birkin, ridiculing him on every point, particularly on his marriage.

'Oh, *don't* make me think of Birkin,' Halliday was squealing. 'He makes me perfectly sick. He is as bad as Jesus. "Lord, *what* must I do to be saved!"'

He giggled to himself tipsily.

'Do you remember,' came the quick voice of the Russian, 'the letters he used to send. "Desire is holy—"'

'Oh yes!' cried Halliday. 'Oh, how perfectly splendid. Why, I've got one in my pocket. I'm sure I have.'

He took out various papers from his pocket book.

'I'm sure I've—*hic! Oh dear!*— got one.'

Gerald and Gudrun were watching absorbedly.

'Oh yes, how perfectly—*hic!*—splendid! Don't make me laugh, Minette, it gives me the hiccup. Hic!—' They all giggled.

'What did he say in that one?' Minette asked, leaning forward, her close fair hair falling and swinging against her face. There was something curiously indecent about her small, longish, fair skull, particularly when the ears showed.

'Wait—oh, do wait! *No-o*, I won't give it to you, I'll read it aloud. I'll read you the choice bits—*hic!* Oh dear! Do you think if I drink water it would take off this hiccup? *Hic!* Oh, I feel perfectly helpless.'

'Isn't that the letter about uniting the dark and the light—and the Flux of Corruption?' asked Maxim, in his precise, quick voice.

'I believe so,' said Minette.

'Oh, is it? I'd forgotten—*hic!*—it was that one,' Halliday said, opening the letter. '*Hic!* Oh yes. How perfectly splendid! This is one of the best. "There is a phase in every race—" ' he read in the sing-song, slow, distinct voice of a clergyman reading the Scriptures, ' "when the desire for destruction overcomes every other desire. In the individual, this desire is ultimately a desire for destruction in the self"—*hic!*—' he paused and looked up.

'I hope he's going ahead with the destruction of himself,' said the quick voice of the Russian. Halliday giggled, and lolled his head back, vaguely.

'There's not much to destroy in him,' said Minette. 'He's so thin already, there's only a fag-end to start on.'

'Oh, isn't it beautiful! I love reading it! I believe it has cured my hiccup!' squealed Halliday. 'Do let me go on. 'It is a desire for the reduction-process in oneself, a reducing back to the origin, a return along the Flux of Corruption, to the original rudimentary conditions of being—!" Oh, but I *do* think it is wonderful. It almost supersedes the Bible—'

'Yes—Flux of Corruption,' said the Russian, 'I remember that phrase.'

'Oh, he was always talking about Corruption,' said Minette. 'He must be corrupt himself, to have it so much on his mind.'

'Exactly!' said the Russian.

'Do let me go on! Oh, this is a perfectly wonderful piece! But do listen to this. "And in the great retrogression, the reducing back of the created body of life, we get knowledge, and beyond knowledge, the phosphorescent ecstasy of acute sensation." Oh, I do think these phrases are too absurdly wonderful. Oh, but don't you think they *are*—they're nearly as good as Jesus. "And if, Julius, you want this ecstasy of reduction with Minette, you must go on till it is fulfilled. But surely there is in you also, somewhere, the living desire for positive creation, relationships in ultimate faith, when all this process of active corruption, with all its flowers of mud, is transcended, and more or less finished—" I do wonder what the flowers of mud are. Minette, you are a flower of mud.'

'Thank you—and what are you?'

'Oh, I'm another, surely, according to this letter! We're all flowers of mud—*Fleurs—hic! du mal!* It's perfectly wonderful, Birkin harrowing Hell—harrowing the Pompadour—*Hic!*'

'Go on—go on,' said Maxim. 'What comes next? It's really very interesting.'

'I think it's awful cheek to write like that,' said Minette.

'Yes—yes, so do I,' said the Russian. 'He is a megalomaniac, of course, it is a form of religious mania. He thinks he is the Savior of man—go on reading.'

'Surely,' Halliday intoned, ' "surely goodness and mercy hath followed me all the days of my life—" ' he broke off and giggled. Then he began again, intoning like a clergyman. ' "Surely there will come an end in us to this desire—for the constant going apart—this passion for putting asunder—everything—ourselves, reducing ourselves part from part—reacting in intimacy only for destruction—using sex as a great reducing agent, reducing the two great elements of male and female from their highly complex unity—reducing the old ideas, going back to the savages for our sensations—always seeking to *lose* ourselves in some ultimate black sensation, mindless and infinite—burning only with destructive fires, ranging on with the hope of being burnt out utterly—" '

'I want to go,' said Gudrun to Gerald, as she signalled the waiter. Her eyes were flashing, her cheeks were flushed. The strange effect of Birkin's letter read aloud in a perfect clerical sing-song, clear and resonant, phrase by phrase, made the blood mount into her head as if she were mad.

She rose, whilst Gerald was paying the bill, and walked over to Halliday's table. They all glanced up at her.

'Excuse me,' she said. 'Is that a genuine letter you are reading?'

'Oh yes,' said Halliday. 'Quite genuine.'

'May I see?'

Smiling foolishly he handed it to her, as if hypnotized.

'Thank you,' she said.

And she turned and walked out of the Café with the letter, all down the brilliant room, between the tables, in her measured fashion. It was some moments before anybody realized what was happening.

From Halliday's table came half articulate cries, then somebody booed, then all the far end of the place began booing after Gudrun's retreating form. She was fashionably dressed in blackish-green and silver, her hat was brilliant green, like the sheen on an insect, but the brim was soft dark green, a falling edge with fine silver, her coat was dark green, lustrous, with a high collar of grey fur, and great fur cuffs, the edge of her dress showed silver and black velvet, her stockings and shoes were silver grey. She moved with slow, fashionable indifference to the door. The porter opened obsequiously for her, and at her nod, hurried to the edge of the pavement and whistled for a taxi. The two lights of a vehicle almost immediately curved round towards her, like two eyes.

Gerald had followed in wonder, amid all the booing, not having caught her misdeed. He heard Minette's voice saying:

'Go and get it back from her. I never heard of such a thing! Go and get it back from her. Tell Gerald Crich—there he goes—go and make him give it up.'

Gudrun stood at the door of the taxi, which the man held open for her.

'To the hotel?' she asked, as Gerald came out, hurriedly.

'Where you like,' he answered.

'Right!' she said. Then to the driver, 'Wagstaff's—Barton Street.'

The driver bowed his head, and put down the flag.

Gudrun entered the taxi, with the deliberate cold movement of a woman who is well-dressed and contemptuous in her soul. Yet she was frozen with overwrought feelings. Gerald followed her.

'You've forgotten the man,' she said coolly, with a slight nod of her hat. Gerald gave the porter a shilling. The man saluted. They were in motion.

'What was all the row about?' asked Gerald, in wondering excitement.

'I walked away with Birkin's letter,' she said, and he saw the crushed paper in her hand.

His eyes glittered with satisfaction.

'Ah!' he said. 'Splendid! A set of jackasses!'

'I could have *killed* them!' she cried in passion. '*Dogs!*— they are dogs! Why is Rupert such a *fool* as to write such letters to them? Why does he give himself away to such *canaille*? It's a thing that *cannot be borne.*'

Gerald wondered over her strange passion.

And she could not rest any longer in London. They must go by the morning train from Charing Cross. As they drew over the bridge, in the train, having glimpses of the river between the great iron girders, she cried:

'I feel I could *never* see this foul town again—I couldn't *bear* to come back to it.'

29

Continental

U rsula went on in an unreal suspense, the last weeks before going away. She was not herself—she was not anything. She was something that is going to be—soon—soon—very soon. But as yet, she was only imminent.

She went to see her parents. It was a rather stiff, sad meeting, more like a verification of separateness than a reunion. But they were all vague and indefinite with one another, stiffened in the fate that moved them apart.

She did not really come to until she was on the ship crossing from Dover to Ostend. Dimly she had come down to London with Birkin, London had been a vagueness, so had the train journey to Dover. It was all like a sleep.

And now, at last, as she stood in the stern of the ship, in a pitch-dark, rather blowy night, feeling the motion of the sea, and watching the small, rather desolate little lights that twinkled on the shores of England, as on the shores of nowhere, watched them sinking smaller and smaller on the profound and living darkness, she felt her soul stirring to awake from its anaesthetic sleep.

'Let us go forward, shall we?' said Birkin. He wanted to be at the tip of their projection. So they left off looking at the faint sparks that glimmered out of nowhere, in the far distance, called England, and turned their faces to the unfathomed night in front.

They went right to the bows of the softly plunging vessel. In the complete obscurity, Birkin found a comparatively sheltered nook, where a great rope was coiled up. It was quite near the very point of the ship, near the black, unpierced space ahead. Here they sat down, folded together, folded round with the same rug, creeping in nearer and ever nearer to one another, till it seemed they had crept right into each other, and become one substance. It was very cold, and the darkness was palpable.

One of the ship's crew came along the deck, dark as the darkness, not really visible. They then made out the faintest pallor of his face. He felt their presence, and stopped, unsure— then bent forward. When his face was near them, he saw the faint pallor of their faces. Then he withdrew like a phantom. And they watched him without making any sound.

They seemed to fall away into the profound darkness. There was no sky, no earth, only one unbroken darkness, into which, with a soft, sleeping motion, they seemed to fall like one closed seed of life falling through dark, fathomless space.

They had forgotten where they were, forgotten all that was and all that had been, conscious only in their heart, and there conscious only of this pure trajectory through the surpassing darkness. The ship's prow cleaved on, with a faint noise of cleavage, into the complete night, without knowing, without seeing, only surging on.

In Ursula the sense of the unrealized world ahead triumphed over everything. In the midst of this profound darkness, there seemed to glow on her heart the effulgence of a paradise unknown and unrealized. Her heart was full of the most wonderful light, golden like honey of darkness, sweet like the warmth of day, a light which was not shed on the world, only on the unknown paradise towards which she was going, a sweetness of habitation, a delight of living quite unknown, but hers infallibly. In her transport she lifted her face suddenly to him, and he touched it with his lips. So cold, so fresh, so sea-clear her face was, it was like kissing a flower that grows near the surf.

But he did not know the ecstasy of bliss in fore-knowledge that she knew. To him, the wonder of this transit was overwhelming. He was falling through a gulf of infinite darkness, like a meteorite plunging across the chasm between the worlds. The world was torn in two, and he was plunging like an unlit star through the ineffable rift. What was beyond was not yet for him. He was overcome by the trajectory.

In a trance he lay enfolding Ursula round about. His face was against her fine, fragile hair, he breathed its fragrance with the sea and the profound night. And his soul was at peace; yielded, as he fell into the unknown. This was the first time that an utter and absolute peace had entered his heart, now, in this final transit out of life.

When there came some stir on the deck, they roused. They stood up. How stiff and cramped they were in the night-time! And yet the paradisal glow on her heart, and the unutterable peace of darkness in his, this was the all-in-all.

They stood up and looked ahead. Low lights were seen down the darkness. This was the world again. It was not the bliss of her heart, nor the peace of his. It was the superficial unreal world of fact. Yet not quite the old world. For the peace and the bliss in their hearts was enduring.

Strange and desolate above all things, like disembarking from the Styx into the desolated underworld, was this landing at night. There was the raw, half-lighted, covered-in vastness of the dark place, boarded and hollow underfoot, with only desolation everywhere. Ursula had caught sight of the big, pallid, mystic letters 'OSTEND' standing in the darkness. Everybody was hurrying with a blind, insect-like intentness through the dark grey air, porters were calling in un-English English, then trotting with heavy bags, their colourless blouses looking ghostly as they disappeared; Ursula stood at a long, low, zinc-covered barrier along with hundreds of other spectral people, and all the way down the vast, raw darkness was this low stretch of open bags and spectral people, whilst, on the other side of the barrier, pallid officials in peaked caps and moustaches were turning the underclothing in the bags, then scrawling a chalk-mark.

It was done. Birkin snapped the hand-bags, off they went, the porter coming behind. They were through a great doorway, and in the open night again—ah, a railway platform! Voices were still calling in inhuman agitation through the dark-grey air, spectres were running along the darkness between the train.

'Köln—Berlin—' Ursula made out on the boards hung on the high train on one side.

'Here we are,' said Birkin. And on her side she saw: 'Elsass—Lothringen—Luxembourg, Metz—Basle.'

'That was it, Basle!'

The porter came up.

'À *Bâle—deuxième classe?—Voilà!*' And he clambered into the high train. They followed. The compartments were already some of them taken. But many were dim and empty. The luggage was stowed, the porter was tipped.

'*Nous avons encore—?*' said Birkin, looking at his watch and at the porter.

'*Encore une demi-heure.*' With which, in his blue blouse, he disappeared. He was ugly and insolent.

'Come,' said Birkin. 'It is cold. Let us eat.'

There was a coffee-wagon on the platform. They drank hot, watery coffee and ate the long rolls, split, with ham between, which were such a wide bite that it almost dislocated Ursula's jaw; and they walked beside the high trains. It was all so strange, so extremely desolate, like the underworld, grey, grey, dirt grey, desolate, forlorn, nowhere—grey, dreary nowhere.

At last they were moving through the night. In the darkness Ursula made out the flat fields, the wet, flat, dreary darkness of the Continent. They pulled up surprisingly soon—Bruges! Then on through the level darkness, with glimpses of sleeping farms and thin poplar trees and deserted high roads. She sat dismayed, hand in hand with Birkin. He pale, immobile like a *revenant* himself, looked sometimes out of the window, sometimes closed his eyes. Then his eyes opened again, dark as the darkness outside.

A flash of a few lights on the darkness—Ghent station! A few more spectres moving outside on the platform—then the bell—then motion again through the level darkness. Ursula saw a man with a lantern come out of a farm by the railway and cross to the dark farm-buildings. She thought of the Marsh, the old, intimate farm life at Cossethay. My God, how far was she projected from her childhood, how far was she still to go! In one lifetime one travelled through aeons. The great chasm of memory from her childhood in the inti-

mate country surroundings of Cossethay and the Marsh
Farm—she remembered the servant Tilly, who used to give
her bread and butter sprinkled with brown sugar in the old
living-room where the grandfather clock had two pink roses
in a basket painted above the figures on the face—and now
when she was travelling into the unknown with Birkin, an
utter stranger—was so great, that it seemed she had no identity, that the child she had been, playing in Cossethay
churchyard, was a little creature of history, not really herself.

They were at Brussels—half an hour for breakfast. They
got down. On the great station clock it said six o'clock.
They had coffee and rolls and honey in the vast desert
refreshment-room, so dreary, always so dreary, dirty, so spacious, such desolation of space. But she washed her face and
hands in hot water and combed her hair—that was a bless-
ing.

Soon they were in the train again and moving on. The
greyness of dawn began. There were several people in the
compartment, large florid Belgian business-men with long
brown beards, talking incessantly in an ugly French she was
too tired to follow.

It seemed the train ran by degrees out of the darkness into
a faint light, then beat after beat into the day. Ah, how weary
it was! Faintly, the trees showed, like shadows. Then a
house, white, had a curious distinctness. How was it? Then
she saw a village—there were always houses passing.

This was an old world she was still journeying through,
winter-heavy and dreary. There was plough-land and pas-
ture, and copses of bare trees, copses of bushes, and home-
steads naked and work-bare. No new earth had come to pass.

She looked at Birkin's face. It was white and still and
eternal, too eternal. She linked her fingers imploringly in his
under the cover of her rug. His fingers responded, his eyes
looked back at her. How dark, like a night, his eyes were,
like another world beyond! Oh, if he were the world as well,
if only the world were he! If only he could call a world into
being, that should be their own world!

The Belgians left, the train ran on, through Luxembourg,
through Alsace-Lorraine, through Metz. But she was blind,
she could see no more. Her soul did not look out.

They came at last to Basle, to the hotel. It was all a drift-ing trance, from which she never came to. They went out in the morning before the train departed. She saw the street, the river, she stood on the bridge. But it all meant nothing. She remembered some shops—one full of pictures, one with orange velvet and ermine. But what did these signify?— nothing.

She was not at ease till they were in the train again. Then she was relieved. So long as they were moving onwards, she was satisfied. They came to Zürich, then, before very long, ran under the mountains that were deep in snow. At last she was drawing near. This was the other world now.

Innsbruck was wonderful, deep in snow, and evening. They drove in an open sledge over the snow: the train had been so hot and stifling. And the hotel, with the golden light glowing under the porch, seemed like a home.

They laughed with pleasure when they were in the hall. The place seemed full and busy.

'Do you know if Mr and Mrs Crich—English—from Paris, have arrived?' Birkin asked in German.

The porter reflected a moment, and was just going to an-swer when Ursula caught sight of Gudrun sauntering down the stairs, wearing her dark glossy coat with grey fur.

'Gudrun! Gudrun!' she called, waving up the well of the staircase. 'Shu-hu!'

Gudrun looked over the rail, and immediately lost her sauntering, diffident air. Her eyes flashed.

'Really—Ursula!' she cried. And she began to move downstairs as Ursula ran up. They met at a turn and kissed with laughter and exclamations inarticulate and stirring.

'But!' cried Gudrun, mortified. 'We thought it was to-morrow you were coming! I wanted to come to the station.'

'No, we've come today!' cried Ursula. 'Isn't it lovely here!'

'Adorable!' said Gudrun. 'Gerald's just gone out to get something. Ursula, aren't you *fearfully* tired?'

'No, not so very. But I look a filthy sight, don't I?'

'No, you don't. You look almost perfectly fresh. I like that fur cap *immensely*!' She glanced over Ursula, who wore a big soft coat with a collar of deep, soft, blond fur and a soft blond cap of fur.

'And you!' cried Ursula. 'What do you think *you* look like!'

Gudrun assumed an unconcerned, expressionless face.

'Do you like it?' she said.

'It's *very* fine!' cried Ursula, perhaps with a touch of satire.

'Go up—or come down,' said Birkin. For there the sisters stood, Gudrun with her hand on Ursula's arm, on the turn of the stairs half-way to the first landing, blocking the way, and affording full entertainment to the whole of the hall below, from the door porter to the plump Jew in black clothes.

The two young women slowly mounted, followed by Birkin and the waiter.

'First floor?' asked Gudrun, looking back over her shoulder.

'Second, Madam—the lift!' the waiter replied. And he darted to the elevator to forestall the two women. But they ignored him, as, chattering without heed, they set to mount the second flight. Rather chagrined, the waiter followed.

It was curious, the delight of the sisters in each other, at this meeting. It was as if they met in exile and united their solitary forces against all the world. Birkin looked on with some mistrust and wonder.

When they had bathed and changed, Gerald came in. He looked shining like the sun on frost.

'Go with Gerald and smoke,' said Ursula to Birkin. 'Gudrun and I want to talk.'

Then the sisters sat in Gudrun's bedroom and talked clothes and experiences. Gudrun told Ursula the experience of the Birkin letter in the café. Ursula was shocked and frightened.

'Where is the letter?' she asked.

'I kept it,' said Gudrun.

'You'll give it me, won't you?' she said.

But Gudrun was silent for some moments before she replied:

'Do you really want it, Ursula?'

'I want to read it,' said Ursula.

'Certainly,' said Gudrun.

Even now she could not admit, to Ursula, that she wanted to keep it as a memento or a symbol. But Ursula knew, and was not pleased. So the subject was switched off.

'What did you do in Paris?' asked Ursula.

'Oh,' said Gudrun laconically—'the usual things. We had a *fine* party one night in Fanny Bath's studio.'

'Did you? And you and Gerald were there! Who else? Tell me about it.'

'Well,' said Gudrun. 'There's nothing particular to tell. You know Fanny is *frightfully* in love with that painter, Billy Macfarlane. He was there—so Fanny spared nothing, she spent *very* freely. It was really remarkable! Of course, everybody got fearfully drunk—but in an interesting way, not like that filthy London crowd. The fact is these were all people that matter, which makes all the difference. There was a Roumanian, a fine chap. He got completely drunk, and climbed to the top of a high studio ladder, and gave the most marvellous address—really, Ursula, it was wonderful! He began in French—*La vie, c'est une affaire d'âmes impériales*—in a most beautiful voice—he was a fine-looking chap—but he had got into Roumanian before he had finished, and not a soul understood. But Donald Gilchrist was worked to a frenzy. He dashed his glass to the ground and declared, by God, he was glad he had been born, by God, it was a miracle to be alive. And do you know, Ursula, so it was—' Gudrun laughed rather hollowly.

'But how was Gerald among them all?' asked Ursula.

'Gerald! On, my word, he came out like a dandelion in the sun! *He's* a whole saturnalia in himself, once he is roused. I shouldn't like to say whose waist his arm did not go round. Really, Ursula, he seems to reap the women like a harvest. There wasn't one that would have resisted him. It was too amazing! Can you understand it?'

Ursula reflected, and a dancing light came into her eyes.

'Yes,' she said. 'I can. He is such a whole-hogger.'

'Whole-hogger! I should think so!' exclaimed Gudrun. 'But it is true, Ursula, every woman in the room was ready to surrender to him. Chanticleer isn't in it—even Fanny Bath, who is *genuinely* in love with Billy Macfarlane! I never was more amazed in my life! And you know, after-wards—I felt I was a whole *roomful* of women. I was no more myself to him than I was Queen Victoria. I was a whole roomful of women at once. It was most astounding! But my eye, I'd caught a Sultan that time—'

Gudrun's eyes were flashing, her cheek was hot, she looked strange, exotic, satiric. Ursula was fascinated at once—and yet uneasy.

They had to get ready for dinner. Gudrun came down in a daring gown of vivid green silk and tissue of gold, with green velvet bodice and a strange black-and-white band round her hair. She was really brilliantly beautiful and everybody noticed her. Gerald was in that full-blooded, gleaming state when he was most handsome. Birkin watched them with quick, laughing, half-sinister eyes, Ursula quite lost her head. There seemed a spell, almost a blinding spell, cast round their table, as if they were lighted up more strongly than the rest of the dining-room.

'Don't you love to be in this place?' cried Gudrun. 'Isn't the snow wonderful! Do you notice how it exalts everything? It is simply marvellous. One really does feel *übermenschlich*—more than human.'

'One does,' cried Ursula. 'But isn't that partly the being out of England?'

'Oh, of course,' cried Gudrun. 'One could never feel like this in England, for the simple reason that the damper is *never* lifted off one, there. It is quite impossible really to let go, in England, of that I am assured.'

And she turned again to the food she was eating. She was fluttering with vivid intensity.

'It's quite true,' said Gerald, 'it never is *quite* the same in England. But perhaps we don't want it to be—perhaps it's like bringing the light a little too near the powder-magazine, to let go altogether, in England. One is afraid what might happen, if *everybody else* let go.'

'My God!' cried Gudrun. 'But wouldn't it be wonderful if all England *did* suddenly go off like a display of fireworks.'

'It couldn't,' said Ursula. 'They are all too damp, the powder is damp in them.'

'I'm not so sure of that,' said Gerald.

'Nor I,' said Birkin. 'When the English really begin to go off, *en masse,* it'll be time to shut your ears and run.'

'They never will,' said Ursula.

'We'll see,' he replied.

'Isn't it marvellous,' said Gudrun, 'how thankful one can be, to be out of one's country. I cannot believe myself, I am so transported, the moment I set foot on a foreign shore. I say to myself: "Here steps a new creature into life." '

'Don't be too hard on poor old England,' said Gerald. 'Though we curse it, we love it really.'

To Ursula there seemed a fund of cynicism in these words.

'We may,' said Birkin. 'But it's a damnably uncomfortable love: like a love for an aged parent who suffers horribly from a complication of diseases, for which there is no hope.'

Gudrun looked at him with dilated dark eyes.

'You think there is no hope?' she asked in her pertinent fashion.

But Birkin backed away. He would not answer such a question.

'Any hope of England's becoming real? God knows. It's a great actual unreality now, an aggregation into unreality. It might be real, if there were no Englishmen.'

'You think the English will have to disappear?' persisted Gudrun. It was strange, her pointed interest in his answer. It might have been her own fate she was inquiring after. Her dark, dilated eyes rested on Birkin, as if she could conjure the truth of the future out of him, as out of some instrument of divination.

He was pale. Then, reluctantly, he answered:

'Well—what else is in front of them but disappearance? They've got to disappear from their own special brand of Englishness, anyhow.'

Gudrun watched him as if in a hypnotic state, her eyes wide and fixed on him.

'But in what way do you mean, disappear?—' she persisted.

'Yes, do you mean a change of heart?' put in Gerald.

'I don't mean anything, why should I?' said Birkin. I'm

an Englishman, and I've paid the price of it. I can't talk about England—I can only speak for myself.'

'Yes,' said Gudrun slowly, 'you love England immensely, *immensely,* Rupert.'

'And leave her,' he replied.

'No, not for good. You'll come back,' said Gerald, nodding sagely.

'They say the lice crawl off a dying body,' said Birkin, with a glare of bitterness. 'So I leave England.'

'Ah, but you'll come back,' said Gudrun, with a sardonic smile.

'Tant pis pour moi,' he replied.

'Isn't he angry with his mother country!' laughed Gerald, amused.

'Ah, a patriot!' said Gudrun, with something like a sneer.

Birkin refused to answer any more.

Gudrun watched him still for a few seconds. Then she turned away. It was finished, her spell of divination in him. She felt already purely cynical. She looked at Gerald. He was wonderful like a piece of radium to her. She felt she could consume herself and know *all,* by means of this fatal, living metal. She smiled to herself at her fancy. And what would she do with herself when she had destroyed herself? For if spirit, if integral being is destructible, Matter is indestructible.

He was looking bright and abstracted, puzzled, for the moment. She stretched out her beautiful arm, with its fluff of green tulle, and touched his chin with her subtle, artist's fingers.

'What are they then?' she asked, with a strange, knowing smile.

'What?' he replied, his eyes suddenly dilating with wonder.

'Your thoughts.'

Gerald looked like a man coming awake.

'I think I had none,' he said.

'Really!' she said, with grave laughter in her voice.

And to Birkin it was as if she killed Gerald, with that touch.

'Ah, but,' cried Gudrun, 'let us drink to Britannia—let us drink to Britannia.'

It seemed there was wild despair in her voice. Gerald laughed and filled the glasses.

'I think Rupert means,' he said, 'that *nationally* all Englishmen must die, so that they can exist individually and—'

'Super-nationally—' put in Gudrun, with a slight ironic grimace, raising her glass.

The next day they descended at the tiny railway station of Hohenhausen at the end of the tiny valley railway. It was snow everywhere, a white, perfect cradle of snow, new and frozen, sweeping up on either side, black crags, and white sweeps of silver towards the blue pale heavens.

As they stepped out on the naked platform, with only snow around and above, Gudrun shrank as if it chilled her heart.

'My God, Jerry,' she said, turning to Gerald with sudden intimacy, 'you've done it now.'

'What?'

She made a faint gesture, indicating the world on either hand.

'Look at it!'

She seemed afraid to go on. He laughed.

They were in the heart of the mountains. From high above, on either side, swept down the white fold of snow, so that one seemed small and tiny in a valley of pure concrete heaven, all strangely radiant and changeless and silent.

'It makes one feel so small and alone,' said Ursula, turning to Birkin and laying her hand on his arm.

'You're not sorry you've come, are you?' said Gerald to Gudrun.

She looked doubtful. They went out of the station between banks of snow.

'Ah,' said Gerald, sniffing the air in elation, 'this is perfect. There's our sledge. We'll walk a bit—we'll run up the road.'

Gudrun, always doubtful, dropped her heavy coat on the sledge, as he did his, and they set off. Suddenly she threw up her head and set off scudding along the road of snow, pulling her cap down over her ears. Her blue, bright dress fluttered in the wind, her thick scarlet stockings were brilliant above the whiteness. Gerald watched her: she seemed to be rushing towards her fate, and leaving him behind. He let her get some distance, then, loosening his limbs, he went after her.

Everywhere was deep and silent snow. Great snow-eaves weighed down the broad-roofed Tyrolese houses that were sunk to the window-sashes in snow. Peasant women, full-skirted, wearing each a cross-over shawl and thick snow-boots, turned in the way to look at the soft, determined girl running with such heavy fleetness from the man who was overtaking her, but not gaining any power over her.

They passed the inn with its painted shutters and balcony, a few cottages, half buried in the snow; then the snow-buried silent saw-mill by the roofed bridge, which crossed the hidden stream, over which they ran into the very depth of the untouched sheets of snow. It was a silence and a sheer whiteness exhilarating to madness. But the perfect silence was most terrifying, isolating the soul, surrounding the heart with frozen air.

'It's a marvellous place, for all that,' said Gudrun, looking into his eyes with a strange, meaning look. His soul leapt.

'Good,' he said.

A fierce electric energy seemed to flow over all his limbs, his muscles were surcharged, his hands felt hard with strength. They walked along rapidly up the snow-road, that was marked by withered branches of trees stuck in at intervals. He and she were separate, like opposite poles of one fierce energy. But they felt powerful enough to leap over the confines of life into the forbidden places and back again.

Birkin and Ursula were running along also over the snow. He had disposed of the luggage, and they had a little start of the sledges. Ursula was excited and happy, but she kept turning suddenly to catch hold of Birkin's arm, to make sure of him.

'This is something I never expected,' she said. 'It is a different world, here.'

They went on into a snow meadow. There they were overtaken by the sledge that came tinkling through the silence. It was another mile before they came upon Gudrun and Gerald on the steep up-climb, beside the pink, half-buried shrine.

Then they passed into a gulley, where were walls of black rock and a river filled with snow, and a still blue sky above. Through a covered bridge they went, drumming roughly over the boards, crossing the snow-bed once more, then slowly up and up, the horses walking swiftly, the driver cracking his long whip as he walked beside, and calling his strange wild *hue-hue!*, the walls of rock passing slowly by till they emerged again between slopes and masses of snow. Up and up, gradually they went, through the cold shadow-radiance of the afternoon, silenced by the imminence of the mountains, the luminous, dazing sides of snow that rose above them and fell away beneath.

They came forth at last in a little high table-land of snow, where stood the last peaks of snow like the heart petals of an open rose. In the midst of the last deserted valleys of heaven stood a lonely building with brown wooden walls and white heavy roof, deep and deserted in the waste of snow, like a dream. It stood like a rock that had rolled down from the last steep slopes, a rock that had taken the form of a house, and was now half buried. It was unbelievable that one could live there uncrushed by all this terrible waste of whiteness and silence and clear, upper, ringing cold.

Yet the sledges ran up in fine style, people came to the door laughing and excited, the floor of the hostel rang hollow, the passage was wet with snow, it was a real, warm interior.

The newcomers tramped up the bare wooden stairs, following the serving woman. Gudrun and Gerald took the first bedroom. In a moment they found themselves alone in a bare, smallish, close-shut room that was all of golden-coloured wood, floor, walls, ceiling, door, all of the same warm gold panelling of oiled pine. There was a window opposite the door, but low down, because the roof sloped. Under the slope of the ceiling were the table with wash-hand-bowl and jug, and across, another table with mirror. On either side the door were two beds piled high with an enormous blue-checked overbolster, enormous.

This was all—no cupboard, none of the amenities of life.

Here they were shut up together in this cell of golden-coloured wood, with two blue checked beds. They looked at each other and laughed, frightened by this naked nearness of isolation.

A man knocked and came in with the luggage. He was a sturdy fellow with flattish cheek-bones, rather pale, and with coarse fair moustache. Gudrun watched him put down the bags in silence, then tramp heavily out.

'It isn't too rough, is it?' Gerald asked.

The bedroom was not very warm, and she shivered slightly.

'It is wonderful,' she equivocated. 'Look at the colour of this panelling—it's wonderful, like being inside a nut.'

He was standing watching her, feeling his short-cut moustache, leaning back slightly and watching her with his keen, undaunted eyes, dominated by the constant passion, that was like a doom upon him.

She went and crouched down in front of the window, curious.

'Oh, but this—!' she cried involuntarily, almost in pain.

In front was a valley shut in under the sky, the last huge slopes of snow and black rock, and at the end, like the navel of the earth, a white-folded wall, and two peaks glimmering in the late light. Straight in front ran the cradle of silent snow, between the great slopes that were fringed with a little roughness of pine trees, like hair, round the base. But the cradle of snow ran on to the eternal closing-in, where the walls of snow and rock rose impenetrable, and the mountain peaks above were in heaven immediate. This was the centre, the knot, the navel of the world, where the earth belonged to the skies, pure, unapproachable, impassable.

It filled Gudrun with a strange rapture. She crouched in front of the window, clenching her face in her hands, in a sort of trance. At last she had arrived, she had reached her place. Here at last she folded her venture and settled down like a crystal in the navel of snow and was gone.

Gerald bent above her and was looking out over her shoulder. Already he felt he was alone. She was gone. She was completely gone, and there was icy vapour round his heart. He saw the blind valley, the great cul-de-sac of snow and mountain peaks under the heaven. And there was no way out. The terrible silence and cold and the glamorous whiteness of the dusk wrapped him round, and she remained crouching before the window, as at a shrine, a shadow.

'Do you like it?' he asked in a voice that sounded detached and foreign. At least she might acknowledge he was with her. But she only averted her soft, mute face a little from his gaze. And he knew that there were tears in her eyes, her own tears, tears of her strange religion, that put him to nought.

Quite suddenly, he put his hand under her chin and lifted up her face to him. Her dark blue eyes, in their wetness of tears, dilated as if she was startled in her very soul. They looked at him through their tears in terror and a little horror. His light blue eyes were keen, small-pupilled and unnatural in their vision. Her lips parted as she breathed with difficulty.

The passion came up in him, stroke after stroke, like the ringing of a bronze bell, so strong and unflawed and indomitable. His knees tightened to bronze as he hung above her soft face, whose lips parted and whose eyes dilated in a strange violation. In the grasp of his hand her chin was unutterably soft and silken. He felt strong as winter, his hands were living metal, invincible and not to be turned aside. His heart rang like a bell clanging inside him.

He took her up in his arms. She was soft and inert, motionless. All the while her eyes, in which the tears had not yet dried, were dilated as if in a kind of swoon of fascination and helplessness. He was super-humanly strong and unflawed, as if invested with supernatural force.

He lifted her close and folded her against him. Her softness, her inert, relaxed weight lay against his own surcharged, bronze-like limbs in a heaviness of desirability that would destroy him, if he were not fulfilled. She moved convulsively, recoiling away from him. His heart went up like a flame of ice, he closed over her like steel. He would destroy her rather than be denied.

But the overweening power of his body was too much for her. She relaxed again, and lay loose and soft, panting in a little delirium. And to him, she was so sweet, she was such bliss of release, that he would have suffered a whole eternity of torture rather than forgo one second of this pang of unsurpassable bliss.

'My God,' he said to her, his face drawn and strange, transfigured, 'what next?'

She lay perfectly still, with a still, child-like face and dark eyes, looking at him. She was lost, fallen right away.

'I shall always love you,' he said, looking at her.

But she did not hear. She lay, looking at him as at something she could never understand, never: as a child looks at a grown-up person, without hope of understanding, only submitting.

He kissed her, kissed her eyes shut, so that she could not look any more. He wanted something now, some recognition, some sign, some admission. But she only lay silent and childlike and remote, like a child that is overcome and cannot understand, only feels lost. He kissed her again, giving up.

'Shall we go down and have coffee and *Kuchen*?' he asked.

The twilight was falling slate-blue at the window. She closed her eyes, closed away the monotonous level of dead wonder, and opened them again to the everyday world.

'Yes,' she said briefly, regaining her will with a click. She went again to the window. Blue evening had fallen over the cradle of snow and over the great pallid slopes. But in the heaven the peaks of snow were rosy, glistening like transcendent, radiant spikes of blossom in the heavenly upper world, so lovely and beyond.

Gudrun saw all their loveliness, she *knew* how immortally beautiful they were, great pistils of rose-coloured, snow-fed fire in the blue twilight of the heaven. She could *see* it, she knew it, but she was not of it. She was divorced, debarred, a soul shut out.

With a last look of remorse, she turned away, and was doing her hair. He had unstrapped the luggage and was waiting, watching her. She knew he was watching her. It made her a little hasty and feverish in her precipitation.

They went downstairs, both with a strange other-world look on their faces, and with a glow in their eyes. They saw Birkin and Ursula sitting at the long table in a corner, waiting for them.

'How good and simple they look together,' Gudrun thought jealously. She envied them some spontaneity, a childish sufficiency to which she herself could never approach. They seemed such children to her.

'Such good *Kranzkuchen*!' cried Ursula greedily. 'So good!'

'Right,' said Gudrun. 'Can we have *Kaffee mit Kranz-kuchen*?' she added to the waiter.

And she seated herself on the bench beside Gerald. Birkin, looking at them, felt a pain of tenderness for them.

'I think the place is really wonderful, Gerald,' he said; '*prachtvoll* and *wunderbar* and *wunderschön* and *unbeschreib-lich* and all the other German adjectives.'

Gerald broke into a slight smile.

'*I* like it,' he said.

The tables, of white scrubbed wood, were placed round three sides of the room, as in a Gasthaus. Birkin and Ursula sat with their backs to the wall, which was of oiled wood, and Gerald and Gudrun sat in the corner next them, near to the stove. It was a fairly large place, with a tiny bar, just like a country inn, but quite simple and bare, and all of oiled wood, ceilings and walls and floor, the only furniture being the tables and benches going round three sides, the great green stove, and the bar and the doors on the fourth side. The windows were double, and quite uncurtained. It was early evening.

The coffee came—hot and good—and a whole ring of cake.

'A whole *Kuchen*!' cried Ursula. 'They give you more than us! I want some of yours.'

There were other people in the place, ten altogether, so Birkin had found out: two artists, three students, a man and wife, and a Professor and two daughters—all Germans. The four English people, being newcomers, sat in their coign of vantage to watch. The Germans peeped in at the door, called a word to the waiter, and went away again. It was not meal-time, so they did not come into this dining-room, but betook themselves, when their boots were changed, to the *Reunion-saal*.

The English visitors could hear the occasional twanging

of a zither, the strumming of a piano, snatches of laughter and shouting and singing, a faint vibration of voices. The whole building being of wood, it seemed to carry every sound, like a drum, but instead of increasing each particular noise, it decreased it, so that the sound of the zither seemed tiny, as if a diminutive zither were playing somewhere, and it seemed the piano must be a small one, like a little spinet.

The host came when the coffee was finished. He was a Tyrolese, broad, rather flat-cheeked, with a pale, pock-marked skin and flourishing moustaches.

'Would you like to go to the *Reunionsaal* to be introduced to the other ladies and gentlemen?' he asked, bending forward and smiling, showing his large, strong teeth. His blue eyes went quickly from one to the other—he was not quite sure of his ground with these English people. He was unhappy too because he spoke no English and he was not sure whether to try his French.

'Shall we go to the *Reunionsaal,* and be introduced to the other people?' repeated Gerald, laughing.

There was a moment's hesitation.

'I suppose we'd better—better break the ice,' said Birkin.

The women rose, rather flushed. And the Wirt's black, beetle-like, broad-shouldered figure went on ignominiously in front, towards the noise. He opened the door and ushered the four strangers into the play-room.

Instantly a silence fell, a slight embarrassment came over the company. The newcomers had a sense of many blond faces looking their way. Then the host was bowing to a short, energetic-looking man with large moustaches, and saying in a low voice:

'Herr Professor, darf ich vorstellen—'

The Herr Professor was prompt and energetic. He bowed low to the English people, smiling, and began to be a comrade at once.

'Nehmen die Herrschaften teil an unserer Unterhaltung?' he said, with a vigorous suavity, his voice curling up in the question.

The four English people smiled, lounging with an attentive uneasiness in the middle of the room. Gerald, who was spokesman, said that they would willingly take part in the entertainment. Gudrun and Ursula, laughing, excited, felt the eyes of all the men upon them, and they lifted their heads and looked nowhere, and felt royal.

The Professor announced the names of those present, *sans cérémonie*. There was a bowing to the wrong people and to the right people. Everybody was there except the man and wife. The two tall, clear-skinned, athletic daughters of the professor, with their plain-cut, dark blue blouses and loden skirts, their rather long, strong necks, their clear blue eyes and carefully banded hair, and their blushes, bowed and stood back; the three students bowed very low, in the humble hope of making an impression of extreme good breeding; then there was a thin, dark-skinned man with full eyes, an odd creature, like a child, and like a troll, quick, detached; he bowed slightly; his companion, a large fair young man, stylishly dressed, blushed to the eyes and bowed very low.

It was over.

'Herr Loerke was giving us a recitation in the Cologne dialect,' said the Professor.

'He must forgive us for interrupting him,' said Gerald, 'we should like very much to hear it.'

There was instantly a bowing and an offering of seats. Gudrun and Ursula, Gerald and Birkin sat in the deep sofas against the wall. The room was of naked oiled panelling, like the rest of the house. It had a piano, sofas and chairs, and a couple of tables with books and magazines. In its complete absence of decoration, save for the big, blue stove, it was cosy and pleasant.

Herr Loerke was the little man with the boyish figure and the round, full, sensitive-looking head, and the quick, full eyes, like a mouse's. He glanced swiftly from one to the other of the strangers, and held himself aloof.

'Please go on with the recitation,' said the Professor suavely, with his slight authority. Loerke, who was sitting hunched on the piano-stool, blinked and did not answer.

'It would be a great pleasure,' said Ursula, who had been getting the sentence ready, in German, for some minutes.

Then, suddenly, the small, unresponding man swung aside, towards his previous audience and broke forth, exactly as he had broken off; in a controlled, mocking voice, giving an imitation of a quarrel between an old Cologne woman and a railway guard.

His body was slight and unformed, like a boy's, but his voice was mature, sardonic, its movement had the flexibility of essential energy, and of a mocking penetrating understanding. Gudrun could not understand a word of his monologue, but she was spell-bound watching him. He must be an artist, nobody else could have such fine adjustment and singleness. The Germans were doubled up with laughter, hearing his strange droll words, his droll phrases of dialect. And in the midst of their paroxysms, they glanced with deference at the four English strangers, the elect. Gudrun and Ursula were forced to laugh. The room rang with shouts of laughter. The blue eyes of the Professor's daughters were swimming over with laughter-tears, their clear cheeks were flushed crimson with mirth, their father broke out in the most astonishing peals of hilarity, the students bowed their heads on their knees in excess of joy. Ursula looked round amazed, the laughter was bubbling out of her involuntarily. She looked at Gudrun. Gudrun looked at her, and the two sisters burst out laughing, carried away. Loerke glanced at them swiftly, with his full eyes. Birkin was sniggering involuntarily. Gerald Crich sat erect, with a glistening look of amusement on his face. And the laughter crashed out again, in wild paroxysms, the Professor's daughters were reduced to shaking helplessness, the veins of the Professor's neck were swollen, his face was purple, he was strangled in ultimate, silent spasms of laughter. The students were shouting half-articulated words that tailed off in helpless explosions. Then suddenly the rapid patter of the artist ceased, there were little whoops of subsiding mirth, Ursula and Gudrun were wiping their eyes, and the Professor was crying loudly.

'*Das war ausgezeichnet, das war famos—*'

'*Wirklich famos,*' echoed his exhausted daughters, faintly.

'And we couldn't understand it,' cried Ursula.

'*Oh leider, leider!*' cried the Professor.

'You couldn't understand?' cried the students, let loose at last in speech with the newcomers. '*Ja, das ist wirklich schade, das ist schade, gnädige Frau. Wissen Sie—*'

The mixture was made, the newcomers were stirred into

the party, like new ingredients, the whole room was alive. Gerald was in his element, he talked freely and excitedly, his face glistened with a strange amusement. Perhaps even Birkin, in the end, would break forth. He was shy and withheld, though full of attention.

Ursula was prevailed upon to sing 'Annie Lowrie', as the Professor called it. There was a hush of *extreme* deference. She had never been so flattered in her life. Gudrun accompanied her on the piano, playing from memory.

Ursula had a beautiful ringing voice, but usually no confidence, she spoiled everything. This evening she felt conceited and untrammelled. Birkin was well in the background, she shone almost in reaction, the Germans made her feel fine and infallible, she was liberated into overweening self-confidence. She felt like a bird flying in the air, as her voice soared out, enjoying herself extremely in the balance and flight of the song, like the motion of a bird's wings that is up in the wind, sliding and playing on the air, she played with sentimentality, supported by rapturous attention. She was very happy, singing that song by herself, full of a conceit of emotion and power, working upon all those people, and upon herself, exerting herself with gratification, giving immeasurable gratification to the Germans.

At the end, the Germans were all touched with admiring, delicious melancholy, they praised her in soft, reverent voices, they could not say too much.

'*Wie schön, wie rührend! Ach, die schottischen Lieder, sie haben so viel Stimmung! Aber die gnädige Frau hat eine wunderbare Stimme; die gnädige Frau ist wirklich eine Künstlerin, aber wirklich!*'

She was dilated and brilliant, like a flower in the morning sun. She felt Birkin looking at her, as if he were jealous of her, and her breasts thrilled, her veins were all golden. She was as happy as the sun that has just opened above clouds. And everybody seemed so admiring and radiant, it was perfect.

After dinner she wanted to go out for a minute, to look at the world. The company tried to dissuade her—it was so terribly cold. But just to look, she said.

They all four wrapped up warmly, and found themselves

in a vague, unsubstantial outdoors of dim snow and ghosts
of an upper-world, that made strange shadows before the
stars. It was indeed cold, bruisingly, frighteningly, unnatu-
rally cold. Ursula could not believe the air in her nostrils. It
seemed conscious, malevolent, purposive in its intense murderous coldness.

Yet it was wonderful, an intoxication, a silence of dim,
unrealized snow, of the invisible intervening between her
and the visible, between her and the flashing stars. She could
see Orion sloping up. How wonderful he was, wonderful
enough to make one cry aloud.

And all around was this cradle of snow, and there was
firm snow underfoot, that struck with heavy cold through
her bootsoles. It was night, and silence. She imagined she
could hear the stars. She imagined distinctly she could hear
the celestial, musical motion of the stars, quite near at hand.
She seemed like a bird flying amongst their harmonious motion.

And she clung close to Birkin. Suddenly she realized she
did not know what he was thinking. She did not know where
he was ranging.

'My love!' she said, stopping to look at him.

His face was pale, his eyes dark, there was a faint spark
of starlight on them. And he saw her face soft and upturned
to him, very near. He kissed her softly.

'What then?' he asked.

'Do you love me?' she asked.

'Too much,' he answered quietly.

She clung a little closer.

'Not too much,' she pleaded.

'Far too much,' he said, almost sadly.

'And does it make you sad, that I am everything to you?'
she asked, wistful. He held her close to him, kissing her, and
saying, scarcely audible:

'No, but I feel like a beggar—I feel poor.'

She was silent, looking at the stars now. Then she kissed
him.

'Don't be a beggar,' she pleaded, wistfully. 'It isn't ignominious that you love me.'

'It is ignominious to feel poor, isn't it?' he replied.

'Why? Why should it be?' she asked. He only stood still, in the terribly cold air that moved invisibly over the mountain tops, folding her round with his arms.

'I couldn't bear this cold, eternal place without you,' he said. 'I couldn't bear it, it would kill the quick of my life.'

She kissed him again, suddenly.

'Do you hate it?' she asked, puzzled, wondering.

'If I couldn't come near to you, if you weren't here, I should hate it. I couldn't bear it,' he answered.

'But the people are nice,' she said.

'I mean the stillness, the cold, the frozen eternality,' he said.

She wondered. Then her spirit came home to him, nestling unconscious in him.

'Yes, it is good we are warm and together,' she said.

And they turned home again. They saw the golden lights of the hotel glowing out in the night of snow-silence, small in the hollow, like a cluster of yellow berries. It seemed like a bunch of sun-sparks, tiny and orange in the midst of the snow-darkness. Behind, was a high shadow of a peak, blotting out the stars, like a ghost.

They drew near to their home. They saw a man come from the dark building, with a lighted lantern which swung golden, and made that his dark feet walked in a halo of snow. He was a small, dark figure in the darkened snow. He unlatched the door of an outhouse. A smell of cows, hot, animal, almost like beef, came out on the heavily cold air. There was a glimpse of two cattle in their dark stalls, then the door was shut again, and not a chink of light showed. It had reminded Ursula again of home, of the Marsh, of her childhood, and of the journey to Brussels, and, strangely, of Anton Skrebensky.

Oh, God, could one bear it, this past which was gone down the abyss? Could she bear, that it ever had been! She looked round this silent, upper world of snow and stars and powerful cold. There was another world, like views on a magic lantern; the Marsh, Cossethay, Ilkeston, lit up with a common, unreal light. There was a shadowy unreal Ursula, a whole shadow-play of an unreal life. It was as unreal, and circumscribed, as a magic-lantern show. She wished the slides could all be broken. She wished it could be gone for ever, like a lantern-slide which was broken. She wanted to have no past. She wanted to have come down from the slopes of heaven to this place, with Birkin, not to have toiled out of the murk of her childhood and her upbringing, slowly, all soiled. She felt that memory was a dirty trick played upon her. What was this decree, that she should 'remember'! Why not a bath of pure oblivion, a new birth, without any recollections or blemish of a past life. She was with Birkin, she had just come into life, here in the high snow, against the stars. What had she to do with parents and antecedents? She knew herself new and unbegotten, she had no father, no mother, no anterior connexions, she was herself, pure and silvery, she belonged only to the oneness with Birkin, a oneness that struck deeper notes, sounding into the heart of the universe, the heart of reality, where she had never existed before.

Even Gudrun was a separate unit, separate, separate, having nothing to do with this self, this Ursula, in her new world of reality. That old shadow-world, the actuality of the past—ah, let it go! She rose free on the wings of her new condition.

Gudron and Gerald had not come in. They had walked up the valley straight in front of the house, not like Ursula and Birkin, on to the little hill at the right. Gudrun was driven by a strange desire. She wanted to plunge on and on, till she came to the end of the valley of snow. Then she wanted to climb the wall of white finality, climb over, into the peaks that sprang up like sharp petals in the heart of the frozen, mysterious navel of the world. She felt that there, over the strange blind, terrible wall of rocky snow, there in the navel of the mystic world, among the final cluster of peaks, there, in the infolded navel of it all, was her consummation. If she could but come there, alone, and pass into the infolded navel of eternal snow and of uprising, immortal peaks of snow and rock, she would be a oneness with all, she would be herself the eternal, infinite silence, the sleeping, timeless, frozen centre of the All.

They went back to the house, to the *Reunionsaal*. She was curious to see what was going on. The men there made her

alert, roused her curiosity. It was a new taste of life for her,
they were so prostrate before her, yet so full of life.

The party was boisterous; they were dancing all together,
dancing the *Schuhplatteln,* the Tyrolese dance of the clapping hands and tossing the partner in the air at the crisis.
The Germans were all proficient—they were from Munich
chiefly. Gerald also was quite passable. There were three
zithers twanging away in a corner. It was a scene of great
animation and confusion. The Professor was initiating Ursula into the dance, stamping, clapping, and swinging her
high, with amazing force and zest. When the crisis came,
even Birkin was behaving manfully with one of the Professor's fresh, strong daughters, who was exceedingly happy.
Everybody was dancing, there was the most boisterous turmoil.

Gudrun looked on with delight. The solid wooden floor
resounded to the knocking heels of the men, the air quivered
with the clapping hands and the zither music, there was a
golden dust about the hanging lamps.

Suddenly the dance finished, Loerke and the students
rushed out to bring in drinks. There was an excited clamour
of voices, a clinking of mug-lids, a great crying of '*Prosit—
Prosit!*' Loerke was everywhere at once, like a gnome, suggesting drinks for the women, making an obscure, slightly
risky joke with the men, confusing and mystifying the
waiter.

He wanted very much to dance with Gudrun. From the
first moment he had seen her, he wanted to make a connexion with her. Instinctively she felt this, and she waited for
him to come up. But a kind of sulkiness kept him away from
her, so she thought he disliked her.

'Will you *schuhplätteln, gnädige Frau*?' said the large,
fair youth, Loerke's companion. He was too soft, too humble
for Gudrun's taste. But she wanted to dance, and the fair
youth, who was called Leitner, was handsome enough in his
uneasy, slightly abject fashion, a humility that covered a certain fear. She accepted him as a partner.

The zithers sounded out again, the dance began. Gerald
led them, laughing, with one of the Professor's daughters.
Ursula danced with one of the students, Birkin with the

other daughter of the Professor, the Professor with Frau Kramer, and the rest of the men danced together, with quite as much zest as if they had had women partners.

Because Gudrun had danced with the well-built, soft youth, his companion, Loerke was more pettish and exasperated than ever, and would not even notice her existence in the room. This piqued her, but she made up to herself by dancing with the Professor, who was strong as a mature well-seasoned bull, and as full of coarse energy. She could not bear him, critically, and yet she enjoyed being rushed through the dance, and tossed up into the air, on his coarse, powerful impetus. The Professor enjoyed it too, he eyed her with strange, large blue eyes, full of galvanic fire. She hated him for the seasoned, semi-paternal animalism with which he regarded her, but she admired his weight of strength.

The room was charged with excitement and strong, animal emotion. Loerke was kept away from Gudrun, to whom he wanted to speak, as by a hedge of thorns, and he felt a sardonic ruthless hatred for this young love-companion, Leitner, who was his penniless dependent. He mocked the youth, with an acid ridicule, that made Leitner red in the face and impotent with resentment.

Gerald, who had now got the dance perfectly, was dancing again with the younger of the Professor's daughters, who was almost dying of virgin excitement, because she thought Gerald so handsome, so superb. He had her in his power, as if she were a palpitating bird, a fluttering, flushing, bewildered creature. And it made him smile, as she shrank convulsively between his hands, violently, when he must throw her into the air. At the end, she was so overcome with prostrate love for him that she could scarcely speak sensibly at all.

Birkin was dancing with Ursula. There were odd little fires playing in his eyes, he seemed to have turned into something wicked and flickering, mocking, suggestive, quite impossible. Ursula was frightened of him, and fascinated. Clear, before her eyes, as in a vision, she could see the sardonic licentious mockery of his eyes, he moved towards her with subtle, animal, indifferent approach. The strangeness of his hands, which came quick and cunning, inevitably to the vital place beneath her breasts, and, lifting with mocking, suggestive impulse, carried her through the air as if without strength, through black magic, made her swoon with fear. For a moment she revolted, it was horrible. She would break the spell. But before the resolution had formed she had submitted again, yielded to her fear. He knew all the time what he was doing, she could see it in his smiling, concentrated eyes. It was his responsibility, she would leave it to him.

When they were alone in the darkness, she felt the strange licentiousness of him hovering upon her. She was troubled and repelled. Why should he turn like this.

'What is it?' she asked in dread.

But his face only glistened on her, unknown, horrible. And yet she was fascinated. Her impulse was to repel him violently, break from this spell of mocking brutishness. But she was too fascinated, she wanted to submit, she wanted to know. What would he do to her?

He was so attractive, and so repulsive at once. The sardonic suggestivity that flickered over his face and looked from his narrowed eyes, made her want to hide, to hide herself away from him and watch him from somewhere unseen.

'Why are you like this?' she demanded again, rousing against him with sudden force and animosity.

The flickering fires in his eyes concentrated as he looked into her eyes. Then the lids drooped with a faint motion of satiric contempt. Then they rose again to the same remorseless suggestivity. And she gave way, he might do as he would. His licentiousness was repulsively attractive. But he was self-responsible, she would see what it was.

They might do as they liked—this she realized as she went to sleep. How could anything that gave one satisfaction be excluded? What was degrading? Who cared? Degrading things were real, with a different reality. And he was so unabashed and unrestrained. Wasn't it rather horrible, a man who could be so soulful and spiritual, now to be so—she balked at her own thoughts and memories: then she added—so bestial? So bestial, they two!—so degraded! She winced. But after all, why not? She exulted as well. Why not be bestial, and go the whole round of experience? She exulted in it. She was bestial. How good it was to be really shameful! There would be no shameful thing she had not experienced. Yet she was unabashed, she was herself. Why not? She was free, when she knew everything, and no dark shameful things were denied her.

Gudrun, who had been watching Gerald in the *Reunionsaal,* suddenly thought:

'He should have all the women he can—it is his nature. It is absurd to call him monogamous—he is naturally promiscuous. That is his nature.'

The thought came to her involuntarily. It shocked her somewhat. It was as if she had seen some new *Mene! Mene!* upon the wall. Yet it was merely true. A voice seemed to have spoken to her so clearly, that for the moment she believed in inspiration.

'It is really true,' she said to herself again.

She knew quite well she had believed it all along. She knew it implicitly. But she must keep it dark—almost from herself. She must keep it completely secret. It was knowledge for her alone, and scarcely even to be admitted to herself.

The deep resolve formed in her, to combat him. One of them must triumph over the other. Which should it be? Her soul steeled itself with strength. Almost she laughed within herself, at her confidence. It woke a certain keen, half contemptuous pity, tenderness for him: she was so ruthless.

Everybody retired early. The Professor and Loerke went into a small lounge to drink. They both watched Gudrun go along the landing by the railing upstairs.

'*Ein schönes Frauenzimmer,*' said the Professor.

'*Ja!*' asserted Loerke, shortly.

Gerald walked with his queer, long wolf-steps across the bedroom to the window, stooped and looked out, then rose again, and turned to Gudrun, his eyes sharp with an abstract smile. He seemed very tall to her, she saw the glisten of his whitish eyebrows, that met between his brows.

'How do you like it?' he said.

He seemed to be laughing inside himself, quite unconsciously. She looked at him. He was a phenomenon to her, not a human being: a sort of creature, greedy.

'I like it very much,' she replied.

'Who do you like best downstairs?' he asked, standing tall and glistening above her, with his glistening stiff hair erect.

'Who do I like best?' she repeated, wanting to answer his question, and finding it difficult to collect herself. 'Why I don't know, I don't know enough about them yet, to be able to say. Who do *you* like best?'

'Oh, I don't care—I don't like or dislike any of them. It doesn't matter about me. I wanted to know about you.'

'But why?' she asked, going rather pale. The abstract, unconscious smile in his eyes was intensified.

'I wanted to know,' he said.

She turned aside, breaking the spell. In some strange way, she felt he was getting power over her.

'Well, I can't tell you already,' she said.

She went to the mirror to take out the hairpins from her hair. She stood before the mirror every night for some minutes, brushing her fine dark hair. It was part of the inevitable ritual of her life.

He followed her, and stood behind her. She was busy with bent head, taking out the pins and shaking her warm hair loose. When she looked up, he saw him in the glass, standing behind her, watching unconsciously, not consciously seeing her, and yet watching, with fine-pupilled eyes that *seemed* to smile, and which were not really smiling.

She started. It took all her courage for her to continue brushing her hair, as usual, for her to pretend she was at her ease. She was far, far from being at her ease with him. She beat her brains wildly for something to say to him.

'What are your plans for tomorrow?' she asked nonchalantly, whilst her heart was beating so furiously, her eyes were so bright with strange nervousness, she felt he could not but observe. But she knew also that he was completely blind, blind as a wolf looking at her. It was a strange battle between her ordinary consciousness and his uncanny, black-art consciousness.

'I don't know,' he replied, 'what would you like to do?' He spoke emptily, his mind was sunk away.

'Oh,' she said, with easy protestation, 'I'm ready for anything—anything will be fine for *me,* I'm sure.'

And to herself she was saying: 'God, why am I so nervous—why are you so nervous, you fool. If he sees it I'm done for for ever—you *know* you're done for for ever, if he sees the absurd state you're in.'

And she smiled to herself as if it were all child's play. Meanwhile her heart was plunging. She was almost fainting. She could see him, in the mirror, as he stood there behind her, tall and over-arching—blond and terribly frightening. She glanced at his reflection with furtive eyes, willing to give anything to save him from knowing she could see him. He did not know she could see his reflection. He was looking unconsciously, glisteningly down at her head, from which the hair fell loose, as she brushed it with wild, nervous hand. She held her head aside and brushed and brushed her hair madly. For her life, she could not turn round and face him. For her life, *she could not.* And the knowledge made her almost sink to the ground in a faint, helpless, spent. She was aware of his frightening, impending figure standing close behind her, she was aware of his hard, strong, unyielding chest, close upon her back. And she felt she could not bear it any more, in a few minutes she would fall down at his feet, grovelling at his feet, and letting him destroy her.

The thought pricked up all her sharp intelligence and presence of mind. She dared not turn round to him—and there he stood motionless, unbroken. Summoning all her strength, she said, in a full, resonant, nonchalant voice that was forced out with all her remaining self-control:

'Oh, would you mind looking in that bag behind there and giving me my—'

Here her power fell inert. 'My what—my what—?' she screamed in silence to herself.

But he had started round, surprised and startled that she should ask him to look in her bag, which she always kept so *very* private to herself. She turned, now her face white, her dark eyes blazing with uncanny, overwrought excitement. She saw him stooping to the bag, undoing the loosely buckled strap, unattentive.

'Your what?' he asked.

'Oh, a little enamel box—yellow—with a design of a cormorant plucking her breast—'

She went towards him, stooping her beautiful, bare arm, and deftly turned some of her things, disclosing the box, which was exquisitely painted.

'That is it, see,' she said, taking it from under his eyes.

And he was baffled now. He was left to fasten up the bag, whilst she swiftly did up her hair for the night, and sat down to unfasten her shoes. She would not turn her back to him any more.

He was baffled, frustrated, but unconscious. She had the whip hand over him now. She knew he had not realized her terrible panic. Her heart was beating heavily still. Fool, fool, that she was, to get into such a state! How she thanked God for Gerald's obtuse blindness. Thank God he could see nothing.

She sat slowly unlacing her shoes, and he too commenced to undress. Thank God that crisis was over. She felt almost fond of him now, almost in love with him.

'Ah, Gerald,' she laughed, caressively, teasingly. 'Ah, what a fine game you played with the Professor's daughter—didn't you now?'

'What game?' he asked, looking round.

'*Isn't* she in love with you—oh *dear,* isn't she in love with you!' said Gudrun, in her gayest, most attractive mood.

'I shouldn't think so,' he said.

'Shouldn't think so!' she teased. 'Why the poor girl is lying at this moment overwhelmed, dying with love for you. She thinks you're *wonderful*—oh marvellous, beyond what man has ever been. *Really,* isn't it funny?'

'Why funny, what is funny?' he asked.

'Why to see you working it on her,' she said, with a half reproach that confused the male conceit in him. 'Really, Gerald, the poor girl—!'

'I did nothing to her,' he said.

'Oh, it was too shameful, the way you simply swept her off her feet.'

'That was *Schuhplatteln,*' he replied, with a bright grin.

'Ha—ha—ha!' laughed Gudrun.

Her mockery quivered through his muscles with curious re-echoes. When he slept he seemed to crouch down in the bed, lapped up in his own strength, that yet was hollow.

And Gudrun slept strongly, a victorious sleep. Suddenly, she was almost fiercely awake. The small timber room glowed with the dawn, that came upwards from the low window. She could see down the valley when she lifted her head: The snow with a pinkish, half-revealed magic, the fringe of pine trees at the bottom of the slope. And one tiny figure moved over the vaguely-illuminated space.

She glanced at his watch; it was seven o'clock. He was still completely asleep. And she was so hard awake, it was almost frightening—hard, metallic wakefulness. She lay looking at him.

He slept in the subjection of his own health and defeat. She was overcome by a sincere regard for him. Till now, she was afraid before him. She lay and thought about him, what he was, what he represented in the world. A fine, independent will, he had. She thought of the revolution he had worked in the mines, in so short a time. She knew that if he were confronted with any problem, any hard actual difficulty, he would overcome it. If he laid hold of any idea, he would carry it through. He had the faculty of making order out of confusion. Only let him grip hold of a situation, and he would bring to pass an inevitable conclusion.

For a few moments she was borne away on the wild wings of ambition. Gerald, with his force of will and his power for comprehending the actual world, should be set to solve the problems of the day, the problem of industrialism in the modern world. She knew he would, in the course of time, effect the changes he desired, he could reorganize the industrial system. She knew he could do it. As an instrument, in these things, he was marvellous, she had never seen any man with his potentiality. He was unaware of it, but she knew.

He only needed to be hitched on, he needed that his hand should be set to the task, because he was so unconscious. And this she could do. She would marry him, he would go into Parliament in the Conservative interest, he would clear up the great muddle of labour and industry. He was so superbly fearless, masterful, he knew that every problem could be worked out, in life as in geometry. And he would care neither about himself nor about anything but the pure working out of the problem. He was very pure, really.

Her heart beat fast, she flew away on wings of elation, imagining a future. He would be a Napoleon of peace, or a Bismarck—and she the woman behind him. She had read Bismarck's letters, and had been deeply moved by them. And Gerald would be freer, more dauntless than Bismarck.

But even as she lay in fictitious transport, bathed in the strange, false sunshine of hope in life, something seemed to snap in her, and a terrible cynicism began to gain upon her, blowing in like a wind. Everything turned to irony with her: the last flavour of everything was ironical. When she felt her pang of undeniable reality, this was when she knew the hard irony of hopes and ideas.

She lay and looked at him, as he slept. He was sheerly beautiful, he was a perfect instrument. To her mind, he was a pure, inhuman, almost superhuman instrument. His instrumentality appealed so strongly to her, she wished she were God, to use him as a tool.

And at the same instant, came the ironical question: 'What for?' She thought of the colliers' wives, with their linoleum and their lace curtains and their little girls in high-laced boots. She thought of the wives and daughters of the pit-managers, their tennis-parties, and their terrible struggles to be superior each to the other, in the social scale. There was Shortlands with its meaningless distinction, the meaningless crowd of the Criches. There was London, the House of Commons, the extant social world. My God!

Young as she was, Gudrun had touched the whole pulse of social England. She had no ideas of rising in the world. She knew, with the perfect cynicism of cruel youth, that to rise in the world meant to have one outside show instead of another, the advance was like having a spurious half-crown instead of a spurious penny. The whole coinage of valuation was spurious. Yet, of course, her cynicism knew well enough that, in a world where spurious coin was current, a bad sovereign was better than a bad farthing. But rich and poor, she despised both alike.

Already she mocked at herself for her dreams. They could be fulfilled easily enough. But she recognized too well, in her spirit, the mockery of her own impulses. What did she care, that Gerald had created a richly-paying industry out of

an old worn-out concern? What did she care? The worn-out
concern and the rapid, splendidly organized industry, they
were bad money. Yet, of course, she cared a great deal,
outwardly—and outwardly was all that mattered, for inwardly was a bad joke.

Everything was intrinsically a piece of irony to her. She
leaned over Gerald and said in her heart, with compassion:
'Oh, my dear, my dear, the game isn't worth even you.
You are a fine thing really—why should you be used on
such a poor show!'

Her heart was breaking with pity and grief for him. And
at the same moment, a grimace came over her mouth, of
mocking irony at her own unspoken tirade. Ah, what a farce
it was! She thought of Parnell and Katherine O'Shea.
Parnell! After all, who can take the nationalization of Ireland
seriously? Who can take political Ireland really seriously,
whatever it does? And who can take political England seriously? Who can? Who can care a straw, really, how the old
patched-up Constitution is tinkered at any more? Who cares
a button for our national ideas, any more than for our national bowler hat? Aha, it is all old hat, it is all old bowler
hat!

That's all it is, Gerald, my young hero. At any rate, we'll
spare ourselves the nausea of stirring the old broth any
more. You be beautiful, my Gerald, and reckless. There *are*
perfect moments. Wake up, Gerald, wake up, convince me of
the perfect moments. Oh, convince me, I need it.

He opened his eyes, and looked at her. She greeted him
with a mocking, enigmatic smile in which was a poignant
gaiety. Over his face went the reflection of the smile, he
smiled, too, purely unconsciously.

That filled her with extraordinary delight, to see the smile
cross his face, reflected from her face. She remembered that
was how a baby smiled. It filled her with extraordinary radiant delight.

'You've done it,' she said.

'What?' he asked, dazed.

'Convinced me.'

And she bent down, kissing him passionately, passionately, so that he was bewildered. He did not ask her of what

he had convinced her, though he meant to. He was glad she was kissing him. She seemed to be feeling for his very heart to touch the quick of him. And he wanted her to touch the quick of his being, he wanted that most of all.

Outside, somebody was singing in a manly, reckless, handsome voice:

> *Mach mir auf, mach mir auf, du Stolze,*
> *Mach mir ein Feuer von Holze.*
> *Vom Regen bin ich nass*
> *Vom Regen bin ich nass—*

Gudrun knew that that song would sound through her eternity, sung in a manly, reckless, mocking voice. It marked one of her supreme moments, the supreme pangs of her nervous gratification. There it was, fixed in eternity for her.

The day came fine and bluish. There was a light wind blowing among the mountain-tops, keen as a rapier where it touched, carrying with it a fine dust of snow powder. Gerald went out with the fine, blind face of a man who is in his state of fulfilment. Gudrun and he were in perfect static unity this morning, but unseeing and unwitting. They went out with a toboggan, leaving Ursula and Birkin to follow.

Gudrun was all scarlet and royal blue—a scarlet jersey and cap, and a royal blue skirt and stockings. She went gaily over the white snow, with Gerald beside her, in white and grey, pulling the little toboggan. They grew small in the distance of snow, climbing the steep slope.

For Gudrun herself, she seemed to pass altogether into the whiteness of the snow, she became a pure, thoughtless crystal. When she reached the top of the slope, in the wind, she looked round, and saw peak beyond peak of rock and snow, bluish, transcendent in heaven. And it seemed to her like a garden, with the peaks for pure flowers, and her heart gathering them. She had no separate consciousness for Gerald.

She held on to him as they went sheering down over the keen slope. She felt as if her senses were being whetted on some fine grindstone that was keen as flame. The snow sprinted on either side, like sparks from a blade that is being sharpened, the whiteness round about ran swifter, swifter, in pure flame the white slope flew against her, and she fused like one molten, dancing globule, rushed through a white intensity. Then there was a great swerve at the bottom when they swung, as it were, in a fall to earth in the diminishing motion.

They came to rest. But when she rose to her feet, she could not stand. She gave a strange cry, turned and clung to him, sinking her face on his breast, fainting in him. Utter oblivion came over her as she lay for a few moments abandoned against him.

'What is it?' he was saying. 'Was it too much for you?'

But she heard nothing.

When she came to, she stood up and looked round, astonished. Her face was white, her eyes brilliant and large.

'What is it?' he repeated. 'Did it upset you?'

She looked at him with her brilliant eyes that seemed to have undergone some transfiguration, and she laughed, with a terrible merriment.

'No,' she cried, with triumphant joy. 'It was the complete moment of my life.'

And she looked at him with her dazzling, overweening laughter, like one possessed. A fine blade seemed to enter his heart, but he did not care, or take any notice.

But they climbed up the slope again, and they flew down through the white flame again splendidly, splendidly. Gudrun was laughing and flashing, powdered with snow-crystals, Gerald worked perfectly. He felt he could guide the toboggan to a hairbreadth, almost he could make it pierce into the air and right into the very heart of the sky. It seemed to him the flying sledge was but his strength spread out, he had but to move his arms, the motion was his own. They explored the great slopes, to find another slide. He felt there must be something better than they had known. And he found what he desired, a perfect long, fierce sweep, sheering past the foot of a rock and into the trees at the base. It was dangerous, he knew. But then he knew also he would direct the sledge between his fingers.

The first days passed in an ecstasy of physical motion, sleighing, ski-ing, skating, moving in an intensity of speed and white light that surpassed life itself, and carried the souls of the human beings beyond into an inhuman abstraction of velocity and weight and eternal, frozen snow.

Gerald's eyes became hard and strange, and as he went by on his skis he was more like some powerful, fateful sigh than a man, his muscles elastic in a perfect, soaring trajectory, his body projected in pure flight, mindless, soulless, whirling along one perfect line of force.

Luckily there came a day of snow, when they must all stay indoors: otherwise Birkin said they would all lose their faculties, and begin to utter themselves in cries and shrieks, like some strange, unknown species of snow-creatures.

It happened in the afternoon that Ursula sat in the *Reunionsaal* talking to Loerke. The latter had seemed unhappy lately. He was lively and full of mischievous humour, as usual.

But Ursula had thought he was sulky about something. His partner, too, the big, fair, good-looking youth, was ill at ease, going about as if he belonged to nowhere, and was kept in some sort of subjection, against which he was rebelling.

Loerke had hardly talked to Gudrun. His associate, on the other hand, had paid her constantly a soft, over-deferential attention. Gudrun wanted to talk to Loerke. He was a sculptor, and she wanted to hear his view of his art. And his figure attracted her. There was the look of a little wastrel about him that intrigued her, and an old man's look that interested her, and then, beside this, an uncanny singleness, a quality of being by himself, not in contact with anybody else, that marked out an artist to her. He was a chatterer, a magpie, a maker of mischievous work-jokes, that were sometimes very clever, but which often were not. And she could see in his brown, gnome's eyes the black look of inorganic misery which lay behind all his small buffoonery.

His figure interested her—the figure of a boy, almost a street arab. He made no attempt to conceal it. He always wore a simple loden suit, with knee breeches. His legs were thin, and he made no attempt to disguise the fact: which was of itself remarkable in a German. And he never ingratiated himself anywhere, not in the slightest, but kept to himself, for all his apparent playfulness.

Leitner, his companion, was a great sportsman, very handsome with his big limbs and his blue eyes. Loerke would go tobogganing or skating in little snatches, but he was indifferent. And his fine, thin nostrils, the nostrils of a pure-bred street arab, would quiver with contempt at Leitner's splothering gymnastic displays. It was evident that the two men who had travelled and lived together, sharing the same bedroom, had now reached the stage of loathing. Leitner hated Loerke with an injured, writhing impotent hatred, and Loerke treated Leitner with a fine-quivering contempt and sarcasm. Soon the two would have to go apart.

Already they were rarely together. Leitner ran attaching himself to somebody or other, always deferring, Loerke was a good deal alone. Out of doors he wore a Westphalian cap, a close brown velvet head with big brown velvet flaps down over his ears, so that he looked like a lop-eared rabbit or a troll. His face was brown-red, with a dry, bright skin, that seemed to crinkle with his mobile expressions. His eyes were arresting—brown, full, like a rabbit's, or a troll's, or like the eyes of a lost being, having a strange, dumb, depraved look of knowledge and a quick spark of uncanny fire. Whenever Gudrun had tried to talk to him he had shied away unresponsible, looking at her with his watchful dark eyes, but entering into no relation with her. He had made her feel that her slow French and her slower German were hateful to him. As for his own inadequate English, he was much too awkward to try it at all. But he understood a good deal of what was said, nevertheless. And Gudrun, piqued, left him alone.

This afternoon, however, she came into the lounge as he was talking to Ursula. His fine, black hair somehow reminded her of a bat, thin as it was on his full, sensitive-looking head, and worn away at the temples. He sat hunched up, as if his spirit were bat-like. And Gudrun could see he was making some slow confidence to Ursula, unwilling, a slow, grudging, scanty, self-revelation. She went and sat by her sister.

He looked at her, then looked away again, as if he took no notice of her. But as a matter of fact, she interested him deeply.

'Isn't it interesting, Prune,' said Ursula, turning to her sister, 'Herr Loerke is doing a great frieze for a factory in Cologne, for the outside, the street.'

She looked at him, at his thin, brown, nervous hands, that were prehensile, and somehow like talons, like *'griffes'*, inhuman.

'What *in*?' she asked.

'Aus was?' repeated Ursula.

'Granit,' he replied.

It had become immediately a laconic series of question and answer between fellow craftsmen.

'What is the relief?' asked Gudrun.

'Alto rilievo.'

'And at what height?'

It was very interesting to Gudrun to think of his making the great granite frieze for a great granite factory in Cologne. She got from him some notion of the design. It was a representation of a fair, with peasants and artisans in an orgy of enjoyment, drunk and absurd in their modern dress, whirling ridiculously in roundabouts, gaping at shows, kissing and staggering and rolling in knots, swinging in swingboats, and firing down shooting-galleries, a frenzy of chaotic motion.

There was a swift discussion of technicalities. Gudrun was very much impressed.

'But how wonderful, to have such a factory!' cried Ursula. 'Is the whole building fine?'

'Oh yes,' he replied. 'The frieze is a part of the whole architecture. Yes, it is a colossal thing.'

Then he seemed to stiffen, shrugged his shoulders, and went on:

'Sculpture and architecture must go together. The day for irrelevant statues, as for wall pictures, is over. As a matter of fact, sculpture is always part of an architectural conception. And since churches are all museum stuff, since industry is our business, now, then let us make our places of industry our art—our factory area our Parthenon, *ecco*!'

Ursula pondered.

'I suppose,' she said, 'there is no *need* for our great works to be so hideous.'

Instantly he broke into motion.

'There you are!' he cried, 'there you are! There is not only *no need* for our places of work to be ugly, but their ugliness ruins the work, in the end. Men will not go on submitting to such intolerable ugliness. In the end it will hurt too much, and they will wither because of it. And this will wither the *work* as well. They will think the work itself is ugly: the machines, the very act of labour. Whereas the machinery and the acts of labour are extremely, maddeningly beautiful. But this will be the end of our civilization, when people will not work because work has become so intolerable to their senses, it nauseates them too much, they would rather starve. *Then* we shall see the hammer used only for smashing, then we shall see it. Yet here we are—we have the opportunity to make beautiful factories, beautiful machine-houses—we have the opportunity—'

Gudrun could only partly understand. She could have cried with vexation.

'What does he say?' she asked Ursula. And Ursula translated, stammering and brief. Loerke watched Gudrun's face to see her judgment.

'And do you think then,' said Gudrun, 'that art should serve industry?'

'Art should *interpret* industry as art once interpreted religion,' he said.

'But does your fair interpret industry?' she asked him.

'Certainly. What is man doing when he is at a fair like this? He is fulfilling the counterpart of labour—the machine works him instead of he the machine. He enjoys the mechanical motion in his own body.'

'But is there nothing but work—mechanical work?' said Gudrun.

'Nothing but work!' he repeated, leaning forward, his eyes two darknesses, with needle-points of light. 'No, it is nothing but this, serving a machine, or enjoying the motion of a machine—motion, that is all. You have never worked for hunger, or you would know what god governs us.'

Gudrun quivered and flushed. For some reason she was almost in tears.

'No, I have not worked for hunger,' she replied, 'but I have worked!'

'*Travaillé—lavorato?*' he asked. '*E che lavoro—che lavoro? Quel travail est-ce que vous avez fait?*'

He broke into a mixture of Italian and French, instinctively using a foreign language when he spoke to her.

'You have never worked as the world works,' he said to her, with sarcasm.

'Yes,' she said. 'I have. And I do—I work now for my daily bread.'

He paused, looked at her steadily, then dropped the subject entirely. She seemed to him to be trifling.

'But have *you* ever worked as the world works?' Ursula asked him.

He looked at her untrustful.

'Yes,' he replied, with a surly bark. 'I have known what it was to lie in bed for three days, because I had nothing to eat.'

Gudrun was looking at him with large, grave eyes that seemed to draw the confession from him as the marrow from his bones. All his nature held him back from confessing. And yet her large, grave eyes upon him seemed to open some valve in his veins, and involuntarily he was telling.

'My father was a man who did not like work, and we had no mother. We lived in Austria, Polish Austria. How did we live? Ha!—somehow! Mostly in a room with three other families—one set in each corner—and the w.c. in the middle of the room—a pan with a plank on it—ha! I had two brothers and a sister—and there might be a woman with my father. He was a free being, in his way—would fight with any man in the town—a garrison town—and was a little man too. But he wouldn't work for anybody—set his heart against it, and wouldn't.'

'And how did you live then!' asked Ursula.

He looked at her—then, suddenly, at Gudrun.

'Do you understand?' he asked.

'Enough,' she replied.

Their eyes met for a moment. Then he looked away. He would say no more.

'And how did you become a sculptor?' asked Ursula.

'How did I become a sculptor—' He paused. *'Dunque—'* he resumed in a changed manner, and beginning to speak French—'I became old enough—I used to steal from the market-place. Later I went to work—imprinted the stamp on clay bottles before they were baked. It was an earthenware bottle factory. There I began making models. One day I had had enough. I lay in the sun and did not go to work. Then I walked to Munich—then I walked to Italy—begging, begging everything.

'The Italians were very good to me—they were good and honourable to me. From Bozen to Rome, almost every night I had a meal and a bed, perhaps of straw, with some peasant. I love the Italian people with all my heart.

'Dunque, adesso—maintenant— I earn a thousand pounds in a year, or I earn two thousand—'

He looked down at the ground, his voice tailing off into silence.

Gudrun looked at his fine, thin, shiny skin, reddish-brown from the sun, drawn tight over his full temples; and at his thin hair—and at the thick, coarse, brush-like moustache, cut short about his mobile, rather shapeless mouth.

'How old are you?' she asked.

He looked up at her with his full, elfin eyes startled.

'Wie alt?' he repeated. And he hesitated. It was evidently one of his reticencies.

'How old are *you?'* he replied, without answering.

'I am twenty-six,' she answered.

'Twenty-six,' he repeated, looking into her eyes. He paused. Then he said:

'Und Ihr Herr Gemahl, wie alt ist er?'

'Who?' asked Gudrun.

'Your husband,' said Ursula, with a certain irony.

'I haven't got a husband,' said Gudrun in English. In German she answered:

'He is thirty-one.'

But Loerke was watching closely, with his uncanny, full, suspicious eyes. Something in Gudrun seemed to accord with him. He was really like one of the 'little people' who have no soul, who has found his mate in a human being. But he suffered in his discovery. She too was fascinated by him, fascinated, as if some strange creature, a rabbit or a bat, or a brown seal, had begun to talk to her. But also, she knew what he was unconscious of, his tremendous power of understanding, of apprehending her living motion. He did not know his own power. He did not know how, with his full, submerged, watchful eyes, he could look into her and see her, what she was, see her secrets. He would only want her to be herself—he knew her verily, with a subsconscious, sinister knowledge, devoid of illusions and hopes.

To Gudrun, there was in Loerke the rock bottom of all life. Everybody else had their illusion, must have their illusion, their before and after. But he, with a perfect stoicism, did without any before and after, dispensed with all illusion. He did not deceive himself in the last issue. In the last issue he cared about nothing, he was troubled about nothing, he made not the slightest attempt to be at one with anything. He existed a pure, unconnected will, stoical and momentaneous. There was only his work.

It was curious, too, how his poverty, the degradation of his earlier life, attracted her. There was something insipid and tasteless to her in the idea of a gentleman, a man who had gone the usual course through school and university. A certain violent sympathy, however, came up in her for this mud-child. He seemed to be the very stuff of the underworld of life. There was no going beyond him.

Ursula too was attracted by Loerke. In both sisters he commanded a certain homage. But there were moments when to Ursula he seemed indescribably inferior, false, a vulgarism.

Both Birkin and Gerald disliked him, Gerald ignoring him with some contempt, Birkin exasperated.

'What do the women find so impressive in that little brat?' Gerald asked.

'God alone knows,' replied Birkin, 'unless it's some sort of appeal he makes to them, which flatters them and has such a power over them.'

Gerald looked up in surprise.

'*Does* he make an appeal to them?' he asked.

'Oh yes,' replied Birkin. 'He is the perfectly subjected be-

CONTINENTAL 483

ing, existing almost like a criminal. And the women rush towards that, like a current of air towards a vacuum.'

'Funny they should rush to that,' said Gerald.

'Makes one mad, too,' said Birkin. 'But he has the fascination of pity and repulsion for them, a little obscene monster of the darkness that he is.'

Gerald stood still, suspended in thought.

'What *do* women want at the bottom?' he asked.

Birkin shrugged his shoulders.

'God knows,' he said. 'Some satisfaction is basic repulsion, it seems to me. They seem to creep down some ghastly tunnel of darkness, and will never be satisfied till they've come to the end.'

Gerald looked out into the mist of fine snow that was blowing by. Everywhere was blind today, horribly blind.

'And what *is* the end?' he asked.

Birkin shook his head.

'I've not got there yet, so I don't know. Ask Loerke, he's pretty near. He is a good many stages farther than either you or I can go.'

'Yes, but stages farther in what?' cried Gerald, irritated.

Birkin sighed, and gathered his brows into a knot of anger.

'Stages farther in social hatred,' he said. 'He lives like a rat in the river of corruption, just where it falls over into the bottomless pit. He's farther on than we are. He hates the ideal more acutely. He *hates* the ideal utterly, yet it still dominates him. I expect he is a Jew—or part Jewish.'

'Probably,' said Gerald.

'He is a gnawing little negation, gnawing at the roots of life.'

'But why does anybody care about him?' cried Gerald.

'Because they hate the ideal also in their souls. They want to explore the sewers, and he's the wizard rat that swims ahead.'

Still Gerald stood and stared at the blind haze of snow outside.

'I don't understand your terms, really,' he said in a flat, doomed voice. 'But it sounds a rum sort of desire.'

'I suppose we want the same,' said Birkin. 'Only we want

to take a quick jump downwards, in a sort of ecstasy—and he ebbs with the stream, the sewer stream.'

Meanwhile Gudrun and Ursula waited for the next opportunity to talk to Loerke. It was no use beginning when the men were there. Then they could get into no touch with the isolated little sculptor. He had to be alone with them. And he preferred Ursula to be there, as a sort of transmitter to Gudrun.

'Do you do nothing but architectural sculpture?' Gudrun asked him one evening.

'Not now,' he replied. 'I have done all sorts—except portraits—I never did portraits. But other things—'

'What kind of things?' asked Gudrun.

He paused a moment, then rose and went out of the room. He returned almost immediately with a little roll of paper, which he handed to her. She unrolled it. It was a photogravure reproduction of a statuette, signed F. Loerke.

'That is quite an early thing—*not* mechanical,' he said, 'more popular.'

The statuette was of a naked girl, small, finely made, sitting on a great naked horse. The girl was young and tender, a mere bud. She was sitting sideways on the horse, her face in her hands, as if in shame and grief, in a little abandon. Her hair, which was short and must be flaxen, fell forward, divided, half covering her hands.

Her limbs were young and tender. Her legs, scarcely formed yet, the legs of a maiden just passing towards cruel womanhood, dangled childishly over the side of the powerful horse, pathetically, the small feet folded one over the other, as if to hide. But there was no hiding. There she was exposed naked on the naked flank of the horse.

The horse stood stock still, stretched in a kind of start. It was a massive, magnificent stallion, rigid with pent-up power. Its neck was arched and terrible, like a sickle, its flanks were pressed back, rigid with power.

Gudrun went pale, and a darkness came over her eyes, like shame, she looked up with a certain supplication, almost slave-like. He glanced at her and jerked his head a little.

'How big is it?' she asked in a toneless voice, persisting in appearing casual and unaffected.

'How big?' he replied, glancing again at her. 'Without pedestal—so high'—he measured with his hand—'with pedestal, so—'

He looked at her steadily. There was a little brusque, turgid contempt for her in his swift gesture, and she seemed to cringe a little.

'And what is it done in?' she asked, throwing back her head and looking at him with affected coldness.

He still gazed at her steadily, and his dominance was not shaken.

'Bronze—green bronze.'

'Green bronze!' repeated Gudrun, coldly accepting his challenge. She was thinking of the slender, immature, tender limbs of the girl, smooth and cold in green bronze.

'Yes, beautiful,' she murmured, looking up at him with a certain dark homage.

He closed his eyes and looked aside, triumphant.

'Why,' said Ursula, 'did you make the horse so stiff? It is as stiff as a block.'

'Stiff?' he repeated, in arms at once.

'Yes. *Look* how stock and stupid and brutal it is. Horses are sensitive, quite delicate, and sensitive, really.'

He raised his shoulders, spread his hands in a shrug of slow indifference, as much as to inform her she was an amateur and an impertinent nobody.

'*Wissen Sie,*' he said, with an insulting patience and condescension in his voice, 'that horse is a certain *form,* part of a whole form. It is part of a work of art, a piece of form. It is not a picture of a friendly horse to which you give a lump of sugar, do you see—it is part of a work of art, it has no relation to anything outside that work of art.'

Ursula, angry at being treated quite so insultingly *de haut en bas,* from the height of esoteric art to the depth of general exoteric amateurism, replied, hotly, flushing and lifting her face.

'But it *is* a picture of a horse, nevertheless.'

He lifted his shoulders in another shrug.

'As you like—it is not a picture of a cow, certainly.'

Here Gudrun broke in, flushed and brilliant, anxious to

avoid any more of this, any more of Ursula's foolish persistence in giving herself away.

'What do you mean by "it is a picture of a horse"?' she cried at her sister 'What do you mean by a horse? You mean an idea you have in *your* head, and which you want to see represented. There is another idea altogether, quite another idea. Call it a horse if you like, or say it is not a horse. I have just as much right to say that *your* horse isn't a horse, that it is a falsity of your own make-up.'

Ursula wavered, baffled. Then her words came.

'But why does he have this idea of a horse?' she said. 'I know it is his idea. I know it is a picture of himself, really—'

Loerke snorted with rage.

'A picture of myself!' he repeated in derision. *'Wissen Sie, gnädige Frau,* that is a *Kunstwerk,* a work of art. It is a work of art, it is a picture of nothing, of absolutely nothing. It has nothing to do with anything but itself, it has no relation with the everyday world of this and other, there is no connexion between them, absolutely none, they are two different and distinct planes of existence, and to translate one into the other is worse than foolish, it is a darkening of all counsel, a making confusion, everywhere. Do you see, you *must not* confuse the relative work of action with the absolute world of art. That you *must not do.'*

'That is quite true,' cried Gudrun, let loose in a sort of rhapsody. 'The two things are quite and permanently apart, they have nothing to do with one another. *I* and my art, they have *nothing* to do with each other. My art stands in another world, I am in this world.'

Her face was flushed and transfigured. Loerke, who was sitting with his head ducked, like some creature at bay, looked up at her swiftly, almost furtively, and murmured:

'Ja—so ist es, so ist es.'

Ursula was silent after this outburst. She was furious. She wanted to poke a hole into them both.

'It isn't a word of it true, of all this harangue you have made me,' she replied flatly. 'The horse is a picture of your own stock, stupid brutality, and the girl was a girl you loved and tortured and then ignored.'

He looked up at her with a small smile of contempt in his eyes. He would not trouble to answer this last charge.

Gudrun too was silent in exasperated contempt. Ursula *was* such an insufferable outsider, rushing in where angels would fear to tread. But then—fools must be suffered, if not gladly.

But Ursula was persistent too.

'As for your world of art and your world of reality,' she replied, 'you have to separate the two, because you can't bear to know what you are. You can't bear to realize what a stock, stiff, hide-bound brutality you *are* really, so you say "it's the world of art". The world of art is only the truth about the real world, that's all—but you are too far gone to see it.'

She was white and trembling, intent. Gudrun and Loerke sat in stiff dislike of her. Gerald too, who had come up in the beginning of the speech, stood looking at her in complete disapproval and opposition. He felt she was undignified, she put a sort of vulgarity over the esotericism which gave man his last distinction. He joined his forces with the other two. They all three wanted her to go away. But she sat on in silence, her soul weeping, throbbing violently, her fingers twisting her handkerchief.

The others maintained a dead silence, letting the display of Ursula's obtrusiveness pass by. Then Gudrun asked, in a voice that was quite cool and casual, as if resuming a casual conversation:

'Was the girl a model?'

'*Nein, sie war kein Modell. Sie war eine kleine Malschülerin.*'

'An art student!' replied Gudrun.

And how the situation revealed itself to her! She saw the girl art student, unformed and of pernicious recklessness, too young, her straight flaxen hair cut short, hanging just into her neck, curving inwards slightly, because it was rather thick; and Loerke, the well-known master-sculptor, and the girl, probably well brought up and of good family, thinking herself so great to be his mistress. Oh, how well she knew the common callousness of it all. Dresden, Paris, or London, what did it matter? She knew it.

'Where is she now?' Ursula asked.

Loerke raised his shoulders to convey his complete igno-
rance and indifference.

'That is already six years ago,' he said, 'she will be twenty-
three years old, no more good.'

Gerald had picked up the picture and was looking at it. It
attracted him also. He saw on the pedestal that the piece was
called 'Lady Godiva.'

'But this isn't Lady Godiva,' he said, smiling good-
humouredly. 'She was the middle-aged wife of some Earl or
other, who covered herself with her long hair.'

'À la Maud Allan,' said Gudrun, with a mocking grimace.

'Why Maud Allan?' he replied. 'Isn't it so? I always thought
the legend was that.'

'Yes, Gerald dear, I'm quite sure you've got the legend
perfectly.'

She was laughing at him, with a little, mock-caressive
contempt.

'To be sure, I'd rather see the woman than the hair,' he
laughed in return.

'Wouldn't you just!' mocked Gudrun.

Ursula rose and went away, leaving the three together.

Gudrun took the picture again from Gerald, and sat looking at it closely.

'Of course,' she said, turning to tease Loerke, now, 'you
understood your little Malschülerin.'

He raised his eyebrows and his shoulders in a complacent
shrug.

'The little girl?' asked Gerald, pointing to the figure.

Gudrun was sitting with the picture in her lap. She looked
up at Gerald, full into his eyes, so that he seemed to be
blinded.

'Didn't he understand her!' she said to Gerald in a slightly
mocking, humourous playfulness. 'You've only to look at
the feet—aren't they darling, so pretty and tender—oh,
they're really wonderful, they are really—'

She lifted her eyes slowly, with a hot, flaming look into
Loerke's eyes. His soul was filled with her burning recognition, he seemed to grow more uppish and lordly.

Gerald looked at the small, sculptured feet. They were

turned together, half covering each other in pathetic shyness and fear. He looked at them a long time, fascinated. Then, in some pain, he put the picture away from him. He felt full of barrenness.

'What was her name?' Gudrun asked Loerke.

'Annette von Weck,' Loerke replied, reminiscent. *'Ja, sie war hübsch.* She was pretty—but she was tiresome. She was a nuisance—not for a minute would she keep still—not until I'd slapped her hard and made her cry—then she'd sit for five minutes.'

He was thinking over the work, his work, the all important to him.

'Did you really slap her?' asked Gudrun coolly.

He glanced back at her, reading her challenge.

'Yes, I did,' he said, nonchalant, 'harder than I have ever beat anything in my life. I had to, I had to. It was the only way I got the work done.'

Gudrun watched him with large, dark-filled eyes for some moments. She seemed to be considering his very soul. Then she looked down in silence.

'Why did you have such a young Godiva then?' asked Gerald. 'She is so small, besides, on the horse—not big enough for it—such a child.'

A queer spasm went over Loerke's face.

'Yes,' he said. 'I don't like them any bigger, any older. Then they are beautiful at sixteen, seventeen, eighteen—after that, they are no use to me.'

There was a moment's pause.

'Why not?' asked Gerald.

Loerke shrugged his shoulders.

'I don't find them interesting— or beautiful—they are no good to me, for my work.'

'Do you mean to say a woman isn't beautiful after she is twenty?' asked Gerald.

'For me, no. Before twenty, she is small and fresh and tender and slight. After that—let her be what she likes, she has nothing for me. The Venus of Milo is a bourgeoise—so are they all.'

'And you don't care for women at all after twenty?' asked Gerald.

'They are no good to me, they are of no use in my art,' Loerke repeated impatiently. 'I don't find them beautiful.'

'You are an epicure,' said Gerald, with a slight sarcastic laugh.

'And what about men?' asked Gudrun suddenly.

'Yes, they are good at all ages,' replied Loerke. 'A man should be big and powerful—whether he is old or young is of no account, so he has the size, something of massiveness and—and stupid form.'

Ursula went out alone into the world of pure, new snow. But the dazzling whiteness seemed to beat upon her till it hurt her, she felt the cold was slowly strangling her soul. Her head felt dazed and numb.

Suddenly she wanted to go away. It occurred to her like a miracle, that she might go away into another world. She had felt so doomed up here in the eternal snow, as if there were no beyond.

Now suddenly, as by a miracle she remembered that away beyond, below her, lay the dark fruitful earth, that towards the south there were stretches of land dark with orange trees and cypress, grey with olives, the ilex trees lifted wonderful plumy tufts in shadow against a blue sky. Miracle of miracles!—this utterly silent, frozen world of the mountain-tops was not universal! One might leave it and have done with it. One might go away.

She wanted to realize the miracle at once. She wanted at this instant to have done with the snow world, the terrible, static ice-built mountain-tops. She wanted to see the dark earth, to smell its earthy fecundity, to see the patient wintry vegetation, to feel the sunshine touch a response in the buds.

She went back gladly to the house, full of hope. Birkin was reading, lying in bed.

'Rupert,' she said, bursting in on him. 'I want to go away.'

He looked up at her slowly.

'Do you?' he replied mildly.

She sat by him and put her arms round his neck. It surprised her that he was so little surprised.

'Don't *you*?' she asked troubled.

'I hadn't thought about it,' he said. 'But I'm sure I do.'

She sat up, suddenly erect.

'I hate it,' she said. 'I hate the snow, and the unnatural-ness of it, the unnatural light it throws on everybody, the ghastly glamour, the unnatural feelings it makes everybody have.'

He lay still and laughed, meditating.

'Well,' he said, 'we can go away—we can go tomorrow. We'll go tomorrow to Verona, and find Romeo and Juliet, and sit in the amphitheatre—shall we?'

Suddenly she hid her face against his shoulder with per-plexity and shyness. He lay so untrammelled.

'Yes,' she said softly, filled with relief. She felt her soul had new wings, now he was so uncaring. 'I shall love to be Romeo and Juliet,' she said. 'My love!'

'Though a fearfully cold wind blows in Verona,' he said, 'from out of the Alps. We shall have the smell of the snow in our noses.'

She sat up and looked at him.

'Are you glad to go?' she asked, troubled.

His eyes were inscrutable and laughing. She hid her face against his neck, clinging close to him, pleading:

'Don't laugh at me—don't laugh at me.'

'Why how's that?' he laughed, putting his arms round her.

'Because I don't want to be laughed at,' she whispered.

He laughed more, as he kissed her delicate, finely per-fumed hair.

'Do you love me?' she whispered, in a wild seriousness.

'Yes,' he answered, laughing.

Suddenly she lifted her mouth to be kissed. Her lips were taut and quivering and strenuous, his were soft, deep, and delicate. He waited a few moments in the kiss. Then a shade of sadness went over his soul.

'Your mouth is so hard,' he said, in faint reproach.

'And yours is so soft and nice,' she said gladly.

'But why do you always grip your lips?' he asked, regret-ful.

'Never mind,' she said swiftly. 'It is my way.'

She knew he loved her; she was sure of him. Yet she could not let go a certain hold over herself, she could not bear him to question her. She gave herself up in delight to being loved by him. She knew that, in spite of his joy when she abandoned herself, he was a little bit saddened too. She could give herself up to his activity. But she could not be herself, she *dared* not come forth quite nakedly to his nakedness, abandoning all adjustment, lapsing in pure faith with him. She abandoned herself to *him,* or she took hold of him and gathered her joy of him. And she enjoyed him fully. But they were never *quite* together, at the same moment, one was always a little left out. Nevertheless she was glad in hope, glorious and free, full of life and liberty. And he was still and soft and patient, for the time.

They made their preparations to leave the next day. First they went to Gudrun's room, where she and Gerald were just dressed ready for the evening indoors.

'Prune,' said Ursula, 'I think we shall go away tomorrow. I can't stand the snow any more. It hurts my skin and my soul.'

'Does it really hurt your soul, Ursula?' asked Gudrun, in some surprise. 'I can believe quite it hurts your skin—it is *terrible*. But I thought it was *admirable* for the soul.'

'No, not for mine. It just injures it,' said Ursula.

'Really!' cried Gudrun.

There was a silence in the room. And Ursula and Birkin could feel that Gudrun and Gerald were relieved by their going.

'You will go south?' said Gerald, a little ring of uneasiness in his voice.

'Yes,' said Birkin, turning away. There was a queer, indefinable hostility between the two men, lately. Birkin was on the whole dim and indifferent, drifting along in a dim, easy flow, unnoticing and patient, since he came abroad, whilst Gerald on the other hand, was intense and gripped into white light, agonistes. The two men revoked one another.

Gerald and Gudrun were very kind to the two who were departing, solicitous for their welfare as if they were two children. Gudrun come to Ursula's bedroom with three pairs of the coloured stockings for which she was notorious, and she threw them on the bed. But these were thick silk stockings, vermilion, cornflower blue, and grey, bought in Paris. The grey ones were knitted, seamless, and heavy. Ursula was in raptures. She knew Gudrun must be feeling *very* loving, to give away such treasures.

'I can't take them from you, Prune,' she cried. 'I can't possibly deprive you of them—the jewels.'

'*Aren't* they jewels!' cried Gudrun, eyeing her gifts with an envious eye. '*Aren't* they real lambs!'

'Yes, you *must* keep them,' said Ursula.

'I don't *want* them, I've got three more pairs. I *want* you to keep them—I want you to have them. They're yours, there—'

And with trembling, excited hands she put the coveted stockings under Ursula's pillow.

'One gets the greatest joy of all out of really lovely stockings,' said Ursula.

"One does,' replied Gudrun; 'the greatest joy of all.'

And she sat down in the chair. It was evident she had come for a last talk. Ursula, not knowing what she wanted, waited in silence.

'Do you *feel*, Ursula,' Gudrun began, rather sceptically, 'that you are going-away-for-ever, never-to-return, sort of thing?'

'Oh, we shall come back,' said Ursula. 'It isn't a question of train journeys.'

'Yes, I know. But spiritually, so to speak, you are going away from us all?'

Ursula quivered.

'I don't know a bit what is going to happen,' she said. 'I only know we are going somewhere.'

Gudrun waited.

'And you are glad?' she asked.

Ursula meditated for a moment.

'I believe I am *very* glad,' she replied.

But Gudrun read the unconscious brightness on her sister's face, rather than the uncertain tones of her speech.

'But don't you think you'll *want* the old connexion with the world—father and the rest of us, and all that it means, England and the world of thought—don't you think you'll *need* that, really to make a world?'

Ursula was silent, trying to imagine.

'I think,' she said at length, involuntarily, 'that Rupert is right—one wants a new space to be in, and one falls away from the old.'

Gudrun watched her sister with impassive face and steady eyes.

'One wants a new space to be in, I quite agree,' she said. 'But *I* think that a new world is a development from this world, and that to isolate oneself with one other person isn't to find a new world at all, but only to secure oneself in one's illusions.'

Ursula looked out of the window. In her soul she began to wrestle, and she was frightened. She was always frightened of words, because she knew that mere word-force could always make her believe what she did not believe.

'Perhaps,' she said, full of mistrust, of herself and everybody. 'But,' she added, 'I do think that one can't have anything new whilst one cares for the old—do you know what I mean?—even fighting the old is belonging to it. I know, one is tempted to stop with the world, just to fight it. But then it isn't worth it.'

Gudrun considered herself.

'Yes,' she said. 'In a way, one is of the world if one lives in it. But isn't it really an illusion to think you can get out of it? After all, a cottage in the Abruzzi, or wherever it may be, isn't a new world. No, the only thing to do with the world, is to see it through.'

Ursula looked away. She was so frightened of argument.

'But there *can* be something else, can't there?' she said. 'One can see it through in one's soul, long enough before it sees itself through in actuality. And then, when one has seen one's soul, one is something else.'

'*Can* one see it through in one's soul?' asked Gudrun. 'If you mean that you can see to the end of what will happen, I don't agree. I really can't agree. And anyhow, you can't suddenly fly off on to a new planet, because you think you can see to the end of this.'

Ursula suddenly straightened herself.

'Yes, she said. 'Yes—one knows. One has no more connexions here. One has a sort of other self, that belongs to a new planet, not to this. You've got to hop off.'

Gudrun reflected for a few moments. Then a smile of ridicule, almost of contempt, came over her face.

'And what will happen when you find yourself in space?' she cried in derision. 'After all, the great ideas of the world are the same there. You above everybody can't get away from the fact that love, for instance, is the supreme thing, in space as well as on earth.'

'No,' said Ursula, 'it isn't. Love is too human and little. I believe in something inhuman, of which love is only a little part. I believe what we must fulfil comes out of the unknown to us, and it is something infinitely more than love. It isn't so merely *human*.'

Gudrun looked at Ursula with steady, balancing eyes. She admired and despised her sister so much, both! Then, suddenly she averted her face, saying coldly, uglily:

'Well, I've got no further than love, yet.'

Over Ursula's mind flashed the thought: 'Because you never *have* loved, you can't get beyond it.'

Gudrun rose, came over to Ursula and put her arm round her neck.

'Go and find your new world, dear,' she said, her voice clanging with false benignity. 'After all, the happiest voyage is the quest of Rupert's Blessed Isles.'

Her arms rested round Ursula's neck, her fingers on Ursula's cheek for a few moments. Ursula was supremely uncomfortable meanwhile. There was an insult in Gudrun's protective patronage that was really too hurting. Feeling her sister's resistance, Gudrun drew awkwardly away, turned over the pillow, and disclosed the stockings again.

'Ha—ha!' she laughed, rather hollowly. 'How we do talk indeed—new worlds and old—!'

And they passed to the familiar worldly subjects.

Gerald and Birkin had walked on ahead, waiting for the sledge to overtake them, conveying the departing guests.

'How much longer will you stay here?' asked Birkin, glancing up at Gerald's very red, almost blank face.

'Oh, I can't say,' Gerald replied. 'Till we get tired of it.'

'You're not afraid of the snow melting first?' asked Birkin, Gerald laughed.

'Does it melt?' he said.

'Things are all right with you then?' said Birkin.

Gerald screwed up his eyes a little.

'All right?' he said. 'I never know what those common words mean. All right and all wrong, don't they become synonymous, somewhere?'

'Yes, I suppose. How about going back?' asked Birkin.

'Oh, I don't know. We may never get back. I don't look before and after,' said Gerald.

'*Nor* pine for what is not,' said Birkin.

Gerald looked into the distance, with the small-pupilled, abstract eyes of a hawk.

'No. There's something final about this. And Gudrun seems like the end to me. I don't know—but she seems so soft, her skin like silk, her arms heavy and soft. And it withers my consciousness, somehow, it burns the pith of my mind.' He went on a few paces, staring ahead, his eyes fixed, looking like a mask used in ghastly religions of the barbarians. 'It blasts your soul's eye,' he said, 'and leaves you sightless. Yet you *want* to be sightless, you *want* to be blasted, you don't want it any different.'

He was speaking as if in a trance, verbal and blank. Then suddenly he braced himself up with a kind of rhapsody, and looked at Birkin with vindictive, cowed eyes saying:

'Do you know what it is to suffer when you are with a woman? She's so beautiful, so perfect, you find her *so good,* it tears you like a silk, and every stroke and bit cuts hot—ha, that perfection, when you blast yourself, you blast yourself! And then—' he stopped on the snow and suddenly opened his clenched hands—'it's nothing—your brain might have gone charred as rags—and—' he looked round into the air with a queer histrionic movement—'it's blasting—you understand what I mean—it is a great experience, something final—and then—you're shrivelled as if struck by electricity.' He walked on in silence. It seemed like bragging, but like a man in extremity bragging truthfully.

'Of course,' he resumed, 'I wouldn't *not* have had it! It's a complete experience. And she's a wonderful woman. But—how I hate her somewhere! It's curious—'

Birkin looked at him, at his strange, scarcely conscious face. Gerald seemed blank before his own words.

'But you've had enough now?' said Birkin. 'You have had your experience. Why work on an old wound?'

'Oh,' said Gerald, 'I don't know. It's not finished—'

And the two walked on.

'I've loved you, as well as Gudrun, don't forget,' said Birkin bitterly. Gerald looked at him strangely, abstractedly.

'Have you?' he said, with icy scepticism. 'Or do you think you have?' He was hardly responsible for what he said.

The sledge came. Gudrun dismounted and they all made their farewell. They wanted to go apart, all of them. Birkin took his place, and the sledge drove away leaving Gudrun and Gerald standing on the snow, waving. Something froze Birkin's heart, seeing them standing there in the isolation of the snow, growing smaller and more isolated.

30

Snowed Up

When Ursul and Birkin were gone, Gudrun felt herself free in her contest with Gerald. As they grew more used to each other, he seemed to press upon her more and more. At first she could manage him, so that her own will was always left free. But very soon, he began to ignore her female tactics, he dropped his respect for her whims and her privacies, he began to exert his own will blindly, without submitting to hers.

Already a vital conflict had set in, which frightened them both. But he was alone, whilst already she had begun to cast round for external resource.

When Ursula had gone, Gudrun felt her own existence had become stark and elemental. She went and crouched alone in her bedroom, looking out of the window at the big, flashing stars. In front was the faint shadow of the mountain-knot. That was the pivot. She felt strange and inevitable, as if she were centred upon the pivot of all existence, there was no further reality.

Presently Gerald opened the door. She knew he would not be long before he came. She was rarely alone, he pressed upon her like a frost, deadening her.

'Are you alone in the dark?' he said. And she could tell by his tone he resented it, he resented this isolation she had drawn round herself. Yet, feeling static and inevitable, she was kind towards him.

'Would you like to light the candle?' she asked.

He did not answer, but came and stood behind her, in the darkness.

'Look,' she said, 'at that lovely star up there. Do you know its name?'

He crouched beside her, to look through the low window.

'No,' he said. 'It is very fine.'

'*Isn't* it beautiful! Do you notice how it darts different coloured fires—it flashes really superbly—'

They remained in silence. With a mute, heavy gesture she put her hand on his knee, and took his hand.

'Are you regretting Ursula?' he asked.

'No, not at all,' she said. Then, in a slow mood, she asked:

'How much do you love me?'

He stiffened himself further against her.

'How much do you think I do?' he asked.

'I don't know,' she replied.

'But what is your opinion?' he asked.

There was a pause. At length, in the darkness, came her voice, hard and indifferent:

'Very little indeed,' she said coldly, almost flippant.

His heart went icy at the sound of her voice.

'Why don't I love you?' he asked, as if admitting the truth of her accusation, yet hating her for it.

'I don't know why you don't—I've been good to you. You were in a *fearful* state when you came to me.'

Her heart was beating to suffocate her, yet she was strong and unrelenting.

'When was I in a fearful state?' he asked.

'When you first came to me. I *had* to take pity on you. But it was never love.'

It was that statement 'It was never love', which sounded in his ears with madness.

'Why must you repeat it so often, that there is no love?' he said in a voice strangled with rage.

'Well you don't *think* you love, do you?' she asked.

He was silent with cold passion of anger.

'You don't think you *can* love me, do you?' she repeated almost with a sneer.

'No,' he said.

'You know you never *have* loved me, don't you?'

'I don't know what you mean by the word "love",' he replied.

'Yes, you do. You know all right that you have never loved me. Have you, do you think?'

'No,' he said, prompted by some barren spirit of truthfulness and obstinacy.

'And you never *will* love me,' she said finally, 'will you?' There was a diabolic coldness in her, too much to bear.

'No,' he said.

'Then,' she replied, 'what have you against me?'

He was silent in cold, frightened rage and despair. 'If only I could kill her,' his heart was whispering repeatedly. 'If only I could kill her—I should be free.'

It seemed to him that death was the only severing of this Gordian knot.

'Why do you torture me?' he said.

She flung her arms round his neck.

'Ah, I don't want to torture you,' she said pityingly, as if she were comforting a child. The impertinence made his veins go cold, he was insensible. She held her arms round his neck, in a triumph of pity. And her pity for him was as cold as stone, its deepest motive was hate of him, and fear of his power over her, which she must always counterfoil.

'Say you love me,' she pleaded. 'Say you will love me for ever—won't you—won't you?'

But it was her voice only that coaxed him. Her senses were entirely apart from him, cold and destructive of him. It was her overbearing *will* that insisted.

'Won't you say you'll love me always?' she coaxed. 'Say it, even if it isn't true—say it Gerald, do.'

'I will love you always,' he repeated, in real agony, forcing the words out.

She gave him a quick kiss.

'Fancy your actually having said it,' she said with a touch of raillery.

He stood as if he had been beaten.

'Try to love me a little more, and to want me a little less,' she said, in a half contemptuous, half coaxing tone.

The darkness seemed to be swaying in waves across his mind, great waves of darkness plunging across his mind. It seemed to him he was degraded at the very quick, made of no account.

'You mean you don't want me?' he said.

'You are so insistent, and there is so little grace in you, so little fineness. You are so crude. You break me—you only waste me—it is horrible to me.'

'Horrible to you?' he repeated.

'Yes. Don't you think I might have a room to myself, now Ursula has gone? You can say you want a dressing-room.'

'You do as you like—you can leave altogether if you like,' he managed to articulate.

'Yes, I know that,' she replied.'So can you. You can leave me whenever you like—without notice even.'

The great tides of darkness were swinging across his mind, he could hardly stand upright. A terrible weariness overcame him, he felt he must lie on the floor. Dropping off his clothes, he got into bed, and lay like a man suddenly overcome by drunkenness, the darkness lifting and plunging as if he were lying upon a black, giddy sea. He lay still in this strange, horrific reeling for some time, purely unconscious.

At length she slipped from her own bed and came over to him. He remained rigid, his back to her. He was all but unconscious.

She put her arms round his terrifying, insentient body, and laid her cheek against his hard shoulder.

'Gerald,' she whispered. 'Gerald.'

There was no change in him. She caught him against her. She pressed her breasts against his shoulders, she kissed his shoulder, through the sleeping jacket. Her mind wondered, over his rigid, unliving body. She was bewildered, and insistent, only her will was set for him to speak to her.

'Gerald, my dear!' she whispered, bending over him, kissing his ear.

Her warm breath playing, flying rhythmically over his ear, seemed to relax the tension. She could feel his body gradually relaxing a little, losing its terrifying, unnatural rigidity. Her hands clutched his limbs, his muscles, going over him spasmodically.

The hot blood began to flow again through his veins, his limbs relaxed.

'Turn round to me,' she whispered, forlorn with insistence and triumph.

So at last he was given again, warm and flexible. He turned and gathered her in his arms. And feeling her soft against him, so perfectly and wondrously soft and recipient, his arms tightened on her. She was as if crushed, powerless in him. His brain seemed hard and invincible now like a jewel, there was no resisting him.

His passion was awful to her, tense and ghastly, and impersonal like a destruction, ultimate. She felt it would kill her. She was being killed.

'My God, my God,' she cried, in anguish, in his embrace, feeling her life being killed within her. And when he was kissing her, soothing her, her breath came slowly, as if she were really spent, dying.

'Shall I die, shall I die?' she repeated to herself.

And in the night, and in him, there was no answer to the question.

And yet, next day, the fragment of her which was not destroyed remained intact and hostile, she did not go away, she remained to finish the holiday, admitting nothing. He scarcely ever left her alone, but followed her like a shadow, he was like a doom upon her, a continual 'thou shalt,' 'thou shalt not'. Sometimes it was he who seemed strongest, whilst she was almost gone, creeping near the earth like a spent wind; sometimes it was the reverse. But always it was this eternal see-saw, one destroyed that the other might exist, one ratified because the other was nulled.

'In the end,' she said to herself, 'I shall go away from him.'

'I can be free of her,' he said to himself in his paroxysms of suffering.

And he set himself to be free. He even prepared to go away, to leave her in the lurch. But for the first time there was a flaw in his will.

"Where shall I go?' he asked himself.

'Can't you be self-sufficient?' he replied to himself, putting himself upon his pride.

'Self-sufficient!' he repeated.

It seemed to him that Gudrun was sufficient unto herself.

closed round and completed, like a thing in a case. In the calm, static reason of his soul, he recognized this, and admitted it was her right, to be closed round upon herself, self-complete, without desire. He realized it, he admitted it, it only needed one last effort on his own part, to win for himself the same completeness. He knew that it only needed one convulsion of his will for him to be able to turn upon himself also, to close upon himself as a stone fixes upon itself, and is impervious, self-completed, a thing isolated.

This knowledge threw him into a terrible chaos. Because, however much he might mentally *will* to be immune and self-complete, the desire for this state was lacking, and he could not create it. He could see that, to exist at all, he must be perfectly free of Gudrun, leave her if she wanted to be left, demand nothing of her, have no claim upon her.

But then, to have no claim upon her, he must stand by himself, in sheer nothingness. And his brain turned to nought at the idea. It was a state of nothingness. On the other hand, he might give in, and fawn to her. Or, finally, he might kill her. Or he might become just indifferent, purposeful, dissipated, momentaneous. But his nature was too serious, not gay enough or subtle enough for mocking licentiousness.

A strange rent had been torn in him; like a victim that is torn open and given to the heavens, so he had been torn apart and given to Gudrun. How should he close again? This wound, this strange, infinitely-sensitive opening of his soul, where he was exposed, like an open flower, to all the universe, and in which he was given to his complement, the other, the unknown, this wound, this disclosure, this unfolding of his own covering, leaving him incomplete, limited, unfinished, like an open flower under the sky, this was is cruellest joy. Why then should he forgo it? Why should he close up and become impervious, immune, like a partial thing in a sheath, when he had broken forth, like a seed that has germinated, to issue forth in being, embracing the unrealized heavens.

He would keep the unfinished bliss of his own yearning even through the torture she inflicted upon him. A strange obstinacy possessed him. He would not go away from her whatever she said or did. A strange, deathly yearning carried him along with her. She was the determining influence of his very being, though she treated him with contempt, repeated rebuffs and denials, still he would never be gone, since in being near her, even, he felt the quickening, the going forth in him, the release, the knowledge of his own limitation and the magic of the promise, as well as the mystery of his own destruction and annihilation.

She tortured the open heart of him even as he turned to her. And she was tortured herself. It may have been her will was stronger. She felt, with horror, as if he tore at the bud of her heart, tore it open, like an irreverent persistent being. Like a boy who pulls off a fly's wings, or tears open a bud to see what is in the flower, he tore at her privacy, at her very life, he would destroy her as an immature bud, torn open, is destroyed.

She might open towards him, a long while hence, in her dreams, when she was a pure spirit. But now she was not to be violated and ruined. She closed against him fiercely.

They climbed together, at evening, up the high slope, to see the sun set. In the finely breathing, keen wind they stood and watched the yellow sun sink in crimson and disappear. Then in the east the peaks and ridges glowed with living rose, incandescent like immortal flowers against a brown purple sky, a miracle, whilst down below the world was a bluish shadow, and above, like an annunciation, hovered a rosy transport in mid-air.

To her it was so beautiful, it was a delirium, she wanted to gather the glowing, eternal peaks to her breast, and die. He saw them, saw they were beautiful. But there arose no clamour in his breast, only a bitterness that was visionary in itself. He wished the peaks were grey and unbeautiful, so that she should not get her support from them. Why did she betray the two of them so terribly, in embracing the glow of the evening? Why did she leave him standing there, with the ice-wind blowing through his heart, like death, to gratify herself among the rosy snow-tips?

'What does the twilight matter?' he said. 'Why do you grovel before it? Is it so important to you?'

She winced in violation and in fury.

'Go away,' she cried, 'and leave me to it. It is beautiful, beautiful,' she sang in strange, rhapsodic tones. 'It is the most beautiful thing I have ever seen in my life. Don't try to come between it and me. Take yourself away, you are out of place—'

He stood back a little, and left her standing there, statue-like, transported into the mystic glowing east. Already the rose was fading, large white stars were flashing out. He waited. He would forgo everything but the yearning.

'That was the most perfect thing I have ever seen,' she said in cold, brutal tones, when at last she turned round to him. 'It amazes me that you should want to destroy it. If you can't see it yourself, why try to debar me?' But in reality, he had destroyed it for her, she was straining after a dead effect.

'One day,' he said, softly, looking up at her, 'I shall destroy *you*, as you stand looking at the sunset; because you are such a liar.'

There was a soft, voluptuous promise to himself in the words. She was chilled but arrogant.

'Ha!' she said. 'I am not afraid of your threats!'

She denied herself to him, she kept her room rigidly private to herself. But he waited on, in a curious patience, belonging to his yearning for her.

'In the end,' he said to himself with real voluptuous promise, 'when it reaches that point, I shall do away with her.' And he trembled delicately in every limb, in anticipation, as he trembled in his most violent accesses of passionate approach to her, trembling with too much desire.

She had a curious sort of allegiance with Loerke, all the while now, something insidious and traitorous. Gerald knew of it. But in the unnatural state of patience, and the unwillingness to harden himself against her, in which he found himself, he took no notice, although her soft kindliness to the other man, whom he hated as a noxious insect, made him shiver again with an access of the strange shuddering that came over him repeatedly.

He left her alone only when he went ski-ing, a sport he loved, and which she did not practise. Then he seemed to sweep out of life, to be a projectile into the beyond. And often, when he went away, she talked to the little German sculptor. They had an invariable topic, in their art.

They were almost of the same ideas. He hated Mestrovic, was not satisfied with the Futurists, he liked the West African wooden figures, the Aztec art, Mexican and Central American. He saw the grotesque, and a curious sort of mechanical motion intoxicated him, a confusion in nature. They had a curious game with each other, Gudrun and Loerke, of infinite suggestivity, strange and leering, as if they had some esoteric understanding of life, that they alone were initiated into the fearful central secrets, that the world dared not know. Their whole correspondence was in a strange, barely comprehensible suggestivity, they kindled themselves at the subtle lust of the Eygptians or the Mexicans. The whole game was one of subtle inter-suggestivity, and they wanted to keep it on the plane of suggestion. From their verbal and physical nuances they got the highest satisfaction in the nerves, from a queer interchange of half-suggested ideas, looks, expressions and gestures, which were quite intolerable, though incomprehensible, to Gerald. He had no terms in which to think of their commerce, his terms were much too gross.

The suggestion of primitive art was their refuge, and the inner mysteries of sensation their object of worship. Art and Life were to them the Reality and the Unreality.

'Of course,' said Gudrun, 'life doesn't *really* matter—it is one's art which is central. What one does in one's life has *peu de rapport,* it doesn't signify much.'

'Yes, that is so, exactly,' replied the sculptor. 'What one does in one's art, that is the breath of one's being. What one does in one's life, that is a bagatelle for the outsiders to fuss about.'

It was curious what a sense of elation and freedom Gudrun found in this communication. She felt established for ever. Of course Gerald was *bagatelle.* Love was one of the temporal things in her life, except in so far as she was an artist. She thought of Cleopatra—Cleopatra must have been an artist: she reaped the essential from a man, she harvested the ultimate sensation, and threw away the husk; and Mary Stuart, and the great Rachel, panting with her lovers after the theatre, these were the exoteric exponents of love. After all, what was the lover but fuel for the transport of this subtle knowledge, for a female art, the art of pure, perfect knowledge in sensuous understanding.

One evening Gerald was arguing with Loerke about Italy and Tripoli. The Englishman was in a strange, inflammable state, the German was excited. It was a contest of words, but it meant a conflict of spirit between the two men. And all the while Gudrun could see in Gerald an arrogant English contempt for a foreigner. Although Gerald was quivering, his eyes flashing, his face flushed, in his argument there was a brusqueness, a savage contempt in his manner, that made Gudrun's blood flare up, and made Loerke keen and mortified. For Gerald came down like a sledge-hammer with his assertions, anything the little German said was merely contemptible rubbish.

At last Loerke turned to Gudrun, raising his hands in helpless irony, a shrug of ironical dismissal, something appealing and child-like.

'Sehen Sie, gnädige Frau—' he began.

'Bitte sagen Sie nicht immer, gnädige Frau,' cried Gudrun, her eyes flashing, her cheeks burning. She looked like a vivid Medusa. Her voice was loud and clamorous, the other people in the room were startled.

'Please don't call me Mrs Crich,' she cried aloud.

The name, in Loerke's mouth particularly, had been an intolerable humiliation and constraint upon her these many days.

The two men looked at her in amazement. Gerald went white at the cheek-bones.

'What shall I say, then?' asked Loerke, with soft, mocking insinuation.

'Sagen Sie nur nicht das,' she muttered, her cheeks flushed crimson. 'Not that, at least.'

She saw, by the dawning look on Loerke's face, that he had understood. She was *not* Mrs Crich! So-o, that explained a great deal.

'Soll ich Fräulein sagen?' he asked malevolently.

'I am not married,' she said, with some hauteur.

Her heart was fluttering now, beating like a bewildered

bird. She knew she had dealt a cruel wound, and she could not bear it.

Gerald sat erect, perfectly still, his face pale and calm, like the face of a statue. He was unaware of her, or of Loerke or anybody. He sat perfectly still in an unalterable calm. Loerke, meanwhile, was crouching and glancing up from under his ducked head.

Gudrun was tortured for something to say, to relieve the suspense. She twisted her face in a smile and glanced knowingly, almost sneering, at Gerald.

'Truth is best,' she said to him, with a grimace.

But now again she was under his domination; now, because she had dealt him this blow; because she had destroyed him, and she did not know how he had taken it. She watched him. He was interesting to her. She had lost her interest in Loerke.

Gerald rose at length and went over in a leisurely still movement to the professor. The two began a conversation on Goethe.

She was rather piqued by the simplicity of Gerald's demeanour this evening. He did not seem angry or disgusted, only he looked curiously innocent and pure, really beautiful. Sometimes it came upon him, this look of clear distance, and it always fascinated her.

She waited, troubled throughout the evening. She thought he would avoid her, or give some sign. But he spoke to her simply and unemotionally, as he would to anyone else in the room. A certain peace, an abstraction possessed his soul.

She went to his room, hotly, violently in love with him. He was so beautiful and inaccessible. He kissed her, he was a lover to her. And she had extreme pleasure of him. But he did not come to, he remained remote and candid, unconscious. She wanted to speak to him. But this innocent, beautiful state of unconsciousness that had come upon him prevented her. She felt tormented and dark.

In the morning, however, he looked at her with a little aversion, some horror and some hatred darkening into his eyes. She withdrew on to her old ground. But still he would not gather himself together against her.

Loerke was waiting for her now. The little artist, isolated

in his own complete envelope, felt that here at last was a
woman from whom he could get something. He was uneasy
all the while, waiting to talk with her, subtly contriving to be
near her. Her presence filled him with keenness and excitement, he gravitated cunningly towards her, as if she had
some unseen force of attraction.

He was not in the least doubtful of himself, as regards
Gerald. Gerald was one of the outsiders. Loerke only hated
him for being rich and proud and of fine appearance. All
these things, however, riches, pride of social standing, handsome physique, were externals. When it came to the relation
with a woman such as Gudrun, he, Loerke, had an approach
and a power that Gerald never dreamed of.

How should Gerald hope to satisfy a woman of Gudrun's
calibre? Did he think that pride or masterful will or physical
strength would help him? Loerke knew a secret beyond
these things. The greatest power is the one that is subtle and
adjusts itself, not one which blindly attacks. And he, Loerke,
had understanding where Gerald was a calf. He, Loerke,
could penetrate into depths far out of Gerald's knowledge.
Gerald was left behind like a postulant in the ante-room of
his temple of mysteries, this woman. But he, Loerke, could
he not penetrate into the inner darkness, find the spirit of the
woman in its inner recess, and wrestle with it there, the central serpent that is coiled at the core of life?

What was it, after all, that a woman wanted? Was it mere
social effect, fulfillment of ambition in the social world, in
the community of mankind? Was it even a union in love and
goodness? Did she want 'goodness'? Who but a fool would
accept this of Gudrun? This was but the street view of her
wants. Cross the threshold, and you found her completely,
completely cynical about the social world at its advantages.
Once inside the house of her soul, and there was a pungent
atmosphere of corrosion, an inflamed darkness of sensation,
and a vivid, subtle, critical consciousness, that saw the world
distorted, horrific.

What then, what next? Was it sheer blind force of passion
that would satisfy her now? Not this, but the subtle thrills of
extreme sensation in reduction. It was an unbroken will reacting against her unbroken will in a myriad subtle thrills of

reduction, the last subtle activities of analysis and breaking down, carried out in the darkness of her, whilst the outside form, the individual, was utterly unchanged, even sentimental in its poses.

But between two particular people, any two people on earth, the range of pure sensational experience is limited. The climax of sensual reaction, once reached in any direction, is reached finally, there is no going on. There is only repetition possible, or the going apart of the two protagonists, or the subjugating of the one will to the other, or death.

Gerald had penetrated all the outer places of Gudrun's soul. He was to her the most crucial instance of the existing world, the *ne plus ultra* of the world of man as it existed for her. In him she knew the world, and had done with it. Knowing him finally she was the Alexander seeking new worlds. But there *were* no new worlds, there were no more *men*, there were only creatures, little, ultimate *creatures* like Loerke. The world was finished now, for her. There was only the inner, individual darkness, sensation within the ego, the obscene religious mystery of ultimate reduction, the mystic frictional activities of diabolic reducing down, disintegrating the vital organic body of life.

All this Gudrun knew in her subconsciousness, not in her mind. She knew her next step—she knew what she should move on to when she left Gerald. She was afraid of Gerald, that he might kill her. But she did not intend to be killed. A fine thread still united her to him. It should not be *her* death which broke it. She had farther to go, a farther, slow, exquisite experience to reap, unthinkable subtleties of sensation to know, before she was finished.

Of the last series of subtleties, Gerald was not capable. He could not touch the quick of her. But where his ruder blows could not penetrate, the fine, insinuating blade of Loerke's insect-like comprehension could. At least, it was time for her now to pass over to the other, the creature, the final craftsman. She knew that Loerke, in his innermost soul, was detached from everything, for him there was neither heaven nor earth nor hell. He admitted no allegiance, he gave no adherence anywhere. He was single and, by abstraction from the rest, absolute in himself.

Whereas in Gerald's soul there still lingered some attachment to the rest, to the whole. And this was his limitation. He was limited, *borné,* subject to his necessity, in the last issue, for goodness, for righteousness, for oneness with the ultimate purpose. That the ultimate purpose might be the perfect and subtle experience of the process of death, the will being kept unimpaired, that was not allowed in him. And this was his limitation.

There was a hovering triumph in Loerke, since Gudrun had denied her marriage with Gerald. The artist seemed to hover like a creature on the wing, waiting to settle. He did not approach Gudrun violently, he was never ill-timed. But carried on by a sure instinct in the complete darkness of his soul, he corresponded mystically with her, imperceptibly, but palpably.

For two days, he talked to her, continued the discussions of art, of life, in which they both found such pleasure. They praised the bygone things, they took a sentimental, childish delight in the achieved perfections of the past. Particularly they liked the late eighteenth century, the period of Goethe and of Shelley, and Mozart.

They played with the past, and with the great figures of the past, a sort of little game of chess, or marionettes, all to please themselves. They had all the great men for their marionettes, and they two were the God of the show, working it all. As for the future, that they never mentioned except one laughed out some mocking dream of the destruction of the world by a ridiculous catastrophe of man's invention: a man invented such a perfect explosive that it blew the earth in two, and the two halves set off in different directions through space, to the dismay of the inhabitants: or else the people of the world divided into two halves, and each half decided *it* was perfect and right, the other half was wrong and must be destroyed; so another end of the world. Or else, Loerke's dream of fear, the world went cold, and snow fell everywhere, and only white creatures, Polar bears, white foxes, and men like awful white snow-birds, persisted in ice cruelty.

Apart from these stories, they never talked of the future. They delighted almost either in mocking imaginations of destruction or in sentimental, fine marionette shows of the past. It was a sentimental delight to reconstruct the world of Goethe at Weimar, or of Schiller and poverty and faithful love, or to see again Jean-Jacques in his quakings, or Voltaire at Ferney, or Frederick the Great reading his own poetry.

They talked together for hours, of literature and sculpture and painting, amusing themselves with Flaxman and Blake and Fuseli, with tenderness, and with Feuerbach and Böcklin. It would take them a lifetime, they felt, to live again, *in petto,* the lives of the great artists. But they preferred to stay in the eighteenth and the nineteenth centuries.

They talked in a mixture of languages. The ground-work was French, in either case. But he ended most of his sentences in a stumble of English and a conclusion of German, she skillfully wove herself to her end in whatever phrase came to her. She took a peculiar delight in this conversation. It was full of odd, fantastic expression, of double meanings, of evasions, of suggestive vagueness. It was a real physical pleasure to her to make this thread of conversation out of the different-coloured strands of three languages.

And all the while they two were hovering, hesitating round the flame of some invisible declaration. He wanted it, but was held back by some inevitable reluctance. She wanted it also, but she wanted to put it off, to put it off indefinitely, she still had some pity for Gerald, some connexion with him. And the most fatal of all, she had the reminiscent sentimental compassion for herself in connexion with him. Because of what *had* been, she felt herself held to him by immortal, invisible threads—because of what *had* been, because of his coming to her that first night, into her own house, in his extremity, because—

Gerald was gradually overcome with a revulsion of loathing for Loerke. He did not take the man seriously, he despised him merely, except as he felt in Gudrun's veins the influence of the little creature. It was this that drove Gerald wild, the feeling in Gudrun's veins of Loerke's presence, Loerke's being, flowing dominant through her.

'What makes you so smitten with that little vermin?' he asked, really puzzled. For he, man-like, could not see anything attractive or important *at all* in Loerke. Gerald expected to find some handsomeness or nobleness to account for a woman's subjection. But he saw none here, only an insect-like repulsiveness.

Gudrun flushed deeply. It was these attacks she would never forgive.

'What do you mean?' she replied. 'My God, what a mercy I am *not* married to you!'

Her voice of flouting and contempt scotched him. He was brought up short. But he recovered himself.

'Tell me, only tell me,' he reiterated in a dangerous, narrowed voice—'tell me what it is that fascinates you in him.'

'I am not fascinated,' she said, with cold, repelling innocence.

'Yes, you are. You are fascinated by that little dry snake, like a bird gaping ready to fall down its throat.'

She looked at him with black fury.

'I don't choose to be discussed by you,' she said.

'It doesn't matter whether you choose or not,' he replied, 'that doesn't alter the fact that you are ready to fall down and kiss the feet of that little insect. And I don't want to prevent you—do it, fall down and kiss his feet. But I want to know what it is that fascinates you—what is it?'

She was silent, suffused with black rage.

'How *dare* you come brow-beating me,' she cried, 'how dare you, you little squire, you bully. What right have you over me, do you think?'

His face was white and gleaming, she knew by the light in his eyes that she was in his power—the wolf. And because she was in his power, she hated him with a power that she wondered did not kill him. In her will she killed him as he stood, effaced him.

'It is not a question of right,' said Gerald, sitting down on a chair. She watched the change in his body. She saw his clenched, mechanical body moving there like an obsession. Her hatred of him was tingled with fatal contempt.

'It's not a question of my right over you—though I *have* some right, remember. I want to know, I only want to know what it is that subjugates you to that little scum of a sculptor downstairs, what it is that brings you down like a humble maggot, in worship of him. I want to know what you creep after.'

She stood over against the window, listening. Then she turned round.

'Do you?' she said, in her most easy, most cutting voice. 'Do you want to know what it is in him? It's because he has some understanding of a woman, because he is not stupid. That's why it is.'

A queer, sinister, animal-like smile came over Gerald's face.

'But what understanding is it?' he said. 'The understanding of a flea, a hopping flea with a proboscis. Why should you crawl abject before the understanding of a flea?'

There passed through Gudrun's mind Blake's representation of the soul of a flea. She wanted to fit it to Loerke. Blake was a clown too. But it was necessary to answer Gerald.

'Don't you think the understanding of a flea is more interesting than the understanding of a fool?' she asked.

'A fool!' he repeated.

'A fool, a conceited fool—a *Dummkopf*,' she replied, adding the German word.

'Do you call me a fool?' he replied. 'Well, wouldn't I rather be the fool I am than that flea downstairs?'

She looked at him. A certain blunt, blind stupidity in him palled on her soul, limiting her.

'You give yourself away by that last,' she said.

He sat and wondered.

'I shall go away soon,' he said.

She turned on him.

'Remember,' she said, 'I am completely independent of you—completely. You make your arrangements, I make mine.'

He pondered this.

'You mean we are strangers from this minute?' he asked.

She halted and flushed. He was putting her in a trap, forcing her hand. She turned round on him.

'Strangers,' she said, 'we can never be. But if you *want* to make any movement apart from me, then I wish you to know you are perfectly free to do so. Do not consider me in the slightest.'

Even so slight an implication that she needed him and was depending on him still was sufficient to rouse his passion. As he sat a change came over his body, the hot, molten stream mounted involuntarily through his veins. He groaned inwardly, under its bondage, but he loved it. He looked at her with clear eyes, waiting for her.

She knew at once, and was shaken with cold revulsion. *How* could he look at her with those clear, warm, waiting eyes, waiting for her, even now? What had been said between them, was it not enough to put them worlds asunder, to freeze them for ever apart! And yet he was all transfused and roused, waiting for her.

It confused her. Turning her head aside, she said:

'I shall always *tell* you, whenever I am going to make any change—'

And with this she moved out of the room.

He sat suspended in a fine recoil of disappointment, that seemed gradually to be destroying his understanding. But the unconscious state of patience persisted in him. He remained motionless, without thought or knowledge, for a long time. Then he rose and went downstairs to play at chess with one of the students. His face was open and clear, with a certain innocent *laisser-aller* that troubled Gudrun most, made her almost afraid of him, whilst she disliked him deeply for it.

It was after this that Loerke, who had never yet spoken to her personally, began to ask her of her state.

'You are not married at all, are you?' he asked.

She looked full at him.

'Not in the least,' she replied, in her measured way. Loerke laughed, wrinkling up his face oddly. There was a thin wisp of his hair straying on his forehead, she noticed that his skin was of a clear brown colour, his hands, his wrists. And his hands seemed closely prehensile. He seemed like topaz, so strangely brownish and pellucid.

'Good,' he said.

Still it needed some courage for him to go on.

'Was Mrs Birkin your sister?' he asked.

'Yes.'

'And she *was* married?'

'She was married.'

'Have you parents, then?'

'Yes,' said Gudrun, 'we have parents.'

And she told him, briefly, laconically, her position. He watched her closely, curiously, all the while.

'So!' he exclaimed, with some surprise. 'And the Herr Crich, is he rich?'

'Yes, he is rich, a coal owner.'

'How long has your friendship with him lasted?'

'Some months.'

There was a pause.

'Yes, I am surprised,' he said at length. 'The English, I thought they were so—cold. And what do you think to do when you leave here?'

'What do I think to do?' she repeated.

'Yes. You cannot go back to the teaching. No'—he shrugged his shoulders—'that is impossible. Leave that to the *canaille* who can do nothing else. You, for your part— you know, you are a remarkable woman, *eine seltsame Frau*. Why deny it—why make any question of it? You are an extraordinary woman, why should you follow the ordinary course, the ordinary life?'

Gudrun sat looking at her hands, flushed. She was pleased that he said, so simply, that she was a remarkable woman. He would not say that to flatter her—he was far too self-opinionated and objective by nature. He said it as he would say a piece of sculpture was remarkable, because he knew it was so.

And it gratified her to hear it from him. Other people had such a passion to make everything of one degree, of one pattern. In England it was chic to be perfectly ordinary. And it was a relief to her to be acknowledged extraordinary. Then she need not fret about the common standards.

'You see,' she said, 'I have no money whatsoever.'

'Ach, money!' he cried, lifting his shoulders. 'When one is grown up, money is lying about at one's service. It is only

when one is young that it is rare. Take no thought for
money—that always lies to hand.'

'Does it?' she said, laughing.

'Always. The Gerald will give you a sum if you ask him
for it—'

She flushed deeply.

'I will ask anybody else,' she said, with some difficulty—
'but not him.'

Loerke looked closely at her.

'Good,' he said. 'Then let it be somebody else. Only don't
go back to that England, that school. No, that is stupid.'

Again there was a pause. He was afraid to ask her outright
to go with him, he was not even quite sure he wanted her;
and she was afraid to be asked. He begrudged his own isolation, was *very* chary of sharing his life, even for a day.

'The only other place I know is Paris,' she said, 'and I
can't stand that.'

She looked with her wide, steady eyes full at Loerke. He
lowered his head and averted his face.

'Paris, no!' he said. 'Between the *religion d'amour,* and
the latest 'ism, and the new turning to Jesus, one had better
ride on a carrousel all day. But come to Dresden. I have a
studio there—I can give you work—oh, that would be easy
enough. I haven't seen any of your things, but I believe in
you. Come to Dresden—that is a fine town to be in, and as
good a life as you can expect of a town. You have everything there, without the foolishness of Paris or the beer of
Munich.'

He sat and looked at her coldly. What she liked about him
was that he spoke to her simple and flat, as to himself. He
was a fellow craftsman, a fellow being to her, first.

'No—Paris,' he resumed, 'it makes me sick. Pah—
l'amour. I detest it. *L'amour, l'amore, die Liebe*—I detest it
in every language. Women and love, there is no greater tedium,' he cried.

She was slightly offended. And yet this was her own basic
feeling. Men and love—there was no greater tedium.

'I think the same,' she said.

'A bore,' he repeated. 'What does it matter whether I
wear this hat or another. So love. I needn't wear a hat at all,

only for convenience. Neither need I love except for convenience. I tell you what, *gnadige Frau*—' and he leaned towards her—then he made a quick, odd gesture, as of striking
something aside—'*gnadiges Fraulein,* never mind—I tell
you what, I would give everything, everything, all your love,
for a little companionship in intelligence—' his eyes flickered darkly, evilly at her. 'You understand?' he asked, with
a faint smile. 'It wouldn't matter if she were a hundred years
old, a thousand—it would be all the same to me, so that she
can *understand.*' He shut his eyes with a little snap.

Again Gudrun was rather offended. Did he not think her
good-looking, then? Suddenly she laughed.

'I shall have to wait about eighty years to suit you at that,'
she said. 'I am ugly enough, aren't I?'

He looked at her with an artist's sudden, critical, estimating eye.

'You are beautiful,' he said, 'and I am glad of it. But it
isn't that—it isn't that,' he cried, with emphasis that flattered her. 'It is that you have a certain wit, it is the kind of
understanding. For me, I am little, *chétif,* insignificant.
Good! Do not ask me to be strong and handsome, then. But
it is the *me*'—he put his fingers to his mouth oddly—'it is
the *me* that is looking for a mistress, and my *me* is waiting
for the *thee* of the mistress, for the match to my particular
intelligence. You understand?'

'Yes,' she said, 'I understand.'

'As for the other, this *amour*'—he made a gesture, dash-
ing his hand aside, as if to dash away something
troublesome—'it is unimportant, unimportant. Does it matter
whether I drink white wine this evening or whether I drink
nothing? It *does not matter,* it does not matter. So this love,
this *amour,* this *baiser.* Yes or no, *soit ou soit pas,* today, tomorrow, or never, it is all the same, it does not matter—no
more than the white wine.'

He ended with an odd dropping of the head in a desperate
negation. Gudrun watched him steadily. She had gone pale.

Suddenly she stretched over and seized his hand in her
own.

'That is true,' she said, in rather a high, vehement voice,
'that is true for me too. It is the understanding that matters.'

He looked up at her almost frightened, furtive. Then he nodded a little sullenly. She let go his hand: he had made not the lightest response. And they sat in silence.

'Do you know,' he said, suddenly looking at her with dark, self-important, prophetic eyes, 'your fate and mine, they will run together till—' and he broke off in a little grimace.

'Till when?' she asked, blanched, her lips going white. She was terribly susceptible to these evil prognostications, but he only shook his head.

'I don't know,' he said, 'I don't know.'

Gerald did not come in from his ski-ing until nightfall, he missed the coffee and cake that she took at four o'clock. The snow was in perfect condition, he had travelled a long way, by himself, among the snow ridges, on his skis, he had climbed high, so high that he could see over the top of the pass five miles distant, could see the Marienhütte, the hostel on the crest of the pass, half buried in snow, and over into the deep valley beyond, to the dusk of the pine trees. One could go that way home; but he shuddered with nausea at the thought of home;—one could travel on skis down there, and come to the old imperial road, below the pass. But why come to any road? He revolted at the thought of finding himself in the world again. He must stay up there in the snow for ever. He had been happy by himself, high up there alone, travelling swiftly on skis, taking far flights and skimming past the dark rocks veined with brilliant snow.

But he felt something icy gathering at his heart. This strange mood of patience and innocence which had persisted in him for some days was passing away, he would be left again a prey to the horrible passions and tortures.

So he came down reluctantly, snow-burned, snow-estranged, to the house in the hollow, between the knuckles of the mountain-tops. He saw its lights shining yellow, and he held back, wishing he need not go in to confront those people, to hear the turmoil of voices and to feel the confusion of other presences. He was isolated as if there were a vacuum round his heart, or a sheath of pure ice.

The moment he saw Gudrun something jolted in his soul. She was looking rather lofty and superb, smiling slowly and

graciously to the Germans. A sudden desire leapt in his heart
to kill her. He thought, what a perfect voluptuous fulfilment
it would be to kill her. His mind was absent all the evening,
estranged by the snow and his passion. But he kept the idea
constant within him, what a perfect voluptuous consummation it would be to strangle her, to strangle every spark of
life out of her, till she lay completely inert, soft, relaxed for
ever, a soft heap lying dead between his hands, utterly dead.
Then he would have had her finally and for ever; there
would be such a perfect voluptuous finality.

Gudrun was unaware of what he was feeling, he seemed
so quiet and amiable, as usual. His amiability even made her
feel brutal towards him.

She went into his room when he was partially undressed.
She did not notice the curious, glad gleam of pure hatred,
with which he looked at her. She stood near the door, with
her hand behind her.

'I have been thinking, Gerald,' she said, with an insulting
nonchalance, 'that I shall not go back to England.'

'Oh,' he said, 'where will you go then?'

But she ignored his question. She had her own logical
statement to make, and it must be made as she had thought
it.

'I can't see the use of going back,' she continued. 'It is
over between me and you——'

She paused for him to speak. But he said nothing. He was
only talking to himself, saying: 'Over, is it? I believe it is
over. But it isn't finished. Remember, it isn't finished. We
must put some sort of a finish on it. There must be a conclusion, there must be finality.'

So he talked to himself, but aloud he said nothing whatever.

'What has been, has been,' she continued. 'There is nothing
that I regret. I hope you regret nothing——'

She waited for him to speak.

'Oh, I regret nothing,' he said, accommodatingly.

'Good then,' she answered, 'good then. Then neither of us
cherishes any regrets, which is as it should be.'

'Quite as it should be,' he said aimlessly.

She paused to gather up her thread again.

'Our attempt has been a failure,' she said. 'But we can try again elsewhere.'

A little flicker of rage ran through his blood. It was as if she were rousing him, goading him. Why must she do it?

'Attempt at what?' he asked.

'At being lovers, I suppose,' she said, a little baffled, yet so trivial she made it all seem.

'Our attempt at being lovers has been a failure?' he repeated aloud.

To himself he was saying, 'I ought to kill her here. There is only this left, for me to kill her.' A heavy, overcharged desire to bring about her death possessed him. She was unaware.

'Hasn't it?' she asked. 'Do you think it has been a success?'

Again the insult of the flippant question ran through his blood like a current of fire.

'It had some of the elements of success, our relationship,' he replied. 'It—might have come off.'

But he paused before concluding the last phrase. Even as he began the sentence, he did not believe in what he was going to say. He knew it never could have been a success.

'No,' she replied. 'You cannot love.'

'And you?' he asked.

Her wide, dark-filled eyes were fixed on him like two moons of darkness.

'I couldn't love *you*,' she said, with stark, cold truth.

A blinding flash went over his brain, his body jolted. His heart had burst into flame. His consciousness was gone into his wrists, into his hands. He was one blind, incontinent desire to kill her. His wrists were bursting, there would be no satisfaction till his hands had closed on her.

But even before his body swerved forward on her, a sudden, cunning comprehension was expressed on her face, and in a flash she was out of the door. She ran in one flash to her room and locked herself in. She was afraid, but confident. She knew her life trembled on the edge of an abyss. But she was curiously sure of her footing. She knew her cunning could outwit him.

She trembled, as she stood in her room, with excitement

and awful exhilaration. She knew she could outwit him. She could depend on her presence of mind, and on her wits. But it was a fight to the death, she knew it now. One slip, and she was lost. She had a strange, tense, exhilarated sickness in her body, as one who is in peril of falling from a great height, but who does not look down, does not admit the fear.

'I will go away the day after tomorrow,' she said.

She only did not want Gerald to think that she was afraid of him, that she was running away because she was afraid of him. She was not afraid of him, fundamentally. She knew it was her safeguard to avoid his physical violence. But even physically she was not afraid of him. She wanted to prove it to him. When she had proved it, that, whatever he was, she was not afraid of him; when she had proved *that,* she could leave him for ever. But meanwhile the fight between them, terrible as she knew it to be, was inconclusive. And she wanted to be confident in herself. However many terrors she might have, she would be unafraid, uncowed by him. He could never cow her, nor dominate her, nor have any right over her; this she would maintain until she had proved it. Once it was proved, she was free of him for ever.

But she had not proved it yet, neither to him nor to herself. And this was what still bound her to him. She was bound to him, she could not live beyond him. She sat up in bed, closely wrapped up, for many hours, thinking endlessly to herself. It was as if she would never have done weaving the great provision of her thoughts.

'It isn't as if he really loved me,' she said to herself. 'He doesn't. Every woman he comes across he wants to make her in love with him. He doesn't even know that he is doing it. But there he is, before every woman he unfurls his male attractiveness, displays his great desirability, he tries to make every woman think how wonderful it would be to have him for a lover. His very ignoring of the women is part of the game. He is never *unconscious* of them. He should have been a cockerel, so he could strut before fifty females, all his subjects. But really, his Don Juan does *not* interest me. I could play Dona Juanita a million times better than he plays Juan. He bores me, you know. His maleness bores me. Nothing is so boring, so inherently stupid and stupidly conceited.

Really, the fathomless conceit of these men, it is ridiculous—the little strutters.

'They are all alike. Look at Birkin. Built out of the limitation of conceit they are, and nothing else. Really, nothing but their ridiculous limitation and intrinsic insignificance could make them so conceited.

'As for Loerke, there is a thousand times more in him than in Gerald. Gerald is so limited, there is a dead end to him. He would grind on at the old mills for ever. And really, there is no corn between the millstones any more. They grind on and on, when there is nothing to grind—saying the same things, believing the same things, acting the same things. Oh, my God, it would wear out the patience of a stone.

'I don't worship Loerke, but at any rate, he is a free individual. He is not stiff with conceit of his own maleness. He is not grinding dutifully at the old mills. Oh God, when I think of Gerald, and his work—those offices at Beldover, and the mines—it makes my heart sick. What *have* I to do with it—and him thinking he can be a lover to a woman! One might as well ask it of a self-satisfied lamp-post. These men, with their eternal jobs—and their eternal mills of God that keep on grinding at nothing! It is too boring, just boring. However did I come to take them seriously at all!

'At least in Dresden, one will have one's back to it all. And there will be amusing things to do. It will be amusing to go to these eurhythmic displays, and the German opera, the German theatre. It *will* be amusing to take part in German Bohemian life. And Loerke *is* an artist, he is a free individual. One will escape from so much, that is the chief thing, escape so much hideous boring repetition of vulgar actions, vulgar phrases, vulgar postures. I don't delude myself that I shall find an elixir of life in Dresden. I know I shan't. But I shall get away from people who have their own homes and their own children and their own acquaintances and their own this and their own that. I shall be among people who *don't* own things and who haven't got a home and a domestic servant in the background, who *haven't* got a standing and a status and a degree and a circle of friends of the same. Oh God, the wheels within wheels of people, it makes one's head tick like a clock, with a very madness of dead mechanical monotony and meaninglessness. How I *hate* life, how I hate it. How I hate the Geralds, that they can offer one nothing else.

'Shortlands!—Heavens! Think of living there, one week, then the next, and *then the third*—

'No, I won't think of it—it is too much—'

And she broke off, really terrified, really unable to bear any more.

The thought of the mechanical succession of day following day, day following day, *ad infinitum,* was one of the things that made her heart palpitate with a real approach of madness. The terrible bondage of this tick-tack of time, this twitching of the hands of the clock, this eternal repetition of hours and days—oh God, it was too awful to contemplate. And there was no escape from it, no escape.

She almost wished Gerald were with her to save her from the terror of her own thoughts. Oh, how she suffered, lying there alone, confronted by the terrible clock, with its eternal tick-tack. All life, all life resolved itself into this: tick-tack, tick-tack, tick-tack; then the striking of the hour; then the tick-tack, tick-tack, and the twitching of the clock-fingers.

Gerald could not save her from it. He, his body, his motion, his life—it was the same ticking, the same twitching across the dial, a horrible mechanical twitching forward over the face of the hours. What were his kisses, his embraces. She could hear their tick-tack, tick-tack.

Ha—ha—she laughed to herself, so frightened that she was trying to laugh it off—ha—ha, how maddening it was, to be sure, to be sure!

Then, with a fleeting self-conscious motion, she wondered if she would be very much surprised, on rising in the morning, to realize that her hair had turned white. She had *felt* it turning white so often, under the intolerable burden of her thoughts, and her sensations. Yet there it remained, brown as ever, and there she was herself, looking a picture of health.

Perhaps she was healthy. Perhaps it was only her unabateable health that left her so exposed to the truth. If she were sickly she would have her illusions, imaginations.

As it was, there was no escape. She must always see and know and never escape. She could never escape. There she was, placed before the clock-face of life. And if she turned round as in a railway station, to look at the bookstall, still she could see, with her very spine, she could see the clock, always the great white clock-face. In vain she fluttered the leaves of books, or made statuettes in clay. She knew she was not *really* reading. She was not *really* working. She was watching the fingers twitch across the eternal, mechanical, monotonous clock-face of time. She never really lived, she only watched. Indeed, she was like a little, twelve-hour clock, vis-à-vis with the enormous clock of eternity—there she was, like Dignity and Impudence, or Impudence and Dignity.

The picture pleased her. Didn't her face really look like a clock dial—rather roundish and often pale, and impassive. She would have got up to look in the mirror, but the thought of the sight of her own face, that was like a twelve-hour clock dial, filled her with such deep terror, that she hastened to think of something else.

Oh, why wasn't somebody kind to her? Why wasn't there somebody who would take her in their arms, and hold her to their breast, and give her rest, pure, deep, healing rest. Oh, why wasn't there somebody to take her in their arms and fold her safe and perfect, for sleep. She wanted so much this perfect enfolded sleep. She lay always so unsheathed in sleep. She would lie always unsheathed in sleep, unrelieved, unsaved. Oh, how could she bear it, this endless unrelief, this eternal unrelief.

Gerald! Could he fold her in his arms and sheathe her in sleep? Ha! He needed putting to sleep himself—poor Gerald. That was all he needed. What did he do, he made the burden for her greater, the burden of her sleep was the more intolerable, when he was there. He was an added weariness upon her unripening nights, her unfruitful slumbers. Perhaps he got some repose from her. Perhaps he did. Perhaps this was what he was always dogging her for, like a child that is famished, crying for the breast. Perhaps this was the secret of his passion, his for ever unquenched desire for her—that he needed her to put him to sleep, to give him repose.

What then! Was she his mother? Had she asked for a child, whom she must nurse through the nights, for her lover. She despised him, she despised him, she hardened her heart. An infant crying in the night, this Don Juan.

Ooh, but how she hated the infant crying in the night. She would murder it gladly. She would stifle it and bury it, as Hetty Sorrell did. No doubt Hetty Sorrell's infant cried in the night—no doubt Arthur Donnithorne's infant would. Ha—the Arthur Donnithornes, the Geralds of this world. So manly by day, yet all the while, such a crying of infants in the night. Let them turn into mechanisms, let them. Let them become instruments, pure machines, pure wills, that work like clockwork, in perpetual repetition. Let them be this, let them be taken up entirely in their work, let them be perfect parts of a great machine, having a slumber of constant repetition. Let Gerald manage his firm. There he would be satisfied, as satisfied as a wheel-barrow that goes backwards and forwards along a plank all day—she had seen it.

The wheel-barrow—the one humble wheel—the unit of the firm. Then the cart, with two wheels; then the truck, with four; then the donkey-engine, with eight, then the winding-engine, with sixteen, and so on, till it came to the miner, with a thousand wheels, and then the electrician, with three thousand, and the underground manager, with twenty thousand, and the general manager with a hundred thousand little wheels working away to complete his make-up, and then Gerald, with a million wheels and cogs and axles.

Poor Gerald, such a lot of little wheels to his make-up! He was more intricate than a chronometer-watch! But oh heavens, what weariness! What weariness, God above! A chronometer-watch—a beetle—her soul fainted with utter ennui, from the thought. So many wheels to count and consider and calculate! Enough, enough—there was an end to man's capacity for complications, even. Or perhaps there was no end.

Meanwhile Gerald sat in his room, reading. When Gudrun was gone, he was left stupefied with arrested desire. He sat on the side of the bed for an hour, stupefied, little strands of consciousness appearing and reappearing. But he did not move, for a long time he remained inert, his head dropped on his breast.

Then he looked up and realized that he was going to bed. He was cold. Soon he was lying down in the dark.

But what he could not bear was the darkness. The solid darkness confronting him drove him mad. So he rose, and made a light. He remained seated for a while, staring in front. He did not think of Gudrun, he did not think of anything.

Then suddenly he went downstairs for a book. He had all his life been in terror of the nights that should come, when he could not sleep. He knew that his would be too much for him, to have to face nights of sleeplessness and of horrified watching the hours.

So he sat for hours in bed, like a statue, reading. His mind, hard and acute, read on rapidly, his body understood nothing. In a state of rigid unconsciousness, he read on through the night, till morning, when, weary and disgusted in spirit, disgusted most of all with himself, he slept for two hours.

Then he got up, hard and full of energy. Gudrun scarcely spoke to him, except at coffee when she said:

'I shall be leaving tomorrow.'

'We will go together as far as Innsbruck, for appearance's sake?' he asked.

She said 'Perhaps' between the sips of her coffee. And the sound of her taking her breath in the word, was nauseous to him. He rose quickly to be away from her.

He went and made arrangements for the departure on the morrow. Then, taking some food, he set out for the day on the skis. Perhaps, he said to the Wirt, he would go up to the Marienhütte, perhaps to the village below.

To Gudrun this day was full of a promise like spring. She felt an approaching release, a new fountain of life rising up in her. It gave her pleasure to dawdle through her packing, it gave her pleasure to dip into books, to try on her different garments, to look at herself in the glass. She felt a new lease of life was come upon her, and she was happy like a child, very attractive and beautiful to everybody, with her soft, luxuriant figure, and her happiness. Yet underneath was death itself.

In the afternoon she had to go out with Loerke. Her to-morrow was perfectly vague before her. This was what gave her pleasure. She might be going to England with Gerald, she might be going to Dresden with Loerke, she might be going to Munich, to a girl-friend she had there. Anything might come to pass on the morrow. And today was the white, snowy iridescent threshold of all possibility. All possibility—that was the charm to her, the lovely, iridescent, indefinite charm—pure illusion. All possibility—because death was inevitable, and *nothing* was possible but death.

She did not want things to materialize, to take any definite shape. She wanted, suddenly, at one moment of the journey tomorrow, to be wafted into an utterly new course, by some utterly unforeseen event, or motion. So that, although she wanted to go out with Loerke for the last time into the snow, she did not want to be serious or business-like.

And Loerke was not a serious figure. In his brown velvet cap, that made his head as round as a chestnut, with the brown velvet flaps loose and wild over his ears, and a wisp of elf-like, thin black hair blowing above his full, elf-like dark eyes, the shiny, transparent brown skin crinkling up into odd grimaces on his small-featured face, he looked an odd little boy-man, a bat. But in his figure, in the greeny lo-den suit, he looked *chétif* and puny, still strangely different from the rest.

He had taken a little toboggan, for the two of them, and they trudged between the blinding slopes of snow, that burned their now hardening faces, laughing in an endless se-quence of quips and jests and polyglot fancies. The fancies were the reality to both of them, they were both so happy, tossing about the little coloured balls of verbal humour and whimsicality. Their natures seemed to sparkle in full inter-play, they were enjoying a pure game. And they wanted to keep it on the level of a game, their relationship: *such* a fine game.

Loerke did not take the tobogganing very seriously. He put no fire and intensity into it, as Gerald did. Which pleased Gudrun. She was weary, oh so weary of Gerald's gripped intensity of physical motion. Loerke let the sledge go wildly, and gaily, like a flying leaf, and when, at a bend, he pitched both her and him out into the snow, he only waited for them both to pick themselves up unhurt off the keen white ground, to be laughing and pert as a pixie. She knew he would be making ironical, playful remarks as he wandered in hell—if he were in the humour. And that pleased her immensely. It seemed like a rising above the dreariness of actuality, the monotony of contingencies.

They played till the sun went down, in pure amusement careless and timeless. Then, as the little sledge twirled riskily to rest at the bottom of the slope:

'Wait!' he said suddenly, and he produced from somewhere a large thermos flask, a packet of Keks, and a bottle of Schnapps.

'Oh, Loerke,' she cried. 'What an inspiration! What a *comble de joie* indeed! What is the Schnapps?'

He looked at it, and laughed.

'*Heidelbeer!*' he said.

'No! From the billberries under the snow. Doesn't it look as if it were distilled from snow. Can you—' she sniffed, and sniffed at the bottle—'can you smell billberries? Isn't it wonderful? It is exactly as if one could smell them through the snow.'

She stamped her foot lightly on the ground. He kneeled down and whistled, and put his ear to the snow. As he did so his black eyes twinkled up.

'Ha! Ha!' she laughed, warmed by the whimsical way in which he mocked at her verbal extravagances. He was always teasing her, mocking her ways. But as he in his mockery was even more absurd than she in her extravagancies, what could one do but laugh and feel liberated.

She could feel their voices, hers and his, ringing silvery like bells in the frozen motionless air of the first twilight. How perfect it was, how *very* perfect it was, this silvery isolation and interplay.

She sipped the hot coffee, whose fragrance flew around them like bees murmuring around flowers, in the snowy air, she drank tiny sips of the *Heidelbeerwasser,* she ate the cold, sweet, creamy wafers. How good everything was! How perfect everything tasted and smelled and sounded, here in this utter stillness of snow and falling twilight.

'You are going away tomorrow?' his voice came at last.

'Yes.'

There was a pause, when the evening seemed to rise in its silent, ringing pallor infinitely high, to the infinite which was near at hand.

'*Wobin?*'

That was the question—*wobin?* Whither? *Wobin?* What a lovely word! She *never* wanted it answered. Let it chime for ever.

'I don't know,' she said, smiling at him.

He caught the smile from her.

'One never does,' he said.

'One never does,' she repeated.

There was a silence, wherein he ate biscuits rapidly, as a rabbit eats leaves.

'But,' he laughed, 'where will you take a ticket to?'

'Oh heaven!' she cried. 'One must take a ticket.'

Here was a blow. She saw herself at the wicket, at the railway station. Then a relieving thought came to her. She breathed freely.

'But one needn't go,' she cried.

'Certainly not,' he said.

'I mean one needn't go where one's ticket says.'

That struck him. One might take a ticket, so as not to travel to the destination it indicated. One might break off, and avoid the destination. A point located. That was an idea!

'Then take a ticket to London,' he said. 'One should never go there.'

'Right,' she answered.

He poured a little coffee into a tin can.

'You won't tell me where you will go?' he asked.

'Really and truly,' she said, 'I don't know. It depends which way the wind blows.'

He looked at her quizzically, then he pursed up his lips, like Zephyrus, blowing across the snow.

'It goes towards Germany,' he said.

'I believe so,' she laughed.

Suddenly, they were aware of a vague white figure near

them. It was Gerald. Gudrun's heart leapt in sudden terror, profound terror. She rose to her feet.

'They told me where you were,' came Gerald's voice, like a judgement in the whitish air of twilight.

'*Maria!* You come like a ghost,' exclaimed Loerke.

Gerald did not answer. His presence was unnatural and ghostly to them.

Loerke shook the flask—then he held it inverted over the snow. Only a few brown drops trickled out.

'All gone!' he said.

To Gerald, the smallish, odd figure of the German was distinct and objective, as if seen through field glasses. And he disliked the small figure exceedingly, he wanted it removed.

Then Loerke rattled the box which held the biscuits.

'Biscuits there are still,' he said.

And reaching from his seated posture in the sledge, he handed them to Gudrun. She fumbled, and took one. He would have held them to Gerald, but Gerald so definitely did not want to be offered a biscuit, that Loerke, rather vaguely, put the box inside. Then he took up the small bottle and held it to the light.

'Also there is some Schnapps,' he said to himself.

Then suddenly, he elevated the bottle gallantly in the air, a strange, grotesque figure leaning towards Gudrun, and said:

'*Gnädiges Fräulein,*' he said, '*wobl—*'

There was a crack, the bottle was flying, Loerke had started back, the three stood quivering in violent emotion.

Loerke turned to Gerald, a devilish leer on his bright-skinned face.

'Well done!' he said, in a satirical demoniac frenzy. '*C'est le sport, sans doute.*'

The next instant he was sitting ludicrously in the snow, Gerald's fist having rung against the side of his head. But Loerke pulled himself together, rose, quivering, looking full at Gerald, his body weak and furtive, but his eyes demoniacal with satire.

'*Vive le héros, vive—*'

But he flinched as, in a black flash, Gerald's fist came

upon him, banged into the other side of his head, and sent him aside like a broken straw.

But Gudrun moved forward. She raised her clenched hand high, and brought it down, with a great downward stroke on to the face and on to the breast of Gerald.

A great astonishment burst upon him, as if the air had broken. Wide, wide his soul opened, in wonder, feeling the pain. Then it laughed, turning, with strong hands outstretched, at last to take the apple of his desire. At last he could finish his desire.

He took the throat of Gudrun between his hands, that were hard and indomitably powerful. And her throat was beautifully, so beautifully soft, save that, within, he could feel the slippery cords of her life. And this he crushed, this he could crush. What bliss! Oh what bliss, at last, what satisfaction, at last! The pure zest of satisfaction filled his soul. He was watching the unconsciousness come into her swollen face, watching the eyes roll back. How ugly she was! What a fulfillment, what a satisfaction! How good this was, oh how good it was, what a God-given gratification, at last! He was unconscious of her fighting and struggling. The struggling was her reciprocal lustful passion in this embrace, the more violent it became, the greater the frenzy of delight, till the zenith was reached, the crisis, the struggle was overborne, her movement became softer, appeased.

Loerke roused himself on the snow, too dazed and hurt to get up. Only his eyes were conscious.

'*Monsieur!*' he said, in his thin, roused voice: '*Quand vous aurez fini—*'

A revulsion of contempt and disgust came over Gerald's soul. The disgust went to the very bottom of him, a nausea. Ah, what was he doing, to what depths was he letting himself go! As if he cared about her enough to kill her, to have her life on his hands!

A weakness ran over his body, a terrible relaxing, a thaw, a decay of strength. Without knowing, he had let go his grip, and Gudrun had fallen to her knees. Must he see, must he know?

A fearful weakness possessed him, his joints were turned

to water. He drifted, as on a wind, veered, and went drifting away.

'I didn't want it, really,' was the last confession of disgust in his soul, as he drifted up the slope, weak, finished, only sheering off unconsciously from any further contact. 'I've had enough—I want to go to sleep. I've had enough.' He was sunk under a sense of nausea.

He was weak, but he did not want to rest, he wanted to go on and on, to the end. Never again to stay, till he came to the end, that was all the desire that remained to him. So he drifted on and on, unconscious and weak, not thinking of anything, so long as he could keep in action.

The twilight spread a weird, unearthly light overhead, bluish-rose in colour, the cold blue night sank on the snow. In the valley below, behind, in the great bed of snow, were two small figures; Gudrun dropped on her knees, like one executed, and Loerke sitting propped up near her. That was all.

Gerald stumbled on up the slope of snow, in the bluish darkness, always climbing, always unconsciously climbing, weary though he was. On his left was a steep slope with black rocks and fallen masses of rock and veins of snow slashing in and about the blackness of rock, veins of snow slashing vaguely in and about the blackness of rock. Yet there was no sound, all this made no noise.

To add to his difficulty, a small bright moon shone brilliantly just ahead, on the right, a painful brilliant thing that was always there, unremitting, from which there was no escape. He wanted so to come to the end—he had had enough. Yet he did not sleep.

He surged painfully up, sometimes having to cross a slope of black rock, that was blown bare of snow. Here he was afraid of falling, very much afraid of falling. And high up here, on the crest, moved a wind that almost overpowered him with a sleep-heavy iciness. Only it was not here, the end, and he must still go on. His indefinite nausea would not let him stay.

Having gained one ridge, he saw the vague shadow of something higher in front. Always higher, always higher. He knew he was following the track towards the summit of the slopes, where was the Marienhütte, and the descent on the other side. But he was not really conscious. He only wanted to go on, to go on whilst he could, to move, to keep going, that was all, to keep going, until it was finished. He had lost all his sense of place. And yet in the remaining instinct of life, his feet sought the track where the skis had gone.

He slithered down a sheer snow slope. That frightened him. He had no alpenstock, nothing. But having come safely to rest, he began to walk on in the illuminated darkness. It was as cold as sleep. He was between two ridges in a hollow. So he swerved. Should he climb the other ridge or wander along the hollow? How frail the thread of his being was stretched! He would perhaps climb the ridge. The snow was firm and simple. He went along. There was something standing out of the snow. He approached with dimmest curiosity.

It was a half-buried crucifix, a little Christ under a little sloping hood at the top of a pole. He sheered away. Somebody was going to murder him. He had a great dread of being murdered. But it was a dread which stood outside him like his own ghost.

Yet why be afraid? It was bound to happen. To be murdered! He looked round in terror at the snow, the rocking, pale, shadowy slopes of the upper world. He was bound to be murdered, he could see it. This was the moment when the death was uplifted, and there was no escape.

Lord Jesus, was it then bound to be—Lord Jesus! He could feel the blow descending, he knew he was murdered. Vaguely wandering forward, his hands lifted as if to feel what would happen, he was waiting for the moment when he would stop, when it would cease. It was not over yet.

He had come to the hollow basin of snow, surrounded by sheer slopes and precipices, out of which rose a track that brought one to the top of the mountain. But he wandered unconsciously, till he slipped and fell down, and as he fell something broke in his soul, and immediately he went to sleep.

31

Exeunt

When they brought the body home the next morning, Gudrun was shut up in her room. From her window she saw men coming along with a burden over the snow. She sat still and let the minutes go by.

There came a tap at her door. She opened. There stood a woman, saying softly, oh, far too reverently:

'They have found him, madam!'

'*Il est mort?*'

'Yes—hours ago.'

Gudrun did not know what to say. What should she say? What should she feel? What should she do? What did they expect of her? She was coldly at a loss.

'Thank you,' she said, and she shut the door of her room. The woman went way mortified. Not a word, not a tear—ha! Gudrun was cold, a cold woman.

Gudrun sat on in her room, her face pale and impassive. What was she to do? She could not weep and make a scene. She could not alter herself. She sat motionless, hiding from people. Her one motive was to avoid actual contact with events. She only wrote out a long telegram to Ursula and Birkin.

In the afternoon, however, she rose suddenly to look for Loerke. She glanced with apprehension at the door of the room that had been Gerald's. Not for worlds would she enter there.

She found Loerke sitting alone in the lounge. She went straight up to him.

'It isn't true, is it?' she said.

He looked up at her. A small smile of misery twisted his face. He shrugged his shoulders.

'True?' he echoed.

'We haven't killed him?' she asked.

He disliked her coming to him in such a manner. He raised his shoulders wearily.

'It has happened,' he said.

She looked at him. He sat crushed and frustrated for the time being, quite as emotionless and barren as herself. My God! this was a barren tragedy, barren, barren.

She returned to her room to wait for Ursula and Birkin. She wanted to get away, only to get away. She could not think or feel until she had got away, till she was loosed from this position.

The day passed, the next day came. She heard the sledge, saw Ursula and Birkin alight, and she shrank from these also.

Ursula came straight up to her.

'Gudrun!' she cried, the tears running down her cheeks. And she took her sister in her arms. Gudrun hid her face on Ursula's shoulder, but still she could not escape the cold devil of irony that froze her soul.

'Ha, ha!' she thought, 'this is the right behaviour.'

But she could not weep, and the sight of her cold, pale, impassive face soon stopped the fountain of Ursula's tears. In a few moments, the sisters had nothing to say to each other.

'Was it very vile to be dragged back here again?' Gudrun asked at length.

Ursula looked up in some bewilderment.

'I never thought of it,' she said.

'I felt a beast, fetching you,' said Gudrun. 'But I simply couldn't see people. That is too much for me.'

'Yes,' said Ursula, chilled.

Birkin tapped and entered. His face was white and expressionless. She knew he knew. He gave her his hand, saying:

'The end of *this* trip, at any rate.'

Gudrun glanced at him, afraid.

There was silence between the three of them, nothing to be said. At length Ursula asked in a small voice:

'Have you seen him?'

He looked back at Ursula with a hard, cold look, and did not trouble to answer.

'Have you seen him?' she repeated.

'I have,' he said coldly.

Then he looked at Gudrun.

'Have you done anything?' he said.

'Nothing,' she replied, 'nothing.'

She shrank in cold disgust from making any statement.

'Loerke says that Gerald came to you when you were sitting on the sledge at the bottom of the Rudelbahn, that you had words, and Gerald walked away. What were the words about? I had better know, so that I can satisfy the authorities, if necessary.'

Gudrun looked up at him, white, childlike, mute with trouble.

'There weren't even any words,' she said. 'He knocked Loerke down and stunned him, he half strangled me, then he went away.'

To herself she was saying:

'A pretty little sample of the eternal triangle!' And she turned ironically away, because she knew that the fight had been between Gerald and herself and that the presence of the third party was a mere contingency—an inevitable contingency perhaps, but a contingency none the less. But let them have it as an example of the eternal triangle, the trinity of hate. It would be simpler for them.

Birkin went away, his manner cold and abstracted. But she knew he would do things for her, nevertheless, he would see her through. She smiled slightly to herself, with contempt. Let him do the work, since he was so extremely *good* at looking after other people.

Birkin went again to Gerald. He had loved him. And yet he felt chiefly disgust at the inert body lying there. It was so inert, so coldly dead, a carcase, Birkin's bowels seemed to turn to ice. He had to stand and look at the frozen dead body that had been Gerald.

It was the frozen carcase of a dead male. Birkin remembered a rabbit which he had once found frozen like a board on the snow. It had been rigid like a dried board when he picked it up. And now this was Gerald, stiff as a board, curled up as if for sleep, yet with the horrible hardness somehow evident. It filled him with horror. The room must be made warm, the body must be thawed. The limbs would break like glass or like wood if they had to be straightened.

He reached and touched the dead face. And the sharp, heavy bruise of ice bruised his living bowels. He wondered if he himself were freezing too, freezing from the inside. In the short blond moustache the life beneath was frozen into a block of ice beneath the silent nostrils. And this was Gerald!

Again he touched the sharp, almost glittering fair hair of the frozen body. It was icy-cold, hair icy-cold, almost venomous. Birkin's heart began to freeze. He had loved Gerald. Now he looked at the shapely, strange-coloured face, with the small, fine, pinched nose and the manly cheeks, saw it frozen like an ice pebble—yet he had loved it. What was one to think or feel? His brain was beginning to freeze, his blood was turning to ice water. So cold, so cold, a heavy, bruising cold pressing on his arms from outside, and a heavier cold congealing within him, in his heart and in his bowels.

He went over the snow slopes to see where the death had been. At last he came to the great shallow among the precipices and slopes, near the summit of the pass. It was a grey day, the third day of greyness and stillness. All was white, icy, pallid, save for the scoring of black rocks that jutted like roots sometimes, and sometimes were in naked faces. In the distance a slope sheered down from a peak, with many black rock-slides.

It was like a shallow pot lying among the stone and snow of the upper world. In this pot Gerald had gone to sleep. At the far end, the guides had driven iron stakes deep into the snow-wall, so that, by means of the great rope attached, they could haul themselves up the massive snow-front, out on to the jagged summit of the pass, naked to heaven, where the Marienhütte hid among the naked rocks. Round about, spiked, slashed snow-peaks pricked the heaven.

Gerald might have found this rope. He might have hauled himself up to the crest. He might have heard the dogs in the Marienhütte, and found shelter. He might have gone on down the steep, steep fall of the south side, down into the dark valley with its pines, on to the great Imperial road leading south to Italy.

He might! And what then? The Imperial road! The south? Italy? What then? Was it a way out? It was only a way in again. Birkin stood high in the painful air, looking at the peaks and the way south. Was it any good going south, to Italy? Down the old, old Imperial road?

He turned away, Either the heart would break or cease to care. Best cease to care. Whatever the mystery which has brought forth man and the universe, it is a non-human mystery, it has its own great ends, man is not the criterion. Best leave it all to the vast, creative, non-human mystery. Best strive with oneself only, not with the universe.

'God cannot do without man.' It was a saying of some great French religious teacher. But surely this is false. God can do without man. God could do without the ichthyosauri and the mastodon. These monsters failed creatively to develop, so God, the creative mystery, dispensed with them. In the same way the mystery could dispense with man, should he too fail creatively to change and develop. The eternal creative mystery could dispose of man, and replace him with a finer created being. Just as the horse has taken the place of the mastodon.

It was very consoling to Birkin to think this. If humanity ran into a cul-de-sac, and expended itself, the timeless creative mystery would bring forth some other being, finer, more wonderful, some new, more lovely race, to carry on the embodiment of creation. The game was never up. The mystery of creation was fathomless, infallible, inexhaustible, for ever. Races came and went, species passed away, but ever new species arose, more lovely, or equally lovely, always surpassing wonder. The fountain-head was incorruptible and unsearchable. It had no limits. It could bring forth miracles, create utterly new races and new species in its own hour, new forms of consciousness, new forms of body, new units of being. To be man was as nothing compared to the possibilities of the creative mystery. To have one's pulse beating direct from the mystery, this was perfection, unutterable satisfaction. Human or inhuman mattered nothing. The perfect pulse throbbed with indescribable being, miraculous unborn species.

Birkin went home again to Gerald. He went into the room and sat down on the bed. Dead, dead and cold!

> Imperial Caesar dead, and turned to clay
> Would stop a hole to keep the wind away.

There was no response from that which had been Gerald. Strange, congealed, icy substance—no more. No more!

Terribly weary, Birkin went away, about the day's business. He did it all quietly, without bother. To rant, to rave, to be tragic, to make situations—it was all too late. Best be quiet, and bear one's soul in patience and in fullness.

But when he went in again, at evening, to look at Gerald between the candles, because of his heart's hunger, suddenly his heart contracted, his own candle all but fell from his hand, as, with a strange whimpering cry, the tears broke out. He sat down in a chair, shaken by a sudden access. Ursula, who had followed him, recoiled aghast from him as he sat with sunken head and body convulsively shaken, making a strange, horrible sound of tears.

'I didn't want it to be like this—I didn't want it to be like this,' he cried to himself. Ursula could but think of the Kaiser's: *'Ich habe es nicht gewollt.'* She looked almost with horror on Birkin.

Suddenly he was silent. But he sat with his head dropped to hide his face. Then furtively he wiped his face with his fingers. Then suddenly he lifted his head and looked straight at Ursula with dark, almost vengeful eyes.

'He should have loved me,' he said. 'I offered him.'

She, afraid, white, with mute lips, answered:

'What difference would it have made!'

'It would!' he said. 'It would.'

He forgot her and turned to look at Gerald. With head oddly lifted, like a man who draws his head back from an insult, half haughtily, he watched the cold, mute, material face. It had a bluish cast. It sent a shaft like ice through the heart of the living man. Cold, mute, material! Birkin remembered how once Gerald had clutched his hand with a warm, mo-

mentaneous grip of final love. For one second—then let go
again, let go for ever. If he had kept true to that clasp, death
would not have mattered. Those who die, and dying still can
love, still believe, do not die. They live still in the beloved.
Gerald might still have been living in the spirit with Birkin,
even after death. He might have lived with his friend, a further life.

But now he was dead, like clay, like bluish, corruptible
ice. Birkin looked at the pale fingers, the inert mass. He remembered a dead stallion he had seen: a dead mass of maleness, repugnant. He remembered also the beautiful face of
one whom he had loved, and who had died still having the
faith to yield to the mystery. That dead face was beautiful,
no one could call it cold, mute, material. No one could remember it without gaining faith in the mystery, without the
soul's warming with new, deep life trust.

And Gerald! The denier! He left the heart cold, frozen,
hardly able to beat. Gerald's father had looked wistful, to
break the heart: but not this last terrible look of cold, mute
Matter. Birkin watched and watched.

Ursula stood aside watching the living man stare at the
frozen face of the dead man. Both faces were unmoved and
unmoving. The candle-flames flickered in the frozen air in
the intense silence.

'Haven't you seen enough?' she said.

He got up.

'It's a bitter thing to me,' he said.

'What—that he's dead?' she said.

His eyes just met hers. He did not answer.

'You've got me,' she said.

He smiled and kissed her.

'If I die,' he said, 'you'll know I haven't left you.'

'And me?' she cried.

'And you won't have left me,' he said. 'We shan't have
any need to despair, in death.'

She took hold of his hand.

'But need you despair over Gerald?' she said.

'Yes,' he answered.

They went away. Gerald was taken to England to be
buried. Birkin and Ursula accompanied the body, along with

one of Gerald's brothers. It was the Crich brothers and sisters who insisted on the burial in England. Birkin wanted to leave the dead man in the Alps, near the snow. But the family was strident, loudly insistent.

Gudrun went to Dresden. She wrote no particulars of herself. Ursula stayed at the Mill with Birkin for a week or two. They were both very quiet.

'Did you need Gerald?' she asked one evening.

'Yes,' he said.

'Aren't I enough for you?' she asked.

'No,' he said. 'You are enough for me, as far as a woman is concerned. You are all women to me. But I wanted a man friend, as eternal as you and I are eternal.'

'Why aren't I enough?' she said. 'You are enough for me. I don't want anybody else but you. Why isn't it the same with you?'

'Having you, I can live all my life without anybody else, any other sheer intimacy. But to make it complete, really happy, I wanted eternal union with a man too: another kind of love,' he said.

'I don't believe it,' she said. 'It's an obstinacy, a theory, a perversity.'

'Well,' he said.

'You can't have two kinds of love. Why should you!'

'It seems as if I can't,' he said. 'Yet I wanted it.'

'You can't have it, because it's false, impossible,' she said.

'I don't believe that,' he answered.

Meyers, Jeffrey. *D. H. Lawrence: A Biography.* New York: Alfred A. Knopf, 1990.

Moore, Harry T. *The Priest of Love: A Life of D. H. Lawrence.* Revised Edition. Carbondale and Edwardsville: Southern Illinois University Press, 1974; New York: Penguin Books, 1974.

Murry, John Middleton. *Son of Woman: The Story of D. H. Lawrence.* New York: Jonathan Cape & Harrison Smith, 1931.

Nehls, Edward, ed. *D. H. Lawrence: A Composite Biography.* Volume One, 1885–1919; Volume Two, 1919–1925; Volume Three, 1925–1930. Madison: The University of Wisconsin Press, 1957, 1958, 1959.

Nin, Anaïs. *D. H. Lawrence, An Unprofessional Study.* Denver: Alan Swallow, 1964.

Ross, Charles L. *The Composition of The Rainbow and Women in Love: A History.* Charlottesville: Published for the Bibliographical Society of the University Press of Virginia, 1979.

Smith, Anne. *Lawrence and Women.* Plymouth and London: Vision Press, 1978.

Worthen, John. *D. H. Lawrence: The Early Years 1885–1912.* Cambridge: Cambridge University Press, 1991.

BIBLIOGRAPHY

Aldington, Richard. *Portrait of a Genius But ...* New York: Duell, Sloan and Pearce, 1950.

Delany, Paul. *D. H. Lawrence's Nightmare: The Writer and His Circle in the Years of the Great War.* New York: Basic Books, 1978.

Delavenay, Emile. *D. H. Lawrence: The Man and His Work. The Formative Years: 1885–1919.* Translated from the French by Katherine M. Delavenay. London: Heinemann, 1972.

DeSalvo, Louise. *Conceived with Malice: Literature as Revenge in the Lives and Works of Virginia and Leonard Woolf, D. H. Lawrence, Djuna Barnes, and Henry Miller.* New York: Dutton, 1994.

Feinstein, Elaine. *Lawrence and the Women: The Intimate Life of D. H. Lawrence.* New York: HarperCollins, 1993.

Lawrence, D. H. *Fantasia of the Unconscious and Psychoanalysis and the Unconscious.* London: Penguin, 1977.

———*The Letters of D. H. Lawrence.* Volume II, June 1913–October 1916, ed. by George J. Zytaruk and James T. Boulton and Andrew Robertson; Volume III, October 1916–June 1921, ed. by James T. Boulton and Andrew Robertson; Volume IV, June 1921–March 1924, ed. by Warren Roberts, James T. Boulton, and Elizabeth Mansfield; Volume V, March 1924–March 1927, ed. by James T. Boulton and Lindeth Vasey. Cambridge: Cambridge University Press, 1981, 1984, 1987, 1989.

Lawrence, Frieda. *"Not I, But the Wind ..."* New York: Alfred A. Knopf, 1956.

Lucas, Robert. *Frieda Lawrence: The Story of Frieda von Richthofen and D. H. Lawrence.* Translated from the German by Geoffrey Skelton. New York: The Viking Press, 1973.